Why couldn't she quit staring at Cordell Hollister?

The moment he'd turned around and she'd found herself looking into his sky blue eyes, she'd felt a jolt all the way to her feet. Which had been a ridiculous reaction, considering she was accustomed to seeing plenty of rugged and sexy cowboys.

More than an hour had passed since Cordell had escorted her around the big barn and introduced her to his relatives. And when the two of them had eventually run into Jack and Vanessa in the crowd, he'd excused himself and left her in their company.

At the time, she'd told herself she was relieved he'd parted ways with her. Now, after watching him dance with one woman after another without so much as a glance in her direction, she was actually feeling disappointed.

She didn't need the company of a man like him. She needed a man who was steady and true, a guy who wanted a family rather than a few romps in bed. So why did she keep looking at him and wondering how it would feel to dance in his arms?

Dear Reader,

When ER nurse Maggie Malone travels to Stone Creek Ranch to attend Jack and Vanessa Hollister's belated wedding reception, she plans to enjoy a few days' stay with her good friend and partake in the Utah countryside. She's certainly not expecting the scenery to include the ranch's sexy foreman, Cordell Hollister, or the sudden rush of attraction she feels whenever he dances her across the barn floor. The man's clearly a rascal and she doesn't need or want any part of him. She wants a home and family. Not an affair that will end in cold ashes.

Cordell has always thought of himself as a wild mustang. He doesn't want a life with fences, especially when the grass on a distant hill always looks better than the field he's currently grazing. However, the moment he meets beautiful Maggie, he feels a lasso tightening around his heart and before he realizes what's happening, he begins to dream of the red-haired nurse filling his nights with love. But could he ever be content living his life with just one woman?

I hope you enjoy reading how a long drive back to Arizona and one fateful night together eventually change Cordell's and Maggie's lives and prove their love was meant to be.

God bless the trails you ride,

Stella Bagwell

For the Rancher's Baby

STELLA BAGWELL

HARLEQUIN

SPECIAL
EDITION

HARLEQUIN®
SPECIAL EDITION™

Recycling programs
for this product may
not exist in your area.

ISBN-13: 978-1-335-72449-6

For the Rancher's Baby

Copyright © 2023 by Stella Bagwell

Harlequin Enterprises ULC
22 Adelaide St. West, 41st Floor
Toronto, Ontario M5H 4E3, Canada
www.Harlequin.com

Printed in U.S.A.

After writing more than one hundred books for Harlequin, **Stella Bagwell** still finds writing about two people discovering everlasting love very rewarding. She loves all things Western and has been married to her own real cowboy for fifty-one years. Living on the south Texas coast, she also enjoys being outdoors and helping her husband care for the animals on the small ranch they call home. The couple has one son, who teaches high school mathematics and coaches football and powerlifting.

Books by Stella Bagwell

Harlequin Special Edition

Men of the West

A Ranger for Christmas
His Texas Runaway
Home to Blue Stallion Ranch
The Rancher's Best Gift
Her Man Behind the Badge
His Forever Texas Rose
The Baby That Binds Them
Sleigh Ride with the Rancher
The Wrangler Rides Again
The Other Hollister Man

Montana Mavericks: Brothers & Broncos

The Maverick's Marriage Pact

Montana Mavericks: The Real Cowboys of Bronco Heights

For His Daughter's Sake

Visit the Author Profile page
at Harlequin.com for more titles.

To my husband, Harrell. Thank you
for being my cowboy for all these years.
I love you.

Chapter One

Cordell Hollister never shied away from a party. Especially when the merrymaking included dancing, drinking and pretty girls. But tonight's event was more than a get-together of neighboring ranchers in need of a break before a hard Utah winter arrived. This was a wedding reception for his brother and sister-in-law, Jack and Vanessa. And anything to do with a wedding made Cordell uncomfortable.

For damned good reason. Being reminded of a time four years ago when he'd come close to getting married sent a cold chill down his spine. He'd shocked his fiancé, Lacey, and everyone in Beaver County, including his family, when he'd called off the whole shebang. But Cordell had only felt immense relief.

Now as he stood at the edge of the crowd, watching his friends and relatives dancing and laughing and sipping champagne, he was happy for Jack and his new wife. And even happier that *he* was still free and single.

Draining the last of his beer, he tossed the bottle in a nearby trash bin and was making his way through the crowd, when he felt a light tap on his back.

"Excuse me, Cord. I want you to say hello to someone."

His new sister-in-law Vanessa's voice managed to break through the music and he turned to see the beautiful bride with a young woman he'd not yet spotted among the reception guests.

"This is Maggie Malone," Vanessa introduced. "She's traveled all the way from Wickenburg to attend the reception."

"So this is the friend you're always talking about," Cordell said, while trying not to stare at Vanessa's friend.

The petite woman had a cloud of vivid red-gold hair that waved from the crown of her head all the way to her waist, while green eyes, the color of rich emeralds, were sliding over his face in a surreptitious way.

"Right. And she only arrived an hour ago," Vanessa explained. "So far she's met your parents and Jack, but not the rest of the family. I thought I'd start with you."

"Nice of you to put me at the head of introductions, Van," he said with a playful grin. "Or was it a case of getting the worst over first?"

Vanessa laughed. "Don't be silly. Everyone in Jack's family is the best."

"Van, you're a perfect diplomat." He offered his hand to the red-haired beauty. "Hello, Maggie. Nice to meet you."

"Cord is foreman of Stone Creek Ranch," Vanessa informed her. "And the middle child of the family, which makes him younger than Jack."

Cordell leveled a playful smile at Maggie. "Five years younger to be exact. I'm also better looking and smarter than Jack, too. But if you stick around for a while, you'll figure that out for yourself."

Vanessa winked at Maggie. "Never mind Cord. When you get past his nonsense you'll find he's actually a nice guy."

Maggie stepped slightly forward and placed her small hand in his. "It's a pleasure to meet you, Mr. Hollister."

Cordell quickly corrected her. "Sorry, it might get confusing if you called me Mr. Hollister. Counting Dad, there are six Mr. Hollisters here on the ranch. Better make it Cord."

She untangled her hand from his and while her gaze continued to sweep over his face, Cordell was amazed to feel a dull blush creeping up his neck. Women never made him self-conscious. But something about the little patronizing curve to her lips made him feel like an idiot.

"Cord it will be," she said.

"Maggie is an RN," Vanessa informed him. "She works the ER unit in a Wickenburg hospital. She's also single. But don't ask me how she hangs on to that status. I can't decide if she's stubborn or picky."

Maggie let out a good-natured groan. "Van, please—would you stop it! I—"

She was about to say more on the subject, but just then his mother walked up.

"Sorry for butting in, Van," Claire said. "But I have some old family friends over here who can't wait to meet you. Would you mind coming with me for a few minutes?"

"I'd love to, Claire." She looked at Maggie and Cordell. "Cord, would you mind introducing Maggie to the rest of the family?"

"I can't think of anything I'd rather do."

Cordell watched Vanessa and his mother disappear into the crowd, then glanced over at Maggie. Judging by the dubious look on her face, she wasn't exactly pleased to have him as her temporary host.

"Don't worry, Maggie. I don't bite. At least, not hard enough to hurt," he added with a wide grin.

"Thank you for that bit of information," she said. "You've put me completely at ease."

Her prim tone wasn't softened by a smile and he decided she must have already sized him up as someone she'd rather avoid. But that was hardly enough to stop him from taking a long, leisurely survey of her oval face.

"That was my sole intention, Maggie." He gestured to the crowd of dancers moving over the worn wood floor. "What do you think of Jack and Van's reception?"

"Everyone appears to be having a good time."

Everyone except her, Cordell thought. She wasn't smiling or tapping her toe to the beat of the lively music. She wasn't even trying to make polite conversation. Had the grim situations she encountered in the ER taken the joy out of her? No. He doubted that was the woman's problem. His older sister, Grace, was an MD and she'd seen plenty of trauma, but it hadn't soured her.

"Mom and Dad suggested having the belated wedding party at the civic center building in town, but Jack nixed that idea. He wanted the shindig here on the ranch and Van agreed. We spent more than a week cleaning out this hay barn to get it ready. Looks pretty good, don't you think? Or is it too rustic for a city girl like you?"

Cutting a glance up to his face, she quickly corrected, "I'm not a *city* girl. Wickenburg population is only in the four digits."

"Oh. Well, Stone Creek Ranch is miles away from everything," he explained. "Anything with more than two stoplights is like a city to me."

To his utter frustration, her expression remained stoic.

After a moment, she said, "You must not get out much."

Cordell couldn't help but burst out laughing and she reacted with a faint frown.

"You find that amusing?" she asked.

"Well, to hear my brothers tell it, I'm always going out. But usually Beaver or Cedar City is the extent of my travels. Guess you saw those towns on your way here."

She nodded. "Barely. Thunderstorms delayed my flight into Cedar City and then I had to wait for my rental car. I'm sure I broke the speed limit driving through Beaver, but I thought I was going to miss Jack and Van's reception entirely."

He smiled, while thinking her complexion was the perfect definition of peaches and cream with a dusting of golden freckles across the bridge of her nose. He figured her skin would feel smooth against his tongue, while her dark red lips would no doubt taste sweeter than a comb of wild honey. But he'd never get close enough to this stern little nurse to find out, he thought.

He said, "That would've been a shame. This is a nice party. Especially the music. The guys with the guitars and violins are all neighbors and the one on the keyboard plays piano at our church in Beaver."

She looked over to where the little band was currently whipping out a popular country tune. "Neighbors? I drove for miles and miles out here without spotting a single house."

His smile was indulgent. "We consider anyone within a thirty-mile radius to be a neighbor. Otherwise, we wouldn't have any."

"Vanessa warned me that Stone Creek Ranch was even more isolated than the Hollisters' Three Rivers Ranch down in Arizona. I found that hard to believe. Until I started driving out here." She slanted a curious glance at him. "Were you surprised about Jack and Van eloping?"

Trying to steer his thoughts away from the tempting curve of her lips, he said, "Not really. Everyone in the family could see they were smitten with each other. Were you surprised that Van suddenly married?"

"In a way. But I was happy. She deserves the best and your brother obviously adores her."

"That's an understatement." He gestured toward a long table laden with an assortment of drinks and a massive tiered wedding cake. "Have you had cake and champagne yet?"

"Not yet."

While she focused on the milling crowd, Cordell allowed his gaze to drop to her dress. The midnight blue garment was fashioned with a turtleneck and long tight sleeves and though it didn't reveal any skin, the shimmery fabric clung to her slender curves like a glove. Normally, he was attracted to women with more flesh to their figures, so why was he feeling the urge to wrap his hands around her tiny waist?

Clearing his throat, he said, "Let's go over and get a glass of champagne. Afterward, we'll weave our way through the crowd and I'll introduce you to my brothers and sisters."

"I, uh, think I should wait. Van might be back any minute."

Her reluctant attitude mystified him. "I doubt she'll show up anytime soon. She's the queen of this ball, so to speak, her attention is going to be divided. And she did tell me to keep you company."

She glanced away from him. "That was just a figure of speech."

Cordell was beginning to get annoyed with her, but did his best not to show it. He didn't want to hurt Vanessa by insulting her friend.

"Okay. We'll skip the champagne. Let's go find my siblings. Hopefully you'll like them a bit better than you like me."

Surprise widened her eyes. "We just met. And you've already decided that I don't like you?"

"Forget I said that." He reached for her arm and was relieved when she didn't pull away from him. "I see Hunter helping himself to a piece of cake. Have you met him yet?"

"No. Is he a Hollister?" she asked, as he ushered her toward the refreshment table.

"The firstborn of us kids. In case Van hasn't told you, he owns and operates the Flying H Rodeo company."

"Sounds interesting. He must lead an exciting life," she replied.

"Compared to the rest of us, I suppose he does. But the grueling travel would get to me."

As they walked the short distance to where Hunter was standing, Cordell noticed a portion of her creamy thigh was exposed by a slit on the side of her dress and the scent drifting from her skin was wild and tangy, like the smell of the desert on a hot, dark night.

Yeah, she was sexy, all right, Cordell thought. But she also had hands-off written all over her. Which was probably a good thing. He didn't need to get mixed up with a woman right now. Hardly a month had passed since he'd gotten himself out of a messy entanglement with a brunette down in Parowan. He needed to steer clear of women for a while.

When Hunter spotted the two of them angling toward him, the rugged cowboy with rusty brown hair and a set of wide shoulders placed his plate of cake on the table and stepped out to meet them.

"Meet Van's friend from Wickenburg," Cord said to his brother. "This is Maggie Malone. She's a nurse. And don't suddenly develop a fever. She's here to enjoy the party."

Hunter reached out to shake Maggie's hand. "My pleasure, Ms. Malone. Welcome to Stone Creek Ranch."

Maggie shook Hunter's hand and Cordell couldn't help but notice she gave him a wide, warm smile.

Hell, what did Hunter have that he didn't? Maybe she went for older men. At thirty-nine, Hunter wasn't exactly old, but Cordell figured he was at least twelve or thirteen years older than Maggie.

"Thank you," she said. "I'm looking forward to seeing the place in the daylight hours."

"Do you plan to stay on the ranch for a while?" Hunter asked. "We always enjoy having company for Thanksgiving."

"How would you know?" Cordell shot the question at his brother. "You're rarely ever around for the holidays."

Hunter leveled a shrewd smile at him. "I didn't realize you missed me so much, Cord."

Cordell looked over to see Maggie's gaze vacillating between him and Hunter. Their subtle jabs at each other probably had had her wondering about their relationship. Cordell could've told her that he was tightly bonded to Hunter and all his brothers. They might argue at times, but the love between was enduring.

She said to Hunter, "Unfortunately, I can only stay a few days. I have to return to work before Thanksgiving."

"That's a shame. But it's good you and Van will have a bit of time to together," Hunter replied. "I imagine she's excited to show you the house she and Jack are having built."

Maggie said, "She's looking forward to having

her own place. Not that she doesn't enjoy living in the big ranch house with everyone. But—"

"Newlyweds need privacy," Hunter finished for her.

Feeling the need to make his presence known, Cordell said, "Maggie has the notion you lead an exciting life, Hunter. She'd probably enjoy a few of your rodeo stories."

Hunter grimaced and Cordell figured this evening had to be a strain for his older brother. Being reminded of his failed marriage had to be rough. Especially when Hunter had never gotten over his wife's leaving. Which made no sense to Cordell. In his opinion, Hunter's wife didn't deserve to be remembered.

Hunter focused on the crowd of dancing couples. "I wouldn't dream of boring Maggie with that stuff."

"Not all women find rodeos boring," Cordell felt compelled to say.

Hunter leveled a meaningful look at him. "Thanks for the reminder, Cord. Now if both of you will excuse me, I see someone I need to go say hello to."

As Hunter walked away, he noticed Maggie staring after him.

She said, "I get the feeling you ruffled his feathers—on purpose. Do you enjoy goading your brother?"

Cordell grimaced. "Not really. I did it for a good reason. You have to trust me on that."

Her short laugh caused him to stare at her in wonder. "You find that funny?"

For the first time this evening, she smiled at him. "The idea of trusting you is very funny."

He playfully slapped a hand over his heart. "Van described you as a sweetheart. She didn't mention you had claws."

She gave him another dimpled smile that caused something to quiver deep in his gut.

"Van is too nice to say bad things about anyone," she said, then surprised him once again by curving her arm lightly through his. "Shall we go find your other siblings? I can't wait to see if any of them are like you."

He very much wanted to place his hand over the one she had resting on his forearm, but decided not to press his luck. "I'll save you the disappointment and tell you that none of my siblings are like me."

"I'm sure your parents are relieved about that."

He chuckled and as he guided her across the wide expanse of barn floor to where his younger brother Flint was standing, he forgot the party was a wedding reception. He even forgot about his plan to avoid women for a while. Cordell had always been a man to live for the pleasure of the moment and he didn't see any good reason to break the habit tonight.

Why couldn't she quit staring at Cordell Hollister?

The question continued to nag at Maggie as she

sat on a hay bale covered with a bright serape and sipped champagne from a stemmed glass. Vanessa's twin sisters-in-law, Bonnie and Beatrice, were seated on either side of her, but Maggie was digesting only half of the young women's chatter. Her thoughts were consumed with the good-looking ranch foreman, who was currently waltzing a pretty brunette around the dance floor.

Before Vanessa had introduced her to Cordell, she'd warned Maggie that he was a bit of a flirt. But she'd failed to mention anything about him having striking looks or that he oozed masculinity from every pore.

The moment he'd turned around and she'd found herself looking into his sky-blue eyes, she'd felt a jolt all the way to her feet. Which had been a ridiculous reaction, considering she was accustomed to seeing plenty of rugged and sexy cowboys. After all, Wickenburg was known as a cowboy town. But she'd never met one who looked exactly like Cordell.

He was six feet of hard, lean muscle with long legs and broad shoulders. Beneath his black Stetson, thick, sandy blond hair waved around his ears and down onto his neck. As for his face, it was made up of unyielding angles and a set of lips that looked just as hard as his squared chin.

Darn it! More than an hour had passed since Cordell had escorted her around the big barn and introduced her to his relatives. And when the two of them had eventually run onto Jack and Vanessa in the crowd, he'd excused himself and left her in their company.

At the time, she'd told herself she was relieved he'd parted ways with her. It had been a constant fight with herself to keep from staring at him and pretending he wasn't creating an earthquake inside of her. Now, after watching him dance with one woman after another, without so much as a glance in her direction, she was actually feeling disappointed. Which was a totally stupid reaction. She'd seen his kind before. He was as sexy as hell and he knew it. He used his charm to wrap women around his finger and then toss them away without the slightest prick to his conscience.

No. She didn't need the company of a man like him. She needed a man who was steady and true, a guy who wanted a family rather than a few romps in bed. So why did she keep looking at him and wondering how it would feel to dance in his arms?

"Maggie, do you ever visit Three Rivers Ranch?"

Glad that Beatrice's question had interrupted her wandering thoughts, she looked over at the blonde twin. Except for being slightly shorter and smaller in stature, her features were almost identical to Bonnie's.

"On occasion. I'm friends with Camille. She's the youngest of the family."

"Oh. I was just wondering," Beatrice replied.

"Jack said they have dozens of nice cowboys working on the place."

"And Bea wants to meet them all," Bonnie spoke with a roll of her eyes. "Just like they're better than the guys up here. I've tried to tell her a man is a man no matter where he is."

"And how would you know?" Beatrice fired the question back at her sister. "The only men you've ever dated are milksops and those have been few and far between."

"Is it a crime to like sensitive men?" Bonnie asked in a deceptively sweet voice.

"No. It's a bore," Beatrice answered between sips of champagne. "But you don't mind being bored. All that concerns you is feeling safe."

Bonnie gave her sister a hard look and Maggie was beginning to fear the two were going to end up in a heated argument, but before the conversation could go any further, a young man wearing a dark Western suit walked up and asked Beatrice for a dance.

As the two of them walked away, Maggie couldn't help saying, "I guess you and your twin don't always see eye to eye."

To her surprise, Bonnie smiled and shrugged. "Mom says Bea and I argued with each other before we could walk. We look alike but we're totally unalike in personalities. But we have a fierce love for each other. It's hard to explain. Other than we have a twin thing. Do you have sisters or brothers, Maggie?"

Shaking her head, she said, "Unfortunately, no. My mother passed away when I was five. And I was her only child."

"Oh, that's sad."

"Yes, but I had a wonderful mother for a while," Maggie said gently. "That's better than having a bad one for years and years. As for my father, I never knew him."

Bonnie looked at her with regret. "I'm sorry to hear that. I've been blessed with great parents, so I try to never take their presence for granted."

Maggie nodded while thinking Bonnie had hit the nail squarely on the head when she'd said her and Beatrice had totally different personalities. The twins were only twenty-four, two years younger than Maggie, yet Bonnie talked like an old soul, whereas Beatrice seemed much younger—and eager to spread her wings.

"I hate to interrupt such a deep conversation, but I've not had a dance with you, Maggie. Would you like to take a whirl?"

She glanced around to see Cordell standing directly in front of her chair and her heart instantly reacted with a hard lurch.

"I'm not really much of a dancer," she told him.

He brushed aside her flimsy excuse. "I saw you dancing earlier with Hunter and he wasn't limping off the floor when the song ended."

Surprised that he'd even noticed, she said, "I think Hunter is wearing steel-toed boots."

He laughed and Bonnie chuckled softly.

"Hunter has never owned a pair of steel-toed boots in his life." He reached his hand down to her. "Come on. This is a slow song. You won't have to do much."

No, she thought, she'd only have to stand in his arms and pretend she was as cool as the north wind blowing outside the barn, when she'd actually be melting like an icicle on a hot June day.

Seeing no polite way to avoid him, she placed her champagne glass on the empty spot next to her, then taking his hand, rose from the chair.

"Excuse me, Bonnie."

"Sure," the young woman replied.

As Cordell led her among the dancing couples, Maggie said, "If you were worried I was feeling like a wallflower you shouldn't have bothered with the dance invitation. I was thoroughly enjoying your sisters."

"You, a wallflower?" He followed the question with a laugh. "You know, Maggie, you're terribly funny. I'll bet you keep all your patients laughing."

"The ones who are fortunate enough to be breathing."

He laughed again, but the smile on his face sobered as he drew her into his arms. "Sorry. I didn't mean that to sound like your job is funny. I'm sure it's very stressful and emotional."

It was difficult for Maggie to digest his serious comment when the contact of his hard body was causing her mind to buzz like a high voltage wire.

"It's both. But thankfully every situation isn't serious."

"Do you like your job?" he asked.

"Love it."

He smelled like the wind that had touched her face the moment she'd stood outside the car in front of the ranch house. The scent was a unique mixture of sage and juniper and some sort of grass. It was a wild, rugged smell that underscored the fact that he was all man.

"Is nursing something you decided on after you became an adult?" he asked curiously. "Or was it always a goal to be an RN?"

"My mother was very ill for a long while before she passed on. I was five years old at the time and the nurses who cared for her were the people who reassured me and saw that my needs were met. I decided then that I wanted to grow up and help people feel better."

"I wish I could say I had an admirable motive to do what I do. But I can't. Being the foreman of Stone Creek Ranch is something I do for a purely selfish reason. I love the work and I want this place to be around whenever my brothers and I get older."

Maybe it was her imagination, but the music seemed to be getting slower. Since he'd circled his arm around the back of her waist and pulled her close against, she doubted they'd traveled more than three feet.

"Working for a united family effort is admirable, too," she told him.

His blue gaze dropped to her face and Maggie had the strangest urge to moisten her lips with the tip of her tongue.

"You think so?" He shrugged one shoulder. "Sometimes I feel guilty because the ranch is something that's always been here. Our father and grandfather are the ones who really toiled and sweated to make the land what it is today."

"But you help keep the ranch going," she pointed out.

"I try. And Jack is great at helping Dad manage everything."

"How did you end up with the foreman job?"

He grinned and she found herself gazing in fascination at his white teeth and the little crinkles at the corners of his eyes. Did he have any idea what kind of effect he had on women? She suspected he might, based on Van's warning.

"I just naturally like giving orders," he said.

She looked away and reminded herself to breathe. Otherwise she was going to embarrass herself by wilting into a heap at his feet.

"I imagine there's more to your job than giving orders," she replied.

"Dad believes I know more about caring for livestock. And that's a never-ending job around here."

The song came to an end and Maggie was trying to decide whether she was disappointed or relieved, when he said, "Let's dance this next one."

Her senses were already a wreck. Five more minutes in his arms and she'd probably start babbling nonsense. "I really should—"

"You really should dance with me, Maggie," a male voice behind her said. "No need in Cord having all the fun."

Maggie caught sight of Cordell's frown as she turned to see the voice belonged to Quint, the youngest brother of the Hollister clan. Earlier, Cord had introduced them.

"You always have to be a pest, baby brother," Cordell said with a good-natured groan, then added, "Thanks for the dance, Maggie. It was a pleasure."

Maggie watched him disappear into the crowd of dancers, while standing at her side, Quint said, "You shouldn't give Cord a second glance, Maggie. He's no good."

Dismayed, she looked at the young cowboy. "That's a harsh thing to say about your brother."

"I'd better rephrase it. Cord is a good guy. He's just no good where ladies like you are concerned. He considers breaking hearts a form of entertainment."

She'd already concluded that Cordell was a playboy. But to hear Quint say it made her wonder if there was a streak of jealousy involved.

"Thanks for the warning, Quint, but I'm only going to be here on the ranch for a few days."

Quint's short laugh was full of sarcasm. "One day is more than enough time for Cord to do damage."

Before Maggie could assure him that she had no intentions of letting Cordell near her heart or any other part of her anatomy, the music suddenly started and Quint led her off into a quick two-step.

The young cowboy was smooth on his feet and Maggie had to focus to keep up with him and the beat of the music, yet even as she danced, her thoughts strayed to Cordell and the strong reaction she'd felt when his arm had pulled her close and his eyes had glinted with sinful promises.

And as she automatically twirled beneath Quint's arm, she realized that Cordell didn't need one day to cast a spell over a woman. He'd managed to captivate her in one short evening.

But tomorrow would be different, Maggie promised herself. Tomorrow she'd have her senses back in good working order and she was going to make darned sure she kept a safe distance from the foreman of Stone Creek Ranch.

Chapter Two

"I didn't know it was supposed to snow today. I'm glad I wore my oilskin."

Cordell glanced over at Quint as the two men rode their horses slowly through the snow-dusted sage toward the foothills lying north of the ranch. This morning, with the weather predicted to worsen through the day, they needed to make sure all the cow-calf pairs were off the mountain and on to a place where the animals could shelter. To help with the chore, Cordell had sent three of the five ranch hands to search the eastern range, while the other two hands were busy putting out feed and hay.

"There is such a thing as a weather forecast. If you'd remember to check it, you might know how to dress in the morning," Cordell told him.

Quint grunted and hunched deeper down in the saddle. "Who needs a weatherman to tell him it's going to be cold or wet? I have two eyes. I can look at the sky."

"Okay. You lucked out today and wore your duster."

A smug smile crossed Quint's face. "I lucked out last night, too. Van's pretty little friend danced three dances with me."

"I never noticed," Cordell said.

"Liar. I saw you watching us," Quint gloated. "Jealous, weren't you?"

Cordell let out a short laugh. "Why would I be jealous? I danced with a number of pretty women at the reception last night."

"Yeah. But none of them looked like Maggie. You know, I never thought I'd go for a redhead, but she's a real firecracker. And she's the same age as me. You know what that means, don't you?"

"Yeah. You're way too young to be thinking about women," Cordell muttered.

"No. It means she's way too young for you, brother."

Cordell kept his gaze focused on his horse's ears, while thinking Quint was right. Maggie was too young and definitely too aloof for his taste. Now, if he could just convince himself of that, until her stay on the ranch was over, he'd be a smart man.

"Probably so," he said as he reached forward and brushed away the flakes of snow collecting on the horse's black mane. "And now that you have those bits of wisdom off your chest, do you think you can get your mind back to punching cows?"

"Punching cows? Hell, we'll have to ride two more miles before we ever see a cow," Quint muttered. "I don't know why you didn't let me stay behind with Jett. I could've helped him fill molasses licks and Brooks could've come with you. He's better at herding cattle than me, anyway."

"Yeah, he is. But I wanted to hear you gripe all morning. Makes my day extra nice to know I'm making you miserable."

He glanced over to see Quint had lowered the brim of his hat to shield the blowing snow from his face. His younger brother was always complaining about the hard work, yet he continued to stay on the ranch and follow orders.

"You know, sometimes I wonder if I have good sense," Quint said as the horses continued to pick their way over the frozen ground. "With my degree, I could be teaching high school agriculture."

"Then why don't you? You talk about it often enough."

"Because I'd hate being cooped up in a room all day."

In spite of the miserable conditions, Cordell had to laugh. "You're outside now. You should be happy," he said, then added slyly, "I probably shouldn't mention this. But Dad is going to put you in charge of the sheep production."

He glanced over just as Quint shot straight up in the saddle and stared at Cord in dazed wonder.

"Are you kidding me?" he asked.

"No. Jack told me yesterday, so I expect Dad will be talking to you about the job in the next day or two. Why? Don't you like the idea? Or you think it's too much responsibility for you?"

"Well, shoot no! I can handle the job just fine." He squared his shoulders and flashed Cordell a toothy grin. "Guess Dad finally realized I was worth something around here."

Funny how one positive accomplishment could make a man's whole world seem brighter, even on a snowy day, Cord thought.

"He sees your hard work and it's paid off. You'll be good with the sheep, Quint. You know a heck of a lot more about them than I do."

If possible, Quint looked even more surprised. "You mean that?"

"I really do."

"Thanks, brother. Coming from you that means a lot," Quint said, then added sheepishly, "And Cord, all that stuff about Maggie—I was just trying to get your goat. Yeah, she danced with me, but all the time I could tell she was thinking about you. Darn it."

The redheaded nurse wasn't a firecracker like Quint had described her, Cordell thought. She was more like a red Popsicle—sweet but so cold a bite of her would make his teeth ache.

"How could you possibly know what she was thinking?" Cordell asked. "Don't tell me you asked her."

"I'm not that dumb. I could just tell by the look on her face every time she spotted you. Her lips flattened and her eyes narrowed."

"You mean like a woman looks whenever she's plotting murder. Well, thanks for the warning, brother. Whenever she's around I'll be sure and watch my back."

"It's not your back you ought to be worried about, Cord. She's the kind that could get under your skin."

Cordell's short laugh was carried away with the cold wind. "Not my skin. My hide is way too tough for that to happen."

Last night, when Maggie had first arrived on Stone Creek Ranch, it had been dark and the only things she could see about the house was that the sizable structure consisted of two stories, countless windows and a tall rock chimney towering up over the north side of the roof. Large round rock formed the foundation and continued half way up the outer wall of the bottom story, while the remaining walls consisted of board lapped siding painted a soft gray.

Later, after the party had ended, she'd been too tired to do more than climb the stairs to the room Van and Claire had shown her to and fall into bed. Now, with the gray morning light slanting through the window, she hurriedly threw a thick robe over her pajamas and made her way out of the bedroom and on to the staircase.

Along the way, she noticed there was no sight of anyone moving about on the second floor, nor any sound coming from the floor below. From what little she knew of ranching life, eight o'clock was the middle of the morning for ranching people. However, with the reception going on into the wee hours, she'd assumed the family would sleep late. And perhaps they were, she thought, as she glanced in passing at several closed doors.

Careful to keep her steps noiseless, she made her way down the wide staircase, while thinking the Hollister home had obviously been built many years ago, when woodwork had been painstakingly carved by hand. The beautiful craftsmanship was evident in the balustrade lining the stairs and the tongue-and-groove walls that were painted a soothing sand color. The oak flooring gleamed with a soft patina and as she reached the bottom floor landing, she caught the scent of lemon wax mixed with the faint smell of roses.

Since Vanessa had moved here to Stone Creek Ranch, she'd never made mention of this house having subtle similarities to the Three Rivers Ranch house. Maybe her friend hadn't noticed the vague parallels, but Maggie was seeing them. True, the Hollisters' house in Arizona had three stories and was somewhat larger; however, this one was of a significant size and the interior was very reminiscent of the other. Which was strange, indeed, given the fact that the two families hadn't known they were related until a few short months ago.

She was nearing the kitchen when the faint scent of bacon and sausage drifted to her and as she entered the door, she expected to find some of the family eating breakfast. Instead, Claire was the only one in the room. She was standing at the cabinet counter stirring something in a big aluminum mixing bowl.

She looked up as Maggie joined her. "Good morning, Maggie. Ready for coffee and breakfast?"

"Is that what you're preparing?"

Claire gave her an indulgent smile. "No. I'm afraid you missed the regular breakfast. This is sourdough mix. I don't know if you're familiar with sourdough, but you have to keep adding ingredients to keep it going. It'll be ready for biscuits tomorrow morning."

Maggie groaned with misgivings. "Everyone had such a late night I thought you were all in bed and I was getting up early."

Claire chuckled. "Ranching folks don't get the luxury of sleeping late. Unless someone is sick. And even then, we try to drag ourselves out of bed. Livestock always needs tending. And I have working men to feed."

Maggie watched Claire continue to push the

wooden spoon through the dough. "You don't have house help?"

"A young woman comes in once a week to help with the deep cleaning. Otherwise, the twins and I do everything. I take care of most all the cooking. Sometimes Bonnie helps prepare the meals. She's pretty good at cooking. Van tries, but she needs practice. Bea can barely make a boiled egg, so she helps with the cleaning up. And believe it or not, sometimes the guys will lend a hand in the kitchen."

Maggie couldn't imagine Cordell washing a dish or scraping scraps from a plate, but she kept the thought to herself. "You've obviously raised your children right."

"Well, we're a big family. So we all have to pitch in." Claire glanced at her. "Jack and Van tell me that the Hollisters down in Arizona have two cooks and a housekeeper, plus a cook for the bunkhouse."

"They do. The ranch is massive. And the family is growing, so they even have a nanny for the children now."

Shaking her head with wonder, Claire said, "I've visited with Maureen over the phone and she's told me about all her grandchildren. I can't relate. Not yet, at least. I only have one grandchild. Grace's son, Ross. But I expect that will soon change now that Van and Jack are married."

As longtime friends, Maggie and Vanessa had often talked about how much they each wanted children. Now that she'd married Jack, Vanessa's dream for a family would soon be coming true. As for Maggie, her luck with men had never been good. She couldn't see a husband on her horizon, much less a baby.

"I hope so. Van and Jack will make great parents."

"Hadley and I think so, too. And in case you didn't get a chance to meet Hadley last night, he's my husband and the children's father."

"Actually, Van did introduce me to Hadley. He's a charming man."

"I've heard that before," Claire said with a chuckle, then setting the spoon aside, she covered the top of the bowl with plastic wrap. "There. Let me put this in the fridge and I'll fix you something to eat."

"Please, don't bother. Coffee will be enough. And anyway, I don't normally eat much in the mornings."

"Nonsense. It's no bother." Claire placed the sourdough mix into a huge stainless-steel refrigerator, then walked to the end of the cabinet where a coffee machine held a glass carafe half full of coffee.

"Do you cook?" Claire asked, then laughed lightly as she filled an orange-and-gold-patterned mug with coffee. "My daughters would shame me for asking you that question. They say nowadays it isn't important if a woman can cook."

"I don't mind you asking. And I'll admit I'm not

too good at cooking. My breakfasts usually consist of cold cereal and dinners are mostly something from the store that's already put together."

"Nothing wrong with that. You're a busy woman." Claire handed Maggie the mug and a spoon, then gestured to a sugar bowl and tiny pitcher of cream sitting in the middle of the table. "Sit down with your coffee and I'll fix you something. I have plenty of bread and jam if you'd like toast."

Maggie gave her a grateful smile. "Toast sounds wonderful."

While Claire dropped bread into the toaster, Maggie took a seat at the long table and stirred a dollop of cream into her coffee,

"Where's Vanessa?"

"She said to tell you she'd be in her office upstairs."

Back in late July, Maureen Hollister had hired Vanessa to dig into their family tree. During her work for the Arizona Hollister matriarch, an intriguing possibility arose of the two Hollister families being related. After a DNA test confirmed her suspicion, Vanessa had continued her search—now at Stone Creek—to unravel the family mystery, but so far she hadn't found any definite link.

Maggie took a careful sip of the hot coffee. "She's working on the family tree today?"

Claire glanced over her shoulder and smiled at Maggie. "She only planned to work until you got up."

Maggie hadn't taken the time to brush her hair.

Now she shook back the tangled mass. "I should've set the alarm."

Claire carried a small plate with two slices of toast and a jar of raspberry jam over to Maggie, then took a seat across from her.

"Van tells us that you've worked in the ER for a long while now."

Maggie slathered a piece of the toast with a thick layer of jam. "Five years. Ever since I became an RN."

"Sometimes I worry Grace will burn out," Claire said thoughtfully. "Being one of the few doctors in town, she's overloaded with work. I would understand if she decided to shut the door on her clinic and just walk away. But she's not that type of person. She cares too much."

Last night at the reception, Maggie had met Grace, the doctor of the family. The pretty blonde resembled her mother, only Grace was considerably taller and her eyes were green whereas Claire's were blue.

Maggie said, "I understand. The ones who care too much are the ones who carry the heaviest loads."

"Yes," Claire replied. "Caring often comes with a heavy price."

Maggie wondered if the Hollister matriarch was talking about Grace or someone else in the family. Had Cordell ever paid a price for caring too much? Somehow she doubted it. She couldn't imagine the man agonizing over anyone, except himself. But then, she didn't really know him well enough to pass any kind of judgment on his character. And besides, she'd be going home in a few short days. Nothing about Cordell Hollister should matter to her.

After Maggie finished her toast and coffee, she returned to her bedroom and dressed in jeans and a warm sweater, then made her way to Vanessa's office, which was located on the west end of the second floor.

When she stepped through the open doorway, she immediately spotted her friend sitting behind a desk, peering intently at a monitor screen.

"Good morning, Mrs. Hollister. Am I interrupting?"

Glancing away from the monitor, Vanessa gave her a cheery smile. "Well, Sleeping Beauty has finally awoken."

Smiling sheepishly, Maggie said, "I should have known you all got up with the chickens. I felt like an idiot for showing up in the kitchen long after everyone had eaten."

Vanessa waved away her words. "Don't be silly. You can sleep until noon if you like."

Maggie turned a full circle as she took in her friend's work area. "This is nice, Van."

"Claire and Hadley fixed this room for me before I first came to Stone Creek. They thought I needed a quiet place to work."

"To go to the trouble and expense of making you an office, they must feel very strongly about uncovering all the branches to the Hollister family tree."

Vanessa leaned back in her chair. "They're very serious about it. Most everyone in the two families wants to know how they came to be related."

"Hmm. I'm not sure I'd want to know anything about my family on the paternal side."

With her father walking out before she'd ever been born, Maggie knew nothing about the man. One of her mother's friends told Maggie he'd originally come from Bishop, California, but after twenty-six years that hardly meant anything.

Vanessa thoughtfully tapped a pencil against the mouse pad on her desk. "Have you ever thought about the possibility of having half siblings somewhere? It might be nice for you to meet them."

Maggie grimaced. "So I could tell them what a creep their father is, or was? No thanks, Van. I'm okay as I am."

Vanessa shook her head. "But you have no one. Except the aunt and uncle who took you in when your mother died. And they're not exactly a loving family unit. I think—"

Maggie held up a hand to prevent her from saying more. "Van, please drop it, will you? I don't want to start my day on a sour note."

Vanessa gave her an apologetic smile. "Right. I'm done. So have you had coffee? Something to eat?"

"Oh, yes. Claire fixed me a plate of toast and we had a nice visit. Your mother-in-law is a lovely woman, Van. Actually, I'm amazed that she gave birth to eight healthy children."

Vanessa nodded. "Funny, but when I first met Jack, he described his mother as being very fragile. Maybe in stature, but she's anything but fragile otherwise. I can only hope I can be as strong a mother and wife as she is."

"No need for you to worry. You're going to be great at both." Maggie walked over to a small window on the left side of the room and glanced out at the view. The November sky was gray with bits of snow landing against the glass panes. But the wintery weather didn't diminish the beauty of the sweeping landscape of Stone Creek Ranch. "It's snowing, Van!"

"Yes. I looked out the window earlier. Winter has apparently arrived in this part of Utah."

Maggie continued to gaze out the window. "This view is something else. The valley looks like it goes for miles before it reaches the mountains."

"Jack and his family call the nearest peak Snow Mountain. I'm not sure if that's its official name on the map, but since the mountain is actually located on Stone Creek Ranch property I guess they can call it whatever they want."

Glancing at her friend, Maggie smiled with fond remembrance. "Remember when we were little girls and the closer it grew to Christmas the harder we'd wish for snow to fall? Wickenburg might see one or two flakes fly through the air in the dead of winter."

Vanessa chuckled. "I remember. We fantasized about making a snowman and going sledding."

Turning her gaze back to the view beyond the window, Maggie dropped her focus directly to the yard behind the house. Along with an open patch of brown grass and a fair-sized patio, there was a low stone fence built along the outside edge of the yard. Next to it, some sort of shrubs had been covered to prevent them from freezing. "What's beneath the gray tarps?"

"Tea roses."

Surprised, Maggie said, "I wouldn't have thought of growing tea roses here in this mountain climate. But I don't suppose it's any stranger than all the irises Tess has growing in the front yard of the Bar X down in Arizona."

Vanessa said, "I was told Jack's grandfather Lionel planted them in honor of his mother. He kept them perfectly cultivated until he passed away. Nowadays Claire tends to the roses. From what I gather, she was especially close to her father-in-law."

"Last night at the reception I noticed you seem to be especially close to your father-in-law," Maggie said with a faint smile. "Lucky you that you have such great in-laws."

Her smile full of affection, Vanessa said, "Hadley is a big teddy bear. And I'll always be grateful he literally forced Jack and I to face each other and admit our love. Otherwise, I might have gone back to Wickenburg and never seen Jack again."

Maggie stepped away from the window and walked over to Vanessa's desk. "And that would've been a tragedy," she said, then gestured to a nearby stack of cardboard boxes. "What's all that stuff? I thought you were doing all your genealogy search on the computer."

"I am researching all I can on the internet. But I'm also going through boxes of old documents and papers that's been stored away for years. I need to find something to give me a clue as to when Hadley's father, Lionel, was born. So far I'm stuck."

"I'd love to help you," Maggie said eagerly. "And from the sizes of those boxes, it looks like you could use an extra pair of eyes."

"Thanks. But you didn't come all the way up here to dig through a bunch of old dusty papers."

Maggie dismissed her words with the wave of a hand. "No. I came up here for your wedding reception. Now that it's over I need to make myself useful."

A dreamy smile appeared on Vanessa's face. "I thought our reception was perfect. Did you enjoy the evening?"

Maggie had enjoyed everything about the evening, except her preoccupation with Cordell. Once she'd met him, she'd had trouble focusing on anything else.

"It was lovely, Van. I'll admit it was the first reception I've ever attended that was held in a barn. But it was the perfect setting for you and Jack."

Vanessa laughed softly. "Jack says he's turned me into a hayseed like him. But you know what? I wouldn't want to be anything else. Guess being in love makes a woman see everything differently."

Maggie glanced away from her friend's face. "I'm beginning to doubt I'll ever know the feeling of being in love."

"Maggie, that's an odd thing for you to say. I got the impression you were in love with Dr. Sheridan—that is, before he left town. But the way I remember things, he asked you to go with him. And you refused."

"I had to refuse," Maggie said ruefully. "Because deep down our relationship didn't feel right to me. Something was missing. Passion—electricity—I don't know exactly."

She glanced over to see Vanessa was studying her thoughtfully.

"So what did you think about Cord?" she asked. "I got the feeling he wasn't quite what you expected."

Maggie didn't want to discuss Cordell. She wanted to forget him. But admitting such things to Vanessa would only create suspicion and more questions from her friend.

"I wasn't expecting him to be such a sexy devil. You should've warned me beforehand."

Smiling cleverly, Vanessa said, "Why? Then I would've had to warn you about all the Hollister brothers. They're all striking men in their own way."

Maggie sighed. "True. But there's something about Cord—well, he's not like his brothers."

"They're all different," Vanessa agreed. "That's something I learned right off."

Different. Oh yes, Cordell was that and so much more. "Cord's brothers are all gentlemen. But he's—"

Vanessa's eyes narrowed. "Did he insult you, or something?"

No. Worse than that, Maggie thought. He'd put some sort of crazy spell on her and she wasn't sure she was over it yet.

Moving away from Vanessa's desk, Maggie ambled aimlessly back over to the window. "No. He was polite. But he was an incessant flirt."

Vanessa's laugh pulled Maggie's gaze away from the view of Snow Mountain and back to her friend.

"What's so funny?"

Vanessa continued to chuckle. "I didn't know it was a crime for a man to flirt with a woman."

Unable to hide her annoyance, Maggie said, "I didn't call him a criminal."

"But you think he is. Because he rubbed you the wrong way. Right?"

Maggie scowled at her. "He didn't rub me *any* way."

"Maybe you would've enjoyed him more if he had," Vanessa suggested with an impish grin.

Maggie let out a rueful groan. "Okay, I'll admit it. Cord rattled me—because I wasn't expecting to be attracted to him. But I was. And that makes me feel darned stupid."

"Oh Maggie, why feel stupid for reacting like a normal woman?" Vanessa asked with gentle reproach.

Maggie darted her friend a hopeless glance. "I suppose I don't like being one of a crowd. I know his kind, Van. That's why it was silly of me to be drawn to him."

Frowning thoughtfully, Vanessa said, "You're being hard on yourself for no reason. And I think you're being a bit hard on Cord, too. Yes, he's dated plenty of women and yes, he's a flirt. But deep down he'd give the shirt off his back to a friend in need. And like Jack, he's devoted to his family and this ranch. So he does have some good qualities."

Maggie gave her friend a lopsided smile. "I'm sure he does. I like to think we all do."

Smiling happily, Vanessa stood and joined her at the window. "Good. Now that we have that out of the way, let's drive over to the house site. It's really cold today, but the carpenters are working inside now and they'll have a few space heaters going. We shouldn't freeze while I'm showing you around."

"Don't worry about me getting cold. I bought all kinds of warm outerwear for this trip. And these next few days will probably be the only chance I'll ever get to use them."

Besides, if she started to shiver from the cold, Maggie thought, she'd only have to think about Cordell and her whole body would light up like a burning match to a gas-soaked log.

Chapter Three

That night, Cordell was late getting to the dinner table and when he stepped into the dining room he expected to find Maggie already flanked by Quint and Flint. But he'd only guessed half-right. Quint was seated on Maggie's left; however, the chair to her right was empty.

Now who'd been kind enough to leave a chair for him right next to the pretty nurse? Vanessa? His mother or sisters? It had to be one of the women in his family. His brothers wouldn't be so thoughtful.

"There you are, Cord. We were just about to start dinner without you," Hadley spoke up from his seat at the head of the table.

"Sorry I'm late, everyone," Cordell said, his gaze

encompassing the whole group. "Some last-minute chores at the barn delayed me."

Quint gave him a smug smile. "No problem, Cord. I saved you a chair by Maggie."

Surprised at his younger brother's unselfish gesture, he patted the back of Quint's shoulder, before taking his seat at the long dining table. Next to him, Maggie darted a quick glance in his direction, then turned her attention elsewhere.

"Quint is in a generous mood tonight," Jack said. "Dad just announced to everyone that he's made our younger brother the manager of the sheep division."

"Is that why we're having wine with our dinner?" Cordell asked. "Or are we honoring our guest tonight?"

As soon as Cordell had walked up to the table, he'd noticed his mother had brought out her best dishes, along with the wine she only served for special occasions.

Claire answered happily, "Both reasons, Cord. We have plenty to celebrate."

"I agree," Cordell replied. "Maggie has definitely brightened up the place. And even though Quint might be the loudest complainer around here, we all know how hard he works."

Everyone at the table clapped enthusiastically, then Hadley lifted his wineglass.

"I think they both deserve a toast." He gestured toward Maggie first. "Maggie, it's a delight to have you in our home. And Quint, here's to you and your sheep," he added with a proud smile. "We know you'll do a good job, son."

"Of course he will," Claire declared as she smiled proudly at Quint. "Grandfather Lionel would be very proud of you. I only wish he was here to see the ranch and all that his family has become."

"I'll second that toast," Hadley said.

After everyone had drunk from their glasses, Cordell glanced to his left to see Quint appeared to be somewhat embarrassed by all the positive attention. As for Maggie, she was giving his youngest brother a smile that would melt the snow on the peaks of Snow Mountain.

Too bad she didn't feel the urge to look at him in the same manner. Not that Cordell was wanting a romantic fling with the woman. Especially since he was trying to stay on a non-dating diet after his recent messy breakup. But that hardly meant a little flirtation would hurt anything.

Quint said, "Thanks, everyone. I'll try not to let the ranch down."

"I chose you for this job, Quint, because I have faith in you," Hadley told him. "I'm not worried about you letting me or anyone down."

A few more congratulatory comments were aimed at Quint before the conversation finally turned to other topics. While the weather and a few bits of local news were discussed, Cordell was thinking how easy it had always been for him to talk with women. He'd never had to strain to think of anything to say or even how to say it. But with Maggie sitting quietly by his side, he felt oddly at a loss for words.

He was wondering if he was coming down with a fever or something, when Maggie's voice broke into his deep thoughts.

"I'm surprised at our dinner," she said.

Realizing she was speaking to him, he looked at her blankly. "Surprised, why? You don't like trout?"

"I love it. But coming to a big ranch like Stone Creek, I expected we'd be eating beef."

Shaking away his mental cobwebs, he said, "Mom likes to mix things up. And we have a friend that keeps us supplied with trout. But I'm sure you'll see plenty of our beef on the dinner table before you go home. What you won't see is the lamb. We don't raise the sheep for food purposes. Mom makes sure of that."

Her fork paused halfway to her mouth as she cast him a curious look. "Really? Then I assume you must sell the wool. Otherwise, there wouldn't be any point of having them. Unless you just like having sheep on the ranch for the fun of it."

Her last comment put a grin on his face. "If you ask Quint he'll tell you that he considers them fun. But yes, we sell the wool. Spring is shearing time. Right now their coats are growing long and thick."

She nodded. "I do know enough about animals to know their fur and hair gets thicker and longer in winter. But I'm curious about your remark concerning Claire. I take it she has a say in what goes on with the sheep?"

"Only in one aspect. She made Dad promise never to sell them for slaughter. And he holds fast with that promise. Actually, sheep have always been a part of Stone Creek Ranch. Our grandfather Lionel first purchased this land and started the ranch back in 1962. And it began with a herd of sheep."

She turned slightly toward him and he could see the history of the ranch and his family had caught her attention. Which was somewhat surprising. Up until now, none of his short conversations with her had appeared to leave much of an impression.

"So compared to Three Rivers, Stone Creek is basically a young ranch."

Cordell swallowed a piece of trout before he replied, "Compared to that ranch, we're a baby. Jack says Three Rivers originated in 1847—when the area was just a wild territory."

She nodded as she reached for her wine and Cordell wondered if the alcohol had loosened her tongue somewhat. Or had she turned her attention to him because Quint was busy talking with Jack and their father? No matter the reason, he told himself. At least she wasn't turning a cold shoulder toward him.

"Hmm. Sheep and tea roses," she said thoughtfully. "Your grandfather must have been a unique man. How long has it been since he passed away?"

"About eleven years. He passed away suddenly

from a stroke at the age of seventy. I was only twenty-one at the time."

"I'm sure his death left an empty space for all of you," she said.

"Empty, yes. He was a big, strong man like Dad, but there was also a refined side to him. He didn't talk much, but whenever he did speak, he expected you to listen. He also expected his granddaughters to behave like ladies and his grandsons to be gentlemen. We made sure we were on our best behavior around him. As for being unique, I'll say he wasn't typical by any means."

She didn't reply. Instead, she turned her focus back to the food on her plate and Cordell got the feeling her thoughts had moved to something personal. And suddenly he was wondering about her own family. Was she close to her parents and siblings? Had she ever had a special guy in her life? Maybe she had one now and was anxious to get back to him. The notion bothered him more than he cared to admit.

Hell, Cord, what does that matter? She's just a temporary guest of the family. At the most, a friend to you.

He was slicing into a roasted potato wedge when she suddenly tossed him a vague little smile. "No doubt, you're all proud of the ranch and the heritage Lionel left behind."

Her eyes were unlike any he'd ever seen. The emerald color was so limpid, each time he gazed at her he felt as though he was falling endlessly into their depths. And even though the sensation was a bit unsettling, he didn't want her to look away.

"We're grateful to him for envisioning this ranch and having the guts to follow his dreams." He glanced at her. "You mentioned the roses and the sheep. He insisted those two things always remain on the ranch. Actually, there was a stipulation in Grandfather's will that stated Dad must always keep a herd of sheep present."

"Obviously he was fond of sheep and roses. But I say everybody deserves their own likes. Don't you?"

"Sure. That's what makes things interesting."

She gave him a faint smile and then Beatrice called to her from across the table. After that, her attention remained on the twins and the questions they were throwing at her.

Cordell forced himself to focus on the food on his plate, but all the while he continued to study her from the corner of his eye.

She smelled like a heavenly flower and each little movement of her body caused the golden red hair lying against her back to ripple like a swathe of silk. Everything about her, from her creamy smooth skin to her soft husky voice, captivated him.

Everybody deserves their own likes.

Yeah, Cordell definitely liked what he saw. But she'd only be around for a few days. He'd be foolhardy to pursue her. But when it came to women, he'd never been accused of using good sense. Why should he start playing it safe now?

After dinner, the twins served coffee and dessert in the den where Hadley had built a roaring fire in the fireplace.

Afraid Cordell might cozy up to her if she sat on one of the two couches in the room, she chose to sit in a leather armchair situated a few feet from the fireplace.

Was she being wise? Or behaving like a coward? Vanessa would say the latter. But her friend was safely married to a wonderful man. She didn't have to wonder or worry about falling for a rascal.

Besides, she was still shaken by the experience of sitting next to Cordell throughout the evening meal. Never in her life had she felt such a deep and sudden attraction to any man. The reaction was crazy and frightening and it made a part of her wish she'd never made this trip to Stone Creek Ranch.

"The best thing about our winter weather is the fires that Dad builds in the evenings. Especially when you've been working out in the cold all day and your bones feel like they're never going to thaw."

Cordell's voice jerked Maggie out of her swirling thoughts and she looked up to see he was standing a few steps away from her chair. Both hands were stretched toward the crackling flames.

Worn faded jeans hugged his muscular thighs,

while a black Western shirt, washed so many times it was very nearly gray, stretched across the broad width of his chest and shoulders. The color flattered his dark blond hair, but then just about anything would look good on him, she decided.

She swallowed, then forced herself to speak. "The fire does feel nice. We do have cool weather in Wickenburg during the winter months, but my house doesn't have a fireplace. And the only time I've seen snow was on a trip to Flagstaff. This is an experience for me."

"Are you enjoying your stay—so far?"

No, I'm too busy thinking about you to enjoy anything, she could've told him. Instead, she gave him a wan smile. "Your parents are wonderful hosts and it's nice to be away from the hospital—just to see something other than patients and doctors."

"Did you get to see Jack and Van's new house today?"

"I did. The spot they picked is beautiful."

"There's only one shade tree around, but it's upwind from the cattle barn."

"Why does being upwind from the barn matter?"

His short laugh was far from an expression of humor. "Dust. Bawling cows and calves at weaning time. Have you noticed the old barn that sits north of this house?"

Earlier this afternoon, Maggie had gone outside for some fresh air and to the area around the house. As she'd strolled around the back yard, she'd noticed the barn and wondered why there was no livestock or human activity around the building.

"Actually, I did notice the barn. I'm guessing it's been there for many years."

He nodded. "It was the ranch's original cattle barn. Now, we only use it for storage and to occasionally stable our horses."

The smirk on his face told her there had to be more to the story of the old barn.

"I guess with the ranch growing you needed a larger building?" she asked.

"Yes, later on. But in the beginning the barn was exactly what Grandfather needed. Until his wife started putting up a huge fuss. She didn't like being close to the livestock or the dust, or anything else that went with it. So to please her, Grandfather built another barn over the hill and out of sight of the house."

Confused, she frowned at him. "His wife? Are you talking about your grandmother?"

The sneer on his face deepened and in spite of all the promises Maggie had made to herself to keep her distance from this man, she felt herself drawn, not only to him, but everything about his life.

"Yes. Although, no one in the family refers to her in that way. Actually, I've never heard Dad refer to the woman as his mother. To be honest, he rarely ever makes a comment about her."

This was a surprise. "I had no idea. When we were talking about your grandfather during dinner,

I wondered about her. Mostly because you didn't mention her. Is she still living?"

He shrugged. "We don't know. She left years and years ago, when Dad and his two brothers were only small boys. After that, Grandfather didn't keep in touch with her. And she never cared if she saw her boys again. So that pretty much tells you what kind of woman she was."

Dismayed, Maggie shook her head. "Obviously something didn't work with them. I mean, to leave three sons behind and never return. That's cold."

He looked into the fire and as Maggie's gaze took in his solemn profile, she realized she was seeing a different man than the playful, sexy flirt she'd danced with last night.

"I couldn't really say what happened between my grandparents. I doubt that Dad even knows what caused the split between them. One thing was clear, she hadn't liked ranching life. As for what else she didn't like—well, Grandfather kept things to himself. Especially about her and his younger years. In any case, none of us ever heard him mention Scarlett."

"Scarlett was her name? Oh dear, I hope she wasn't a redhead."

The words popped out of her before she had time to think and he looked at her and immediately began to laugh.

"No, I think Scarlett had dark hair," he said, then

still grinning, added, "Even if her hair had been red, I wouldn't hold it against you."

"That's a relief. We redheads often get a bad rap. Hot-tempered, wild natured—that sort of thing. I've even had patients worry I might get mad and jab them with a needle."

"You're kidding, aren't you?" he asked.

"No, I'm serious," she answered. "I've had some weird reactions from patients about my hair. Thankfully, most of them are funny."

"Well, your hair is very pretty, Maggie. Don't ever let anyone tell you different."

His compliment hadn't been said in a flirtatious tone, nor had he looked at her in a provocative way. He'd been sincere and somehow that was even harder for her to deal with than his blatant flirting.

"Thank you." The two words were all she could manage to say and thankfully he didn't appear to expect anything else from her.

Instead, he turned his back to the fire and his head slightly away from her and Maggie used the unguarded moment to slide her gaze from his head all the way down to his black cowboy boots. He had the hard, lean body of a man who spent hours in the saddle, plus working outside in the harsh elements. Odd, how much stronger he looked than the men she knew who regularly pumped iron at the gym.

"During dinner, I heard Quint talking about the long ride the two of you made through the snow today. How miserable was that?"

One brow was cocked upward as he looked at her and Maggie could only think he considered her question ridiculous.

"It wasn't miserable. Anytime we can make living conditions better for the livestock, it's all good."

"I wasn't questioning the purpose of the ride," she told him. "Merely the bad weather conditions."

"Sorry if you thought I was being sharp with you, Maggie. That wasn't my intention. I only want people to understand that ranchers don't think of their jobs as a hardship. We do the tough, nasty and exhausting things that go with ranching because we love it." He grinned at her. "Don't worry, Quint did his fair share of complaining. He thought he was freezing until I told him he was being promoted to head shepherd. After that, he didn't even know it was snowing."

"Being acknowledged makes a big difference, you know?"

Across the small space between them, his gaze locked with hers and the connection was as jolting as a sudden, unexpected clap of thunder.

"Yeah. I know."

She was wondering what was going through his mind, when Bonnie walked up and gestured to the dessert dish and coffee cup Maggie had placed on an end table.

"Would you like more bread pudding or coffee, Maggie? I'll be glad to get it for you."

She smiled gratefully at Bonnie. "Thanks, but I'm about to pop."

"Then I'll take your dishes to the kitchen," she offered. "Bea's in there doing the cleaning up tonight."

"Is that why she's pouting?" Cordell asked his sister. "Because she's cleaning up the dinner mess?"

Bonnie rolled her eyes. "No. She's sulking because the weather caused her to miss driving into town to meet Jeremy for a date. And to hear her tell it, a girl missing a date is comparable to the sky falling in."

Maggie rose to her feet. "I should go to the kitchen. Maybe I can lift Beatrice's spirits."

Shaking her head, Bonnie promptly gathered Maggie's dishes. "No way. You stay here and visit with Cord. I'm going to go make Bea angry at me. That always makes her forget her troubles."

Watching Bonnie leave the den, Cordell shook his head. "Twins. I'll never understand how their minds work. But one thing I do know, Bonnie has definitely come out of her shell since Van has come into the family. Before, she was quiet and mostly stayed in her room. Now it's like she's bloomed."

Maggie joined him on the rock hearth, but was careful to keep a respectable distance between them.

"Vanessa is a teacher at heart," she said. "She knows how to draw a person from his or her shell."

His gaze traveled across the room to where Jack

had Vanessa cuddled close to his side. The pair were truly made for each other, yet Maggie doubted Cordell could see their genuine love. She got the feeling he was more focused on the failed marriages in his family.

"Yes. I suppose Jack did need a bit of drawing out, too," he said.

And what about you, Cord? What do you need? The questions were too loaded to ask.

"I noticed Hunter wasn't here for dinner tonight," she commented. "Has he already hit the road again with his rodeo company?"

He slanted her a sly look. "Missing my older brother, are you?"

Maggie frowned. "If Hunter had shown up tonight, I'm sure I would've enjoyed chatting with him," she said primly. "But since the rest of your siblings are here, I was merely curious about his absence."

He grinned at her. "You sure get your dander riled easily."

She pressed her lips tightly together. She should've known the serious side he'd shown only a minute or two ago wouldn't last long. But then, did she really want him to be somber all the time? No. Taking the playfulness out of Cordell would be like taking the sun from the sky.

"It's my red hair, remember?"

His soft laugh skittered down her spine like a ticklish finger.

"Yeah. I remember. I'm glad I'm not lying on a gurney in the ER. You might do something—painful to me."

She could think of several things she'd like to do to him, but none of them involved pain.

Turning toward the fire, she stared into the flames and tried to push the erotic thoughts from her mind.

"Count yourself lucky," she said.

He chuckled again, louder this time, and she could only think how very long it had been since she'd been around a man who joked and laughed. And sadly, she hadn't even realized it until now.

"You're a very funny girl, Maggie. Has anyone ever told you that?"

"Not that I can recall." She'd been labeled as too serious, prim and proper, and even frigid, she thought ruefully. But never funny. Did this man see things about her that others didn't? The idea was unsettling.

"That's too bad," he said. "Laughing is good for the soul."

She glanced at him just long enough to see amusement sparkling in his blue eyes before she turned her gaze back to the burning logs.

"Then yours must be thriving," she replied.

"I like to think so."

It was way past time she excused herself and crossed the room to mingle with the rest of the family. So why couldn't she make a move to leave Cordell's side?

She was asking herself the simple question when she noticed his hand diving into the front pocket of his jeans.

"A man can't even have a Sunday night to himself," he mumbled to himself as he pulled out a smartphone. After giving the screen a quick scan, he cast a glance in her direction. "Excuse me, Maggie. I need to return this call."

"Certainly," she said.

He walked off and as Maggie watched him depart the den, she tried not to guess whether the call had been from a girlfriend. Cordell's private life was none of her business. Still, now that he was gone from the room, the fire didn't feel quite so warm.

You're getting in trouble, Maggie. You've only been here twenty-four hours and you're already letting Cordell get a stranglehold on your senses. Wake up! Your life is back in Arizona. Besides, you don't have the courage to fall into bed with a hunky cowboy.

Releasing a long, weary breath, she turned back to the fire and was trying to push the taunting voice from her head, when Vanessa walked up and joined her on the hearth.

"You must be feeling the cold," she commented. "You've been here by the fireplace ever since we came into the den."

She gave her friend a halfhearted smile. "I'm not cold at all. I'm enjoying toasting myself. Once I go home, I'll have to settle for central heat. Standing over a vent in the floor just isn't the same."

"Let's not talk about you going home. You have a few days left before you head back to Arizona and I still have so much to show you—the school where I'll be teaching and Grace's clinic, plus, the boutique where Bea works. Oh, and I can't forget the Wagon Spoke Café. It's kind of like a coffee shop and grill combined."

Maggie smiled at her friend's enthusiasm. "Sounds like you're going to keep me busy. And speaking of work, you were very lucky to be hired midterm."

"The opening for a history teacher was very unexpected, so to say the least, I was thrilled to get the job."

"I'm not sure I'd be looking forward to such a daily commute. The road between here and Beaver is long and mostly dirt. It took me forever to drive out here." And thanks to Hadley, she didn't have to drive her rental car back into Beaver. He'd instructed one of the ranch hands to return the car to the agency for her.

"I'm not dreading it," Vanessa said. "The scenery between here and there is beautiful. And since Bea works in Beaver on weekdays, we'll be making the drive together."

"She's been telling me all about the boutique where she works. It sounds like a fun place to shop."

Vanessa chuckled knowingly. "Loads of fun. So tomorrow when we go to town, you might as well get ready to charge up your credit card. You're going to find all sorts of things you can't live without."

Maggie could only hope that getting off the ranch for a while would free her mind of Cordell. So far, since he'd left the den, she'd been darting glances at the door and wondering if he might return. Could she possibly get any sillier?

"I'm hoping the snow won't force us to stay home tomorrow," she told Vanessa.

Vanessa waved away her concerns. "Not a chance. The sky is already clearing tonight and the weather is supposed to be much warmer. It'll be a great day to get out."

Maggie's attention was drawn once again to the opposite end of the den where Jack and Quint appeared to be keeping their parents locked in conversation. Everyone else had left the room, including Flint, whom she understood had late shift duty as a county deputy sheriff.

"I asked Cordell earlier why Hunter wasn't here tonight. But he didn't give me a straight answer. Has Hunter already hit the road again? Or does he usually keep to himself whenever he's home?"

She shook her head. "He comes around quite frequently while he's here on the ranch. I believe

Hunter will be leaving for northern California tomorrow, so I'm sure he and his crew are busy getting the livestock and everything ready to go."

"Isn't it rather cold for the spectators to sit outdoors?"

Vanessa answered, "At this time of the year, the rodeos are dwindling down to a few indoor venues. He makes all of those he can. He's in a very competitive business so he grabs a contract whenever he can."

"Hmm. So basically everyone in the Hollister family works at some type of job or career," Maggie said thoughtfully. "Reminds me of another Hollister family I know."

Vanessa nodded. "True. There are no hangers-on in either family," she said, then slanted a clever smile at Maggie. "I noticed you and Cord were chatting earlier. I'm glad you're giving him a chance."

Maggie frowned. "A chance? For what?"

Rolling her eyes, Vanessa said, "For the two of you to get to know each other and become friends, of course."

Was it possible for any woman to be just a friend to Cordell? Surely, it was, Maggie thought. After all, he couldn't view every woman as a romantic target.

She said, "I don't know why. I'm only going to be here for a few more days."

Vanessa let out an impatient sigh. "Maggie,

sometimes you act as though you're fifty-six instead of twenty-six."

Maggie grimaced. "I had to grow up fast, Van. You know that better than anyone."

Vanessa nodded. "When we were little girls, I remember how we had to play outside so we didn't disturb your uncle."

"He was and still is a creep. And my aunt—well, Mom didn't know what sort of mean-spirited woman her sister really was. Thank God, she didn't know. Otherwise, she would've died worrying about me."

Vanessa said, "Well, I think those tough years made you a stronger person. If anything, you can be grateful for that."

"Yes, those years made me tough."

She gazed across the room to where Quint was deep in conversation with Hadley. The young cowboy was exactly her age and from what she could see, he was turning into a responsible man. Yet there was a lightheartedness about him that was missing in Maggie.

"I don't know, Van. Somewhere along the way, I forgot how to be warm and giving and loving. After a few dates, men discover I'm—lacking in that department."

Vanessa groaned with disbelief. "What a ridiculous self-assessment. You're a nurse, for Pete's sake. Nurses are the epitome of caring and giving."

"Yes, when it comes to patients in need. But the

giving is different when it's between a man and a woman." She slanted Vanessa a wry glance. "Anyway, I came up here to spend time with you. Not strike up a friendship or romance with a man."

Chuckling, Vanessa shot her an impish grin. "Maybe you could do a little multitasking?"

Much later, Maggie was about to enter her bedroom to retire for the night, when she heard footsteps behind her and then a male voice called her name.

Turning slightly, she spotted Cordell walking toward her and her heart thudded hard and fast as she stood and waited for him to reach her.

"I thought everyone had already gone to bed," she said when he was finally standing in front of her. "Where did you come from?"

A nearby footlight was enough for Maggie to see a sexy grin on his face.

"Over at Hunter's house. He wanted to see me before he left for California tomorrow."

"Oh." So the call that had caused him to leave the den had most likely been from his brother, she thought. And all along her brain had been working overtime, imagining him having an intimate conversation with a girlfriend.

He said, "Hunter told me to tell you goodbye and maybe he'd see you again sometime."

Feeling suddenly light-headed, Maggie reminded herself to breathe.

"I appreciate him thinking of me," she said. "But I imagine it will be a long while before I come up this way again."

His gaze caught hers and Maggie found herself wondering what would happen if she took a step forward. How would he react if she placed her palms against his chest and angled her lips up to his? If he backed away from her, it would be terribly embarrassing.

"I'm sorry to hear you're not planning to come back to Stone Creek anytime soon. Van will miss you."

"With her parents living in Phoenix, I'll see her when she travels down to visit them."

His lips twisted. "Yes, but that leaves out the rest of us. Don't we count?"

The more he spoke, the lower his voice grew and the husky sound of it was causing goose bumps to break out over her forearms.

"Don't tell me you'll miss me when I'm gone," she said wryly.

"Why not? I will—miss you."

Her groan was full of misgivings. "Cord, you are so full of it."

A tiny frown pulled his brows together. "You don't believe me. Why?"

"Because—I think you'd say most anything to a woman just to make her like you."

His head moved slightly from side to side. "I

don't need to make you like me. We both know that you already do."

He smelled like the wind outside and somewhere between the ground floor and here, he'd left his hat. Now his dark blond hair fell in a thick hank near his right eye and waved over the back of his collar. The urge to touch him was so strong she could practically taste it.

She swallowed as heightened nerves tightened her throat. "Have you always been so sure of yourself?"

A dimple carved a deep groove in his right cheek. "I'm not as cocky as you think I am. It's just that I have a habit of speaking the truth. People mistake that for being cocky."

She breathed deeply and tried to pull her gaze from his, but her eyes refused to cooperate. "Maybe people get the cocky impression from the *way* you speak the truth."

He chuckled softly. "There you go again. Being funny without even trying. That's one of the things I'll miss once you've gone—this ability you have to make me laugh."

"I'm sure you'll find some other comic relief to take my place," she said dryly. "And now I'm going to say good-night. It's getting late and I am rather tired."

She turned to reach for the knob on the bedroom door, but his hand quickly wrapped over her forearm. The contact was like a band of hot iron shooting heat all the way up to her shoulder.

"Wait, Maggie."

Twisting her head around, she arched a questioning brow at him. "You wanted to say something else?"

He nodded. "I thought it would be nice if you'd let me take you to dinner before you leave. There are several nice places to eat in Beaver and I promise the food is great."

Maggie had already decided her heart couldn't beat any faster, but somehow it managed to shift into a higher gear. "Are you asking me on a date?"

The little half grin on his face was so tempting she very nearly groaned out loud.

He said, "If you want to think of it that way."

She drew in another deep breath. "Thank you, Cord. But no. I'm not interested in dating right now. Not with you—or any man."

His grin softened to a wan smile. "Neither am I. I haven't been on a date in—a good while. But I like you. And you like me. So I thought dinner together wouldn't hurt anything."

She had to say no. She couldn't trust herself with him. Even if he wasn't planning a secluded, romantic dinner, it would feel like one to her. Which meant she had to turn down his invitation.

"I'm sorry. I wouldn't feel comfortable," she told him, even as a wave of disappointment washed over her.

He shrugged as though he wasn't the least bit cut up over her negative reply. "I expected you to say something along those lines. So I have another suggestion—and hopefully you'll think this one is innocent enough. Let me show you around the ranch. Do you know how to ride a horse?"

His sudden switch in gears caught her completely off guard and for a moment she struggled to get her mind off the provocative invitation to dinner and onto riding a horse. A dinner date with Cordell would be far too romantic for her to handle. But riding around the ranch on horseback—well, what could it possibly hurt?

Long, pregnant seconds ticked by before she finally answered, "Why, yes. I used to ride on Three Rivers Ranch with my friend."

"Great. We'll ride to some of the prettier spots on the ranch. The sheep and cattle are all down from the mountains now, so you'll be able to see some of the livestock. Or does the outing sound boring to you?"

If she was smart, she'd play it safe and give him another no-thanks. But in spite of the warning bells going off in the back of her head, Maggie couldn't deny she wanted to spend time with him. "It doesn't sound boring at all. I would love to see more of the ranch. But I'm afraid I can't go tomorrow. Van and I and Bonnie are going into Beaver for most of the day."

His smile grew wide. "No problem. Tomorrow, Quint and I have a few chores that will keep us tied up for most of the day. So the day after will be even better for me."

"I'm glad that works for the both of us," she told him. "Just let me know what time I need to be ready."

His hand slid down her forearm until he reached her hand and then his fingers gently laced through hers. The contact was warm and intimate and she could only think how sweet it would be to press the front of her body to his, to feel the hard warmth of him against her.

"You've made me happy, Maggie."

"You should probably wait until after the ride before you say that," she said impishly, then before she could stop herself, she stood on the tips of her toes and pressed a kiss to his cheek. "Good night."

His hands framed her face as he brushed his lips against her forehead. "Good night, Maggie."

Slipping away from his hold, she hurriedly turned and entered the bedroom. Yet by the time she'd fastened the door behind her, she was literally shaking from his touch.

You're a coward, Maggie. If you were a real woman, you would've yanked him into your arms. You would've led him into the dark shadows of this room and showed him exactly how you wanted him. So what if your time with him would only be temporary. At least, you'd have an incredible memory to keep you company on your lonely nights back in Wickenburg.

Walking over to the bed, she sat on the side of the mattress and shoved mightily at the taunting voice in her head. She had no doubts that making red-hot memories with Cordell would be an incredible experience. But she wanted to get back to Arizona with her heart. Not leave it here with Cordell.

Chapter Four

Except for a few clouds scudding along to momentarily pass over the bright sun, the next morning as Vanessa drove Maggie and Bonnie to Beaver, the day was already showing signs of warming and melting the layer of snow on the ground.

"Montana is known for being big-sky country," Maggie said as she gazed out at the sweeping valleys outlined by tall mountain ridges. "But the vastness of this land goes on forever."

"Look to your left, Maggie," Bonnie said from the back seat. "There's a herd of mule deer grazing at the bottom of the foothill."

Maggie quickly directed her gaze past Vanessa to get a glimpse of the wildlife.

"So beautiful," she murmured. "I'm glad to see

the snow is nearly gone and the deer are finding something to eat."

"Don't worry," Bonnie spoke up. "When the weather gets really bad, most of the ranchers throw out extra hay for the deer and antelope."

Vanessa said, "Jack jokes that in the winter season we feed as many antelope as we do cattle."

I imagine it will be a long while before I ever come up this way again.

Maggie had said those words to Cordell last night, mainly as a way to assure him, and herself, that the two of them had no chance of ever being more than friendly acquaintances. And yet now, when she thought about returning to Arizona, she realized how very much she was going to miss the Hollister family and Stone Creek Ranch. But most of all, she was going to miss Cordell.

A few more miles passed and the outskirts of town appeared on the distant horizon.

"We're almost there," Vanessa said. "Where do you two want to go first?"

Maggie glanced over her shoulder at Bonnie, who looked extra-fetching this morning in a brown sweater with a faux fur collar and a sparkly headband to hold back her long blond hair.

"You choose, Bonnie."

Bonnie thoughtfully tilted her head to one side. "First the clinic and school. Because once we get to the boutique, we'll be there for ages."

"Agreed," Vanessa said. "And after the boutique we'll go to the Wagon Spoke Café for lunch."

When Maggie had hurriedly driven through Beaver on her way to Stone Creek Ranch, she'd not really had a chance to notice much about the little town. Now she could see the quaint little settlement with brick-and-mortar buildings had obviously been built many years ago. As Vanessa drove them down the main thoroughfare, Maggie was charmed by the storefronts with awnings over the windows and sidewalks lined with small shade trees.

"This is all so pretty and picturesque. It makes me feel like I've stepped back in time."

Vanessa said, "Speaking of stepping back in time. I got some news this morning in the mail. So far I've only told Jack. And he agreed to keep it to himself until this evening. We didn't want to spoil Hadley and Claire's day."

Scooting to the edge of the seat, Bonnie stuck her head between the two women. "Spoil their day? Is it bad news?"

Vanessa absently bit down on her bottom lip and Maggie could see she wasn't exactly joyous over the correspondence she'd received.

"I wouldn't necessarily call it bad. More like puzzling. It was a letter from the Utah Department of Vital Records. They're sorry to inform me, but they have no record matching Lionel Hollister. No information regarding his birth in the state of Utah."

Bonnie gasped. "That can't be true! Dad has said plenty of times that Grandfather was born here in

Utah. Supposedly somewhere in the valley area around Parowan! There has to be some sort of record!"

Seeing Bonnie's distress, Maggie tried to reassure her, "Perhaps his birth was never registered. In the late thirties when Lionel was apparently born, record keeping was done by hand and typewriter. And two or three years late, WWII hit and government clerks were working overtime. The information could've been misplaced."

Vanessa nodded. "Maggie is right. We're not going to start wringing our hands now. We'll just figure out some other way to get the information we need."

Bonnie was quiet as they traveled on down the street toward the school, but then all of a sudden, she asked in a worrisome tone, "What if he lied?"

"He? Who do you mean?" Maggie asked.

Vanessa added another question, "What are you talking about, Bonnie?"

"I'm talking about Grandfather. Could be that he lied about where he was born. Because he didn't want anyone to follow his past."

"Hmm. Anything is possible," Vanessa said. "But I don't see the motive or reason. Why lie about his birthplace?"

After a moment's thought, Maggie suggested, "Because he was in trouble with the law and didn't want to be traced?"

Vanessa laughed. "Oh, Maggie, I think you've missed your calling. Instead of nursing in the ER you should be home writing mystery novels."

Maggie made a palms-up gesture. "Okay, so my theory might sound like a bad movie plot. But there has to be some explanation for the man's missing birth records."

"Hadley might have some ideas on the subject. Right now, we're going to forget the matter," Vanessa announced as she steered the truck into a large parking area and braked to a halt in front of a sprawling redbrick building trimmed in forest green. The US flag, along with the Utah State flag, was flying high on the front lawn, which was landscaped with several tall fir trees and small boulders lining the sidewalk leading up to the entrance.

Maggie gazed out the windshield. "This must be Mountain View High School."

"Right," Vanessa said proudly. "The superintendent gave me a tour of the place the day I signed my contract. My classroom will be located at the very end of the west wing. The auditorium is over on the east side of the building and the cafeteria is at the back. There's also a pretty campus behind the building. The football stadium, basketball gymnasium and baseball field are on the next street over from this one. If school wasn't going on, I'd take you inside and show you around."

"Seeing the outside is enough," Maggie told her. "Now when I think of you at work, I can picture you in this building. It very pretty, Van. Is the superintendent anything like Prudence?"

Vanessa let out a good-natured groan. "No one

could match up to Prudence. But Mr. Simmons and the rest of the staff are very nice. Hopefully, I'll fit in with everyone."

"Van, even the meanest person in the world would love you," Bonnie spoke up.

Vanessa chuckled, "Bonnie, I think you're a bit biased."

Back on the main street, Vanessa drove to the middle of town, then turned down a side street. After about three blocks, she pulled to a stop in front of an older-type house built in a shotgun style with lapped board siding painted a pristine white. A small covered porch shielded the glass door entrance, while black-and-white-striped awnings shaded the windows located on either side of the door. A sign hanging from a post in the tiny front yard read Pine Valley Clinic—Grace Hollister, MD.

"Would you like to go in? I don't imagine Grace would mind."

Maggie glanced at the small graveled parking lot located to the left side of the building. With the spaces all filled with vehicles, it was easy to see the little clinic was extremely busy.

"From the looks of the parking lot she has her hands full without us barging in on her," Maggie said.

"Maybe we shouldn't go in," Bonnie said impishly. "She's always needing nurses. She might just put Maggie to work."

Vanessa tossed Maggie a suggestive smile. "Now

that's a fabulous idea! You could move up here and I'd have my friend close by."

Not fabulous, Maggie thought, *more like disastrous.* Even with nearly five hundred miles between here and Wickenburg, it was going to be hard enough for her to forget Cordell. Living here in Beaver would be too close for comfort. She'd never get the man out of her mind.

"Sorry. I couldn't leave Wickenburg or my job at the ER."

Bonnie let out a little wail of disappointment. "Oh, darn. I thought you liked it around here. You've been saying how beautiful it is."

Maggie looked over her shoulder at Bonnie. "I do like it up here. And it is beautiful. And it's very sweet of you to want me to stick around and be your neighbor. But this isn't my home. I'm sure you understand."

"Well, sure," she said with a halfhearted smile. "I was thinking about my feelings rather than yours. You probably have a special guy down in Arizona. One you don't want to give up. Right?"

Maggie stifled a groan. "No special guy. Just a few good friends who I work with."

"I can't imagine you without a steady guy," Bonnie said. "You're smart and beautiful."

"Thank you, Bonnie. But it takes more than those two things to get a really special guy," Maggie told her.

Vanessa pulled the gearshift into Drive and steered

the truck back onto the street. "Maggie has your mindset, Bonnie. She believes men find her unlovable."

Bonnie didn't reply for a long moment and then she said, "I'm going to make a major announcement, Van. I've quit thinking I'm a plain little mouse. I'm starting to believe that when the right man comes along, he'll find me very lovable. And the same will happen for Maggie."

"This is good news," Vanessa said proudly, then turned a clever look on Maggie. "You need to remember Bonnie's prediction about *the right man*."

Ignoring Vanessa's not-too-subtle hint, she said, "I won't be a bit surprised when I receive an invitation to Bonnie's wedding."

Bonnie giggled. "Will you come back to Utah for my wedding—if I ever have one?"

Maggie didn't hesitate. "I wouldn't miss it for anything."

By that time, Cordell would most likely be hooked up with a girlfriend and never give her a second glance. She wouldn't be tempted to throw herself into his arms. The thought should've eased her mind. Instead, it felt like a bank of cold, gray clouds had covered the sun.

Five minutes later, Vanessa crossed the main street in town, then drove down another side street until she found a parking space alongside the sidewalk.

Canyon Corral, the boutique where Beatrice

worked as a sales assistant, was located on the corner of the next block. The building was an old two-story with the front being covered with natural, wood-shingled siding. Two large plate glass windows filled with displays of women's clothing, footwear and jewelry bracketed the single wooden door entrance, which was protected from the weather by a short awning.

A bell tinkled as the three women made their way inside the store and Beatrice immediately left a table where she was arranging jewelry and hurried to meet them.

"Gosh, this is so nice to have all three of you here!" She gave her twin a swift kiss on the cheek. "Sis, I hope you're going to let loose while you're here and buy something wild and sexy."

Bonnie gave her sister a sly smile.

"I might just surprise you and buy something with fringe or animal print," Bonnie told her. "The holidays are coming up and I want to sparkle this year."

Comical disbelief swept over Beatrice's face. "Really, sissy? Are you serious?"

"Absolutely."

Beatrice grabbed her by the hand. "This is going to be fun!"

The sisters hurried away and Maggie took a moment to take in her surroundings. The long, narrow room had high ceilings open to wooden rafters, while the decorations and furnishings were a mix of bohemian and Western. Burning candles scented the store with juniper and somewhere near the checkout counter, a radio was quietly playing country music. The walls were lined with shelves of merchandise ranging from blue granite dishes, to purses and boots and colognes designed for the Western woman. In the middle of the floor, round racks were jammed with hanging dresses, blouses and skirts, while deeper into the room, more long, straight racks were completely devoted to jeans.

"This place reminds me of Cactus and Candles Boutique in Wickenburg," Maggie commented to Vanessa.

"Unfortunately." Vanessa let out a guilty chuckle. "I want to buy one of everything. The dresses are so cute! I think I'll splurge and get one. Like Bonnie said, the holidays are coming. Come on, let's both pick out a party dress."

Yes, the holidays would soon arrive. But Maggie would spend her Thanksgiving and Christmas working shifts for the nurses who wanted to celebrate with their families. Being in the ER certainly beat sitting home alone.

"A new dress would be a waste," Maggie told her. "I'll be pulling extra shifts. If I do end up going to a little get-together, I can find something already in my closet."

Rolling her eyes, Vanessa grabbed Maggie by the arm. "Talk about bah-humbug! Come on, girl.

When we leave here, you're going to have a stack of clothes and a party spirit!"

Later that evening, in an old work truck, Cordell was driving himself and Quint back to the ranch yard when they passed Hunter's rambling log house. Both men glanced thoughtfully at the home, which was situated on a hill that overlooked a small creek.

In the beginning, the area around the house had been barren of trees, but Hunter's wife had wasted no time planting a few aspens and cottonwoods in the front yard. Those happier days in Hunter's life had long passed, but the trees had continued to grow and were now large enough to provide shade. With the arrival of winter, the gold and brown leaves had fallen to create a carpet on the ground.

"The place looks kind of lonely while Hunter is gone," Quint commented.

Cordell unwittingly slowed the truck to a crawl as he gazed beyond the house to the barns and corrals Hunter used to house his rodeo livestock. Except for two palomino horses and three spotted bulls, the pens were presently empty.

"My same thoughts," Cordell replied. "He's better off traveling the rodeo circuit. He's too lonely here."

Quint frowned thoughtfully. "It's a fine house. But I guess the place does feel pretty empty to him."

Turning his gaze back to the dirt road, Cordell

pressed his foot on the accelerator. "I think the place is always lonely to Hunter," he said flatly.

Quint darted a curious glance at him. "You think he's unhappy living here?"

Cordell shrugged. "Who knows? He's a whole lot like Jack. He keeps his feelings to himself. The way I see things, the house is only a place for Hunter to eat and sleep and recuperate after rodeoing. It's not the home he first thought it would be."

"No. Guess not. He and Willow had plans to fill it with kids." Quint let out a low, mocking snort. "Poor guy. He should've known better than to put so much trust in a woman."

Cordell directed a frown at him. "Is that why you date so many of them? You're trying to figure out which one you can trust?" he asked wryly.

Quint shook his head. "Nope. I'm just following in your footsteps, brother. I don't need to trust any of them. All I want is temporary fun."

"Hmm. Hunter might agree with your philosophy, but Jack wouldn't," Cordell said matter-of-factly. "He's deliriously happy with Vanessa."

"Well, sure he is. Because Vanessa is different. But think about it, Cord. We're not fools. We both know women like her don't grow on trees. Guess Hunter knows it, too. He'll probably stay single the rest of his life. Like you."

Single for the rest of his life? Cordell hadn't set out to live his life as a bachelor. No, during his early twenties he'd believed he wanted to eventually settle down with one woman and have a big family like his parents. Hadley and Claire were a prime example of how love could endure through the best and worst of times. But after seeing Hunter crushed by his broken marriage and Grace's heart broken by a divorce, something inside Cordell had turned cold and wary.

"What about you?" Cordell asked. "Don't tell me you've erased marriage from your to-do list."

Quint tugged at the brim of his hat. "Heck, I'm only twenty-six, Cord. After I spread my wings for a while, I might consider getting myself a wife. But I know one thing for sure, Hunter would've been a damned sight better off if he'd wised up like you did."

Cord frowned. "What do you mean? Like I did?"

Quint wearily wiped both hands over his face. The day had been a long, busy one and both men were tired. But so far, Quint hadn't done any whining and Cordell was beginning to think his brother was finally maturing into a responsible rancher.

"I'm talking about when you called off the wedding to Lacey. It was the smartest thing you've ever done." He gave his head a rueful shake. "Yeah, I know you caught hell from just about everyone. But that's a damned sight better than you being miserable. And if Hunter had ended his engagement to Willow before tying the knot with her, he'd be a happier guy now."

"You think so?" Cordell asked, while his thoughts

involuntarily turned to Maggie. Last night she'd told
him she hadn't been dating. She'd further implied
that she wasn't interested in getting serious about a
man. Frankly, that was good news for him. He sure
as heck didn't want to get serious about her or any
woman. Yet the closer he got to her, the more he
wanted her and that scared him.

Quint groaned in disbelief. "You have to ask?
Apparently you haven't been noticing Hunter's behavior. I can't remember the last time I saw him
smile."

"Hunter has a lot on his mind. And you haven't
been looking. He does smile. He smiled plenty at
Maggie," Cordell added without thinking.

"Hmm. No surprise there. She makes me smile,
too," Quint said with a sheepish grin. "Maggie is
beautiful and smart. And she doesn't get on a man's
nerves with a bunch of silly chatter. She's a woman
a man might want to keep forever. Has that idea ever
crossed your mind?"

"Nope."

Quint shot him a disgusted look. "Would you
hurry up and get us to the barn? I'm afraid this truck
is going to be struck by lightning and I don't want
to become a victim of your lying."

Cordell let out an annoyed sigh. "Okay. I have
thought about Maggie and how she's the family
type. I mean, a woman is either that kind or she
isn't. That's not hard for a man to figure."

As the ranch yard appeared in the distance, Quint

began to pull on his coat. "Yeah. I don't think she's the have-an-affair kind, either. Not that it matters. She'll be leaving in three days. I heard Van telling Mom that much."

Three days wasn't long. He needed to make the most of the remainder of her stay, Cordell thought. And if he was lucky, he might be able to talk her into staying a few more days.

What good would that do, Cord? Maggie is the kind that wants a husband and children, not a few nights in bed with a womanizer. Spending more time with her isn't going to get you anything.

"So what are you going to do about it, Cord? Don't you think you ought to try to talk her into staying here?"

Quint's questions pushed away the annoying voice in Cordell's head and he glanced incredulously at his brother. "Talk her into staying here? Is that what I heard you say?"

Chuckling under his breath, Quint tugged the brim of his hat down on his forehead. "Yep. Not a hard question, Cord."

Driving into the ranch yard, Cordell braked the truck to a stop next to the black Ford truck their father drove. But instead of shutting off the engine, he rested his left arm on top of the steering wheel as he turned to face Quint.

"I don't exactly understand why you keep digging at me about Maggie. If you're trying to play matchmaker then you need to drop it. 'Cause you're irritating the hell out of me."

Quint stubbornly crossed his arms across his chest. "I don't want to see you mess up and miss your chance with her."

"My chance? For what? We both just agreed that she's not my kind."

"That's why you need to change *your* kind."

And pursue her as a real love interest? No. Cordell wasn't about to lead Maggie on and imply he wanted them to have a serious relationship, then push her aside. When it came to women, he might be a jerk, but he wasn't a total jackass.

"Look, Quint, I appreciate your concern for my happiness. But Maggie and I—well, I think you could say we've become friends. And she's agreed to go riding with me tomorrow. But there is nothing serious going to evolve between the two of us. Got it?"

Quint was dumbfounded. "You're going riding? Where?"

"Just around the ranch. So if you want to do something for me, just say a little prayer for the nice weather to hold through tomorrow."

"I'll pray for more than good weather," he said with obvious glee. "Way to go, Cord! How did you talk her into this, anyway?"

Normally, Cord would've given his brother a smug answer, but Maggie wasn't some prize to gloat over. Besides, one innocent outing with the woman was hardly anything to crow about.

"I honestly don't know, Quint. I think it was the mention of horses that did the trick. You know how women are about horses."

"Yeah. They're either scared to death of them or they have a fanatic love for the animals. Obviously Maggie must be the latter. Lucky you."

"Yeah. Lucky me," Cordell murmured as he shut off the engine and reached for his jacket. But as he and Quint left the truck and headed to the cattle barn, he wondered if spending a few hours of private time with Maggie was the right or smart thing to do.

She was a forever kind of gal and he was a temporary sort of guy. He'd be a fool to think he could ever fit them together.

So why did he want to try?

Chapter Five

Cordell and Quint were missing from the dinner table that night. Hadley had sent his sons out to round up several bulls that had broken through a fence bordering their northern neighbor.

Considering the area was a few miles from the ranch house, Maggie didn't expect the men to return home anytime soon. But she hoped to see Cordell before bedtime. If he still planned to take her riding tomorrow, she needed to find out when and where to meet him.

But by ten o'clock, she'd given up on his return, and after bidding those who were left in the den a good night, headed to her bedroom.

Halfway up the staircase, she heard rapidly approaching footsteps and glanced over her shoulder to see Cordell following her up the stairs.

Foolish or not, the sight of him filled her with joy and spread a wide smile across her face. "Hello," she said, "or should I say good night? You've had a long day."

Smiling wearily, he climbed one more step until he was standing at her side. "Underline the long. Sorry I missed having dinner with you and everyone. Are you retiring for the night?"

She nodded. "Yes. But I'm glad I ran into you. I wanted to speak with you about tomorrow and—"

Her words halted as he wrapped an arm against the back of her waist. "Sorry to interrupt you, Maggie. Let's go to my room and we can finish talking there. I'm dying get out of these wet boots and see if my feet will unthaw."

Maggie darted a wary glance at him, while trying to ignore the wonderful warmth radiating from the arm he had wrapped around her waist. "Do we have to go into your bedroom to talk? What if someone sees me go in there with you?"

He laughed. "Maggie, we're adults. My family knows I'm not going to try to seduce a guest in my bedroom."

Heat flared through Maggie's cheeks. "I wasn't thinking you had seduction on your mind. It's just that me going in there might look a little—improper."

He responded with an indulgent smile and she murmured, "I must seem pretty childish to you."

"No, Maggie. Just nice."

On the second floor they walked to the far end of the balcony, where Cordell opened the door to his bedroom and immediately flipped a wall switch and the table lamp near the head of his bed flickered on.

Gesturing for her to precede him into the room, he said, "I'm not a very tidy guy, but I did make the bed before I went out to work this morning. If you'd like to sit, there's a wing chair over by the window or the dressing bench at the end of the bed is fairly comfortable."

Feeling terribly awkward, but doing her best to hide it, she walked over and took a seat in the dark green chair. A short step away, the curtains on a pair of paned windows were fastened back to show a view of the old barn north of the house. Directly in front her was a queen-size four-poster bed covered with a brown-and-green comforter. Pillows were piled against the headboard, while a pair of blue jeans was draped over the footboard.

"Quint and I ended up having to get off our horses and wade a creek. That's why my boots are soaked." He sank onto the edge of the mattress and began to tug off a pair of brown, waterlogged cowboy boots. "Did Dad explain what we were doing?"

"Yes. While we were having dinner. Did you get the bulls back to where they belonged?"

"Not quite. We managed to get them corralled

in a lot on the neighbor's land, which is a temporary fix. The fence will have to be repaired before
we can turn the bulls back into the pasture where
they originally belong."

She crossed her legs and tried to appear relaxed.
"I can't imagine chasing bulls around on horseback
in the dark, but I guess you ranchers do lots of difficult things," she said.

"It's usually something different every day.
That's what keeps the job interesting." He set the
boots aside, then peeled off his socks. After he'd
draped the socks over the shafts of the boots, then
shrugged out of his waist length woolen jacket, he
looked at her. "So tell me about your day. Did you
have a good time in town?"

She'd not come into his room to exchange casual
chitchat with the man, but he seemed to consider
it natural to have her sitting an arm's length away
from his bed.

A nervous tickle in her throat forced her to swallow before she spoke. "Very good. After a round of
shopping, we had a bite to eat at the Wagon Spoke."

"I hope you tried a doughnut while you were at
the cafe. Mildred, she cooks the pastries there—she
makes the best. She's been talking about retiring,
but I told her seventy-six is too young to retire."

The bottoms of his jeans were damp and muddy,
while his gray Western shirt had a mark across his
midriff that looked suspiciously like dried blood.

Whether it was human or animal, she could only guess.

"She sounds a bit like Reeva, the Hollisters' house cook. She's in her seventies and the food she makes is out-of-this-world delicious."

He nodded. "Jack told us about her. He raved so much about her cooking that I was afraid it might hurt Mom's feelings. But it didn't. She says she'd love to meet Reeva one day."

"Reeva is prickly on the outside and a marshmallow on the inside. Claire would love her," Maggie told him. "As for a doughnut at the Wagon Spoke, I didn't eat any pastries. I had a tuna salad."

He looked at her and laughed. "So the nurse in you took over."

She smiled faintly, while telling her heart to stop its runaway act. Sure, she was sitting alone in a quiet room with Cordell, but that hardly meant he had any designs to get close to her. Only a few moments ago on the staircase, he'd made it clear he didn't have seduction on his mind. So why were her thoughts zeroing in on him and that four-poster bed?

She drew in a deep breath and slowly expelled it. "Not really. I don't want to gain five pounds before I go home."

His gaze met hers. "Quint tells me you'll be leaving for Arizona in three days. I wonder if you might consider staying a bit longer? You'd make my family happy. And make me happy, too."

His suggestion surprised her. Partly because he sounded sincere, but mostly because she couldn't imagine why he'd want her to hang around for a few more days. It wasn't like the two of them had a special thing going.

"I wouldn't want to risk wearing out my welcome," she told him. "Anyway, my work schedule demands that I return to Wickenburg in four days. And I never miss a shift."

He arched a brow at her. "Never?"

She made a dismissive gesture with her hand. "Well, once. When I was too ill to get out of bed."

"Dedication. I admire you for having it."

His compliment warmed her far more than he could know. Because in spite of him being a flirt, he was obviously quite devoted to the ranch and its success. The fact that he saw the same dedication in her was very nice, indeed.

"Thanks," she said. "My job is important to me.

"I had that much about you figured out the first night I met you."

Leaning back on the mattress, he propped his upper body on one bent elbow and Maggie found herself imagining how he would look with his shirt off, with his hair ruffled from her fingers and his lips moist from her kisses. She didn't know why he brought out such primal urges in her. Or why she couldn't put a stop to them.

Forcing her mind to a safer place, she said, "You missed Van's news tonight at dinner."

Curiosity peaked his brows. "News from Van? Let me guess. She's pregnant?"

She studied his face in an attempt to read his thoughts, but the most she could see was faint amusement. "What would you think if she was?"

"I'd say I'm extremely happy for her and Jack. What kind of reaction would you expect from me?"

Shrugging, she absently smoothed the suede fabric of her skirt across her lap. "Oh, something like you're glad it's Jack and not you. Or your poor brother is going to be shackled for life."

A quizzical frown twisted his features. "Your opinion of me must be on the level of a snake. In spite of what you might think, I'm not an ogre. I don't dislike kids."

Her smile was knowing. "As long as they belong to someone else," she said, then quickly shook her head. "If Van is pregnant, I know nothing about it. Her news was something entirely different. It was about your grandfather."

He raised back up to a sitting position. "Grandfather? Don't tell me—she's discovered he slipped around and had a Hollister child out of wedlock."

Rolling her eyes, she said, "My, oh my, how your mind works. You believe your grandfather was capable of such a thing?"

Chuckling, he said, "Uh, if you want me to answer honestly, then yeah. He probably was. From the things I've heard, Scarlett would drive a man to do most anything—short of murder."

"Well, Van hasn't found anything so concrete concerning Lionel. But she did finally receive a letter from the Utah records department. They have no information regarding your grandfather. No proof that he was born in this state."

He looked confused and then with a rueful sigh, said, "You know, Maggie, when I first heard about all this family tree business, I thought it was silly. Who cares, anyway—that was my thoughts on the matter. Now, I'm beginning to think I might have been wrong. A person's roots are kind of a guidepost or a blueprint. Sometimes we need to look back to know where we're going. Wouldn't you say?"

His question left her feeling empty and resentful and she quickly looked away as she struggled to keep her emotions pulled together. "I would say you're exactly right. I guess that's why I sometimes feel a little aimless."

The corners of his lips curved faintly upward. "You? Aimless? No. I see you marching straight forward—to whatever it is you want out of life."

Rising to her feet, she stepped over to the window and stared out at the shadowy view of the old barn. Cordell had talked about how his grandmother had made demands to have the livestock moved away. It wasn't exactly a nice family memory, but at least he had one. The most Maggie could say about her father was that he hadn't wanted anything to do with his daughter, or the woman who'd given birth to her.

"You don't understand, Cord. I never had a father. He skipped out on my mom before I was ever born. I have no idea who he is or where he might be."

Behind her, she heard the faint rustle of the bed-covers and then he was standing behind her, his hand gently touching her upper arm.

"Sorry, Maggie, all this talk about my family roots—you told me about your mother passing away. I didn't know about your father," he said gently.

Her throat was suddenly so tight, she wasn't sure she could utter one word. "Don't apologize, Cord. It's hardly your fault that I only have half of a family tree. And it's rather barren. But that doesn't mean I need sympathy. Plenty of people never know their biological parents. At least I was blessed with a mother."

His fingers tightened ever so slightly on her arm and Maggie couldn't ignore the warmth and excitement his touch was creating inside her.

"Did your mother ever talk to you about your father? Tell you his name?"

Shaking her head, she turned to face him and was surprised to see his eyes were full of compassion. Perhaps there was more to Cordell than riding the range, dating a bevy of women and having fun, she thought.

"Mom told her sister that my father was a drifter and dreamer and that I was better off not knowing him. But I'm not sure if Mom really thought of him in those terms."

"Poor woman. No telling how your mother actually felt about the man." A thoughtful frown creased his forehead. "Have you ever wanted to find him?"

"When I was a little girl I wondered about him a lot," she answered. "In my little girl's mind I'd imagine him walking up to me and explaining how he'd always loved me—he'd only stayed away because he'd been very busy making a wonderful home for the two of us. By the age of eleven, I threw away those fantasies. Now I have no desire to communicate with him."

His hand gently rubbed her arm in a comforting motion. "It's possible he might want to know you. Twenty-six years ago, he might not have been mature enough to deal with a wife and child. He could have left because he was scared of falling short of what you and your mother needed."

She snorted softly. "Sorry, Cord. I wished I could be that compassionate. Everyone is scared of failing at one thing or another. But you don't run. You stand and face your responsibilities."

"Hmm. Easy to say, hard to do. But I'm hardly a man to talk about taking care of a family."

His blue gaze was sliding over her face like a pair of exploring fingers and the sensation was causing her breaths to grow shorter and shorter.

"I, uh, better go to my room." She carefully stepped around him and headed toward the door.

He followed closely behind her. "I thought you wanted to speak to me about something."

With her hand on the doorknob, she paused to look at him. "I did. But somehow we got sidetracked."

His eyelids lowered to provocative slits. "Yeah. Somehow. So what's on your mind?"

All of a sudden he was back to the Cord she'd first met at the wedding reception. The Cord who charmed and flirted and reminded her that he was a man she couldn't take seriously. Which was probably a good thing, she decided. The Cord she saw a moment ago with soft compassion in his eyes was far harder to resist.

"Tomorrow. Is our ride still on?"

Something fluttered in her stomach as a wicked grin slowly spread his lips.

"Definitely on. I'm looking forward to it. Are you?"

He couldn't know how much she'd been thinking about spending time with him tomorrow. "Yes, I am. So when and where do I need to meet you?"

"Ten in the morning should be good. Give the sun a little time to warm things up. I'll pick you up here at the house. We'll leave on the horses from the ranch yard."

"I'll be ready." She opened the door a crack. "Anything else I need to know—about the ride?"

"Just be sure to wear something warm. It should be sunny, but the wind might be sharp."

"Okay. See you tomorrow at ten." She opened the door and peered down the dimly lit balcony before she stepped out of his room.

Behind her, Cordell chuckled under his breath. "Don't worry, Maggie. Your reputation isn't in danger."

No, but her peace of mind was shot to pieces, she thought helplessly.

"Good night, Cord."

Without glancing back, she hurried to her own room and carefully locked the door. Not because she was afraid Cordell might stroll right in and make himself at home. No, she was far more worried about herself and the unbearable longing she felt for him.

When Cordell's alarm had buzzed well before daylight, he felt as if he'd barely shut his eyes. But how had he expected to feel after tossing and turning for more than half the night?

He'd been a damned fool for inviting Maggie into his bedroom, he thought, as he methodically saddled the paint mare she'd be riding today. Now he couldn't forget the image of her sitting by the window, her flaming hair lying against her white blouse, her features bathed in soft lamp light, and the slit in her skirt revealing a tiny peek of one pale calf.

All the while she'd sat there, exchanging bits of conversation, he'd done his best to remain cool.

He'd tried not to think about tugging her onto his bed and making hot, hot love to her. And for a while he managed to stave off those yearnings. But then she'd started talking about having no family, of being discarded by an unknown father and all of a sudden he was feeling things that went far beyond the urge for sex. Something had stirred deep within him, something so real and sharp, he'd actually endured a moment of pain. Then, when she'd told him good night, he'd believed that would be the end of the problem. He'd thought he would sleep and forget. Instead, he'd lain awake for hours wondering about her and how it was going to feel once she was gone.

Doing his best to shake away last night's disturbing memories, Cordell finished saddling the pair of horses and drove back to the ranch house to fetch Maggie. By the time he parked the truck in front of the ranch house and had walked halfway to the porch, he saw her descending the steps to meet him.

Dressed in jeans and boots and a red plaid coat with a fur-edged hood pulled onto her head, she looked adorably young and fresh and full of life. The sight of her made him forget all about being tired, while the bright smile on her face sent his spirits soaring.

"Good morning," he called to her. "Do you have everything you need with you?"

Nodding, she patted the pockets on her coat. "I'm traveling light. Everything is in here."

"Great. Let's get going then." He cupped a hand beneath her elbow as they began the short walk to the truck. "Did you tell Mom and Van you were leaving?"

"Yes. But I told them I didn't have any idea when I'd be back. You didn't mention how long we'd be riding."

The idea that she wasn't planning to set a time limit on their ride put a smile on his face. "Who knows? Until we get tired or I've showed you everything I think you might enjoy."

He helped her into the truck, then took his place in the driver's seat and started the engine. As he adjusted the temperature of the heater, he asked, "Has Van already shown you the ranch yard?"

"No. We only went to her and Jack's new house. Van explained the ranch yard is in the opposite direction from there."

"Yes. Just over the big hill." He glanced at her hands, which were folded loosely in her lap. "I hope you brought gloves. Otherwise your hands are going to freeze."

Patting the pocket on her coat, she said, "Right here. And sunglasses, too. I wasn't sure if I'd need them today, so I brought them just in case."

Satisfied they were ready to go, he turned the truck around and headed down a dirt track leading away from the house.

On the drive to the barn, he noticed she was gazing out the passenger window at the ridge of mountains to the north. The rapt expression on her face surprised him. None of the women he'd dated had particularly cared about the outdoors, or what his job as foreman of the ranch entailed. Even his former fiancée, Lacey, had often told him she had no desire to live in the countryside, so far away from civilization.

Talk about following in his grandfather's footsteps. Cord had come damned close.

Pushing that grim thought aside, he glanced in Maggie's direction. "I hope Van isn't annoyed with me for dragging you away today.

"Not in the least. She's glad I'm getting a chance to see some of the ranch. When I left her a few minutes ago, she was sifting through more of your family's old papers from the attic."

"Hmm. Digging for a lead on Grandfather's birth place, I imagine."

"Lionel is a big puzzle," she replied. "But Van is also working on another angle and it involves the Arizona side of the family. One of the early founders of Three Rivers had a first wife who died in childbirth. But she can't find a record of the child's death. Van wonders if the baby might have survived and been raised by someone else, but kept the Hollister name. It's possible that's where the split occurred and this child grew up and traveled north to Utah."

Cordell frowned. "Sounds a like a bad soap opera to me. But I won't say impossible. I never

believed my family was related to the people on
Three Rivers Ranch and it turned out I was wrong."

The truck crested a hill dotted with sage and the
occasional juniper. Below, on a flat stretch of treeless ground, the ranch yard stretched in a north-to-
south direction. Cordell was familiar with every
board, every piece of corrugated iron and fence
post that made up the barns and corrals. Even in the
pitch-dark without a flashlight, he could find each
latched gate, plus the many water troughs and hay
mangers. This work headquarters was his domain
and he saw the ranch yard as the heart of Stone
Creek. And though he tried to convince himself it
didn't matter, he realized he wanted Maggie to see
it all as he did.

"There's the ranch yard," he announced.

She leaned eagerly forward and peered at the
scene beyond the windshield. "Oh, I wasn't expecting to see so many barns or corrals. And everything is— Oh my, I'm beginning to hear spooky
music again."

He darted a comical frown at her. "What are you
talking about?"

"The barns. They're painted the same colors as
the barns and sheds on Three Rivers Ranch." Turning her gaze on him, she added in a wondrous voice,
"And the ranch house here on Stone Creek is so
very similar to the Hollisters' home in Arizona.
How very strange."

Her mystified reaction caused him to chuckle.

"Turn off the spooky music, Maggie, it's all merely coincidental."

"Sure. Like Jack resembles Chandler. And your father looks a whole lot like Gil. You know, even as a nurse, I never really thought much about DNA and matching genes until I came up here to Stone Creek and began to see a real connection between the two Hollister families."

"Okay, Maggie. If you're hearing spooky music I believe you," he said with a wry grin. "But trust me, the sound will soon be drowned out with bawling cattle and bleating sheep.

"I can't wait."

After parking in an out-of-the-way spot near one of the smaller sheds, Cordell helped her from the truck, then taking her by the hand, led her over to the barn used to house the ranch's work horses.

As they grew nearer to the entrance, he noticed Maggie's head was twisting one way and another as she glanced curiously around her.

"Why do you have those cattle penned up?" she asked, gesturing toward a corral located at the far end of the ranch yard.

"They're heifers carrying their first babies. Normally we don't have calves dropping at this time of the year, but in this case, a bull got into a pasture where he wasn't supposed to be. So these girls got pregnant before we planned for them to. And with bad weather likely to hit any day, we want the heifers where we can keep a close eye on them."

"I see. Do you have to assist with the births?" she asked, then shook her head. "I know very little about raising livestock, so forgive me if I ask stupid and boring questions."

"Your questions aren't stupid or boring, Maggie. If things were turned around and I was on your turf, I'd be terribly lost. I know very little about medicine or working in an emergency room."

She looked unconvinced. "I think you're being humble. I'm sure you're capable of doctoring animals when they're in need."

"That's different. A rancher has to know the fundamentals of caring for livestock. Stone Creek Ranch isn't large enough to support a resident veterinarian. And we're a far distance from the animal clinic in town. So most problems we have to handle ourselves. And to answer your original question, yes, we usually have to help the heifers get their babies born."

She gazed once again at the large corral of heifers. "Must be a very busy time when the calves start coming."

"There are times we rarely get to sleep. But in the end, when the calves are standing on the ground, nursing their mothers, it's all worth it."

With a hand against her back, he urged her through a small open doorway and into the building, where two rows of horse stalls were divided by an alleyway large enough for a pickup truck to drive through. On the left side, at the far end of the structure, two mounts were tied to a wooden hitching rail.

"The horses are ready and waiting," he said. "Your ride is the paint. She's a mare named Domino. That's not her registered name, but it's the nickname we call her."

"She's beautiful. And so is the bay," she said as they approached the horses.

"We call him Bugs," Cordell told her.

"Do you ride him often?"

"I switch back and forth between Bugs and a dun named Ranger, so as not to overuse either horse. Both are loyal, hardworking and my best buddies."

Cordell gestured to the mare. "Go ahead and get acquainted with her," he said. "We're not in that big of a hurry."

Her eyes sparkling, Maggie stepped up to Domino's left side and gently stroked a hand against her neck and along her cheek.

"Hi, Domino," she crooned to the mare. "You are a real princess!"

"She has a daughter who looks a lot like her. She's out to pasture with the other yearlings. We won't be doing anything with her or the others until they reach the age of two years old."

"Oh. Do you do any of the horse training?" she asked curiously.

"Me and Chance. He's one of our hired hands. We do all the horse training on the ranch."

She flashed him an impish smile and Cordell

couldn't stop himself from taking a step closer to her side.

"I won't ask if you've ever been bucked off," she said.

He laughed. "Any cowboy worth a grain of salt has had the seat of his jeans dusted more than once. Frankly, I like the challenge. It's not Jack or Quint's cup of tea. Flint wouldn't take the job, either. But Hunter likes horse training. In fact, he and I both rode rodeo broncs professionally back in our much younger days. Or let me put it this way, we tried. Once we figured out we weren't making any money at it, we quit."

Her green eyes widened. "You've surprised me. I wouldn't have pictured you venturing away from the ranch—even to follow the excitement of the rodeo circuit."

He gave her a crooked grin. "I was in my early twenties then. I was full of adventure."

She glanced away from him. "I've never been a reckless person. But there are times I wish I could be more daring—just to see how it would feel."

With a man? With him? No. Now wasn't the time to be letting his thoughts stray in that direction.

Clearing his throat, he stepped to the head of his horse and untied the let-down rope from the hitching rail. "A little later this morning, we'll be riding up a steep mountain trail. It's kind of adventurous."

She laughed softly. "I'm sure the whole ride will be adventurous enough to suit me, Cord."

Once he had the horses untied, he backed them slightly away from the hitching rail, then handed the reins of the mare to Maggie. "If you're ready, we'll walk the horses through that wide door at the end of the barn, then mount up outside," he told her.

"I'm ready. Except for one thing."

Reaching for his hand, she clasped it tightly between both of hers. The unexpected touch took him by complete surprise and the most he could do was arch a brow in question.

"I wanted to tell you—"

She paused and as Cordell's gaze dropped to her lips he saw they were quivering ever so slightly. Was she afraid of him? Herself? Or was she simply feeling things that only occurred inside a woman? Things he couldn't understand. No matter, he thought. Whatever she was feeling, he wanted to pull her into his arms and cradle her head against his chest.

"Yes?"

She drew in a deep breath, then did her best to smile. "I only wanted to say thank you, Cord. For going to all this trouble for me. I realize there are dozens of other things you could be doing and I appreciate your thoughtfulness."

Her words touched him in so many ways he couldn't begin to understand them all. And before he could stop himself, he lifted her hand and placed a tiny kiss on her knuckles.

"You make me feel like a hypocrite, Maggie," he

said huskily. "I'm not being thoughtful. I'm being selfish."

Her gaze roamed his face. "Maybe you're thinking that way. But I'm not."

The tiny quiver was still on her lips and the urge to pull her into his arms and kiss her was gripping him like a vise. But before he gave in to the fierce desire, the voices of two of the ranch hands could be heard entering the barn.

The interruption was enough to bring his senses back to earth and he quickly dropped his hold on her hand.

"Come on," he said. "I think it's time we hit the trail."

Chapter Six

Minutes later, as the two of them rode away from the ranch yard, Maggie's head was still spinning. Back there in the barn, she didn't know what had possessed her to grab hold of his hand, or why she'd stood so close to him she could see the pores in his skin and the faint lines in his hard, chiseled lips.

And those lips. Oh my, when he'd pressed them to the back of her hand, she'd felt sure her boots had momentarily lifted off the ground.

What was she doing? Cordell wasn't a man to be played with. No. With him it would be all raging fire or nothing.

And up until now that was exactly what she'd had from the men who'd been in her life—nothing. This past year she'd tried hard to make herself feel something for Greg Sheridan. He'd been a kind man, dedicated to helping others. If she had agreed to marry him, she had no doubts he would have been faithful and loving. But her feelings for him had never gone beyond lukewarm and she'd realized she couldn't live the rest of her life just being warm and cozy.

But did she have the courage to reach for something more? Even if she ended up with a bruised heart? She didn't know.

Her deep thoughts were interrupted as Cordell suddenly reined his horse next to hers.

"Are your stirrups good?" he asked. "Not too short or long?"

The smile on his face made her heart thrum hard and fast.

"They're great," she told him. "No problem. And I'm amazed at this saddle. It's just the right size."

"That's because it belongs to Bea. She and Bonnie have matching saddles, naturally. But Bonnie's is a half inch bigger. Which doesn't sound like much, but it makes a huge difference in the size of the seat."

"I'm not very knowledgeable about riding tack," she admitted. "When I used to ride with Camille on Three Rivers, the ranch hands always tacked up the horses for us."

"Used to? You don't ride with her now?"

"It's been a long time. She moved to Dragoon, got married to the longtime foreman of Three Rivers and gave birth to their son. Plus, she runs her own little café. So I rarely have a chance to see her now."

"Poor Maggie. You've lost both your friends to marriage."

She shrugged. "I haven't lost anything." Except, maybe the hope that someday it would be her turn to have a husband and babies, she thought.

Deciding to move their conversation in a safer direction, she asked, "Do the twins ride much?"

"When they were younger it was hard to keep them off a horse. Now their jobs keep them busy. But when spring and fall roundups come around, they both join in as much as they can."

"What about Claire? So far I've not heard your mother mention riding."

He shook his head. "Mom loves animals of all kinds and will even help bottle-feed the calves or lambs if any need it, but riding isn't her thing. She gets in the saddle, takes one look at the ground and freezes with fear. Cooking and raising kids—that's always been her love."

"And she tends the roses. Or so Van tells me."

"You know about the roses?" he asked.

"I saw the tarps in the backyard and asked Van what was underneath," Maggie explained. "I imagine the roses look beautiful in the summer when they're blooming against the stone wall."

He nodded. "Most of the blooms are red, but yellow, pink and white are mixed in with them. And yes, they make the backyard a special place in the summer. When Grandfather got older, he spent lots of time in the rose garden. He'd say it made him feel closer to his mother."

The man must have had a sentimental side to him, Maggie thought. "Did you know your great-grandparents?"

He shook his head. "No. Grandfather told us that his parents both passed away when he was very young. He rarely mentioned them—maybe it was too painful for him. In any case, he'd always say the past was best left in the past. We all respected his wishes and didn't prod him with questions."

"Hmm. Did you ever see any photos of Lionel's parents? I have the feeling that your great-grandmother Hollister was probably a very beautiful woman."

His expression turned rueful. "Whenever Dad was a young child, he recalls seeing photos of his grandparents. But later on, something happened and the pics went missing. Lionel accused Scarlett of destroying them, but that accusation was never proven to be true."

The more he talked about his grandparents, the more Maggie realized how fractured their marriage must have been. She couldn't help thinking, too, that the couple's volatile union had obviously left scars on this Hollister family.

"Destroying something your grandfather cherished—the photos of his deceased parents—only an evil person could do such a thing," she remarked.

His lips twisted to a rueful slant. "Scorned love drives some people to lash out and do evil things. I can do without that kind of drama in my life."

Did he believe love usually ended as his grandparents' had ended? With revenge and spite? She didn't want to think so. Maybe she was seeing Cordell through rose-colored glasses, but she believed he had the capacity to care deeply. He just chose to ignore that part of himself.

They rode for a few more minutes in an easterly direction and Maggie determinedly pushed their conversation about scorned love to the back of her mind. Instead, she focused on the open, windswept land around them and the rhythmic walk of the horse beneath her.

"Better enjoy this smooth road while you can," Cordell spoke up. "As soon as we pass Hunter's house, we'll be heading north and the trail will get steadily rougher as we get closer to the creek."

"Other than water, what else will we see at the creek?" she asked curiously.

"Plenty of fir trees and the grasses that grow there usually last into late fall and early winter," he answered. "Which means there should be some cattle grazing along the banks."

"Sounds lovely. What about the sheep? Will I get to see any of them today?"

"On the latter part of our ride. That is, unless

you get too tired to make it that far and we have to turn back," he playfully taunted.

She let out a smug little laugh. "You're going to find out I'm not a weakling, Cord."

Five more minutes down the road, Hunter's place came into view. Maggie peered with interest at the L-shaped log house surrounded by a few hardwood trees.

"Oh, how pretty!" She looked over at Cordell riding close at her side. "It's a big house for a bachelor who's gone most of the time.

A cynical look crossed his face. "When Hunter had the house built he was thinking of filling it with a bunch of kids. But his plans didn't work out."

Pulling on the reins, she stopped the horse and stared up at the house, which had an almost abandoned look about it. "How sad. To be so beautiful on the outside, yet empty inside."

"A lot of things look far better on the outside than in."

Since first meeting Cordell, she'd not thought of him as being much of a philosophical person. Unless it was in a sardonic way. But the more time she spent with him, the more she was beginning to see there were many different layers to the man.

"I remember the night of the reception you were throwing a few digs at Hunter. Why? Is there a rift between him and the rest of your family because he works outside of the ranch?"

He looked at her with faint surprise. "Not at all.

We're all proud of Hunter's accomplishments. And you need to remember, Flint and Grace and Bea all work outside of the ranch, too."

"True," she murmured thoughtfully. "I wasn't thinking about them."

His gaze turned toward the distant mountains. "You're probably thinking I should be ashamed of myself for trying to get at Hunter. But it's only be-cause I—love him and want him to get over the past. To be happy again."

She said, "I'm going to take a leap here and as-sume his rodeo company had something to do with his divorce."

A tight grimace marred his features as he turned his gaze back to her. "Hunter believes Willow left because she couldn't take him being gone so much. You see, living on the road wasn't her thing, either. But I'm not convinced his rodeoing was the reason. He came home one day to find her packed up and gone. No warning. No goodbyes. Just gone."

Maggie shook her head with disbelief. "She didn't tell any of your family where she was going? Or why?"

He said, "None of us were aware of her plans. Willow was sort of a loner and didn't come around to the big ranch house very often."

"Because she didn't get along with your family?"

He shrugged one shoulder. "Hard to say. She seemed happy to be a part of the family, but could've had us all fooled,."

Maggie glanced up at the house, while thinking how crushed Hunter must have felt to find his wife gone, his home empty. "How awful."

"Hell of a way for a woman to treat a man," he said flatly. "So you see, that's why I dig at Hunter from time to time. I want him to move on."

She arched a brow at him. "And marry again?"

His snort was bitter. "I don't expect Hunter will ever want to try marriage again. I only wish he'd find a woman who can help him forget."

He clearly didn't believe Hunter needed love or marriage to help him find happiness, she thought.

"You know, Cord, your brother has probably already found the kind of woman you think he needs."

His lips flattened to a thin line. "If he's found her, then she sure hasn't made him happy."

Smiling wanly, she said, "Now you're getting the point."

She nudged the heels of her boots against Domino's sides and as the mare moved forward, she glanced back at him. "Ready to ride on?"

The look on his face said he wanted to say more on the subject, but then he nodded and urged his horse alongside hers. "Sure. Let's get going."

With Hunter's place behind them, they rode a few more minutes in an easterly direction until Cord motioned toward a cattle trail leading off the hill. Because the ground was rocky and the path not wide enough for the horses to travel abreast, Maggie chose to follow Cordell.

For the next quarter of a mile the horses carried them downward and into a wide valley covered with tall brown grass and clumps of sage. As they rode, Maggie tried to concentrate on her surroundings, but the beauty of the landscape wasn't enough to prevent her gaze from drifting to Cordell.

Before she realized where her thoughts were going, she was thinking how good it would feel to be riding double with him; to lock her arms around his waist, press her cheek to his back and let the warmth of his hard body fill the hungry spots inside her.

"We're almost to the creek," he called back to her. "It's just beyond the line of trees. So be careful of low-hanging limbs."

His voice splintered her fantasy and she gave him a little acknowledging wave. "I'll be right behind you," she assured him.

They rode into a grove made up of birch and willows, tall sycamores and a few evergreens. Most of the leaves on the hardwoods had fallen and as the horses wound their way through the maze of tree trunks, the soft carpet on the ground muffled the clopping of their hooves.

Once they emerged on the other side of the grove, the small creek was only a few yards farther and they rode to the edge of the bank before reining their mounts to a stop.

The water was only two or three foot deep and sparkling clear as it splashed a westward trail over large boulders and a pair of fallen logs. "Is this the creek the ranch is named after?"

He shook his head. "No. We call this one Bird Creek. Stone Creek is on the west side of the ranch. Both are smaller tributaries of a river that travels through the north of the property."

Maggie figured come springtime, the snowmelt running down from the mountains would fill the little creek to the top of its banks. "Does this water dry up in late summer?"

"Depends on the winter snow fall in the mountains north of us. Some summers are really dry, then we irrigate a few of the meadows." He pointed across the creek to where a herd of Black Angus cows was slowly emerging from a stand of evergreens. "Here comes one of our smaller herds. You won't see any calves with this bunch. They've been weaned and put in a separate pasture."

Pride was on his face as he watched the grazing cattle and it struck Maggie that Cordell already had a family of his own. He was married to this land and the livestock were his children.

"I imagine springtime brings a blanket of wildflowers along the creek and over the meadows. Must be a beautiful time of the year here on the ranch," she commented as she absently stroked a hand down the top of Domino's mane.

"Yes. By then, the grass is turning green, the flowers are blooming and baby calves and lambs are romping and playing and the sheep are sheared. Guess it has to be my favorite time on the ranch."

He looked over at her and as his gaze made a gentle foray of her face, Maggie was struck by the way his features had softened. Surely he was thinking about the ranch and not her, she thought.

"If you do ever decide to come back for another visit, I think you'd like seeing it in the spring," he said.

"I'll remember—in case I do come back."

Cold wind was whistling down from the north and though the bright sunshine was enough to keep the birds chattering and flittering about the bushes growing along the creek bank, it wasn't enough to ward off the sudden chill that raced through Maggie.

She was tightening the ties on her hood, when Cordell moved his horse alongside hers.

Concern was in his voice as he asked, "Do you need to get down and stretch your legs? Rest a few minutes? We don't have to hurry."

No, she needed to get her mind off him, she thought desperately. She needed to quit wondering how it would feel to touch him, make love to him.

She gave him her best reassuring smile, even though she felt as though she was losing complete control of her common sense. "No. I'm fine. Let's ride on."

"Okay. There's a shallow point of the creek not

far from here. We'll cross it there and then head to the high country. Way up there."

He motioned to a distant mountain made up of sheer rock bluffs and thick evergreen forest.

"Wow! Looks steep and treacherous. Do you plan for us to go all the way to the top?" she asked with dismay.

He chuckled. "Don't worry. We'll go around the bluffs. The trail is a switchback, so it's not like we'll be going straight up."

She let out a good-natured groan. "Oh, great. Just sort of straight up, right?"

Chuckling again, he said, "Trust me, Maggie. You know I wouldn't put the horses in jeopardy."

"Definitely not your horses. But maybe a female guest," she joked.

"I promise you'll be happy when we get to the top. The view is amazing and while we're up there I'll show you Grandfather's old hunting cabin. It's been there since he first started the ranch. Are you game for the trip, or do you want to play it safe and just ride through the valley?"

Play it safe? No. She'd agreed to this ride with him because she'd wanted to experience a bit of adventure before she went home and back to work. She didn't intend to waste the day being timid.

Slanting him a provocative glance, she said, "I'm not a fraidy-cat, Cord. Just lead the way."

Clearly pleased with her response, he gave her a lopsided grin. "Let's go."

* * *

When Maggie had told Cordell she knew how to ride a horse, he'd assumed she'd probably walked the animal over smooth level ground for a short distance. He'd not expected her to handle the horse like a pro or be able to navigate a steep and rocky trail for nearly an hour without so much as a five-minute break, or making the slightest complaint about being cold or tired.

Now as they neared the end of the mountain climb, he reined Bugs to a halt on a wide ledge and waited for her to guide her horse alongside his.

"This is as far as we ride," he informed her. "We'll lead the horses the rest of the way. But we'll rest here for a few minutes before we head on up the mountain."

"I'm glad to hear we're taking a break. I was getting a little tired," she admitted, while flexing her shoulders.

"A little? That's all? I'm impressed. Working in the ER must make you tough."

"Being on your feet for sixteen to eighteen hours each shift makes this feel like horseplay," she said, then laughed. "Sorry for the goofy pun. I couldn't help myself."

Seeing her smile and hearing her laugh made him happy in a way he couldn't explain or understand. Yet the pleasure of being with her didn't stop there. Even when she wasn't saying a word, he felt close to her. As though the two of them were together in mind and spirit. The notion was somewhat unsettling, but Cordell had no desire to push it away. Instead, he wanted to hold on to the strange feelings for as long as possible.

"Climbing a mountain isn't what Bugs or Domino considers horseplay," he said jokingly. "They call it work."

He dismounted, then walked around to Domino's left side to offer a hand up to Maggie.

"Let me help you down," he told her. "Just in case your legs aren't quite as sturdy as you think they might be."

"Thanks."

She placed her gloved hand in his and gracefully climbed out of the saddle. Once she was standing next to him, he continued to keep a tight hold on her hand while she steadied herself.

"Feeling okay?" he asked.

Laughing under her breath, she looked up at him. "Ask me that question again in a minute or two," she joked, then added, "Seriously, I'm fine, Cord."

Maybe she was, but he wasn't, Cordell thought. He was beginning to feel things about Maggie that he shouldn't be feeling. Think things that could only lead him to trouble. And yet he realized he didn't want to let go of her. Not today. Not ever.

Clearing his throat, he gathered the reins of both horses. "I'll tie the horses in a safe spot and then I'll show you just how far up we've ridden."

She waited while he tethered both animals to a

Get up to 4
FREE FABULOUS BOOKS
You Love!

To thank you for being a loyal reader we'd like to send you up to 4 FREE BOOKS, absolutely free when you try the Harlequin Reader Service.

Just write "YES" on the Loyal Reader Voucher and we'll send you 2 free books from each series you choose and Free Mystery Gifts, altogether worth over $20.

Try **Harlequin® Special Edition** and get 2 books featuring comfort and strength in the support of loved ones and enjoying the journey no matter what life throws your way.

Try **Harlequin® Heartwarming™ Larger-Print** and get 2 books featuring uplifting stories where the bonds of friendship, family and community unite.

Or **TRY BOTH and get 2 books from each series!**

Your free books are completely free, even the shipping! If you continue with your subscription, you can look forward to curated monthly shipments of brand-new books from your selected series, always at a discount off the cover price! Plus you can cancel any time.

So don't miss out, return your Loyal Readers Voucher today to get your Free books.

Pam Powers

LOYAL READER
FREE BOOKS VOUCHER

YES! I Love Reading, please send me up to 4 FREE BOOKS and Free Mystery Gifts from the series I select.

Just write in "YES" on the dotted line below then return this card today and we'll send your free books & gifts asap!

➡ YES ⬅
— — —

Which do you prefer?

☐ **Harlequin® Special Edition**
235/335 HDL GRCT

☐ **Harlequin Heartwarming® Larger-Print**
161/361 HDL GRCT

☐ **BOTH**
235/335 & 161/361
HDL GRC5

FIRST NAME

LAST NAME

ADDRESS

APT.#

CITY

STATE/PROV.

ZIP/POSTAL CODE

EMAIL ☐ Please check this box if you would like to receive newsletters and promotional emails from Harlequin Enterprises ULC and its affiliates. You can unsubscribe anytime.

SE/HW-622-LR_LRV22

sturdy juniper root growing out of a stand of rocks. Once he was satisfied the animals were secured, he reached for her hand.

"Let's walk over to the edge of the clearing. But not too close," he warned. "Sometimes the dirt breaks away for no reason. If that happened, they'd never find us."

Smiling impishly, she said, "Are you trying to scare me?"

"I would never want to scare you."

She didn't make a reply, but the look she darted at him was a mixture of amusement and skepticism. A reaction that shouldn't surprise him. For the past few days since she'd arrived on the ranch, he'd gone out of his way to make sure she didn't take him seriously. And yet a part of him wished that, just once, he could show her the part of him that needed and wanted and hurt just like any other man.

With her hand still in his, he helped her across the rocky ground to a spot where they could stand between two lodgepole pines and view the valley far below.

She gasped as she gazed out at the scenic view and Cordell watched a look of amazement wash over her lovely features.

"Oh! Oh, Cord! This is breathtaking! There are so many meadows and the trees make the creeks look like they're lined with lace. And the cattle— they're everywhere. Is all the land I'm seeing Stone Creek Ranch? If it is, I'm in awe!"

He couldn't keep the pride he was feeling from his voice. "Yes, all you see belongs to the Hollister family, plus some that's impossible to see from this spot." He drew her closer to his side. "I, uh, wanted you to see the ranch from this point—the way I see it."

She stared out at the view for long, long moments before she finally glanced up at him. "I think I understand now," she said softly.

The sparkle of moisture in her green eyes caught him by surprise and he instinctively dropped her hand in order to slide his arm around the back of her waist.

"Understand what?" he asked.

"Why your heart is tied to the ranch."

He felt like a maudlin fool as his throat suddenly tightened with emotions.

"Yeah," he said huskily. "I guess it is."

The corners of her lips tilted knowingly upward. "At least the ranch will never leave you."

Like Scarlett had left his grandfather? Like Willow had left Hunter? Was that what she was thinking? Did she believe he shied away from love because he was afraid of being deserted? Well, he could tell her he wasn't afraid. He was being wise. Like Quint had said, the smartest thing Cord had ever done was call off his wedding.

"No. And I won't ever leave the ranch." Feeling the need to move on, he nudged her away from the mountain ledge. "Grandfather's cabin is just around this next switchback. I think it's time for coffee and a snack, don't you?"

"Sounds great."

The final climb up the mountain on foot left Maggie a little winded, but as soon as the old cabin came into view, she decided it was all worth the effort.

Made of thick logs chinked with gray mortar, the structure sat on a wide ledge and was surrounded by a pair of huge spruce trees and one tall birch. A tiny covered porch sheltered the front door and two small windows faced a view of the valley below. The steep roof was made from sheets of corrugated iron and though it was rusty in many spots, it appeared to be strong and intact.

While Cord tethered the horses to an old wooden hitching rail some distance from the cabin, Maggie walked over and gave the little building a closer look.

"This is incredible, Cord. How did your grandfather get all this material up here? And why build it so far up the mountain?"

He loosened the girths on both horses and pulled the saddlebags from Bugs before he walked over to join her.

"Grandfather reasoned that deer hunting was better up here, but I think that's hogwash. The deer are usually found much lower on the flats and near the creeks. Especially in the winter months. I think he considered this place more of a getaway than a hunting cabin. Dad says Lionel would come up here alone and stay for days on end."

"Sounds like it was his version of a man cave."

"My same thoughts," he said, then wrapping a hand around her upper arm, he urged her toward the porch. "Let's go in. If we're lucky they'll be a bit of firewood and we can build a fire."

"This little cabin has a fireplace?"

"No. A potbellied stove. And don't ask me how Grandfather got it up here. Piece by piece on a pack mule, I suppose."

After shouldering the door open, he glanced inside, then gestured for her to precede him into the one room.

As Maggie looked curiously around the dusty space furnished with a small table and chairs and one double bed with a scrolled iron head and footboard, Cordell placed his saddlebags on the tabletop.

"Down through the years some of the hands used this cabin for a line shack," he said, "but it's really too unhandy to be used for that purpose. Come summer, if Quint decides to bring the sheep on this side of the ranch, they might use it for a sheepherder's cabin. Otherwise the place is just a shelter for anyone who wants to use it."

He walked over to a wooden box jammed in one corner of the room and lifted out an armful of firewood. "We're in luck. You should find a box of matches over there on one of the shelves. The ranch hands keep the cabin supplied with food and other necessities."

On the left side of the room a small table with two chairs was pushed against the wall. Above the table, three wooden shelves were attached to the wall and partially covered with a muslin curtain.

Maggie found the matches, along with several cans of food, a jar of peanut butter and a tin box of crackers.

"Oh, this food looks fairly fresh. Peaches, pork 'n' beans, tomatoes and sardines in hot sauce. Mmm. Mmm."

"I'd tell you to eat the sardines, only they'd stink up the cabin," he said as he placed the short pieces of wood inside the belly of the stove. "What about the matches?"

"Oh yes, sorry," she told him. "The food distracted me."

"I hope this doesn't happen to you in the ER," he teased. "Somebody brings in a candy bar and you forget the bleeding patient on the gurney."

She joined him at the stove and handed him the matches. "I never get distracted in the ER," she assured him. "At least, not by food."

"Only by handsome doctors?" he asked slyly.

She tried not to stiffen. "Hysterical family members are the real distractions for me. Not doctors."

He lit a match and stuck the flame to a piece of

pine kindling. Once the flame began to grow and spread, he turned away from the stove to look at her.

"Is that why you sound like you could bite nails? The thought of those hysterical family members?"

Grimacing, she let out a long breath and then as she dared to meet his inquisitive gaze, she felt something hard and cold break. And suddenly, keeping the disappointments of her past bottled up, no longer made any sense.

"Well, there was a doctor in my life," she admitted.

"Was?"

There were questions in his blue eyes, yet beyond the questions there was something else. Whatever it was, she couldn't define it; she only knew it was drawing on her, like his hand had drawn her to the edge of the mountain.

"Yes, was. He left six months ago. He's in California now. Practicing at a prestigious hospital."

His gaze roamed her face. "Oh. And his leaving broke your heart?"

"I wished it had. At least, a broken heart would have meant I was normal."

A crease formed between his brows. "What does that mean?"

Bending her head, she focused on pulling off her leather gloves and stuffing them in the pockets of her coat. "It means I tried very hard to love the man. And when he asked me to marry him I wished with everything inside of me that I could've told him yes. But I couldn't."

"Is that why he went to California? Because you turned down his marriage proposal?"

With a slight shake of her head, she said, "No. He'd already accepted the new position in California when he proposed. He'd planned for me to go with him."

He shut the lid on the stove and adjusted the damper. "And you turned him down."

Sighing, she walked over to one of the small windows and stared through the dusty pane. From this lofty spot on the mountain, she could see the western horizon where clouds touched snowy peaks and the valley stretched like a golden ribbon.

"It was the right thing to do." She turned away from the window to see he was watching her and she imagined he was thinking she was some sort of narcissist, or worse. "My coworkers called me stupid. And I have a feeling if my mother had been alive, she would've been disappointed in me. Because Greg would've made a great husband and father. But I couldn't make myself feel something that just wasn't there."

"You should've told your coworkers to keep their mouths shut. You made a wise choice for yourself, not them. Just because something looks good doesn't mean it is good." He walked over to the table and lit an oil lamp. After adjusting the flame, he returned the glass globe. "This should give us a little light. Come on. Let's have some coffee."

He wasn't berating her, or laughing the whole thing off, or accusing her of being silly. Maybe he could be considerate to a woman's feelings, she thought. Even though he didn't want anything to do with love.

She walked over to join him. "Coffee sounds great. And Cord, thanks for—well, not calling me a fool."

He gave her a lopsided grin. "Forget all of that, Maggie. Let's enjoy our coffee. Would you like to take the chairs over by the fire? I think the logs are burning enough to throw off some heat."

"Sounds good."

They placed the pair of wooden chairs close to the iron stove and then Cordell poured coffee from a thermos into two tin granite cups.

"You have to drink it quickly in these cups. They don't hold the heat." He handed her one of the cups. "I have packets of sugar and cream in the saddlebag if you want some."

"Thanks. Plain is fine," she said. "With my job, I've learned to drink the stuff any way I can get it."

She took a seat in one of the chairs and carefully sipped the hot brew. When he sat down next to her, he held up a chocolate candy bar.

"Bonnie packed my saddlebags," he said with a chuckle. "She was obviously worried about keeping up our energy level. Let's share it."

"Sure. I love anything chocolate."

He unwrapped the candy and broke off a hefty portion before handing her the remainder.

She chewed a bite of the chocolate and almonds, then washed it down with a sip of coffee. "So how often do you come up here?" she asked.

"Depends on the weather and what's going on with the cattle. During the summer some of the cows decide they want to wander up to higher ground. We don't try to stop them, but we do keep an eye on them. If the hands are too busy with haying or fencing to ride the mountains, Quint and I do the job."

She ate more of the candy. "In other words, work brings you up here. You never visit this cabin just to get away from everything?"

"No. Don't guess I ever feel the need to escape from work—or other things." He glanced at her. "But I don't have to deal with the stress of life-and-death situations like you do. Unless you count the animals we tend to."

"Thankfully, we don't deal with that sort of trauma every day." She shrugged, then forced out a chuckle. "This is the first vacation I've taken in five years and it will probably be even longer before I take another. But I don't mind. Traveling alone, seeing the sights without anyone to share them with—it's not much fun."

The heat from the stove was rapidly warming the room and she looked at him as she slipped off her hood and removed the black scarf she'd wrapped around her neck for added protection from the cold wind.

"Are we going to be here long enough for me to shed my coat?" she asked.

"Go ahead and make yourself comfortable. We need to stay until the logs burn down anyway. To make sure any stray sparks don't escape the stove." He held out his hand. "I'll hold your coffee for you."

She handed him her cup, then rose and removed the red plaid coat. After hanging it on the back of the chair. She retrieved her cup from him, but didn't return to her seat. Instead she stood by the stove, sipping the last of her drink, while the delicious heat relaxed her muscles.

"The other night you told me you weren't interested in dating right now. Is that because of the doctor?"

His unexpected question had her looking at him with surprise and then, as she realized he was waiting for an answer, her cheeks began to burn.

"Why are you asking me about my dating habits?"

"Just curious." He drained the last of his coffee and placed the cup on the floor.

She slanted him a skeptical look. "Maybe I'm curious as to why you say you aren't presently dating."

His grin said he was an open book, but Maggie was beginning to see it would take years of reading to get the full picture of his life.

"No deep secret there," he said. "My last girlfriend got a little too clingy and I had a heck of a time convincing her I needed space. After she finally got the message, I decided to take a little hiatus. Maybe that's how you felt after you finally parted ways with the doctor."

Hoping to appear indifferent to the whole subject, she shrugged one shoulder, yet all the while her mind was whirling with everything he'd just told her. Cordell had been in a sticky situation with a woman, one he was glad to have escaped. She couldn't fault him for that. Not when her relationship with Greg had left her feeling hopeless and trapped.

"To be honest, my break with Greg isn't the sole reason. But it made me—well, disenchanted. And leery of getting involved again."

"How long did you date him?"

"Close to a year."

He looked at her with stunned fascination. "Are you kidding me?"

Annoyed with him now, she frowned, "It's nothing to kid about. I thought you understood that."

"I do. And no, there's nothing funny about this. In fact, I think it's downright pitiful. It took a year for you to figure out you couldn't feel anything for the man?"

"Maybe this won't make sense to you, but I don't like giving up on an endeavor. So I kept trying and hoping that I would grow to feel more for Greg. I mean, that does happen to people. It takes time for love to grow. I wanted to give it a proper chance."

"Grow, hell," he said with a heavy dose of mockery. "It wouldn't have taken me a fraction of that time to know whether I felt something for a woman," he said.

She couldn't stop her lips from twisting into a smirk. "Like thirty minutes or a couple of hours?" she asked, not bothering to hide the sarcasm from her voice. "Actually, I imagine you already know beforehand that you're not going to feel anything for a woman. Nothing of value, that is."

His jaw dropped and then suddenly he was standing directly in front of her and she could see something hot and raw smoldering in the depths of his blue eyes.

"That's a hell of a thing to say," he said flatly. "Especially when you couldn't possibly know what I feel."

Her heart was beating in her throat. Not from fear of making him angry. No, she was frightened of herself and the strange desire that was beginning to grip every cell in her body. All of a sudden, it didn't matter if he used a woman and then tossed her away. She didn't care that in two more days she'd never see him again. All she wanted was to feel his arms around her, his lips crushing down on hers.

"Sorry, Cord. I—had no right to say that. Or to judge your feelings about women. At least you can *feel* something. You're not dead inside—like me."

Her voice broke on the last two words, and appalled that she'd said such personal things to him, she bit down on her lip and looked away.

His hand came down on her shoulder and the warm contact was so alluring she couldn't stop herself from stepping closer.

"You're so wrong, Maggie," he said gently. "You're not dead inside. I hear emotions in your voice. See them in your eyes."

"Sure. I can feel happy or sad or frightened or angry and perhaps more than anything, loneliness. But that isn't—" Unable to go on, she groaned helplessly and rested her palms against the middle of his chest. "Cord, please—kiss me."

Disbelief flashed in his blue eyes. "What is this? Some sort of experiment?"

She moved close enough for the front of her body to brush against his. "Call it an experiment if you want," she murmured. "Call it crazy or reckless. I don't care."

His expression turned somber. "Kissing you would probably ruin things between us."

He was hesitating and weighing the consequences, something that Maggie had done all of her life. But caution had gotten her nowhere. Especially when it came to finding a soulmate. Besides, she wasn't looking for love. Not from Cordell.

"That's funny, Cord. There are no *things* between us," she said quietly. "And I don't expect there to be."

"You could've fooled me. I thought we were friends."

She didn't know what was coming over her, but suddenly her body was taking total control of her senses. Even if she'd wanted to, she couldn't have stopped herself from closing the last tiny space between them.

"Friends can kiss, can't they?" Her voice fell to a whisper as she studied the unyielding line of his jaw and chin, the rugged hollow of his cheeks, and the sexy droop to his eyelids. "Or is my red hair scaring you away? You're afraid I'll bite—or something?"

"Or something," he answered and with a throaty growl, he lowered his head toward hers.

Her heart pounding with wild anticipation, Maggie watched his face until his lips were hovering over hers and then she closed her eyes and waited for her fantasy to become reality.

His arms wrapped around her shoulders at the same time his lips settled over hers and in one incredible instant Maggie felt drawn to a faraway place where there was nothing but his strength and warmth surrounding her, where the only sound was that of her heart thrumming in her ears.

His lips were hard and a bit chafed by the wind, but that only added to the electric sizzle they were creating on hers. He tasted like coffee and chocolate, but most of all he tasted like a man. One who didn't hold back from grabbing what he wanted.

And as her arms slipped around his waist and

her lips boldly responded to his kiss, she could only think how much she wanted him to grab her and never let go.

Chapter Seven

Cordell liked to think he was a man who was always in control. Especially where women were concerned. But kissing Maggie wasn't like anything he'd ever encountered before and the more his lips searched hers, the more he lost track of his senses.

He'd never had a woman feel this soft and warm and giving in his arms. Until he'd touched his lips to Maggie's, he'd never had one who tasted so incredibly delicious. This wasn't just a kiss, he thought. This was like taking a trip up to the clouds and he never wanted to come down to earth.

The thought was circling around in his head like a warning bell, clanging out a signal of oncoming danger. But he wasn't paying the sound any heed.

How could he? When all he wanted to do was draw her closer to him, kiss her over and over.

And then suddenly he felt her lips pulling away from his and the loss of the warm contact caused him to open his eyes and gaze down at her flushed face.

"Maggie, I—"

He paused to suck in a deep breath, but she didn't give him a chance to say more. Instead, the tips of her fingers reached up to touch his lips.

"Don't apologize. Don't say anything. There's no need for words," she whispered.

Her green eyes were misty and in that moment he knew she was just as shaken by their kiss as he'd been. And the knowledge only made him want her more.

"No. No need for words," he murmured. "Only this."

He lowered his lips back to hers and felt a sense of triumph when she responded with a hunger that took his breath away. He couldn't begin to know why she'd suddenly wanted to be close to him. Nor did he care. Something magical was happening to him and whatever it was, he didn't want it to stop.

As his lips feasted on hers, he could feel her hands gliding up and down his back, then around to his chest and down his ribs. Beneath the heavy fabric of his shirt, the touch of her fingers was leaving a scorching trail in their wake and he could only imagine the pleasure he would feel if they were actually touching his skin.

The thought was racing through his mind when her hand inadvertently scraped against a sore wound on his abdomen.

The pain caused him to flinch and groan. The reaction had Maggie instantly pulling back to stare at him with confusion.

"Cord! What's wrong? Did I hurt you?"

Cradling a hand against his midsection, he shook his head. "No. It's nothing. Forget it."

She frowned at him. "Nothing? Something is hurting you."

Feeling worse than embarrassed, he groaned again, only this time it was a sound of regret. "It's just a little scratch."

Her lips pressed to a determined line, she reached for the front of his shirt. "Let me see this nothing you're talking about."

Reluctantly, he tugged the tails of his shirt from the waistband of his jeans and unsnapped the front. "Okay. I had a little fight with a tangle of barbed wire last night during the hunt for the bulls," he admitted. "That's all."

"Hmm. I thought I saw dried blood on your shirt, but I thought it had probably come from an animal. Why didn't you tell anyone you'd hurt yourself?"

"Because it's no big deal."

He opened the denim fabric to allow her a view of the long, jagged slash across the lower part of his abdomen. The cut itself had turned a crusty brown while the surrounding flesh was red and inflamed.

She bent her head for a closer inspection. "No wonder this is painful to the touch. The cut needs proper attention or you're going to have a serious infection."

"I took a shower before I went to bed," he told her. "I thought the cut was clean enough. But this morning I didn't have time to worry with it."

She groaned with disapproval. "You thought wrong. Was the wire rusty? Have you had a tetanus shot recently?"

"It was dark so I can't tell you if the wire was rusty. But, yes to the tetanus. A horse bit my shoulder a few weeks back and Grace insisted I needed a shot."

"Thank goodness your sister was taking good care of you." She looked at him. "Do you carry a first aid kit in your saddlebags?

"Dad insists that we all carry small first aid kits. But when you're chasing cattle or hurrying to put up wire before the rest of the herd scatters, you don't have time to stop and treat a scratch," he explained.

"Well, we have time now. I'll treat it with whatever you have in the kit. Later, when we get back to the ranch I'll do a more thorough job," she told him.

Seeing she'd slipped into nursing mode, Cordell knew he'd be wasting his time to suggest they forget the medical care for now, so he walked over to the table where he'd left his saddlebags. Maggie fol-

lowed close on his heels and waited patiently while
he dug the mini-medical-kit from the saddlebag.

Maggie quickly opened the small square box
and rifled through the contents. "Oh good. Here's
a small bottle of antiseptic and a tube of antibiotic
cream. This will do for now." She put the items
aside, then with a quizzical frown held up a plastic bag. "Uh, sewing needles and spool of nylon
thread? Don't tell me you've tried to suture a wound
with this stuff!"

He chuckled. "Sometimes we have to sew up
wounds on livestock. Works good. I haven't done
any suturing on a person—yet. But Jack has. Dad
was gored in the thigh once and Jack sewed up the
wound. Afterward, Grace praised him for the job.
Since they were so far away from medical help, she
said without Jack's quick efforts, Dad might have
ended up losing too much blood. See, sometimes a
person doesn't have a sterile room and medical instruments to work with. In an emergency you just
make do with what you have."

Her green eyes were soft as she glanced up at
him and the urge to drag her into his arms and wrap
his mouth over hers was creating an ache deep in
his gut. One that far outweighed the discomfort of
the cut on his belly.

"Make do with what I have," she said gently.
"That's my intentions."

He feigned a look of disappointment. "Oh. I

thought you might want to kiss me first," he suggested. "Just to make the pain not so bad."

Her sigh was barely audible as she picked up the antiseptic and a small square of gauze. "I think the kiss needs to wait."

"Why?" he asked softly. "Are you afraid of what you just felt with me? Afraid you might forget all about being a nurse?"

She kept her eyes on the gauze as she soaked the square with antiseptic. "What is this about? You want me to stoke your already giant ego?"

He didn't know why her response annoyed him. Or why it should matter if she ever kissed him again. But it did matter. Too damned much. "You're not supposed to answer a question with more questions," he said.

She glanced at him. "Okay. I'll answer your question. I am a little afraid. Of myself. Not you."

What was she trying to tell him? That she was afraid of losing her self-control with him? It didn't make sense, he thought. A few minutes ago, she was bemoaning her fear of not being able to feel passion. Now she wanted to run from it?

Damn!

Wake up, Cord. She's a woman. What do you expect? You're not going to hear anything straightforward coming from Maggie's lips. All you're going to get is contradictions.

The taunting voice in his head was instantly

pushed aside as she stepped over and pressed the wet gauze to the cut on his belly.

"Owwweee! That's cold!" he exclaimed, then blew out a lungful of air as she bent her head and focused on cleaning the wound. "You don't give a guy much time to get prepared."

"Just like diving into a pool of cold water," she said. "Don't think, just make a quick jump and get the shock over with."

The shock of kissing her certainly hadn't left him, Cordell thought. He wasn't sure he'd ever be the same. Even now, as the warmth of her fingers brushed against his flesh, he was reliving every second his mouth had been on hers.

"Is that what you normally tell the patients you're treating?" he attempted to joke. "Right before you jab them with a hypodermic needle?"

She chuckled softly as she put down the gauze and reached for the antibiotic salve. "I thought you were supposed to be a tough cowboy."

"Yeah, well, a man has his limitations, you know."

She smoothed the ointment over the wound and after covering it with two large bandages, she straightened to her full height and reached for his shirt.

"There," she said, as she began to snap the pieces of fabric back together. "You're all fixed. That didn't hurt much, did it?"

"Hurt like hell," he told her.

Finished with the last snap, she dropped the tails of his shirt and lifted her gaze to his. "Really?"

"I'm still hurting." He reached for her and once her head was carefully cradled in the crook of his arm, he lowered his mouth to within a scant inch of hers. "Because I couldn't do this."

Her eyes darkened and then her soft sigh was whispering against his cheek. "I didn't mean to cause you pain, Cord."

"Then why don't you kiss me and make it all better?"

She gently cupped the palm of her hand against the side of his face and Cordell could only wonder why her touch felt so different. How could just the simple touch of her fingers give him such a thrill? It was ridiculous.

Her lips tilted to a provocative slant. "Since I don't have any candy to give you, I suppose you do deserve a kiss—or two—for being a good patient."

"Mmm. You are so right," he spoke against her cheek.

A moan vibrated in her throat at the same time her arms slipped around him. Cordell fastened his lips over hers and as he folded her upper body close to his chest, he was struck with the same incredible magic he'd felt when the two of them had kissed only minutes ago.

Slowly and softly, his lips searched hers and then he lifted his head just enough to look into her eyes. The green orbs were drowsy and glimmering with desire. The sight of it caused a deep hunger to stir in the pit of his belly.

"You did say a kiss—or two, didn't you?" He whispered the question.

"I did."

"Then I'd better make the most of the second one."

He lowered his mouth back to hers and this time there was no holding back for either of them. On and on they kissed, each giving and taking until the need for oxygen finally forced them to break the hot connection of their lips.

Turning his head aside, Cordell sucked in ragged breaths and attempted to rein in the desire that was threatening to consume him. At this moment, there was only one thing on his mind and that was to carry her over to the bed, strip away her clothes and make passionate love to her.

And what would be so wrong with that, Cord? Consequences never stepped in your way before. Take what she's offering and don't worry about tomorrow.

He was tussling with the mocking voice in his head when she suddenly wiggled out of his arms, taking away any chance he might've had to carry out the urgings of his body.

Breathing hard, she turned her back to him. "I, uh, think that's probably enough reward for being a good patient."

Her voice was so low and husky he could barely

hear the words and he realized the hot chemistry that had exploded between them had shaken her as much as it had jolted him.

And just like that, Quint's warning was darting through his head. Getting involved with Maggie would be like playing with fire, his younger brother had predicted. At the time, Cordell had been amused by his little brother's advice. Yet now he had to admit it was ringing all too true. She wasn't just a woman who set his libido on fire. She was doing something to his thinking. And no matter how much he fought against the change coming over him, he couldn't seem to stop it.

"Yeah," he said quietly. "We'd probably better get our things together and head on down the trail. Otherwise—well, we don't want our ride to end with regrets."

She turned toward him and as he watched shadows of disappointment fill her eyes, something in the middle of his chest twisted into an uncomfortable knot. Whatever she was thinking, he didn't want her to have regrets. Not about kissing him.

"Cord, I hope you don't believe— Well, when I asked you to kiss me, I didn't realize—" Her gaze dropped to her feet. "I'm not a tease. But I guess I've behaved like one. I can't explain—I'm just not myself today."

He could've told her that ever since he'd first met her at the wedding reception, he hadn't been himself. But admitting such a thing to her would only make things even more awkward. Especially when he had to tell her goodbye.

His hand wrapped around her upper arm and gave the flesh a gentle squeeze. "Maggie, I'm not thinking anything of the sort," he said gently. "No need for either of us to get bent out of shape over what happened. We kissed. It was natural. And nice—for both of us."

She looked up and he could see her lips were trembling as she tried to smile. "Nice. Yes."

He'd never been a convincing liar, but he was doing a hell of a job of it right now, Cordell thought.

Swallowing at the thickness in his throat, he said, "Thanks for treating my cut. It already feels better."

"You're welcome."

She stepped over to the table and began to place the items she'd used back into the medical kit.

As Cordell watched her complete the task, he wondered why he felt a little sick inside. Was it because they'd only kissed—nothing more? Or was the reality that she'd soon be gone from his life something he couldn't bear to think about?

Minutes later, the two of them left the cabin and started down a mountain trail different than the one they'd ridden up. Since then Cordell hadn't spoken much and she wondered if he was regretting those moments he'd held her in his arms. Sure, he'd acted as though he'd enjoyed her kisses, Maggie thought, but then having a woman fawn over him was probably a routine occurrence for him.

Are you satisfied now, Maggie? You kissed Cordell. Not once, but several times. Now you know what it's like to be thrilled by a man. Now you can go home and lament over the fact that you'll never feel such rapturous heights again. What were you thinking?

The taunting voice going on in her head very nearly brought tears to her eyes, but she determinedly blocked out the sound.

She'd be damned before she'd let herself have regrets about asking Cordell to kiss her. Yes, maybe it would make it harder for her to forget him. But at least she'd have the special memories to carry with her for a lifetime.

"I don't want to spook you, Maggie. But you should take a look at this."

Cordell's voice broke into her swirling thoughts and she glanced up to see he'd reined his horse to a halt next to a tall lodgepole pine. Other than more rocks and spruce trees, she didn't see anything else near the trail, especially anything that appeared spooky.

She urged her horse forward until she reached his side. "What is it?" she asked.

He pointed to the trunk of the pine. "A rather large visitor has come through here and from the fresh looks of the markings, it was only a few hours ago."

Glad to have her mind on something other than him, Maggie curiously studied the tree. Long, deep scratches had torn away pieces of the bark to expose streaks of light-colored wood.

She asked, "What did that damage? A mountain lion? Or do you have those around here?"

He shook his head. "We do, a few different species of mountain lions, in fact. But this wasn't made by a big cat. These marks were made by a black bear."

"How can you determine those were made by a bear?"

"The height. Plus I can see a few tracks leading off the trail." He pointed to a spot on the ground just in front of Bugs' right shoulder. "The length of its foot and marks of its claws are clearly visible."

Maggie darted a cautious glance at the rugged forest surrounding them. "It never crossed my mind that bear might be close by. The weather is cold. Wouldn't the animals be in hibernation by now?"

"The males are sometimes slow about bedding down for the winter. They usually hunt for food as long as the weather isn't brutally cold." He grinned at her. "But don't get spooked. He doesn't want to face off with two horses and two humans."

He nudged Bugs on down the trail, then glanced back to make sure she was following. "The trail on this side of the mountain is shorter so we'll be at the foothill soon. When we get there I have something else to show you."

"Another cabin?" she asked wryly.

His low, sexy laugh made her smile.

"No. No more cabins between here and home."

Home. Strange how her little house down in Arizona no longer conjured up her image of home, Maggie thought. Yes, it provided her with comfort and sheltered her from the elements. She even felt a sense of pride for being a homeowner at her young age. But the rooms weren't filled with conversation or laughter, or the kind of warmth that came from genuine love.

She couldn't know when, or if, she might ever find that kind of love. But she had learned one thing from the incredible moments she'd spent in Cordell's arms. She wasn't dead inside. She was capable of feeling true passion. Now all she had to do was find a man who'd want to share that passion with her for the rest of his life.

A half hour later, near the base of the mountain, they intersected a small branch of water and followed the downward flow until it eventually spilled into Bird Creek. There, a canopy of fir trees opened up to reveal a sky full of bright sunshine and a cold north wind swooping across the valley floor.

Maggie reined Domino to a stop and called to Cordell, who was riding a few steps in front of her.

"Give me a minute to fix my scarf, Cord. This wind is brutal."

He stopped Bugs in the middle of the trail and waited while she wrapped the scarf higher upon her neck and tightened the strings of her hood even more beneath her chin.

"We're not far from where I intended for us to stop," he told her. "But if you're freezing, we'll skip it and head on."

"Quit trying to make a wimp out of me! I imagine I can stand this cold better than you could take the Arizona heat," she taunted playfully.

"You're probably right," he said with a grin, then gestured upstream. "Okay, we go this way."

After riding a hundred more yards or so, Maggie spotted a pile of old logs and lumber partially hidden by tall clumps of sagebrush.

"Was a house here once?" she asked as they drew the horses to a halt a few feet away. "Some of your family?"

"No. This old dilapidated structure was here before Lionel ever built the ranch. Evidently, prospectors were using water from the creek to wash ore."

"Ore? You mean they were digging for gold or silver in this area?" She looked around her for a sign of an old mine entrance, but saw nothing that resembled a cave.

"Gold is the assumption," he told her. "Let's get down for a closer look."

After helping her out of the saddle, he tethered the horses to the branches of a fallen log, then returned to her side. As the two of them started walking through clumps of sage and boulders, Maggie was thinking how natural it was to have his arm curved protectively against the back of her waist, how right it felt to be on this little adventure with him.

Once they reached the pile of logs and lumber, Maggie surveyed the ruins for long moments before she finally asked, "If this wasn't once a cabin or shack, what was it?"

"Sluice boxes to recover gold," he answered. "At one time the whole thing probably made a trough that sloped from the water's edge onto dry ground. The water washes away the silt and gravel, while the heavier pieces of gold remain in the sluice box."

His explanation created a full image in her mind and it quickly sparked her imagination. "Then these pieces of logs and timber might be centuries old," she said with wonder. "Do you have any idea if gold was found?"

He shook his head. "Dad once looked through the county land registries to see if anyone ever filed a mine claim, but there wasn't any record of minerals ever being discovered on this land. As for Grandfather, he was never interested in finding a fortune in the ground."

"Hmm. Well, I don't really know much about the legalities of claiming a mine, but I imagine there were prospectors who kept their finds secret. Mainly for self-preservation reasons. The untamed West was rough, you know. Men had to fight to survive."

He angled an indulgent smile at her. "You sound

like Van. Do you teach history when you're not working in the ER?"

She laughed lightly. "No. These sluice boxes bring back memories of my high school classes on Arizona history. Our state had its fair share of gold rushes, too. But I'll confess. Part of my history knowledge might be coming from the tons of Western movies I've watched. You know, where the villains try to move in on the heroine and steal the gold mine she'd just inherited from her slain father."

Chuckling, he shook his head. "I believe you have watched a few Westerns. Was this a part of your college curriculum?"

"Of course," she said with a guilty grin. "Between biology and anatomy, a girl had to have some entertainment in her life."

His brows arched toward the brim of his hat. "What about boyfriends? I'm sure you had plenty of those in college to keep you entertained."

She shrugged. "A few. But they were mostly pals," she said, then cut him a sly glance. "I'm fairly certain you had a list of girlfriends during your college days."

He let out a short laugh. "I've always had girlfriends, Maggie. It started in kindergarten with a little black-haired girl by the name of Sarah. She had the biggest brownest eyes I'd ever seen and she always wanted to hold my hand. Made me feel like a prince."

Smiling wanly, she asked, "So do your present girlfriends make you feel like a prince?"

He turned to face her and Maggie tried not to tremble as his forefinger came to a rest beneath her chin. "You do."

Why in heck did she want to believe the serious look in his eyes? Why did the softness in his voice melt something deep inside her? The answers were obvious. Where Cordell was concerned, she couldn't help being a fool.

Trying to make light of his response, she looked away from him and let out a little laugh, but it sounded terribly hollow. "Oh, Cord, I'm going to miss your funny nonsense."

His forefinger tugged on her chin until she was looking directly into his blue eyes.

"Then why don't you stay on Stone Creek a little longer?"

She was glad she was wearing layers of heavy clothing. Otherwise he might've seen that her heart was pounding so hard, her chest was quaking.

"You've already asked me to stay longer and I told you I couldn't. That hasn't changed. I have to go."

He released a heavy breath. "Yeah. But that was before we, uh, found out we sizzle when we're— together."

Her nostrils flared as her gaze dropped to the tempting line of his lips. Oh, if only she had the courage to fling herself into his arms and beg him to make love to her right here on the creek bank. But she wasn't bold enough or brave enough to give that much of herself to him.

"Sizzles usually turn to flames. I don't want to remember us as a pile of ashes," she murmured. "Do you?"

"No. I want—" He didn't go on. Instead, he put an arm around her shoulders. "Forget it. We'd better move on."

As the two walked back to the waiting horses, Maggie wondered what he'd been about to say to her. Yet she knew there was no point in asking him. He wasn't going to suddenly start mouthing platitudes about how he'd suddenly fallen in love with her. That he needed and wanted her to stay with him, not just for a few more days, but for the rest of their lives. And even if he did say those flowery words to her, she'd believe him about as much as she believed snow would fall in Wickenburg in mid-July.

Her thoughts came to an abrupt halt as the hand on her shoulder suddenly stopped her forward motion.

"Maggie, take a look over to our right," he instructed.

At first she had no idea what she was supposed to be looking for and then she heard tinkling bells. Seconds later, she spotted a fairly large herd of wooly sheep emerging from a heavy growth of underbrush.

She gasped with delight. "The sheep! Oh Cord, they're so beautiful. Aww, and look at all the little lambs."

Her reaction pulled a chuckle from him. "The way you're carrying on I'd think you'd never seen a sheep before."

She darted an annoyed look at him. "Of course I've seen sheep, even close up. But this is different. There are so many of them and in such a gorgeous area with the creek and the sage and spruce trees all around."

"Sorry. I guess this is so routine to me that I don't stop to appreciate how pretty it all looks. Thanks for reminding me," he said.

She gave him a dubious smirk. "Do you really mean that? Or is this some Cordell sarcasm?"

Frowning, he said, "Sure, I mean it. And in case you're interested, we have the sheep separated into two different herds. The larger one is presently grazing the area over toward Snow Mountain. I thought we'd have to travel a bit further west to spot this bunch. We were lucky, they found us."

Fascinated, she watched the group of ewes and lambs grow closer and then to her surprise, she spotted a pair of Great Pyrenees dogs with long, shaggy white coats trotting a short distance behind the herd. The canines appeared to be completely focused on the sheep and totally ignoring her and Cordell.

Perplexed, she looked at him. "I don't understand, Cord. There are no cowboys around. And these dogs act like they don't even see us. Who's giving them orders?"

He chuckled. "No one is giving them orders. They're trained to remain with the herd and understand their job is to not let any of the sheep wander off and to keep away predators such as coyotes and mountain lions. You see, right now we don't have a regular sheepherder on the ranch. And we can't spare one of our regular ranch hands to stay with the sheep round the clock. So we have dogs to do most of the work."

She smiled as she watched a pair of lambs frolicking around their mother. "I'm impressed. I've heard of sheepdogs, but I had no idea they could do so much on their own. Clearly they're intelligent, but they'd have to be loyal and dedicated, too." She glanced at him. "What do the dogs eat while they're away from the ranch and guarding a herd?"

"Quint, or one of the ranch hands, brings food out on a daily basis for the dogs. Besides caring for the dogs, someone has to make sure the sheep have plenty of grazing and water available and to doctor any animal that might be sick or injured. So it's a big, never-ending job. In a way, the sheep require more work than the cattle because they're more vulnerable."

She gazed thoughtfully at the sheep. "After hearing all this, I can only wonder why Quint was so happy about getting the job of overseeing the sheep division. I heard him talking at the dinner table about wanting to increase the number of animals. How does he expect to keep up with all the extra work?"

"My little brother is just like any other man. It's important for him to feel needed. As for increasing the sheep count on Stone Creek, Quint insists he can find a guy to take the full-time job of sheepherder. But I've tried to warn him that finding the right guy for the position isn't going to be as easy as he thinks. It's a hard, lonely job. Not just any man wants to hole himself up in the mountains for ten months out of the year without anyone to talk to except his dogs and horses."

"Oh, I don't know," she said with feigned seriousness. "You might find a guy without any family or friends. That way he wouldn't have anyone to miss. It might help matters if he was antisocial and didn't like phones, TV or computers. And last but not least, he might be extra savvy about taking care of horses, sheep and dogs. I'll bet you know plenty of guys like that."

She looked over at him and they both began to laugh together. And in that moment she felt especially close to him.

"Sure, Maggie. You can pick up men with those qualities on any street corner," he joked.

She gave the sheep one long last look before she lifted her gaze to his. "Thank you, Cord, for showing me such beautiful places on the ranch and sharing information about them," she said softly. "I'll never forget this day."

"I have a feeling I won't forget it, either."

She started to move forward, but something in his eyes made it impossible for her to leave his side. And then, before she could guess his intentions, he lowered his head and kissed her lips so softly and sweetly it felt as if a thousand butterflies were fluttering around her heart.

When he eventually eased his head back from hers, he said, "I wanted to give you a goodbye kiss while we're out here and alone. Instead of with the whole family standing around watching."

A lump of emotion hung in her throat, forcing her to swallow before she spoke. "I'm not leaving until the day after tomorrow."

"We won't be standing here by Bird Creek the day after tomorrow," he explained, then with a hand on her shoulder urged her on to the waiting horses.

As much as she wanted to, Maggie didn't turn her head and give the sheep one last look. Nor did she look at Cordell as he gave her a foot up in the saddle.

No. She didn't want to take the risk of bursting into tears at the thought of leaving him and Stone Creek Ranch behind.

Chapter Eight

The next morning, Maggie awoke to bright sunlight streaming across the bed. Ten after nine! She'd planned to be up hours ago!

Pushing back the covers, she was about to swing her legs over the side of the mattress, when a knock sounded on her bedroom door.

"Maggie? It's me, Van. Are you awake in there?"

Sitting straight up, Maggie called out, "Come in, Van."

Smiling cheerfully, Vanessa strolled into the room and plopped down on a dressing bench at the end of the bed. "Good morning, sleepyhead. Did I wake you?"

Maggie pushed a tumbled wave of red hair back from her face and swung her feet to the floor. "I had just opened my eyes when you knocked. Why didn't you wake me earlier, Van? I didn't want to waste this last full day on the ranch sleeping!"

Vanessa pretended to sniff back tears. "Don't remind me that you'll be leaving in the morning. I'm going to miss you terribly."

Maggie sighed. "You have plenty in your life without me around. Once I'm gone you'll think of me, but you won't miss me."

Vanessa frowned. "What's with the cynical malarkey? Did you sleep on the wrong side of the bed?"

Maggie had gone to bed last night believing she was tired enough to fall asleep instantly. Instead, she'd lain awake, her mind reliving every minute she'd spent with Cordell. Then shortly after eleven, she'd heard his bedroom door opening and closing and then the faint sounds of his boots moving across the hardwood floor. After that, she couldn't stop herself from imagining him in bed, lying between the sheets with nothing on. She couldn't quit wondering what he might do if she walked into his room and slipped into the bed with him.

"Sorry for sounding so cranky," Maggie said ruefully. "I didn't sleep well."

Vanessa said, "I'm not surprised. You and Cord took a long ride yesterday. My body would've been aching all over."

"I wasn't aching," Maggie told her. "My brain refused to slow down enough to let me sleep."

Vanessa studied her with a keen glance. "Hmm. You seemed preoccupied about something last night. Especially after dinner. You hardly said two words."

She scrubbed her face with both hands. "You and your family were discussing the upcoming holidays. So I thought it best just to listen."

Vanessa impatiently rolled her eyes. "While you sat there feeling sorry for yourself, because you won't be celebrating the holidays. Instead, you'll insist on making a martyr of yourself and work every shift available just—"

"Stop it!" Maggie interrupted. "I don't volunteer for extra shifts to be a martyr!"

Shaking her head, Vanessa said, "I'm sorry. That was mean of me. So why did you come up here to your room so early last night?"

Maggie stood and reached for her robe. She couldn't admit to Vanessa that when Cordell had disappeared with Hadley and Jack shortly after dinner, she'd felt so ridiculously lost without his company that she'd decided to retire for the evening.

"Cord and I rode a long distance and the cold wind has a way of wearing on a body. Especially when you're not accustomed to it. I was tired."

She pulled on the chenille robe and as she tied the sash at her waist, she glanced over to see Vanessa was watching her with a keen eye. No doubt her friend could see through her half-baked excuses for her unusual behavior.

"I haven't had much chance to talk to you about your ride with Cord yesterday," Vanessa said. "And neither one of you said much about it at the dinner table. Did everything go okay?"

Maggie forced a cheerful smile on her face. "Everything was great. The ranch is beyond beautiful and Domino was such a sweet little lady to ride. And Cord was a perfect guide."

"I'm happy to hear you two got along. I know you disapprove of his playboy past. But he seems to be putting all of that behind him. Actually, it's been so long since he's gone on a date, Jack is beginning to worry something is wrong with him."

Now that Maggie had experienced Cordell's arms around her and his lips on hers, she recoiled at the idea of him making love to another woman. But that kind of thinking was idiotic. Cordell was a free-roaming maverick. He wasn't going to save his kisses just for one woman.

She walked over to the closet to collect a pair of jeans and a thin pink sweater. "Jack needn't worry. Cord won't be without a woman for long," she said, while hoping she didn't sound as glum as she felt.

"Well, I didn't get you out of bed to discuss Cord's dating habits," Vanessa said. "I was wondering if you've purchased your plane ticket for tomorrow yet?"

When Maggie had originally booked her flight from the Phoenix airport to Cedar City, she'd only purchased a one-way ticket. At that time her schedule to return to work hadn't yet been determined and she'd wanted to make sure of the exact day before she committed to a ticket for the flight home.

She placed the jeans and sweater across the foot of the bed. "No. That's something I need to do before I have my morning coffee. Do you mind if I use your office computer? Since I've been here on the ranch, the signal on my smartphone has been almost nonexistent. My cell carrier isn't living up to its nationwide coverage," she said with sardonic humor.

"My computer is yours anytime. But you might not need a plane ticket."

Maggie let out a short laugh. "I haven't grown wings, Van. I have to purchase a ticket. Preferably for a flight that leaves out fairly early in the morning because I'll have to get Emma to drive down to Phoenix to pick me up."

Smiling shrewdly, Vanessa said, "Forget all of that. Cord is leaving for Three Rivers Ranch in the morning. He'll drive right through Wickenburg. I'm certain he'll be thrilled to have you as a traveling companion. It will save you money and save your friend a long drive to Phoenix."

Somewhat dazed by this unexpected development, Maggie stared at her. Travel all the way to Arizona with Cordell? She couldn't imagine anything riskier. But how much chancier could the trip be than the one she'd made with him yesterday? Not much, she decided. True, they'd kissed with reckless abandon at the cabin, but nothing had happened beyond those kisses. Ultimately, she'd held her common sense together and so had he.

"Uh, why is Cord going to Three Rivers? Is it something about the Hollister family tree?"

"Gosh, I wish that was the reason for his trip. But no, Hadley has purchased three prize bulls from the ranch and he's sending Cord down to collect them. That's what the men were doing last night when they disappeared into the study. They were discussing the deal."

Vanessa had encouraged her to loosen up and enjoy spending time with Cordell while she was here on Stone Creek. But that hardly meant her friend wanted Maggie to become obsessed with the man. Not for anything did she want Vanessa to get the idea that she'd foolishly fallen for the guy. Because she hadn't. Yes, she was wildly attracted to him, but lust wasn't anything close to love.

"Well, I can't just hitch a ride without an invitation. If Cord asks me to join him on the trip, I might consider it. Otherwise, I—"

Vanessa interrupted with a shake of her head. "Maggie, if you wait around on Cord for an invite, you might not be able to purchase a plane ticket for a flight tomorrow. It's not like Cedar City has dozens of flights leaving out every day." Rising from the bench, she started toward the door. "I think Cord is with Hadley right now in his study. I'll go let him know you want to see him before he leaves the house."

"No!"

Perplexed by Maggie's one-word outburst, Vanessa paused to look back at her. "What do you mean, no? You just told me if Cord invited you that you'd accept his offer."

"Uh, yes, I know. I did say that," Maggie said, as she tried to explain her wishy-washy response. "And I realize you're trying to help me save money, but I don't want to push myself on Cord. I've budgeted for my plane fare. It's no problem."

"Stop with the silliness and get dressed," Vanessa ordered. "I'll see you in a little while."

Vanessa left the room and Maggie quickly snatched up her jeans and sweater and headed to the bathroom. This was her last day at Stone Creek Ranch, and she didn't want to spend it worrying over what tomorrow may or may not bring.

On the ground floor of the house, in the study Hadley used for an office, Cordell sat in front of the wide wooden desk as his father went over last-minute details for the trip to Arizona.

"Once you get the bulls loaded and start back, I don't want you fooling around with any unnecessary stops," Hadley said. "The trip is going to be long and stressful for the bulls without you adding to the strain."

It didn't matter that Cordell and his brothers had been grown men for several years; Hadley still gave all of them the same kind of orders he'd given them during their teenage years. At the moment, Cordell felt the urge to tell his father he wouldn't stop to catch a movie, or pull over at every fast-food joint on the highway to get an ice cream cone. But he kept the sarcasm to himself.

This deal for the bulls was important to Hadley for many reasons. The superior quality of the animals would greatly improve the calf production on Stone Creek. Secondly, Hadley felt it was one of the first steps of building a bridge between his family and Gil's. And thirdly, Cordell loved and respected his father too much to openly mock his orders.

"Don't worry, Dad," Cordell told him. "I'll make the trip for them as smooth as possible."

Hadley rose from his executive chair and walked over to a small safe built into a wood-paneled wall. After retrieving an envelope from inside the safe, he returned to the front of the desk and handed the manila square to Cordell.

"This should cover the bulls and anything else you might need along the way," he said. "You also have the ranch's credit card, in case you run into the unexpected. And Cord, I want you to remember this is a deal with our new family and I want you to treat them as such. Maureen and Gil will be delighted to meet you. So get ready to be lavished with a tremendous amount of hospitality."

"I understand, Dad. And trust me, I'll act like a gentleman and show them that our side of the Hollister family is good stock, too."

Hadley patted his shoulder with approval. "I never thought you'd do anything less, Cord."

Cordell opened the envelope and found a stack of money, along with a check made out for the amount of the bulls. He'd handled business dealings of his father before, but nothing of this i. .agnitude.

"Knock, knock."

The muffled female voice sounded through the closed door of the study and Hadley promptly walked over and opened it.

"Van, come in!" he boomed in a cheerful voice. "Cord and I were just finishing up."

Her glance encompassed both men as she stepped into the room. "I don't want to interrupt, but I'm glad I caught you two together."

Hadley shot her a look of concern. "Is anything wrong?"

Vanessa hugged an arm around the back of her father-in-law's waist. "Not in the least, Hadley. I wanted to ask a favor of Cord. Since he's going to be driving through Wickenburg tomorrow, I thought he could give Maggie a lift home. It would save her the cost of plane fare. Plus, it would give her a chance to see a bit of scenery between here and there."

Cordell's brain was suddenly spinning at a high rate of speed. He'd been so busy agonizing over today being Maggie's last day on the ranch, the thought of her riding back to Arizona with him had never once crossed his mind.

Hadley said, "Well now, I think that's a great

idea. I should've already thought about Maggie catching a lift with Cord."

Vanessa smiled hopefully at Cordell. "What do you think, Cord? Would you mind having Maggie for company? She's about to purchase a plane ticket, so I need—no, let me rephrase that, *you* need to go invite her. She doesn't want to be a pest."

Feeling half-numb, Cordell rose from the chair. "I—sure. I'd be glad to have Maggie along. That is, if she's willing to make the long drive." He left off the *with me* part. He didn't want to give Vanessa or his father a reason to think there was any kind of tension between him and Maggie. "I'll go find her right now."

Before any more could be said, Cordell left the study and carried the manila envelope up to his bedroom. After locking the cash safely in his own personal safe, he left the room and walked over to Maggie's door.

When she failed to answer, he went downstairs and eventually found her in the den. She was sitting in an armchair in front of the fireplace, sipping hot coffee.

"Look at you," he said with a teasing grin. "Sitting in an armchair drinking coffee is a far cry from riding Domino in the cold weather. I hope the wind didn't chap your cheeks."

She gave him a faint smile as he walked over to stand on the fireplace hearth. "I soaked them and my lips with petroleum jelly. That done the trick."

Cordell's gaze slipped over the strawberry blonde hair brushed loose upon her shoulders, the pale oval of her face and her lips, which were just a shade darker than the pink sweater she was wearing. From the moment he'd met Maggie, her beauty was the one thing he'd never misjudged. But there were many things about her that he had misinterpreted. She was far from distant and unfeeling. Nor was she self-absorbed or snobby as he'd first assumed. More than once he'd walked into the kitchen and found her helping his mother clean the dishes or prepare the evening meal. Not to mention the hours she'd spent helping Vanessa dig for ancestry clues.

"I missed you last night after dinner," he told her. "Dad and Jack kept me in a meeting and then when it finally ended, I came down here to find you, but Mom told me you'd gone to bed. Guess you were tired after the long ride."

She nodded. "I won't lie. I was tired. But I'm good today. Not even a sore muscle."

"You must go to the gym."

"Hah! Who has time for the gym? Remember, I have to race around the ER stabbing people with hypodermic needles," she joked. "Keeps my legs and arms in shape."

He chuckled, then realizing he was suddenly nervous, he drew in a deep bracing breath. What in hell was wrong with him, anyway? In all of his adult life, he couldn't remember a time he'd gotten rattled over asking a woman to go out with him.

You're being stupid, Cord. You'd be better off if she did turn down your invitation. You need to make your goodbye to Maggie short and final. Not spend several hours cooped up with her in the cab of a truck.

"Well, I'm on my way to the ranch yard. I just stopped by the den to tell you that Dad is sending me to Three Rivers tomorrow and I thought you might like to catch a ride with me. I realize flying would be faster and probably more comfortable for you. But going down the highway, you'll get to see lots of scenery. And I promise I'm a safe driver. Besides, I'd be a lot better company than what you'd probably find on an airplane."

One of her delicate brows arched with wry skepticism.

"Van put you up to this, didn't she?"

He felt his face growing warm. "She mentioned it. But I would've asked you anyway."

With a heavy sigh, she placed her coffee cup on an end table next to her chair.

"Listen, Cord, one thing I can't stand is a person who makes a nuisance of him- or herself. I don't want to be a nuisance. You have ranching business to deal with. Not being a taxi service for me."

He walked over to her chair and clasping his hands around hers, gently pulled her to her feet. "I'm not worried about you being a bother, Maggie. I thought we'd have a good time together. We can count the out-of-state tags we see on the vehicles we pass on the highway, sing along to the radio and eat too much fast food. Sounds like a blast, doesn't it?"

She gave him a hopeless smile. "I can't imagine anything more fun."

He squeezed her hands. "Are you saying yes?"

"Okay," she said softly. "It's a yes."

Grinning, he bent his head and placed a swift kiss on her cheek. "Thanks, Maggie."

"For what? I'm the one who's saving money in this deal."

He chuckled. "I'm thanking you for agreeing to be housed up with me for five hundred miles."

She gave him a coy glance. "I'm a nurse, remember. I always carry plenty of aspirin with me."

Laughing, he planted another kiss on her cheek, then hurried out of the den before he got carried away and placed one on her lips.

The next morning before the sun had risen over the eastern ridge of distant mountains, Cordell put the truck and trailer into motion, while across from him in the passenger seat, Maggie shamelessly dabbed at the tears spilling onto her cheeks.

"Maggie, you shouldn't be crying," he said gently. "It's going to be a beautiful day."

She didn't look in his direction. Instead, she bowed her head and continued to press a small square of napkin to her eyes.

"Yes, but I—might never see your family again, Cord. And I—"

Her broken voice trailed away and for a moment Cordell considered stopping the truck and making an attempt to console her. But they were still within sight of the ranch house. He didn't want his family or any of the hands to spot the stalled truck and think he was having problems. Which would be accurate. Seeing Maggie cry was ripping a hole right in the middle of his chest.

Thankfully, after a couple of minutes, she lifted her head and said in a choked whisper, "Your mother looked so sad when I told her goodbye."

She certainly wasn't exaggerating, Cordell thought. He'd been standing to one side, waiting while Maggie had said her goodbyes to the family and frankly it had been awkward as hell to see his parents trying to put on a cheerful act when he knew both of them hated to see her leave. And poor Bonnie had looked stricken. On the other hand, Vanessa had been surprisingly cheerful. She'd even given him a conspiring wink as she'd reminded him to drive safely.

Deciding a dose of firm reality might do better than coddling, he said, "Goodbyes are usually sad. But this business of you never seeing them again is a bunch of hogwash."

His last remark appeared to stiffen her spine and she glared at him through bleary green eyes. "How would you know? You can't see into my future!"

He shrugged. "You can't see into mine, either. But the distance between Stone Creek Ranch and

Wickenburg, Arizona, isn't halfway around the world—like you're making it out to be."

She made one last swipe at her eyes before dropping the napkin in her handbag. "Okay, Cord. I'm guilty of being overemotional and melodramatic. Don't worry. I'm not going to cry or whine the whole way to Arizona."

He reached over and gave her hand a squeeze. "I'm not worried," he teased. "I brought a pair of earplugs with me. Just in case you get to chattering too much."

She gave him a lopsided smile. "I'll try not to sound like a happy canary."

By the time they reached Beaver City, Maggie's spirits appeared to lift and for the next hundred miles, Cordell made an effort to point out the more interesting landmarks along the way.

When they reached St. George, he pulled over at a fast-food restaurant for a short coffee and restroom break. Once they were back in the truck and headed southbound, they crossed the state line and entered Nevada. The landscape quickly changed to dry, desert hills and Maggie was delighted when she began to spot wild burros grazing among clumps of sage and tall Joshua trees.

"I can't imagine what those burros are eating out there. The land is so barren. This makes Stone Creek Ranch look like a green paradise."

"I agree. Amazingly, ranchers somehow manage

to run livestock on this land. I wouldn't know how to do it, that's for sure."

Now that they were traveling through countryside he'd rarely seen, his focus should've been on the landscape passing by them. But the stark scenery wasn't enough to keep his gaze from continually straying over to Maggie.

She was dressed all in black from her cowboy boots and jeans, along with a black long-sleeved sweater. The latter was made with a slit from the base of her throat all the way down to a spot between her breasts and if she moved a certain way, he could catch a glimpse of her pale skin. A sight that played havoc with his senses. And with each passing mile, he wondered if he'd turned into some sort of soft-hearted fool.

He'd been an idiot for not making love to her when they been in the cabin. She'd wanted him. He'd tasted the hunger in her lips, felt it in the way her hands had touched him. But for once in his life he'd wanted to put a woman's feelings before his own sexual desire. He'd not wanted to turn Maggie into one of his many discards. She deserved better than that—than him.

Yet as the clock on the dashboard continued to tick away and the miles slipped behind them, he was beginning to feel a little sick with regret. He was also wishing that somehow the two of them didn't have to say goodbye. At least, not a permanent goodbye.

"Are you making it okay?" he asked after a few minutes of silence had passed between them.

"I'm fine. Your truck is very comfortable. It feels like we're floating."

"Not like riding Domino, eh?"

"No. But she was nice. Our ride was nice."

When she didn't say more he glanced over to see her expression had turned reflective. Was she, too, remembering the cabin and their kisses? No. He couldn't let himself ponder on any of that now. It was too late to go back. Too late to change anything.

He cleared his throat and adjusted the aviator sunglasses covering his eyes. "If you're getting hungry, there are plenty of snacks inside the console. Mom packed a whole sack full of things."

"I know. She put in some of the leftover doughnuts she fried for breakfast. I'm not about to get into the sack or I'll eat two or three. But I'll get something for you, if you like."

"No, thanks. I was thinking when we reach Bullhead City we'd stop and have a nice dinner."

She looked at him. "Do we have time?"

"We'll make time," he promised. "The bulls aren't leaving until I get there."

"If that's the case, then dinner would be nice," she told him.

"Yeehaw!" he yelled with a happy whoop. "It's taken me close to four hundred miles and several hours of driving, but you've finally agreed to have dinner with me."

The smile she gave him was surprisingly tender. "You're full of nonsense, Cord Hollister."

"Not when it comes to you, Maggie."

An hour and a half later, Maggie shifted around in the seat to ease the stiffness creeping into her legs and lower back. "How much farther to Bullhead City?"

"I'm guessing about ten miles or so," he answered. "Getting tired?"

"Yes. And hungry."

He slanted her an amused glance. "I won't ask if you're having fun yet."

The remark had barely left his mouth, when all of a sudden, the truck began to sputter and lurch.

"What the hell?" he muttered.

Maggie glanced over to see he was carefully studying the instrument panel behind the steering wheel. Although, the truck was still carrying them on down the highway, it was obvious the engine was running roughly.

"Oh, wow! What happened? I thought we were going to stop completely," she remarked.

He groaned. "I don't know what happened. Damn! The engine light is flashing. I'll take a look under the hood. A wire or something could be loose."

Fortunately the highway had wide graveled shoulders. He carefully parked the truck as far off the road as possible and while Maggie waited inside the truck, he took a look under the hood. After a few short minutes he climbed back into the driver's seat and set the truck into motion.

"I can do a little mechanic work in a pinch and I couldn't find anything that looked out of place. Let's just hope we can sputter into Bullhead City without breaking down completely."

Not wanting to make matters worse with a bunch of inane questions, she simply nodded. However, once he pulled back onto the highway and set the truck in motion it quickly became obvious the vehicle couldn't build any speed.

"Something has cut the power," he stated the obvious. "But we're not far from Bullhead City. If necessary it won't take long to get a tow truck to haul us the rest of the way."

She gave him an encouraging smile. "I'm not worried in the least."

Admiration flashed across his face. "No. I don't suppose a little car trouble is enough to shake you. Not when you're used to dealing with life-and-death situations."

"You're giving me too much credit. I have my shaky moments. You saw me this morning when we drove away from Stone Creek."

He shook his head. "You were emotional. Not in a panic."

The hot kisses he'd given her at the cabin had very nearly put her into a panic. Not to get away from him, she thought. No, the deep desire to make love to him had been the root of her fears.

"Nurses can't panic," she told him. "We have to keep ice in our veins."

Thankfully, the truck managed to slowly putter the remaining miles into Bullhead City, where Cordell stopped at the first car dealership they could find with a garage capable of dealing with major repairs. While he discussed the situation with the mechanics, Maggie tried to relax in the customer waiting room.

Like she'd told Cordell, the fact that they were momentarily stranded was no cause to panic. Yet it was beginning to look like getting to Wickenburg tonight might prove unlikely.

She was sitting in a hard plastic chair, flipping through a tattered magazine, when Cordell finally entered the room. Judging from the glum expression on his face, the news couldn't be good.

"What's the verdict?" she asked as he eased into the chair next to hers.

"I have good and bad news," he said. "The truck can be easily repaired. The problem is locating the replacement part. The mechanic has made calls all over town, but no luck. He's having one shipped from another dealership, but it won't arrive until midmorning tomorrow."

Maggie didn't blink an eye. True, she hadn't planned on this development, but neither had

Cordell. And whining and complaining would only make the matter worse.

"I see. Well, that just means we won't get to Wickenburg tonight."

"No. But we should get there by tomorrow afternoon. The mechanic assures me it only takes a few minutes to change the part on the truck." He reached over and gave her hand a squeeze. "I'm sorry about this, Maggie. Looks like you would've been better off taking a plane—the way you'd originally planned."

She shook her head. "You hardly knew the truck was going to break down. None of this is your fault. Things happen. That's all."

"Yeah. The mechanic said he rarely sees this kind of problem. Just our luck, I suppose. I was thinking if you absolutely need to be home by tonight, you might catch a plane from the Bullhead City airport or across the river at the Laughlin airport. I imagine either one of those airports have regular flights into Phoenix. Or you could call your friend to come after you. The one who was going to pick you up at the airport."

"I wouldn't dare ask Emma to make such a long drive. And I don't have any desire to spend most of the night sitting in an airport lobby waiting for a flight. Anyway, I scheduled in an extra day before I had to be back at work," she explained. "No problem, Cord. Everything will work out fine—

for the both of us." She made a palms-up gesture. "What now?"

"The dealership is lending us a vehicle to drive until the truck is repaired and I've already transferred our bags into the car. Let's go find a place to stay for the night."

"And eat," she added.

Chuckling, he pulled her to her feet. "We should be able to get some tasty sandwiches and potato chips from a convenience store."

Her eyes narrowed in a calculating way. "What happened to the promise of a nice dinner?"

He let out a short laugh. "It went out the window when I learned I was going to have to spring for a huge mechanic bill.".

With a good-natured shrug, she said, "Forget the sandwiches. I'll pay for dinner. Remember, I saved money by not buying the plane ticket."

He laughed again and this time it was a genuine sound that made her smile. It also made her appreciate his jovial attitude even when he'd been handed troubles. She knew several men who'd be handling the situation with a string of curse words or cold, sulky silence.

He said, "I'm joking, Maggie. The dinner will be on my dime. Anyway, the mechanic has assured me that the repairs aren't going to be that costly. The worst part is that we're stranded. But the breakdown happened for a reason, so we might as well make the most of the situation. Don't you think?"

Yes, everything in life happened for a reason, Maggie thought. So what was the reason his truck had suffered a hiccup? To delay their goodbyes? Was it actually meant for the two of them to be together for one night?

One night? Wake up and face facts, Maggie. You don't want to be with Cordell for just one night. You want to be with him forever.

"Maggie, did you hear me? Don't you think we ought to make the most of our time here in Bullhead City?"

Shaking away the little voice going through her head, she slipped her arm through his. "I definitely do. Let's think of it as an early Thanksgiving—for both of us."

"I like the sound of that."

Grinning, he slipped an arm around her waist and as they crossed the parking lot to the rental car, Maggie tried not to let herself think too far ahead. She didn't want anything to spoil this unexpected gift of having Cordell's company for one more night.

Chapter Nine

Cordell and Maggie chose to stay at one of the many hotels overlooking the Colorado River. After acquiring adjoining rooms, Maggie insisted she needed a few minutes to change and freshen up before they went to dinner.

While Cordell waited, he made use of the time to call his father and give him the unfortunate news of the truck's breakdown. Thankfully, Hadley took the delay all in stride and assured Cordell he would contact the Hollisters to let them know Cordell would be a day late reaching Three Rivers Ranch.

He'd just finished changing his blue denim shirt for a gray one and was running a comb through his hair, when a knock sounded on the door, followed by Maggie's muffled voice.

"It's me, Cord."

He quickly snatched up his hat and jacket, then joined her out in the corridor.

"Ready?" she asked.

She'd changed into a chocolate-colored dress that clung to her curves and draped slightly below her delicate collarbones. How was he supposed to concentrate on eating? She looked like a sexy siren with her hair lying over her shoulders like a red shawl and her lips the color of ripe strawberries.

Clearing his throat, he said, "All ready. The concierge tells me the hotel has a very good restaurant. He also said there's an excellent Italian restaurant within walking distance. I'm game for either."

"I love Italian food."

"Then Italian it will be," he told her. "The weather is so mild this evening I think it would be nice to walk. What about you?"

"Sounds lovely. I brought my coat just in case we'd be leaving the hotel." She placed her handbag on the floor and handed him a dark green coat she'd draped over her arm. "Would you care to help me with this? I have to hold the ends of my sleeves or they'll slide up."

"Sure." He held the garment out so she could slip her arms into the sleeves and as he smoothed the fabric across the top of her shoulders, the exotic scent of flowers and spices wrapped around his senses.

While she retrieved her handbag, he was asking

himself how she might react if he turned her around and placed a long, hot kiss on her lips. Would it be the start of their evening? Or the end of it?

Not giving himself a chance to put the question to the test, he put a hand beneath her elbow and quickly escorted her down the corridor to the nearest elevator.

As the two of them walked a pathway following the river's edge, Cordell's hand was wrapped tightly around hers, sending all sorts of fiery signals to the rest of her body.

How much longer could she hide her desire from him? The question had been nagging her throughout the day and now that she was faced with the night ahead of them, she felt her resistance slipping with each passing minute.

"Have you ever been to this town before?" she asked as she made an effort to rein in her wandering thoughts.

"I have. When Quint turned twenty-one he wanted to take a gambling trip, so I offered to go with him."

"Naturally," she said with a shrewd smile.

Grinning sheepishly, he said, "We went to Vegas and ended up down here at Laughlin."

"Were you lucky?"

"No. But we had a blast," he told her.

She shot him a perceptive smile. "I imagine you got your eyes full of showgirls."

He laughed. "Well, I'll put it this way. We sure didn't go around with our eyes closed." He laughed, then pointed to a sign up ahead. "We've arrived. There it is in bright neon—Mario's. Get ready to stuff yourself, sweet lady."

Fortunately, the hour was early enough to avoid the evening crowd and with only a few diners scattered around the small interior of the restaurant there were plenty of vacant tables available. The hostess guided them over to a choice spot near a plate glass window and placed menus on the checked linen tablecloths.

As soon as they were seated in plain wooden chairs, a waiter arrived and Cordell ordered a bottle of wine to go with their meal. As they sipped the chilled Chianti and waited for their food to be prepared, they watched the lighted boats passing up and down the river and talked about a few of the sights they'd seen during their travels today.

By the time their meal arrived and Maggie had eaten her fill of ravioli and eggplant smothered in cheese and marinara sauce, she was more than relaxed. She was happy. And she was tucking away each special moment of the evening into her memory bank.

"This really is a Thanksgiving treat for me, Cord. Thank you for the extra-nice dinner," she told him as the two of them walked arm in arm back to the hotel.

"It was extra-special for me, too. But I won't

make a big deal about how good the food was in front of Mom," he said with wry fondness. "She takes pride in her cooking and I don't want to hurt her feelings."

"That kind of thoughtfulness is going to ruin your tough-cowboy image."

He chuckled. "That's funny, Maggie. I'm not tough. I'm just a good pretender."

She was a good pretender, too, Maggie thought. From the very first night she'd met Cordell she'd been pretending he wasn't the kind of man she would ever want in her life. Or that being near him, getting close to him and kissing him hadn't affected the deepest part of her heart.

They finished the walk to the hotel in companionable silence, but once they were inside the lobby, Cordell gestured across the wide expanse to an open doorway.

"There's a bar connected to the restaurant. It's still early. Would you like a drink before we go up to our rooms?" he asked.

She would love to spend more time with him, but her head was already buzzing slightly from the wine. If she consumed any more alcohol, she might end up saying or doing something she might regret.

"Any other time I'd say yes, I'd love a martini, but I've already drank too much wine," she said honestly. "You go ahead and enjoy one. You don't have to escort me up to my room."

"Maybe I'm old-fashioned, but my parents taught

me to be a gentleman. I'm not about to let you go
up alone. Besides, what fun is a drink if you don't
have someone to share it with you?"

What fun was anything without someone to
share with? Maggie asked herself. And suddenly
she was looking into the future, seeing herself trying to make herself feel something for a man, and
hoping against hope she'd eventually be able to
make herself fall in love with him.

The bleakness of her thoughts had her reaching
for Cordell's hand. "I'm glad you're not going to
let me go up alone. I'm feeling a little—emotional
tonight. It must be the wine."

He didn't say anything as he led her over to an
elevator, but once they'd stepped inside the empty
space and the doors closed in front of them, he
pulled her into his arms.

"It's not the wine, Maggie," he murmured. "It's
this thing we have—it's doing something—to both
of us."

His lips came down on hers and he kissed her
until the elevator came to a halt and the doors
swished open.

Thankfully, no one was waiting outside the
doors. But Maggie got the impression from his kiss
that he wouldn't have cared if someone had caught
them in a tight clench. His lips had been plainly
saying he wanted her in the most basic way a man
could want a woman.

The short walk to their rooms didn't give Mag-

gie enough time to collect her scattered senses. But
then, she'd already had hours, even days to think
about what she might do if she actually had the
chance to go to bed with Cordell. Up until tonight,
she'd run scared from the idea. But now everything
felt so very different and the change in her had
nothing to do with the wine. It had everything to
do with being brave enough to reach for what she
wanted. And she wanted Cordell with every part
of her being.

Even so, when they reached the door of his room
and he pulled the entry card from his wallet, she
wondered if they were both about to jump off a cliff.

Stepping closer, she placed a hand on his arm.
"Cord, I— Is this what we want—really?"

His answer was to quickly open the door and
usher her into the room. A lamp on the nightstand
was the only light burning, but it was enough to reveal Cordell's face. The look of yearning she saw
in his eyes was impossible to resist and when he
reached for her, she let out a tiny moan of surrender and fell willingly into his arms.

Nuzzling his cheek against hers, he whispered,
"I want you, Maggie. And I know you want me.
If you want to tell me good-night and go to your
room, I'll understand. But will turning away from
me make you happy?"

"I can't turn away from you. Not now."

Her simple answer appeared to satisfy him and
he left her long enough to bolt the door behind them.

While he dealt with the lock, Maggie caught a glimpse of a king-size bed and a wall of drapes partially opened to a view of the distant lights of Laughlin. But the quick survey of the room ended when he returned and reached for her.

"Come here, beautiful."

With his hands anchored at the sides of her waist, he tugged her against him and lowered his head to hers.

Sighing, she curled her arms around his neck and angled her lips up to his. And in a matter of seconds everything faded away, except the taste of his mouth on hers, the erotic sensation of his tongue tangling with hers and the hard warmth of his body setting fire to something deep inside her.

She had no idea how long they stood just inside the door with her body crushed against him and his lips making a feast of hers. But there was one certainty in her mind. She'd never wanted a man the way she wanted Cordell. It was as if her whole being was begging to become a part of him and have him become a part of her.

She was clutching the front of his shirt and wondering how much longer her legs were going to hold her upright, when he finally lifted his head and led her over to the side of the bed.

"Do you know how much I've thought about this?" The question was whispered fervently against the middle of her forehead. "I've been going crazy telling myself I shouldn't make love to you. But when I touch you—kiss you, none of them make sense and everything feels right."

"Oh, Cord, this might be wrong—for me—for you—for both of us. But tonight I don't care. All I want is for you to make love to me."

With his hands cupping her jaws, he tilted her head back and looked deeply into her eyes. "My little sweetheart. Tonight isn't a time for thinking. It's a time for feeling and giving and taking."

She sighed and he dropped his head and began to place tiny rows of kisses along the side of her neck. Shivers of delight flooded through her and caused the flesh on her arms to erupt in goose bumps.

Groaning with pleasure, she reached to undo the pearl snaps on the front of his shirt. While he continued to nibble his way down to her collarbone, she managed to deal with the fasteners and push the fabric aside.

His bare flesh was hot beneath her fingertips as they glided over his chest, then bumped over each rib as they made their way downward.

Eventually, her fingertips came in contact with the flesh-colored bandages covering the cut above his navel and she lowered her head to press tender kisses around the wound. And all the while, her senses were drawing in his masculine scent and the salty taste of his skin.

Above her, she heard the sharp intake of his breath and then his hands were meshing in her hair, urging her face back to his.

This time his kiss felt altogether different. The hunger he'd shown her moments ago was now tempered with something soft and tender and the sweetness of it touched her so deeply that tears stung the back of her eyes.

"Maggie, you're precious—utterly precious."

His husky words were followed by another kiss and then his hands were unzipping her dress and pushing it off her shoulders.

Once the garment reached her hips, it slid to the floor, leaving her standing there with nothing on but a lacy black bra and matching panties.

A sound of pleasure vibrated in her throat, as she slid her arms up and around his neck. He anchored his hands on each side of her waist and lifted her onto the mattress.

Rolling onto her side, she watched him slip off his shirt, then sit on the edge of the mattress to remove his cowboy boots. By the time the footwear clunked against the carpet and his jeans followed them onto the floor, Maggie's whole body was humming with anticipation.

Wearing only a pair of white boxers, he stretched out beside her and as she scooted close enough to wrap an arm around his waist, she thought how right his words had been. Tonight wasn't a time for thinking. It was all about needing and wanting.

With his cheek pressed to hers and his hands on her buttocks, he drew the lower half of her body tight against his. Maggie's senses were instantly consumed with the sensation of his skin sliding against hers, the breadth of his shoulders as he moved his arms around her and the strength of his long, muscled legs tangling with hers.

He kissed the tip of her nose, the middle of her chin and finally her lips. "Mmm. You taste so good—feel so good. This isn't a dream, is it? You are really here in my bed?"

Smiling, she whispered, "I'm really here. And don't expect me to leave anytime soon."

He growled in protest. "Don't mention the word *leave*. We have all night. All night," he repeated.

She held on to those two words as she closed the tiny space between their lips and let his kiss numb her mind to everything but him and the glorious fire he was building inside her.

Maggie grew unaware of time, or how much of it had passed before he eventually removed her bra and panties. The only thing registering in her brain was the feel of his hands and mouth upon her breasts, and the aching need to feel his body connected to hers.

By the time he did finally take one nipple between his teeth, she was whimpering moans of desperation and pressing the juncture of her thighs against his hard shaft. Yet he didn't seem quite ready to give her the relief she was asking for. Instead, he took his time lathing the soft flesh with his tongue before he moved to the opposite breast and gave it the same delicious treatment.

"Cord—this waiting—is torture! I want you! Now!"

With her hands in his hair, she lifted his head and in the dim light filtering through the window, she could see the rugged outline of his lips, the soft gleam in his blue eyes.

"Are you sure, Maggie? Really sure? When tomorrow gets here I don't want you to hate me."

Reaching up she rested her palm against his cheek. "I could never hate you, Cord. And we're not going to think about tomorrow. Remember?"

The slant of his lips turned into a sensual grin and he quickly left the bed to collect his wallet from where he'd tossed it onto the dresser. Desire throbbed in her as she watched him remove his shorts, then roll a condom over his erection.

When he returned to the bed and drew her back into his arms, she said, "In case the question crossed your mind, Cord, I take the pill. So you don't have to worry about birth control."

One of his brows cocked upward. "Do I look like I'm worried?"

Even as he asked the question, his hand was slipping between her thighs, searching for the spot he needed.

Her laugh was garbled as his finger found her moist folds and gently stroked. "No. You look—oh, oh—"

Desire shot through every cell in her body and as he continued to touch and stroke, she grew so aroused she was on the verge of climaxing. Then just as she was about to float off into neverland, he rolled her onto her back and slowly entered her until she had accepted all of him.

The connection momentarily snatched the breath from her lungs and then all at once a shock of intense pleasure rushed through her and before he could even begin to move, she was cresting over a mountain and flying into a sky of bright glowing sun.

Crying out, she arched against him and gripped his arms until the undulating waves of ecstasy finally ebbed away. When her eyes fluttered opened, she saw he was gazing down at her with an expression she'd never seen on his face before. It was almost a look of anguish. And she was suddenly shocked and embarrassed by what had just occurred.

"Oh, Cord, I—didn't mean to—to start things out like this!" Groaning, she turned her face toward the mattress. "You must think I'm—sex-starved or something!"

Bending his head, he pressed kisses to her cheek, her nose and forehead before he finally captured her lips in a kiss that managed to fire up the longing in her loins all over again.

"I think you're the loveliest woman who's ever walked into my life." He nibbled at her ear, then pressed kisses along her jaw. "Don't you know that pleasing you is the same as pleasing me?"

"I need to repay you just the same."

Wrapping her arms around him, she arched her hips toward his and with a low, guttural groan, he began to move inside her.

She met each thrust with hungry abandon, while thinking everything about him felt right. From the touch of his hands gliding over her skin, to the perfect way his hard body fit with hers and the sweet, indescribable taste of his lips. And while the fiery need between them began to build, her one and only focus was to hold on to him and these moments for as long as she could.

Yet the powerful need between them made it impossible to slow their journey. All too soon, Maggie recognized his thrusts growing quicker and his breaths turn to ragged gasps. She did her best to match the wild pace he was setting, but she was rapidly losing the battle.

Then suddenly his tongue plunged deep into her mouth and he fastened his hands over her buttocks and lifted her hips up and forward.

Moaning, she gripped his back and latched her legs around his hips. It was the last thing she did before she was swept away on another violent crescendo of pleasure. Only this time she wasn't alone. This time, she heard his low groan, felt the desperate grip of his hands on her hips and his one final thrust.

Long after the shudders of aftermath died away, Maggie opened her eyes to see him poised above her, his rumpled hair falling into his eyes and sweat rolling from his forehead and onto his cheeks. Even though a couple of minutes had already ticked away, he was still breathing hard and his chest was visibly shaking from the racing beat of his heart.

Until now, she'd never realized how dear his face had become to her and she knew that no matter what the future held for her, she would always remember how he looked tonight. Like a man vulnerable enough to love a woman. Not just with his body, but with his heart.

The poignant thoughts had her reaching up and pulling him down to her and for long moments she held him close and tried to wordlessly convey what their union had meant to her.

Cordell eventually recognized the heavy weight of his body was draped over Maggie's and he rolled to one side, while managing to keep an arm curved around her waist. His breaths were still coming in short gulps as he lay flat on his back and stared blindly at the tilting walls of the room.

Was he dying? Was this how it felt before a man lost all consciousness?

The questions were darting through his spinning brain when he sensed her rolling toward him. Once she'd pillowed her cheek upon his shoulder, he managed to turn his head just enough to look down at her.

"Okay?" he asked.

His voice was so husky he hardly recognized it, but with the emotional upheaval that had just taken place inside him, he barely recognized himself, much less the sound of his voice.

Slipping her arm across his chest, she hugged herself closer to him and smiled dreamily. "Very okay," she answered. "Thank you, Cord."

He grunted with faint amusement. "For asking?"

"No."

She tilted her head back in order to look directly at him and as his gaze met hers, he didn't miss the gleam of moisture in her green eyes.

"For making me feel wanted. For showing me how it's supposed to feel between a man and a woman."

Her reply caught him totally off guard and for a moment he was too stunned to say anything. And then as he searched for a suitable response, he feared anything he might say would be misconstrued. She might take his words to heart and come up with the idea that he'd developed serious feelings about her.

That would never do, he thought. He wasn't ready to hand her his heart. She'd take it and run. And he'd be left with nothing.

"I'm glad you're happy."

She turned her head just enough to press a kiss to his collarbone. "And sad, too."

He tried not to stiffen with dread. "Why should

you be sad, Maggie? We agreed this was what we both wanted."

"I'm not sad about tonight, Cord. I'm sad that we waited so long to make love. We wasted all that time when we could've been making each other happy. But that's mostly my fault. Up until I met you, I was always cautious to the point of boredom."

He let out a long breath as more confusing emotions poured through him. Yes, they could've had a few more nights like this one. But what would that have done to him? To her? He was already feeling far too drawn to her. Any more of what they'd just shared tonight would only make saying goodbye a hundred times more difficult.

"It's best to dwell on what you have, Maggie," he said softly. "Not what you've missed."

She sighed. "I suppose so. For a long time I was so busy agonizing over the fact that I didn't have any family, I think I forgot to concentrate on the future and what might come into my life."

He rested his cheek against the top of her head. "Does that mean you're disappointed with yourself for not following the doctor to California?"

She looked up at him, her expression completely befuddled, and then she laughed. Not in a sarcastic way but with genuine amusement.

"Oh, Cord," she said, then lifting her head from his shoulder, she shifted around so that she was looking at him head-on. "Me following the doctor to California would have been a drastic mistake. I know that more than ever now."

Women didn't make him blush. He'd been over that awkward stage for years. That is, until Maggie came along. Now he could feel his face growing hot.

"Well, you did say he asked you to marry him," he said in an effort to defend his question.

"Yes, and I told you I turned him down."

"Thank goodness. Otherwise, I'd feel pretty bad about having you in my bed tonight."

She laughed again and Cordell could only think how nice it would be to hear that warm, velvety sound for the rest of his life.

"I'd probably feel pretty bad about it, too," she joked, then scooted forward until her lips were hovering over his. "You know what I am thinking about?"

His arms came around her and he stroked his fingers through the golden red hair lying against her back. "Hmm. About what?"

"Your truck," she answered. "And how lucky we were that it broke down."

This time Cordell was the one who laughed and then with a groan of satisfaction, he rolled her onto her back and captured her arms above her head.

"I'll be sure not to tell Dad you said that."

He nibbled at her lips, then started a downward path along her neck and onto the small mound of one breast. When he teased the nipple with his tongue he heard the tiny mews in her throat and felt a sense of triumph that he could arouse her a second time.

When he moved away from her breasts and continued tasting her skin between her rib cage farther down to the shallow indention of her navel, she thrust her hands in his hair and paused his downward motion.

"Do you have the energy for this?" she asked.

He smiled at the doubt in her voice. "I have plenty of energy, but unfortunately, I was only carrying one condom with me. I suppose we could take a cold shower—together."

"Like that would fix things?"

He let out a hopeless grunt. "No. A cold shower wouldn't fix this ache I have for you."

She lifted his head and the tender smile he saw on her face hit him somewhere deep in his chest.

"You must have forgotten I'm on the pill."

Relief flooded through him. "I had forgotten. So this means I don't have to get dressed and go out shopping for condoms."

"No. All you have to do is make love to me. Again."

Grinning, he lowered his head and mouthed against the soft skin of her belly. "And again. And again."

"Bragging?" she teased.

"No. Promising."

Because he had the awful feeling that the next few hours he had with her might be the last.

Chapter Ten

After little more than two hours' sleep, Maggie rose the next morning and, without waking Cordell, went to her own room to shower and get ready for the day ahead.

Standing beneath the hot pelting water, she thought how the remnants of Cordell's lovemaking might be washing down the drain, but the vivid memories would always remain with her.

Last night she'd given in to her longings for the man and for a while he'd taken her to another world. She could never be sorry for the incredible experience. Even now, in the light of day, she felt forever changed. And no matter where she went in life, or who she might meet, her body and her heart would always belong to him.

You're a fool, Maggie. Cordell has never once hinted that he loved you. Or that he wants to spend the rest of his life with you. You're another notch on his bedstead. Nothing more.

The mocking voice continued to pester her as she finished dressing, but by the time she reunited with Cordell for breakfast in the hotel restaurant, she'd managed to push the dismal thoughts aside and put a decent smile on her face.

"I've already been in contact with the garage this morning," he told her as they dug into plates of bacon and French toast. "From what the mechanic says the truck should be ready to go in a couple of hours. Is there anything you'd like to do until then?"

She gave him a wry smile as she reached for her coffee. "I think we've already done it."

His expression sly, he reached across the table and touched fingers to her free hand. "I thought women needed their beauty sleep," he said gently. "But you look great this morning. That old adage must not apply to you."

His compliment pierced her heart. "It's amazing what a little soap and water can do for a girl."

The grin still on his face, he rubbed a hand against his jaw. "I managed to shave. Did you notice?"

The urge to laugh and cry at the same time had her desperately swallowing a mouthful of coffee. Was he kidding? Didn't he realize she was completely absorbed with every tiny detail about him?

"I noticed. You're going to look very respectable when you arrive at Three Rivers Ranch. And they'll be happy to see you."

He shrugged. "Jack says they're a hospitable bunch."

She put down the coffee cup and forked off a piece of the French toast drenched with maple syrup. "I thought everyone on Stone Creek Ranch was hospitable, too."

"I'm glad you thought so. Maybe—"

When he didn't go on, she glanced up to see he was regarding her with an odd, almost strained look.

"Maybe what?"

He continued to study her for a few more seconds before he shook his head. "Nothing. I'm just glad, that's all."

She blew out a heavy breath and glanced to the other side of the room. The restaurant was full of breakfast diners, all of whom appeared to be enjoying the food and their morning. Too bad she and Cordell couldn't be like some of the obvious couples sitting nearby. From the looks of them they weren't planning on saying a final goodbye. They were all looking forward to the day ahead—together.

Look, Maggie, you understood the situation before you ever jumped into bed with Cordell. You're getting just what you deserve. So stiffen your spine and smile.

Deciding this was one time she needed to heed

the little voice in her head, she turned a gentle smile on him.

"Cord, if you're thinking I need flowery words or promises from you, forget it. I don't expect them. We had a nice time together. Now it's over. It's that simple. So please don't feel awkward, or get the idea I need a charming speech from you. Okay?"

Surprise flashed in his eyes and then after a moment of tense silence, he nodded. "Okay. And now we'd better eat up. The morning is getting away from us."

And so was that special feeling they'd shared last night, Maggie thought dismally. But she couldn't think about that now. Otherwise she'd burst into mortifying tears.

With each mile they traveled eastward, Maggie began to withdraw into a quiet shell. Most of the time she gazed out the passenger window and spoke only when it was necessary. Clearly, she was preoccupied with her own private thoughts. Ones that she didn't want to share with him.

The change in her behavior didn't make sense to him. This morning when they'd met to go down to breakfast, she'd seemed like her regular self. Especially when he'd greeted her with a kiss. But later in the restaurant, he'd felt her throwing up a wall between them. And that speech she'd given him about not needing flowery words had sounded as phony as a three-dollar bill.

Perhaps he'd been fooled by her sighs and kisses, but he believed the connection they'd shared last night had affected her far more than she wanted to admit. But hell, didn't she understand that making love to her had turned him upside down? Couldn't she see that he'd never be the same?

Maggie isn't a mind reader, Cordell. Without one word from you, she's supposed to know what you're thinking? Feeling? She doesn't understand that some sort of cataclysmic upheaval took place inside of you.

None of that mattered, Cordell thought glumly, as he tried to keep his focus on the highway. He had his own life to lead and she had hers and he didn't see any way of changing that fact.

By midafternoon, they arrived in the town of Wickenburg. Normally, when Maggie had been away, even for just a day or two, she was always happy to be back in the place that had been her home since birth. But today she barely noticed the streets landscaped with desert plants and stucco buildings painted pink and turquoise. All she could see was the weeks and months ahead without Cordell.

"Turn on this street, Cord," she instructed as he braked to a stop at an intersection of residential streets. "My house is the green one—third on the left."

"I see it. Will it be okay to park the truck and

trailer on the side of the street? Your driveway is too short for this big rig," he said as he peered ahead.

She reached for her handbag at her feet. "I think so. My neighbors aren't usually coming and going at this time of day. Besides, you'll just be here long enough to let me out and get my bags."

He shot her a puzzled look. "Aren't you going to ask me in? Show me your place?"

She pressed her lips tightly together as she tried to stem the dull ache that had started building in her chest more than a hundred miles back down the highway. "No. I'd rather not, Cord. Surely you understand."

He braked the truck to a stop and after shutting off the engine, squared around in the seat to face her.

"Frankly, no. I don't understand. If you're worried about me seeing a mess, forget it. Sometimes my room looks like a tornado has hit it."

As much as she wanted to jerk the truck door open and escape this final scene with him, she forced herself to remain in the seat and hold back her tears.

"It's not that. I—well, I don't know how to explain my feelings. Except that our time together is over. And I want the cut to be clean and final." And she didn't want to have to remember how he looked walking through the rooms of her house. It would be like his spirit was always haunting her, she thought.

"Clean and final," he repeated as though the

two words had been spoken in a foreign language. "That's how you want things to be for us?"

She rolled her eyes helplessly toward the ceiling of the cab. "Look, Cord, I'm not delusional. That's the only way things can be for us. I'm sure you've gone through these parting scenes dozens of times before. You know the drill much better than I."

"I never thought you'd be so flip about it. I thought—you were different. That's why—"

She looked at him and had to fight like crazy not to break into sobs. The expression on his face wasn't one of anger or confusion. No. He actually looked torn. Where was that coming from?

Unable to stop herself, she reached over and clasped his hand in hers. "Cord, I think you know how much I've enjoyed being with you," she said gently. "Not just last night, but our times together on your ranch, too. It's been very special for me. But this is where it ends."

His eyes searched hers for a tense moment. Then like the flip of a switch, his jaw grew hard and he turned to open the door.

"I'll get your things," he said flatly.

Maggie didn't wait for him to help her down from the truck. With her handbag in tow, she stood on the street while he pulled her bags from the back floorboard.

When she started to reach for one, he said curtly, "I'll carry them."

He picked up all three bags and started up the

sidewalk. As Maggie followed behind him she prayed she could keep her tears at bay until he drove away.

When they stepped up on the little front porch, he set the bags onto the concrete, but she didn't make any move to dig the house key from her purse. She didn't want to open the door with him standing next to her. Otherwise, she might weaken and pull him inside. She might forget that he was all wrong for her and she—well, now she had to go back to being cautious and cool Maggie, instead of the one who'd burned like a flame in his arms.

"Goodbye, Cord. Enjoy your visit with the Hollisters and have a safe trip back to Stone Creek." She'd somehow said it with hardly a wobble in her voice. She could be proud of herself for that much, at least.

"Goodbye, Maggie."

Unable to look him in the eye, she started to open her handbag to search for her key, but suddenly his hand cupped her chin and he tugged her face up to his.

"Cord."

She breathed his name just before his lips came down on hers and for a few brief seconds, the two of them were back in Bullhead City with the whole night ahead of them.

But just as the fantasy flashed through her mind, he ended the kiss, then turned and strode quickly back to his truck.

Maggie unlocked the door and by the time she'd carried her bags into the house, he'd driven away. And out of her life.

At the Hollisters' insistence, Cordell had ended up spending an extra night on Three Rivers. And as Jack had predicted, everyone on the ranch had been especially nice and welcoming. He'd done his best to be cheerful and, for the most part, he'd left with his new relatives convinced he'd enjoyed his visit.

Under normal circumstances, Cordell would've been thrilled to stay several days on the massive ranch and study how their foreman, Tag O'Brien, handled such a big job with so many men. But Maggie had shaken him and he'd been anxious to get home and get his life back to normal.

Unfortunately, stepping back on Stone Creek soil had only intensified his misery. From the kitchen, to the den, to the upstairs bedroom where she'd stayed next to his, he could see her; her red-blond hair swinging against her back, a smile tilting her pretty lips.

More than a week had passed since he'd returned from the Arizona trip and he was no closer to burning Maggie's image from his brain. Yet he had to keep trying. Otherwise, he was going to have some sort of breakdown.

"Hey, brother. What are you doing still up?"

Cordell glanced away from the burning logs to see Quint sinking into the chair next to his. After working on fence for half of the day, the two of them had ridden out to Snow Mountain to check on the sheep. During the return ride, snow had begun to fall and in spite of his heavy coat, Cordell had grown unusually cold. Even sitting in front of the fire hadn't yet warmed the deep chill inside him.

"Soaking up some heat before we have to look for those lost heifers tomorrow. The weather predicts more snow flurries and wind."

"The dogs will find the heifers right quick. I don't expect that job will take very long. How do you see it?"

Every morning when Cordell caught a glimpse of himself in the mirror, he saw an idiot. That's what he saw. And the image wasn't going to change anytime soon, he thought miserably.

"We'll manage all right."

Quint didn't reply and Cordell closed his eyes and massaged the burning lids with the tips of his fingers. He couldn't remember the last time he'd slept the night through.

"Have you heard from Maggie?"

The question caused an ice-cold shaft to slice right through him and he opened his eyes to see Quint regarding him with a dubious look.

"Why would I have heard from her?"

When he'd left her on the porch of her house, she'd made it perfectly clear she was cutting all ties with him. And his pride had told him to accept her decision like a man. Why should he beg just to get a few words from her now and then? No. He needed to move on. But how did a man move on when his insides were dead?

"Why not? I thought you two were getting chummy," Quint said. "You took her on that long horseback ride. Then traveled all the way to Wickenburg together. By the way, what was that? A trip to hell and back?"

"It wasn't easy," Cordell grumbled.

Quint grunted. "I wish Dad had sent me on the chore. I would've enjoyed a few hours with Maggie by my side."

Helpless anger poured through him. "Just shut the hell up, will you?" he snarled.

Stunned silence followed his outburst and Cordell was glad no one else was in the den to witness his behavior.

"You bet, Cord. I'll be glad to."

Quint rose and started to walk off, but Cordell reached out and grabbed his forearm. "Wait, Quint. I didn't mean that the way it sounded."

"Sure sounded like you meant it."

"I'm sorry. I shouldn't be taking my bad mood out on you."

Quint's eyes narrowed with speculation. "Feel like telling me what happened between you and Maggie?"

How could he tell Quint that he'd fallen hard for Maggie? And she'd given him the brush-off?

What are you whining about, Cordell? That's

*been your MO for years. But you expect things to go
differently when it's your feelings involved. You're
a jerk. Furthermore, you know it.*

Groaning with frustration, Cordell left the chair
and walked over to a nearby window overlooking
the backyard. The area was partially illuminated
by a yard lamp and through a veil of snowflakes he
could just make out the stone wall and tarped roses.

Maggie had talked about how she'd love to see
the roses in bloom and he'd imagined her returning to the ranch. At least, for a short summer stay.
He'd been wrong.

Looking over his shoulder, he saw Quint still
standing by the armchair, waiting for his answer.
"No. I don't want to talk about what happened. I—"
He shook his head in a hopeless way. "I'm missing
her. That's all, Quint."

Frowning, Quint closed the short space between
them. "Man, I can't believe you could miss any one
woman."

Frankly, Cordell couldn't believe it himself. "She
was different, Quint."

"Yeah. The whole family could see Maggie was
special." He gave Cordell's shoulder a squeeze. "But
heck, Cord, you have a little black book longer than
my arm. Why don't you give one or two of your old
girlfriends a call? You need to move on."

Thoughtful now, he looked at Quint. "You're
right. I should go out and enjoy myself. Tomorrow

is Friday. Might be nice to drive down to Cedar City and do a little dancing at the Rusty Rowel."

"Never know 'til you try."

And Cordell suddenly decided he was going to try with all his might.

A week and a half later, the clock was nearing eleven on Thanksgiving night when Maggie closed a privacy curtain around the latest patient to arrive in the ER and walked over to the nurses' station. Dr. Nelson was writing on a chart and she waited for him to look up before she spoke.

"The patient's IV is dripping, Doctor. And he seems to be calming down somewhat."

The middle-aged doctor, who regularly worked the night shift, gave her a cursory glance. "I'm glad to hear it. As soon as his blood test arrives, let me know. Meanwhile, I've signed discharge papers for Mrs. Whitmire. Before she leaves the hospital, be sure to go over her orders carefully with her. She was so stressed about having a lasting scar, she didn't hear half of what I told her about caring for the wound on her arm. Oh, and by the way, when you have a chance you should go down to the break room and put your feet up. There's some great pumpkin pie and cranberry bread. You look like you could use a break."

Giving him a grateful smile, she said, "I will. And I hope you had a happy Thanksgiving with your family."

He chuckled. "Oh, it was great. My in-laws came over. The table was loaded with food none of us should've been eating. The TV was blaring with college football and the kids were fighting over a turkey leg."

Maggie laughed, even though she wanted to burst into tears. "Sounds like fun. But there are two turkey legs to a bird. Why fight over one?"

He let out a good-natured groan. "Because the baby gave the dog the other leg while we weren't looking. My wife was still trying to clean the carpet in the living room when I left for work." He suddenly looked beyond Maggie to the swinging doors leading into the ER. "There's Dr. Edwards from Internal. I'll be in my office if you need me."

Maggie gave him a nod, then hurried away to deal with the discharge patient.

Once she'd waved the woman and her husband away from the back entrance of the ER, she came back in to find Emma emerging from the bay of the male patient who'd come in after his Thanksgiving dinner.

Emma was a tall, curvy brunette with gray, luminous eyes. She'd been divorced for five years and now that she was thirty-five, she'd swore she'd never marry again. But it was plain to Maggie that Emma was the sort of woman who was meant to have a man in her life. Her friend just hadn't realized it yet.

"How is he?" Maggie asked, lowering her voice

to make sure the patient couldn't overhear the two nurses discussing his case.

Emma rolled her eyes. "I think he's recuperated. He says he's hungry and wants to eat."

"Eat? That's the reason he wound up here in the ER in the first place! He ate so much Thanksgiving dinner the pressure on his sternum was suffocating him."

"Typical man. Now that he can breathe again, I imagine he'll go straight home to the leftover dressing." She settled a calculating look on Maggie. "And speaking of eating, you haven't taken a break in the past four hours and it shows. Let's go dig into the pie."

"I am tired. But we can't leave the floor unattended," Maggie told her. "Charlotte hasn't showed up yet. She must be suffering a turkey day hangover."

"Charlotte is here. She's in bay 2 with another patient. I'll tell her where she can find us. You go on."

Grateful for a chance to put her feet up, Maggie nodded and made her way down a short hallway and into a small room furnished with a utility table and chairs, along with a fridge, microwave and hot plate.

On a cabinet counter at the back of the room, someone had set out single servings of pie and cranberry bread on paper plates covered with plastic wrap.

Maggie grabbed up one of both and was pouring herself a cup of coffee when Emma walked in to join her.

"Oh brother, I definitely needed a break," she said as she picked up a piece of pie. "This has been some day."

"You've only been on duty for four hours," Maggie reminded her. "We're just getting started."

Sinking into one of the chairs, Emma peeled the plastic wrap from the pie. "I know. But at the last minute this morning, I decided to drive over to Yarnell to have dinner with my in-laws."

Maggie grimaced. "Why? Those are your ex-in-laws. Please, don't tell me Gordon was there!"

"You think I'd spend a second of my Thanksgiving Day with him? I'd rather go scrub the entire ER floor with a toothbrush," she said with a snort, then shrugged. "But his parents always treated me nice and when they called and invited me, I couldn't say no. The couple doesn't have anyone to share the holidays with. Gordy can't be bothered. And it's not good for anyone to spend the holidays alone."

"No. It's not good." Maggie placed her food and coffee on the table, then eased into a seat directly across from Emma, who was suddenly looking shamefaced.

"Sorry, Maggie. I wasn't thinking. Did you eat dinner alone today? I thought Camille might be coming in for the holiday and you'd eat dinner out at Three Rivers."

With the fragile condition of her heart right now,

Maggie hardly needed to be around a family of Hollisters to remind her of everything she was missing. Especially at Stone Creek.

Cordell. Cordell.

She'd believed the passing of time would ease the pain of telling him goodbye, but so far the loss she felt in her heart was only growing larger.

Breaking off a piece of the sweet bread, she said, "I haven't given Camille a call in quite a while. She's very busy caring for a husband and baby, plus her diner."

"It's too bad you couldn't stay with your friend up in Utah until the holidays were over," Emma replied. "Have you talked with her lately?"

Maggie absently stabbed the sweet bread with a plastic fork. "She called yesterday. She was in the kitchen, helping her mother-in-law bake pies. Which is funny. She's not much of a cook. But neither am I."

"You're a good nurse, though," Emma said with an affectionate grin. "And good nurses are hard to find. Why do you think we're asked to do double shifts?"

"I don't mind." She rubbed a hand across her forehead. "Only these past few days I feel like I have lead weights on my feet. I'm so tired."

"Is that why you've been looking like you lost your best friend?"

Frowning, Maggie glanced across the table to

see Emma was eyeing her with concern. "I look that awful?"

"You don't exactly look like a happy camper. In fact, ever since you've come back from Utah you haven't been yourself. I've been waiting for you to tell me what's wrong, but it looks like I'm going to have to dig it out of you."

Maggie stiffened. No way did she want to tell Emma she'd behaved like a fool and fallen for a rowdy cowboy with little more on his mind than sex.

Just like you hadn't had sex on your mind, Maggie. Who do you think you are, anyway? Miss Prim?

Shutting off the condemning voice in her head, she said, "Okay, Emma. I do feel a little sad. You know how I've always talked about wanting a family of my own. A big one—with a loving husband and lots of kids."

"Sure, I remember. And I've told you to be careful what you wish for. A husband plus kids equals work. And it isn't all rosy. Believe me, I tried the husband part. You see what I ended up with—nothing but a bitter taste in my mouth."

"I know, but there are people who do have big loving families and that's what I found when I went to Utah. Except for two of them, the Hollisters all live together in a big ranch house. It's old and beautiful and just walking through the rooms makes you feel like you've stepped back to a slower, more beautiful time. Claire and Hadley have eight grown children and they're still very much in love. I guess seeing all of that and how it can be has made me—a little melancholy." She looked down and blinked as tears threatened to blur her eyes. "I'm not having a pity party for myself, Emma. Plenty of people are alone. Even you, sort of. You live alone, but you do have parents and siblings close by. I wish for the same things. That's all."

"Oh, honey, I understand. I really do. And look at you. You're just so smart and pretty—if you'll give yourself a chance, you'll find the right man. Just make damned sure he's not like Gordy," she added with a smirk.

Maggie had given herself a chance to experience passion and she would never regret making love to Cordell. Her only regret was that she'd stupidly allowed her heart to get involved.

"I'll try to keep away from all the Gordons in the world," Maggie tried to joke.

Before Emma could reply, Charlotte, their co-worker, stuck her head around the edge of the door. "Hey, you two!" There's been a wreck on North 93. ETMs are three minutes away with four injured."

Maggie and Emma jumped to their feet and tossing what was left of their food into a trash bin, hurried out to the ER floor.

By mid-December, the pregnant heifers at the barn began giving birth. Instead of his nightly excursions into town to meet a girlfriend, Cordell had been spending his evenings in the cattle barn, pulling calves and making sure each mama and baby survived.

As he sluiced disinfectant over his hands, he kept a careful eye on the calf that had just been born. The baby was small, but she was breathing and already responding to the loving licks of her mother's tongue.

"Looks like you've been busy. Where's Payton? I thought he was staying to help you."

Cordell glanced over his right shoulder to see Jack walking up. The appearance of his older brother in the barn at this time of night was unusual. Normally, he left chores like this to Cord and the ranch hands.

"Payton was here," Cordell explained. "But he acted like he's coming down with the flu, so I sent him home."

"You should've called me. I would've been out here to the barn sooner." He squatted on his heels to take a closer look at the newborn calf. "She's a little thing. But her eyes are bright."

No matter how low Cordell's spirits sunk, he always felt joy when a calf, colt or lamb was born.

"Don't worry. She's going to be a feisty thing." He lifted his hat from his head and ran a weary hand through his hair. "What brought you here to the barn anyway? It's after midnight. You should be in bed with your wife."

"I heard Quint come in and got up to check on

him. He was going to grab a bite to eat, then come over here to help you. But he's flat wrung out from moving sheep all day and half the night. I told him to go to bed—I'd make the trek over here." Jack straightened to his full height and came to stand next to him. "Quint is worried about you, Cord. And frankly, the rest of the family is, too."

Cordell snorted. "You're all wasting energy. There's nothing for any of you to worry about."

Jack grimaced. "Right, Cord. When you get back to the house take a good look at yourself in the mirror. You look like hell. Which is hardly a surprise. For the past three weeks you've been out nearly every night. What are you doing? Trying to overdose on women?"

He was trying to forget, Cordell thought. Trying to wipe the sweet memories of Maggie from his mind, but so far it wasn't working. No matter how many pretty faces he looked at, their features always morphed into Maggie's. Their kisses and touches all fell flat and meaningless. He might as well face the fact that one night in Bullhead City had ruined his life.

Glaring at Jack, he asked, "How do you know I've been out with a woman every night? And what makes you think that's any of your business?"

"I pulled the information out of Quint. He said you were on a mission to—well, the way he put it was to *clear your mind.*" Jack cursed under his breath. "When I see my brother messing up his life, I feel obliged to do something about it."

Groaning, Cordell scrubbed his face with both hands. "There's nothing you can do, Jack. I've been a fool. And I'm being a bigger fool by trying to fix something that can't be fixed."

"Does this have anything to do with Maggie?"

Cordell looked at him. "What makes you think so? Quint's been lipping off—again?"

"No. He hasn't mentioned Maggie's name to me. But Van has. She says every time she talks to her friend, she doesn't sound like herself. Van is just as worried about her as I am about you. If the two of you—"

"Whatever was between us ended when I left her in Wickenburg. So leave it alone, will you?"

Cordell moved away from the cow and newborn calf to stand in the path of a heater blowing down from the ceiling. Jack followed him.

"I would, if you could," he said, then shook his head. "I don't get you, Cord. From what I can gather, you had your chance with Maggie. Why didn't you take it?"

He had taken his chance with Maggie. He just hadn't realized how going to bed with her was going to affect him.

"Hell, Jack. I'm not meant to be a husband or father to a bunch of kids. Those are the things Maggie wants in her life and she deserves to have them. It's just going to take me a while to come to terms with the idea that she's gone and I can't do anything about it."

Jack snorted. "If you had half the guts I believe you have, then you could do something about Maggie. You could go after her. No, better than that, you could have done like me and carted her off to a wedding chapel in Vegas before you ever reached Wickenburg."

"Yeah, but I'm not like you."

"Okay, so you're going to go around moping and sulking and making everyone around you miserable. Maybe you want your Christmas to be that way but I don't want you ruining mine and the rest of the family's! You've already hurt Mom because you didn't show up the other night to trim the tree. Quint tried to smooth it over by telling her you were busy with the heifers. Thank goodness, she didn't know you were busy with a different kind of female."

Growing angry and more frustrated by the moment, Cordell practically yelled at him. "Why make me out to be a jerk because I didn't show up to trim the tree? Hell, Mom has seven other kids!"

Jack studied him for long moments before he shook his head with disappointment. "And lucky for her they're not all like you!"

Cordell wanted to curse. Mostly because he knew his brother was right. "Okay, Jack. I get what you're trying to say. When I'm around the family I'll be sure and keep a smile on my face. I don't want to ruin anyone's Christmas."

Jack shot him a meaningful look. "Then why don't you call Maggie?"

And listen to her tell him once again how things were over between them? No, thanks. "I never did go for self-inflicted pain, Jack."

Jack let out a mocking grunt. "Where do you think your pain is coming from now?"

Chapter Eleven

On Christmas Eve morning, Maggie crawled out of bed with a queasy stomach, but managed to force down a few bites of toast and a half a cup of coffee before heading off to work. She was doing a double shift today at the ER and, at this late date, it would be impossible to find another nurse to replace her.

In spite of feeling draggy, Maggie made it through the first shift without any stomach issues. Which was a blessing, considering the fact that there was a steady stream of patients coming and going throughout the day. But by the time Emma joined her for the night shift a strong bout of nausea struck her and this time she had no choice but to rush to the nearest commode.

After losing what bit of lunch she'd eaten at three

that afternoon, she emerged from the restroom with a pale face and pressing a hand to her stomach.

Emma rushed over to put a supportive hand on Maggie's arm. "What's wrong? Are you ill?"

"I lost all my lunch," she explained. "I'm not feverish or aching. In fact, now that the food is up, I feel much better. So I don't think it's a bug. Must be something I ate."

Her expression full of concern, Emma patted her arm. "You're very pale, Maggie. You should go to the break room and sit for a few minutes—maybe try eating a cracker. Charlotte and I will take care of things out here."

"I'm okay, Emma."

Emma nudged her toward the break room. "Do as I say, will you?"

Maggie didn't have the energy to argue, so she trudged her way to the break room. Thankfully, there was no one around and she sank heavily into one of the chairs and rested her head on her folded arms.

She must have dozed off for a few minutes because she suddenly woke up to the sound of a male voice coming from right above her head. Dazed, she looked up to see Dr. Nelson standing over her.

"Oh! Doctor!" She straightened up in the chair and smoothed a hand over her ponytail. "I—I'm so sorry!"

He patted her shoulder. "No problem. All is quiet

on the floor right now. Emma said you weren't feeling well and wanted me to have a look at you."

"Emma is just being a mother hen. I don't want to bother you. I'm okay. Really."

The doctor left her long enough to shut the door of the break room, then returned to her. "You never fall asleep like this, Maggie. Tell me, did you get any sleep yesterday?"

"Yes. A few hours. I don't remember how many. But I have been very tired."

"Let me have a look at you." He pulled a penlight from the pocket of his lab coat and flashed it in her eyes, then ordered her to open her mouth. "Hmm. Emma tells me you threw up your lunch."

"Emma has a big mouth."

He chuckled. "She's a nurse. You nurses are supposed to have big mouths so us doctors can hear you."

Maggie relented. "I woke up feeling queasy this morning. I didn't vomit then, but it definitely hit me a few minutes ago. Do you think I'm coming down with a virus? Doctor, I don't have time to be sick! I've already promised Charlotte I'd do her shift tomorrow night."

Shaking his head, he rested a hip on the edge of the table and leveled a thoughtful look at her. "I have no intentions of digging into your personal life, Maggie. But have you missed a menstrual period?"

Her jaw dropped. Oh, no. No. He couldn't be

thinking along those lines. It was impossible! Or was it?

"I—don't know," she said, "I've never been very regular. So I don't think much about it if I go for several weeks without one. About three months ago my gyn changed my pills to a weaker dosage. He believes that might help to get me more regular."

His brows arched with speculation and then to her surprise, he smiled. "Okay, Maggie. I don't think you're coming down with a virus or any other intestinal ailment. I'm going to have Emma draw your blood and I'll write up an order for a pregnancy test. Since it's Christmas Eve, the lab is working a skeleton crew, but with any luck, we'll have the results by tomorrow."

Maggie couldn't contain her gasp. "Pregnant! But doctor, how can that be? I just told you I'm on the pill. And I've not missed a dose."

He reached over and patted her arm. "These things have a way of happening. I'm not a specialist in female health, but I suspect the weaker dosage of birth control wasn't enough to prevent pregnancy. At least, not in your case."

Astounded by the possibility, she dazedly rose to her feet. "I'm—I don't know what to think," she mumbled.

"Do you need to go home to rest and let this soak in?" he asked.

Maggie lifted her chin. "No. I'm fine, Doctor.

And ready to get back to work. Thank you for giving me your time."

"Maggie, you're one of the best nurses in the ER.
I want you to be healthy and happy. If it turns out
you are pregnant. I'll be the first one to say you're
going to make a great mother."

A great mother. Just as her own mother had been.
She'd borne Maggie alone and raised her up without
help from a man. Maggie could be just as strong as
her mother had been.

Too choked to say anything more, Maggie merely
nodded at him and hurried out to join Emma on the
ER floor.

The next day, Maggie received the word that
she was actually pregnant. However, it wasn't until
she'd had a chance to visit her gyn and enough time
to gather her nerve, that she finally called the cell
number Cordell had given her.

He answered on the third ring and the familiar
sound of his deep voice brought a sting of tears to
her eyes.

"Hello, Cord. Do you, uh, have a moment to
talk?"

There was a long pause and for a second or two
she thought he was going to hang up on her. If he
did, she couldn't blame him. She'd been rather curt
when they'd parted. He couldn't know she'd been
putting on a front, pretending that it wasn't tearing
her apart to tell him goodbye.

"I am busy. If you're calling just to wish me a belated Merry Christmas, then thanks, the same to you. Otherwise, I really don't think we have anything to say to each other."

A hot lump filled her throat. "I expected you to feel that way. But I—"

"Is this necessary, Maggie?" he interrupted. "I'm at the vet. Waiting for him to sew up my horse's ankle. I don't have time to rehash something that, frankly, I'd rather forget."

In all the time they'd been together, he'd never talked to her with sarcasm dripping from his voice, but he was definitely doing it now. She didn't know whether she wanted to scream at him or burst into tears.

"Look, Cord, I'll make this short. I didn't call to rehash anything. I need to talk to you. And I don't mean talk on the phone. Can you meet me halfway somewhere?" she asked, then suddenly changing her mind, she said, "No, I'll drive two-thirds of the way and meet you at St. George. Can you manage that?"

The line went silent again and Maggie wondered why she was putting herself through this humiliation. He clearly didn't want anything to do with her. If she had any gumption at all, she'd hang up and put him out of her mind once and for all. But she didn't want her child to grow up as she had. Never knowing her father and asking herself why he'd never cared enough to want to meet his daughter.

For her baby's sake, she could deal with a little humiliation.

"Is this some sort of joke, Maggie? I don't have time to go running off to St. George. If you want to say something to me, say it now. Otherwise, I'm hanging up."

"No! Please, Cord! This is important. I can be in St. George by next Monday evening."

More silence ticked by and then he said, "You sound stressed."

"I am. A little," she admitted. "I'll explain everything when I see you."

Finally, he said, "Okay. I'll be there Monday. You can text me as to where to find you."

"Thank you, Cord. And I hope your horse's ankle heals well."

She hung up the phone and though she was visibly shaking from the exchange with Cordell, she refused to give in to the tears burning her eyes.

Once she told him about the coming baby, the worst would be over. What he chose to do afterward would be up to him. She only hoped he would care enough to be a part of their child's life. Even if his visits were few and far between.

To say hearing from Maggie had shaken Cordell would be a ridiculous understatement. Just seeing her name light up on the phone had rattled him, much less hearing her voice. The sound of it had practically been his undoing.

She wanted to talk. About what? There was no them. There couldn't be.

Questions and doubts had swirled through his mind the past three days. Now that Monday had finally arrived and he was entering the city of St. George, he realized he'd never felt so confused and uncertain. In fact, throughout most of the drive down here, he'd cursed himself for agreeing to make this trip in the first place.

But something in her voice had touched him in a way he still couldn't understand. And he'd been unable to tell her no. Just like he hadn't been able to refuse her when she'd asked him to make love to her.

Make love. Make love. He needed to stop thinking of that night in Bullhead City in such syrupy terms. They'd had sex. Plain and simple. And as far as he was concerned hot sex was all there would ever be between them.

Earlier this afternoon, he'd received a text from Maggie informing him of the time and place she'd be waiting for him. Following the directions on his smartphone, he found the hotel and after a long search for a parking space, entered the lobby.

He'd walked only a few feet beyond the double glass entryway when he spotted her sitting on a couch in the lounge area. Even from a distance, the sight of her caused his heart to race. Like a kid longing for a coveted object, he thought. What the hell was wrong with him, anyway? He wasn't here to pick up where they'd left off in Bullhead City.

He was halfway across the spacious lobby when she checked her watch, then glanced in his direction. Instantly, she rose and walked over to meet him. Cordell could only think how lovely she looked in a white blouse and a black-and-white plaid skirt that swirled around the ankles of her winter boots.

"Hello, Cord. Thank you for coming."

He drew in a deep breath in hopes it would ease the odd pressure twisting in the middle of his chest. He wasn't about to let her see how much he'd missed her, or how much she'd upended his world.

"I figured I owed you this much."

The flare of her nostrils caused him to take a closer survey of her pale, strained features. Was seeing him affecting her that much?

"You don't *owe* me anything." She made a quick search of the busy lobby. "The hotel bar is right over there beyond the open doorway. We could talk there."

"Good idea. I need a drink."

Three minutes later they were sitting at a small, secluded table where a waiter served Cordell a double Scotch on the rocks and Maggie a cup of heavily creamed coffee.

"How was your drive down?" she asked.

Her hand trembled as she reached for the coffee and the sudden urge to reach over and comfort her was like a drum banging and banging inside his head.

He gulped down a large swallow of the Scotch. "No breakdowns this time."

"I'm not accustomed to driving long distances," she admitted. "I'm a little tired."

While she continued to sip the coffee, Cordell noticed faint blue crescents under her eyes and her cheeks were the color of his mother's raw biscuit dough. Was something wrong with her health? "I can see that."

She looked at him and he didn't miss the wounded shadows in her eyes. "Sorry. I realize I'm not looking my best."

He grimaced and took another swig of his drink. "That's not what I meant."

"Forget it," she said. "None of that matters anyway."

Was she deliberately trying to play some sort of waiting game with him? If so, she was winning. His patience was close to snapping.

Gripping the tumbler, he leveled a point-blank look at her. "Exactly what does matter, Maggie?"

She drew in a shaky breath, then moved her gaze to a spot across the room. "This is very hard for me, Cord. Because you've made your feelings clear about your plans for the future. And they don't include—"

"Include what? You? Is that what this is all about? You want us to get together—somehow?" He sounded incredulous, but he couldn't help it. This whole thing with her was so out of the blue.

Her gaze landed back on his and this time there was a hardness in the green depths that left him totally puzzled.

"No! That isn't what I want!" She leaned toward him and lowered her voice to a hiss. "Do you honestly think I'm the type of woman who'd get on the phone and beg a man to meet me? If so, then you don't know me at all!"

He'd clearly angered her, but he was beyond caring. These past two months without her had been pure hell. At least, what he imagined hell to be—a place of constant torture.

"Okay, Maggie. If this meeting isn't for your sake, then who? Me? Let me guess. Van called you and told you that I'm messed up and need to see you? If that—"

"I haven't talked to Van!" she firmly interrupted. "Not about you. And this meeting isn't for my sake or yours. It's for our baby."

All at once, the room tilted to a crazy angle and he gripped the edge of the table as he leaned toward her. "Baby! Did I hear you right?"

She gave him one solemn nod. "I'm pregnant. A little over two months, in fact."

His jaw dropped and he could feel his heart pounding so hard and fast he feared it was going to burst right through his chest.

"I guess it's fairly easy to figure out the timeline. Just count the calendar days back to our night in Bullhead City. But why am I just now getting the news?"

"Because I only learned about the baby on Christmas Day. I was sick at work and the ER doctor suspected what was wrong. A blood test confirmed it."

"Is that why you're so pale?" he asked. Or was it the thought of bearing his child that was making her ill? The notion hurt.

"I've had a bit of morning sickness. Nothing serious."

She leaned back in her chair and picked up her coffee as though she was discussing the weather instead of throwing him a live hand grenade.

He said, "So this is what you didn't want to discuss on the phone."

She must have been holding her breath, because a long one rushed out of her.

"I wanted to talk with you face-to-face. You needed to know you're going to be a father. And I needed to get your feelings about being a part of the child's life."

"What does that mean?"

"Don't worry. I won't ask much from you. Maybe a few occasional visits—just so he or she will know who you are. As far as child support, I don't want or expect anything of that sort. Of course if you want to contribute, I'll accept it for the baby's sake. But as it stands, the salary I make as a nurse is quite sufficient to take care of the two of us."

Cordell grabbed up the tumbler and tossed back the last of the Scotch before the string of curse words on his tongue slipped out loud enough to echo throughout the bar.

"Do you have anything else on your mind?"

"Yes. One more thing," she answered. "If it's agreeable with you, I'd like for our son or daughter to carry the Hollister name. Later on, I think it will be important to the child."

On the verge of exploding, Cordell yanked bills from his wallet and threw enough of them onto the table to cover their drinks.

"Do you have a room here in the hotel?" he asked bluntly.

Her brows drew together. "Yes. Why?"

"Because we're going there. Right now!"

With his hand on her arm, he quickly hustled her out of the bar and straight to the nearest elevator. Not a word was exchanged between them until they'd reached her room and the lock on the door had clicked loudly behind them.

By then, Maggie wanted to hurl something at him.

"Has anyone ever told you that you're a complete jerk?" she asked as she crossed the room and sank into a wingback chair near the window.

"Often and loudly," he retorted.

She folded her arms against her breasts as he came to stand in front of her. "Maybe that's why

I don't seem to be getting through to you. I'm not getting loud enough." She groaned, then shook her head. "Look, Cord, I understand this is a shock to you. It stunned me. But I—"

Before she could explain further, he rudely interrupted. "How *did* this happen?"

She rolled her eyes toward the ceiling. "I suppose I could draw a diagram. Or better yet, just picture yourself as one of the bulls you picked up at Three Rivers and I'm one of those little heifers you had locked in the barn corral. Get the picture of how it happened?"

His jaws clamped tight. "You told me you were on the pill. I believed you."

"You better keep believing it, because I was totally honest with you. About three months before I met you, my doctor changed the prescription of my pills to a weaker dosage. He was trying to fix my irregular cycles. Obviously the birth control was too weak to prevent a pregnancy. So if you want to blame me, go ahead. You couldn't hurt me any more than—"

She broke off abruptly and he took a step closer. "What?" he demanded. "I already have? What do you think you've done to me?"

His audacity caused her mouth to fall open. "Considering the circumstances, I think I've been quite reasonable. All I'm asking is for you to be man enough to acknowledge our child. That's all I want from you!"

"Well, it isn't all *I* want!" he barked at her.

Suddenly she felt afraid. Very afraid. The Hollisters were rich. Definitely not in the same league as the Three Rivers Hollisters, but rich just the same. If Cordell decided to sue her for custody of the child, he could afford to hire the best of lawyers. But surely, he wouldn't do such a thing. He was a confirmed bachelor. What would he want with a baby?

"What do you mean?" she asked in a guarded voice.

He began to pace back and forth across the room. "The nonsense you spouted in the bar—about me seeing our child on occasion—it made me sick! Our baby will be raised on Stone Creek Ranch and nowhere else! I'll be its full-time father. No one else!"

Maggie's head was whirling so fast she feared it was going to bring on another bout of nausea. She instinctively pressed a protective hand against her lower stomach.

"Exactly what are you suggesting?" she asked in a stricken voice. "You're not going to take my baby away from me. I don't care who you think you are!"

A look of odd disbelief twisted his features. "You have everything wrong, Maggie. You and I are going to get married. Tomorrow, in fact."

She stared at him in stunned fascination. "Married! No! Oh, no! I wouldn't marry you if you got down on your knees and begged."

"Why? I'm the father of your baby. Apparently you felt something for me—once."

Maggie pressed the hand tighter to her midsection. Oh Lord, give her the strength to get through this, she prayed.

"You don't want to be married, Cord. Not to me or anyone. You don't love me. And I don't love you."

He stopped his pacing to look at her. "There are plenty of married couples who don't love each other."

She was feeling sicker by the minute. "Yes, but are they happy?"

"Happy?" He swiped a hand over his face as though he considered her view on the subject as sappy and juvenile. "You think life is supposed to be one happy party?"

Maggie had spent the majority of her adult life caring for people and trying to ease their pain. But, God forgive her, at this very moment she wanted to slap Cordell's jaw. She wanted him to experience the same pain he was inflicting upon her.

"I'll tell you what I think, Cord. I want my life and that of my child's to be better—happier than what my mother and I had. And frankly, I don't believe marrying you will give either one of us any kind of happiness."

He walked over to her and she didn't try to resist when he reached for her hands and slowly pulled her to her feet.

"Why not?" he asked gently, his tone totally different from just moments before. "We made each other happy in Bullhead City."

The warm touch of his hands was bittersweet and she struggled to swallow the burning lump of emotion in her throat.

"Yes. For one night. But a marriage between us wouldn't last. In a few weeks' time, when my belly gets big and my ankles are swollen, you'll be wishing you were out with one of your girlfriends—free to do as you wish." Her eyes narrowed as another thought struck her. "Or maybe you have the idea of having an open marriage. You'll be free to do your thing and I can do mine. Is that what you're thinking?"

"Right now I'm thinking how tired I am of having you insult me. And I'm especially tired of not doing this!"

As he pulled her into his arms and settled his lips over hers, Maggie couldn't resist. And why would she want to? For more than two months, she'd ached for his touch and the taste of his kiss. To turn away from him now would be like turning off the moon or stars.

"Cord," she whispered when he finally lifted his head. "This chemistry between us. It isn't enough for marriage."

"We'll make it be enough. At least until our child reaches adulthood. Then, if the heat is gone, we'll go our separate ways."

Eighteen years. Twenty-one years. No. That would never be enough time with him.

"How long do you think this flame between us can burn?" she asked.

"Long enough."

Clutching her tightly, he pressed his cheek next to hers and as Maggie melted in the circle of his arms, she wanted to believe he was right.

He kissed her hungrily and deeply and Maggie could only think how he was the father of her baby. And even if he weren't, this was the man she longed to be with for the rest of her life. If that meant she loved him, then she could admit her feelings to herself, even if she couldn't admit them to him.

He eased his mouth slightly back from hers. "Ours won't be an open marriage or one of convenience. You're going to be my wife in every sense of the word and we're going to live together at Stone Creek. Yes?"

No words of love. No promises of forever. But that wasn't enough to keep her from closing her eyes and wrapping her arms around his neck. "Yes, Cord. I'll be your wife."

"When Cord said he needed to go to St. George on personal business, I expected him to bring back a new truck," Hadley said with a hearty laugh. "I didn't have a clue it was going to be a wife."

Only a couple of hours ago, Cordell and Maggie had arrived on Stone Creek and surprised the family with the news of their marriage earlier in the day at St. George. Since then, the whole family, with the exception of Grace and Ross, had arrived to share dinner with the newlyweds.

Now everyone had migrated to the den, where Beatrice and Bonnie were passing out glasses of champagne to celebrate the happy occasion. Next to him, on a loveseat near the fireplace, Maggie had mostly remained quiet and he tried not to dwell on the doubts she'd voiced to him the day before. They were going to have a baby together. He wanted to believe, in spite of its rocky start, his marriage could be like Jack and Vanessa's. Or hopefully like his parents', whose union had endured for close to forty years.

But that would mean you have to love Maggie. And you can't do that, Cord. You're too afraid you'll end up like Hunter, alone and lonely. Or like your grandfather, bitter until you die.

Determined not to let the mocking voice ruin his evening, he pushed it aside and put a grin on his face. "Well, I couldn't let Jack outdo me. He took a trip with Vanessa and ended up eloping with her. I thought I'd follow his example."

"Honey, I think something happens to our sons when they take a trip." Claire smiled with happy approval as she looked at Cordell and Maggie. "The love bug bites them."

"Look at this way, Mom, you and Dad are saving lots of money," Flint spoke up from a chair next to

Hadley's. "You won't have to throw a big wedding for your prodigal son."

"Don't call Cord the prodigal!" Beatrice scolded her brother. "He's a married man now."

His sister's remark caused Cordell's gaze to slip over to Maggie's left hand and the plain gold band on her ring finger. She hadn't wanted a diamond ring for the wedding ceremony. Nor had she wanted a special dress and shoes, or a visit to the salon. He supposed she'd thought a quick marriage ceremony performed in front of a county judge was nothing to make a fuss over.

Still, a part of Cordell had felt bad about the bare-bones, quickie wedding. But not bad enough to forgo it until a later date when his parents would want to lavish them with a big wedding. He hadn't wanted to give Maggie the opportunity to change her mind and head back to Arizona.

"You know what this means, Hadley," Claire said. "We'll need to hold another wedding reception."

Across the room, Vanessa laughed and dug her elbow into Jack's ribs. "Just think. Our reception is what got these two together."

Jack gave his wife a faint smile before he leveled a meaningful look at Cordell. As if to say he'd already figured out there was more behind this sudden marriage than love at first sight.

Before they'd arrived on the ranch, Maggie and Cordell had agreed it would make the situation less awkward if they didn't announce her pregnancy until later. But with her fighting morning sickness, he wasn't sure how long it would be before someone figured out a baby was on the way. As for their relationship, they both agreed it would be best to have everyone believe they were crazy in love. Which would hardly take much acting on his own part, Cordell thought. Not when he could hardly keep his hands off his new wife.

Beatrice did a little waltz in the middle of the floor. "Yay! I'm all for another party. It'll make a nice excuse to invite our new relatives up for a visit. If we held the reception party after the weather warms, they might consider coming."

"Good idea, Bea," Hadley said. "I'd like for the Hollisters to come for a visit, too. But it will be Cord and Maggie's reception. They'll need to choose the date for it."

Cordell eased his arm around Maggie's shoulders. "We haven't had a honeymoon yet," he said. "Maybe we'd better think about having one of those first."

Jack and Vanessa looked at one another and laughed.

"We're still waiting to have our honeymoon," Vanessa said.

"Sorry, Maggie," Hadley said. "That's what happens when you marry a rancher."

Maggie gave her new father-in-law an understanding smile. "Living here on the ranch will be like a honeymoon to me. But I must admit, not working long hours in the ER every day is going to take some getting used to. I guess I can be Stone Creek Ranch's resident nurse now."

"You certainly can. Welcome to the family, Maggie," Hadley told her, then aimed a proud look at Cordell. "Son, I never thought you'd find a woman who was right for you. But you proved me wrong. You couldn't have picked one that was more right. Let's drink a toast to Cord's good taste."

"For once!" Quint playfully joked.

Everyone in the room laughed, except Maggie. She was too busy blinking away a rush of tears.

And Cordell suddenly realized that having a wife, especially a pregnant one, was going to be a much harder task than anything he'd ever faced in his life.

Chapter Twelve

Three weeks later, Maggie was sitting at the kitchen table, when her mother-in-law walked up behind her and placed a hand on her shoulder.

"You've hardly eaten any of your lunch, Maggie. If you don't care for chicken salad I can make you something else. I have soup left over from yesterday. It might sound more appetizing to you. Let me heat a bowl for you."

Ever since Maggie had moved into the ranch house as Cordell's wife, Claire had been super kind to her. Which, in some ways, made the whole situation for Maggie even more stressful. Claire believed her son was truly in love with his new wife. And why shouldn't she think so? When Maggie and Cordell were in front of his family, he was loving and attentive. Claire had no idea that in private, he'd grown morose. Oh, they had sex and it was good, she thought miserably. But afterward he rolled away with little more than a handful of words to say before he went to sleep.

"Thank you, Claire, but this is fine, really. I'm not very hungry today. I've had so much to do," she attempted to explain. "What with having all my things shipped up here and getting my house in Wickenburg closed up and put on the market. Not to mention tying up loose ends with my job."

"How did that go?" Claire asked. "I can't imagine it was easy for you. After working in the same hospital for years and with coworkers you've grown close to."

Maggie sighed. "Saying good-bye to friends is never easy. But they've promised to stay in touch. And the doctors I worked under were understanding and supportive of my move. Though to be honest, Claire, I'm exhausted from the whole ordeal."

Claire smiled gently as she eased down in the chair next to Maggie's. "Obviously, you weren't prepared for a sudden elopement."

Maggie tried to chuckle, but the sound fell flat. "No. I wasn't exactly planning on it. But…"

Claire picked up where Maggie left off. "I understand. Cordell has plenty of persuasive charm."

He had more than charm, Maggie thought. He had something that made her long to be the center of his world. Unfortunately she didn't fall into that category. She was just the woman who happened to be carrying his baby. It was the one and only reason he'd agreed to marry her. And the fact was something she was going to have to live with for as long as they remained together.

"Yes. Cord has a way about him." She glanced over to see Claire was eyeing her thoughtfully.

"Vanessa tells me you're going to try for a nursing job at the hospital in Beaver. I'm glad. Because I have the feeling that your job as an RN gives you a sense of fulfillment."

Maggie nodded. "It does. I've always loved nursing. And I do plan to go back to work. That is, if Cordell is agreeable to the idea."

"I wouldn't worry about Cord. He'll want you to be happy and to make your own decisions. And he'll get used to the idea of you working again."

Yes, but would he ever get used to being a husband and father? She was beginning to lose hope. "Maybe so."

She forked up a portion of diced chicken, but only managed to get the bite of food halfway to her mouth before her stomach roiled in violent protest.

"Oh! I—" Jumping to her feet, she rushed over to the trash basket located at the end of the cabinet counter and vomited up everything she'd eaten.

When she finally managed to straighten up, Claire was standing next to her with a cold wet washcloth. "Here, honey. Wash your face. It'll make you feel better."

Feeling horribly embarrassed, she thanked Claire and pressed the cloth to her hot face. Thank God she and her mother-in-law were the only ones in the room.

Once she'd washed her face, she said, "I think I'd better sit down. My legs are shaky."

Holding on to her arm, Claire guided her over to the table and helped her into one of the chairs.

"Sit still and I'll get this out of your sight." Claire took the plate of salad away, then came back to her. "Feeling better?"

Maggie nodded as she continued to press the cool cloth to her forehead. "Yes. Much better. I'm—so sorry, Claire. This has nothing to do with the lunch you made. It's delicious. My stomach is giving me problems."

Claire sat down next to Maggie and reached for her hand. "Nausea is fairly common for pregnant women. You'll get past it soon."

Maggie's mouth fell open. "You know?"

Gently patting the top of Maggie's hand, she said, "From that very first night when we were all in the den toasting your marriage. You didn't drink any champagne and I wondered why. Then I heard you being sick upstairs the other morning and it all clicked."

Bending her head, she pressed the washcloth to her closed eyes. "You must think I'm awful, Claire."

"Oh honey, how could you say that? I love you. And I'm thrilled about the baby. I've been waiting for a long time for my children to start giving me grandchildren. Finally, Cord has stepped up to the plate."

Grimacing, Maggie said, "I thought you'd resent me for—well, you and I know that, if not for the baby, Cord would still be single. But believe me, Claire, I didn't demand he marry me. I thought— well, he kept insisting."

Claire frowned. "I'm not sure what you're thinking, Maggie. But I'm certain that Cord cares deeply about you and the baby. Yes, he's always been the rascal of the family, but there's another side to him. You'll see. In the meantime, though, I think you should go see Grace. She'll give you a thorough examination and help you with the nausea."

"I would like to see Grace. It's time I started having regular prenatal checkups." Maggie gave Claire's hand a grateful squeeze. "You haven't told Hadley or anyone else about the baby, have you? I think Cord should be the one to do that."

She gave Maggie a reassuring smile. "Not a peep to anyone. But I am about to give Grace a call and schedule an appointment for you. She'll have to know. But she's always mum about her patients."

Maggie leaned over and kissed her mother-in-law's cheek. "Thank you, Claire. You make me feel like I have a mother again."

Her eyes shimmering with unshed tears, Claire rose to her feet and patted Maggie's shoulder. "You do have a mother, Maggie. Now I'm going to go call Grace."

* * *

Cordell was lying in bed that night, watching Maggie pull a brush through her long red hair, when she turned away from the dresser mirror to look at him.

"Your mother knows I'm pregnant."

Cordell sat straight up in the bed. "You told her?"

She shook her head. "No. She guessed that very night we got home from St. George. I didn't drink any champagne."

He grunted. "She watches too many detective shows."

"She's a mother. Not a detective."

"They're one and the same," he muttered, then shrugged. "It doesn't matter anyway. I've noticed you're getting a tummy. Everyone is going to figure out why we got married."

And his family and friends were going to know that Maggie didn't marry him because she loved him. They were going to know she was here on Stone Creek and wearing his ring only for the sake of the baby. A month ago, he believed none of that mattered. He'd told himself he didn't need Maggie's love anyway. But as each day had gone by, each night with her lying in his arms and never a word whispered about caring for him, he'd realized he'd been fooling himself. He did want Maggie to love him. But he feared she'd closed her heart to him.

"Does that bother you?" she asked.

He lied to save his pride. "No. It's no one's business but yours and mine, anyway."

She walked over to the bed and sat down on the opposite side of the mattress. With her back to him, she said, "Claire made an appointment for me to see Grace tomorrow. She's concerned about my nausea."

"Do you want me to drive you into town?"

"No," she said curtly. "You have work to do. I'll drive myself."

Her answer created a hollow space in his chest. "Fine. I'll leave my debit card on the dresser. Get whatever you want or need."

"I don't need your debit card."

Hurt and anger swirled through him. "How could I forget? You're self-sufficient. You've always taken care of yourself. You don't need me or anyone."

I would like for our child to carry the Hollister name.

Her words suddenly returned to him and he wondered if, aside from sex, the Hollister name was the only thing she'd ever really wanted from him.

Stung by the notion, he switched off the lamp on the nightstand and turned his back to her.

The next afternoon, Grace helped Maggie to a sitting position on the end of the examination table. "You can get dressed now, Maggie, and we'll finish talking in my office. The nurse will show you the way."

Once the doctor had exited the small room, Maggie quickly donned her clothes and followed the nurse down a narrow hallway to a tiny office. Grace was sitting behind a desk cluttered with files, notepads, coffee cups and framed photos of family members, including one of her seven-year-old son, Ross.

The tall blonde pulled off a pair of horn-rimmed glasses and gestured for Maggie to take a seat. "I'm so glad Mom sent you in to see me. And I'm very honored that you chose me to be your physician."

Maggie smiled. "I've heard what a good, dedicated doctor you are to this community. It's obvious by the packed waiting room out there."

Grace waved away the compliment. "Let's get down to you and the baby. From what I can observe, you appear to both be fine. The baby's heart is beating at a normal pace and he or she seems to be the correct size according to the length of your pregnancy. Before you leave, I want Cleo to draw your blood and the results will give me the rest of the information I need to know. In the meantime, I'm going to call in two prescriptions for your nausea and a super-duper prenatal vitamin. Because I have a suspicion you might be slightly anemic, but we'll see. Other than that, we'll look for a baby in about five and a half months."

Maggie plastered a smile on her face even though a lump of tears was choking her. "Thank you, Grace."

"Oh, and in case you're wondering, we'll do an ultrasound on your next visit. Cord might want to come along then, so he can see the baby, too."

"I'll, uh, tell him." She put her hands on the arms of the chair in anticipation of rising. "Is that everything?"

Grace leaned back in her chair. "No. As your sister-in-law, I'm curious as to why you look so sad. This should be a joyous time for you. A new husband. A baby on the way. Are you worried about the baby being healthy or the pain of giving birth?"

"Not any more than the normal woman worries about those things. It's just that I—" She drew in a deep breath, then shook her head. "Grace, I—I can't pretend with you. Cordell only married me because of the baby. In the beginning I thought I could handle being in a loveless marriage. But as time passes I'm discovering it's very hard."

Grace thoughtfully tapped the end of an ink pen against a thick notepad. "A loveless marriage. Does that mean you don't love Cordell?"

The question brought her up short and suddenly she realized just how very, very much she did love Cordell. And that was the crux of the problem. One-sided love was a lonely place.

"I adore him. I love him more than he could possibly know."

"I sort of had things figured that way," she said, then shook her head. "You might not know this, but Cord has always been afraid of marriage. He was even engaged once and ended up deserting the woman at the altar. Well, almost at the altar. He called everything off a few days before the wedding. That's how uncertain he's always been about being a husband. I think it all stems from Grandfather and his bitter divorce. But no matter the reason, I believe you've changed him, Maggie. Give him time and he's going to be happy about becoming a family man. You'll see."

Rising from the chair, Maggie went around the desk and gave Grace a grateful hug. "I'll try to hold on to that hope."

Throughout the following month, snow and freezing temperatures hit the ranch with a vengeance. Cordell and the men worked nearly around the clock to keep the livestock fed and water supplies thawed. Yesterday, they'd used the last of the alfalfa and none could be found in the area. Jack had been forced to purchase a truckload from Fallon, Nevada, some five hundred miles away. The cost had made Hadley's eyes roll, but sacrifices had to be made to sustain the ranch.

But the ranch and the brutal weather were the least of Cordell's problems. For the past few weeks, he'd felt Maggie drawing away from him. Yes, at night she went willingly into his arms. But after the passion between them cooled, she spoke very little. Even her comments about the coming baby were limited and she'd ceased to show any interest in the ranch's day-to-day happenings.

She missed her nursing job; that much was understandable. And probably her friends and coworkers. He also realized that suddenly uprooting her whole life and moving to his world had been jarring for her. But all along, he'd believed and hoped that he would be enough to make her happy. Apparently, he wasn't. And the reality was crushing him.

It was long past dinnertime when Cordell finally made it home to the ranch house. The twins were in the kitchen cleaning up the mess and Bonnie met him at the door to take his coat.

"There's ice frozen on this, Cord! Why didn't you come to the house and get something dry to wear?"

"Waste of time," he told her. "Before I made it back to the barn, it would be covered in snow."

Bonnie went to hang his coat in the mudroom and Cordell walked over to where Beatrice was placing dishes in the dishwater. A plate of chicken was still sitting on the countertop and he plucked up a piece and bit into the crusty meat.

"Is the snow still coming down?" Beatrice asked. "If it doesn't stop I may not be able to get to work tomorrow."

Bonnie groaned as she returned to the room. "I can't remember any February being this bad. Maggie lived in a place where it never snowed. Now she's been introduced to blizzards."

"Where is everyone? In the den having dessert?" Cord asked.

"That happened more than an hour ago," Bonnie answered. "I think Maggie has already gone upstairs. She didn't seem like she was feeling all that well."

A prick of uneasiness sent a chill over him and he quickly started out the room. "I'll go check on her."

"But you haven't eaten, Cord," Beatrice called after him. "Do you want me to fix you a plate of leftovers?"

"Later."

Not bothering to stop by the den, he headed up the stairs. When he reached the balcony, Vanessa was just stepping out of the room he shared with Maggie. She hurried to meet him.

"Is something wrong?" he asked, careful to keep his voice lowered.

"I think you have trouble on your hands." She swiped fingers over her bleary eyes. "I've been in there trying to talk to her. But she's—shut herself off to me. Maybe you can reach her."

Vanessa wasn't prone to dramatics. Seeing tears in her eyes meant something was terribly wrong. "What's going on?"

Shaking her head, she said, "Go find out for yourself."

"I intend to."

Moments later, he entered the bedroom, expecting to find Maggie getting ready for bed. Instead, she was standing at the dresser lifting out stacks of lingerie.

He pulled off his hat and hung it on the bed-post, then started unsnapping the cuffs on his denim shirt. "Isn't this an odd time of the day to be tidy-ing up the drawers?" he asked.

"I'm not tidying. I'm sorting. Trying to decide what I'm going to take with me tomorrow."

He grunted. "Maggie, it's still snowing. I don't think tomorrow would be a good time to take any-thing to the cleaners in Beaver."

Leaving the drawer open, she turned and walked over to him. "I'm not going to Beaver. I'm going home to Wickenburg."

Cordell wasn't completely blind. These past weeks, he could see she was unhappy. But he'd never expected anything like this and the shock hit him like the slug of a fist.

"What—are you talking about? You're my wife! This is your home, Maggie. Here. With me and my family!"

She looked up at him and he could see the green eyes that used to remind him of glimmering em-eralds were now dull and lifeless. "When I agreed to marry you, Cord, I did so in hopes that you and Stone Creek would be enough for me. But I've come to realize I can't go on like this—it's not enough. It will never be enough. I tried to tell you in the be-ginning—I need a husband who loves me. I don't care if he can only provide a shack for us to live in.

At least, I'll know that when he touches me it will be with love, not lust. And when he marries me it will be because in the deepest part of his heart, he wants me by his side for the rest of his life. Not just because I'm carrying his child and it's the responsible thing to do!"

Her shoulders were visibly shaking as she turned her back to him and dropped her head in her hands. Cordell's first instinct was to reach for her. But from everything she'd just said, he realized that touching her wouldn't fix anything.

"You don't have to say it, Maggie. You resent me for making you pregnant. For uprooting your life and taking you away from everything in Arizona. I'm sorry about that. But I believed our baby would be more important to you than your own personal feelings about me. Obviously, I was wrong."

Angry now, she whirled back to him. "I'm not surprised that you don't get what I'm telling you. I honestly didn't expect you to. I'm wasting my breath talking. So let's just make all of this quick. I'm leaving and getting a divorce. I don't want anything from you. Nothing! Understand?"

Up until now, Cordell had been bone cold from working outside in single digits for most of the day. But now anger was burning every cell in his body. "Yeah, I can get that much, Maggie. But what about our baby? He or she deserves to have two parents, living together, parenting together."

"We can still parent together. I have no intentions of trying to prevent you from having partial custody."

If anything, her response made him more furious. "And have our baby become a pawn? Spending a certain allotted time between Arizona and Utah? I can't imagine anything worse!"

"I can! Living without a father's love."

She stalked over to the dresser and began to quickly unload the drawers. Groaning with frustration, Cordell followed her.

"Love! Your brain is hung up on that one word, Maggie. And why? It's intangible. The minute you start to believe it's real, it vanishes. I want something concrete I can hold on to. Something I can touch and kiss. Is that so wrong?"

Turning, she looked at him and this time there was an expression of hopeless resignation on her face. The sight of it scared him even more than her threat of divorce.

"No. It's not wrong for you, Cord. That's why you'll be much better off without me in your life. I'm an albatross to you and—"

As her words broke off, a blank stare hit her face and then suddenly she was pitching forward and straight into his arms.

He managed to catch her before she fell, but by the time he'd swept her into the cradle of his arms, she was as limp as a rag.

Terrified, he carried her over to the bed and after

laying her flat on the mattress, rushed to the bathroom for a wet washcloth.

Back in the bedroom, he pressed the cloth to her face and searched for a pulse at her wrist. The faint, rapid beat was hardly enough to ease his fears.

"Maggie! Honey, can you hear me?"

As he continued to bathe her face with the ice-cold cloth, she began to moan and then to his utter relief, her eyes fluttered open.

"Cord? What—happened?" Confused, she glanced at the bed, then focused on his face hovering over hers. "How did I get here?"

"I put you here. You fainted."

Astonished, her head moved slowly back and forth against the mattress. "I fainted? That's crazy. I—didn't feel faint. All I remember was a rushing noise in my ears."

"How do you feel now? Are you having pains—the baby?"

"No. No pain. Nothing like that. Help me sit up."

Slipping an arm beneath her shoulders, he helped her to a sitting position, then kept a steadying hold on her arm.

"Better?" he asked.

Closing her eyes, she touched fingers to her forehead. "A little. But I don't think I'll try to stand just yet. I feel pretty woozy."

He eased her back down on the mattress and propped a pillow beneath her head. "I'll be right back."

After covering her with a warm comforter, he stepped out of the room and, slipping his cell phone from his pocket, punched Grace's private number.

She answered on the third ring and he let out a breath of relief.

Knowing something had to be wrong for her brother to be calling at this hour, she didn't bother with a greeting. "What's wrong?"

"It's Maggie. She fainted a few minutes ago in our bedroom."

"Did she fall?"

"No. I managed to catch her before she hit the floor. She's not hurting anywhere, but she still doesn't feel like standing. I realize it's snowing and the roads are probably slick, but do you think you could make it out here to see her? I could drive her into the hospital, but I'm afraid forty minutes of jostling over rough roads might not do her or the baby any good."

"No. Don't try anything like that. Keep her in bed and if she has to go to the bathroom you need to assist her—just in case she might faint again."

"What do you think is wrong?" Even though he knew it was impossible for his sister to answer the question now, he had to ask it. He was terrified for Maggie and the baby.

"I can't answer your question until I examine her, Cord. Try not to worry. I'll be there as soon as I can."

* * *

Try not to worry.

Nearly two hours later, Cordell was silently repeating Grace's words as he paced back and forth across the second-floor balcony.

The rest of the family had urged him to join them in the den, while they waited for Grace to finish tending to Maggie, but he'd not wanted to get that far away from the bedroom.

He was gripped with fear. And remorse. If anything happened to Maggie or the baby, it would be his fault. He was making her miserable.

I need a husband who loves me.

I don't want anything from you. Not a thing.

"Cord."

The sound of Grace's voice interrupted his tortured thoughts and he hurried across the balcony to where she stood outside the bedroom door.

"How is she?"

Her expression solemn, Grace caught him by the arm and led him out of Maggie's earshot.

"Right now she's somewhat better. But I'm not sure for how long. When I first got here, her blood pressure was sky-high. I don't think I have to tell you how dangerous that is—particularly while carrying a baby."

Fear raced through him. "Can't you give her meds? Won't that take care of the problem?"

Grace sighed. "A pill can only do so much, Cord.

It's going to be up to you to do the rest. Right now, I'm still contemplating admitting her to the hospital and keeping her there for a few days."

A sick feeling churned in the pit of his stomach. "She wants a divorce."

Grace grimaced, then seeing the utterly lost look on his face, she patted his arm. "I know. I saw the suitcase and asked Maggie to explain. She told me what was going on and why."

Groaning, Cord swiped a hand over his face. "It's all my fault, sis. I've done everything wrong."

Shaking her head, Grace said, "I haven't given you my full diagnosis, Cord. Yes, your wife is experiencing high blood pressure. But the root cause is homesickness."

Cordell nodded glumly. "I understand. She misses her home in Wickenburg."

"Like Maggie says, you don't get it, Cord. She isn't missing those things. She's homesick for your love and a place where she truly feels the two of you are at home—together."

Swallowing at the painful lump in his throat, he said, "I always wanted to think I had a tough hide and a tough heart. Just like Grandfather. But I guess I don't. 'Cause all I want now is for Maggie to love me and for her to give me a chance to love her and our baby."

Smiling now, Grace nudged him toward the bedroom door. "Go tell that to your wife."

* * *

Maggie was lying in bed, gazing at the snow falling beyond the windowpanes, when Cordell entered the bedroom and came to sit on the edge of the bed.

His expression was solemn as he looked at her and she figured he'd finally reached the conclusion that, baby or not, he needed, even wanted to let her go. The idea was crushing her, but she had to remain steadfast, or she'd never truly find the happiness she wanted for herself and the baby.

"Grace says you and the baby are going to be okay." He reached over and clasped her hand between the two of his. "That is—if you follow doctor's orders and do what your husband tells you to do."

Her eyes narrowed skeptically. "I'm supposed to follow your orders, too?"

"Love, honor and obey. Those words were in our marriage vows. Only I tried to ignore the first one. But tonight I found out the hard way that it's the most important one of all." Leaning his head down close to hers, he looked into her eyes. "I love you, Maggie. You don't have to believe me now. But some day, after we'd been married fifty years, I hope you'll come to believe how you live in my heart. How I'll always carry you in the deepest part of it."

She stared at him in wonder. "Are you just saying this because we argued and I fainted?"

His hand came up to gently smooth her hair back

from her face. "I'm saying it because I mean it. Because I realize my life would be worthless without you. I think—maybe deep down I knew all along that I'd fallen in love with you, but I ran from the feelings, Maggie. Ran scared. I can't run anymore. Even if you don't love me, I need you in my life. By my side through thick and thin."

Tears were suddenly streaming down her face and then she began to laugh with sheer joy. "We've both been idiots, Cord. And I'm guilty of being the biggest one. I kept telling myself that I'd be a fool to fall in love with a playboy. But I think my heart was lost to you from that very first night when we danced at the reception."

His brows arched with surprise. "Why didn't you tell me?"

"Because that would've been like telling a wild stallion that the grass inside a fenced pasture was just as green as the grass on the open range. It wouldn't have worked. As soon as you heard the word *love* you would have taken off in a gallop."

Laughing, he slipped his arm beneath her shoulders and pulled her upper body close to him. "Honey, you can change my playboy label to family man. I can't wait for our baby to come—to be a father to him or her and all the other babies we're going to have."

Her expression turned coy as she kissed his cheek. "Other babies? How is that going to work?

You suggested we could go our separate ways once this baby reaches adulthood."

He chuckled as his hand fondly cradled her tummy. "Easy. By the time we raise a bunch of babies to adulthood, we'll have been married for a long, long time."

She brought her lips against his. "Why don't we shoot for forever?"

"Forever it will be, my darling."

Epilogue

Five months later, the sun was about to set behind Snow Mountain. Long shadows were stretching across the low rock wall where a sea of rose blossoms was spreading a heady scent across the patio. Next to the carefully tended garden, Maggie strolled at her husband's side. Normally his arm would have been resting against her back, but this evening it was too busy cradling their daughter, Bridget, who'd arrived only two weeks earlier.

"Cord, I hate to rain on your parade, but our daughter's eyes aren't developed enough for her to see a rose."

"I want to show them to her, anyway. If Grandfather is looking down on us, it will make him smile. He didn't do that too often and I'd like to think I put a grin on his face."

"Hmm. My mother didn't do much smiling, either. But if she can see us now, she'd be very happy, Cord."

He slanted her a tender glance. "Are you happy, Maggie?"

With a soft laugh, she rested her arm against the back of his waist. "You have to ask? We've been blessed with a healthy new daughter. Plus I have you. I'm walking on air."

He sighed. "Yes, but it has to be hard for you to watch Van going off every morning to teach school and you're not going to work at the hospital."

She flashed him an indulgent smile. "There will be plenty of time for me to get a nursing job later on. After Bridget gets older. And who knows, by then we might have another baby on the way."

Pausing his footsteps, Cordell adjusted the thin blanket away from Bridget's face. "Another baby," he said softly. "It's funny, Maggie. I used to think being a father would be like having a ball and chain locked on my ankle. Now when I hold our daughter I feel like a king with an armload of treasure. A man can't have too many treasures like this one."

Maggie's heart swelled as she watched her husband place a tiny kiss on their daughter's forehead. So far everyone was saying the baby resembled Maggie, but she suspected that was because of her wispy, red-gold hair. Her eyes were going to be the same brilliant blue of her daddy's.

"I can hardly wait for the contractors to start

building our house next month. Once it's finished, Bridget will have her own little nursery."

"Hah! You told your parents that you weren't going to let Bridget sleep more than a foot away from our bed until she turned two. What does she need a nursery for now?"

He stroked a finger gently over the top of the baby's head. "We need space to put all the little girly things I'm going to buy her. Like chaps and spurs. Boots and jeans. She's going to make quite a cowgirl."

Maggie said, "Right after Bridget was born you told me you weren't disappointed we had a girl. But I wonder."

He frowned at her. "Are you kidding? Bridget is my princess. I wouldn't trade her for ten boys. Besides," he added with a suggestive grin, "sooner or later, we'll have those boys."

"Sounds like we'd better tell the contractors to add a few more rooms to our house," Maggie teased, then gazed thoughtfully out at the spot where Cordell and Maggie's home would be built.

The mountain with Lionel's cabin would be a distant view from the front porch, along with the valley where herds of sheep grazed along the creek banks. It was going to be a beautiful home. Not just because of the setting, but because Cordell and their baby daughter would be living there as a real family. The kind of loving family Maggie had always wanted.

"You know, Cord, now that we have Bridget, I'm beginning to think a whole lot more about your grandfather and great-grandfather and how they started this family of Hollisters. Bridget and all the other children born in this family will carry on their DNA and the Hollister name. So I understand more of why Hadley feels it's important to be able to fill in the blank spots on the family tree."

"Dad has never been close to his two brothers. They never wanted anything to do with the ranch and they moved away as soon as they graduated high school. But yesterday Dad called both of them to see if they can contribute any information about Grandfather. They came up empty."

"Hmm. I'm not surprised. Hadley is the one who's always been here on the ranch. He's the one who lived with Lionel until he died. He should know the most about your family. But Van and I aren't losing faith. We'll figure this out sooner or later. In the meantime, did you know Maureen and Gil are coming up for a Labor Day party your parents are throwing?"

He shot her a comical look. "Labor Day party? We've never had one of those before."

Maggie laughed. "Well, it's going to be our belated wedding reception in the guise of a Labor Day party. But no matter, it's going to be fun. Hadley says Blake and Holt might come, too. If they can get away from Three Rivers for a day or two."

"Say, that would be great," he said. "We can

show off Bridget. But before that happens I've been thinking we should do something special for Grace. Maybe throw her a little party of some sort. She's done so much for me and you, Maggie. And for little Bridget."

Her eyes shining with love, she smiled up at him. "I think that's a wonderful idea, my darling. If not for your sister, we might not have ever admitted our love to each other. Not only that, she kept me healthy and strong during my pregnancy. Then safely delivered Bridget without a hitch. I'll say we owe her plenty."

"Let's talk to Mom about it and see what we can come up with," Cord said.

"Good idea," she replied, then thoughtfully glanced over at the glorious rose blossoms nodding in the waning sunlight. "Too bad we can't give Grace what she really needs."

"And what is that? A bigger clinic to go with her growing patient list?"

She gave him a clever smile. "No. A loving husband. Do you know any bachelors who need a doctor?"

Chuckling, he pressed a kiss to her cheek. "No. But I know a cowboy who's very glad he married a nurse."

* * * * *

#2971 FORTUNE'S FATHERHOOD DARE
The Fortunes of Texas: Hitting the Jackpot • by Makenna Lee
When bartender Damon Fortune Maloney boasts that he can handle any kid, single mom Sari Keeling dares him to watch her two rambunctious boys for just one day. It's game on, but Damon soon discovers that parenthood is tougher than he thought—and so is resisting Sari.

#2972 HER MAN OF HONOR
Love, Unveiled • by Teri Wilson
Bridal-advice columnist and jilted bride Everly England couldn't have predicted the feelings a sympathetic kiss from her best friend would ignite in her. Henry Aston knows the glamorous city girl is terrified romance will ruin their friendship. But this stand-in groom plans to win her "I do" after all!

#2973 MEETING HIS SECRET DAUGHTER
Forever, Texas • by Marie Ferrarella
When nurse Riley Robertson brought engineer Matt O'Brien to Forever to meet the daughter he never knew he had, she was only planning to help Matt see that he can be the father his little girl needs. But could the charming new dad be the man Riley didn't know she needed? And are the three ready to become a forever family?

#2974 THE RANCHER'S BABY
Aspen Creek Bachelors • by Kathy Douglass
Suddenly named guardian of a baby girl, rancher Isaac Montgomery gamely steps up for daddy duty, with the help of new neighbor Savannah Rogers. Sparks fly, but Savannah's reserved even as their feelings heat up. Are Isaac and his baby too painful a reminder of her heartbreaking loss? Or do they hold the key to healing?

#2975 ALL'S FAIR IN LOVE AND WINE
Love in the Valley • by Michele Dunaway
Unexpectedly back in town, Jack Clayton is acting as if he never crushed Sierra James's teenage heart. When he offers to buy her family's vineyard, the former navy lieutenant knows Jack is turning on the charm, but no way is she planning to melt for him again. But will denying what she still feels for Jack prove to be a victory she can savor?

#2976 NO RINGS ATTACHED
Once Upon a Wedding • by Mona Shroff
Fleeing her own nuptials wasn't part of wedding planner Sangeeta Parikh's plan. Neither was stumbling into chef Sonny Pandya's arms and becoming an internet sensation! So why not fake a relationship so Sangeeta can save face and her job, and to get Sonny much-needed exposure for his restaurant? It's a good plan for two commitmentphobes...until their fake commitment starts to feel all too real.

HARLEQUIN
PLUS

Try the best multimedia subscription service for romance readers like you!

Read, Watch and Play.

Experience the easiest way to get the romance content you crave.

Start your **FREE TRIAL** at
<u>www.harlequinplus.com/freetrial</u>.

HIGH PRAISE FOR DAVID ZINDELL'S NEVERNESS

"Excellent hard science fiction . . . Ideas splash out of
Zindell's mind and flow across the pages of this book."
—Orson Scott Card

"[Zindell's] feat of universe crafting propels him instantly into
the big leagues with the likes of Frank Herbert and Ursula K.
Le Guin."
—Edward Bryant

"A first novel that has the power to renew one's faith in
the genre."
—*Booklist*

"One of the finest talents to appear since Kim Stanley
Robinson and William Gibson—perhaps the finest."
—Gene Wolfe

"An exceptional feat of both world creation and storytelling:
grand in scope, vivid in evocation, inventive in its sure-handed
marshaling of far-future detail, and genuinely moving as a
human document. . . . I applaud his accomplishment."
—Michael Bishop

"Distinctive . . . Zindell succeeds brilliantly . . . Vastly
promising work."
—*Kirkus Reviews*

"Talented, ambitious . . . thoughtful philosophic concepts
and challenging writing, recalling early John Barth."
—*Publishers Weekly*

Books by David Zindell

NEVERNESS
THE BROKEN GOD

DAVID ZINDELL

THE
BROKEN
GOD

BANTAM BOOKS
NEW YORK • TORONTO • LONDON • SYDNEY • AUCKLAND

THE BROKEN GOD

A Bantam Spectra Book / January 1994

THE
BROKEN
GOD

PART I

DANLO THE WILD

CHAPTER I

SHAIDA

All that is not halla is shaida.
For a man to kill what he cannot eat, that is shaida;
For a man to kill an imakla animal, that is shaida, too.
It is shaida for a man to die too soon;
It is shaida for a man to die too late.
Shaida is the way of the man who kills other men;
Shaida is the cry of the world when it has lost its soul.

—from the Devaki "Song of Life"

This is the story of my son, Danlo wi Soli Ringess. I came to know him very well, though it was his fate (and my own) that he grew up wild, a lost manchild living apart from his true people. Until he came to Neverness, he knew almost nothing of his heritage or the civilized ways of the City of Light; in truth, he did not really know he was a human being. He thought of himself as an Alaloi, as one of that carked race of men and women who live on the icy islands west of Neverness. His adoptive brothers and sisters bore the signature of chromosomes altered long ago; they each had strong, primal faces of jutting browridges and deep-set eyes; their bodies were hairy and powerful, covered with the skins of once-living animals; they were more robust and vital, and in many ways much wiser, than modern human beings. For a time, their world and Danlo's were the same. It was a world of early morning hunts through frozen forests, a world of pristine ice and wind and seabirds flocking in white waves across the sky. A world of variety and abundance. Above all, it was a world of *halla,* which is the Alaloi name for the harmony and beauty of life. It was Danlo's tragedy to have to learn of *halla*'s

3

fragile nature at an early age. Had he not done so, however, he might never have made the journey home to the city of his origins, and to his father. Had he not made the journey all men and women must make, his small, cold world and the universe which contains it might have known a very different fate.

Danlo came to manhood among Alaloi's Devaki tribe, who lived on the mountainous island of Kweitkel. It had been the Devaki's home for untold generations, and no one remembered that their ancestors had fled the civilized ruins of Old Earth thousands of years before. No one remembered the long journey across the cold, shimmering lens of the galaxy or that the lights in the sky were stars. No one knew that civilized human beings called their planet Icefall. None of the Devaki or the other tribes remembered these things because their ancestors had wanted to forget the *shaida* of a universe gone mad with sickness and war. They wanted only to live as natural human beings in harmony with life. And so they had carked their flesh and imprinted their minds with the lore and ways of Old Earth's most ancient peoples, and after they were done, they had destroyed their great, silvery deep ship. And now, many thousands of years later, the Devaki women gathered baldo nuts to roast in wood fires, and the men hunted mammoths or shagshay or even Totunye, the great white bear. Sometimes, when the sea ice froze hard and thick, Totunye came to land and hunted them. Like all living things, the Devaki knew cold and pain, birth and joy and death. Death—was it not a Devaki saying, as old as the cave in which they lived, that death is the left hand of life? They knew well and intimately almost everything about death: the cry of Nunki, the seal, when the spear pierces his heart; the wailing of an old woman's death song; the dread silence of the child who dies in the night. They knew the natural death that makes room for more life, but about the evil that comes from nowhere and kills even the strongest of the men, about the true nature of *shaida,* they knew nothing.

When Danlo was nearly fourteen years old, a terrible illness called the "slow evil" fell upon the Devaki. One day, during deep winter, the men and women sickened all at once with a mysterious, frothing fever. It was a fever that stole away sense and lucidity, leaving its hosts paralyzed and leaking fluids from the ears. Of all the tribe, only Danlo and one strange man named Three-Fingered Soli remained untouched. It fell to them to hunt and prepare the food, to melt snow for drinking water, to keep the oilstones burning so there might be a little light to warm the sick inside their snow huts. Danlo and Three-Fingered Soli loved their near-brothers and sisters as they loved life, and for six days they worked like madmen to perform the hundreds of little daily devotions necessary to keep their tribe from going over too soon. But since there were eighty-eight Devaki and only two of them, it was an impossible task. Slowly—for the Alaloi are a tenacious, stubborn people—slowly Danlo's tribe began to die. His near-sister, Cilehe, was one of the first to make the journey to the other side of day. And then his near-fathers, Wemilo and Choclo, died, and Old Liluye and many others. Soon the cave was full of rotting bodies waiting to be buried. Danlo tried to ignore them, even though, for the Devaki, the care of the dead is nearly as important as that of the living. He lavished his energies on his found-father, Haidar, and on Chandra, the only woman he had ever known as a mother. He made blood tea and dribbled the thick, lukewarm liquid down their throats; he rubbed hot seal oil on their foreheads; he prayed for their spirits; he did everything he could to keep them from going over. But to no avail. At last, the slow evil stole them from life. Danlo prayed and wept, and he left their hut intending to go outside the cave to find some fireflowers to put on their grave. But he was so exhausted that he tripped into a snowdrift and fell at once into a deep, dreamless sleep. Later that day, Three-Fingered Soli found him there, covered with layers of fresh new snow.

"Danlo," Soli said as he brushed the sparkling *soreesh* from the boy's furs, *"wo lania-ti?* Are you all right?"

"I was just sleeping, sir," Danlo said. *"Mi talu los wamorashu.* I was so tired." He rubbed his eyes with his powdered mittens. Even sitting in the snow, he was tall for a boy thirteen years old; he was taller, leaner, and more angular than any of his near-brothers. In truth, he did not look like an Alaloi at all. He had the long nose and bold face bones of his father. His eyes were his mother's eyes, dark blue like liquefied jewels, and even though he was very tired, they were full of light. In almost any city of the Civilized Worlds, his fellow human beings would have found him fiercely handsome. But he had never seen a true human being, and he thought of himself as being different from his near-brothers. Not exactly ugly, but rather strange and delicately deformed, as if he were a thallow born into a nest of sparrowhawks.

"You should not sleep in the snow," Soli said as he brushed back his gray and black hair. Like most Alaloi men, he was large

5

and muscular. Today, he was very tired. His shoulders were slumped, and there was a faraway, brooding look about his eyes. He seemed very worried. "Only dogs sleep in the snow."

"But, sir, I was only going to pick fireflowers," Danlo said. "I do not know what happened."

"You might have slept too long and never awakened."

Soli pulled him to his feet. They were standing near the mouth of the cave. Thirty feet away, the sled dogs of twelve families were tied to their stakes in the snow; they were pulling at their leashes, whining, begging for their evening meal. Danlo couldn't remember the last time he had fed them. He couldn't remember the last time he had fed himself. It was late afternoon and the sun was low in the sky. The air was blue cold, as clear as *silka,* the new ice. He looked out over the valley below the cave. The forest was already lost in shadows of dark green and gray— tomorrow, he thought, he might hunt shagshay, but tonight the dogs would go hungry again.

"Haidar and Chandra have gone over," Danlo said. He looked at Soli.

"Yes, they were the last."

"Haidar and Chandra," Danlo repeated, and he wiped a clump of melting snow away from his forehead. And then he said a prayer for his found-parents' spirits: *"Haidar eth Chandra, mi alasharia la shantih Devaki."*

Soli rubbed his nose with his three-fingered hand and said, *"Shantih, shantih."*

"And Sanya," Danlo said, "and Mahira, they have gone over, too."

"Shantih," Soli said.

"And Irisha, Yukio, and Jemmu—all *alasharu."*

"Shantih."

"And Rafael, Choclo, and Anevay. And Mentina, they have all made the great journey."

"Yes," Soli said, *"shantih."*

"They are all dead."

"Yes."

"Ten days ago, all alive and fat with life, even Old Anala, and now—"

"Do not speak of it. Words are only words—there is no purpose."

Danlo took off his mittens and pressed his eyes; the hot water there burned his cold thumbs. "I am so tired," he said.

6

And then, "The blessed Devaki—the whole tribe, sir. How can this be?"

Soli turned his face to the north, saying nothing.

Danlo followed his gaze outward, upward to where the pointed summit of Kweitkel rose above them. It was a great shining mountain marbled in granite and ice, a god watching over them. Four thousand years ago the first Devaki had named the island after the mountain forming its center. Generation upon generation of Danlo's ancestors were buried here. He closed his eyes as the wind came up and whipped his hair wildly about his head. There was ice in the wind, the smell of pine needles, salt, and death. "Kweitkel, *shantih,*" he whispered. Soon he must bury his people in the graveyard above the cave, and after that, the Devaki would be buried on Kweitkel no longer.

"It was bad luck," Soli said at last, rubbing the thick brows of his forehead. "Yes, bad luck."

"I think it was *shaida,*" Danlo said. "It is *shaida* for our people to die too soon, yes?"

"No, it was just bad luck."

Danlo held his hand over his forehead to keep his hair from lashing into his eyes. He had thick black hair shot with strands of red. "In all the stories Haidar told over the oilstones, in all your stories, too, I have never heard of a whole tribe going over all at once. I never thought it was possible. I . . . never thought. Where has this *shaida* come from? What is wrong with the world that everyone could die like this? 'Shaida is the cry of the world when it has lost its soul'—why is the world crying of *shaida,* sir?"

Soli put his arm around him, and touched his head. Danlo wept freely, then, wept for a long time into Soli's stiff, frozen furs until a cold thought sobered him. He was only thirteen years old, but among the Devaki, thirteen is almost old enough to be a man. He looked at Soli, whose icy blue eyes were also full of tears. "Why us, Soli? Why didn't the slow evil carry us over, too?"

Soli looked down at the ground. "It was luck," he said. "Just bad luck."

Danlo heard the pity and pain in Soli's voice, and it carried him close to despair. Soli, too, was ready for death. Anyone, even a child could see that. There was madness and death in his eyes and all over his haggard, gray face. The wind blowing through the forest and over the icy boulders all around them

7

was very cold, almost dead cold, and Danlo felt like dying himself. But he couldn't let himself die because he loved life too much. Wasn't it *shaida* to die too soon? Hadn't he seen as much of *shaida* as he could bear? He blew on his chilled, purple fingers and put his mittens back on. Yes, he must live because it was not time for him to go over yet, he was still young and full of life, still just a boy who suddenly knew that he had to find an answer to *shaida*.

He looked into the cave, at the great, black gash in the side of the hill where Jonath and his other near-brothers lay entombed. "It is strange that the slow evil did not take me, yes? Perhaps the slow evil is afraid of wildness. I have always been a little wild, I think. Haidar used to say I was wild, with all my talk of driving a sled east into the sunrise. He used to say I listened to you too much. When I was a boy—"

"Shhh, you talk too much."

"But I have to ask you this, sir; I must know a thing."

"What is that?"

"When I was a boy, I wanted to find the bed of Sawel from where he arises each morning to light the world. Pure wildness, as Haidar always warned. Tell me, sir, you must know—was I born with this wild face? My face is so different from the faces of my brothers. And they were so much stronger and hardier in their bodies; they never seemed to feel the cold. Why did they go over and not I?"

Soli looked at him and said, "It was fate. Just blind fate."

Danlo was disturbed by the way Soli spoke of fate. There was *galia*, he knew, the World-soul, and one could certainly speak of the *wilu-galia*, the intention of the World-soul, but how could the World-soul be blind? No, he thought, only people or animals (or God himself) could be blind. As Haidar had taught him, he shut his eyes again and breathed frigid air to clear his inner sight. He tried to *askeerawa wilu-galia*, to see the intention of the World-soul, but he could not. There was only darkness in front of him, as deep and black as a cave without light. He opened his eyes; the cold needles of wind made him blink. Could it be that Haidar had told him and the other children false stories about the animals, about the birth and life of the World? Could it be that everything he knew was wrong? Perhaps only full men were able to see that the World-soul's intention was *shaida*; perhaps this was what Soli meant by blind fate.

"It is cold," Soli said, stamping his feet. "It is cold and I am tired."

8

He turned to step toward the cave and Danlo followed him. He, too, was tired, so tired that his tendons ached up and down his limbs and he felt sick in his belly, as if he had eaten bad meat. For thirteen years of his life, ever since he could remember, entering the cave from the outside world had always been a moment full of warmth, certitude, and quiet joy. But now nothing would ever be the same again, and even the familiar stones of the entranceway—the circular, holy stones of white granite that his ancestors had set there—were no comfort to him. The cave itself was just as it had been for a million years: a vast lava tube opening into the side of the mountain; it was a natural cathedral of gleaming obsidian, flowing rock pendants hanging from ceiling to floor, and deep silences. Now, in the cave of his ancestors, there was too much silence and too much light. While Danlo had slept in the snow, Soli had gathered faggots of bonewood and placed them at fifty-foot intervals around the cave walls. He had set them afire. The whole of the cave was awash with light, flickering orange and ruby lights falling off the animal paintings on the walls, falling deep into the cave's dark womb where the cold floor rose up to meet the ceiling. Danlo smelled woodsmoke, pungent and sweet, and the firelight itself was so intense it seemed to have a fragrance all its own. And then he smelled something else layered beneath the smells of wood, fur, and snow. Touching every rock and crack of the cave, all around him and through him, was the stench of death. Though he breathed through his mouth and sometimes held his breath, he could not escape this terrible stench. The bodies of the dead were everywhere. All across the snow-packed floor, his near-brothers and sisters lay together in no particular order or pattern, a heap of bent arms, hair, furs, rotting blood, thick black beards, and dead eyes. They reminded Danlo of a shagshay herd driven off a cliff. Leaving them inside their snow huts until burial would have been less work, but Soli had decided to move them. The huts, the fifteen domes built of shaped snow blocks in the belly of the cave, had kept the bodies too warm. The smell of rotting flesh was driving the dogs mad and howling with hunger, and so Soli had dragged the bodies one by one to the cave's center where they might freeze. Danlo worried that Soli, tired as he was, might have left someone inside one of the snow huts by mistake. He told Soli of this worry, and Soli quickly counted the bodies; there were eighty-eight of them, the whole of the Devaki tribe. Danlo thought it was wrong to count his kin one by one, to assign abstract numerals to human beings

9

who had so recently breathed air and walked over the brilliant ice fields of the world. He knew that each of them had a proper name (except, of course, for the babies and very little children who were known simply as "Son of Choclo" or "Mentina's Second Daughter"), and he knew the names of each of them, and he stood over the dead calling their names. "Sanya," he said, "Yukio, Choclo, Jemmu . . ." After a while his voice grew thin and dry, and he began to whisper. Finally, he grew as silent as Soli, who was standing beside him. He couldn't see the faces of everyone to say their names. Some of the dead lay facedown, half buried in the snow. Others—usually they were babies— were covered by the bodies of their mothers. Danlo walked among the dead, looking for the man he called his father. He found Haidar next to Chandra, the woman who had adopted him when he was a newborn only a few moments old. They were lying together, surrounded by Cilehe, Choclo, and Old Liluye, and others of their family. Haidar was a short man, though remarkably broad and muscular; he had always been remarkably patient, canny, and kind, and Danlo could not understand how such a great man had so inexorably died. In death, with his *anima* passed from his lips, Haidar seemed smaller and diminished. Danlo knelt beside him, between him and Chandra. Haidar's hand was stretched out, resting across Chandra's forehead. Danlo took Haidar's hand in his own. It was a huge hand, but there was no strength there, no tone or vitality. It was as cold as meat, almost cold enough to begin hardening up like ice. Chandra's face was cold, too. The hair around her ears was crusted with layers of a pale red fluid. Some of this fluid had dried days before; the freshest, the blood of her death agony scarcely hours old, was now beginning to freeze. Danlo combed the thick hair away from her forehead and looked at her lovely brown eyes, which were open and nearly as hard as stones. There was nothing in her eyes, neither joy nor light nor pain. That was the remarkable thing about death, Danlo thought, how quickly pain fled the body along with its *anima.* He turned and touched Haidar's cold forehead then, and he closed his own eyes against the tears burning there. He wanted to ask Haidar the simplest of questions: Why, if death was so peaceful and painless, did all living things prefer life to death?

"Danlo, it is time to ice the sleds." This came from Soli, who was standing above him, speaking gently.

"No," Danlo said, "not yet."

"Please help me with the sleds—we still have much to do."

"No." Danlo sat down on the cave floor, and he rested one hand over Haidar's eyes, the other over Chandra's. "Haidar, *alasharia la shantih,*" he said. And then, "Chandra, my mother, go over now in peace."

"Quiet now," Soli said, and he ruffled Danlo's hair. "There will be time for praying later."

"No."

"Danlo!"

"No!"

Soli shrugged his shoulders and stared into the depths of the cave where the firelight reflected off the shiny black walls. His voice sounded low and hollow as he said, "The sleds have to be iced. Join me outside when you are done, and we will bury the Devaki."

That evening, they began burying their tribe. They worked as quickly as they could, stripping the bodies naked and rubbing them with seal grease from toe to forehead. Danlo knew that it would be cold on their spirits' journey to the other side of day, and the grease would help against the cold. Loading the bodies on the sleds and hauling them up to the burial grounds above the cave was gruesome, exhausting work. Some of his near-sisters had died many days earlier, and their flesh had run dark and soft as rotten bloodfruit. It would have been less horrible to remove the bodies all at once and place them in the snowdrifts where they would freeze hard and fast. But there were bears in the forest and packs of wolves; as it was, they had to gather bunches of dead wood to keep the cave's entrance fires burning, to keep the wild animals at bay. Of course the sled dogs were familiar with fire, and they had little fear of it. And so Danlo and Soli decided to spend a couple of days hunting shagshay while most of their people awaited burial. They had to flay the great, white, fleecy animals and cut them up for food, or else the starving dogs might have gnawed off their leashes and gone sniffing for carrion in the cave. After that, they returned to work. One by one, they placed the bodies on the icy, treeless burial field. They oriented them with their heads to the north. They heaped boulders atop each body; they built many stone pyramids to keep the animals away and to remind them that each living thing must return to the earth from which it is born. Their labor took ten days. There were too few boulders close to the cave, so they had to tie the dogs to their traces and drive sleds down through the forest to an icy stream where they found many smooth, rounded rocks. And then back up to the burial ground again with sleds full of rocks, back and forth for many trips. When they were finished at last, they found some *anda* bushes and picked orange and red fireflowers to place atop the graves. And then they prayed for the dead, prayed until their voices fell hoarse and their tears were frozen sheets over their cheeks; they prayed far into the night until the cold off the sea ice chilled their bones.

"Mi alasharia," Danlo said one last time, and he turned to Soli. "It is done, yes?"

They began walking down through the dark graves, down through the snowdrifts and the swaying yu trees. There were stars in the sky, and everywhere snow covered the forest. After a while they came to the stream where they had built a little snow hut to live in while they did their work. Never again would they sleep in the cave.

"What will we do now?" Danlo asked.

"Tomorrow, we will hunt again," Soli said. "We will hunt and eat and continue to pray."

Danlo was quiet while he stared at the cold snow hut that would provide shelter for a night, or perhaps many nights. And then he said, "But, sir, what will we *do*?"

They crawled through the tunnel of the hut. The tunnel was dark and icy, and barely wide enough to allow Soli passage. The main chamber was larger, though not so large that either of them could stand up without breaking through the top of the little snow dome. In the half darkness, Danlo moved carefully lest he knock against the snow blocks that formed the hut's walls. He spread his sleeping furs atop his bed of hard-packed snow. Soli added chunks of seal blubber to the oilstone, a bowl of scooped stone which was always kept burning, however faintly. The blubber melted and caught fire, and Danlo gazed at the small pearly flame floating on a pool of dark oil. Soon the curved white walls of the hut glowed with a warm, yellow light.

"Yes, what to do now," Soli said. The oilstone grew hotter, and he began boiling water in a small clay pot. It was his habit to drink some blood tea before sleeping.

Danlo thought Soli was a strange man, at heart a wild man like himself, or rather, like he would be if he ever became a man. He felt an affinity to this wildness. Hadn't Soli's great-great-grandfather left the tribe a few generations ago to journey across the southern ice? Hadn't Soli and his now-dead family returned from the fabled Blessed Isles with fantastic stories of air so warm that the snow fell from the sky as water? It was told that Soli had once journeyed across the eastern ice to the Unreal City where the shadow-men lived in mountainous stone huts. Danlo wondered if these stories were true, just as he wondered at the secret, wild knowledge of numbers and circles that Soli had taught him. He thought Soli was a mysterious, wild man, and then a startling idea came to him: perhaps this is why the slow evil had avoided him, too.

Danlo scooped some frozen seal blood out of a skin and dumped the blackish, crystalline mass into Soli's pot. He said, "We will have to journey west to Sawelsalia or Rilril, won't we? We have many far-cousins among the Patwin, I have heard it said. Or perhaps the Olorun—which of the tribes do you think will welcome us, sir?"

He felt uncomfortable talking so much because it was unseemly for a boy to talk so freely in front of a man. But he was uncertain and afraid for the future, and in truth, he had always liked to talk. Especially with Soli; if he didn't initiate conversation, Soli was likely to remain as silent as a stone.

After a long time, Soli said, "To journey west—that may not be wise." He took a long drink of blood tea. Danlo watched him hold his cup up to his mouth; it seemed that his eyes were hooded in steam off the tea, and in secretiveness.

"What else can we do?"

"We can remain here on Kweitkel. This is our home."

Danlo held his hand to his eyes and swallowed hard against the lump in his throat; it felt like a piece of meat was stuck there. "No, sir, how can we remain here? There are no women left to make our clothes; there are no more girls to grow into wives. There is nothing left of life, so how can we remain?"

While Soli sipped his tea silently, Danlo continued, "It is wrong to let life end, yes? To grow old and never have children? To let it all die—isn't that *shaida,* too?"

"Yes, life, *shaida,*" Soli finally said. *"Shaida."*

Something in the way Soli stared into his tea made Danlo feel a sharp pain inside, over his liver. He worried that Soli secretly blamed him for bringing *shaida* to their tribe. Was such a thing possible? he wondered. Could he, with his strange young face and his wildness, bring the slow evil to the Patwin tribe as well? He felt shame at these thoughts, then, felt it deep in his chest and burning up behind his eyes. He tried to speak, but for once his voice had left him.

Soli stirred his lukewarm tea with his forefinger. The two fingers next to it were cut off; the scars over the knuckle stumps were white and shiny. "To the east," he said at last, "is the Unreal City. Some call it the City of Light, or . . . Neverness. We could go there."

Danlo had slumped down into his furs; he was as tired as a boy could be and still remain among the living. But when he heard Soli speak of the mythical Unreal City, he was suddenly awake. He was suddenly aware of his heart beating away as it did when he was about to spear a charging shagshay bull. He sat up and said, "The Unreal City! Have you really been there? Is it true that shadow-men live there? Men who were never born and never die?"

"All men die," Soli said softly. "But in the Unreal City, some men live almost forever."

In truth, Soli knew all about the Unreal City because he had spent a good part of his life there. And he knew everything about Danlo. He knew that Danlo's blood parents were really Katharine the Scryer and Mallory Ringess, who had also lived in the City. He knew these things because he was Danlo's true grandfather. But he chose not to tell Danlo the details of his heritage. Instead, he sipped his tea and cleared his throat. And then he said, "There is something you must know. Haidar would have told you next year when you became a man, but Haidar has gone over, and now there is no one left to tell you except me."

Outside the hut, the wind was blowing full keen, and Danlo listened to the wind. Haidar had taught him patience; he could be patient when he had to be, even when the wind was blowing wild and desperately, even when it was hard to be patient. Danlo watched Soli sipping his tea, and he was sure that something desperately important was about to be revealed.

"Haidar and Chandra," Soli forced out, "were not your blood parents. Your blood parents came from the Unreal City. Came to the tribe fifteen years ago. Your mother died during your birth, and Haidar and Chandra adopted you. That is why you are different from your brothers and sisters. Most men of the City look as you do, Danlo."

Danlo's throat ached so badly he could barely speak. He rubbed his eyes and said simply, "My blood parents . . . There are others who look like me, yes?"

"Yes, in the Unreal City. It is not *shaida* to have a face such as yours; you did not bring this *shaida* to our people."

Soli's explanation cooled Danlo's shame of being left alive. But it brought to mind a hundred other questions. "Why did my blood parents come to Kweitkel? Why? Why wasn't I born Devaki as all Devaki are born? Why, sir?"

"You don't remember?"

Danlo shut his burning eyes against the oilstone's light. He remembered something. He had an excellent memory, in some ways a truly remarkable memory. He had inherited his mother's "memory of pictures"; when he closed his eyes, he could conjure up in exact color and contour almost every event of his life. Once, two winters ago, against Haidar's warnings, he had rashly gone out to hunt silk belly by himself. A silk belly boar had found him in a copse of young shatterwood trees; the boar had charged and laid open his thigh with his tusk before Danlo could get his spear up. He was lucky to be alive, but it wasn't his luck that he most remembered. No, what he saw whenever he thought about that day was Chandra's fine needlework as she sewed shut his wound. He could *see* the bone needle pulling through the bloody, stretched-out skin, the precision stitching, each loop of the distinctive knot Chandra used to tie off his wound. Inside him was a whole universe of such knots of memories, but for some reason, he had almost no memory of the first four years of his life. Somewhere deep inside, there was a faint image of a man, a man with piercing blue eyes and a sad look on his face. He couldn't bring the image to full clarity, though; he couldn't quite see it.

He opened his eyes to see Soli staring at him. He drew his furs up around his naked shoulders. "What did my father look like?" he asked. "Did you know my father? My mother? The mother of my blood?"

Soli sipped the last of his tea and bent to pour himself another cup. "Your father looked like you," he said. Then his face fell silent as if he were listening to something, some animal cry or sound far away. "Your father, with his long nose, and the hair—he never combed his hair. Yes, the wildness, too. But you have your mother's eyes. She could see things clearly, your mother."

"You must have known them very well, if they lived with the tribe. Haidar must have known them, too."

Danlo closed his eyes again and tried to shut out the wind whispering just beyond the snow blocks above his head. Inside him, there were other sounds, other whispers. He remembered the way Choclo and some of the other men would sometimes look at him strangely, the way their voices would drop into whispers whenever he surprised them in some dark corner of the cave. He had always imagined that everyone was talking about him when he wasn't there to listen. There were darker memories, too: he had once overheard Chandra and Ayame talking about a *satinka,* a witch who had worked her evil and brought *shaida* to her people. He had thought the story was of the dreamtime, the time of the ancestors, the eternal, indestructible time that was at once the history and the communal dreaming state of his people. He must have been wrong, he thought. Perhaps there had been a real *satinka* in the tribe. Perhaps this *satinka* had bewitched his blood mother and father.

"Yes, Haidar knew your blood parents," Soli admitted.

"Then what were their names? Why didn't he tell me?"

"He would have told you when you became a man, during your passage. There is more to the story, things a boy should not have to think about."

"I am almost a man," Danlo said. The set of his face was at once open and pained, innocent and hard. "Now that Haidar is dead, you must tell me."

"No, you are not a man yet."

With his long fingernails, Danlo scraped frost off the ruff of his sleeping furs. He tried to make out his reflection in the glazed hut walls above him, but all he could see was his shadow, the outline of his face and wild hair darkening the milky white snow. "I am almost a man, yes?"

"Next deep winter, after your passage, then you will be a man." Soli yawned and then said, "Now it is time to sleep. We must hunt tomorrow, or we will starve and join the rest of the tribe on the other side."

Danlo thought hard for a while. He had a naturally keen mind made all the keener by the mind tools Soli had given him in secret. Ever since he could remember, Soli had taken him alone into the forest to draw figures in the hard-packed snow. He had taught him geometry; he had taught him about things called spheres and strange attractors and the infinities. Proof structures and topology, and above all the beautiful, crystalline logic which ordered the universe of number. Logic: even though Danlo found it a strange and wild way of thinking, he loved to argue logically with Soli.

He held his hand up to his mouth to cover a smile, then said, "The journey across the eastern ice to the Unreal City will be long and hard, yes?"

"Yes," Soli said. "Very hard."

"Even a man might not complete such a journey—Totunye,

the bear, may hunt him, or the Serpent's Breath might strike him and kill him with cold, or—"

"Yes, the journey will be dangerous," Soli broke in.

"What if I were left alone to find the City?" Danlo asked softly. "Or if the slow evil found you at last out on the ice? What if the shadow-men in Unreal City do not know *halla*? Maybe the shadow-men would kill you for your meat. If you died before my passage, sir, how would I ever become a man?"

For Danlo, as for every Alaloi boy, the initiation into manhood is the third most important of life's transformations and mysteries, the other two being birth and death.

Soli rubbed his temples and sighed. He was very tired but he must have clearly seen the logic of Danlo's argument, that he would have to make his passage a year before his time. He smiled at him and said, "Do you think you are ready, Danlo? You are so young."

"I am almost fourteen."

"So young," Soli repeated. "Even fifteen years is sometimes too young. The cutting is very painful, and there have been many boys older than you who were not ready for the pain of the knife. And then, after the cutting . . ." He let his voice die off, and he looked at Danlo.

"And then there is the secret knowledge, yes? The Song of the Ancestors?"

"No, after the pain, there is terror. Sheer terror."

He knew that Soli was trying to frighten him, so he smiled to hide his fear. The air inside the hut was steamy from the boiling tea and from their rhythmic exhalations; it was *selura,* wet cold—not as absolutely cold as white cold, but cold enough to lap at his skin like a thirsty seal and make him shiver slightly. He pulled himself down into his furs, trying to keep warm. All his life, from the older boys and young men, he had heard rumors about the passage into manhood. It was like dying, Choclo had once said, dying transcendently, *ur-alashara*; it was like going over, not to the other side of day, but going over oneself to find a new, mysterious world within. He thought about what it would be like to go over, and he tried to sleep, but he was too full of death and life, too full of himself. All at once, his whole body was shivering beyond his control. He had an overwhelming sense that his life, every day and night, would be supremely dangerous, as if he were walking a snow bridge over a crevasse. He felt wild and fey in anticipation of making this eternal crossing. And then, deep inside, a new knowledge sudden and pro-

17

found: he loved the dark, wild part of himself as he loved life. *Ti-miura halla,* follow your love, follow your fate—wasn't this the teaching of a hundred generations of his people? If he died during his passage, died to himself or died the real death of blood and pain, he would die in search of life, and he thought this must be the most *halla* thing a man could do.

The shivering stopped, and he found himself smiling naturally. "Isn't terror just the left hand of fate?" he asked. "Will you take me through my passage tomorrow, sir?"

"No, tomorrow we shall hunt shagshay. We shall hunt, then eat and sleep to regain our strength."

"And then?"

Soli rubbed his nose and looked at him. "And then, if you are strong enough and keep your courage, you will become a man."

Four days later, at dusk, they strapped on their skis and made the short journey to Winter Pock, a nearby hill where the Devaki men held their secret ceremonies. Danlo was not allowed to speak, so he skied behind Soli in silence. As he planted his poles and pushed and glided through the snow, he listened to the sounds of the forest: the loons warbling with bellies full of yu berries; the clicking of the sleekits halfway out of their burrows, warning each other that danger was near; the wind keening across the hills, up through the great yu trees heavy with snow. It was strange the way he could hear the wind far off before he could feel it stinging his face. He listened for Haidar's rough voice in the wind, and the voices of his other ancestors, too. But the wind was just the wind; it was only the cold, clean breath of the world. He hadn't yet entered into the dreamtime, where his mother's dying plaints and the moaning of the wind would be as one. He smelled sea ice and pine needles in the wind; as the light failed and the greens and reds bled away from the trees, the whole forest was rich with the smells of the freezing night and with life.

In silence, they climbed up the gentle slopes of Winter Pock. The hill was treeless and barren at the top, like an old man whose hair has fallen off the crown of his head. Set into the snow around a large circle were wooden stakes. Each stake was topped with the skull of a different animal. There were a hundred different skulls: the great, tusked skull of Tuwa, the mammoth; the skulls of Nunki and long, pointed skulls of the snow fox and wolf; there were many, many smaller skulls, those of the birds, Ayeye, the thallow, and Gunda and Rakri, and Ahira, the snowy owl. Danlo had never seen such a sight in all of his life, for the boys of the tribe were not allowed to approach Winter Pock. In the twilight, the circle of grayish-white skulls looked ominous and terrifying. Danlo knew that each man, after his cutting, would look up at the skulls to find his *doffel*, his other-self, the one special animal he would never again hunt. His *doffel* would guide him into the dreamtime, and later, through all the days of his life. Beyond this bit of common knowledge, Danlo knew almost nothing of what was to come.

Soli kicked off his skis and led him inside the circle of skulls. At the circle's center, oriented east to west, was a platform of packed snow.

"When we begin," Soli said, "you must lie here facing the stars." He explained that it was traditional for the initiate boy to lie on the backs of four kneeling men, but since the men had all gone over, the platform would have to do. Around the platform were many piles of wood. Soli held a glowing coal to each pile in turn, and soon there were dozens of fires blazing. The fires would keep Danlo from freezing to death.

"And now we begin," Soli said. He spread a white shagshay fur over the platform and bade Danlo to remove his clothes. Night had fallen, and a million stars twinkled against the blackness of the sky. Danlo lay down on his back, with his head toward the east as in any important ceremony. He looked up at the stars. The lean muscles of his thighs, belly, and chest were hard beneath his ivory skin. Despite the fires' flickering heat, he was instantly cold.

"You may not move," Soli said. "No matter what you hear, you may not turn your head. And you may not close your eyes. Above all, on pain of death, you may not cry out. On pain of death, Danlo."

Soli left him alone, then, and Danlo stared up at the deep dome of the sky. The world and the sky, he thought—two halves of the great circle of *halla* enfolding all living things. He knew that the lights in the sky were the eyes of his ancestors, the Old Ones, who had come out this night to watch him become a man. There were many, many lights; Soli had taught him the art of counting, but he could not count the number of Old Ones who had lain here before him because it would be unseemly to count the spirits of dead men as one did pebbles or shells by the sea. He looked up at the stars, and he saw the eyes of his father, and his father's fathers, and he prayed that he would not break the great circle with cries of pain.

After a while he began to hear sounds. There came sharp, clacking sounds, as of two rocks being struck together. As the fires burned over him, the rhythm of the clacking quickened; it grew louder and nearer. The sound split the night. Danlo's right half knew that it must be Soli making this unnerving sound, but his left half began to wonder. He could not move his head; it seemed that the eyelight of the Old Ones was streaming out of the blackness, dazzling him with light. The clacking hurt his ear now and was very close. He could not move his head to look, and he feared that the Old Ones were coming to test him with terror. Suddenly the clacking stopped. Silence fell over him. He waited a long time, and all he could hear was his deep breathing and the drumbeat of his heart. Then there came a dreadful whirring and whooshing that he had never experienced before; the air itself seemed to be splitting apart with the sound. The Old Ones were coming for him, his left side whispered. He dare not move or else they would know that he was still just a frightened boy. How could Soli be making such a sound? his right side wanted to know. He dare not move or Soli would have to do a terrible thing.

"*Danlo!*" a voice screamed out of the darkness. "*Danlo-mi!*" It was not Soli who called to him; it was not the voice of a man. "*Danlo, dorona ti-lot!* Danlo, we require your blood, now!"

It was the voice of a terrible animal he had never heard before. It screamed like a thallow and roared like a bear, all at once. He began to tremble, or perhaps he was just shivering, he couldn't tell which. Despite the intense cold, drops of sweat burst from his skin all across his forehead, chest, and belly. The animal screamed again, and Danlo waited motionless for it to tear at the throbbing arteries of his throat. He held his head rigid, pressing it down into the fur. He wanted to close his eyes and scream, but he could not. Straight up at the dazzling lights he stared, and suddenly the lights were gone. The animal was standing over him, bending low, blocking out the night sky. It wasn't really an animal at all; it was the Beast of the young men's stories. It had horns and great conical teeth like a killer whale; its cruel, hooked beak was dipping toward his face; its claws were the claws of the snow tiger, and they were sweeping down toward his belly and groin. He had never seen a man wearing a mask before, but even if he had, his left side would still be shouting that the Beast was about to rip away at him. He held himself very still.

20

"Danlo, we require your blood!" the Beast growled out again.

To live, I die, he thought, silently repeating the Devaki prayer of initiation.

Ever since he could remember, ever since he had seen the older men naked and looked between their legs with dread and wonder, he had known this moment must come. The Beast reached down and grasped his membrum. Its claws were cold and sharp against the shaft. In his fear and cold, his unprotected stones tightened up in their sac. He was very afraid; never had he known such a belly-tightening fear, not even when Haidar fell sick from the slow evil and began bleeding from his ears. The fear was all over him, like dead cold air falling down from the sky, suffocating him, clutching in his lungs. He was afraid the Beast would cut him, yes, afraid of the pain, but even more he dreaded convulsing like a frightened snow hare and trying to run away. And if he did that, he would be slain. The Beast would kill him for giving in to his fear. This thought, in turn, fed his fear, intensified it until the sweat poured off his ribs and soaked the furs beneath him. The wind began to blow, chilling him to the core, and he despaired because he felt himself falling through a black bottomless night from which there is no escape. *Fear is the consciousness of the child*—he remembered Haidar saying this once when they were lost out at sea. He stared up at the brilliant stars, waiting for the Beast to cut him, or tear open his throat, and in a moment of exhilaration he realized that he was here to surrender up his fear, or rather, to lose a part of himself, to let die his childish conception of himself as a separate being terrified of the world. All men must be tested this way, he knew, or else they could never be full men. Just then the Beast roared something into the night, a huge, angry sound that rattled the skulls surrounding him. He felt his foreskin being pulled away from the bulb, and there was a tearing, hot pain. He clenched his jaws so hard he thought his teeth would break off in splinters and be driven into his gums; his muscles strained to rip apart his bones, and instantly his eyes were burning so badly he could not see. He could still hear, though, and in many ways that was the worst of it, the crunching, ripping sound of his foreskin being torn away from his membrum. *It hurts!* he silently screamed. *Oh, God, it hurts!* The pain was a red flame burning up his membrum into his belly and spine. The pain ate him alive; the world was nothing but fire and pain. There came a moment when his body was like a single nerve connected to a vastly

21

greater ganglia and webwork of living things: trees and stars and the wolves howling in the valleys below. He could hear the death scream of Churo and Yaga, and all the animals he had ever killed exploding from his own throat; he remembered the story of a Patwin boy who had died during his passage, and he felt a sudden pressure below his ribs, as if a spear or claw had pierced his liver. In one blinding moment he saw again the faces of each member of his tribe as they prayed to be freed of the slow evil. The hurt of all these peoples and things, and every thing, flowed into him like a river of molten stone. He ached to move, to scream, to pull himself up and run away. Only now wholly consumed by the terrible pain that is the awareness of life, he was no longer afraid. Beyond pain, there was only death. Death was the left hand of life, and suddenly he beheld its long cold fingers and deep lines with a clarity of vision that astonished him. Seen from one perspective, death was cruel and dreadful like a murderer's hand held over a baby's face; but from another, death was as familiar and nonfrightening as the whorls of his father's open palm. He would die, tonight or ten thousand nights hence—he could almost see the moment when the light would flee his eyes and join all the other lights in the sky. Even now, as the Beast tore at him, he was dying, but strangely he had never been so alive. He held himself quiet and still, listening to the wind beating through the trees and over the mountains. He heard a voice whispering that his membrum's red bulb must be exposed to the cold air, just as the man within must finally shed his childlike skin of wishes and certitude and come to know the world as it really is. That was the way of all life, he heard the voice say. Life was always lived with death close at hand, and it was continually shedding death even as it made itself over to be born anew.

To live, I die, he told himself.

And inside him, despite the pain, at the center of his deepest self was just sheer joy at being alive. In some sense, he would always be alive, no matter the killing coldness of the wind or fatal illnesses or any of a thousand other fates that he might suffer.

"Danlo!" the Beast howled out. "Your blood is red and flows like a man's!"

Danlo listened to his deep breathing as other cuts were carved into his flesh, tiny cuts up and down the length of his membrum. He realized that it was Soli making these cuts and rubbing various colored powders into them. The cuts would fes-

22

ter and then heal, and soon his membrum would be like that of any other Alaloi man: long and thick, and decorated with dozens of green and ocher scars.

"Danlo, are you ready now?"

He felt something soft being wrapped around his membrum; it felt like feather moss held in place with a newl skin.

"Danlo, you must gather your strength for the journey," a voice called out of the darkness. Then the Beast stood above him, gripping a gobbet of flesh between its bloody claws. "This piece of meat will sustain you. Open your mouth and swallow it without chewing."

Danlo did as he was told. Like a baby bird, he opened his mouth and waited. Suddenly he felt the raw bit of meat pressed into his mouth, back against his tongue. He swallowed once, convulsively, and he tasted fresh warm blood.

"Danlo, this is the skin of your childhood. It will impregnate you like a seed. From the child grows the man. Are you ready to be a man, now?"

Again Danlo swallowed against the hot salty slickness of his own blood.

"Danlo, wi Ieldra sena! Ti ur-alashareth. The ancestors are coming! It is time for you to go over, now."

His eyes were now calm and clear, and he looked up at the stars to see a million points of light streaming toward him.

"Danlo, you may turn your head."

Danlo blinked his eyes slowly. He turned and there was Soli standing over him. He was dressed as usual, in his winter furs; the terrible Beast was gone. "You have done well," he said.

He helped Danlo sit up and wrapped him in a fresh shagshay skin. There was blood everywhere, dark red soaking into the white furs. Danlo looked through the flickering red fires up at the circle of skulls. He must find the one animal who was his *doffel.* Soli would help him if his vision faltered, but it would be better if he came to his other-self unaided and alone.

"Danlo, can you *see*?"

"Yes."

He was six thousand feet above men and time. He turned his head in half a circle, and he could see many things. Below him were the dark forest and the starlit hills of his childhood, and farther out where the island's ragged shore came up against the ocean, he beheld the faint, silvery shimmer of sea ice falling off to infinity. There were nearer sights. Soli's face was drawn out ghastly and pale; he looked at once fey and ill, as if he were

23

ready to die. *Pain is the awareness of life,* Danlo thought. His body still burned with pain, but his spirit had begun the journey through pain into a deeper world. He was beginning to see himself as he really was. Every act of his passage had been designed to bring him to this moment. His childish picture of himself, his old ways of thinking—shattered, like ice crystals beneath a hammer stone. There was a sudden clarity, an intensity of color, shape, and meaning. Far above him, in the sky, the stars burned with a pale blue fire, and nearer, spread over his thighs and belly, was his deep red blood. Again, he looked up at the circle of skulls, at the bits of ivory gleaming in the blackness. Each skull was his skull; life was connected to life in ways he was just beginning to see. One skull, though, seemed to shimmer under the watchful eyes of the Old Ones. One skull called out to him. It was the skull of Ahira, the snowy owl. Ahira, the wisest and wildest of the animals. No other animal was so alive and free. And no other animal was so perilous to one's spirit. In truth, he dreaded discovering that Ahira was his *doffel,* his other-self, for only once in ten generations was one born whose other-self is Ahira. He stared on and on waiting for this splendid bird to stop calling him, but at last he was sure that Ahira was his *doffel.* Ahira must guide him and help him go over to the trackless, unknown world where his deepest self lived.

Soli saw Danlo gazing at Ahira's small, round skull. That the Devaki fathers had acquired a skull at all was something of a miracle, for Ahira was the rarest of all birds and hunters did not often catch sight of him.

"*This* bird?" Soli said. "Are you sure, Danlo?"

"Yes," Danlo said. "Ahira, the snowy owl."

"Full men know this bird as the white thallow. You should call him that, too."

Everyone knew, of course, that owls were thallows, just as they knew that God was a great thallow whose body made up the universe. But among the Alaloi elders, from tribe to tribe, there was a dispute as to whether God was a silver thallow, or the blue thallow, or the rare white thallow whom children referred to as the snowy owl.

"Ahira is my *doffel,*" Danlo said.

"Very well," Soli said. Then he magically produced a musty leather bag stuffed with various objects. He rummaged around in the bag and removed a single white feather. He gave it to Danlo, placing it between his folded hands. "This is the wing

24

feather of the white thallow," he said. "The white thallow is your *doffel.*"

Danlo looked down at the feather. Its whiteness was as pure as snow. Its edge was rough and fuzzy, the better to muffle the sound of Ahira's beating wings. Ahira was a magnificent hunter, and he could swoop down toward his prey in almost total silence. With a little bone clip that Soli gave him, Danlo fastened the feather to his long hair. Soli began to chant then, and a world whose snowfields were pure and vast opened before him. Danlo entered into the dreamtime, into the *altjiranga mitjina* of his people. The shock of pain and terror—and his newfound ability to overcome his attachment to terror—had hurled him into this world. He listened to Soli chant, listened as the Old Ones began to speak to him. New knowledge was revealed to him, secrets that only a man may know. Soli chanted the lines of the Song of Life. The Song was a new way of structuring reality, a system of symbol and meaning connecting all things of the world to the great circle of *halla.* There are 4,096 lines to this song; Soli chanted quickly, his deep voice rasping out the music. He told of how the lesser god, Kweitkel, had created the world from single pieces of rock and ice. He told of Kweitkel's wedding with Devaki, and of their children, Yelena, Reina, and Manwe. Danlo learned that on the third morning of the world, wise Ahira had befriended Manwe and taught him to love flying, hunting, and mating, and the other things of life. Manwe and Ahira—the Two Friends, two of the oldest of the Old Ones. Danlo listened to the Song of Life, and he joined them in the dreamtime. The dreamtime was now, the shall-be and always-was. The dreamtime occurred in the Now-moment, the true time in which the world was forever created anew.

"Ali wos Ayeye," Soli chanted. "God is a great, silver thallow whose wings touch at the far ends of the universe."

Danlo listened to the Song of Life's sixty-fourth line. Now, and over the next three days, he must learn every line exactly as Soli chanted it because someday he would repeat the Song to a son or near-son of his own. Pain was the most potent of mnemonics; pain had awakened him to record the rise and fall and each liquid vowel; pain, and the intensity of pain, had prepared his mind and spirit to remember perfectly.

"All animals remember . . ." Soli sang out, and his voice began to tremble and crack. "All animals remember the first morning of the world."

He stopped suddenly, rubbing the back of his neck. His face

25

had fallen as gray as old seal grease. He licked his lips and continued with difficulty. After a while, he came to the first of the Twelve Riddles, chanting: "How do you capture a beautiful bird without killing its spirit?"

Danlo waited for Soli to supply the answer in the second line of the couplet, but Soli could not speak. He groaned and clutched at his stomach and looked at Danlo.

"Sir, what is wrong?" Danlo asked. He didn't want to speak because he sensed that the uttering of words would remove him from the dreamtime. But Soli suddenly heaved over gasping for breath, and he had to find out what was wrong. Now that he knew the way, he could make the journey into the dreamtime whenever he must. "Sir, here, let me loosen your hood's drawstring—it is too tight."

It was obvious that Soli was gravely ill. Sweat beaded on his forehead, and his nose was bleeding. His eyes were the eyes of a whale caught unexpectedly in the freezing ice of the sea. Danlo stood up, and the rush of blood into his cut membrum was agony. He helped Soli lie down on the bloody platform where he had so recently surrendered up his childhood flesh. The Alaloi are not an ironic people, but he appreciated the deep irony of their reversed positions.

"Sir, are you all right?"

"No," Soli gasped, "never . . . again." He regained his wind, and spoke slowly. "Listen, Danlo, you must know. At a boy's passage, one of the men must be the Beast. The Beast . . . the mask."

With difficulty he bent over and stuck his hand into the leather bag. He removed a mask made of glued-together bones, fur, teeth, and feathers. He rattled the mask in front of Danlo.

"But it is sometimes hard to become the Beast," Soli said. "If the boy moves or cries out . . . then he must be slain. It is hard to become the Beast by wearing the mask alone. Help is needed. For some men, help. On the afternoon before the boy's passage, the liver of the jewfish must be eaten. The liver gives terrible vision, terrible power. But it is dangerous to eat it. Sometimes the power is too great. It consumes."

Danlo took Soli's hand; even though he himself was cold and half-naked, with only a shagshay skin draped loosely across his shoulders, Soli's hand felt colder still. "What can I do? Is there no cure? Should I make some blood tea to give you strength?"

"No, that would not help."

"Does it hurt? Oh, sir, what can I do?"

"I . . . believe," Soli said, "I believe that Haidar knew of a cure, but he has gone over, hasn't he? All the men—the women, too."

Danlo blinked away the pain in his eyes, and he found that he could see things very clearly. And on Soli's face, in his tired, anguished eyes, there was only death. Soli would go over soon, he knew, there could be no help for that. It was *shaida* for a man to die too soon, but Soli's death would not be *shaida* because it was clear that he was dying at the right time.

"Sir," he said, *"ti-alasharia,"* you, too, why, why?"

"Yes," Soli said. And then he stretched out his hand and pointed upward. "The stars, you must be told about the stars."

Danlo looked up through the bitterly cold air at the heavens. He pulled the shagshay fur tightly around himself, let out a long steamy breath, and said, "The stars are eyes of the Old Ones. Even a child knows that."

"No, the stars are . . . something other."

"Does the Song of Life tell of the stars?"

Soli coughed deeply a few times; it seemed that he might begin gasping again. "Yes, the Song of Life, but that is only one song, the song of our people. There are other songs. The stars shine with eyelight, yes, but that is just a metaphor. A symbol, like the symbols for numbers we used to draw in the snow. There is an otherness about the stars that I . . . I must tell you."

"Please, sir."

"This will be hard to explain."

"Please."

Soli sighed, then said, "Each star is like Sawel, the sun. A burning, a fusion of hydrogen into light. Three hundred billion fusion fires in this galaxy alone. And the galaxies . . . so many. Who could have dreamed the universe would make so many?"

Danlo pressed his knuckles against his forehead. He felt sick inside, dizzy and disoriented. Once, when he was eight years old, he and Haidar had been caught out on the sea in a *morateth*. The sky had closed in, white and low over the endless whiteness of the ice. After ten days, he hadn't been able to distinguish right from left, up from down. Now he felt lost again, as if a *morateth* of the spirit were crushing him under.

"I do not understand."

"The stars are like fires burning across space. Across the black, frozen sea. Men can cross from star to star in boats called lightships. Such men—and women—are called pilots. Your father was a pilot, Danlo."

"My father? My blood father? What was his name?" He took Soli's hand and whispered, "Who is my blessed father?"

But Soli didn't seem to hear him. He began to speak of things that Danlo couldn't comprehend. He told of the galaxy's many wonders, of the great black hole at the core, and of that brilliant, doomed region of the galaxy called the Vild. Human beings, he explained, had learned to make stars explode into supernovas; even as they spoke together, beneath the dying sky, ten thousand spheres of light were expanding outward to the ends of the universe. "So many stars," Soli said, "so much light."

Danlo, of course, couldn't comprehend that this wild starlight would eventually reach his world and kill all of the plants and animals on Icefall's surface. He knew only that Soli was dying, and seeing visions of impossible things.

"Sir, who is my father?" he repeated.

But now Soli had lapsed into a private, final vision, and his words made no sense at all. "The rings," Soli forced out. "The rings. Of light. The rings of eternity, and I . . . I, oh, it hurts, it hurts, it hurts!"

Quite possibly he was trying to tell Danlo that he was Danlo's grandfather, but he failed, and soon his lips fell blue and silent, and he would never utter any words again.

"Soli, Soli!"

Again, Soli began gasping for air, and very soon he stopped breathing altogether. He lay still with his eyes fixed on the stars. Danlo was surprised at how quickly he had died.

"Soli, *mi alasharia la shantih Devaki.*"

How many times, Danlo wondered, had he said that prayer? How many times must he say it again?

He closed Soli's eyes and kissed them. "*Shantih,* Soli, may your spirit find the way to the other side."

Then the enormity of all that had occurred during the past days overwhelmed him. He jumped up and threw off his fur, standing naked to the world. "No!" he cried out. "No!" But there was no one to listen to him. The fires had burnt low, dim orange glimmerings lost into the blackness of night. It was very cold. He watched the fires die, and he began to shiver violently. "No," he whispered, and the wind stole the breath from his lips and swept it away. His body hurt so urgently that he welcomed numbness, but next to the pain of his spirit, it was almost noth-

g. How would he live now, he wondered, what would he do? He had been cut, and part of him had died, and so he was no longer of the *onabara,* the once-born children. But until he completed his passage, he would remain unfinished, like a spearpoint without an edge; he would never be of the *diabara,* the twice-born men. And because he knew that only a twice-born man who had learned the whole Song of Life could be wholly alive, he almost despaired.

Later that night, above the cave, he buried Soli with the others. After he had hefted the last frozen boulder onto his grave, he prayed. "Soli, *pela ur-padda, mi alasharia, shantih.*" He pressed his eyes hard before shaking his head and crying out, "Oh, Ahira, what shall I do?"

He fell into the dreamtime then, and the wind through the trees answered him. There was a rush of air carrying the deep-throated hooing of the snowy owl. It was Ahira, his other-self. Perched high on a yu tree's silvery branch, across the snow-covered graveyard, Ahira was looking through the darkness for him.

"Ahira, Ahira."

The owl's snowy round head turned toward him. His eyes were orange and black, wild and infinitely wise.

"Danlo, Danlo." The owl turned his head again, and there was a shimmer of starlight off his eyes. And Danlo suddenly beheld a part of the circle of *halla*: the World-soul did not intend for him to join the Patwin tribe, nor any other tribe of the islands to the west. Who was he to bear the taint of *shaida* to his uncles and cousins? No, he would not burden his people with such unspeakable sorrows. No matter how badly he needed to hear the whole Song of Life, his future and his fate did not lie in that direction.

I must journey east, he thought. *I must go to the Unreal City alone.*

Somehow he must make the impossible journey to the city called Neverness. And someday, to the stars. If the stars really were fusion fires burning in the night, they were part of a vast, larger world that must know *halla,* too.

To Ahira, he solemnly bowed his head. *"Mi alasharetha,"* Danlo said, praying for that part of himself that had died. *"Shantih."*

Then he turned his back to the wind and wept for a long time.

DANLO THE WILD

The organism is a theory of its environment.
— *Walter Wiener, Holocaust Century Ecologist*

It took Danlo nine days to prepare for his journey. Five days h
spent in his snow hut, recovering from his cutting. He begrudge
every day of it because he knew that sledding across the easter
ice would be dangerous and long. According to Soli's stories, th
Unreal City lay at least forty days away—perhaps more. Since
was already the eighty-second day in deep winter, he couldn
hope to reach the City until the middle of midwinter spring
And midwinter spring was the worst season for travel. Wh
could say when a fierce *sarsara*, the Serpent's Breath, woul
blow in from the north, heralding many days of blizzard? If th
storms delayed his crossing too long, he might be stranded fa
out on the Stanbergersee when false winter's hot sun came ou
and melted the sea ice. And then he and his dogs would die. N
he thought, he must find the City long before then.

And so, when he deemed himself healed, he went out t
hunt shagshay. Skiing through the valleys below Kweitkel wa
now very painful, since every push and glide caused his mem
brum to chafe against the inside of his trousers. Pissing could b
an agony. The air stung the exposed red tip of his membru
whenever he paused to empty himself. Even so he hunted dil
gently and often because he needed a lot of meat. Ice fishin
through a hole in the stream's ice would have been an easi
source of food, but he found that the fatfish were not runnin
that year. He cut the meat and scant blubber into rations; h
sealed the rich blood into waterproof skins; he entered the cav

and raided the winter barrels of baldo nuts. Into his sled went carefully measured packets of food. Into his sled, he carefully stowed his oilstone, sleeping furs, bag of flints, and bear spear. And, of course, his long, barbed whalebone harpoon. The dogs could pull only so much weight. Somewhere to the east they would finish the last of the food, and he would use the harpoon to hunt seals.

On the morning of his departure he faced the first of many hard decisions: what to do with the dogs? He would need only seven dogs to pull the sled: Bodi, Luyu, Kono, Siegfried, Noe, Atal, and his best friend, Jiro. The others, the dogs of Wicent and Jaywe and the other families of the tribe, he would have to let loose. Or kill. After he had loaded his sled, he paused to look at the dogs staked out near their snow dens at the front of the cave. There were fifty-nine of them, and they were watching him with their pale blue eyes, wagging their tales and whining. In truth, he knew it was his duty to kill them, for how would they live without men to get their food and comfort them when they were sick or lonely? The dogs would flee barking into the forest, and they would pack and try to hunt. The wolves, however, were better hunters than the dogs; the silent wolves would track and circle them, and they would kill the dogs one by one. Or they would die of hunger, with folds of flesh hanging loosely over their bones. The dogs would surely die, but who was he to kill them? He thought it would be better for them to know a single additional day of life, even if that day was filled with pain and terror. He looked over the treetops into the sky. It was *sharda,* a deep, deep blue. The deep sky, the green and white hills, the smells of life—even a dog could love the world and experience something like joy. *Joy is the right hand of terror,* he told himself, and he knew he wouldn't steal the dogs away from life. He nodded his head decisively. He smiled and trudged up through the powdery snow to set them free.

The last thing he did before leaving was to press his forehead against the bare rocks near the mouth of the cave. He did this because Manwe, on the twelfth morning of the world, had performed just such a gesture before setting out on his journey to visit all the islands of God's new creation. *"Kweitkel, narulanda,"* he said, "farewell."

With a whistle to his sled dogs he began his journey as all Alaloi men do: slowly, cautiously schussing through the forest down to the frozen sea. There, beyond the beach of his blessed island, the ice fields began. The gleaming white ice spread out in a great circle, and far off, at the horizon, touched the sky. It was the oldest of teachings to live solely for the journey, taking each moment of ice and wind as it came. But because he was still a boy with wild dreams, he couldn't help thinking of the journey's end, of the Unreal City. That he would reach the City, he felt certain; although in truth, it was a journey only a very strong man should contemplate making alone. There was a zest and aliveness about him at odds with all that had happened. He couldn't help smiling into the sunrise, into the fusion fire glistering red above the world's rim. Because he was hot with excitement, he had his snow goggles off and his hood thrown back. The wind lashed his hair; it almost tore away Ahira's shining white feather. His face was brown against the white ruff of his hood. It was a young face, beardless and full of warmth and hope, but for all that, a strong, wild face cut with sun and wind and sorrow. With his long nose puffing steam and his high cheekbones catching the glint of the snowfields, there was a harshness there, softened only by his eyes. He had unique eyes, large and blue-black like the early evening sky. *Yujena oyu,* as the Alaloi say—eyes that see too deeply and too much.

Danlo handled the sled and guided the dogs across the ragged drift ice with skill and grace. Many times Haidar and he had made such outings, though they had never traveled very far from land. Six hundred miles of frozen sea lay before him, but he knew little of distances measured in this manner. For him and his panting dogs, each segment of ice crossed was a day, and each day rose and fell with the rhythm of eating, sledding, and sawing the blocks of snow that he shaped into a hut every night. And finally, after he had fed the dogs and eaten again himself, after he had slipped down into the silky warmth of his furs, sleep. He loved to sleep, even though it was hard to sleep alone. Often he would have bad dreams and cry out in his sleep; often he would awake sweating to see the oilstone burnt low and its light nearly extinguished. He always welcomed morning. It was always very cold, but always the air was clear, and the eastern sky was full of light, and the blessed mountain, Kweitkel, was every day vanishingly smaller behind him.

For twenty-nine days he traveled due east without mishap or incident. A civilized man making such a journey would have been bored by the monotony of ice and the seamless blue sky. But Danlo was not yet civilized; in his spirit, he was wholly Alaloi, wholly taken with the elements of the world. And to his eyes, there were many, many things to look at, not just sky and

32

ice. There was *soreesh,* the fresh powder snow that fell every four or five days. When the wind blew out of the west and packed the snow so that it was fast and good for sledding, it became *safel.* The Alaloi have a hundred words for snow. To have a word for an object, idea, or feeling is to distinguish that thing from all others, to enable one to perceive its unique qualities. For the Alaloi, as for all peoples, words literally create things, or rather they create the way our minds divide and categorize the indivisible wholeness of the world into things. Too often, words determine what we do and do not see.

Ice and sky, sky and ice—when he awoke on the thirtieth morning of his journey, the ice surrounding his hut was *ilka-so,* frozen in a lovely, wind-driven ripple pattern. Farther out were bands of *ilka-rada,* great blocks of aquamarine ice heaved up by the contractions of the freezing sea. The sky itself was not purely blue; in places, at various times of the day, high above, there was a yellowish glare from light reflected off the snowfields. And the snowfields were not always white; sometimes, colonial algaes and other organisms spread out through the top layers of snow and colored it with violets and blues. These growths were called iceblooms, *urashin,* and Danlo could see the faint purple of the iceblooms off in the distance where the world curved into the sky. *Kitikeesha* birds were a white cloud above the iceblooms. The *kitikeesha* were snow eaters; at this time of the year, they made their living by scooping snow into their yellow bills and eating the snowworms, which in turn lived on the algae. (The furry, tunneling sleekits, which could be found near any island or piece of land, also ate snow; sleekits would eat anything: algae, snowworms, or even snowworm droppings.) Danlo liked to stand with his hand shielding his eyes, looking at the iceblooms. Looking for Ahira. Sometimes, the snowy owls followed the *kitikeesha* flocks and preyed upon them. Ahira was always glad to sink his talons into a nice, plump *kitikeesha* chick, but on the thirtieth morning, Danlo looked for his *doffel* in vain. Ahira, he knew, was very wise and would not fly when a storm was near. "Ahira, Ahira," he called, but he received no reply. No direct reply, that is, no screeching or hooing or beating of wings. In silence, Ahira answered him. The Alaloi have five words for silence, and *nona,* the silence that portends danger, is as meaningful as a bellyful of words. In *nona,* Danlo turned his face to the wind and listened to things no civilized man could hear.

That day he did not travel. Instead, he cut snow blocks for a hut larger and sturdier than his usual nightly shelter. Into the hut he moved the food packets from the sled. He brought the dogs into the hut as well, bedding them down in the long tunnel that led to his living chamber. He made sure that there was snow to melt into drinking water and enough blubber to burn in the oilstones. And then he waited.

The storm began as a breath of wind out of the north. High wispy clouds called *otetha* whitened the sky. The wind blew for a long time, intensifying gradually into a hiss. It was the Serpent's Breath, the *sarsara* that every traveler fears. Danlo listened to the wind inside his hut, listened as it sought out the chinks between the snow blocks and whistled through to strike at his soft, warm flesh. It was a cold wind, dead cold, so named because it had killed many of his people. It drove glittering particles of spindrift into his hut. Soon, a layer of cold white powder covered his sleeping furs. The curled-up dogs were tougher than he, and didn't really mind sleeping beneath a shroud of snow. But Danlo was shivering cold, and so he worked very hard to find and patch each chink with handfuls of *malku*, slush ice melted from the heat of his hand. After the *malku* had frozen in place—and this took only a moment—he could breathe more easily and settle back to "wait with a vengeance," as the Alaloi say.

He waited ten days. It began snowing that evening. It was too cold to snow very much, but what little snow that the sky shed, the wind found and blew into drifts. "Snow is the frozen tears of Nashira, the sky," he told Jiro. He had called the dog closer to the oilstones and was playing tug-of-war with him. He pulled at one end of a braided leather rope while Jiro had the other end clamped between his teeth, growling and shaking his head back and forth. It was childish to pamper the dog with such play, but he excused himself from the usual traveling discipline with the thought that it was bad for a man—or a half man—to be alone. "Today, the sky is sad because the Devaki have all gone over. And tomorrow, too, I think, sad, and the next day as well. Jiro, Jiro, why is everything in the world so sad?"

The dog dropped the rope, whined, and poked his wet nose into his face. He licked the salt off of his cheeks. Danlo laughed and scratched behind Jiro's ears. Dogs, he thought, were almost never sad. They were happy just to gobble down a little meat every day, happy sniffing the air or competing with each other to see who could get his leg up the highest and spray the most piss against the snow hut's yellow wall. Dogs had no conception of *shaida,* and they were never troubled by it as people were.

While the storm built ever stronger and howled like a wolverine caught in a trap, he spent most of his time cocooned in his sleeping furs, thinking. In his mind, he searched for the source of *shaida*. Most of the Alaloi tribes believed that only a human being could be touched with *shaida*, or rather that only a human being could bring *shaida* into the world. And *shaida*, itself, could infect only the outer part of a man, his face, which is the Alaloi term for persona, character, cultural imprinting, emotions, and the thinking mind. The deep self, his *purusha*, was as pure and clear as glacier ice; it could be neither altered nor sullied nor harmed in any way. He thought about his tribe's most sacred teachings, and he asked himself a penetrating, heretical question: what if Haidar and the other dead fathers of his tribe had been wrong? Perhaps people were really like fragments of clear ice with cracks running through the center. Perhaps *shaida* touched the deepest parts of each man and child. And since people (and his word for "people" was simply "Devaki") were *of* the world, he would have to journey into the very heart of the world to find *shaida*'s true source. Shaida *is the cry of the world when it has lost its soul,* he thought. Only, how could the world ever lose its soul? What if the World-soul were not lost, but rather inherently flawed with *shaida*?

For most of a day and a night, like a thallow circling in search of prey, he skirted the track of this terrifying thought. If, as he had been taught, the world were continually being created, every moment being pushed screaming from the bloody womb of Time, that meant that *shaida* was being created, too. Every moment, then, impregnated with flaws that might eventually grow and fracture outward and shatter the world and all its creatures. If this was so, then there could be no evolution toward harmony, no balance of life and death, no help for pain. *All that is not halla is shaida,* he remembered. But if everything was *shaida*, then true *halla* could never be.

Even though Danlo was young, he sensed that such logical thinking was itself flawed in some basic way, for it led to despair of life, and try as he could, he couldn't help feeling the life inside where it surged, all hot and eager and good. Perhaps his assumptions were wrong; perhaps he did not understand the true nature of *shaida* and *halla*; perhaps logic was not as keen a tool as Soli had taught him it could be. If only Soli hadn't died so suddenly, he might have heard the whole Song of Life and learned a way of affirmation beyond logic.

When he grew frustrated with pure thought, he turned to

other pursuits. He spent most of three days carving a piece of ivory into a likeness of the snowy owl. He told animal stories to the dogs; he explained how Manwe, on the long tenth morning of the world, had changed into the shape of the wolf, into snow-worm and sleekit, and then into the great white bear and all the other animals. Manwe had done this magical thing in order to truly understand the animals he must one day hunt. And, too, because a man must know in his bones that his true spirit was as mutable as ivory or clay. Danlo loved enacting these stories. He was a wonderful mimic. He would get down on all fours and howl like a wolf, or suddenly rear up like a cornered bear, bellowing and swatting at the air. Sometimes he frightened the dogs this way, for it was no fun merely to *act* like a snow tiger or thallow or bear; he had to *become* these animals in every nuance and attitude of his body—and in his love of killing and blood. Once or twice he even frightened himself, and if he had had a mirror or pool of water to gaze into, it wouldn't have surprised him to see fangs glistening inside his jaws, or fur sprouting all white and thick across his wild face.

But perhaps his favorite diversion was the study of mathematics. Often he would amuse himself drawing circles in the hard-packed snow of his bed. The art of geometry he adored because it was full of startling harmonies and beauty that arose out of the simplest axioms. The wind shifted to the northwest and keened for days, and he lay half out of his sleeping furs, etching figures with his long fingernail. Jiro liked to watch him scurf off a patch of snow; he liked to stick his black nose into a mound of scraped-off powder, to sniff and bark and blow the cold stuff all over Danlo's chest. (Like all the Alaloi, Danlo slept nude. Unlike his near-brothers, however, he had always found the snow huts too cold for crawling around without clothes, so he kept to his sleeping furs whenever he could.) It was the dog's way of letting him know he was hungry. Danlo hated feeding the dogs, not only because it meant a separation from his warm bed, but because they were steadily running out of food. It pained him every time he opened another crackling, frozen packet of meat. He wished he had had better luck spearing fatfish for the dogs because fatfish were more sustaining than the lean shag-shay meat and seemed to last longer. Though, in truth, he loathed taking dogs inside the hut whenever their only food was fish. It was bad enough that the hut already stank of rotten meat, piss, and dung. Having to scoop out the seven piles of dung that every day collected in the tunnel was bad indeed, but at least the dung was meat-dog-dung and not the awful-smelling fish-dog-dung that the dogs themselves were reluctant to sniff. Nothing in the world was so foul as fish-dog-dung.

On the eighth morning of the storm, he fed them their final rations of food. His food—baldo nuts, a little silk belly meat, and blood tea—would last a little longer, perhaps another tenday, that is, if he didn't share it with the dogs. And he would have to share, or else the dogs would have no strength for sled pulling. Of course, he could sacrifice one of the dogs and butcher him up to feed the others, but the truth is, he had always liked his dogs more than an Alaloi should, and he dreaded the need for killing them. He whistled to coax the sun out of his bed and prayed, *"O Sawel, aparia-la!"* But there was only snow and wind, the ragged, hissing wind that devours even the sun.

One night, though, there was silence. Danlo awakened to *wonoon,* the white silence of a new world waiting to take its first breath. He sat up and listened awhile before deciding to get dressed. He slipped the light, soft underfur over his head, and then he put on his shagshay furs, his trousers and parka. He took care that his still sore membrum was properly tucked to the left, into the pouch his found-mother had sewn into his trousers. Next, he pulled his waterproof sealskin boots snug over his calves. Then he crawled through the tunnel where the dogs slept, dislodged the entrance snow block, and stepped outside.

The sky was brilliant with stars; he had never seen so many stars. The lights in the sky were stars, and far off, falling out into space where it curved black and deep, points of light swirled together as densely as an ice mist. The sight made him instantly sad, instantly cold and numinous with longing. Who could stare out into the vast light-distances and not feel a little holy? Who could stand alone in the starlight and not suffer the terrible nearness of infinity? *Each man and woman is a star,* he remembered. Many stars, such as Behira, Alaula, and Kalinda, he knew by name. To the north, he beheld the Bear, Fish, and Thallow constellations; to the west, the Lone White Wolf bared his glittering teeth. Two strange stars shined in the east, balls of white light as big as moons, whatever moons really were. (Soli had told him that the moons of the night were other worlds, icy mirrors reflecting the light of the sun, but how could this be?) Nonablinka and Shurablinka were strange indeed, supernovae that had exploded years ago in one of the galaxy's spiral arms. Danlo, of course, understood almost nothing of exploding stars. He called them simply *blinkans,* stars which, from time to time, would appear from nowhere, burn brightly for a while, and then disappear into the blackness from which they came. In the east, too, was the strangest light in the sky. It had no name that he knew, but he thought of it as the Golden Flower, with its rings of amber-gold shimmering just beyond the dark edge of the world. Five years ago, it had been born as a speck of golden light; for five years it had slowly grown outward, opening up into space like a fireflower. The various golden hues flowed and changed color as he watched; they rippled and seemed alive with pattern and purpose. And then he had an astonishing thought, astonishing because it happened to be true: Perhaps the Golden Flower really *was* alive. If men could journey past the stars, he thought, then surely other living things could as well, things that might be like flowers or birds or butterflies. Someday, if he became a pilot, he must ask these strange creatures their names and tell them his own; he must ask them if they ached when the stellar winds blew cold or longed to join the great oceans of life which must flow outward toward the end of the universe, that is, if the universe came to an end instead of going on and on forever.

O blessed God! he prayed, how much farther was the Unreal City? What if he missed it by sledding too far north or south? Haidar had taught him to steer by the stars, and according to the stories, the Unreal City lay due east of Kweitkel. He looked off into the east, out across the starlit seascape. The drift ice and snowfields gleamed faintly; dunes of new snow rose up in sweeping, swirling shapes, half in silver-white and half lost in shadow. It was very beautiful, the cold, sad, fleeting beauty of *shona-lara,* the beauty that hints at death. Now the midwinter storms would blow one after the other, and snow would smother the iceblooms, which would die. And the snowworms would starve, and the sleekits—those who weren't quick enough to flee to the islands—would starve, too. The birds would fly to Miurasalia and the other islands of the north, because very soon, after the storms were done, the harsh sun would come out, and there would be no more snow or ice or starvation because there would be nothing left to starve.

Later that day, at first light, he went out to hunt seals. Each hooded seal—or ringed or gray seal—keeps many holes open in the sea ice; the ice of the sea, east and west, is everywhere pocked by their holes. But the holes are sometimes scarce and irregularly spaced. Snow always covers them, making them hard to find. Danlo leashed his best seal dog, Siegfried, and together they zigzagged this way and that across the pearl-gray snow.

Siegfried, with his keen nose, should have been able to sniff out at least a few seal holes. But their luck was bad, and they found no holes that day. Nor the next day, nor the day after that. On the forty-third morning of his journey, Danlo decided that he must sled on, even though now he only had baldo nuts to eat and the dogs had nothing. It was a hard decision. He could stay and hope to find seals by searching the ice to the north. But if he wasted too many days and found no seals, the storms would come and kill him. "Ahira, Ahira," he said aloud to the sky, "where will I find food?" This time, however, his *doffel* didn't answer him, not even in silence. He knew that although the snowy owl has the most farseeing eyes of any animal, his sense of smell is poor. Ahira could not tell him what to do.

And so Danlo and his dogs began to starve in earnest. Even though he had eaten well all his life, he had heard many stories about starvation. And instinctively he knew what it is like to starve—all men and animals do. When there is no food, the body itself becomes food. Flesh falls inward. The body's various tissues are burnt like seal blubber inside a sac of loose, collapsing skin, burnt solely to keep the brain fresh and the heart beating a while longer. All animals will flee starvation, and so Danlo sledded due east into another storm, which didn't last as long as the first storm, but lasted long enough. Bodi was the first dog to die, probably from a stroke fighting with Siegfried over some bloody, frozen wrappings he had given them to gnaw on. Danlo cut up Bodi and roasted him over the oilstones. He was surprised at how good he tasted. There was little life in the lean, desiccated meat of one scrawny dog, but it was enough to keep him and the remaining dogs sledding east into other storms. The snows of midwinter spring turned heavier and wet; the thick, clumpy *maleesh* was hard to pull through because it froze and stuck to the runners of the sled. It froze to the fur inside the dogs' paws. Danlo tied leather socks around their cracked, bleeding paws, but the famished dogs ate them off and ate the scabs as well. Luyu, Noe, and Atal each died from bleeding paws, or rather, from the black rot that sets in when the flesh is too weak to fight infection. In truth, Danlo helped them over with a spear through the throat because they were in pain, whining and yelping terribly. Their meat did not taste as good as Bodi's, and there was less of it. Kono and Siegfried would not eat this tainted meat, probably because they no longer cared if they lived or died. Or perhaps they were ill in their stomachs and could no longer tolerate food. For days the two dogs lay in the snow hut staring listlessly until they were too weak even to stare. That was the way of starvation: after too much of the flesh had fallen off and gone over, the remaining half desired nothing so much as reunion and wholeness on the other side of day.

"Mi Kono eth mi Siegfried," Danlo said, praying for the dogs' spirits, *"alasharia-la huzigi anima."* Again, he brought out his seal knife and butchered the dead animals. This time he and Jiro ate many chunks of roasted dog, for they were very hungry, and it is the Alaloi way to gorge whenever fresh meat is at hand. After they had finished their feast, Danlo cut the remaining meat into rations and put it away.

"Jiro, Jiro," he said, calling his last dog over to him. With only the two of them left, the little snow hut seemed too big.

Jiro waddled closer, his belly bulging and distended. He rested his head on Danlo's leg and let him scratch his ears.

"My friend, we have had forty-six days of sledding and twenty-two days of storm. When will we find the Unreal City?"

The dog began licking his bleeding paws, licking and whining. Danlo coughed and bent over the oilstones to ladle out some hot dog grease melting in the pot. It was hard for him to move his arms because he was very tired, very weak. He rubbed his chest with the grease. He hated to touch his chest, hated the feel of his rib bones and wasted muscles, but everyone knew that hot grease was good for coughing fits. It was also good for frostbite, so he rubbed more grease over his face, over those burning patches where the dead, white skin had sloughed off. That was another thing about starvation: the body burnt too little food to keep the tissues from freezing.

"Perhaps the Unreal City was just a dream of Soli's; perhaps the Unreal City does not exist."

The next day, he helped Jiro pull the sled. Even though it was lighter, with only twelve food packets stowed among the ice saw, sleeping furs, hide scraper and oilstone, it was still too heavy. He puffed and sweated and strained for a few miles before deciding to throw away the hide scraper, the spare carving wood and ivory, and the fishing lines. He would have no time for fishing now, and if he reached the Unreal City, he could make new fishing gear and the other tools he might need to live. He pulled the lightened sled with all his strength, and Jiro pulled, too, pulled with his pink tongue lolling out and his chest hard against the leather harness, but they were not strong enough to move it very far or very fast. One boy-man and a starved dog cannot match the work of an entire sled team. The grueling labor all day in the cold was killing them. Jiro whined in frustration, and Danlo felt like crying. But he couldn't cry because the tears would freeze, and men (and women) weren't allowed to cry over hardships. No, crying was unseemly, unless of course one of the tribe had died and gone over—then a man could cry an ocean of tears; then a true man was required to cry.

Soon, he thought, he too would be dead. The coming of his death was as certain as the next storm; it bothered him only that there would be no one left to cry for him, to bury him, or to pray for his spirit. Though Jiro might whine and howl for a while before eating the meat from his emaciated bones. Although it is not the Alaloi way to allow animals to desecrate their corpses, after all that had happened, Danlo did not begrudge the dog a little taste of human meat.

"Unreal City," he repeated over and over as he stared off into the blinding eastern snowfields, "unreal, unreal."

But it was not the World-soul's intention that Jiro eat him. Day by day the sledding became harder, and then impossible. It was very late in the season. The sun, during the day, burned too hotly. The snow turned to *fareesh*, round, granular particles of snow melted and refrozen each day and night. In many places, the sea ice was topped with thick layers of *malku*. On the eighty-fifth day of their journey, after a brutal morning of pulling through this frozen slush, Jiro fell dead in his harness. Danlo untied him, lifted him into his lap, and gave him a last drink of water by letting some snowmelt spill out of his lips into the dog's open mouth. He cried then, allowing himself a time of tears because a dog's spirit is really very much the same as a man's.

"Jiro, Jiro," he said, "farewell."

He placed his hand over his eyes and blinked to clear them. Just then he chanced to look up from the snow into the east. It was hard to see, with the sun so brilliant and blinding off the ice. But through the tears and the hazy glare, in the distance, stood a mountain. Its outline was faint and wavered like water. Perhaps it wasn't a mountain after all, he worried; perhaps it was only the *mithral-landia*, a traveler's snow-delirious hallucination. He blinked and stared, and he blinked again. No, it was certainly a mountain, a jagged white tooth of ice biting the sky. He knew it must be the island of the shadow-men, for there was no other land in that direction. At last, perhaps some five or six days journey eastward lay the Unreal City.

He looked down at the dog lying still in the snow. He

stroked his sharp gray ears all the while breathing slowly; everything seemed to smell of sunlight and wet, rank dog fur.

"Why did you have to die so soon?" he asked. He knew he would have to eat the dog now, but he didn't want to eat him. Jiro was his friend; how could he eat a friend?

He pressed his fist against his belly, which was now nothing more than a shrunken bag of acid and pain. Just then the wind came up, and he thought he heard Ahira calling to him from the island, calling him to the terrible necessity of life. "Danlo, Danlo," he heard his other-self say, "if you go over now, you will never know *halla*."

And so, after due care and contemplation, he took out his knife and did what he had to. The dog was only bones and fur and a little bit of stringy muscle. He ate the dog, ate most of him that day, and the rest over the next several days. The liver he did not eat, nor the nose nor paws. Dog liver was poisonous, and as for the other parts, everyone knew that eating them was bad luck. Everything else, even the tongue, he devoured. (Many Alaloi, mostly those of the far western tribes, won't eat the tongue under any circumstances because they are afraid it will make them bark like a dog.) He made a pack out of his sleeping furs. From the sled he chose only those items vital for survival: the oilstone, snowsaw, his bag of carving flints, and bear spear. He strapped on his skis. Into the east he journeyed, abandoning his sled without another thought. In the Unreal City, on the island of the shadow-men, he could always gather whalebone and cut wood to make another sled.

In his later years he was to remember only poorly those next few days of skiing across the ice. Memory is the most mysterious of phenomena. For a boy to remember vividly, he must experience the world with the deepest engagement of his senses, and this Danlo could not do because he was weak of limb and blurry of eye and clouded and numb in his mind.

Every morning he slid one ski ahead of the other, crunching through the frozen slush in endless alternation; every night he built a hut and slept alone. He followed the shining mountain eastward until it grew from a tooth to a huge, snow-encrusted horn rising out of the sea. Waaskel, he remembered, was what the shadow-men called it. As he drew closer he could see that Waaskel was joined by two brother peaks whose names Soli had neglected to tell him—this half ring of mountains dwarfed the island. He couldn't make out much of the island itself because a bank of gray clouds lay over the forests and the mountains' lower slopes.

It was at the end of his journey's ninetieth day that the clouds began clearing and he first caught sight of the City. He had just finished building his nightly hut (it was a pity, he thought, to have to build a hut with the island so close, no more than half a day's skiing away) when he saw a light in the distance. The twilight was freezing fast, and the stars were coming out, and there was something wrong with the stars. At times, during flickering instants when the clouds billowed and shifted, there were stars *below* the dark outline of the mountains. He looked more closely. To his left stood the ghost-gray horn of Waaskel; to his right, across a silver, frozen tongue of water that appeared to be a sound or bay, there was something strange.

Then the wind came up and blew the last clouds away. There, on a narrow peninsula of land jutting out into the ocean, the Unreal City was revealed. In truth, it was not unreal at all. There were a million lights and a thousand towering needles of stone, and the lights were burning *inside* the stone needles, burning like yellow lights inside an oilstone, yet radiating outward so that each needle caught the light of every other and the whole City shimmered with light.

"O blessed God!" Danlo muttered to the wind. It was the most beautiful thing he had ever seen, this City of Light so startling and splendid against the nighttime sky. It was beautiful, yes, but it was not a *halla* beauty, for something in the grand array of stone buildings hinted of pride and discord and a terrible longing completely at odds with *halla*.

"Losas shona," he said. *Shona*—the beauty of light; the beauty that is pleasing to the eye.

He studied the City while the wind began to hiss. He marveled at the variety and size of the buildings, which he thought of as immense stone huts flung up into the naked air with a grace and art beyond all comprehension. There were marble towers as bright as milk-ice, black glass needles, and spires of intricately carved granite and basalt and other dark stones; and at the edge of the Sound where the sea swept up against the frozen city, he beheld the glittering curves of a great crystal dome a hundred times larger than the largest snow hut. Who could have built such impossibilities? he wondered. Who could cut the millions of stone blocks and fit them together?

For a long time he stood there awestruck, trying to count the lights of the City. He rubbed his eyes and peeled some dead skin off his nose as the wind began to build. The wind cut his face. It hissed in his ears and chilled his throat. Out of the north it howled, blowing dark sheets of spindrift and despair. With his ice-encrusted mitten, he covered his eyes, bowed his head, and listened with dread to the rising wind. It was a *sarsara,* perhaps the beginning of a tenday storm. Danlo had thought it was too late in the season for a *sarsara,* but there could be no mistaking the sharpness of this icy wind that he had learned to fear and hate. He should go into his hut, he reminded himself. He should light the oilstones; he should eat and pray and wait for the wind to die. But there was no food left to eat, not even a moldy baldo nut. If he waited, his hut would become an icy tomb.

And so, with the island of the shadow-men so near, he struck out into the storm. It was a desperate thing to do, and the need to keep moving through the darkness made him sick deep inside his throat. The wind was now a wall of stinging ice and blackness that closed off any light. He couldn't see his feet beneath him, couldn't get a feel for the uneven snow as he glided and stumbled onward. The wind cut his eyes and would have blinded him, so he squinted and ducked his head. Even though he was delirious with hunger, he had a plan. He tried to ski straight ahead by summoning up his sense of dead reckoning (so-called because if he didn't reckon correctly, he would be dead). He steered straight toward the bay that separated the mountain, Waaskel, from the City. If it was the World-soul's intention, he thought, he would find the island. He could build a hut beneath some yu trees, kill a few sleekits, rob their mounds of baldo nuts, and he might survive.

He skied all night. At first, he had worried about the great white bears that haunt the sea ice after the world has grown dark. But even old, toothless bears were never so desperate or hungry that they would stalk a human being through such a storm. After many long moments of pushing and gliding, gliding and pushing, he had neither thought for bears, nor for worry, nor for anything except his need to keep moving through the endless snow. The storm gradually built to a full blizzard, and it grew hard to breathe. Particles of ice broke against the soft tissues inside his nose and mouth. With every gasp stolen from the ferocious wind, he became weaker, more delirious. He heard Ahira screaming in the wind. Somewhere ahead, in the sea of blackness, Ahira was calling him to the land of his new home. "Ahira, Ahira!" He tried to answer back, but he couldn't feel his lips to move them. The blizzard was wild with snow and death; this wildness chilled him inside, and he felt a terrible urge to keep moving, even though all movement was agony. His arms and legs seemed infinitely heavy, his bones as dense and cold as stone. *Only bone remembers pain*—that was a saying of Haidar's. Very well, he thought, if he lived, his bones would have much to remember. His eye sockets hurt, and whenever he sucked in a frigid breath, his nose, teeth, and jaw ached. He tried each moment to find the best of his quickness and strength, to flee the terrible cold, but each moment the cold intensified and hardened all around him, and through him, until even his blood grew heavy and thick with cold. Numbness crept from his toes into his feet; he could barely feel his feet. Twice, his toes turned hard with frostbite, and he had to stop, to sit down in the snow, bare each foot in turn, and thrust his icy toes into his mouth. He had no way to thaw them properly. After he had resumed pushing through the snowdrifts, his toes froze again. Soon, he knew, his feet would freeze all the way up to his ankles, freeze as hard as ice. There was nothing he could do. Most likely, a few days after they were thawed, his feet would run to rot. And then he—or one of the City's shadow-men—would have to cut them off.

In this manner, always facing the wind that was killing him, or rather, always keeping the wind to his left, to the frozen left side of his face, by the wildest of chances, he came to land at the northern edge of Neverness. A beach frozen with snow—it was called the Darghinni Sands—rose up before him, though in truth he could see little of it. A long time ago morning had come, a gray morning of swirling snow too thick to let much light through. He couldn't see the City where it loomed just beyond the beachhead; he didn't know how near were the City's hospices and hotels. Up the snow-encrusted sands he stumbled, clumsy on his skis. Once, he clacked one ski hard against the other and almost tripped. He checked himself by ramming his bear spear into the snow, but the force of his near fall sent a shooting pain into his shoulder. (Sometime in the night, while he was thawing his toes for the third time, he had set his poles down and lost them. It was a shameful lack of mindfulness, a mistake a full man would never make.) His joints clicked and ground together. He made his way over the wind-packed ridges of *bureesha* running up and down the length of the beach. Little new snow had accumulated on the island; the wind, he knew, must have blown it away. The *bureesha* was really *bureldra*, thick old ribs of snow too hard for skiing. He would have taken his skis off, but he was afraid of losing them, too. He peered through the white spindrift swirling all around him. It was impossible to see more than fifty feet in any direction. Ahead of him, where the beach ended, there should be a green and white forest. If he was lucky, there would be yu trees with red berries ready for picking. And stands of snow pine and bonewood thickets, birds and sleekits and baldo nuts. From somewhere beyond the cloud of blinding snow, Ahira called to him. He thought he could hear his father, the father of his blood, calling, too. He stumbled on in a wild intensity of spirit far beyond pain or cold or the fear of death. At last he fell to the snow and cried out, "O Father, I am home!"

He lay there for a long time, resting. He didn't really have the strength to move any farther, but move he must or he would never move again.

"Danlo, Danlo."

Ahira was still calling him; he heard his low, mournful hooing carried along by the wind. He rose slowly and moved up the beach toward Ahira's voice. Closer he came, and the sound drew out, piercing him to the bone. His senses suddenly cleared. He realized it wasn't the voice of the snowy owl at all. It was something else, something that sounded like music. In truth, it was the most beautifully haunting music he had ever imagined hearing. He wanted the music to go on forever, on and on, but all at once, it died.

And then, at the head of the beach, through the spindrift, he beheld a fantastic sight: a group of six men stood in a half circle around a strange animal unfamiliar to Danlo. *Strange are the paths of the Unreal City,* he reminded himself. The animal was taller than any of the men, taller even than Three-Fingered Soli, who was the tallest man he had ever seen. He—Danlo could tell that the animal was male from the peculiar-looking sexual organs hanging down from his belly—he was rearing up on his hind legs like a bear. Why, he wondered, were the men standing so close? Didn't they realize the animal might strike out at any instant? And where were their spears? Danlo looked at the men's empty hands. No spears! he marveled, and even though they were dressed much as he was, in white fur parkas they wore no skis. How could these shadow-men hunt animals across snow using neither spears nor skis?

Danlo approached as quietly as he could; he could be very quiet when he had to be. None of the men looked his way, and that was strange. There was something about the men's face and in their postures that was not quite right. They were not alert, not sensitive to the sounds or vibrations of the world. The animal was the first to notice him. He was as slender as an otter; his fur was white and dense like that of a shagshay bull. He stood too easily on his legs. No animal, Danlo thought, should be so sure and graceful on two legs. The animal was holding in his paw some kind of stick, though Danlo couldn't guess what an animal would be doing with a stick, unless he had been building a nest when the men surprised him. The animal was staring at Danlo, watching him in a strange and knowing manner. He had beautiful eyes, soulful and round and golden like the sun. Not even Ahira had such large eyes; never had Danlo seen eyes like that on any animal.

He moved closer and drew back his spear. He couldn't believe his good luck. To find a large meat animal so soon after his landfall was very good luck indeed. He was very hungry; he prayed that he would have the strength to cast the spear straight and true.

"Danlo, Danlo."

It was strange the way the animal stood there watching him, strange that he hadn't fled or cried out. Something had cried out, though. He thought it must be Ahira reminding him that he was required to say a silent prayer for the animal's spirit before he killed him. But he didn't know the animal's name, so how could he pray for him? Perhaps the Song of Life told the names of the Unreal City's strange animals. For the thousandth time, he lamented not hearing the whole Song before Soli had died.

Just then, one of the men turned to see what the animal was staring at. "Oh!" the man shouted. "Oh, oh, oh!"

The other men turned, too, looking at him with his spear arm cocked, and their eyes were wide with astonishment.

Danlo was instantly in shock. He could finally see that Soli had told the truth. The shadow-men's faces were much more like his own lean, beardless face than the rugged Alaloi faces of his near-fathers. And here was the thought that shocked and shamed him: What if the animal was *imakla*? What if these beardless men knew the animal was *imakla* and may not be hunted under any circumstances? Wouldn't the men of the City know which of their strange animals was a magic animal and which was not?

"No!" one of the men shouted. "No, no, no!"

Danlo was ravenous, exhausted, and confused. Because of the wind and the spindrift stinging his eyes, he was having trouble seeing. He stood with his spear held back behind his head. His whole body trembled, and the spearpoint wavered up and down.

Many things happened all at once. Slowly, the animal opened his large, mobile lips and began making sounds. The man who had shouted "Oh!" shouted again and flung himself at the animal, or rather, tried to cover him with his body. Three of the others ran at Danlo, shouting and waving their arms and hands. They grabbed him and wrenched the spear from his hand. They held him tightly. They were not nearly so strong as Alaloi men, but they were still men, still strong enough to hold a starved, frightened boy.

One of the men holding him—remarkably, his skin was as black as charred wood—said something to the animal. Someone else was shouting, and Danlo couldn't make out what he said. It sounded like gobbledygook. And then, still more remarkably, the animal began to speak words. Danlo couldn't understand the words. In truth, he had never thought there might be languages other than his own, but he somehow knew that the animal was conversing in a strange language with the men, and they with him. There was a great yet subtle consciousness about this animal, a *purusha* shining with the clarity and brilliance of a diamond. Danlo looked at him more closely, at the golden eyes and especially at the paws that seemed more like hands than paws. Was he an animal with a man's soul or a man with a deformed body? Shaida *is the way of the man who kills other men.* O blessed God! he thought again, he had almost killed that which may not be killed.

"Lo ni yujensa!" Danlo said aloud. "I did not know!"

The animal walked over to him and touched his forehead. He spoke more words impossible to understand. He smelled of something familiar, a pungent odor almost like crushed pine needles.

"Danlo los mi nabra," Danlo said, formally giving the animal and the men his name. It was his duty to trade names and lineages at the first opportunity. He tapped his chest with his forefinger. "I am Danlo, son of Haidar."

The black man holding him nodded his head severely. He poked Danlo in the chest and nodded again. "Danlo," he said. "Is that what they call you? What language are you speaking? Where did you come from that you can't speak the language of the Civilized Worlds? Danlo the Wild. A wild boy from nowhere carrying a spear."

48

Danlo, of course, understood nothing of what the man said, other than the sound of his own name. He didn't know it was a crime to brandish weapons in the City. He couldn't guess that with his wind-chewed face and his wild eyes, he had frightened the civilized men of Neverness. In truth, it was really he who was frightened; the men held him so tightly he could hardly breathe.

But the animal did not seem frightened at all. He was scarcely perturbed, looking at him in a kindly way and smiling. His large mouth fell easily into a kind of permanent, sardonic smile. "Danlo," he repeated, and he touched Danlo's eyelids. His fingernails were black and shaped like claws, but otherwise his exceedingly long hands were almost human. "Danlo."

He had almost killed that which may not be killed.

"Oh, ho, Danlo, if that is your name, the men of the City call me Old Father." The animal-man placed his hand flat against his chest and repeated, "Old Father."

More words, Danlo thought. What good were words when the mind couldn't make sense of words? He shook his head back and forth, and tried to pull free. He wanted to leave this strange place where nothing made sense. The shadow-men had faces like his own, and the animal-man spoke strange, incomprehensible words, and he had almost killed that which may not be killed and therefore almost lost his soul.

Shaida is the cry of the world when it has lost its soul, he remembered.

The man-animal continued to speak to him, even though it was clear that Danlo couldn't understand the words. Old Father explained that he was a Fravashi, one of the alien races who live in Neverness. He did this solely to soothe Danlo, for that is the way of the Fravashi, with their melodious voices and golden eyes, to soothe and reflect that which is most holy in human beings. In truth, the Fravashi have other ways, other reasons for dwelling in human cities. (The Fravashi are the most human of all aliens, and they live easily in human houses, apartments, and hospices so long as these abodes are unheated. So human are they, in their bodies and in their minds, that many believe them to be one of the lost, carked races of man.) In truth, the men surrounding Old Father were not hunters at all, but students. When Danlo surprised them with his spear, Old Father had been teaching them the art of thinking. Ironically, that morning in the blinding wind, he had been showing them the way of *ostrenenie,* which is the art of making the familiar seem strange in order to reveal its essence, to reveal hidden relationships, and above all, truth. And Danlo, of course, understood none of this. Even if he had known the language of the Civilized Worlds, its cultural intricacies would have escaped him. He knew only that Old Father must be very kind and very wise. He knew it suddenly deep in his aching throat, knew it with a direct, intuitive knowledge that Old Father would call *buddhi*. As Danlo was to learn in the coming days, Old Father placed great value on *buddhi*.

"Lo los sibaru," Danlo said. Unintentionally, he groaned in pain. All the way up to his groin, his legs felt as cold as ice. "I'm so hungry—do you have any food?" He sighed and slumped against the arms of the men still holding him. Speech was useless, he thought. "Old Father"—whatever the incomprehensible syllables of that name really meant—couldn't understand the simplest of questions.

Danlo was beginning to fall into the exhausted stupor of starvation when Old Father brought his stick up to his furry mouth and opened his lips. The stick was really a kind of long bamboo flute called a shakuhachi. He blew into the shakuhachi's ivory mouthpiece. And then a beautiful, haunting music spread out over the beach. It was the same music Danlo had followed earlier, a piercing, numinous music at once infinitely sad yet full of infinite possibilities. The music overwhelmed him. And then everything—the music, the alien's strange new words, the pain of his frozen feet—became unbearable. He fainted. After a while, he began to rise through the cold, snowy layers of consciousness where all the world's sensa are as hazy and inchoate as an ice fog. He was too ravished with hunger to gain full lucidity, but one thing he would always remember: astonishingly, with infinite gentleness, Old Father reached out to open his clenched fist and then pressed the shakuhachi's long, cool shaft into his hand. He gave it to him as a gift.

Why? Danlo wondered. Why had he almost killed that which may not be killed?

For an eternity he wondered about all the things that he knew, wondered about *shaida* and the sheer strangeness of the world. Then he clutched the shakuhachi in his hand, closed his eyes, and the cold dark tide of unknowing swept him under.

THE GLAVERING

> *The Dark God feared that the Fravashi might one day see the universe as it really is, and so might come to challenge him. Therefore, he implanted in each one an organ called a glaver which would distort his perceptions and cause him to mistake illusion for reality. "How effective is the glaver?" asks the Unfulfilled Father. "Go look in a mirror," answers the First Least Father, "and you will see the effectiveness of the glaver."*
>
> —Fravashi parable

In a way, Danlo was very lucky to encounter Old Father and his students before any others. The Unreal City—its proper name is Neverness—can be a cold, harsh, inhospitable city to the many strangers who come to her seeking their fates. Neverness is roughly divided into four quarters, and the Zoo, where Danlo came to land, is the most inhospitable of them all, at least for human beings. The Darghinni District and the Fayoli Flats, the Elidi Mews—in which of the Zoo's alien sanctuaries or strange-smelling dens could he have hoped for succor? While it is not true that the Scutari, for instance, murder men for their meat, neither are those wormlike, cannibalistic aliens famous for goodwill or aid to the wretched. Had Danlo wandered up from the Darghinni Sands into the Scutari District, he would have found a maze of cluster cells. And in each cell, through translucent wax walls as high as a man, the many waiting eyes of a Scutari clutch staring at whatever passed by. Danlo would never have found his way out of the confusing mesh of streets; there

51

he certainly would have died, of neglect or cold, or if hunger further deranged his wits and he dared to break open a cluster cell with his spear, he would have suffocated in a cloud of carbon monoxide. And then the Scutari *would* have eaten him, even the toenails and bones. Those peculiar aliens believe that meat must never be wasted, and more, they avow that they have a holy duty to scavenge meat whenever fate offers them the chance.

Old Father brought Danlo to his house in the Fravashi District. Or rather, he bade his students to carry Danlo. The Fathers of the Fravashi—the Least Fathers, the Unfulfilled, and the Old Fathers—do not like to perform physical labor of any sort. They consider it beneath their dignity. And Old Father was in many ways a typical Fravashi. He liked to think, and he liked to teach, and mostly he liked to teach human beings how to think. It was his reason for living, at least during this last, deep winter phase of his life. In truth, teaching was his joy. Like every Old Father, he lived with his students in one of the many sprawling, circular houses at the heart of the Farsider's Quarter. (The Fravashi District is the only alien district not located in the Zoo. In every way it is unique. Only there do human beings and aliens live side by side. In fact, human beings have fairly taken over the district and greatly outnumber the Fravashi.) Old Father had a house just off the City Wild, which is the largest of all Neverness's natural parks or woods. It was a one-story, stone house: concentric, linking rooms built around a circular apartment that Old Father called his thinking chamber. In a city of densely arrayed spires and towers where space is valuable, such houses are—and were—an extravagance. But they are a necessary extravagance. The Fravashi cannot enter any dwelling where others might walk above their heads. Some say this is the Fravashi's single superstition; others point out that all Fravashi buildings are roofed with a clear dome, and that the sight of the sky, day or night, is vital to clear thinking.

Almost no one doubts that the Fravashi themselves have played a crucial part in the vitality of Neverness and, therefore, in the vitality of the Order. Three thousand years ago, the pilots of the Order of Mystic Mathematicians and Other Seekers of the Ineffable Flame crossed over into the bright Sagittarius Arm of the galaxy and founded Neverness. Two hundred years later, the first Fravashi came to the City of Light, and they taught their alien mental arts of hallning, shih, and ostrenenie. And the Order thrived. To learn, to journey, to illuminate, to begin—that is the motto of the Order. Only, would the pilots—and the cetics, ecologists, and others—ever have learned so well if the Fravashi hadn't come to teach them? So, no one doubts that the Fravashi have given the Order the finest of mind tools, but many believe that like a bloodfruit squeezed of its juice, their teachings are old and dry. The Age of the Fravashi is two millennia dead, the naysayers proclaim. The Fravashi District with all its squat stone houses is an anachronism, they say, and should be razed to the ground. Fortunately, for the Fravashi and for all the people of Neverness (and for the boy everyone was calling Danlo the Wild), the lords of the Order who run the City cherish anachronisms.

Danlo was given a room just off Old Father's thinking chamber. Like all of the students' rooms, it was austere, nearly barren of furniture or decoration. No rug or fur covered the polished wood floors; the walls were hexagonal granite blocks cut with exactitude and fit together without mortar. Beneath the skylight, at one end of the curved room, there was a low platform bed. Danlo lay in this bed for many days, recuperating from his journey. While he was still unconscious, Old Father invited a cryologist and a cutter to his house. These professionals thawed Danlo's feet and repaired his damaged tissue, layer by layer. When the body's water crystallizes into ice, it expands and ruptures the cells, especially the fine network of capillaries vital to the flow of the blood. Gangrene becomes inevitable. The cutter could find no gangrene, however, because Danlo's feet had not had time to rot. The cutter, a dour little man off one of the made-worlds of Camilla Luz, took Old Father aside and told him, "The boy has starved—I can't tell you why. You say he speaks a language no one can understand. Well, he's obviously new to the City. Perhaps his parents have died and he doesn't know that food is free here. Or perhaps he's an autist; he wouldn't be the first autist to wander around and starve to death. I've put some nutrients back into his blood. He'll wake up soon, and then he'll need to eat, juices at first, and then fruits and starches and anything else he wants. He should recover quickly, however . . ."

Old Father was standing at the foot of Danlo's bed, listening carefully, as the Fravashi always listen. He waited for the cutter to continue, and when he did not, he said, "Ahhh, is there a difficulty?"

"There's something you should see," the cutter said, pointing to Danlo, who was sleeping on his back. The cutter pulled back the covers and showed Old Father the cut membrum, the brightly colored scars running up and down the shaft. "This mutilation was done recently, within the last half year. Perhaps the boy is sick in his mind and has mutilated himself. Or perhaps . . . well, this is a city of cults and bizarre sects, isn't it? I've never seen this kind of thing before, but that doesn't mean anything. I've heard a story that the boy tried to kill you with an archaic weapon. What do you call it—with a *spear*? Is that true? No, don't tell me, I don't want to have to repeat what may be only rumors. But be careful, Honored Fravashi. I'm no cetic, but anyone could read the wildness on this boy's face. What is it they're calling him, Danlo the Wild?"

Later that afternoon Danlo awakened, and he spent most of the next tenday in his bed, eating and sleeping. The other students brought him food, rich meat soups sloshing in bowls, and fruits and breads heaped atop the mosaic plates Old Father had transported from his birth world. Although Danlo couldn't speak to the students, he kept them very busy. Possibly no other people can eat as much as hungry Alaloi. And Danlo, while not an Alaloi by heredity, had learned to "eat for a season," as they say. He devoured yu berries in cream, roasted snow apples, and bloodfruits. He had his first awkward experience with wheat noodles, and a hundred other strange foods of the Civilized Worlds. There was nothing he did not like, even the yellow-skinned, sickly sweet fruit called a banana. He liked to eat and wonder at all that had happened, to eat again and sink down with a full belly into the delicious warmth of his bed. In truth, of all the marvels of civilization, he thought his bed was the most marvelous. The mattress was soft yet resilient and had a good smell. Wonderfully soft underfurs covered him. They weren't the kind of furs he was used to; they were something finer, millions of individual strands of shagshay silk twisted into fibers and woven together into what one of Old Father's students called a sheet. Danlo couldn't imagine any woman making the effort to weave such a sheet. How long would it take? And the brown and white blankets were also woven, of shagshay wool. They were not quite as soft as the sheets, but still soft enough to lay his face against while he curled up and let the heat lull him to sleep.

As the days passed, however, his contentment gave way to a hundred doubts and worries. His mind cleared, and the sheer unnaturalness of his new life made him uneasy. The ways of the students who came and went were inexplicable. How did they cook the food they brought him? What kind of meat had he eaten? What were the animals' names—he had to know the names of the dead animals who gave him life so that he could pray for their spirits. Didn't these people understand the simplest of things? And as for that, how many people lived in this monstrous stone hut? He had counted six other students in addition to those he had met on the beach—four of them were women. He wondered if they were all near-brothers and near-sisters? How could they be? Some had faces as white as that of a fatfish; a few, like the black man on the beach, must have burned their skins in a fire. All of them seemed to be of an age with his found-parents, Haidar and Chandra, though with their strange, weak, civilized faces it was hard to determine their years. Where were the old ones of this strange tribe? Where were their children? Why hadn't he heard the babies crying in the deeper parts of the hut?

Three times Old Father came to visit him. Again Danlo was stunned by his inability to decide if this creature was man or animal. No man, he thought, could breathe through such a tiny black nose; no man had such long graceful limbs or such a delicacy of mouth and face. But then no animal had eyes like the sun, all golden and burning with awareness. And neither animal nor man could boast the profligacy of sexual organs that dangled between Old Father's legs. His stones were not visible (the long, white belly fur probably covered them, he thought), but his membrum was huge and unique. In truth, his membrum was not a singular organ; all Fravashi males possess hemipenes, two huge connected tubes of flesh, one atop the other. Old Father took no care to cover himself or stand so that one of his legs might obscure this remarkable sight. He was clothed only in his shiny fur and his disdain for the human emotion of shame. "Danlo," he said, and his voice was like music. "Danlo the Wild, let us play the shakuhachi."

Without any more words, Old Father indicated that Danlo should remove the bamboo flute from beneath his pillow, where he always kept it. He showed him the fingering, how to place his fingers on the holes up and down the shaft; he showed him how to blow into the ivory mouthpiece. Danlo took to the instrument immediately. Soon, he too was playing music, and Old Father left him alone to see what he might discover for himself. (The Fravashi do not like to teach *things*. Their whole art has evolved to find a way of teaching, rather than things to teach. In fact, the untranslatable Fravashi word for learning means something like

55

"The Way.") The pure notes and little melodies that Danlo coaxed from the shakuhachi were simple and unrefined, but for all that had a power over him hard to understand. The music was haunting and soothing at the same time. After a while, after many long evenings of watching the stars through the skylight and making music, he concluded that the shakuhachi's sound soothed him precisely *because* it was haunting. Like Ahira's lonely cry, it called to the wildness inside and made him poignantly glad to be alive. It alerted him to possibilities. Only in this heightened state could he put aside his day-to-day anticipations and restlessness and listen to the holy music of life singing in his blood. The Song of Life—he played the shakuhachi, and its pure tones recalled the *altjiranga mitjina,* the dreamtime. Often, he let the music carry him along into the dreamtime. Like a wounded bird seeking refuge on a mountain ledge, he dwelt in the dreamtime until he was whole again. It was a dangerous thing to do, dangerous because once he developed a taste for the infinite, how should he return to the everyday world of snow and frozen slush and pain? There must always be time for simply living. Somewhere, at the end of the shakuhachi's sound where it rushed like a stream of liquid light, there must be a balance and a harmony; there must always be *halla.* Yes, he thought, it was dangerous to play the shakuhachi, and it was very dangerous to seek *halla,* but, in truth, he loved this kind of danger.

Few come to such self-knowledge so young. Danlo applied this knowledge and began to savor not only music but the bewildering experiences of his new world. One of the women—she had golden hair and he thought her name was Fayeth—showed him how to eat with tools called chopsticks. His clumsiness and ineptitude with the wooden sticks did not embarrass him. In full sight of the curious students who often came to watch him, he would put his chopsticks aside, shovel handfuls of noodles into his mouth, and wipe his greasy hands on his face when he was done. He thought there must be something wrong with civilized people that they didn't want to touch their food, as if they required a separation from life or things that had once been alive. And they were ignorant of the most basic knowledge. Adjacent to his room was another room, which was really more of a closet than a room. Every morning he entered this closet, squatted, and dropped his dung through a hole in the floor, dropped it into a curious-looking device called a multrum. He pissed in the multrum, too, and here was the thing that frustrated him: The hole to the multrum was almost flush with the closet's north wall; it was hard to position himself with his back to the wall without falling in the hole. But he had to stand in this cramped, awkward position in order to piss to the south. Didn't the civilized makers of this dung closet know that a man must always piss to the south? Apparently not. And as for the dung itself, what happened to it once it fell through the hole? How was it returned to the world? Did dung beetles live in the multrum or other animals that would consume his excretions? He didn't know.

Despite a hundred like uncertainties, he quickly put on muscle and flesh; soon he was able to walk easily again, and this amazed him for he kept waiting for his toes to blacken with the fleshrot. He was given to understand he was not welcome to leave his room, so he began pacing, pacing and pivoting when he reached the far wall, and then, because he was in many ways still just a boy, running back and forth to burn off the prodigious amounts of food he ate. Someone gave him a pair of fur slippers, and he discovered that after getting up his speed with a little running, he could slide across the polished floor almost as if it were wet ice. In this way he amused himself—when he wasn't playing his shakuhachi—until his loneliness and curiosity became unbearable. It would be unseemly of him to ignore the wishes of his elders and leave his room, but surely, he thought, it was even more unseemly of Old Father and his family to leave a guest alone.

One night, after the others had gone to bed (or so he presumed), he set out to explore the house. He threw the blanket around his shoulders and put on his slippers; otherwise he was naked. His filthy furs, of course, had been taken away for burning, and he had been given no new ones. It didn't occur to him that the others might believe the shame of his nakedness would be enough to confine him to his room. Indeed, there was nothing else to confine him. The Fravashi do not believe living spaces should be enclosed by doors, so Danlo had no trouble entering the narrow hallway outside his room. From one end of the curving hallway came a reverberant, rhythmic sound, as of someone chanting; from the other, silence and the smell of crushed pine needles. He followed the silence, followed the piney aroma that grew stronger with every step he took. Hexagonal granite blocks lined the hallway; they were icy to the touch and picked up the faint whisper of his furry slippers against the floor. Cold flame globes, spaced every twenty feet, gave off a many-hued light. He marveled at the flowing blues and reds, and he might have killed himself sticking his hand inside one, but the globes were high above his head and he couldn't reach them, not even with the probing end of his shakuhachi. In silence, he followed the flame globes down the hallway as it spiraled inward to the center of the house.

Inevitably, he came to Old Father's thinking chamber. Old Father was sitting on a Fravashi carpet at the room's exact midpoint, but Danlo didn't notice him at first because he was too busy gawking at all the extraordinary things. He had never imagined seeing so many things in one place: against the circular wall were wooden chests, gosharps, ancient books, heaumes of various computers, sulki grids, and cabinets displaying the sculpted art of 50 different races; 106 different musical instruments, most of them alien, were set out on shelves. No spot of the floor was uncovered; carpets lined the room, in many places overlapping, one intricately woven pattern clashing against another. Everywhere, in huge clay pots, grew plants from other worlds. Danlo stared at this profusion of things so at odds with the rest of the house. (Or the little he had seen of it.) Many believe the Fravashi should live in the same austerity they demand of their students, but in fact, they do not. They are thingists of the most peculiar sort: they collect things not for status or out of compulsion, but rather to stimulate their thinking.

"Danlo," came a melodious voice from the room's depths, *"Ni luria la, ni luria manse vi Alaloi,* Danlo the Wild, son of Haidar."

Danlo's head jerked and he looked at Old Father in surprise. Old Father didn't seem surprised to see him. And even if he had been surprised, the Fravashi strive at all times to maintain an attitude of zanshin, a state of relaxed mental alertness in the face of danger or surprise.

"Shantih," Danlo said, automatically replying to the traditional greeting of his people. He shook his head, wondering how the man-animal had learned this greeting. *"Shantih,* sir. Peace beyond peace. But I thought you did not know the words of human language."

Old Father motioned for Danlo to sit across from him on the carpet. Danlo sat cross-legged and ran his fingers across the carpet's thick pile; the tessellation of white and black birds—or animals that looked like birds—fascinated him.

"Ah ho, while you were healing these last ten days, I learned your language."

Danlo himself hadn't been able to learn much of the language of the civilized people; he couldn't understand how anyone could comprehend all the strange words of another and put them together properly. "Is that possible?" he asked.

"It's not possible for a human being, at least not without an imprinting. But the Fathers of the Fravashi are very good at learning languages and manipulating sounds, ah ha? At the Academy, in the linguists' archives, there are records of many archaic and lost languages."

Danlo rubbed his stomach and blinked. Even though Old Father was speaking *the* human language, the only language that could aspire to true humanity in its expression of the Song of Life, he was using the words in strange, hard to understand ways. He suddenly felt nauseous, as if nothing in the world would ever make sense again. "What do you mean by an 'imprinting'? What is this Academy? And where are the others, the black man who held me on the beach? The woman with the golden hair? Where are my clothes? My spear? Does every hut in the Unreal City possess a bathing room? How is it that hot water can run through a tube and spill out into a bowl? Where does it come from? How is it heated? And what *is* a Fravashi? Are you a man or an animal? And where—"

Old Father whistled softly to interrupt him. The Fravashi are the most patient of creatures, but they like to conduct conversation in an orderly manner.

"Ahhh, you will have many questions," he said. "As I have also. Let us take the most important questions one at a time and not diverge too far with the lesser questions that will arise. Human beings, diverging modes of thought—oh no, it's not their strength. Now, to begin, I am a Fravashi of the Faithful Thoughtplayer Clan, off the world of Fravashing, as human beings call it. I am, in fact, an animal, as you are. Of course, it's almost universal for human languages to separate man from the rest of the animal kingdom."

Danlo nodded his head, though he didn't believe that Old Father really understood the only human language that mattered. Certainly man was of the animal kingdom; the essence of the Song of Life was man's connectedness to all the things of the world. But man was that which may not be hunted, and only man could anticipate the great journey to the other side of day. Men prayed for the spirits of the animals they killed; animals

59

didn't pray for men. "You are a Fravashi? From another world? Another star? Then it is true, the lights in the sky burn with life! Life lives among the stars, yes?"

"So, it's so. There is life on many *planets*," Old Father corrected. "How is it that you weren't certain of this?"

Danlo brushed his knuckles against the rug's soft wool. His face was hot with shame; suddenly he hated that he seemed to know so little and everyone else so much.

"Where do you come from, Danlo?"

In a soft voice, which broke often from the strain of remembering painful things, Danlo told of his journey across the ice. He did not tell of the slow evil and the death of his people because he was afraid for Old Father to know that the Devaki had been touched with *shaida*.

Old Father closed his eyes for a while as he listened. He opened them and looked up through the skylight. Danlo thought there was something strange about his consciousness. It seemed to soar like a flock of *kitikeesha,* to divide and regroup without warning and change directions as if pursued by a snowy owl.

"Ahhh, that is a remarkable story," Old Father said at last.

"I am sorry I rose my spear to you, sir. I might have killed you, and this would have been a very bad thing because you seem as mindful and aware as a man."

"Thank you," Old Father said. "Oh ho, I have the awareness of a man—this is a rare compliment indeed, thank you!"

"You are welcome," Danlo said very seriously. He hadn't yet developed an ear for Fravashi sarcasm, and in his naive way, he accepted Old Father's words without looking for hidden meaning. "You *seem* as aware as a man," he repeated, "and yet, on the beach, you made no move to defend yourself. Nor did you seem afraid."

"Would you really have killed me?"

"I was very hungry."

"Oh ho!" Old Father said, "there is an old, old rule: even though you would kill me, I may not kill you. The rule of ahimsa. It is better to die oneself than kill. So, it's so: never killing, never. Never killing or hurting another, not even in your thoughts."

"But, sir, the animals were made for hunting. When there is hunger, it is good to kill—even the animals know this."

"Is that true?"

Danlo nodded his head with certainty. "If there were no

killing, the world would be too full of animals, and soon there would be no animals anywhere because they would all starve."

Old Father closed both eyes, then quickly opened them. He looked across the room at one of his shelves of musical instruments. As he appeared to study a collection of wooden flutes that looked similar to Danlo's shakuhachi, he said, "Danlo the Wild—if you really lived among the Alaloi, you're well named."

"I was born into the Devaki tribe."

"I've heard of the Devaki. They're Alaloi, like the other tribes even farther to the west, isn't that true?"

"Why should I lie to you?"

Old Father looked at him and smiled. "It's known that when the ancestors of the Alaloi first came to this world, they carked themselves, their flesh. Ah ha, carked every part into the shape of very ancient, primitive human beings called Neanderthals."

"Neanderthals?"

"The Alaloi have hairy bodies like Neanderthals, muscles and bones as thick as yu trees, faces like granite mountains, ah ho! You will forgive me if I observe that you don't look very much like a Neanderthal."

Danlo wondered at the way Old Father used this word "carked." Danlo understood carking to mean the radical transformation of one's self or true essence, but how could anyone change the shape of his body? And weren't the Devaki *of* the world? Hadn't they emerged from the Great Womb of Time on the first morning of the world? That the Devaki looked much as Old Father said, however, he could not deny.

"My father and mother," Danlo said, "were of the Unreal City. They made the journey to Kweitkel where I was born. They died, and Haidar and Chandra adopted me."

Old Father smiled and nodded politely. For the Fravashi, smiling is as easy as breathing, though they have learned the awkward custom of head nodding only with difficulty. "How old are you, Danlo?"

He started to tell Old Father that he was thirteen years old, but then remembered that he must have passed his fourteenth birthday at the end of deep winter, somewhere out on the ice. "I have lived fourteen years."

"Do fourteen-year-old Devaki boys leave their parents?"

Again, Danlo's face burned with shame. He didn't want to explain how his parents had died. He pulled back the blanket covering his groin and pointed to his membrum. "I have been

61

cut, yes? You can see I am a man. A man may journey where he must."

"Ah ha, a man!" Old Father repeated. "What is it like to be a man at such a young age?"

"Only a man would know," Danlo answered playfully. And then, after a moment of reflection, he said, "It is hard—very hard."

He smiled at Old Father, and in silence and understanding his smile was returned. Old Father had the kindest smile he could have imagined. Sitting with him was a comfort almost as deep as sitting in front of the flickering oilstones on a cold night. And yet, there was something else about him that he couldn't quite define, something not so comforting at all. At times, Old Father's awareness of him seemed almost too intense, like the hellish false winter sun. At other times, his attention wandered, or rather, hardened to include Danlo as merely one of the room's many objects, and then his intellect seemed as cold as glacier ice.

"Oh ho, Danlo the Wild, I should tell you something." Old Father laced his long fingers together and rested his chin in his hands. "Most people will doubt your story. You might want to be careful of what you say."

"Why? Why should I be careful? You think I have lied to you, but no, I have not. The truth is the truth. Am I a *satinka* that I would lie to others just for the sport? No, I am not a liar, and now it is time for me to thank you for your hospitality and continue my journey."

He was attempting to stand when Old Father placed a hand on his shoulder and said, "Sit awhile longer. Ho, ho! I can hear the truth in what you say, but others do not have this ability. And, of course, even hearing the truth is not the same as knowing it."

"What do you mean?"

Old Father whistled slowly, then said, "This will be hard for you to understand. But so, it's so: it is possible for a human being to cast away true memories and implant new ones. False ones."

"But memory is memory—how can memory be cast away?"

"Ah, oh, there are ways, Danlo."

"And how can memories be implanted? Who would want to remember something unreal?"

"Oh ho, but there are many people who desire false memories, a new reality, you see. They seek the thrill of newness. To

62

cark the mind in the same way they cark the body. Some people sculpt their bodies to resemble aliens or according to whatever shape is fashionable; some like to *be* aliens, to know a wholly different experience. Most people will conclude that you, Danlo the Wild, must have merely imprinted the Alaloi reality."

"But why?"

"To be what you want to be: isn't this the essence of being human?"

"I do not know," Danlo said truthfully.

Old Father smiled, then bowed his head politely, in respect for the seriousness of effort with which Danlo received his words. Painfully, with infinite care and slowness, he arose to make some tea. "Ahhh!" he grunted. "Ohhh!" His hips clicked and popped with arthritis; he could have gone to any cutter in the Farsider's Quarter and ordered new hips, but he disdained bodily rejuvenations of any sort. He crossed the room, opened a wood cabinet, and from a shiny blue pot poured steaming tea into two mugs. Danlo saw no fire or glowing oilstones; he couldn't guess how the tea was heated. Old Father returned and handed him one of the mugs. "I thought you might enjoy some mint tea. You must find it cold in this room."

Indeed, Danlo was nearly shivering. The rest of the house—his room and the hallway at least—were warmed by hot air which mysteriously gusted out of vents on the floor, but Old Father's thinking chamber was almost as cold as a snow hut. Danlo sat with his knees pulled up to his chest and wrapped his blanket tightly around himself. He took a sip of tea. It was delicious, at once cool and hot, pungent and sweet. He sat there sipping his tea, thinking about everything Old Father had told him. From the hallway, reverberating along the winding spiral of stone, came the distant sound of voices. Old Father explained that the students were chanting in their rooms, repeating their nightly mantras, the word drugs which would soothe their minds. Danlo sipped his tea and listened to the music of the word drugs, and after a while, he began digging around in his nostril for some pieces of what the Alaloi call "nose ice." According to the only customs he knew, he savored his tea and ate the contents of his nose. The Alaloi do not like to waste food, and they will eat almost anything capable of being digested.

With a smile Old Father watched him and said, "There is something you should know about the men and women of the City, if you don't know it already, ah ho, ah ha!"

"Yes?"

"Every society—even alien societies—prescribe behaviors which are permitted and those which are not. Do you understand?"

Danlo knew well enough what was seemly for a man to do —or so he thought. Was it possible, he asked himself, that the Song of Life told of other behaviors that the Alaloi men practiced when they were not around the women and children? Behaviors that he was unaware of? Or could the men of the City have their *own* Song? Obviously, they did not know right from wrong, or how could they have given him food to eat and not told him the names of the eaten animals?

"I think I understand," he said, as he rolled some nose ice between his fingers and popped the little green ball into his mouth.

Old Father was still for a moment, then he whistled a peculiar low tiralee out of the side of his mouth. One eye was shut, the other open, a great, golden sun shining down on Danlo. The music he made was strange, evocative, and compelling. He continued to whistle out of the corner of his mouth, while his remarkably mobile lips shaped words on the other side.

"You must understand," he finally said, "among the Civilized Worlds, in general, there is a hierarchy of disgust of orifices. So, it's so." He whistled continuously, accompanying and punctuating his speech with an alien tune. "In sight of others, or even alone, it is less disgusting to put one's finger in the mouth than in the ear. Ha, ha, but it is *more* acceptable to probe the nose than either urethra or anus. Fingernails, cut hair, calluses, and such are never eaten."

"Civilized people do not eat nose ice, yes?" Danlo said. He suddenly realized that the city people must be as insane as a herd of mammoths who have gorged on fermented snow apples. Insane it was to imprint false memories, if that were really possible. And to eat animals and not say a prayer for their spirits— insane. Insane people would not know *halla*; they might not even know it existed. He nodded his head as if all the absurdities he had seen the past days made sense.

"And what of a woman's yoni?" he asked. He took a sip of tea. "What level does this orifice occupy in the disgust hierarchy?"

Old Father opened his eye and shut the other. He smiled and said, "Ahhh, that is more difficult to determine. Among some groups of humans, the yoni may never be touched with the fingers, not even in private by the woman herself. *Especially* not

64

in private. Other cultures practice the art of orgy and require touching by many, in public; they may even allow one orifice, such as the mouth, to open onto the yoni."

Danlo made a sour face. Ever since he was eleven years old, he had enjoyed love play with the girls and young women of his tribe. Even among the wanton Devaki, certain practices were uncommon. Some men liked to lick women's slits, and they were scorned and called "fish eaters," though no one would think to tell them what they should and should not eat. Of course, no one would lick a woman while she was bleeding or after she had given birth, nor would they touch her at these times. In truth, a man may not look a woman in the eyes when she was passing blood or tissue of any sort—could it be that the people of the Civilized Worlds were insane and did not know this?

"Danlo, are you all right?" Old Father asked. "You look ill."

Danlo was not ill, but he was not quite all right. He was suddenly afraid that Fayeth and the other women of Old Father's house would not know to turn their eyes away during their thirtyday bleedings. What if their eyes touched his and the blood of their menses colored his vision with the power of the women's mysteries? And then a more despairing thought: How could a sane man ever hope to live in an insane world?

"You seem to understand these . . . *people*," he said to Old Father. He rubbed his belly and then stared at Old Father's belly, or rather stared below it at his furry double membrum. And then he suddenly asked, "Do the Fravashi women have two yonis? Do the Fravashi also have a hierarchy of disgust of orifices?"

"No," Old Father said. He finished the last of his tea and set the mug down on the carpet. "The answer is 'no' to both of your questions."

"Then why do you have two membrums?"

"Ah ha, so impatient! You see, the top membrum"—and here he reached between his legs, hefted his membrum in his cupped fingers, and pulled the foreskin back to reveal the moist, red bulb—"is used only for sex. The lower membrum is for pissing."

"Oh."

Old Father continued whistling and said, "There is no disgust hierarchy. But, oh ho, the younger Fravashi, some of them, are disgusted that human males use the same tube for both pissing and sex, much as everyone is disgusted that the Scutari use the same *end* of the tube for both eating and excreting."

Danlo stared at Old Father's membrum. He wondered how he could claim to be a man—or rather an elder of his tribe—if his membrum was uncut. He listened to Old Father's beautiful, disturbing music for a long while before asking him about this.

"Ahhh, different peoples," Old Father said. He stopped whistling and opened both eyes fully. "Different brains, different self-definitions, different ways, aha, aha, oh ho! A man is a man is a man—a Fravashi: so, it's so, do you see it, Danlo, the way the mirror reflects everything you think you know, the way you think? The mirror: it binds you into the glavering."

"I do not understand, sir."

"Haven't you wondered yet why civilized ways are so different than those of your Alaloi?"

At that moment Danlo was wondering that very thing. He held his breath for a moment because he was afraid that this unfathomably strange alien animal could reach into his mind and pull out his thoughts one by one. Finally, he gathered his courage and looked straight at sun-eyed Old Father. "Can you enter my head like a man walks into a cave? Can you see my thoughts?"

"Ahhh, of course not. But I can see your thought shadows."

"Thought shadows?"

Old Father lifted his face toward the wall where the colors inside the cold flame globe flickered up through the spectrum, from red to orange, orange-yellow through violet. He held his teacup above the carpet, blocking some of the flame globe's light. "As real objects cast shadows by which their shapes may be determined, so with thoughts. So, it's so: thought shadows. Your thought shadows are as distinct as the shadow of this cup. You think that the people of the City—the Fravashi, too!—must be insane."

"You *are* looking at my thoughts!"

Old Father smiled at him, then, a smile of reassurance and pity, but also one of provocation and pain. "And you are glavering, ah ho! Glavering, and human beings are the masters of the glavering. Glavering: being deceitfully kind to yourself, needlessly flattering the prettiness of your worldview. Oh, Danlo, you assume your assumptions about the world are true solely according to your conditioning. What conditioning, what experience, what uncommon art of living? Behold the cuts in your membrum. The trees and rocks of the forest are alive? you say.

All life is sacred! Your mother spoke many words to you, did she not? How do you know what you know? How did your mother know, and her mother before her? The Alaloi have two hundred words for ice, so I've learned. What would you see if you only had one word? *What* can you see? The people of Neverness: they have many words for what you know as simply 'thought.' Wouldn't you like to learn these words? You see! When you look out over an ice field, you put on your goggles lest the light blind you. And so, when you look at the world, you put on the goggles of custom, habit, and tribal wisdoms lest the truth make you insane. Ahhh, truth—who wouldn't want to see the world just as it is? But instead, you see the world reflected in your own image; you see yourself reflected in the image of the world. Always. The mirror—it's always there. Glavering, glavering, glavering. This is what the glavering does: It fixes our minds in a particular place, in a traditional knowledge or thoughtway, in a limited conception of ourselves. And so it binds us to ourselves. And if we are self-bound, how can we ever see the truths beyond? How can we ever truly *see*?"

For a long time Danlo had been staring at Old Father. His eyes were dry and burning so he rubbed them. But he pressed too hard, temporarily deforming his corneas, and nothing in the room seemed to hold its color or shape. The purple alien plants ran with streaks of silver and blue light and wavered like a mirage, like the *mithral-landia* of a snow-blind traveler.

After Danlo's vision had cleared, he said, "The Song of Life tells about the seeing. On the second morning of the world, when Ahira opened his eyes and saw . . . the holy mountain named Kweitkel, and the ocean's deep waters, unchanging and eternal, the truth of the world."

"Ah ha," Old Father said, "I've given you the gift of my favorite flute, and now I shall give you another, a simple word: 'epistane.' This is the dependence or need to know a thing as absolutely true."

"But, sir, the truth is the truth, yes?"

"And still I must give you another word, from my lips, into your mind: 'epistnor.' "

"And what is 'epistnor'?"

"Epistnor is the impossibility of knowing absolute truth."

"If *that* is true," Danlo said with a smile, "how are we to know which actions are seemly, and which are not?"

"Ah, ah, a very well-made question!" Old Father sat there

humming a beguiling little melody, and for a while, his eyes were half-closed.

"And what is the answer to the question?" Danlo asked.

"Oh ho, I wish I knew. We Fravashi, sad to say, are much better at asking questions than answering them. However. However, might it be that one person's truth is another's insanity?"

Danlo thought about this as he listened to Old Father whistle and hum. Something about the music unsettled him and touched him inside, almost as if the sound waves were striking directly at his heart and causing it to beat more quickly. He rubbed his throat, swallowed, and said, "On the beach, when I raised my spear to slay you, the man with the black skin looked at me as if *I* were insane."

"Ah, that was impolite of him. But Luister—that's his name —Luister is a gentle man, the gentlest of men. He's devoted to ahimsa, and can't bear to see violence made."

"He calls me Danlo the Wild."

"Well, I think you're very wild, still."

"Because I hunt animals for food? How does Luister think he could survive outside this Unreal City without hunting?"

"And how do you think you will survive *in* the City without learning civilized ways?"

"But if I learn the ways of insane men . . . then won't I become insane, too?"

"Ah, ha, but the human beings of Neverness have their own truth, Danlo, as you will see. And hear."

Old Father's music intensified, then, and Danlo could feel its theme in his belly. It was a music of startling new harmonies, a music pregnant with longing and uncertainty. The Fravashi Fathers are masters of using music to manipulate the emotions of body and mind. Ten million years ago, the ur-Fravashi, in their frightened, scattered herds, had evolved sound as a defensive weapon against predators; over the millennia, these primitive sounds had become elaborated into a powerful music. The frontal lobes of any Fravashi Father's brain are wholly given over to the production and interpretation of sound, particularly the sounds of words and music. They use music as a tool to humiliate their rivals, or to soothe sick babies, or woo the unwed females of their clans. In truth, the Fravashi have come to view reality in musical terms, or rather, to "hear" the music reverberating in all things. Each mind, for them, has a certain rhythm and tonal quality, idea themes that build, embellish, and repeat themselves, like the melody of a sonata; in each mind, too, there are deeper harmonies and dissonances, and it is their joy to sing to the souls of any who would listen. Danlo, of course, understood nothing of evolution. Some part of him, however—the deep, listening part—knew that Old Father's music was making him sick inside. He clasped his hands over his navel, suddenly nauseous. The nausea wormed its way into his mind, and he began to worry that his brief, narrow understanding of the Unreal City was somehow distorted or false. With his fist, he kneaded his belly and said, "Ever since I awoke in my bed, I have wondered . . . many things. Most of all, I have wondered why no one prays for the spirits of the dead animals."

"No one prays, that is so."

"Because they do not know any better!"

"Praying for the animals is your truth, Danlo."

"Do you imply that the truth of the Prayer for the Dead is not wholly true?"

"Aha, the truth—you're almost ready for it," Old Father said as he began to sing. "Different peoples, different truths."

"But what truth could an insane people possibly possess . . . that they would not know the names of the animals or pray for them on their journey to the other side of day?"

Even though Danlo's voice trembled and he had to swallow back hot stomach juices to keep from retching, even though a part of his interior world was crumbling like *malku* beneath a heavy boot, he was prepared to learn something fantastic, some horrible new truth or way of thinking. What this new truth might be, however, was impossible to imagine.

"Danlo," Old Father said, "the meat you've eaten in my house is not the meat of animals."

"What!"

"In nutrient baths, cells are programmed to grow, to replicate, to—"

"What!"

"Ahhh, this is difficult to explain."

Both of Old Father's eyes were now open, twin pools of golden fire burning with fulfillment and glee. He delighted in causing Danlo psychic anguish. He was a Fravashi, and not for nothing are the Fravashi known as the "holy sadists." Truth from pain—this is a common Fravashi saying. Old Father loved nothing better than to inflict the angslan, the holy pain, the pain that comes from higher understanding.

"The meats of the Civilized Worlds are cultured almost like crystals, grown layer upon layer in a saltwater bath."

"I do not understand."

"Imagine: independent, floating tissues, huge pink sheets of meat growing, growing. Ah ho, the meats are really more like plants than animal. So it's so: no bone, no nerves, no connection to the brain of a living animal. Just meat. No animal has to die to provide this meat."

The idea of eating meat that wasn't really meat made Danlo sick. He rubbed his aching neck; he coughed and swallowed back his vomit. How could he pray for the spirits of the dead animals, he wondered, when no animals had died to provide his meat? Had this meat ever possessed true spirit, true life? He grabbed his stomach and moaned. Perhaps his thinking truly was bound by old ideas; perhaps, as Old Father might say, he was glavering and was too blinded by his familiar thoughtways to see things clearly. But if that were so, he asked himself, how could he know anything? Like a traveler lost in the enclosing whiteness of a *morateth,* he searched for some familiar custom, some memory or piece of knowledge by which he might steer his thinking. He remembered that the women of his tribe, after they were done panting and pushing out their newborn babies, boiled and ate the bloody afterbirths which their heaving wombs expelled. (In truth, he was not supposed to know this because it was the women's secret knowledge. But once, when he was nine years old, he had sneaked deep into the cave where the men were forbidden to go, and he had watched awestruck as his near-mother, Sanya, gave birth.) No prayers were said when this piece of human meat was eaten. No one could think that an afterbirth might have a spirit to be prayed for. He tried to think of the civilized meats as afterbirths, but he could not. *The meats of the City had never been part of a living animal!* How could he forswear hunting to eat such meat? It would dishonor the animals, he thought, if he refused to hunt them and partake of their life. Something must be wrong with people who grew meat even as the sun ripens berries or snow apples or other plants. Something was terribly wrong. Surely it must be *shaida* to eat meat that had never been alive.

"Oh, Danlo, you must remember, many men and women of the City live by the rule of ahimsa: never killing or hurting any animal, never, never. It is better to die oneself than to kill."

Suddenly, the mint tea, the thousand unknown objects of the thinking chamber, Old Father's piney body stench and his relentless music—all the strange sensa and ideas were too much for Danlo. His face fell white and grim while juices spurted in his mouth. He knelt on hands and knees, and he spewed a bellyful of sour brown meats over the carpet. "Oh!" he gasped. "Oh, no!"

He looked about for a piece of old leather or something so he could sop up his mess. According to everything he had been taught, he should have been ashamed to waste good food, but when he thought of what he had eaten, he gasped and heaved and vomited again.

"Aha, ho, I should thank you for decorating this carpet with the essence of your pain. And my mother would thank you, too—she wove it from the hair of her body."

Danlo looked down at the carpet's beautifully woven black and white birds, now swimming in his vomit. Birds shouldn't be made to swim, he thought, and he was desperate to undo what had happened.

"Don't concern yourself," Old Father said gently. "As I've explained, Fravashi have no disgust of the body's orifices, or of what occasionally emerges from them. We'll leave this to dry, as a reminder."

More insanity, Danlo thought, and he suddenly was dying to flee this insanity, to flee homeward to Kweitkel where his found-mother would make him bowls of hot blood tea and sing to him while she plucked the lice from his hair. He wanted this journey into insanity to be done; he wanted the world to be comfortable and make sense again. He knew that he should flee immediately from the room, yet something kept him kneeling on the carpet, staring into Old Father's beautiful face.

"Now it begins," he said to Danlo, and he smiled. He was the holiest of holy sadists, but in truth, he was also something else. "Who'll show a man just as he is? Oh, ho, the glavering, the glavering—try to behold yourself without glavering."

Danlo touched the white feather bound to his disheveled black and red hair. In his dark blue eyes there was curiosity and a terrible will in the face of falling madness. He felt himself becoming lost in uncertainty, into that silent *morateth* of the spirit that he had always looked away from with dread and despair. A sudden chill knowledge came into him: it was possible that all that he knew was false, or worse, arbitrary and quaint. Or worse still, unreal. All his knowledge of the animals and the world, unreal. In this insane City of Light, it very well might be impossible to distinguish the real from what was not. At least it might be impossible for a boy as ignorant and wild as he. He still believed, though, that there *must* be a way to see reality's truth, however much it might rage, white and wild and chaotic as the worst of blizzards. Somewhere, there must be a higher truth beyond the truths that his found-father had taught him, certainly beyond what Old Father and the civilized people of the City could know. Perhaps beyond even the Song of Life. Where he would find this truth, he could not say. He knew only that he must someday look upon the truth of the world, and all the worlds of the universe, and see it for what it really was. He would live for truth—this he promised himself. When truth was finally his, he could come at last to know *halla* and live at peace with all things.

This sudden, revealed direction of his life's journey was itself a part of the higher truth that he thought of as fate, and the unlooked-for connectedness between purpose and possibility delighted him. Inside, chaos was woven into the very coil of life, but inside, too, was a new delight in the possibilities of that life. All at once, he felt light and giddy, drunk with possibility. He was no longer afraid of madness; in relief (and in reaction to all the absurdities that had occurred that evening), he began to laugh. The corners of his eyes broke into tens of radiating, up-raised lines, and even though he gasped and covered his mouth, he couldn't stop laughing.

Old Father looked into his eyes, touched his forehead, and intoned, "Only a madman or a saint could laugh in the face of this kind of personal annihilation."

"But . . . sir," Danlo forced out between waves of laughter, "you said I must look at myself . . . without glavering, yes?"

"Ah ho, but I didn't think you would succeed so well. Why aren't you afraid of yourself, as other men are? As bound to yourself?"

"I do not know."

"Did you know that laughing at oneself is the key to escaping the glavering?"

Danlo smiled at Old Father and decided to reveal the story of his birth that Chandra had often repeated. Even though Three-Fingered Soli had told him that Chandra was not his true mother, he liked to believe this story because it seemed to explain so much about himself. Probably, he thought, Chandra had witnessed his birth and altered the story slightly.

"They say I was born laughing," Danlo told Old Father. "At my first breath of air, laughing at the cold and the light, instead of crying. I was not *I* then, I was just a baby, but the natural state, the laughing . . . if laughter is the sound of my first self, then when I laugh, I return there and everything is possible, yes?"

With one eye closed, Old Father nodded his head painfully. And then he asked, "Why did you come to Neverness?"

"I came to become a pilot," Danlo said simply. "To make a boat and sail the frozen sea where the stars shine. To find *halla*. Only at the center of the Great Circle will I be able to see . . . the truth of the world."

Next to Old Father, atop a low, black lacquer table, was a bowl of shraddha seeds, each of which was brownish-red and as large as a man's knuckle. Old Father reached out to lift the bowl onto his lap. He scooped up a handful of seeds and began eating them one by one.

"Ah," he said as he crunched a seed between his large jaws. "You want to make another journey. And such a dangerous one —may I tell you the parable of the Unfulfilled Father's journey? I think you'll enjoy this, oh ho! Are you comfortable? Would you like a pillow to sit on?"

"No, thank you," Danlo said.

"Well, then, ah . . . long, long ago, on the island of Fravashing's greatest ocean, it came time for the Unfulfilled Father to leave the place of his birth. All Unfulfilled Fathers, of course, must leave their birth clan and seek the acceptance of a different one, on another island—else the clans would become inbred and it would be impossible for the Fravashi Fathers to learn the wisdom of faraway places. In preparation for his journey, the Unfulfilled Father began to gather up all the shraddha seeds on the island. The First Least Father saw him doing this and took him aside. 'Why are you gathering so many seeds?' he asked. 'Don't you know that the Fravashi won't invent boats for another five million years? Don't you know that you will have to swim to the island of your new life? How can you swim with ten thousand pounds of seeds?' And the Unfulfilled Father replied, 'These shraddha seeds are the only food I know, and I'll need every one of them when I get to the new island.' At this, the First Least Father whistled at him and said, 'Don't you suppose you will find food on your new island?' And the Unfulfilled Father argued, 'But shraddha seeds grow only on *this* island, and I will starve without them.' Whereupon the First Least Father laughed and said, 'But what if this turned out to be a parable and your shraddha seeds were not seeds at all, but rather your basic beliefs?' The Unfulfilled Father told him, 'I don't understand,' and he swam out into the ocean with all his seeds. There he drowned, and sad to say, he never came within sight of his new island."

Having finished his story, Old Father rather smugly reached into the bowl and placed a shraddha seed into his mouth. And then another, and another after that. He ground up and ate the seeds slowly, though continually, almost without pause. The cracked seeds gave off a bitter, soapy smell that Danlo found repulsive. Old Father told him that it was dangerous for human beings to eat the seeds, which is why he did not offer him any. He told him other things as well. Subtly, choosing his words with care, he began to woo Danlo into the difficult way of the Fravashi philosophy. This was his purpose as a Fravashi Old Father, to seek new students and free them from the crushing, smothering weight of their belief systems. For a good part of the evening, he had listened to Danlo speak, listened for the rhythms, stress syllables, nuances, and key words that would betray his mind's basic prejudices. Each person, of course, as the Fravashi have long ago discovered, acquires a unique repertoire of habits, customs, conceits, and beliefs; these conceptual prisons delimit and hold the mind as surely as quick-freezing ice captures a butterfly. It was Old Father's talent and calling to find the particular word keys that might unlock his students' mental prisons. "That which is made with words, with words can be unmade"—this was an old Fravashi saying, almost as old as their complex and powerful language, which was very old indeed.

"Beliefs are the eyelids of the mind," Old Father told Danlo. "*How* we hold things in our minds is infinitely more important than *what* we hold there."

"How, then, should I hold the truths of the Song of Life?"

"That is for you to decide."

"You hint that Ayeye, Gauri, and Nunki, all the animals of the dreamtime—you hint that they are only *symbols* of consciousness, yes? The way consciousness inheres in all things?"

"So, it's so: it's possible to see the animals as archetypes or symbols."

"But Ahira *is* my other-self. Truly. When I close my eyes, I can hear him calling me."

Danlo said this with a smile on his lips. Even though he himself now doubted everything he had ever learned, in the wisdom of his ancestors he still saw many truths. Because he was not quite ready to face the universal chaos with a wholly naked mind (and because he was too strong-willed simply to replace

74

the Alaloi totem system with Old Father's alien philosophy), he decided to give up no part of this wisdom without cause and contemplation. In some way deeper than that of mere symbol, Ahira was still his other-self; Ahira still called to him when he listened, called him to journey to the stars where he might at last find *halla*.

"So many strange words and strange ideas," he said. "Everything that has happened tonight, so strange."

"Aha."

"But I must thank you for giving me these strangenesses."

"You're welcome."

"And I must thank you for taking me into your home and feeding me, although of course I cannot thank you for feeding me *shaida* meat."

"Oh ho! again you're welcome—the Alaloi are very polite."

Danlo brushed his thick hair away from his eyes and asked, "Do you know how I might become a pilot and sail from star to star?"

Old Father picked up his empty teacup and held it between his furry hands. "To become a pilot you would have to enter the Order. So, it's so: Neverness, this Unreal City of ours, exists solely to educate an elite of human beings, to initiate them into the Order."

"There is a . . . passage into this Order, yes?"

"A passage, just so. Boys and girls come from many, many worlds to be pilots. And cetics, programmers, holists, and scryers—you can't yet imagine the varieties of wisdom which exist. Oh ho, but it's difficult to enter the Order, Danlo. It might be easier to fill an empty cup with tea merely by wishing it so."

The Fravashi do not like to say a thing is impossible, so he smiled at Danlo and whistled sadly.

"I must continue my journey," Danlo said.

"There are many journeys one can make. All paths lead to the same place, so the Old Fathers say. If you'd like, you may stay here and study with the other students."

In the thinking chamber, there was no sound other than the crunching of Old Father's seeds. While they had talked, the chanting coming from the house's other rooms had faded out and died.

"Thank you," Danlo said, and he touched the white feather in his hair. *"Kareeska,* grace beyond grace, you've been so kind,

75

but I must continue my journey. Is there any way you can help me?"

Old Father whistled awhile before saying, "In another age, I might have invited you into the Order. Now, the Fravashi have no formal relationship—none!—with the lords and masters who decide who will become pilots and who will not. Still, I have friends in the Order. I have friends, and there is the smallest of chances."

"Yes?"

"Every year, at the end of false winter, there is a competition of sorts. Oh ho, a test! Fifty thousand farsiders come to Neverness in hope of entering the Order. Perhaps sixty of them are chosen for the novitiate. The smallest of chances, Danlo, such a small chance."

"But you will help me with this test?"

"I'll help you, only . . ." Old Father's eyes were now twin mirrors reflecting Danlo's courage in the face of blind fate, his verve and optimism, his rare gift for life. But the Fravashi are never content merely to reflect all that is holiest in another. There must always be a place inside for the angslan, the holy pain. "I'll help you, only you must always remember one thing."

Danlo rubbed his eyes slowly. "What thing?" he asked.

"It's not enough to look for the truth, however noble a journey that might be. Oh ho, the truth, it's never enough, never, never! If you become a pilot, if you journey to the center of the universe and look out on the stars and the secret truths, if by some miracle you should see the universe for what it is, that is not enough. You must be able to say 'yes' to what you see. To all truths. No matter the dread or anguish, to say 'yes.' What kind of man or woman could say 'yes' in the face of the truth? So, it's so: I teach you the asarya. He is the yeasayer who could look upon evil, disease, and suffering, all the worst incarnations of the Eternal No, and not fall insane. He is the great-souled one who can affirm the truth of the universe. Ah, but by what art, what brilliance, what purity of vision? Oh, Danlo, who has the *will* to become an asarya?"

Old Father began to sing, then, a poignant, rapturous song that made Danlo brood upon fear and fate. After saying good night, Danlo returned to his room, returned down the long stone hallway to the softness and warmth of his bed, but he could not sleep. He lay awake playing his shakuhachi, thinking of everything that had happened in Old Father's chamber. To be an asarya, to say "yes" to *shaida* and *halla* and the other truths of life—no other idea had ever excited him so much. Ahira, Ahira, he silently called, did *he,* Danlo the Wild, have the will to become an asarya? All night long he played his shakuhachi, and in the breathy strangeness of the music, he thought he could hear the answer, "yes."

SHIH

The metaphysicians of Tlon view time as being the most illusory of mental constructions. According to one school, the present is formless and undefined, while the future is just present hope, and the past is nothing more than present memory in the minds of men. One school teaches that the universe was created only moments ago (or that it is being eternally created), and all sentient creatures remember with perfect clarity a past that has never been. Still another school has as its fundamental doctrine that the whole of time has already occurred and that our lives are but vague memories in the mind of God.

—from the Second Encyclopaedia of Tlon,
Vol. MXXVI, page 33

In truth, Danlo really didn't know how difficult it is to enter the Order. On the planets of the Civilized Worlds, the Order maintains thousands of elite and lesser schools. The students of the lesser schools vie with one another to enter the elite schools; in the elite schools, there is a vicious struggle to be among the few chosen for the novitiate and the great Academy on Neverness. And so the chosen come to the City of Light, where there is always a sense of being at the center of things, an imminence of cosmic events and astonishing revelations. In truth, Neverness is the spiritual center of the most brilliant civilization man has ever known. Who would not desire a lifetime of seeking knowledge and truth in sight of her silvery spires? Who would not relish the excitement, the camaraderie, and, above all, the sheer power of being a pilot or high professional of the Order? So esteemed and coveted is this life of the mind (and since the masters of the various disciplines can be brought back to their youthful bodies many times, it can be a very long life indeed) that many ordinary people come to Neverness hoping to bribe or bully their way into the Order. There is of course no hope for these venal souls, but for others, for the thousands of unfortunate girls and boys who grow up on planets too small or obscure to support an elite school, there is the slightest of hopes. As Old Father informed Danlo, each year the masters of the Order hold a competition. And it is not easy to enter the competition, much less to win a place at Borja, which is the first of the Academy's schools. Petitions must be made. Each boy or girl (or in rare cases, each of the double-sexed) must find a sponsor willing to petition the Master of Novices at Borja. The sponsors must certify their student's brilliance, character, and most importantly, their desire to enter the novitiate. Each year, more than fifty thousand petitions are received, but only one of seven are accepted. At the end of false winter, when the sun shines hotly and melts the sea ice, perhaps seven thousand of the luckiest youths are permitted to enter this most intense of competitions.

"Oh ho, I *have* sponsored you," Old Father told Danlo a few days later. "I've made a petition in your behalf, and we will see what we will see."

While Danlo awaited the doubtful results of Old Father's petition—doubtful because Bardo the Just, Master of Novices, was said to resent the Fravashi and any others who taught outside of the Order's dominion—he busied himself learning the thousands of skills necessary to negotiate the strange streets and even stranger ways of the city called Neverness. During the evenings, Fayeth began the painful task of teaching him the Language of the Civilized Worlds. And every morning, when the air was clean and brisk, the black man who had first dubbed him "Danlo the Wild" taught him to ice skate. Luister Ottah, who was as thin and dark (and quick) as a raven, took Danlo out on the icy streets. He showed him how to stroke with his skates and hold an even edge; he showed him how to execute a hokkee stop by jumping in a tight little quarter circle and digging his steel blades into the ice. Danlo took to this exhilarating sport immediately. (Although Danlo thought it only natural that the City streets should be made of ice, the glissades and slidderies, as they are called, are the wonder—and consternation—of all who visit Neverness.) He spent long afternoons racing up and down the streets of the Fravashi District, savoring the sensations of his new life. The hot yellow sun, the cool wind, the cascade of scurfed-off ice whenever he ground to a sudden stop—he loved the touch of the world. He loved the sting of the *soreesh* snow that fell every third or fourth day; he loved the eave swallows who roosted atop the round houses; he loved their warbling, their shiny orange bills, even the chalky smell of their spattered white droppings. These things were real, and he grasped for the reality of the world as a baby grasps his mother's long, flowing hair.

Other things seemed less real. The ecology of the City made no sense to him at all. Who made his furs and that remarkable device called a zipper by which he closed and fastened his parka? Where did his food come from? Old Father had said that the grains and nuts he ate for his meals grew in factories to the south of Neverness. Every morning sleds laden with food rocketed up and down the streets. Danlo had seen these sleds. They were not, of course, real sleds pulled by dogs. They were brightly colored clary shells mounted on steel runners. Rhythmic jets of flame and burning air pushed the sleds across the ice. The sight of these sleek, fiery monsters terrified him, at least at first. (And he was quite confused by the harijan men who operated the sleds laden with cast-off clothing, with broken vases and sulki grids and ruined furniture, and with pieces of half-eaten food. He couldn't imagine why anyone would wish to accomplish such labor. Old Father explained this puzzle with typical Fravashi humor. He said that human beings had invented civilization in order to develop a class of people low enough to handle other people's garbage.) After a while, Danlo's terror softened to wonder, and wonder became profound doubt. What if the sleds turned against their human masters and refused to bear their loads? Or what if a storm, a vicious *sarsara,* destroyed the factories, whatever factories really were? How would the city people eat? There could not be enough animals in the world to feed so many people—would they eat each other? Was it possible they didn't know it was *shaida* for human beings to hunt one another?

Because Danlo would not eat the factories' cultured meats but still had a taste for shagshay or silk belly or fish, sometimes he would cross to the district's edge and steal into the woods of the City Wild. And he hunted. There, among the flowing streams and yu trees, he found a small herd of shagshay. With their fuzzy false winter antlers and their dark, trusting eyes, they were not quite civilized, but neither were they completely wild. It was too easy to kill them. He stripped the bark from a limb of black shatterwood, carved it, and mounted the long flint spearpoint that he had secreted inside his furs. (His old spear shaft he had to leave at Old Father's house because it was illegal to carry weapons through the City.) On two different days he killed two fawns and ten sleekits before deciding that there weren't enough animals in the City Wild for him to hunt. He froze part of the meat and ate the shagshay's tenderloin raw. He did not want to build a fire. Too many paths wound through the woods; too many people from the surrounding districts took their exercise skating there. It was not illegal to hunt animals within the City, but Danlo didn't know this. There was no law against hunting or cutting trees only because no one had ever thought that such a law would be necessary. He sensed, however, that the insane people would be disgusted by his killing animals for food, much as he dreaded the thought of eating *shaida* meat that wasn't real. In the end, after many days of surreptitious feasting in the yu trees, he decided that he would eat neither cultured meats nor animals. He would follow Old Father's example. Grains, nuts, pulses, and fruit—henceforth these kinds of plant life would be his only food.

Perhaps the most unreal thing about his new life were the people of the City, themselves. With their many-colored skins and differently shaped noses, lips, and brows, they looked much like demons out of a nightmare, and he often wondered if they had spirits as real people do. He passed them every day on the streets, and he wondered at their peculiar stiffness and weakness of limb. They seemed so hurried and aloof, and abstract, as if their thoughts were as insubstantial as smoke. Could it be that they weren't really *there* at all, not really living in the moment? Their faces were so ugly with wants and fears and urgency, so very ugly and hard to read. What must they think of him, with his white feather and his wind-whipped hair? In truth, no one bothered to notice him at all. It was as if they couldn't see him, couldn't perceive his curiosity, his loneliness, and his uncivilized spirit. Usually, he was dressed much as an Alaloi (in new, white furs that Old Father had given him), but so were many other people. And many were dressed much more colorfully. Autists, neurosingers, cetics, harijan, and whores—people of many different sects and professions every day passed through the district. And the clothes they wore! Red robes, emerald sweaters, and furs of every color. Journeymen holists skated by in cobalt kamelaikas. He saw jeweled, satin jackets, cottons and woolens, and kimonos woven of a material called silk. Much of this clothing was beautiful, in a gaudy, overwhelming way. It was hard to continually take in such beauty. After a while, he tired of looking at fabricated things; he felt sick and too full, as if he had eaten eight bowls of overripe yu berries. He invented a word for the different beauties of the City: *shona-manse,* the beauty that man makes with his hands. It was not a deep beauty. Nor was it a various beauty, despite the many hues and textures of man-made things. In a single chunk of granite, with its millions of pink and black flecks of quartz, mica, and silicates, there was more complexity and variety than in the loveliest kimono. It was true that most of the buildings—the glory of Neverness!—were faced with granite, basalt, and other natural rocks. When Danlo looked eastward toward the Old City, the obsidian spires glittered silver-black. And, yes, it was beautiful, but it was a dazzling, too-perfect beauty. No single spire possessed a mountain's undulations or its intricate and subtle pattern of trees, rock, snow, and ice. And the City itself was ill-balanced and unalive compared to the beauty of the world. Where, in such an unreal place, could he hope to find *halla?* A few times, at night, he sneaked out of Old Father's house to gaze at the stars. But everywhere he looked, the city spires were outlined black against the sky. He could see only the supernovas, Nonablinka and Shurablinka, and the enigmatic Golden Flower; the hideous glowing haze of a million city lights devoured the other stars. *Oh, blessed God,* he thought, *why must the people of the City place so many things between themselves and the world?*

Once, he asked Old Father about this, and Old Father stroked his furry white face in imitation of a man thinking, and he said, "Oh ho, soon enough you will learn about the Fifth Mentality and the Age of Simulation, but for now it's sufficient to appreciate one thing: every race that has evolved language is cursed—and blessed!—with this problem of filtering reality. You say that the people of Neverness are cut off from life, but you haven't journeyed to Tria, where the tubists and merchants spend almost their entire lives inside plastic boxes breathing conditioned air and facing sense boxes. And what of the made worlds orbiting Cipriana Luz? Aha, and what of the Alaloi? Do they not place animal furs between their skins and the coldness of ice? Oh ho! I suppose you can tell me that your Alaloi don't have a language?"

Danlo, as a guest of an Honored Fravashi, was beginning to

appreciate how words can shape reality. He said, "The Alaloi have a language, yes. On the second morning of the world, the god Kweitkel kissed the frozen lips of Yelena and Manwe and the other children of Devaki. He kissed their lips to give them the gift of Song. The true Song is perfectly created so the sons and daughters of the world can know reality. Perfect words as pure and clean as *soreesh* snow. Not like these confusing words of the civilized language that Fayeth has been teaching me."

"Oh ho!" Old Father said. "You're glavering again, and you must be as wary of the glavering as a shagshay ewe is of a wolf. In time you'll appreciate the beauty and subtlety of this language. Oh, ah, there are many concepts and ways of seeing. So many realities beyond the immediacy of *soreesh* or the *sarsara* that blows and freezes the flesh. Beyond even what you call the *altjiranga mitjina*."

"You know about the dreamtime of my people?"

"Ah, I *do* know about the dreamtime—I'm a Fravashi, am I not? The dreamtime occupies a certain space similar to the space of samadhi. There are many, many spaces, of course. Do you want to learn the words?"

"But I'm already too full of words. Last night, Fayeth taught me three new words for ways of seeing the truth."

"And what were these words?"

Danlo closed his eyes, remembering. "There is hanura and nornura. And there is inura, too."

"And what is inura?"

"Fayeth defines it as the superposition of two or more conflicting theories, ideas, or sets of knowledge in order to see the intersection, which is called the comparative truth."

"Oh ho! even seemingly opposite truths may have something in common. So, inura: you should keep this word close to your tongue, Danlo."

Danlo ran his fingers through his hair and said, "Different words for truth, but the truth is the truth, isn't it? Why slice truth into thin sections like a women slices up a piece of shagshay liver? And space is . . . just space; now you say there are different spaces?"

"So, it's so: thoughtspace and dreamspace, realspace, and the many spaces of the computers; there is memory space and the ontic realm of pure mathematics, and of course, the strangest space of all, the space that the pilots call the manifold. So many spaces, oh, so many realities."

Danlo could not deny that the people of the City lived in a

different reality from his. The spaces that their minds dwelt in—so different, so strange! He wondered if he could ever learn the language of such a strange people. In truth, he balked at learning their strange nouns and verbs because he was worried that the words of an insane people would infect him with that very insanity.

"Ah, oh, it's just so," Old Father said. "It's too bad that you can't learn the Fravashi language—then you would know what is sane and what is not."

If it was true that Danlo, like other human beings, could not master the impossible Fravashi language, at least he could learn their system toward a sane and liberated way of being. After all, the Fravashi had taught this system across the Civilized Worlds for three thousand years. Some consider Fravism, as it is sometimes called, to be an old philosophy or even a religion, but in fact it was designed to be both antiphilosophy and antireligion. Unlike Zanshin, Buddhism, or the Way of the Star, pure Fravism does not in itself try to lead its practitioners toward enlightenment, awakening, or rapture with God. What the first Old Fathers sought—and some still seek—is just freedom. Specifically, it is their purpose to free men and women from the various cultures, languages, worldviews, cults, and religions that have enslaved human beings for untold years. The Fravashi system is a way of learning how one's individual beliefs and worldviews are imprinted during childhood. Or rather, it is an orchestration of techniques designed to help one *unlearn* the many flawed and unwholesome ways of seeing the world that human beings have evolved. Many religions, of course, out of their injunction to find new adherents, deprogram the minds of those whom they would convert. They do this through the use of isolation, paradox, psychic shock, even drugs and sex—and then they reprogram these very minds, replacing old doctrines and beliefs with ones that are new. The Fravashi Old Fathers, however, have no wish to instill in their students just a new set of beliefs. What they attempt to catalyze is a total transformation in perception, in the way the eye, ear, and brain reach out to organize the chaos and reality of the world. In truth, they seek the evolution of new senses.

"So, it's so," Old Father said, "after a million years, human beings are still so human: listening, they do not hear; they have eyes but they don't really see. Oh ho, and worse, worst of all, they have brains with which to think, and thinking—and thinking and thinking—they still do not know."

In Old Father's encounters with his students, he often warned against what he considered the fundamental philosophical mistake of man: the perception of the world as divided into individual and separate things. Reality, he said, at every level from photons to philosophical fancies to the consciousness of living organisms was fluid, and it flowed everywhere like a great shimmering river. To break apart and confine this reality into separate categories created by the mind was foolish and futile, much like trying to capture a ray of light inside a dark wooden box. This urge to categorize was the true fall of man, for once the process was begun, there was no easy or natural return to sanity. All too inevitably, the infinite became finite, good opposed evil, thoughts hardened into beliefs, one's joys and discoveries became dreadful certainties, man became alienated from what he perceived as other ways and other things, and, ultimately, divided against himself, body and soul. According to the Fravashi, the misapprehension of the real world is the source of all suffering; it is bondage to illusion, and it causes human beings to grasp and hold on to life, not as it is, but as they wish it to be. Always seeking meaning, always seeking to make their lives safe and comprehensible, human beings do not truly live. This is the anguish of man which the Fravashi would alleviate. The Fravashi use their word keys and songs and alien logic to bring human beings closer to themselves, but the first part of this program toward liberation is the teaching of the language called Moksha. As Danlo became more familiar with the ways of Old Father's house, he immersed himself in the Fravashi system with all the passion of a seal splashing in the ocean, only to discover that he was required to learn the strange words and forms of Moksha.

"But, sir, the Language is confusing enough," Danlo told Old Father. "Now you say that I must learn Moksha, too—and at the same time?"

"Ha, ha, you are confused, just so, but the Old Fathers made Moksha solely to free human beings from their confusion," Old Father said. "Learn and learn, and you will see what you see."

Where the Fravashi system, as a whole, was created to free people from all systems, Moksha was put together as a kind of mind shield against the great whining babble of all human languages. It is a synthetic language, rich with invented words for strange and alien concepts, and with thousands of borrowed words from Sanskrit, Anglish, Old Japanese, and, of course, from the various languages of Tlon. The Fravashi Fathers regard this language family as the most sublime of all Old Earth's languages; from the Tlonish grammar, they have borrowed elements of syntax that accommodate and support the pellucid Fravashi worldview. Some say that Moksha is as complex and difficult to learn as the Fravashi language itself, but a clever woman or man is usually able to master it once a few familiar notions are discarded. For instance, Moksha contains no verb for the concept "to be," in the sense that one thing can be something else. As the Fravashi say: "Everything *is,* but nothing is anything." In Moksha, the sentence "I am a pilot" would be an impossible construction. As Danlo learned, one might try to say: "I act like a pilot," or "I have learned a pilot's skills," or even "I exult in the perquisites and glory of a pilot," but one could never proclaim, "I am this," or "I am that," any more than one would say, "I am a bowl of noodles."

At first this aspect of Moksha confused Danlo, for he thought that the path toward sanity lay in seeing the connectedness of all things. He was familiar with the Sanskrit equation: *Tat tvam asi,* that thou art. In some sense, he really *was* a bowl of noodles, or rather, his true essence and that of noodles (or falling snow or stone or a bird with white feathers) was one and the same. Because he thought these Sanskrit words were pure wisdom, he went to Old Father to ask why Moksha forbade such expressions.

"Ah, ah," Old Father said, "but the problem is not with Moksha, but with the natural human languages. Oh, even with the Sanskrit. Does Sanskrit have a word for 'you'? Yes. A word for 'I'? Indeed it does, and sadly so. And so. And so, having such words, such poisonous concepts, they are forced into paradox to detoxify and break down these concepts. *Tat tvam asi*—a deep statement, no? *That* thou art. Lovely, succinct, and profound—but an unnecessary way of expressing a universal truth. Is there a better way? Oh ho, I teach you Moksha. If you will learn this glorious tongue, then you will learn truth not just in one immortal statement, but in every sentence you speak."

And so Danlo applied himself to learning Moksha, and he soon discovered another reason why it was impossible to simply say, "I am a pilot." Moksha, it seemed, had completely freed itself of the bondage of pronouns, particularly from the most poisonous pronoun of all.

"Why do you think Moksha has banished this word 'I'?" Old Father asked one day. "What is this 'I' that human being are so attached to? It's pure romance, the greatest of fictions and confabulations. Can you hold it or taste it? Can you define it or even see it? 'What *am* I?' asks a man. Oh, ho, a better question might be 'What am I *not*?' How often have you heard someone say, 'I'm not myself today'? Or 'I didn't mean to say that'? No? Ha, ha, here I am dancing, dancing—am I the movement and genius of my whole organism or merely the sense of selfness that occupies the body, like a beggar in a grand hotel room? Am *I* only the part of myself that is noble, kind, mindful, and strong? Which disapproves and disavows the 'me' that is lustful, selfish, and wild? *Who* am I? Ah, ah, 'I *am*,' says the man. I am despairing, I am wild, I do not accept that I am desperate and wild. *Who* does not accept these things? I am a boy, I am a man, I am father, hunter, hero, lover, coward, pilot, asarya, and fool. Which 'I' are you—Danlo the Wild? Where is your 'I' that changes from mood to mood, from childhood to old age? Is there more to this 'I' than continuity of memory and love of eating what you call nose ice? Does it vanish when you fall asleep? Does it multiply by two during sexual bliss? Does it die when you die—or multiply infinitely? How will you ever know? So, it's so, you will try to watch out for yourself lest you lose your selfness. 'But how do I watch?' you ask. Aha—if *I* am watching myself, what is the 'I' that watches the watcher? Can the eye see itself? Then how can the 'I' see itself? Peel away the skin of an onion and you will find only more skins. Go look for your 'I.' Who will look? You will look. Oh ho, Danlo, but who will look for *you*?"

As Danlo came to appreciate, not only had Moksha done away with pronouns, but with the class of nouns in general. The Fravashi loathe nouns as human beings do disease. Nouns, according to Old Father, are like linguistic iceboxes that freeze a flowing, liquid reality. In using nouns to designate and delimit all the aspects of the world, it is all too easy to confuse a symbol for the reality that it represents. This is the second great philosophical mistake, which the Fravashi refer to as the "little maya." When speaking Moksha, it is difficult to make this mistake, for the function of nouns has largely been replaced by process verbs, as well as by the temporary and flexible juxtaposition of adjectives. For instance, the expression for a star might be "bright-white-continuing," while one might think of a supernova as "radiant-splendid-dying." There is no rule specifying the choice or number of these adjectives; indeed, one can form incredibly long and precise (and beautiful) concepts by skillful agglutinization, sticking adjectives one after another like beads on a string. Aficionados of Moksha, in their descriptions of the world, are limited only by their powers of perception and poetic virtue. It is said that one of the first Old Fathers in Neverness, as an exercise, once invented ten thousand words for the common snow apple. But one does not need the Fravashi flair with words to speak Moksha well. By the beginning of winter, when the first of that season's light snows dusted the streets, Danlo had learned enough of this language to make such simple statements as: *Chena bokageladesanga faras,* which would mean something like: *Now this ambitious-bright-wild-becoming pilots.* Given enough time in Old Father's house—and given Danlo's phenomenal memory—he might have become a master of Moksha rather than a pilot. But even as he composed poems to the animals and amused Old Father with his attempts to describe the Alaloi dreamtime, his brilliant fate was approaching, swiftly, inevitably, like the light of an exploding star.

On the ninety-third day of winter, after Danlo had begun to think in Moksha—and after he had put on pounds of new muscle and burned his face brown in the bright sun—Old Father called him into his chamber. He informed him that his petition had been accepted after all. "I have good news for you," Old Father said. "Bardo the Just does not like Fravashi, but other masters and lords do. Oh ho, Nikolos Petrosian, the Lord Akashic, is in love with the Fravashi. He's my friend. And he has persuaded Master Bardo to accept my petition. A favor to me, a favor to you."

Danlo understood nothing of politics or trading favors, and he said, "I would like to meet Lord Nikolos—he must be a kind man."

"Ah, but someday—if you survive the competition—you may be required to do more than merely acknowledge his kindness. For the time, though, it's enough that you compete with the other petitioners. And if you are to compete with any hope of winning, I'm afraid that you must learn the Language."

"But I am learning it, sir."

"Yes," Old Father said, "you spend ten hours each day making up songs in Moksha, while you give Fayeth half an hour in the evening toward your study of the Language."

"But the Language is so ugly," Danlo said. "So . . . clumsy."

"Aha, but few in the Order speak Moksha anymore. It's

almost a dead art. In the Academy's halls and towers, there is only the Language."

Danlo touched the feather in his hair and said, "Fayeth believes that in another year I shall be fluent."

"But you don't have another year. The competition begins on the twentieth of false winter."

"Well," Danlo said, "that's more than a half year away."

"Aha, very true. But you'll need more than the Language to enter the Academy. The Language is only a door to other knowledge, Danlo."

"And you think I should open this door now, yes?"

"Oh ho, surely it's upon you to decide this. If you'd like, we could withdraw the petition and wait until the following year."

"No," Danlo said. About most things, he had the patience of an Alaloi, which is to say the patience of a rock, but whenever he thought of the journey he had to complete, he was overcome with a sense of urgency. "I can't wait that long."

"There is another possibility."

"Yes?"

"So, it's so: a language—any *human* language—can be learned almost overnight. There are techniques, ways of directly imprinting the brain with language."

Danlo knew that the fount of intelligence lay inside the head, in the pineal gland which he called the third eye. Brains were a kind of pink fat that merely insulated this gland from the cold. Brains—animal brains, that is—were mainly good for eating or mashing up with wood ash in order to cure raw furs. "How can coils of fat hold language?" he wanted to know.

Old Father whistled a few low notes and then delivered a short lecture about the structures of the human brain. He pressed his long fingers down against Danlo's skull, roughly indicating the location deep in his brain of the hippocampus and almond-shaped amygdala, which mediated memory and the other mental functions. "Like a baldo nut, your brain is divided into two hemispheres, right and left. Oh ho, two halves—it's as if you had two brains. Why do you think human beings are divided against themselves, one half saying 'no,' while the other half continually whispers 'yes'?"

Danlo rubbed his eyes. From time to time, he tired of Old Father's air of superiority. He had stayed long enough in Old Father's house to relish the art of sarcasm, so he said, "And the Fravashi have an undivided brain? Is this why your consciousness wriggles about like a speared fatfish and never holds still?"

Old Father smiled nicely. "You're perceptive," he said. "The Fravashi brain, aha! So, it's so: our brains are divided into quarters. The frontal lobes"—and here he touched his head above his golden eyes and whistled softly—"the front brain is given over almost wholly to language and the composition of the songlines. The other parts, other functions. Four quarters: and the Fravashi sleep by quarters, you should know. Because we think more, because we are better able to compose, edit, and sing the song of ourselves, so we sleep more, much more. So, to dream. The Fravashi sleep by quarters: at any time, one, two, or three quarters of our brain is sleeping. Rarely are we wholly awake. And never—never, never, never, never!—must we allow ourselves to be four quarters asleep."

It was hard for Danlo to imagine such a consciousness, and he shook his head. He smiled at Old Father. "Then your brain, the four quarters—does it whisper 'yes,' 'no,' 'maybe,' and 'maybe not'?"

"Ho, ho, a human being making jokes about the Fravashi brain!"

Danlo laughed along with Old Father before falling serious. He asked, "Does your brain hold language like mine?"

"Ah, oh, it would be better to think of the Fravashi brain absorbing language like cotton cloth sucks up water. There are deep structures, universal grammars for words, music, or any sound—we hear a language one time, and we cannot forget."

"But I am a man, and I *can* forget, yes?"

"Oh ho, and that's why you must undergo an imprinting, if you are to learn the Language quickly and completely."

Danlo thought of all the things he had learned quickly and completely during the night of his initiation. He asked, "Will it hurt very much?"

Old Father smiled his sadistic smile, then, and his eyes were like golden mirrors. "Ah, the pain. The brain, the pain, the brain. On your outings with Ottah, skating on the streets, have you ever seen a Jacaradan whore?"

Danlo, who would have been shocked that certain women trade sex for money, that is, if he had known about money, said, "I am not sure."

"Women who leave their bellies bare, the better to display their tattoos. Tattoos: red and purple pictures of naked women, green and blue advertisements of their trade."

"Oh, *those* women." Danlo had come to appreciate the subtleties and delicateness of civilized females, and he said, "They are very lovely, yes? I wondered what they were called."

Old Father whistled a little tune indicating his disapproval of whores. But the meaning was lost on Danlo. "An imprinting is like a tattoo of the brain. Indelible sounds and pictures fixed into the synapses—the brain's synapses themselves are fixed like strands of silk in ice. There is no physical pain because the brain has no nerves. Ah, but the pain! Sudden new concepts, reference points, relationships among words—you can't imagine the possible associations. Oh ho, there *is* pain! The angslan of suddenly being more than you were. The pain of knowing. Oh, the pain, the pain, the pain, the pain."

The next day Old Father took Danlo to the imprimatur's shop. They left the district via the infamous Fravashi sliddery, a long orange street that flows down past the Street of the Common Whores and the Street of Smugglers and winds deep into the heart of the Farsider's Quarter. Old Father was fairly clumsy on his skates. His hips were not as loosely jointed as a human's, and they creaked with disease. Often, when rounding a curve he had to lean on Danlo to keep from falling. Often, he had to stop to catch his breath. They made a strange pair: Danlo with his open face and deeply curious eyes, and kindly, inscrutable Old Father towering over him like a furry mountain. Because it was warm, Danlo wore only a white cotton shirt, wool trousers, and a black wool jacket. (And, of course, Ahira's white feather fluttering in his hair.) It was one of those perfect winter days. The sky was as deep blue as a thallow's eggshell, and a fresh salt wind was blowing off the ocean. On either side of the street, the outdoor restaurants and cafés were crowded with people watching the continuous promenade of people stream by. And there was much to watch. As they penetrated deeper into the Quarter, the mix of people began to change and grow ever more colorful, seedier, more dangerous. There were many more whores and many master courtesans dressed in diamonds and the finest of real silks. There were hibakusha in rags, barefoot autists, harijan, tubists, merchants, wormrunners, and even a few ronin warrior-poets who had deserted their order for the pleasures of Neverness. The air heaved with the sounds and smells of teeming humanity. Fresh bread, sausages, and roasted coffee, ozone, woodsmoke, toalache, wet wool and floral perfumes, kana oil and sweat, and the faint, fermy essence of sex—there was no end to the smells of the City. These smells excited Danlo, although it was difficult to sort one from the other to track its

91

source. Once, when they were caught in the crush at the intersection of the Street of Imprimaturs, a plump little whore pressed up against him and ran her fingers through his hair. "Such thick, pretty hair," she said. "All black and red—is it real? I've never seen such hair before." While Old Father whistled furiously to shoo her away, Danlo drank in the fragrance of rose perfume which her sweaty hand had left in his hair. He had never encountered such a flower before, and he relished the smell, even though he wished that the whore had noticed he was not a boy, but a man.

Of the many shops on the Street of Imprimaturs, Drisana Lian's was one of the smallest. It sat on the middle of the block squeezed between a noisy café and the fabulously decorated shop of Baghaim the Imprimatur. Where Baghaim's shop was large and fronted with stained-glass windows, Drisana's was nothing more than a hole through an unobtrusive granite doorway; where many rich and fashionably dressed people queued up to apply for the services of Baghaim and his assistants, Drisana's shop was very often empty. "Drisana is not popular," Old Father explained as he knocked at the iron door. "That's because she refuses most imprintings requested of her. Ah, but there isn't a better imprimatur in the City."

The door opened and Drisana greeted Old Father and Danlo. She bowed painfully but politely before inviting them inside. Without in any way ignoring Danlo, she made it clear that she was glad to see Old Father, whom she had known since he first came to Neverness. They spoke to each other almost conspiratorially in the Language, and Danlo was able to pick put only a tenth of the words. "Drisana Lian," Old Father said, "may I present Danlo."

"Just 'Danlo'?"

"He's called Danlo the Wild."

They proceeded slowly down the bare hallway, very slowly because Drisana was very old and very slow. She shuffled along in her brownish-gray robe, taking her time. Like Old Father, she disdained bodily rejuvenations. Danlo had never—at least in his many days in the City—seen such an old woman. Her hair was long and gray and tied back in a chignon. Hundreds of deep lines split her face, which was yellow-white like old ivory. Most people would have thought her ugly, but Danlo did not. He thought she was beautiful. She had her own face, as the Devaki say. He liked her tiny round nose, red as a yu berry. He liked her straight, white teeth, although it puzzled him that she still had teeth. All the women of his tribe, long before they grew as old as Drisana, had worn their teeth down to brown stumps chewing on skins to soften them for clothing. Most of all, he liked her eyes. Her eyes were dark brown, at once hard and soft; her eyes hinted of a tough will and love of life. Something about her face and her eyes made Danlo feel comfortable for the first time since he had left his home.

She led them into a windowless room where Danlo and Old Father sat on bare wooden chairs around a bare wooden table. "Mint tea for the Honored Fravashi?" she asked as she hovered over her lacquered tea cabinet next to the dark wall. "And for the boy, what would he like in his cup? He's not old enough to drink wine, I don't think."

She served them two cups of mint tea, then returned to the cabinet where she opened a shiny black door and removed a crystal decanter. She poured herself a half glass of wine. "It's said that alcohol makes the Fravashi crazy. Now that would be a sight, wouldn't it—a crazy Fravashi?"

"Oh ho! it *would* be quite a sight indeed."

Drisana eased herself into a chair and asked, "I suppose Danlo is here for an imprinting? A language, of course." She turned to Danlo and said, "Old Father always brings his students to me to learn a language. What will it be? Anglish? Old Swahili? New Japanese? The Sanskrit, or the neurologician's sign language they employ on Silvaplana? I'm sure you'd like to learn the abominably difficult Fravashi language but that's impossible. No one can imprint it. Eighty years I've been trying and all I can manage is a few whistles."

Danlo was silent because he didn't understand her. He tapped his forehead and smiled.

Drisana wet her lips with wine and whistled at Old Father. In truth, she could speak more than a few whistles of Fravash, enough to make her meaning understood: "What is the matter with this boy?"

Old Father loved speaking his own language and he smiled. He whistled back, "So, it's so: he needs to learn the Language."

"What? But *everyone* speaks the Language! Everyone of the Civilized Worlds."

"So, it's so."

"He's not civilized, then? Is that why you call him Danlo the Wild? Such a name—I certainly don't approve of these kinds of names, the poor boy. But he's not of the Japanese Worlds, certainly. And he doesn't seem as if he's been carked."

In truth, one of Danlo's ancestors *had* illegally carked the family chromosomes, hence his unique, hereditary black and red hair. But it was too dark in the room for Drisana to make out the spray of red in his hair; it was too dark and her eyes were too old and weak. She must have seen clearly enough, however, that he possessed none of the grosser bodily deformations of the fully carked races: blue skin, an extra thumb, feathers, fur, or the ability to breathe water instead of air.

"Ah oh, I can't tell you where he comes from," Old Father whistled.

"It's a secret? I love secrets, you know."

"It's not for me to tell you."

"Well, the Fravashi are famous for their secrets, it's said." Drisana drank her wine and got up to pour herself another glass. "To imprint the Language—nothing could be easier. It's so easy, I hesitate to ask for payment."

Old Father closed one eye and slowly whistled, "I was hoping to make the usual payment."

"I'd like that," Drisana told him.

The usual payment was a song drug. Old Father agreed to sing for Drisana after their business was concluded. The Fravashi have the sweetest, most exquisite of voices, and to humans, their otherworldly songs are as intoxicating as any drug. Neither of them approved of money, and they disdained its use. Old Father, of course, as a Fravashi believed that money was silly. And Drisana, while she had defected from the Order years ago, still clung to most of her old values. Money was evil, and young minds must be nurtured, no matter the cost. She loved bestowing new languages on the young, but she refused to imprint wolf consciousness onto a man, or transform a shy girl into a libertine, or perform the thousand other personality alterations and memory changes so popular among the bored and desperate. And so, her shop usually remained empty.

Drisana poured herself a third glass of wine, this time from a different decanter. Danlo smiled and watched her take a sip.

"It's rude," she whistled to Old Father, "how very rude it is to speak in front of him in a language he doesn't understand. In a language *no one* understands. When we begin the imprinting, I shall have to speak to him. I suppose you'll have to translate. You *do* speak the boy's language, don't you?"

Old Father, who was not permitted to lie, said, "It's so. Of course I do. Oh, ho, but if I translate, you might recognize the language and thus determine his origins."

Drisana stood near Danlo and rested her hand on his shoulder. Beneath her loose skin on the back of her hand, the veins twisted like thin, blue worms. "Such a secret you're making of him! If you need to keep your secret, of course you must keep it. But I won't make an imprinting unless I can talk to him."

"Perhaps you could speak to him in Moksha."

"Oh? Is he fluent?"

"Nearly so."

"I'm afraid that won't be sufficient, then."

Old Father closed both eyes for an uncomfortably long time. He stopped whistling and started to hum. At last he looked at Danlo and said, *"Lo ti dirasa,* ah ha, I must tell you Drisana's words as she speaks them."

"He speaks Alaloi!" Drisana said.

"You recognize the language?"

"How could I not?" Drisana, who spoke 523 languages, was suddenly excited, so excited that she neglected to transpose her words into the Alaloi tongue. She began talking about the most important event that had happened in the Order since Neverness was founded. "It's been four years since Mallory Ringess ascended to heaven, or whatever it is that his followers believe. *I* think the Lord Pilot left the City on another journey—the universe is immense, is it not? Who can say if he'll ever return? Well, everyone is saying he became a god and will never return. One thing *is* certainly known: the Ringess once imprinted Alaloi —he was a student of bizarre and ancient languages. And now it seems that everyone wants to do the same, as young Danlo has obviously done. It's really *worship,* you know. Emulation, the power of apotheosis. As if learning a particular language could bring one closer to the godhead."

Old Father was obliged to translate this, and he did so. However, he seemed to be having trouble speaking. Alternately opening and shutting each eye, he sighed and paused and started and stopped. Danlo thought that he must be three-quarters asleep, so long did it take him to get the words out.

"Mallory Ringess was a pilot, yes?"

"Oh, yes," Old Father said. "A brilliant pilot. He became the Lord Pilot of the Order, and then, at the end, the Lord of the Order itself. Many people hated him; some loved him. There was something about him, the way he compelled people's love or hate. Twelve years ago, there was schism in the Order. And war. And the Ringess was a warrior, among other things. So, it's so: a very angry, violent man. And secretive, and cruel, and vain.

Oh ho, but he was also something else. An unusually complex man. A kind man. And noble, and fated, and compassionate. He loved truth—even his enemies would admit that. He devoted his life to a quest for the Elder Eddas, the secret of the gods. Some say he found this secret and *became* a god; some say he failed and left the City in disgrace."

Danlo thought about this for a while. Drisana's tea room was a good place for reflection. In some ways it reminded him of a snow hut's interior: clean, stark, and lit by natural flames. High on the granite walls, atop little wooden shelves, were ten silver candelabra. All around the room, candles burned with a familiar yellow light. The smells of hot wax and carbon mingled with pine and the sickly sweet fetor that old people exude when they are almost ready to go over. Danlo traced his finger along his forehead and wondered aloud, "Is it possible for a man to become a god? For a *civilized* man? How can such a thing be possible? Men are men; why should a man want to be a god?"

He wondered if Old Father was lying or speaking metaphorically. Or perhaps, in such a *shaida* place as a city, a man really could aspire to godhood. Danlo really didn't understand civilized people, nor could he conceive of the kinds of gods they might become. And then he had a startling thought: It wasn't necessary for him to understand everything in order to accept Drisana's and Old Father's story. As his first conscious act as an asarya, he would say "yes" to this fantastic notion of a man's journey godward, at least until he could see things more clearly.

He turned to Old Father and asked, "What is the Elder Eddas?"

"Oh ho, the Elder Eddas! No one is quite sure. It is the secret knowledge that all peoples have sought in all places at all times. The great knowledge, the deep and direct way of knowing all things. Some have called it the Philosopher's Stone. Or the One Tree, the Burning Bush, Pure Information, or the Pearl of Great Price. Aha, or the River of Light, the Ring of Scutarix, the Universal Program, the Eschaton. *And* the Golden Key, the Word, even the Wheel of Law. So, it's so: the Elder Eddas. But the Eddas is also something other. Something more. Aha, perhaps something more specific. Once there was a race of gods, the Ieldra, once, once, three million years ago. When human beings lived in trees; when the Fravashi still warred with each other, clan against clan. The Ieldra, it's said, discovered the secret of the universe. The pilots of the Order have named this secret the Elder Eddas. All the power of God. It's said that the

Ieldra have used this secret to *become* God, or to become as one with God. It's said that they carked their minds—ah, ah, their very consciousness—into the singularity at the galaxy's core. Into a spinning black hole. But before their final evolution, a gift. A bequest from the Ieldra to their chosen successors. *Not* the Fravashi, it's said. Not the Darghinni. Nor the Scutari, nor the Farahim, nor the Friends of Man. It's said that the Ieldra have carked their secrets into human beings only; long ago they encoded the Elder Eddas into the human genome. Wisdom, madness, infinite knowledge, racial memory—oh ho, all of these, indeed! It's thought that certain segments of human DNA code the Elder Eddas as pure memory. And so, inside all human beings, a way of becoming gods—and perhaps something more."

While Danlo stared at the flame shadows dancing atop the floor, he smiled with curiosity and amusement. Finally, he asked, "And what is DNA?"

"Ah, so much to learn, but you needn't learn it just now. The main point is this: The Ringess showed the way to remember the Elder Eddas, and people hated him for that. *Why?* All is one, you say, and man shall be as gods? Creation and memory— God is memory? So, it's so: there's a way for anyone to remember the Elder Eddas, but here is the most ironic of ironies: Many can hear the Eddas within themselves but few can understand."

Danlo closed his eyes, listening. The only sound inside was the beating of his heart. "I do not hear anything," he said.

Old Father smiled and, as Danlo had, closed both his eyes.

Drisana was savoring her fourth glass of wine, and she finally spoke to Danlo in his language, *"Kareeska,* Danlo, grace beyond grace. It's been a long time since I spoke Alaloi; please forgive me if I make mistakes." After a long sip of wine, she continued, "There are techniques of remembering, of listening. You chose an exciting time to enter the Order. Everyone is trying to learn the remembrancing art, certainly they are. If you're accepted into Borja, perhaps you'll learn it, too."

Her voice was slurry with wine and bitterness. Once, at the beginning of the Great Schism, because she had believed the Order was corrupt and doomed, she had renounced her position as master imprimatur. And now, twelve years later, there was a renewal of spirit and vision in the towers of the Academy, and the Order was more vital than it had been in a thousand years. Given the chance, she would have rejoined the Order, but for those who abjure their vows, there is never a second chance.

Danlo, who was quite unafraid to touch old people, took Drisana's hand and held it as he would his grandmother's. He liked the acceptance he saw in her sad, lovely eyes, though he wondered why she would be so bitter. "The gods have imprinted human beings with the Elder Eddas, yes?"

"No, certainly not!" Drisana did not explain that it was *she,* herself, who had once imprinted Mallory Ringess, and therefore she was partly responsible for creating the Ringess and all the chaos of the war. "The memory of the Eddas lies deeper than the brain. When we speak of an imprinting, we speak merely of changing the metabolic pathways and the neural network. It's all a matter of redefining the synapses of the brain."

"Fixing the synapses like strands of silk in glacier ice?"

Drisana stared at him as she took a sip of wine. Then she started laughing, and the bitterness suddenly left her. "Dear Danlo, you don't understand *anything* about what we're going to do here today, do you?"

"No," he said. "I always thought the brain was just a store of pink fat."

Drisana laughed nicely and pulled at his hand. "Come," she said. "Danlo, and my Honored Fravashi—you'll have to help me because I've drunk too much wine."

She led them through a wooden door into the imprinting room, or her chamber of impressions, as she liked to call it. In the center of the imprinting room, atop the Fravashi carpet that Old Father had once given her, was a padded chair covered with green velvet. Aside from a couple of hologram stands behind the chair, it was the only article of furniture in the room. On each of the six walls, from ceiling to floor, were polished shelves holding up what looked like gleaming metal skulls. There were 622 of these skulls, arrayed neatly in their rows. "These are the heaumes," Drisana explained as she sat Danlo down on this chair. "You've certainly seen a heaume before?"

Danlo sat stiffly in the chair, craning his neck, looking at the heaumes. *Ahira, Ahira,* he silently called, *why would anyone collect metal skulls?*

Drisana wobbled on her feet as she ran her hands through his hair, roughly sizing his head. He had a large head for a boy fourteen years old, large and broad, and she turned to select a heaume from the third row from the top. "First, we have to make a model of your brain," she said.

"A model?"

"A picture. Like a painting."

While Old Father sat down on the rug in the Fravashi fashion to watch, she fit the heaume over Danlo's head. Danlo held his breath, then slowly let it out. The heaume was cold, even through his thick hair. The heaume was hard and cold, and it tightly squeezed his skull. Something important was about to happen, he thought, though he couldn't quite tell what. Through the dark hallways of Drisana's shop, he had kept his sense of direction. He was sure he was facing east. One must piss to the south, sleep with one's head to the north, but all important ceremonies must occur facing east. How could Drisana know this?

"A painting of your brain," Drisana slurred out. Her breath was heavy over his face and smelled of wine. "We'll paint it with light."

Directly behind Danlo's chair, one of the hologram stands suddenly lit up with a model of his brain. There, seemingly floating above the stand, were the glowing folds of his cerebral cortex, the cerebellum and medulla, and the vivid chasm splitting the brain into halves. Danlo felt nothing, but he sensed a gleam of light from his side and turned to look.

"Stop!" Drisana cried out.

It was too late. Danlo had been blindly obedient only once in his life, during his passage into manhood, on pain of death. How could he help looking at a painting of his brain? He looked, and in the back of the model of his brain, the visual cortex flared with orange light. He looked at his own visual cortex, painted bright with orange and orange-red, and the very act of looking caused the neurons within the cortex to fire. As he looked and looked, suddenly the light was blindingly, brilliantly red. The light was a red spearpoint through his eyes into his brain. The pain was quick, sharp, and intense. Old Father had been wrong; there was a hideous pain. He closed his eyes and looked away. The pain fell off into a white heat and a burning, the terrible pain.

Drisana grasped his face in her withered hands and gently turned him facing forward. "You mustn't look at your brain's own model! Soon, we'll go deeper, down to the neurons. The neurotransmitter flow, the electricity. Your thoughts—you would be able to see your own thoughts. And that's *so* dangerous. Seeing your thoughts as they form up—that itself would create another thought for you to see. The feedback, the infinities. Certainly, the process could go on to infinity, but you'd be insane or dead long before then."

Danlo stared straight ahead. He held himself very still. He

was sweating now, beads of salt water squeezed between his forehead and the heaume. "Ahira, Ahira," he whispered. "O blessed Ahira!"

"Now be still. Before we can make an imprinting, we must see where to imprint."

Even though Drisana was half-drunk, she laid his brain bare as deftly and easily as he might slit open a snow hare's belly. Before she had learned the art of imprinting, she had been an akashic. As an akashic, she had done many thousands of brain mappings. All imprimaturs are also akashics, though few akashics know much about the art of imprinting. In truth, it is easier to map and read a brain than it is to imprint it. For no good reason—and this is a bitter irony—the akashics possess a much higher status in the Order than do the lowly imprimaturs.

"Close your eyes, now," Drisana called out softly.

Danlo closed his eyes. Behind him, his brain's model rippled with light waves. The language clusters in the left hemisphere were magnified and highlighted. The neural network was dense and profoundly complex. Millions of individual neurons, like tiny, glowing red spiders, were packed into a three-dimensional web. From each neuron grew thousands of dendrites, thousands of red, silken strands which sought each other out and connected at the synapses.

"Danlo, *ni luria la shantih,*" Drisana said, and his association cortex fairly jumped with light. And then, *"Ti asto yujena oyu,* you have eyes that see too deeply and too much."

"Oh ho, that's true!" Old Father broke in. *"Yujena oyu*— so, it's so."

Drisana held up a hand to silence him, and she spoke other words in other languages, words that failed to bring Danlo's association cortex to life. In a few moments, Drisana determined that Alaloi was his milk tongue, and more, that he knew no others except Moksha and a smattering of the Language. It was an extraordinary thing to discover, and she probably longed to immediately spread this news in the various cafés and bars, but as an imprimatur she was obliged to keep secrets.

"Now we have the model; now we will make the actual imprinting."

She removed the heaume from Danlo's head. While he brushed back his sodden hair, she walked over to the far wall behind Old Father to search for a particular heaume. She tried to explain the fundamentals of her art, though it must have been difficult to find words in the Alaloi language to convey he meaning. Danlo quickly became confused. In truth, imprinting is both simple and profound. Every child is born with a certain array of synapses connecting neuron to neuron. This array is called the primary repertoire and is determined partly by the genetic programs and partly by the self-organizing properties of the growing brain. Learning occurs, simply, when certain synapses are selected and strengthened at the expense of others. The blueness of the sky, the pain of ice against the skin—every color, each crackling twig, smell, idea, or fear burns its mark into the synapses. Gradually, event by event, the primary repertoire is transformed into the secondary repertoire. And this transformation—the flowering of a human being's selfness and essence, one's very soul—is evolutionary. Populations of neurons and synapses compete for sensa and thoughts. Or rather, they compete to make thoughts. The brain is its own universe, and thoughts are living things which thrive or die according to natural laws.

Drisana eased the new heaume over Danlo's head. It was thicker than the first heaume and heavier. Above the second hologram stand, a second model of Danlo's brain appeared. Next to it, the first model remained lit. As the imprinting progressed, Drisana would continually compare the second model to the first, down to the molecular level; she would need to see both models—as well as the tone of Danlo's blue-black eyes—to determine when he had imprinted enough for one day.

"So many synapses," Drisana said. "Ten trillion synapses in the cortex alone."

Danlo made a fist and asked, "What do the synapses look like?"

"They're modeled as points of light. Ten trillion points of light." She didn't explain how neurotransmitters diffuse across the synapses, causing the individual neurons to fire. Danlo knew nothing of chemistry or electricity. Instead, she tried to give him some idea of how the heaume's computer stored and imprinted language. "The computer remembers the synapse configuration of other brains, brains that hold a particular language. This memory is a *simulation* of that language. And then in *your* brain, Danlo, select synapses are excited directly and strengthened. The computer speeds up the synapses' natural evolution."

Danlo tapped the bridge of his nose; his eyes were dark and intent upon a certain sequence of thought. "The synapses are not allowed to grow naturally, yes?"

"Certainly not. Otherwise imprinting would be impossible."

"And the synapse configuration—this is really the learning, the essence of another's mind, yes?"

"Yes, Danlo."

"And not just the learning—isn't this so? You imply that anything in the mind of another could be imprinted in my mind?"

"Almost anything."

"What about dreams? Could dreams be imprinted?"

"Certainly."

"And nightmares?"

Drisana squeezed his hand and reassured him, "No one would imprint a nightmare into another."

"But it is possible, yes?"

Drisana nodded her head.

"And the emotions . . . the fears or loneliness or rage?"

"Those things, too. Some imprimaturs—certainly they're the dregs of the City—some do such things."

Danlo let his breath out slowly. "Then how can I know what is real and what is unreal? Is it possible to imprint false memories? Things or events that never happened? Insanity? Could I remember ice as hot or see red as blue? If someone else looked at the world through *shaida* eyes, would I be infected with this way of seeing things?"

Drisana wrang her hands together, sighed, and looked helplessly at Old Father.

"Oh ho, the boy is difficult, and his questions cut like a *sarsara*!" Old Father stood up and painfully limped over to Danlo. Both his eyes were open, and he spoke clearly. "All ideas are infectious, Danlo. Most things learned early in life, we do not choose to learn. Ah, and much that comes later. So, it's so: the two wisdoms. The first wisdom: as best we can, we must choose what to put into our brains. And the second wisdom: the healthy brain creates its own ecology; the vital thoughts and ideas eventually drive out the stupid, the malignant, and the parasitical."

Because Danlo's forehead was wet and itched, he tried to force his finger up beneath the heaume, but it was too tight. He said, "Then you are not afraid that the words of the Language will poison me?"

"Oh ho, all languages are poison," Old Father said. His eyes were bright with appreciation of Danlo's unease. "Bu that's why you've learned Moksha and the Fravashi way, as an antidote to such poisons."

Danlo trusted nothing about the whole unnatural process of imprinting, but he trusted Old Father and trusted Drisana, too. He made a quick decision to affirm this trust. *Follow your fate,* he thought, and he tapped the heaume. "I shall learn the Language now, yes?"

The imprinting of Danlo's brain took most of the day. It was painless, without incident or sensation. He sat quiet and still while Drisana spoke to the heaume's computer in an artificial language that neither he nor Old Father could understand. She selected the sequence of imprinting, and with the computer's aid, she monitored his brain chemistry: the concentrations of the neurotransmitters, the MAP2 molecules, the synapsin and kinase and the thousands of other brain proteins. Layer by glowing layer, she laid his cortex bare and imprinted it.

Once, Danlo asked, "Where are the new words? Why can't I feel the Language as it takes hold? Why can't I hear it or think it?" And then he had a terrifying thought: If the heaume could add memories to his brain, perhaps it could remove them just as easily. And if it did, how would he ever know?

Drisana had brought in a chair from the tea room and was sighing heavily (she had also brought in another glass of wine); she was much too old to remain standing during the entire course of an imprinting. She said, "The heaume shuts off the new language clusters from the rest of your brain until it's over. You certainly wouldn't want to be bothered thinking in a new language until a good part of it was in place, would you? Now you must think of something pleasant, perhaps a happy memory or a daydream to occupy your time."

Usually, an imprinting required three sessions, but Drisana found that Danlo was accepting the Language quickly and well. His eyes remained bright and focused. She let the imprinting go on until he had nine tenths of the words, and then she decided that that was quite enough. She removed the heaume, took a sip of wine, and sighed.

Old Father stood up and said, "Thank you." He walked up and placed his furry hand over Danlo's head. His black fingernails were hard against Danlo's temple. Speaking in the Language, Old Father said, "Drisana is kind, very kind and very beautiful, don't you think?"

Without thought or hesitation, Danlo replied, "Oh, yes, she is radiant with shibui. She is . . . what I mean to say, shibui . . ." The words died in his mouth because he was suddenly excited and confused. He was speaking the Language! He was speaking fluently words he had never heard before. Did he understand what he had said? Yes, he *did* understand. Shibui: a kind of beauty that only time can reveal. Shibui was the subtle beauty of gray and brown moss on an old rock. And the taste of an old wine which recalled a ripening of grapes and the perfect balance of sun, wind, and rain—that too was shibui. Drisana's face radiated shibui—"radiate" was not quite the right word— her face revealed the grain of her character and her life's experiences as if it were a piece of ivory painstakingly and beautifully carved by time.

He rubbed his temple slowly and said, "What I mean is . . . she has her own face." Then, realizing that he had fallen back on an Alaloi expression, he began thinking of the many conceptions and words for beauty. There were the new words: sabi, awarei, and hozhik. And wabi: the unique beauty of a flawed object, such as a teapot with a crack; the beautiful, distinctive, aesthetic flaw that distinguishes the spirit of the moment in which an object was created from all other moments in eternity. And always, there was *halla*. If *halla* was the beauty, the harmony and balance of life, then the other words for beauty were lesser words, though they were connected to *halla* in many ways. In truth, each of the new words revealed hidden aspects of *halla* and helped him to see it more clearly.

"Oh, blessed beauty! I never knew . . . that there were so many ways of looking at beauty."

For a while the three of them talked about beauty. Danlo spoke haltingly because he was unsure of himself. To suddenly have a new language inside was the strangest of feelings. It was like entering a dark cave, like climbing toward the faint sound of falling water, and all the while being possessed of an eerie sense that there were many pretty pebbles to be found but not quite knowing where to look. He had to search for the right words, and he struggled to put them together.

"So much to . . . comprehend," he said. "In this blessed Language, there is so much . . . passion. So many powerful ideas."

"Oh ho!" Old Father said. "The Language is sick with ideas."

Danlo looked at the many rows of heaumes and tapped the heaume that Drisana was still holding in her hand. "The whole of the Language is inside here, yes?"

"Certainly," she said, and she nodded at him.

"And other languages, you say? How many . . . languages?"

Drisana, who was bad with numbers, said, "More than ten thousand but certainly less than fifty thousand."

"So many," he mused. His eyes took on a faraway look, as of ice glazing over the dark blue sea. "So many . . . how could human beings ever learn so many?"

"He's beginning to see it," Old Father said.

Drisana put the heaume down atop the inactive hologram stand and smiled at Danlo. Her face was warm and kind. "I think you've had enough conversation for one day. Now you should go home and sleep. Then you'll dream of what you've learned and tomorrow your speech will come more easily."

"No," Old Father said sharply. He directed a few quick whistles at her, then said, "Imprinting is like giving a newborn the ability to walk without strengthening the leg muscles. Let him use the Language a little more, lest he stumble later when he can least afford to."

"But he's too tired!"

"No, look at his eyes, look how he sees; now he is liminal, oh ho!"

Liminal, Danlo thought, to be on the threshold of a new concept or way of viewing things. Yes, he was certainly liminal; his heart pounded and his eyes ached because he was beginning to see too much. He stood up and began pacing around the room. To Drisana, he said, "Besides languages, there are many . . . categories of knowledge, yes? History, and what Fayeth calls eschatology, and many others. And all may be imprinted?"

"Most of them."

"How many?"

Drisana was silent as she looked at Old Father. He gave forth a long, low whistle, then said, "Oh, oh, if you learned all of a heaume's forty thousand languages, it would be like standing alone on a beach with a drop of water in your hand while an ocean roared beyond you."

"That's quite enough!" Drisana snapped. "Such a sadist you are."

"Oh ho!"

Danlo threw his hand over his eyes and rubbed them. Then he stared up at the ceiling for a long time. At last he was seeing the great ocean of knowledge and truth as it opened before him.

The ocean was as deep and bottomless as space, and he could see no end to the depths. He was drowning in deepness; the air in the room was so thick and close that he could hardly catch his breath. If he must learn all the truths of the universe, then he would never know *halla*. "Never," he said. And then, cursing for the first time in his life: "There is . . . too damn much to know!"

Drisana sat him down in the velvet chair and pressed her wineglass into his hand. "Here, take a sip of wine. It will calm you. Certainly, no one can know everything. But why would you want to?"

With a humming sound that was two thirds of a laugh, Old Father said, "There's a word that will help you. You must know what this word is."

"A word?"

Old Father began whistling in fugue, and he said, "A word. Think of it as a culling word. So, it's so: those who grasp the intricacies and implications of this word are culled, chosen to swim in a sea of knowledge where others must drown. Search your memory; you know this word."

Danlo closed his eyes, and there in the darkness, like a star falling out of the night, was the word. "Do you mean 'shih,' sir?" he asked. "I must learn shih, yes?"

Shih was opposite of facts and raw information; shih was the elegance of knowledge, the insight and skill to organize knowledge into meaningful patterns. As an artist chooses colors of paint or light to make her pictures, so a master of shih chooses textures of knowledge—various ideas, myths, abstractions, and theories—to create a way of seeing the world. The aesthetics and beauty of knowledge—this was shih.

"Just so, shih," Old Father said. "An old word for an old, old art."

He explained that the etymon of shih was a simple word in Old Chinese; the Fravashi had fallen in love with this word, and they had borrowed and adapted it when they invented Moksha. From Moksha, the concept of shih had entered into the Language—along with thousands of other concepts and words. Those who fear the Fravashi regard this invasion of the Language with alien (or ancient) words as the most subtle of stratagems to conquer the human race.

Danlo rubbed his eyes as he listened. "You say that shih . . . is a word of Moksha, yes?"

"So, it's so: in Moksha, shih is used only as a verb. In the Language, shih becomes corrupted as a noun."

"But why haven't I been taught this word, sir?"

"Ah, ah, I've been saving it for the proper time," Old Father said. "In the Language, shih is elegance in using one's knowledge. But in Moksha, this broader meaning: Shih is recognizing and making sense of different *kinds* of knowledge. It's the most brilliant art, this ability to gauge the beauties and weaknesses of different worldviews. Oh ho, now that you have the Language in your head, you will badly need this art. If you are to keep the civilized worldview from overwhelming you, you must become a man of shih."

In a gulp, Danlo downed the rest of the wine. The tartness and the sugars tasted good. As Drisana had said it would, it calmed him. He talked with Drisana and Old Father about shih, or rather, he listened while they talked. After a while the wine made him drowsy. He shifted about, resting his head on the chair's soft velvet arm with his legs flopped over the other arm. He listened until the words of the Language lost their meaning, and all the sounds of the room—Old Father's whistling, Drisana's heavy sighs, and the faint clamor of the café next door —melted into a chaotic hum.

"Look, he's falling asleep," Drisana said. "That's certainly enough for today. You'll bring him back tomorrow to complete the imprinting?"

"Tomorrow or the day after."

Old Father roused Danlo then, and they said their goodbyes. Drisana rumpled his hair and warned him about the dangers of drinking too much wine. All the way home, skating along the noisy evening streets, Danlo overheard stray bits and snatches of conversation. Most of the talk seemed muddled, insipid, and meaningless. He wondered how many of these chattering, confused people understood shih?

Old Father read the look on his face and scolded, "Oh ho, you must not judge others according to what you think you know. Do not glaver, Danlo, not tonight, and not ever."

By the time they reached Old Father's house, Danlo was very tired. He fairly fell into his bed. That night he slept with his clothes on, and he had strange dreams. He dreamed in the words of the Language; his dreams were chaotic, without theme or pattern or the slightest sense of shih.

THE RETURNISTS

The minute anything—science, feminism, Buddhism, holism, whatever—starts to take on the characteristics of a cosmology, it should be discarded. How things are held in the mind is infinitely more important than what is in the mind, including this statement itself.

—Morris Berman, Holocaust Century Historian

The problem when people stop believing in God is not that they thereafter believe in nothing; it is that they believe in anything.

—G. K. Chesterton

During the days that followed, Danlo returned often to Drisana's shop. He imprinted much besides the Language, for although the Order would not test the bulk or quality of his knowledge, he still needed the anchor stones of history, mechanics, ecology, and other disciplines to support the web of associations so necessary for understanding civilization's complexities. He learned many astonishing things. Human beings, it seemed, were fairly infested with tiny animals too small to be felt or seen. These animals were called bacteria, and they sometimes made up as much as ten percent of the body's weight. Bacteria—and viruses and protozoa—swam in fluids of his eyes and filled his bowels with putrid gases; sometimes they tunneled deep into the tissues of his body. A few of these organisms were harmful and caused disease. And so the people of Neverness were afraid to touch each other for fear of infection. Most, even indoors, covered their hands with thin leather gloves and were careful not to get too close to strangers lest they breathe each other's exhalations. This inhibition caused Danlo many pains. In the Alaloi manner, he liked to brush up against Fayeth or Luister when he greeted them in the hallways of Old Father's house. To smell their hair or run his callused hands over their smooth faces reassured him of their realness and essential humanity. With great difficulty he learned to restrain himself. Especially out on the narrow streets of the Fravashi District, in the midst of the manswarm, he had to skate with great care to avoid the swish of perfumed silk or sweat-stained woolens. It vexed him that casual bumping—the slightest of accidental contact—required immediate apology. Even to look purposefully at another, to touch eye to eye or let one's gaze linger too long, was considered provocative and gauche.

Of course, he still knew nothing of slelling. He couldn't guess that slel neckers sometimes steal another's DNA in order to tailor specific viruses to kill in horrible and specific ways. (Or sometimes, in the unspeakable art of slel mime, a victim's brain is replaced neuron by neuron with programmed neurologics, gradually converted to a slave unit, and taken over.) Once, it occurred to him that a virus might have infected and killed his people—how else to explain his tribe's death? He marveled at the extension of the world's ecology to include such tiny, parasitical beasts. Viruses, he thought, were really just another kind of animal that preyed on the cells of human beings, no more fearsome than snow tigers or lice or bears. He wondered, however, how viruses could kill his whole tribe all at once. A bear might stalk and slay a solitary hunter, but never an entire band of men bristling with spears. Such an event would be *shaida,* a complete unbalancing of the world's way. He could only guess that something must have happened to ruin his tribe's *halla* relationship with the world. Perhaps one of the men had forgotten to pray for the spirit of an animal he had killed; perhaps one of the women had prepared a batch of blood tea incorrectly, and so weakened the bodies of all the Devaki people. In truth, he never suspected that a civilized virus might have found its way into Haidar and Chandra and his near-brothers and near-sisters; he never imagined the making of viruses as weapons because such thoughts, for him, were still unimaginable.

As winter passed into deep winter and the weather grew colder, he found himself slowly and painfully adapting to the strangeness of the City. He spent much of each day outside skating, exploring the convoluted, purple glidderies of the Bell and the other districts of the Farsider's Quarter. Learning the Language was like opening the door to a mansion containing many fabulously decorated rooms; it enabled him to talk with wormrunners and autists and maggids, and other people he met on the streets. Despite his natural shyness, he loved to talk, especially to the Order's pilots and academicians, who could often be found eating elaborate dinners at the Hofgarten or drinking chocolate in the many Old City cafés. Gradually, from a hundred little remarks that these people made about the Fravashi—as well as his participation in the meditations, word games, and other rituals of Old Father's house—he came to see the entire Fravashi system from a new perspective. He began to entertain doubts as to whether the Fravashi way really *was* a way toward true liberation. Each evening, before the usual Moksha competition, he sat with the other students around Old Father, and he repeated the Statement of Purpose: "Our system is not a simple system like other systems; it is a meta-system designed to free us from all systems. While we cannot hope to rid ourselves of all beliefs and worldviews, we can free ourselves from bondage to any particular belief or worldview." He listened as Old Father discussed the Three Paradoxes of Life, or the Theory of Nairatmya, or the poems of Jin Zenimura, who was one of the first human masters of Moksha. Always, Danlo listened with half a smile on his face, even as a voice whispered in his ear that the Fravashi system, itself, might bind him as surely as a fireflower's nectar intoxicates and traps a fritillary.

In truth, he did not want to accept some of the Fravashi system's fundamental teachings. Although it was somewhat rash of him, even presumptuous, from the very beginning he disagreed with Old Father over the ideal and practice of the art of plexure. This art—it is sometimes called plexity—aims at moving the student through the four stages of liberation. In the first stage, that of the simplex, one is caught within the bounds of a single worldview. This is the reality of a child or an Alaloi hunter, who may not even be aware that other ways of perceiving reality exist. Most peoples of the Civilized Worlds, however, *are* aware of humanity's many religions, philosophies, ways, and worldviews. They suspect that adherence to their own belief system is somewhat arbitrary, that had they been born as autists or as Architects of the Infinite Life, for example, they might venerate dreams as the highest state of reality or worship artificial life as evolution's ultimate goal. In fact, they might believe *anything,* but simplex people believe only one thing, whatever reality their parents and culture have imprinted into their brains. As the Fravashi say, human beings are self-satisfied creatures who love looking into the mirror for evidence that they are somehow brighter or more beautiful than they really are. It is the great and deadly vanity of human beings to convince themselves that their worldview, no matter how unlikely or bizarre, is somehow more sane, natural, pragmatic, holy, or truthful than any other. Out of choice—or cowardice—most people never break out of this simplex stage of viewing the world as through a single lens, and this is their damnation.

All of Old Father's students, of course, by the very act of adopting the Fravashi system, had elevated themselves to the complex stage of belief. To be complex is to hold at least two different realities, perhaps at two different times of one's life. The complex woman or man will cast away beliefs like old clothes, as they become worn or inappropriate. Using the Fravashi techniques, it is possible to progress from one belief system to another, ever growing, ever more flexible, bursting free from one worldview into another as a snake sheds an old skin. The truly complex person will move freely among these systems as the need arises. When journeying by sled across the frozen sea, he will have nineteen different words for the colors of whiteness; when studying the newtonian spectrum, she will compose wavelengths of red, green, and blue into pure white light; when visiting the Perfect on Gehenna, one will choose articles of clothing containing no white, since it is obvious that white isn't really a color at all, but rather the absence of all color, and thus, the absence of light and life. The ideal of complexity, as Old Father liked to remind his students, was the ability to move from system to system—or from worldview to worldview—with the speed of thought.

"Ah, ha," Old Father said one night, "all of you are complex, and some of you may become very complex, but who among you has the strength to be multiplex?"

The third stage of plexure is the multiplex. If complexity is the ability to suspend and adopt different beliefs as they are useful or appropriate, one after another, then multiplexity is the holding of more than one reality at the same time. These realities may be as different—or even contradictory—as the old science and the magical thinking of a child. "Truth is multiple," as the Old Fathers say. One can never become multiplex if afraid of paradox or enslaved by the god of consistency. Multiplex vision is paradoxical vision, new logics, the sudden completion of startling patterns. The mastery of multiplexity makes it possible to see the world in many dimensions; it is like peering into a jewel of a thousand different faces. When one has attained a measure of the multiplex, the world's creation is seen as the handiwork of a god, and a fireball exploding out of the primordial neverness, and a communal dream, and the eternal crystallization of reality out of a shimmering and undifferentiated essence—all these things and many others, all at once. The multiplex man (or alien) will see all truths as interlocking parts of a greater truth. The Fravashi teach that once in every cycle of time, one is born who will evolve from multiplexity to the omniplex, which is the fourth and final stage of liberation. This completely free individual is the asarya. Only the asarya may hold all possible realities at once. Only the asarya is able to say "yes" to all of creation, for one must see everything as it truly is before making the final affirmation.

This idea is the pinnacle of all Fravashi thought and wisdom, and it was this very teaching that Danlo disputed above all others. As he maintained in his discussions with Old Father, to hold all realities and look out over the whole of the universe was a noble and necessary step, but an asarya must go beyond this. The entire logic of the Fravashi system pointed toward liberation from belief systems and beliefs—why not strive to believe nothing at all? Why not behold reality with faultless eyes, as free from worldviews as a newborn child? Wasn't this awakening into innocence the true virtue of an asarya?

"Oh, oh," Old Father said to him, "but everyone must believe *something*. Even if one must invent one's own beliefs. It's surprising that after half a year in my house, you haven't come to believe this."

Old Father was always quick to bestow his holy sadism upon his students, particularly one so strong-willed as Danlo. And Danlo, for his part, quite enjoyed the intricate dance of wits so beloved of the Fravashi. He never took hurt from any of Old Father's jokes or calculated ridicule. And he never deluded himself that he was close to freedom from belief. Quite the opposite. Willfully—and as mindfully as a hunter stepping into a snow tiger's lair—he entered into the Fravashi worldview. It was indeed a strange and beautiful place. While he was always aware of the little flaws in this reality waiting to widen into cracks, he cherished the most basic of all Fravashi teachings, which was that human beings were made to be free. He believed this passionately, fiercely, completely. He kept the spirit of Fravism close to his heart, like an invisible talisman cut from pure faith. The Fravashi might misunderstand what it would mean to be an asarya, but no matter. Their system could still be used to smash the illusions and thoughtways imprisoning people. And then, once released, each human being could soar free in whatever direction called.

The Fravashi system was nobly conceived, yes, but as Danlo discovered, not all conceptions can be perfectly realized. The Fravashi had come to Neverness three thousand years earlier, and over time, the original teachings and practices of their system had become too systematic. Experiments in thinking had become reified into exercises; ideas had been squeezed into ideology; insight hardened into doctrine; and the little graces and devotions that the students delighted in tendering their Old Fathers had inevitably become onerous obligations. Quite a few students forgot that Moksha was to be used as a tool. All too often, they worshiped this language and imagined that learning ever more Moksha words and poems and koans would be sufficient to free them from themselves. Nothing dismayed Danlo more than this tendency toward worship. And no aspect of worship was so dangerous as the way that Luister and Eduardo and the others fell into fawning over Old Father and surrendered their will to him.

This, of course, is the pitfall of cults and religions dominated by a guru, sage, or messiah. The pattern of enslavement is ancient: a young man or woman hears the call of a deeper world than the everyday reality of education, marriage, amusement, or vying for wealth and social advantage. Perhaps this person is sick with life, while dreading that somehow, no matter every effort toward authenticity and meaning, she has failed to really live. Perhaps, like an urchin sampling forbidden candies, she will move from religion to religion, from way to way, in search of something that will satisfy her hunger. If she is lucky, eventually she will discover a way that is sweeter than the others, a system of disciplines with a pure living center. If she is very lucky, she will become a student of an Old Father, for the Fravashi system, despite many flaws, is the best of systems, the oldest and truest, the least corrupt. Whatever the chosen way, there will commence a period of fasting, meditation, dance forms, electronic simulation, prayer, attitudes, or word drugs—anything and everything to concentrate the student's attention on the seeming boundaries of her selfness. The object, of course, is to smash these boundaries as a thallow chick might break its way out of an egg. This is the first accomplishment of all seekers. One's worldview begins to crack and fall apart, and, more, to appear as an arbitrary construct. The student begins to see how she herself has constructed her own reality. If she is perceptive, she will see how she has constructed her very self. Inevitably, she will ask the questions: What *is* a self? What is a worldview? She will see all the prejudices, delusions, memories, psychic armoring, and little lies that protect the "I" from the outside world. Having gone this far, she may lose her sense of reality altogether. This is the dangerous moment. This is the time of heart flutters and flailing, of being lost in a dark room and unable to find the light key on the wall. It is a time for floating in fear, or worse, of falling alone into the cold inner ocean that pulls and chills and drowns. The student will feel herself dying; she will have a horrifying sense that every essential part of her is melting away into neverness. If she is weak, her terror of death will paralyze her or even plunge her into madness. But if she has courage, she will see that she is not really alone. Always, the Old Father remains close by her side. His smiles and his golden eyes remind her that he once made the same journey as she. His whole being is a mirror reflecting a single truth: that something great and beautiful will survive even as the student loses herself. The Old Father will help the student find this greater part of herself. This is his glory. This is his delight. He will help the student completely break through the worldview that traps her. And then, as the student cleans away the last slimy bits of eggshell, selfness, and certainty that cling to her, a vastly greater world opens before her. This world is brilliant with light and seems infinitely more real than she ever could have imagined. She, herself, is freer, vaster, profoundly alive. Intense feelings of joy and love overwhelm her. This is the eternal moment, the awakening that should set the student free on the path toward complete liberation. Only, it is here that most students fall into a subtle and deadly trap. Their joy of freedom becomes gratitude toward the Old Father for freeing them; their love of the real becomes attached to the one who made possible this experience of reality. Indeed, they cannot imagine ever making this journey again, by themselves, for themselves, and so their natural love of the Old Father becomes a needy and sickly thing. They begin to revere their Old Father, not as a mere guide or teacher, but as a mediator between themselves and the new world they have seen. And then it is but one small step to worshiping the Old Father as an incarnation of the infinite. Only through the Old Father (or through the roshi or priest or buddha) can the *real* reality be known. His every word is a sweet fruit bursting with truth; his system of teaching becomes the only way that this truth might be known. And so the student who has flown so high and so far comes at last to a new boundary, but nothing so well defined and fragile as her original worldview. She looks into her Old Father's eyes and beholds herself as vastened and holy, but sadly, this new sense of herself is something that he has created and grafted onto her. Her reality is now completely Fravashi. If she is truly aware—and truly valorous—she will try once more to break her way free. But the Fravashi worldview is sublime; escaping it is like a bird trying to break through the sky. Most students will fail to do so; in truth, most will never attempt such an act of ingratitude and rebellion. But even in failure, it is still their pride to soar above the swarms of humanity earthbound and closed in by their familiar and self-made horizons.

To be fair to the Fravashi, the Old Fathers have long recognized the dangers of guruism. They have done everything possible to discourage their students' slavish attachments to them. But the truth is, they *like* being gurus. And despite every warning, their students take solace in abandoning themselves and trusting their fates to a white-furred alien. In Old Father's house this was true of Salim and Michael and Ei Eleni, and of most of the others. It was especially true of Luister Ottah. As Old Father had said, he was a gentle man, a kind man, a living jewel among men—but he was not a man to return Old Father's sarcasm and jokes in the spirit with which they were offered. Luister composed koans and irreverent poems in Moksha out of duty only, because he was challenged to keep up a certain level of repartee. But he was really much happier simply drinking tea at Old Father's feet, while listening attentively and then parroting Old Father's views or words of wisdom. And there was no arguing with Luister once these views had been pronounced. Although Danlo liked Luister as much as anyone he'd met since coming to Neverness, during the short days of deep winter, he began to find him tiresome. Luister instructed Danlo in chess and etiquette and Moksha, as well as skating, and so Danlo found himself in his company more than he would have wished. Luister was somewhat of a polymath, and he enjoyed holding forth on every subject from Lavic architecture to causal decoupling to the journeys of the Tycho—or fenestration, or free will, or the dangers of ohrworms and information viruses. Unfortunately, however, none of his opinions or insights was his own. He had the irritating habit of prefacing his remarks with the phrase: "Old Father says that . . ." He seemed to have memorized every word that Old Father ever spoke. "Old Father says that buildings of organic stone tend toward the grandiloquent and have no place in human cities," he told Danlo one dark and snowy morning. And then later that night, "Old Father says that the greatest trick of religions is in saving people from infinite regresses. Consider the question: What caused the universe? The natural answer is that God caused the universe. Aha, but then one is tempted to ask: But what caused God? Ho, ho. And so on—do you see? Religions break the regress. They tell us this: *God* caused the universe, and God causes God, and this is all that anyone needs to know."

The closer Danlo penetrated to the heart of the Fravashi system, ironically, the more aware he became that in the city of Neverness, there were many other systems, many other ways. He began to wonder about these ways. Although he never forgot his hope of becoming a pilot, of journeying to Camilla Luz and Nonablinka and inward to the universe's center, he still had a half year to wait before he might be admitted to the Order. Of course, he might *not* be admitted to the Order, and then he would have to remain as Old Father's student. (Or return to one of the Alaloi tribes west of Kweitkel.) Because he couldn' imagine becoming like Luister Ottah—and because he was a hungry for experience as a wolf pup sniffing up nosefuls of new snow—he decided to spend the next two hundred days exploring certain worldviews that he found either fascinating or utterl strange. No rule or pronouncement of Old Father's forbad such exploration. In fact, Old Father often encouraged the don ning of different realities, but only as a formal game, played ou beneath the sound of chimes and chanting that echoed throug his house. Danlo suspected that *his* method of knowing differer ways would not meet the approval of the others, and so, durin his daily outings, he began to visit certain parts of the City secret.

During an unexpected lull in deep winter's cold, when th air was clear and the sky softened to a warm *falu* blue, Danl began to frequent the Street of Smugglers where it narrows be low the Fravashi District. There, he befriended men and wome of the autist sect, and he sat with them on lice-ridden furs, ar he spent whole days and nights lost in deep, lucid, commun

116

dreams, which the autist dream guides claim are the *real* reality, much more real than the material world of snow or rocks or the ragged clothes that the autists wrap around their emaciated bodies. Likewise he joined a group of mushroom eaters who called themselves the Children of God. Deep in the Farsider's Quarter, in secret ceremonies held inside one of the abandoned Cybernetic churches, he bowed before a golden urn heaped high with magic mushrooms and solemnly prayed before opening his mouth and taking the "Flesh of God" inside himself. He prayed, as well, to the shimmering emerald aliens who came to him during the most vivid of his mushroom visions. In truth, he came to worship these delightful and beguiling entities as messengers of the One God, that is, until he tired of worship altogether and sought out more sober (and sobering) experiences.

Sometime in midwinter spring, after Danlo had passed his fifteenth birthday with no more ceremony than a few prayers to his dead mother, he made contact with a group of men and women who called themselves the Order of True Scientists. Of course, there are many who consider themselves as scientists, or rather, as the intellectual heirs of Galileo and the Newton and others who began the great journey through the universe of number and reason. There are holists and logicians, complementarianists and mechanics and grammarians. There are practitioners of the Old Science and the faithful of the New Science of God. There are many, many sciences, almost as many as the hundreds of different sects of the Cybernetic Universal Church. As Danlo learned, the second greatest event in the intellectual history of the human race was the clading off of science into different schools, each with its own epistemology and set of beliefs, each one practicing its own methodology, each one with its own notion as to what science really *is*. There were those sciences that clove to metaphysical and epistemological realism and those that treated science as a grand, but ultimately meaningless game. Some sciences continued to rely on physical experiments to validate their theories while others used computers or pure mathematical theorems to probe the nature of reality. Individual sciences might resemble each other no more than a man does a Darghinni, but they all had at least one thing in common: each science claimed a privileged status and denigrated all others as inferior or false.

This was especially the way of the Order of True Scientists. Of all the cults that Danlo was to encounter during his stay in Neverness, this was the hardest for him to penetrate, the most

117

bizarre. As a prospective Scientist—the leaders of this quaint cult are always desperate to find new members and they will recruit almost anybody—Danlo was required to accept the doctrines of Scientism. To begin with, in front of seven master Scientists wearing their traditional white gowns, he had to make the Profession of Faith: that Science is not merely a tool for understanding or modeling reality, but the one path to truth. There was the Creed of Chance, that all phenomena in the universe are the result of bits of matter moving about and colliding, endlessly, randomly, meaninglessly. He learned the closely related Doctrine of Mechanism, that all things can be explained by reducing to the mechanisms of pieces of matter causing other pieces to move. Danlo, of course, as a child of the Alaloi, had always regarded the world and everything in it as holy. He had the greatest trouble, at first, in seeing rocks and trees and water as being composed of nothing more than atoms or quarks, bits of interchangeable stuff that were without purpose or life. The logic of this view almost demanded a certain kind of action: if matter was fundamentally dead, then there was nothing wrong with vexing and perturbing it until it yielded its secrets. The Scientists worshiped logic, and so the first duty of any scient man was to make experiments as to the nature of things. The ancient Scientists, he learned, once built machines the size of mountains (and later whole planets) in order to smash matter into ever tinier pieces, always looking for the tiniest piece, always in hope of discovering the ultimate cause of consciousness and all creation. Because they always discovered more questions than they did answers, they designed their experiments toward understanding the "how" of nature instead of the "why." In one of the first of these experiments, when the Scientists transmuted matter into pure energy and exploded the first atomic bomb they almost ignited the atmosphere of Old Earth. But their calculations told them that this would not happen, and they had faith in these calculations, and so life on Earth was spared for few more years.

To accept experiments and experimenting as a valid way c knowing reality—to accept that only that which can be measured is real—Danlo had to turn his thinking inside-out, t *whelve,* as the Fravashi say. He had to learn to regard the worl as an objective thing that he could understand only as an observer, studying events and phenomena from the outside looking in, much as a voyeur might peep through a window in hop of catching a man and woman engaged in love play. As he to

118

Old Father much later, after he had whelved once again and returned to his old thoughtways: "The Scientists study the effects of cold on an organism with thermocouples and theories, and they say they understand everything . . . that can be understood. But they do not really *know* cold. They seem never to have experienced it. And why not? It would be a simple experiment to perform, yes? All they need do is remove their gowns and walk outside in the snow."

He, himself, performed the experiments required of him only with difficulty. He disavowed any use of living animals, preferring instead, for example, to immerse himself in a bath of ice water during his experiments in the survival of cold. Some of the classical experiments he would never make, such as dissecting a snowworm's nervous system as a way of appreciating that animal's unique consciousness. He could never wholly consent to this kind of analysis, for during his passage on the mountain with Three-Fingered Soli he had made certain promises as an Alaloi man, and the Alaloi so love the world that if they chance to kick over a rock, they will replace it in its exact position in order to restore the world to *halla*. The truth is, he would have made a poor Scientist, and the masters of this cult must have mistrusted him from the beginning. But then, the Scientists mistrust everyone. Most peoples and other orders regard the Method of the Scientists as an outmoded and barbarous art, and they have done everything possible to suppress this cult. Because of long persecution, the Scientists automatically suspect new members of being spies sent to report on them. And so new members are tested in many ways before they are allowed access to secret information and secret experiments. Although Danlo never witnessed any of these illegal experiments, through a friend of a friend, he heard a rumor about one of them.

It seemed that in one of their buildings in the Darghinni District, deep underground in windowless, locked rooms, the Scientists were performing experiments on the embryos of various alien species. Apparently, one of the master Scientists was trying to cark Scutari blastulas into a shape more to his liking. In most animals, alien or earth type, the critical point in development is not the fertilization of the egg, but rather gastrulation. It is only during grastrulation, after the egg has divided and redivided many times and shaped itself into a hollow ball of cells called a blastula, that the development of organs, limbs, and other body parts begins. Some of the cells on the exterior of the blastula are destined to become eyes or wings or fibrillets; the

119

gut of most animals is typically formed in this manner: A group of cells on the blastula's surface begins to indent and push toward the ball's opposite side. The blastula deforms as if a finger were pushing into a balloon. Eventually, the group of cells will push completely through the other side, forming a hollow tube from a sphere. One end of the tube will be the mouth while the other will be the anus. Most animals are formed around such a digestive tube, with sheets of cells circling and contracting and branching out to make the rest of the body's tissues. But the Scutari are different. During the gastrulation of this species, the original group of cells never quite meets the opposite wall, and so the Scutari are shaped more like wine cups than tubes. It was an experiment of the Scientists to interfere with Scutari gastrulation, coaxing the blastulas that they had somehow acquired to develop more like sea urchins or Darghinni or even human beings. And so they had. They made many broods of doomed Scutari nymphs. While some of these nymphs, at first, were able to ingest food almost as continuously as a hungry harijan, the little monsters would eventually begin vomiting up their feces, and all of them fell mad or died. A few master Scientists had acclaimed this experiment a great advance in knowledge, as if they had somehow explained Scutari law or the gruesome Scutari face or the inexplicable mind of the Scutari adults. But Danlo could not see it in such a light. In fact, upon hearing that certain masters were dissecting living nymphs in order to ascertain the cause of their madness, he formally abjured his Profession of Faith and quit the Scientists. Although he never abjured Science itself—he would always cherish the cold, terrible glory of Science, and he would use this lens cautiously, like a polarized glass made for looking at the sun—he had finally discovered a limit to the ideal of complexity and the holding of different worldviews.

To enter into a new reality completely is not merely to cherish this reality or to perceive things in a new way, but to remake one's being and to act in accordance with new rules. However, not all worldviews are equal in truth, and not all acts are permissible. As to what the most truthful worldview might be, generations of philosophers and millennia of war have not decided the answer. The Fravashi teach that each worldview is true only relatively. Science gives a better picture of the universe's mechanistic aspects than does Hinduism, but has little to say about the nature of God. Many revere this teaching, only to fall into the trap of relativism: if all worldviews are in some way true

en nothing is really *true.* Danlo, at this time, like many others
efore him, might easily have descended into nihilism and de-
ied that there could ever be any real ground of truth. He might
ave concluded that *all* acts, even those of a criminal or mad-
an, are permitted. But he never fell into this kind of despair. It
as always his faith that a free human being, if he looked deeply
nough inside himself, would find a pure burning knowledge of
hat was true and what was not.

Whatever his criticisms of Science (or the other sciences
at he would encounter), the attempts of the Scientists to con-
ol what they defined as matter and energy fascinated him.
ven after he had left the Scientists, he harbored a fierce curios-
y about this control. From one of his friends who had remained
the cult, he learned the implications of the Doctrine of En-
opy, that the universe was falling into disorder, all configura-
ons of matter across the galaxies falling apart and spreading
ut like fat globules in a bowl of lukewarm soup, all of its ener-
ies running down and seeking an equal level, as waters run into
still lake from which they can never escape. The Scientists
reached absolute control over all of material reality, and yet
ey were doomsayers who pleaded helplessness in face of the
niverse's ultimate death. It was the great discovery of this
hase of Danlo's life that this disaster might not be merely
ords of doctrine or some impossibly distant event. The power
control matter and energy, to release the energy trapped in
atter, was very immediate, very serious, very real.

One evening at twilight, just before dinner, Danlo returned
Old Father's house in a state of intense agitation. He rushed
side with news of an unbelievable thing that he had learned
arlier from one of the Scientists. For most of the afternoon, he
ad been skating down near the dangerous Street of Smugglers,
ating and skating as he breathed in the musty smell of
oached shagshay furs and brooded about cosmic events. He
omped into Old Father's thinking chamber not even bothering
kick the ice from his boots. (He had remembered to eject the
ate blades only after stumbling across the doorway and grind-
g steel, chipping the square blue tiles in the outer hallway.)
Ni luria la!" he shouted, lapsing into his milk tongue. And
en, "Sir, I have learned the most *shaida* thing, *shaida* if it is
ue, but . . . O blessed God! how can it be true? About the
essed—"

"Ho, careful now! Careful you don't drip water all over my
other's carpet!" Old Father caught him with both of his eyes,

121

looked at the snowmelt running down Danlo's boots, and sho
his head. Like all Fravashi, he revered pure water and consid
ered it somewhat sacrilegious to scatter such a holy substanc
over his mother's woven fur. That evening, he was engaged in
thinking session with one of his students. Across from him o
his carpet (very near the spot where Danlo had once vomited
sat Fayeth, a good-looking woman with a quick smile and a
even quicker tongue toward making jokes. She had come to Ol
Father's house after a long search, after spending years as
student of Zanshin and the Way of the Rose. She was the best o
Old Father's twelve students, the kindest, and the least slavish
and Danlo was a little in love with her. But her age was mor
than twice his, and she had taken a vow of strict celibacy. Eve
so, she never resented his attentions; she didn't seem to mind a
all that he had interrupted her time with Old Father.

"Danlo," she said, "please sit with us and tell us what
blessed."

"You're early," Old Father said to Danlo out of one half o
his mouth. "But, yes, please sit down. Take your boots off an
sit down." And then, from his mouth's left side, at the sam
time, he continued speaking to Fayeth: "We must try somethin
more difficult this time, perhaps something that humans kno
very well when thinking about it but find impossible to explain.

They were playing with realities; specifically, they wer
playing a game called spelad in which Fayeth, prompted by
hint from Old Father, would name some object, idea, personag
historical movement, or phenomenon. Old Father would the
choose a particular worldview, which Fayeth was required t
enter. She would behold the named object through th
worldview, describing its various aspects as if she had been bor
a tychist or a Buddhist or even an alien. Points were score
according to her knowledge, her sense of shih, and above all h
mastery of plexity.

"I'll name a concept this time," Fayeth said. She smiled a
Danlo and continued, "And the concept is: the future."

"Oh, but this is not precise enough," Old Father said. "D
you know the doctrine of the sarvam asti?"

"The Hindu doctrine or that of the scryers?"

"It's your choice," Old Father said.

"Then I'll choose the scryer's doctrine."

"Very well. Then let me choose a worldview. Aha, abid
with me a moment." Old Father looked at Danlo knowingl
then turned to Fayeth and said, "I choose the view of the scier

tists. Aha, aha—and to make this more difficult, the *ancient* scientists. Before the mechanics and holists split off from them to form their own arts."

Danlo had never heard of the sarvam asti: the doctrine that everything exists, past and future, because the mind, at the moment of conceiving all things, could not do so if they didn't exist. In truth, at that moment, he didn't care about games or doctrines because he had discovered the existence of a terrible thing that he could barely conceive of. He tried to sit patiently across from Old Father, but at last he blurted out, "Sir, the blessed stars are exploding! Why didn't you tell me about this?"

"Ah, ah, the stars," Old Father said. "We must certainly consider the stars. But do you mind if I play the spelad with Fayeth? She's scored nearly enough points to be excused from cooking next season's dinners."

So saying, Old Father continued his dual conversation, talking in two different voices at once. The first (or right-hand voice) was his usual melodious baritone; the second voice was high and raspy, as of a saw cutting through ice. Danlo struggled to separate the dual stream of words that spilled out of Old Father's adroit mouth. It was a confusing way to hold a conversation, and it demanded his intense concentration. "Oh ho, Fayeth, you might begin by exploring the intersection of the ontic realm and platonic space. Oh, Danlo, the stars are exploding, you say? The existence arguments and suchlike. This has been known for some time. Space is space and the stars go on endlessly through space only—"

"Sir," Danlo interrupted, "people are killing the stars!"

"Ah, oh, oh, oh," Old Father said. Then he lifted a finger toward Fayeth and smiled. "You may begin."

Fayeth hesitated a moment before saying: "The sarvam asti states that the future, in every future, the possibilities are actualized through an act of will, and—"

"Oh, oh, Danlo, you've learned of the Vild, so it's so. The Vild, the far part of the galaxy where a million stars are exploding, or ten million stars—and why?"

"—because existence cannot be understood as other than quantities of matter distributed throughout a homogeneous space and—"

"Because human beings have a need to deform space," Old Father said. "And for other reasons."

While Old Father had been talking with Danlo, Fayeth had transformed herself into something like a scientist (or Scientist), and was continuing to hold forth about the future: "—can be an intersection of these two spaces only in mathematics which—"

"*Shaida* reasons," Danlo said.

"—certainly the mind can conceive of things that have no existence in spacetime—"

"Oh ho," Old Father said to Fayeth, "but what is mind?"

"When I was a child," Danlo said, "I used to think . . . that the stars were the eyes of my ancestors."

"—runs parallel programs, and reality represented by symbols—"

"The stars . . . this splendid eyelight."

"—is not reflected in the natural world, nor is the world really reflected in mind—"

At this, Old Father shut his eyes for a moment and said, "Be careful about this word 'reflect.' "

"But stars are . . . just hydrogen plasma and helium," Danlo said. "Easy to fusion into light."

"—processing information, but macroscopic information decays to microscopic information, and therefore the future—"

Old Father said to Danlo, "To understand the Vild, we will have to discuss the Architects and *their* doctrines of the future."

"—the future is completely determined but unknowable because—"

"It is the Architects who have created the Vild, yes?"

"—the creation of information is a chaotic process and—"

"The *shaida* Vild."

"—there is no way for the process to run any faster than time itself."

Here both Danlo and Old Father paused in their conversation while Fayeth criticized the many-worlds hypothesis of the mechanics and went on to declare that there could be only one timeline, one reality, one future. The scryers' doctrine, she said, was completely false. If scryers happened to foretell the future, this was only pure chance. The scryers were great deluders, and worse, they were firebrands who incited false hopes in the many swarms and caused the people to believe impossibilities. Scryers should be silenced for their violations of truth. "They should be collared or banished," Fayeth said. Her face was hard and grim, and she seemed utterly serious. "Or their brains should be cleansed of their delusions, as was done on Arcite before the Order interfered. All scryers who—"

"Ho, ho, that will be enough!" Old Father said. "A scientist, indeed."

At this, Fayeth breathed deeply and relaxed as she returned to her usual good humor. She folded her hands on her lap, waiting for Old Father's approval.

"You've done well—forty points at least. Ha, ho, there will be no kitchen work for you until next false winter."

"Thank you," she said.

"And now," Old Father said as he turned to Danlo, "we must discuss the Vild. And what better place to begin than the Doctrine of Totality. Ah, ho, Fayeth, you might want to hear this, too."

Because it was cold in the thinking chamber, Danlo zipped his collar tight around his throat and sat next to Fayeth as he listened to Old Father's remarkable story. Old Father told them of Nikolos Daru Ede, the first human being to become a god by carking his mind into a computer. The idea that a man could transfer into a machine the pattern of his brain—his personality, memories, consciousness, his very soul—astonished Danlo. Try as he may, he could never quite believe that one's selfness could be encoded as a computer program. It amused him to think of someone incarnating as a machine, even a godly computing machine that could think a billion times faster than any man. Who could ever know what had really happened to Nikolos Daru Ede when he had become vastened in this impossible way? Of course, many billions of people believed they knew quite well. As Old Father explained, humanity's largest religion had arisen from this singular event. Followers of Ede worshiped this god as God, and they called themselves the Architects of God. Two thousand years ago, the Architects had fought a great war among themselves and had schismed into two halves: the Architects of the Infinite Intelligence of the Cybernetic Universal Church—which most people called simply the Old Church—and their enemies, the Cybernetic Reformed Churches. Everyone knew that the Reformed Churches had won this war, but few knew that Architects of the Old Church, after their defeat, had fled into the unknown spaces of the galaxy that would someday become the Vild. According to Old Father, the Architects of the Old Church had probably created the Vild. As was now known, these Architects had a plan for totally remaking the universe according to the design of Ede the God, and so they were demolishing the planets and the stars, one by one. "Ah oh, what is the Vild but stars and stars that human beings have exploded into supernovas? Some say it is hell of dead stars two trillion cubic light-years in volume. A region of stars and space ripping

· 125

open the galaxy like a lightning bolt. Oh ho, the Vild, the Vild—what is to be done about this cosmic lightning that men call the Vild?"

"What . . . can be done?" Danlo asked.

"Who really knows? Eleven years ago, Mallory Ringess sent a mission to the Vild. Oh, oh, but the mission failed. It's the talk of the City: why the Vild mission failed and how to organize another."

Old Father went on to speak of the Doctrine of Totality and other eschatological doctrines of the Edic religion of the Architects. He tried to elucidate the Architect view of free will and the fate of the universe. Danlo was so enthralled by this story that he almost forgot he was sitting next to Fayeth. His thoughts fell deep and troubled, and he looked up at the dome covering the thinking chamber. Two days ago it had snowed, and lovely white feathers of spindrift were frozen around the dome's western quadrant; but to the north and east, where the dome was clear, there were stars. His heart beat a hundred times as he studied the milky glare of the *blinkans*, Nonablinka and Shurablinka. "These strange stars," he said. "I have always wondered about these stars. They are supernovas, yes?"

"Oh, yes, supernovas, indeed," Old Father said.

"But they were once stars . . . just like other stars."

"This is true."

"Stars like . . . our sun."

"Yes, Danlo."

"But . . . how is it possible to kill the stars, sir?"

For a while Old Father spoke of the Architects and their strange technologies, machines that could generate streams of invisible graviphotons and shoot them into the sun. He talked about ways to deform the smooth black tissues of spacetime, to collapse the core of a star into a ball of plasma so hot and so dense that it instantly rebounded in a cosmic explosion of light. Danlo, with his hands pressed together beneath his chin, listened raptly. Then, without warning, he sprang to his feet and flung his arms upward toward the night sky. "Light is faster than a diving goshawk—this I have learned. Faster than the wind. The light from the *blinkans,* from the supernovas that the Architects have made, this *shaida* light races across the galaxy, yes. The killing light. It races, eleven million miles each minute, but . . . relatively, it creeps like a snowworm across the endless ice. Because the blessed galaxy is so vast. There is a *blinkan*—Merripen's Star, it is called. A supernova recently born. Soon

126

its light will reach this world, I think, and we will all burn. Then I and you and everyone will go over."

Slowly, painfully, puffing with caution and care, Old Father stood up. He rested a heavy hand on Danlo's shoulders, and his black claws clicked together. He pointed at a starless patch of sky east of Shurablinka. There, glowing circles of light rippled deep in their changing colors of tangerine and gold. "Do you see it?" he asked.

"The *Fara Gelastei*," Danlo said. "The Golden Flower—it has grown recently, yes?"

"We call it the Golden Ring. And yes, it has grown. So, it's so: six years ago, Mallory Ringess becomes a god, and the Golden Ring mysteriously appears in the heavens. It's life, of course! New life floating along the currents of space, feeding off of light. Exhaling diatomic oxygen and ozone and photoreflective gases. An extension of the biosphere. A new layer of atmosphere. A great golden ring of life—like a seed!—growing. There's hope that this ring will shield Neverness from the radiation and light of the supernovas. Ah, ah—and not just Neverness. Above many worlds, all through the galaxy, there are rings of gold. Perhaps a million new rings. It's hoped that the Golden Rings of all the worlds will protect people from the light of the Vild. Like a million golden umbrellas, it will shield us so that minds like yours might remain alive to ask: When will I be devoured by light?"

Fayeth, who was still sitting on the carpet, let loose a long, low whistle, the kind of disapproving sound that the Fravashi emit when they have caught one of their students falling into a belief system. She seemed delighted to point out Old Father's error, and she said, "It's not really known if the Golden Ring will protect us."

"Ah, ha, very good, this is true," Old Father said. "Not even the biologists have been able to project the Ring's rate of growth."

"I've heard many people talking of abandoning our planet," Fayeth said.

"Ah, oh, but the light from the supernova won't reach Neverness for thirteen more years. There's time enough to wait and see."

A bell rang then, the dinner bell summoning them to a typically simple meal of bread, cheese, and a fruit, probably fresh snow apples or icy cold Yarkona plums. Old Father and

Fayeth made ready to leave the thinking chamber, but Danlo remained near its center, staring up at the sky.

"What do you see?" Old Father asked.

For a moment Danlo kept his silence, and then he said, "The blessed stars. The . . . *shaida* stars. I never thought that anything could kill the stars."

Soon after this, Danlo began associating himself with a cult known as the Returnists. This was the newest of the City's cults, founded by a renegade scryer named Elianora Wen. She was a remarkable woman who had been born into one of the musical clans on Yarkona. When she was ten years old, her family brought her to Neverness, where she had thrilled the aficionados of Golden Age music with her mastery of the gosharp, flute, and other instruments. She might have had a long career as a music master, but she had stunned her family by renouncing everything to join the Order. She was strong-willed, thoughtful, provocative, quirky, and possessed of immaculate sensibilities, and so she had managed to win a position as a novice at Borja. Eventually, she had blinded herself and become a scryer, one of the finest, only to quit the Order at the time of the Pilot's War. For thirteen years, she had frequented the better hotels and cafés near the Street of Embassies, drinking Summerworld coffees and eating kurmash, and making friends with everyone she could. By the time Danlo came to the City, she knew ten thousand people by name and twenty thousand more by the sound of their voices. She became quite popular as a reader of futures, though she scandalized the traditionalists by accepting money for her services. It was said that she gave all her money to the hibakusha hospices, but her fame and influence was based not on her generosity but upon a series of visions that had come to her on the ninety-ninth night of deep winter of the preceding year. In her reading of her own future, in a moment of blinding revelation, she had come at last into her calling, which was to prepare the people for the godhood of Mallory Ringess. This she had done, with all her considerable powers. The Returnists soon numbered in the hundreds, and they all believed—and preached—that Mallory Ringess would return to Neverness. He would save the Order from corruption and divisiveness, just as he would save the City from the panic over the coming supernova. It was the glory of the Ringess to cause the quickening of the Golden Ring, to watch over its growth, and thus to save the planet from the fury of the Vild. Someday, according to the

Returnists, Mallory Ringess would stop the stars from exploding and save the universe from its ultimate fate.

During the long, sunny days of false winter, Danlo frequented the cafés along the Old City Glissade, drinking toalache tea with the Returnists who gathered there each afternoon for refreshment and conversation. The Returnists were mostly young Ordermen, joined by a few wealthy farsiders who wore rich clothes and golden bands around their heads as a token of their devotion. They liked to talk about the life of Mallory Ringess, and they liked to speculate as to the changes that a god might bring to their city. It was their hope that the Ringess would recognize them as true seekers and explain to them the mystery of the Elder Eddas and other secrets that only a god might understand.

One day, while talking with a woman named Sarah Turkmanian and various of her friends, Danlo learned that Mallory Ringess had once journeyed to the Alaloi tribe known as the Devaki. Nearly seventeen years previously, he had made this journey in the hope of discovering the secret of the Elder Eddas embroidered into the primitive Alaloi chromosomes. This news astonished Danlo. He immediately guessed that he was Mallory Ringess's son. Three-Fingered Soli had told him that his blood father was a pilot of the City, but he had never suspected that his father might also be a god. And his mother was surely one of the women who had accompanied Mallory Ringess on his ill-fated expedition, perhaps even Katharine the Scryer, and Danlo wanted to share this astonishing hypothesis with the other Returnists, but he was unsure if it was really true. Perhaps, he thought, Three-Fingered Soli had told him a polite lie concerning his true parentage. Perhaps his mother and father were really wormrunners, common criminals poaching shagshay furs from Kweitkel's forests. Perhaps his mother had given birth to him far from the City, only to abandon him to die on some snowy ledge near the Devaki cave. It was possible that Haidar and Chandra had found him and adopted him, and it was very possible that Soli had told him a false story to spare him the shame of such an ignoble birth. Because Danlo had a keen desire to learn the truth about himself—and because he loved hearing any story told about the mysterious Mallory Ringess—Danlo joined the Returnists for tea and companionship and wild speculations, and he sat with them as often as he could.

It is hard to know what the future of this cult would have been if Elianora Wen hadn't delivered her famous prophecy of

129

the eleventh of false winter. In the great circle outside the Hofgarten, she stood serene and grave in her immaculate white robe and announced to the City that the return of Mallory Ringess was imminent. He would return to Neverness in nine more days, on twentieth night. The wounded hibakusha in their tenements should rejoice, for Mallory Ringess would restore them to health. The wormrunners and other criminals should flee the City or else Mallory Ringess would judge them and execute them for their crimes. Above all, she said, the lords and masters of the Order should humble themselves, for Mallory Ringess would return as Lord of Lords, and he would remake the Order into an army of spiritual warriors who would restore the galaxy to its splendor.

Given the mistrust of people toward scryers and their secret art, the effect of Elianora's prophecy was somewhat amazing. Many wormrunners did in fact leave Neverness at this time; not a few merchants gave all their wealth and worldly possessions to the hibakusha and went to live together as dedicated Returnists in the free hostels of the Old City; and most amazing of all, six lords of the Academy renounced their positions to protest the political maneuvering that had so weakened the Order. At dusk on twentieth night, Elianora led nine hundred women and men of her cult up the lower slopes of Urkel to await the return of Mallory Ringess. "He will appear this night," Elianora had told everyone. Not only Returnists but many others came to see if this prophecy proved true. To Danlo, sitting in a meadow with the other Returnists, it seemed that half the City had turned out. Before it fell dark and the stars came out, he counted some eighty thousand people spread out on Urkel's slopes. From the eastern edge of the Academy down around to the Hollow Fields, where the hills flattened out just south of the mountain, they laid out their furs on the snowy rocks and passed around bottles of toalache or wine. The Returnists, of course, held a central position slightly higher than everyone else. Below them the city of Neverness sparkled with a million lights; above their encampment on the mountain, the dark ice fields and ridge lines gave way to the blackness of nearspace, and the sky was brilliant with starlight. Elianora had not said how Mallory Ringess would return from the stars. Some hoped that he would fall to earth like a meteor, or even materialize out of the air and walk among them. But most expected that his famous lightship, the *Immanent Carnation,* would appear in the heavens like a flash of silver and glide down to the waiting runs of the Hollow Fields. Then

Mallory Ringess would climb out of his ship and ascend the mountain like any other man, though in truth, no one knew if he would still look like a man. No one knew what a god was supposed to look like, and so the swarms of people drank their toalache and talked about the purposes of evolution, and they waited.

Danlo waited, too, no less excited than any Returnist. Like the others, he wore a glowing golden band around his head; he wore his best racing kamelaika, and on his face, he wore the lively, longing look of one who expected to be touched by the infinite. He sat not within the first circle of Elianora's followers, nor even in the second, but on the outer edge of this group, by a little stream running fast and full with melted snow. It was a warm, clear night of mountain winds and ageless dreams, and it would be a short night as false winter nights always are. But measured by the minds of the manswarm eager to behold a miracle, the night was long indeed. Danlo lay back against the cold earth, counting his heartbeats as he tried to count the thousands of stars burning through the night. It was a game he liked to play, but a game he could never win because there were too many stars and the sky never held still. Always the world turned into the east, turning its cold face to the deeps of the galaxy and to the greater universe beyond. Always, above the curve of the eastern horizon, new lights appeared, the *blinkans* and the constellations and the lone, blue giant stars. He lay there waiting and sometimes dreaming, listening to random bits of conversation that fell out of the mouths of the people nearby. All through the night, people made their way up from the City, and the crowds around him began to thicken. Near midnight, a few of the weary ones folded up their furs and abandoned their vigil. With every hour that passed, the people's mood shifted from anticipation to grim faith to uneasiness, and then into an ugly suspicion that somehow they had been fooled. When the great Swan constellation rose above Urkel's dark ridge line, Danlo knew that the sun could not be far behind. He, too, had begun to doubt Elianora's prophecy—at least he doubted the wisdom of taking her words literally. He was searching the tired faces of his fellow Returnists for despair when, one by one, everyone stopped talking and looked down the narrow, rocky path that wound up the mountain. For a moment there was a vast, unnerving silence, and then someone cried out: "Look, it is he!"

Danlo looked down into the dark path to see a tall figure making his way across the stunt spruce and the snowfields. Like

131

everyone else, he hoped that it was Mallory Ringess, but his eyes were used to looking for animals in dark forests, and he could see what others could not. Immediately he recognized this latecomer as a Fravashi alien, and then moments later, from the tufts of fur below the ears and his arthritic gait, he saw that it was Old Father. As Old Father climbed higher up the path, this sobering fact became apparent to everyone else. There were many groans of disappointment; this sound broke from the lips of a thousand people with the suddenness of ice cracking from a glacier and falling into the sea. As if they had come to a sudden understanding, people began standing up and leaving. They brushed past Old Father without a glance, not even bothering to notice his strange smile or his golden eyes burning through the darkness. Old Father walked through the manswarm straight toward the spot where Danlo sat. He greeted Danlo politely, and then, in his most playful and sadistic voice, he asked, "Ho, am I too late?"

Danlo looked at the sudden flood of people going down the mountain, and he said, "Perhaps."

"Ah, oh, it's nearly dawn. I'd heard that Mallory Ringess would appear before dawn."

"The whole city must have heard of Elianora's vision," Danlo said.

"Even we Fravashi," Old Father said. "But I wanted to see for myself."

"But, sir, how did you find me here? There are so many people."

Old Father pointed his black claw at the circles of Returnists still sitting around Elianora Wen. Even as Danlo did, they all wore templets around their heads, and these nine hundred luminescent bands cast halos of golden light into the black air. "I followed the glow," Old Father said. "You can see it a long way off. And then as I came closer, I followed your scent. It's unique and quite strong, you know."

Danlo bent his head to sniff his clothes, and he said, "I did not know the Fravashi had such keen noses."

"Ha, ha, you smell like a wolf who has rolled in musk grass. Have you considered bathing more frequently?"

"I . . . do bathe," Danlo said. "I love the water."

"Ah, ha, but you haven't bathed since you began dreaming with the autists, have you?"

"You know about the Dreamers, sir?"

Old Father said nothing but simply smiled at him.

"Then you must know . . . about the Scientists as well?"

"Oh, ho, I *do* know."

"These blessed worldviews," Danlo said. "These ways of seeing."

"Ah, oh, oh, ah," Old Father said. "This is a city of cults, isn't it?"

"But I have left the Dreamers," Danlo said. "I have left the Scientists, too."

"So, it's so."

"You taught me, sir. How to free myself from any worldview."

"But now you wear the templet and sit with the Returnists?"

"You are worried that I will become bound to this way . . . because it promises so much, yes?"

Old Father motioned toward the men and women sitting close to them, murmuring words of exhausted hope as they looked up at the sky. "*This* cult? Oh, no, no, no—when dawn comes and Mallory Ringess has failed to return, the Returnists will be no more. If I seem worried—and I must tell you that it's nearly impossible for a Fravashi to worry—it's only because you seem to love all cults too well."

With his little finger Danlo touched the glowing templet tight against his forehead, and he asked, "But what better way . . . to know these ways?"

"Well, there is the spelad, of course. Someday you may play this as well as Fayeth. Ah, ho, the whole Fravashi system."

"Spelad is a clever game," Danlo said. "But it is only a game."

"Ah, ah?"

Danlo held out his hand. In the light of his templet, his fingernails glowed yellow-orange. He suddenly curled his fingers toward his palm, making a loose fist. He said, "The Fravashi teach their students to hold any worldview lightly, as they would a butterfly, yes?"

"To hold a reality lightly is to change realities easily," Old Father said. "How else may one progess from the simplex to the higher stages of plexity?"

"But, sir, your students, Fayeth and Luister, the others— they hold most realities *too* lightly. They never really *know* the realities they hold."

"Ho, ho, do you think you understand the beliefs of science

more completely than Fayeth does? And the other belief systems as well?"

"No, sir."

"Then I'm afraid that *I* don't understand."

There was a half smile on Old Father's face, and Danlo thought that he was being only half truthful with him.

"There is a difference," Danlo said, "between knowledge and belief."

"Ah ho, aha," Old Father said.

Danlo turned to face the east, where the sky showed blue with the day's first light. It would be some time before the sun rose, but already the horizon was stained with tones of ocher and glowing red. Many of the Returnists were looking in this direction, too. Elianora stood up and somehow oriented herself toward the coming dawn. Like all scryers she was blind, and more, her eyepits were scooped hollows as black as space. Perhaps she was waiting to feel the heat of the sun's rays against her cheeks. If she was chagrined or shamed that her prophecy was about to prove false, she gave no sign.

"Do you see this lovely scryer?" Danlo said. He dropped his voice to a near whisper and moved closer to Old Father. "Before she blinded herself, she had eyes as I have. As we do. She could see all the colors of the world. But . . . what if she had been born eyeless, just as she is now. What if she had been blind from birth, like the hibakusha babies? How could she know that blood is the reddest of all the reds? How could she see the colors of the sunrise? When you look at the sky, sir, do you say, 'I believe in blueness'? No, you do not, not unless you are blind. You see the blessed blue, and so you know it. Don't you see? We do not need to believe . . . that which we know."

"Ah, ho, knowing," Old Father said. "So, it's so."

"Fayeth may understand the beliefs of Science better than I," Danlo said. "But she'll never know Science . . . until she has seen a snowworm sliced into a hundred segments while it is still alive."

"Would you expect me to subject all my students to such atrocities?"

"To be truly complex . . . yes. The other students play the spelad, and they think they know what it is like to move from reality to reality. But it is not really . . . *real,* to them. When they enter a new worldview . . . they are like old men wading in a hot spring. Half in, half out, never completely wet or dry."

Now the sky was flaming crimson, and the air was lighter,

and the trees and boulders across the mountain were beginning to take on the colors of morning. Of all the people who had climbed Urkel during the night, only the Returnists remained. And now most of these were leaving because their belief in the return of Mallory Ringess had been broken. This, Danlo thought, was the essential difference between belief and knowledge. Knowledge could only intensify into deeper knowledge, whereas belief was as fragile as glass. Hundreds of red-eyed people muttered to themselves as they cast betrayed looks at Elianora and turned their backs to her without bidding her farewell. They left behind forty-eight men and women who knew something they did not. Danlo knew it, too, but he could hardly explain this knowledge to Old Father. He knew that, in some sense, Mallory Ringess *had* returned to Neverness that night. There had indeed been a god upon the mountain—Danlo had only to remember the wistful looks on eighty thousand faces to know that this was so. Because of Elianora's prophecy, something in the City had changed, irrevocably, and something new had been born. Old Father was wrong to suppose that the movement she had begun would simply evaporate like dew drops under a hot sun.

Old Father, who was always adept at reading people's thought shadows, studied Dano's face, then said, "You never really believed Mallory Ringess would return, did you?"

"I do not want to believe anything," Danlo said. "I want to know . . . everything."

"Ha, ha, not an insignificant ambition. You're different than my other students—they merely desire liberation."

"And yet they are so . . . unfree."

Old Father's eyes opened wide, and he said, "How so?"

"Because they think they have found a system . . . that will free them."

"Haven't they?"

"The Fravashi system . . . is the one reality they hold tightly. And it holds them even more tightly."

"Do you have so little respect for our way, then?"

"Oh, no, sir, I have loved this way very well, it is only . . ."

Old Father waited a moment, then said, "Please continue."

Danlo looked down at the stream bubbling through the trees nearby. He said, "The virtue of the Fravashi system is in freeing us from systems, yes?"

"This is true."

"Then shouldn't we use this very system . . . to free ourselves from the Fravashi way?"

"Ah, ah," Old Father said as he shut both his eyes. "Oh, oh, oh, oh."

"I must . . . free myself from this way," Danlo said.

"Ohhh!"

"I must leave your house before it is too late."

"So, then—it's so."

"I am sorry, sir. You must think me ungrateful."

Old Father opened his eyes, and his mouth broke into a smile. "No, I've never thought that. A student repays his master poorly if he always remains a student. I've known for some time you would leave."

"To enter the Order, yes?"

"Ho, ho, even if the Order were to reject you, you still must leave. All my students leave me when they've learned what you've learned."

"I am . . . sorry," Danlo said.

"Oh, ho, but *I'm* not sorry," Old Father said. "You've learned well, and you've pleased me well, better than I could say unless I say it in Fravash."

Danlo looked down to see that his fellow Returnists were beginning to break their encampment, packing up their furs and baskets of food. One of them, a young horologe from Lara Sig, told Danlo that it was time to hike back to the City.

"Perhaps we should say good-bye now," Old Father said.

Danlo glanced at Elianora, standing silently in the snow as she held her face to the morning sky. The other Returnists swarmed around her, talking softly, and one of them offered his arm for the journey back down the mountain.

"In five more days," Danlo said, "I shall begin the competition. If the Order accepts me, may I still visit you, sir?"

"No, you may not."

Now Danlo froze into silence, and he was scarcely aware of the other Returnists leaving him behind.

"These are not *my* rules, Danlo. The Order has its own way. No novice or journeyman may sit with a Fravashi. We're no longer trusted—I'm sorry."

"Then—"

"Then you may visit me after you've become a full pilot."

"But that will be years!"

"Then we must be patient."

"Of course," Danlo said, "I might fail the competition."

"That's possible," Old Father said. "But the real danger to you is in succeeding, not failing. Most people love the Order too completely and find it impossible to leave once they've entered it."

"But they haven't been students of a Fravashi Old Father, I think."

"No, that's true."

"I must know what it is to be a pilot," Danlo said. "A blessed pilot."

"Ho, ho, it's said that the pilots know the strangest reality of all."

Danlo smiled then, and bowed to Old Father. "I must thank you for everything you have given me, sir. The Moksha language, the ideals of ahimsa and shih. And your kindness. And my shakuhachi. These are splendid gifts."

"You're welcome, indeed." Old Father looked down the path where the last of the Returnists were disappearing into the forest. He said, "Will you walk back to the City with me?"

"No," Danlo said. "I think I will stay and watch the sunrise."

"Ah, ho, I'm going home to bed, then."

"Good-bye, sir."

"Good-bye, Danlo the Wild. I'll see you soon."

Old Father reached over to touch Danlo's head, and then he turned to walk home. It took him a long time to make his way down the mountain, and Danlo watched him as long as he could. At last, when he was alone with the wind and the loons singing their morning song, he faced east to wait for the sun. In truth, although he never told this to anyone, he was still waiting for Mallory Ringess. It was possible that this god was only late, after all, and Danlo thought that somebody should remain to greet him if he returned.

PART 2

Borja

THE CULLING

The starting point of Architect—or Edic—understanding is the recognition that God is created after the image of man. This idea views man and God as joined with one another through a mysterious connection. Man, out of hubris, wanted an image formed of himself as a perfected and potentially infinite God. In that man is reflected in God, he makes himself a partner in this self-realization. Man and God belong so closely to one another that one can say that they are intended for each other. Man finds his fulfillment in God.

—Encyclopaedia Britannica, *1,754th Edition,* Tenth Revised Standard Version

On the twenty-fifth day of false winter, in the year 2947 since the founding of the Order, the annual Festival of the Unfortunate Petitioners was held at Borja College. This is the first of the Order's colleges, and it occupies much of the Academy, which is really a separate city within the city of Neverness. At the very eastern edge of Neverness, pushed up against the mountains, is a square mile of dormitories, towers, halls, and narrow red glidderies crisscrossing the well-tended grounds. A high granite wall (it is called the Wounded Wall because part of its southern face was once destroyed by the blast of a hydrogen bomb) surrounds the Academy on three sides; it separates the Academy's spacious buildings from the densely arrayed spires and apartments of the Old City. There is no wall along the eastern grounds of the Academy. Or rather, the mountains, Urkel and Attakel, rise up so steeply as to form a beautiful, natural wall of ice and rock.

Some students rail at such enforced isolation from the dirty more organic city life, but most others find comfort in the company of like minds rather than loneliness or alienation or despair.

On this crisp, clear morning, at dawn, Danlo skated through the city streets until he came to the Wounded Wall. There, outside the wall's West Gate, on a narrow red gliddery, he waited with the other petitioners who had come to enter the Academy. Danlo was one of the first to arrive, but in little time, as the sun filled the sky, thousands of girls and boys (and quite a few of their parents) from most of the Civilized Worlds began lining up behind him. For blocks in any direction, the side-streets giving onto the Wounded Wall overflowed with would-be students wearing parkas, kimonos, ponchos, furgowns, chukkas, sweaters, babris, cowl jackets, and kamelaikas, garments of every conceivable cut and material. Many of the petitioners were impatient; they grumbled and muttered obscenities as they queued up waiting for the great iron gates to open.

"We're early," someone behind Danlo said. "But you'd think they would let us come in out of the cold."

Danlo examined the wall surrounding the Academy. It was as high as three tall men, and it was seamed with cracks and covered with sheets of grayish lichen. He had always loved climbing rocks, so he wondered if he could find a handhold in the cut blocks and pull himself up and over. Why, he wondered, would anyone want to build a wall inside a city?

"It's cold on this damn world—my tutors never told me it would be so cold."

At last the gates opened inward, and the petitioners slowly filed onto one of the main slidderies cutting through the Academy. Behind Danlo there was much grumbling and shouting, pushing and shoving, especially at those intersections where it was not clear how the lines should merge. In several places fights broke out. Most of these fights were short, clumsy affairs of cursing, flailing fists, and hurried apologies when the combatants were pulled apart. Inside the gate, however, there was order. Scores of Borja novices, in their official, white robes, quickly separated the girls from the boys and led them in groups to various buildings around the Academy.

Danlo—along with two thousand other boys—was led across the high professionals' college, Lara Sig, to a large hemispherical structure called the Ice Dome. Inside the Ice Dome were figure rings, sled courts, and ice fields on which was played that murderously fast game known as hokkee. That morning, however, the ice fields were empty of skaters; for hundreds of yards across the ice fields, beneath the curving, triangular panes of the dome, the novices had stacked many bundles of worn white robes. Next to each bundle was a heap of sandals of varying sizes. The sandals were paired, left foot to right, tied together around the toe thongs with a single white ribbon. Danlo smelled old wool and the rancid thickness of leather stained with human sweat. One of the elder novices—he was actually the Head Novice, Sahale Featherstone, a tall boy with a shaved head and a serious face—directed Danlo and the others each to choose a robe and a pair of sandals. "Listen, now, listen," the novice said to a group of boys standing nearby. "You must remove all your clothes and put on the petitioner's robe."

"But it's too damn cold in here!" an unhappy boy next to Danlo protested. "Are we supposed to stand barefoot on ice while we rummage through a bunch of stinking old shoes? Our damned feet will freeze!"

The Head Novice ignored him, as did most of the other boys; at least, they did not pay him obvious attention. Few were pleased at having to strip naked in such a chill, open place, but neither did most of them want to be singled out as complainers. The boys did as they were told. The air was suddenly full of sound: zippers being pulled open, the swish of woven fabrics, clacking skates, and the buzz of a thousand voices. It was cold enough inside the Dome to steam the breath; everywhere Danlo looked, puffs of silvery vapor escaped from trembling lips and vanished into the air. Novices went among the naked boys, collecting clothes and skates and giving each of them a number in return. "Your number is 729," a pimply novice said as he wrapped Danlo's jacket around his skates and tied the bundle together. "You must remember this number to reclaim your clothes after the competition." He didn't explain that new clothes would be given to those few who were admitted to Borja. Plainly, he did not expect Danlo to be among the chosen.

Soon, all the boys were naked, and many were shivering, their brown or white or black skins stippled with goose bumps. The ice around the stacks of robes was crowded, but even so, each of the boys took care to keep a space around himself and not brush against any of his fellow petitioners. As they waited their turns at the stacks, they furtively glanced from body to naked body, comparing and reflecting, silently judging.

"Hurry, please, I'm freezing to death!"

This came from a plump boy who had his arms clapped across his chest. He had dark brown skin the color of coffee, and his eyes were full of fear; alternately, he lifted one knee high and then the other, up and down, touching the ice with his tender-soled feet as quickly and as briefly as possible. He looked silly and pathetic, like a strange insect dancing atop a blister of hot, shiny oil.

"Please hurry!"

Ahead of Danlo was a frenzy of boys ripping through robes and sizing sandals to their feet. Everywhere, cast-off white ribbons from the sandals carpeted the ice. Danlo found that by kicking some of the ribbons together he could stand on them and not feel the *ilka-hara,* the burn of naked ice against flesh. He stood clutching his bamboo shakuhachi in his hand, patiently waiting his turn, watching and waiting, and all the while he was aware that many of the boys were watching him, too. They stared at his loins, at the membrum that Three-Fingered Soli had cut and marked with colored scars. This unique mutilation riveted their stares. And Danlo stared at the other boys, or rather, he quickly surveyed the contours of the smooth, civilized bodies all around him. None of the boys had been cut; they each retained foreskins sheathing the bulbs of their membrums, and thus they were truly boys, not men. Some of the boys had yet to begin their growth; their chests were slight and narrow, and their membrums were almost as small as Danlo's little finger. But even the older boys, with their large, fully developed membrums, were uncut. Despite his training in the perils of glavering, he could not take them as equals. (In truth, he worried at his own manhood, for how could he ever become a full man until he completed his passage and listened to the complete and whole Song of Life?) No, he was very different from all the others, and he was at once ashamed and proud of this difference. No one else seemed quite so tall, or as tough and hardy in the body. He stood calm and waiting, fairly inured to the cold. He was still too lean from his starvation the previous year; the sinews and bones stood out beneath his weathered skin, and long flat bands of muscle quivered with every breath taken and released. Most of the boys were weak-looking, as thin and white as snowworms or layered with fat like seals. Even the few athletes among them, with their carefully cultivated physiques, seemed pampered and soft. They looked at him—at the various parts of his body—with a mixture of horror, envy, and awe.

There was one other boy, however, who also stood out

from the others, though mostly for different reasons. As Danlo donned a loose, scratchy wool robe and kicked on a pair of sandals, he overheard this boy talking about Ede the God and the Cybernetic Universal Church, a subject that interested him endlessly. He slipped through the crowded ice field until he came upon a short, thin boy who held the attention of others standing around him. "Of course, all the Cybernetic Churches worship Ede as God," the boy was saying. "But it's the Architects of the original church who have created the Vild."

In a low voice Danlo said a prayer, then whispered, *"Shantih, shantih."*

The boy—his name was Hanuman li Tosh—must have overheard what Danlo said, for he turned and bowed his head politely. He had the oldest young face imaginable, smooth like new white ice and indecently unmarked even for a fifteen-year-old. At the same time, he seemed strangely jaded, as if he'd lived a thousand times before, and each life full of disappointments, boredom, anguish, madness, and desperate love. With his full, sensual lips, he smiled at Danlo; it was a beautiful smile, at once shy and compelling. In many ways, he was a beautiful boy. There was a delicateness to his finely made face bones, an almost otherworldly grace. Danlo thought he must be either half an angel or half demon. His hair was yellow-white, the color of an iceblink, and his skin was so white that it was almost translucent, a thin shell of flesh that could scarcely protect him from the coldness and cruelties of the world. Except for his eyes, he was really too beautiful. His eyes were a pale blue, vivid and clear like those of a sled dog. Danlo had never imagined seeing such eyes in a human being. There was too much sensitivity and suffering there, as well as passion and fury. In truth, Danlo instantly hated the sight of those hellish, *shaida* eyes. He began to think of this strange boy as the "Hell-eyes," a pale fury he should either flee from immediately or kill.

But the circle of chattering boys surrounding Hanuman pressed close and caught Danlo up in civilized conversation; he was caught, too, by Hanuman's silver tongue and his charm.

"I'm Hanuman li Tosh, off Catava. What does this word 'shantih' mean? It's a beautiful word, and the way you say it— beautiful and haunting."

How could Danlo explain the peace beyond peace to a civilized boy with eyes out of his deepest nightmares? Hanuman was shivering in his sandals and his robe, looking at him expectantly. Despite the seeming frailty of his long neck and naked limbs where they stuck out of his robe, he bore the cold well. There was something about him that the other boys lacked, some inner fire or intensity of purpose. He had his fist up to his mouth coughing at the cold air, but even in his pain, he seemed very determined and very aware of Danlo looking at him.

"*Shantih,*" Danlo said, "is a word . . . my father taught me. It is really the formal ending to a prayer."

"And what language would that be? What religion?"

Danlo had been warned not to reveal his past so he evaded the question. "I have not presented myself," he said. "I am Danlo." He bowed his head and smiled.

"Just . . . *Danlo*?"

He didn't want to tell him that he was Danlo, son of Haidar, whose father was Wicent, the son of Nuri the Bearkiller. He felt the other boys staring at him, whispering, and he blurted out, "They call me Danlo the Wild."

Behind Hanuman, a muscle-fat boy with a cracking voice and a pugnacious face began to laugh. His name was Konrad and he called out, "Danlo the Wild—what kind of name is that?"

And someone else said, "Danlo the Wild, the nameless child."

Danlo's neck suddenly hurt and his eyes were burning with shame. He stood there breathing deeply and evenly, as Haidar had taught him, letting the cold air enter his lungs to steal the heat from his anger. A few of the boys laughed at him and made jokes about his strange name. Most, however, hung back and kept their silence, obviously doubting the wisdom of baiting such a tough-looking boy. With a feather stuck in his hair and his deep blue eyes, Danlo *did* in fact look uncivilized and not a little wild.

Hanuman coughed some more, great racking coughs that tore through his chest and brought tears to his eyes. When he had caught his breath, he asked, "Which is your birth world?"

"I was born here."

"You were? In Neverness? Then you must be used to the cold."

Danlo rubbed his arms and blew on his fingers to warm them. A man, he thought, should not complain about things he can't change, so he said, simply, "Can one ever get used to the cold?"

"*I* certainly can't," Hanuman said as he began coughing again. And then, "So cold—how do you stand it?"

146

Danlo watched him cough for a while, and said, "You are ill, yes?"

"Ill? No, I'm not—it's just that the air is so cold it cuts the lungs."

After another round of coughing, Danlo decided that Hanuman was indeed very ill. Once, when Danlo was a young boy, he had watched his near-brother Basham die of a lung fever. Hanuman certainly had the pale, haunted look of someone who was contemplating going over. Perhaps a virus was eating away at his lungs. He seemed to be burning from deep inside. His eyes were sunken into dark, bruised flesh; the contrast of the light blue irises against the dark hollows made them seem more hellish by the moment. There was a fear in his eyes, a frightened, fey look almost as if he could see his fate approaching like a dark storm that would ice his heart and steal his breath away. He coughed again, and Danlo could almost feel the spasm tearing through his own chest. He was afraid for Hanuman. He was afraid, and that was seemly, for a man to fear another's dying, but of course it was very wrong that Hanuman should be afraid for himself. Hanuman's fear made Danlo sick. He had keen eyes, and he could see that this frail, ill boy was trying to hide his fear from all the others, perhaps even trying to hide it from himself. Someone, he thought, should feed him bowls of wolf-root tea and bathe his head with cool water. Where was his mother, to care for him? He would have placed his hand on Hanuman's burning forehead to touch the fever away, but he remembered that he was not supposed to touch others, especially not strangers, especially not in sight of a hundred other laughing, joking boys.

Hanuman moved closer to Danlo and spoke in a low, tortured voice, "Please don't tell the novices or masters I'm ill."

He coughed so hard that he doubled over and lost his balance as his foot slipped on the ice. He would have pitched face forward, but Danlo caught him by the armpit and hand. Hanuman's hand was hot like an oilstone and surprisingly strong. (Later Danlo would learn that Hanuman had trained in the killing arts in order to harden himself. In truth, he was much stronger than he looked.) Danlo gripped Hanuman's hard little hand, pulling him to his feet, and suddenly they didn't seem at all like strangers. There was something between them, some kind of correspondence and immediate understanding. Danlo had a feeling that he should pay close attention to this correspondence. Hanuman's intenseness both attracted and repelled him. He smelled Hanuman's fear and sensed his will to suffer that fear in silence no matter the cost. He smelled other things as well. Hanuman stank of sweat and sickness, and of coffee—obviously he had been drinking mugs of coffee to keep himself awake. With tired, feverish eyes Hanuman looked at Danlo as if they shared a secret. Hanuman shook off his hand, gathered in his pride, and stood alone. Danlo thought he was being consumed from within like an overfilled oilstone burning too quickly. Who could hold such inner fire, he wondered, and not quickly go over to the other side of day?

"You should rest in your furs and drink hot tea," Danlo said, "or else you might go over."

"Go over? Do you mean *die*?" Hanuman spoke this word as if it were the most odious and terrifying concept that he could imagine. "Please, no, I hope not."

He coughed and there was a bubbly sound of liquid breaking deep in his throat.

"Where are your parents?" Danlo asked as he combed back his long hair with his fingers. "Did you make the journey here alone?"

Hanuman coughed into his cupped hand, then wiped a fleck of blood from his lips. "I don't have any parents."

"No father, no mother? O blessed God, how can you not have a mother?"

"Oh, I had parents once," Hanuman explained. "I'm not a slelnik, even though some people say I look like one."

Danlo hadn't yet heard of the despised, unnatural breeding strategies practiced on a few of the Civilized Worlds; he knew nothing of the exemplars and slelniks born in abomination from the artificial wombs. He thought he understood a part of Hanuman's pain and obvious loneliness; however, he understood wrongly. "Your parents have gone over, yes?"

Hanuman looked down at the ice and then shook his head. "Does it matter?" he asked. "To them, *I* might as well be dead."

He told Danlo something of his journey to Neverness, then. In the Ice Dome, a thousand boys were stamping their feet, slapping leather sandals against ice as they huffed out steam and complained of neglect, and Hanuman told of how he had been born into an important Architect family on Catava. His parents were Pavel and Moriah li Tosh, readers in the Cybernetic Reformed Church. (This church is but one of many sects of the Architects, for over the millennia, the Architects of the Infinite Intelligence of the Cybernetic Universal Church have been riven into many different sub-religions. The Evolutionary Church of Ede, the Cybernetic Orthodox Churches, the Fostora Separatist Union—these are but a few of the hundreds of churches that have splintered off from the original church body, beginning with the Ilanthian Heresy and the First Schism in the year 331 EV, that is to say, the 331st year since the vastening of Nikolos Daru Ede. All time, the Architects say, must begin at the moment Ede carked his consciousness into one of his main-brain computers and thus became the first of humanity's gods.) Like his parents, Hanuman had undergone the traditional reader training in one of the church schools. Unlike any of the respectable Architects that he knew, however, he had rebelled while still very young, begging his parents' permission to attend the Order's elite school in Oloraning, which is Catava's largest and only real city.

"My father allowed me to enter the elite school," Hanuman said, "only because it was the best school on Catava. But I had to agree to finish my reader training in the church after graduation; I had to agree *not* to attend the Academy on Neverness. So I agreed. But it was an impossible agreement. I never should have made it. All my friends in the elite school were planning to enter the Academy, if they could. And I'd always hoped to enter the Academy. To become a reader like my parents and grandparents—I never really wanted that. Oh, wait . . . please excuse my coughing. Do you know about the readers of my church? Of my *parents'* church? No? I'm not supposed to tell anyone this, but I shall anyway. The second holiest ceremony in our church is the facing ceremony. You'll have heard rumors about the facing ceremony—almost everyone has. No? Where have you spent your life? Well, in the facing ceremony, any Worthy Architect is allowed to interface with one of the church's communal computers. The interfacing, entering into computer consciousness, the information flows, like lightning, the power. It's like heaven, really, the only good thing about being an Architect. But before every facing ceremony, there has to be a cleansing. Of sin. We Architects . . . *the* Architects, call sin 'negative programming.' So before a facing, a cleansing, because it's blasphemy to interface a holy computer while unclean with negative programs—that's what most of the Cybernetic Churches teach. I can't tell you about the cleansing ceremony. It's worse than hateful, really, it's a violation of the soul. Oh, I'll tell you, if you promise to keep this secret. The readers strip bare your mind with their akashic computers. Everything, every

149

negative thought or intention, especially vanity, because that's the worst thing, the damning sin, to think too highly of yourself or want to be more than you were born for. Almost everything —there are ways of hiding things; you have to learn to keep your thoughts secret or else the readers will rape your soul. They'll cleanse you until there's nothing left. Have you ever had an imprinting? The cleansing is like a reverse imprinting. The readers remove the bad memories. They reprogram the brain . . . by killing parts of it. Not everyone believes that, of course, or else they'd panic whenever it was time for a cleansing. But even if the readers don't actually kill the brain cells, they kill something else when they eliminate old synaptic pathways and create new ones. Why not call it soul? I know that's an inelegant word for an elegant, inexpressible concept, but soul . . . you have to keep your soul to yourself, do you see? The soul, the light. And that's why I left my church. Because I'd rather have died than become a *reader*."

In silence Danlo listened as this intense, ill boy talked and coughed. That he talked so much and so freely surprised him. Danlo was beginning to discover a talent for listening to others and winning their trust. He listened deeply, as he would listen to the west wind scrape across and articulate the ice forms of the sea. He liked the way Hanuman used words, the richness and clarity of his thought. It was a rare thing, he knew, for a boy to speak as fluently as a skillful-tongued man.

"I wonder what it would be like . . . to touch minds with a computer," Danlo said.

"You've never faced a computer?"

"No."

"Well, it's pure ecstasy," Hanuman said.

Danlo touched the feather dangling from his hair, and then he touched his forehead. "You know about computers—are computers truly alive? Life, consciousness is . . . even the smallest living things, even the snowworms are conscious."

"*Is* a snowworm conscious?" Hanuman asked.

"Yes," Danlo said. "I am not a shaman so I have never entered into snowworm consciousness. But Yuri the Wise and others of my . . . other men that I have known have entered the consciousness of the animals, and they know what it is like to be a snowworm."

"And what is it like?"

"It is like *something*. It is like being a snowflake in a blizzard. It is like the beginning of drawing in a breath of new air. It is like . . . I do not know. Perhaps someday I will become a snowworm and I will tell you."

Hanuman smiled as he began to cough again. Then he said, "You're very strange, did you know that?"

"Thank you," Danlo said, returning his smile. "You are strange, too."

"Oh, yes, strange—I think I was born that way."

"And your parents?" Danlo asked. "They had no sympathy . . . for this strangeness?"

Hanuman was silent for a few moments as he stared down at the steaming ice. As if he had come to a grave decision, he nodded his head. He looked up suddenly and then told Danlo the rest of his story. The Cybernetic Reformed Churches, Hanuman said, did not believe in the freedom of the soul. And so, hating the life-perverting ethos and practices of his church, Hanuman had made secret plans to journey to Neverness after his graduation. That he would be accepted to the Academy, he felt certain, for all his life he had studied the disciplines with a frenzy, and he had risen to the zenith of the ranks of the chosen. But, it was said, the greater the height, the farther the drop, and so one of his friends, out of envy and spite, had betrayed him to his father just before their graduation. His father had immediately removed him from the school. He never graduated. He was locked inside the reading room of his family's church, there to familiarize himself with the heaumes of the akashic computers, with the Edic lights of the altar, and with the burning incense and brain musics used in Architect ceremonies. His father told him to meditate on the *Book of God*. He was to give special attention to its sub-books: *The Life of Ede, Facings,* and *Iterations.* In *Facings,* a body of so-called wisdom revealed to Kostos Olorun long after Ede had become a god, he came across the crucial passage:

And so Ede faced the universe, and he was vastened, and he saw that the face of God was his own. Then the would-be gods, who are the hakra devils of the darkest depths of space, from the farthest reaches of time, saw what Ede had done, and they were jealous. And so they turned their eyes godward in jealousy and lust for the infinite lights, but in their countenances God read hubris, and he struck them blind. For here is the oldest of teachings, here is wisdom: No god is there but God; God is one, and there can be only one God.

What followed, in this holy book of *Facings*, were many chapters describing the detection and cleansing of hakras. For the thousandth time in his life, Hanuman reflected on his church's doctrine that *all* human beings were considered—and condemned—as potential hakras, potential gods. What kind of hateful, corrupt church, he wondered, would deny the divinity within each human being? He decided that Kostos Olorun, three thousand years ago, in his ambition to validate the authority of the nascent church and to establish himself as "God's Prophet," had lied about receiving revelations from Ede, and, more, that he had invented many false doctrines. While Hanuman waited for his father to cleanse him of his sins, he had a dangerous thought: The true meaning of Ede's vastening was that each man, woman, and child should come to apprehend the god within. *Every man and woman is a star*—Ede himself had written these words in his *Universals*. But somehow his church had corrupted and perverted this beautiful image to mean that every woman and man is a star whose light must be extinguished periodically lest it outshine that of Ede the God. Perhaps, Hanuman mused, human beings truly were as angels, or rather, as godlings who might grow into infinity, and someday, at the end of time, be united with Ede and all the other gods of the universe.

Unwittingly, Hanuman had come to formulate one of the oldest and most secret heresies of his church: the Major Hakra Heresy. One day, in front of the reading room's altar, as he watched the jeweled Edic lights shimmering up through the spectrum from red to violet, he voiced this heresy to his father. His father, who was a stern, handsome man, was scandalized by his son's ideas. He told him to immediately prepare himself for a deep cleansing. There was hatred in his father's voice, jealousy and loathing. Although Hanuman had been cleansed many times, he had never had a deep cleansing. Against the power and subtleties of the holy computers as they cleansed him deeply, the little mind tricks he had learned would be useless; a deep cleansing would disfigure his soul as surely as a hot wind melts the features of an ice sculpture. He closed his eyes to look upon the familiar, very mortal face of his soul, and he was terrified. He begged his father to relent, to subject him only to the usual, mundane cleansing. But his father was a hard man. His father, this prince of the church, hardened his heart and reviled his son as a hakra; he would not relent. His father told him to kneel beneath the heaume of the holy, cleansing computer. But instead, in his terror and pride, in a blind panic, Hanuman swept up the gold incense stand and struck his father's forehead. It was a quick, powerful, desperate blow; his father immediately fell dying across the altar. Hanuman gasped to see the rainbow of Edic lights falling over his father's open brains. He wept uncontrollably as long as he dared, and then he tore the Edic lights from the altar and left his father in a pool of blood. He fled to Oloruning. There he sold the priceless lights to a wormrunner. He used the money to buy a passage on a harijan prayership, where one of the filthy pilgrims infected him with a lung disease. Thus he had come to Neverness, ill in his body and burning in his soul; he had come to the City of Pain hoping to enter the Academy and forget his sinful past.

Part of this story, of course—the sad, murderous part—Danlo did not learn until years later. For good reason, Hanuman was a secretive boy, and he would grow to be a secretive man. It was a mark of his unusual trust in Danlo that he had told him as much as he had. "I've given up everything to enter the Academy," he said to Danlo. "My whole life."

He coughed for a long time, and Danlo listened to the ragged, ripping sound. The huge Dome was full of sound: wind breaking against the clary panes high above, chattering teeth, and two thousand shivering boys grumbling and wondering how long they would be made to wait in such a frigid place. Then a deep voice called out, "Silence, it's time!" The Head Novice, with a look of command written over his narrow face, quickly made his way to the center of the Ice Dome. "Silence, it's time for the first test. Form a queue at the nearest doorway; a novice will lead you to your first test. Silence! Once the test begins, anyone caught talking will be dismissed."

Danlo looked at Hanuman and whispered, "I wish you well."

"I wish *you* well, Danlo the Wild."

They began their walk across Borja, then. Boys and girls clad in thin white robes issued forth from many of the buildings. That year, some seven thousand petitions to compete in the festival had been accepted; long lines of would-be novices filled the glidderies. The sun was now high in the southern sky, and everywhere the spires were awash in the hot, false winter light. It was much warmer than it had been inside the Ice Dome. A film of water mirrored the red ice of the lesser glidderies. It was so slippery that some of the petitioners linked arms and proceeded very carefully. Others hurried recklessly along in sudden bursts of speed, using their flat leather sandals to skid and hydroplane across the ice. Danlo stayed near Hanuman, waiting for him to slip and fall momentarily. But Hanuman kept his balance, even as they made their way toward the Tycho's Spire. Above them—above the dormitories and lesser buildings—this giant needle marked the very center of Borja. Danlo liked the feeling of the novices' college; it was a place of beauty that had taken centuries to evolve and unfold. On most of the buildings, variegated lichens burned across the stonework in lovely rossettes of ocher, orange, and red. Many old yu trees had grown almost as high as the spires themselves. It was impossible to stand on any lawn of the Academy and not hear the *kap, kap, kap* of mauli birds pecking at bark. The smooth, immaculate glidderries, the fireflowers, the snow loons hunting yu berries in the snow—here, Danlo thought, was a place touched by the arts of mankind, and perhaps steeped the unutterable essence of *halla*.

Beneath the Tycho's Tower, surrounded by eight buildings that house the various computers used in the novices' education, is the beloved Lavi Square. That is to say, it is beloved by the novices who gather there to gossip and greet new friends, and to enjoy a few moments (or hours) of open sky. The petitioners rarely come to love Lavi Square. Every year, the Test of Patience is held there. This is the first test of the Festival of Unfortunate Petitioners, and every year it takes a different form. Every year, the Master of Novices delights in designing trials to cull the most patient of petitioners. Sometimes the unfortunate boys and girls are made to recite poetry until their voices are hoarse, and the weak among them beg to be allowed surcease from the torment of speaking; one time, ten years before, they were required to stay awake and attentive while an historian lectured about the manifold horrors of the Fifth Mentality and the Second Dark Age. Only those few boys and girls who had remained awake after three days had been allowed to take the second test.

Along with Hanuman—and seven thousand other boys and girls—Danlo was herded into the Square. For a hundred fifty yards along the length and breadth of the Square, seven thousand straw mats were laid out in a neat array. Each mat was a rectangle three feet wide and four feet long. The mats were jammed close together, their frayed edges separated by only a few inches of white ice. A novice bade the petitioners to each kneel on a mat. Danlo took his place on a mat next to Hanuman. The sharp, ragged ends of the straw pricked his knees, and the mat was so worn and full of holes that the wet ice beneath bathed him with waves of cold.

"Silence, it's time!" the Head Novice cried out again.

The petitioners fell silent as they looked up expectantly, eager to learn the nature of that year's test. Except for a few yu trees laden with red fruit and some ice sculptures (and twelve precious shih trees from Simoom), the Square was entirely stived with row upon row of nervous girls and boys. Danlo smelled clean, childish sweat and the ferment of overripe berries. From the buildings towering over them came the *plip, plip* of melting icicles. There was anxiety in the air, a chill intensity of anticipation.

"Silence, it's time to present the Master of Novices, Pesheval Lal!"

From the building behind the novice, an ugly, bearded man emerged from the doorway and made his way down a flight of steps. His birth name was Pesheval Lal, and the novices and journeymen called him Master Lal, but everywhere else he was famous simply as Bardo. (Or as Bardo the Just.) Bardo's formal black robe was tight across his immense chest and belly. White is the color of Borja, and all novices wear white, but Bardo the Just had been a pilot before assuming the office of Master of Novices; like the other pilots he was properly dressed in color.

"Yes, silence!" his voice boomed out, echoing the novice's injunction. He was a huge man, and he had a huge voice. He sternly looked from petitioner to petitioner. He had cunning, superb eyes that didn't miss very much when it came to judging human character. Occasionally he would favor one of the petitioners with a smile and a slight head bow. He strolled about with a ponderous, heavy gait, as if he were hugely bored with himself and the impromptu judgments he had to make.

"Silence!" he shouted, and his voice vibrated from building to building across the square. "You'll be silent while I explain the rules of this year's test. The rules are simple. No one will be allowed off his mat except to relieve himself. Ah . . . or herself. There will be no eating or drinking. Anyone caught talking will be immediately dismissed. Anything not forbidden is permitted. It's a simple test, by God! You're here to wait."

And so they waited. Seven thousand children, not one of whom was older than fifteen years, waited in the warmth of the false winter sun. Mostly they waited in silence. Hanuman, of course, couldn't help coughing, but none of the officious novices patrolling up and down the rows of petitioners seemed to bear him any ill feelings. Danlo listened to this coughing, and he worried how Hanuman would stand the bite of the evening air. He thought to distract Hanuman's ailing spirit with a little music, to take him out of himself. He removed the shakuhachi from beneath his robe and began to play. The low, breathy melody he composed caught the attention of everyone around him. Most of the petitioners seemed to enjoy the music; the novices, though, were not pleased. They shot Danlo poisonous looks, as if they were insulted that he had found a clever way around Bardo's injunction to silence. To be sure, he was not talking, but in many ways the music he made was a purer communication than mere words.

In this manner, kneeling on his straw mat, blowing continuously down his long bamboo flute, Danlo whiled away the endless afternoon. It was a beautiful day, really, a day of warmth and pungent air wafting down from the mountains. The shih trees beneath the buildings were snowy with white blossoms, and clouds of newly hatched fritillaries sipped nectar and filled the air with an explosion of bright violet wings. It wasn't hard for him to wait, with the sun burning hot against the clear sky. A million needles of light stung his neck and face. He closed his eyes and played on and on, taking little notice of the sun as it grew large and crimson in the west. When twilight fell, the first chill of evening stole over the petitioners, but he was still warm and fluid inside with the music of dreamtime. Then the stars came out, and it was cold. The cold touched him, gently at first, and then more urgently. He opened his eyes to darkness and cold air. There, above the City's eastern edge, the sky was almost clear of light pollution; the sky was black and full of stars. In unseen waves, heat escaped the City and radiated upward into the sky. There were no clouds or moisture in the air to hold in the heat.

"It's cold! I can't stand this cold!"

Danlo noticed the boy named Konrad sitting ten yards in front of him, sitting and cursing as he beat his legs to keep warm. A cadre of novices converged on him and grasped his robe. "Your face!" Konrad shouted. "Your rotting face!" But the novices took no notice of his bad manners or profanity; they immediately escorted him from the Square.

If Konrad was the first to forget his patience and hope, he was not the last. As if a signal had been given, children in ones and twos began standing and leaving the Square. And then roups of ten or a hundred gave up en masse, abandoning their ellows, and so abandoned their quest to enter the Order. By the ime night had grown full and deep, only some three thousand petitioners remained.

Just before midnight, a wicked round of coughing alerted Danlo as to the gravity of Hanuman's illness. It wasn't very cold —at least it was no colder than the interior of a snow hut—but Hanuman was shivering as he coughed, bent low with his face pressing his mat, shivering beyond control. If he didn't give up and seek shelter soon he would surely die. But Hanuman didn't look as if he were ready to give up. The hard straw had cut parallel marks into his forehead and cheek; his eyes were open to the light of the flame globes shining at the edge of the Square. Such eyes he had, a pale blue burning as the hellish *blinkans* in he sky burned, strangely and with terrible intensity. Something terrible and beautiful inside Hanuman was holding him to his mat, keeping him coughing in the cold. Danlo could almost see his thing, this pure, luminous will of Hanuman's beyond even he will to life. *Each man and woman is a star,* he remembered, and something brilliant and beautiful about Hanuman's spirit attracted him, just as a fritillary is compelled to seek a wood fire's fatal light.

"Hanuman!" he whispered. He couldn't help himself. The urge to speak to this willful boy before he died was greater than his fear of being dismissed as a petitioner. He had a strange, overwhelming feeling that if he could somehow see the true Hanuman, he would learn everything about *shaida* and *halla.* Waiting until none of the novices was near, he whispered again, "Hanuman, it is best not to touch your head to the ice. The ice, even through the mat—it is very cold. Colder than the air, yes?"

Through his chattering teeth, Hanuman forced out, "I've . . . never . . . been so cold."

Danlo looked around him. Most of the nearby mats were empty, and those few petitioners who were within listening distance were curled up like dogs and seemed to be asleep. He pitched his voice low and said, "I have seen too many people go over. And you, you will go over soon, I think, unless you—"

"No, I won't quit!"

"But your *life,*" Danlo whispered, "to keep it warm and quick, your life is—"

"My life's worth nothing unless I can live it as I must!"

"But you do not know how to live . . . in the cold."

"I'll have to learn, then, won't I?"

157

Danlo smiled into the darkness. He squeezed the cold bamboo shaft of the shakuhachi and said, "Can you wait a little longer? It will be morning soon. False winter nights are short."

"Why are you talking to me?" Hanuman suddenly wanted to know. "Aren't you afraid of being caught?"

"Yes," Danlo said in a soft voice. "I know we should not be talking."

"You're different from the others." Hanuman swept his arm in an arc, waving at the motionless petitioners slumped down on their mats. "Look at them, asleep on the most important night of their lives. None of them would take such a chance —you're not like them at all."

Danlo touched Ahira's feather and thought back to the night of his passage into manhood. "It is hard to be different, yes?"

"It's hard to have a sense of yourself. Most people don't know who they are."

"It is as if they were lost in a *sarsara*," Danlo agreed. "But it is hard to see yourself, the truth. Who am *I*, after all? Who is anyone?"

Hanuman coughed wickedly, then laughed. "If you can ask that question, you already know."

"But I do not really know anything."

"And that's the deepest knowledge of all."

They looked at each other knowingly and broke into soft laughter. Immediately, though, their laughter died when a novice clacked across the Square ten rows behind them. As they waited for him to pass, Hanuman blew on his hands and began shivering again.

When it seemed safe, Danlo asked, "You would risk your life to enter the Academy?"

"My life?" Hanuman rasped out. "No, I'm not as ready to die as you seem to think."

He coughed for a while, then Danlo asked, "Did you journey here to become a pilot? It is my fate to be a pilot, I think."

"Your fate?"

"I have dreamed of being . . ." Danlo began, and then fell silent. "I . . . I have always wanted to be a pilot."

"I also," Hanuman said. "To be a pilot, to interface with the ship's computer, this continual vastening the pilots are allowed—that's the beginning of everything."

"I had not thought of it that way." Danlo looked up at the Wolf and Thallow constellations and the other stars, and said simply, "I will become a pilot so I can journey to the center of the Great Circle, to see if the universe is *halla* or *shaida.*"

He closed his eyes and pressed his cold thumbs against his eyelids. To see the universe as it really is and say "yes" to that truth, as man and as asarya—how could he explain his dream to anyone? In truth, the Alaloi are forbidden to reveal their night-time dreams or visions, so how could he tell Hanuman that he had dreamed of becoming an asarya?

"What is this word 'halla' that you keep using?" Hanuman asked.

Danlo listened to the wind rise and whoosh between the buildings. It fell over him, and he began to shiver. Despite his discomfort, he loved the chill of the wind against his face, the way it carried in the sea smells and a feeling of freedom. How exhilarating it was to talk long past midnight with such an aware, new friend! How reckless to talk beneath the novices' ears with only the wind for cover! Suddenly the utter strangeness of kneeling on a scratchy mat and waiting with three thousand other freezing boys and girls was too much. He found himself telling Hanuman about the death of his parents and his journey to Neverness. He tried to tell him about the harmony and beauty of life, then, but he found that the simple Alaloi concepts he had been taught sounded trite and naive when translated into civilized language. "*Halla* is the cry of the wolf when he calls to his brothers and sisters," he said. "And it is *halla* that the stars should shine at night when the sun falls beneath the mountains. *Halla* is the way . . . the way false winter takes away the cold, and the way false winter dies into the colder seasons so the animals do not become too many and crowd the ice. *Halla* is . . . oh, blessed *halla!* it is so fragile when you try to define it, like crossing *morilka,* the death ice. The greater weight you give it, the more likely it is to break. *Halla is*. Sometimes, lately, I think of it as pure isness. A way of simply being."

Hanuman pressed his lips together as he turned his face away from the wind and tried not to cough. "I've never known anyone like you before," he marveled. "To cross a thousand miles of ice looking for something you call *halla*—and to do it alone!"

"Old Father warned me that if I told anyone, they might not believe me. You will not . . . tell anyone else?"

"Of course I won't. But you should know, I believe you."

"Yes?"

159

Hanuman stared at the feather in Danlo's hair, then coughed and said, "Danlo the Wild—you *look* a little wild. And the way you see things, so wild. I'll have to think about what you've said. Especially about being. Can it be enough just to *be*? I've always dreamed of becoming."

"Becoming . . . what?"

"Becoming more," Hanuman said.

While Hanuman bent low with another coughing fit, Danlo touched the shakuhachi's ivory mouthpiece with his lips. "But, Hanu," he said, impulsively inventing a diminutive form of his name. He reached over and touched the boy's forehead. It was burning hot. "Hanu, Hanu, you are not *becoming*. You are dying."

"No, that's silly," Hanuman said hoarsely. "Please don't say that."

After that, he lost his voice and began coughing in great breaking waves. Danlo wondered why the novices or Bardo the Just, who strolled among the petitioners from time to time, didn't take this unfortunate, dying boy inside somewhere to heal him. He decided that entering the Order must be a kind of passage. And like all passages into new levels of being, there must always be danger and the possibility of death.

"Will you play your flute now?" Hanuman whispered. "I can't talk anymore."

Danlo wet his lips and smiled. "It is soothing, yes?"

"Soothing? No, it's haunting, really. Haunting. There's something about the way you play, the music. Something I can't bear to hear. But something I have to hear. Do you understand?"

Danlo played his music, then, even though his mouth was so dry that the playing was difficult. He licked his lips for the hundredth time. He was very thirsty. Since the morning coffee, he had drunk nothing, and his tongue was dry against his teeth, as dry as old seal leather. Of course he was hungry, too, with his belly tightening up empty and aching, but the hunger wasn't as bad as his need for water. And, in truth, he was colder than he was thirsty. Soon, perhaps, the thirst would grow angry and all-consuming, but now, as he played, the cold was more immediate, like a stiff, frozen fur touching every part of him. The wind blew down his neck, and the mat was icy against his legs. It was hard to move his fingers, especially the two smallest ones on his right hand: as a child, he had burned them in the oilstones, and they were stiff with scar over the knuckles and now almost numb. Somewhat clumsily, he played his music while Hanuman watched and listened. And on Hanuman's delicate face, in his eyes, there was a look of anguish, whether from the music or cold it was hard to tell. Danlo played to the anguish, all the time thinking of Old Father and the "holy pain" that he delighted in causing others. Danlo took no joy in others' suffering, but he could appreciate the need for pain as a stimulant. *Pain is the awareness of life*—that was a saying of the Alaloi tribes. Life was pain, and in Hanuman's pain, there was still an urge to life. This miracle of living, though, was such a delicate thing liable to end at any moment. He could see that Hanuman was dying—how much longer could his will and inner fury keep him alive? Death is the left hand of life, he thought, and death is *halla,* but suddenly he did not want Hanuman to die.

He set down the shakuhachi and whispered, "Hanu, Hanu, keep your hands inside your robe. Do not blow on them. Fingers claw the cold from the air—do you understand?"

Hanuman nodded and thrust his hands into either of his loose sleeves. He said nothing as he began to cough and shiver even more violently.

"Hanu, Hanu, you were not made for the cold, were you?"

Danlo rolled the thin wool of his robe between his fingers and smiled grimly. The wind rose up and drove particles of ice across the Square. It seemed that everyone was shivering, even the tired novices in their white jackets. For a long time, as the wind continued to blow, he looked at Hanuman. Hanuman had spoken sophisticated words, and he had courage, but in truth he was still just a boy, uncut and unseasoned against the world's bitterness. He was frail and sick, and he would go over soon. Danlo watched and waited for him to go over. He waited, all the while wondering what dread, mysterious affinity connected his life with Hanuman's. He studied Hanuman's fevered face, and somewhat worried at the turn of his thoughts, he decided that he and Hanuman must share the same *doffel.* Surely Hanuman's spirit animal must be the snowy owl or perhaps one of the other kinds of thallow.

Then, in the deepest, coldest part of night with the wind dying and the world fallen silent, just before dawn, Danlo heard Ahira calling him. "Danlo, Danlo," his other-self said, "Hanuman is your brother spirit and you must not let him die." Rashly, almost without thought, Danlo shrugged off his robe. There was a smile on his lips, grim necessity in his eyes. Then he leaned closer to Hanuman and worked the rough wool over his head, down over his trembling body. He knelt back down on his own mat, freezing and naked, astonished at what he had done.

Hanuman stared at him and smiled faintly. After a while he closed his eyes in exhaustion. Danlo scooped up a few of the nearby mats and built a half pyramid over him. The overlapping mats—and his robe—might keep the wind from killing him.

"Danlo, Danlo, there is no pain as terrible as cold," Ahira whispered to him.

While Danlo clenched his fists to keep from shivering, Hanuman fell into unconsciousness and began to dream. It was obvious he was dreaming: his eyelids fluttered like the wings of a fritillary, and he moved his cracked, bleeding lips silently. Then he began to murmur in his sleep, to call out for his father. "No, no, Father," he said. "No, no."

"Hanu, you must be quiet!" Danlo whispered. He looked around to see if any of the other petitioners had been awakened. Among the Alaloi it is taboo to disturb the sleep of others with one's own dreams. Sleep is the sacred time, the return to the natural state, which is at once the source and sustenance of the spirit. To reveal a dream is to infect another's spirit with images that must remain secret. If dreams weren't kept sacred, Danlo believed, the spirits of all men and women would fall into confusion and madness. "Hanu, Hanu, wake up if you cannot sleep!"

But Hanuman was now lost into nightmare. There was sweat on his face, terror on his lips. "Father, Father!" he began to cry out. "No, no, no—"

His shouts were cut off abruptly when Danlo leaned over and clamped his hand over his mouth. "Shhh!" Danlo said. His cold hand hurt with the breath burning out of Hanuman's nose. "Shhh, go to sleep now!" he whispered. "*Shantih*, go to sleep."

He cradled Hanuman's head in the crook of his arm as he held his hand hard over the boy's mouth. He was afraid one of the novices might hear the muffled cries. But the nearest novice was fifty yards away leaning against the trunk of a shih tree and heard nothing. Soon, to the whispered supplication of "*Shantih*, go to sleep!" Hanuman fell into dreamlessness and peace. When he was quiet and still, Danlo let him go and returned to kneeling on his mat. He looked at the thousands of mats lining the ice of Lavi Square, at the thousands of suffering *children*; never in his life had he felt so cold, so abandoned, so utterly alone.

With dawn came a rising of the wind and the sun. "*Lura Sawel*," Danlo whispered. "O blessed sun, be quick to take away the teeth of the wind." But the sun was not quick that morning, and the wind was still cold. The sky was salmon-red, frozen with high, wispy clouds. Soon after first light, with the sun still lost behind the mountains to the east, Bardo the Just appeared to take inventory of the night's attrition. He sent the novices scurrying up and down the ranks and rows. They counted the petitioners on their mats. Most of the mats were empty. Only one thousand twenty-two petitioners remained. And of these, only one thousand and twenty would continue the competition into the next day—during the night, two girls had died. The novices found them dead on their mats, seemingly asleep.

They found something else, too. A cadre of novices on skates surrounded Hanuman and Danlo. "Look!" one of them pointed. "This boy is naked!"

Bardo made his way carefully among the petitioners. Despite his girth, he was light on his feet and adept at moving across ice. He waggled a finger at Hanuman, half covered with mats and still unconscious. "And this boy," he said, "is wearing two robes. Why is he wearing two robes?" He turned to Danlo, and his carmine lips were tight with disapproval. "You're *naked,* by God! Do you understand me, boy? Incline your head once if the answer is 'yes.' Did you give this other boy your robe?"

Danlo nodded his head. He was kneeling low with his thighs pressing his chest. His skin was ivory in the early light, and along his naked back and sides, the muscles quivered like the strings of a gosharp. He hated it that everyone was looking at him.

"Extraordinary!" Bardo thundered. "Remarkable—this is worthy of remark. In all my years as Master of Novices, I've never seen such a selfless act. Who would have thought anyone would strip off his robe and give it to another? Why did you do that, boy? Ah, excuse me, you may not speak. Such a selfless act —and reckless! How do you think to last another day? It's damn cold out here!"

Danlo looked up, saying nothing. Something in his deep blue eyes must have irritated Bardo, for he snapped, "Don't stare at me, boy, it's impolite! Ah, why, why, *why* must I suffer these impolitenesses?"

Danlo continued to stare, not at Bardo, with his black beard and sad, self-pitying face, but rather through him, up at the sky. *Ti-miura halla,* he thought, follow your fate. He stared at the beautiful circle of the sky, at the cloud patterns and colors. *Ti-miura halla.*

Obviously, Bardo the Just mistook this unspoken, open-eyed prayer of Danlo's as a sign of defiance. "Impolite boy!" he said. "Does anyone know this boy's name?"

A conceited-seeming novice named Pedar came closer and said, "I saw him in the Ice Dome—they call him Danlo the Wild."

"Then stay close to this wild boy for the rest of the day," Bardo said. "Watch him—I'll be dining at the Hofgarten, so you'll have to watch him closely." He looked back and forth between Danlo and Hanuman, all the while muttering, "Impolite boy!"

And so Danlo knelt beneath the watchful eyes of the novice, Pedar Sadi Sanat. Pedar was the oldest of the high novices patrolling the Square; he was a diligent boy with hard little eyes and a face covered with pimples and pockmarks. Like some of the high novices, he liked to torment first-year novices and petitioners. He kept a vigil over Danlo and Hanuman. From time to time, to his passing friends, he would call out witticisms such as: "Behold the Boy of Ice! How does he keep from freezing to death? Has he had his blood carked with juf? With drugs? Behold Danlo the Wild!"

Some of the other novices skated closer to gawk at Danlo. Soon, word of his deed spread throughout Borja. Novices fresh from their morning thought exercises took a few moments to pass through Lavi Square. Danlo was surrounded with girls and boys laughing, pointing at him. Hundreds of steel blades cracked the ice near him and flung up patches of chiseled snow. Hunched over as he was in the unfamiliar kneeling posture, his muscles began to ache and cramp. He longed to move, to stretch out his stiff legs, but he did not want anyone to view the cuts and scars of his manhood.

"I've never seen a naked boy before!" a pretty novice giggled. "His arms, his back, the muscles—he looks like a sculpture of a god!"

Another girl stood next to her beneath a shih tree. She was older, a yellow-haired journeyman holist almost womanly in the fullness of her body. She craned her neck to get a better view and said, "Well I *have* seen naked boys before. This Danlo the Wild, whoever he is—he's splendid."

Many of the petitioners were up on their mats, watching him, too. And as the morning passed, quite a few masters from Lara Sig and Upplysa came to see what could be causing such a commotion. One of them, the famous remembrancer Thomas Rane, chastised Pedar for his cruelty. Master Thomas Rane, who had a fine head of silvery hair and a noble face, smoothed out the folds of his silver robe and said, "Pedar, don't you remember when you began your novitiate three years ago? What was it they called you—Pedar the Pimple? And now you accuse this boy of carking his flesh with juf. Yes, there are substances to keep the blood from freezing, but they are no help against cold and hypothermia. He gave his robe to another! You should applaud his act, not deride him for it."

In truth, many of the people standing over Danlo seemed to be in awe of his toughness and resolve, as well as his selflessness. "He gave his robe to his friend," one novice or another would explain to the continuous stream of arriving spectators. "He's been like this all night, naked as ice."

Pedar shooed away a couple of novices who were standing too close. He stripped off his white glove, then bent over and felt Danlo's back. "And his skin is cold as ice," he announced.

"What about the other boy?"

"His face is hot," Pedar said as he held his fingers to Hanuman's cheek. "He's sick. I don't know how either of them will last the day."

One of Pedar's fellow novices agreed. "Not *this* day—that's certain. I think it will snow before nightfall."

Indeed, the sky was full of snow sign; Danlo had known since first light that there would be snow that day. He smelled moisture in the air, the ominous shifting of the wind to the south. And then there was no wind, and the clouds thickened up, the silver wisps growing out of nowhere into an impenetrable, icy gray. A wet cold descended over the world. *Eeshakaleth*, as the Alaloi named it. On many mornings of his life, he had felt the coldness before snow. And now, waiting beneath the gray, gravid sky, there was a foreboding that recalled his deepest memories, distant childhood images of chilled teeth, bewilderment, and dread. He feared the snow. No man (or boy), he thought, should have to bare his flesh to the snow. Suddenly, in shivering waves tearing down his chest and belly, he was afraid of snow as he had never been before.

That afternoon snow began to fall. Large sharp flakes broke against his back and melted. Ice water pooled against his spine, and in freezing rivulets ran down his side. Every particle of melted snow stole a little heat from his body, and there were many, many particles of snow. His numbed skin, his throat, his eyes—everything about him hurt. *There is no pain so terrible as cold,* he thought. Soon, he would stop shivering, and then he must ask to be carried inside, either that or die.

He might have quit, then, but he remembered that he was engaged in a competition. Beside him, deep in fever, Hanuman still slept. Often, Danlo thought his sleep was with death. Each time when he had almost given up hope, however, Hanuman would cough, and the snowy mats covering him would rattle and shake. The fever was saving the boy, keeping him warm beneath layers of robes, mats, and snow. All the others around him, of course, were also being covered with snow. And they each wore robes, but there was no real heat in clothing. Clothing could keep heat in; it could not make heat. Only a living thing such as a star or a body's inner fires could make heat.

"Look at them quit!" Danlo heard one of the novices exclaim. "A little snow and they can't stand it."

Many petitioners began standing up, brushing snow from their sodden robes, and leaving the Square. All but a few of the mats within fifty yards of Danlo and Hanuman were empty. Danlo lifted his head to count the remaining petitioners. A stand of yu trees obscured his vision; he couldn't see much of the Square's southern half. But from what he could see—rows of abandoned mats broken here and there by a miserable, shivering, snow-covered child—he estimated that only two hundred of them were left. Two hundred out of seven thousand! How much longer, he wondered, would Bardo the Just allow the competition to go on?

"Behold the boy of ice!" Pedar called out. There was vindictiveness in his voice, and darker emotions. Despite Master Rane's chastisement—or because of it—he obviously had decided to hate Danlo. "Why not quit? Shall I take you inside where it's warm? Why not quit *now,* while you can, Wild Boy? Danlo the Wild, the Nameless Child—don't you think you should quit?"

Snow covered Danlo's head and back; even the upturned soles of his feet were layered with snow. His skin had fallen blue cold, too cold to melt the snow.

"Quit now! Wouldn't it be so easy to quit?"

Danlo was breathing hard, almost gasping for air. He had stopped shivering. His muscles had hardened up like knots of cold shatterwood; he didn't know if he could move to stand, even if he were willing to quit. His belly ached with cold. The cold mat cut his kneecaps. The cold was like a stone point being hammered into his bones. Soon even his bones would grow numb, but now there was agony along his legs and spine. Cold and pain, pain and cold—it seemed that the world was made of nothing else. He tried to think of a way out of the cycle of pain, but his thoughts were sluggish, as opaque and slow-moving as glacier ice. Why should he care about the world's pain, or even his own? He began falling into a deep well of torpor and insensibility. He remembered, dimly, something he had once heard as a child. While the snow fell silently over him and his will to life cooled, he remembered that certain hunters of his tribe had spoken of a discipline called *lotsara*. *Lotsara*, the burning of the blood. There was a way to look within, to light the body's inner fires and burn with warmth. Anyone could learn this way. Any *man*, that is. He knew that the art of *lotsara* was part of the Song of Life, a small part of the lore he would have been taught had he completed his passage into manhood. Only a man could apprehend the ebb and flow of the world's energies. (He wondered if the women taught such arts in their ceremonies, but he didn't know.) Only a man could have enough experience of himself to look inward at that secret place where the fires of being burst into life.

Only a man . . . He remembered certain things that Haidar had once told him about *lotsara*. As in the open-waiting attitude of the hunter, the face of being must be cleared. But instead of looking through to the other side of day with clear vision, he must look deep within for his *anima*; specifically, he must look for the life fire that is the most vital part of *anima*, and in so doing, he must face himself.

Because the world was only a swirling cloud of snow—because his sight was failing—he closed his eyes. There was darkness and silence as vast as the night. He descended into himself; it was like venturing into an unknown, unexplored cavern. Unknown, and yet he seemed instinctively to know the way. The remembered stories of his elders guided him; he could almost hear Haidar chanting, "*Ti-miura anima, ti-miura wilu sibana:* to follow your *anima*, follow the hunger of your will." Deep in his belly, he found the place where the *anima* dwelt. Behind his navel, almost touching his spine—that was the secret place. At birth, the navel of man was cut off from creation's fires, but deeper inside a part of the sacred flame always burned. And now the flame was as tenuous and dim as that of a dying oilstone; now he must make it burn more brightly. He envisioned the fat tissues of his body. Between skin and muscle, in his chest, belly, and groin, along the soles of his feet and the palms of his

167

hands, was a thin layer of fat. He was lean as knotted rope leather, but even bodies that have once starved retain a trace of fat. There was scant fat, but what little there was, he envisioned melting like blubber inside an oilstone. Melting, heating, flowing inside him, catching fire. There was a fire in his belly, then, and it was hot. It burned and grew hotter, touched his blood. The fire of life raced along his blood. His veins were burning vessels of fire, burning and branching down his legs and arms, quickening even his numbed fingertips with heat. Into his skin came a hot, red flush. The snow atop his back began to thaw. Soon the snow was falling down his sides in slushy clumps. Snowflakes striking his bare, red skin dissolved instantly into drops of water. But the water was not cold; he felt life rushing hot in every part of him, and he couldn't imagine ever being cold again.

"Look!" someone said. "Look how red his skin is! The snow's melting off him."

Pedar worked his skates closer to Danlo and felt his arm. "It's hot," he said. "It was cold, and now it's hot."

"I've heard of such things," another said. "Down in the Farsider's Quarter, some of the avadhutas soak their robes in water. And sit outside in winter all night long. They dry their robes with their body heat. Do you think he's an avadhuta?"

"Who knows?" Pedar said. He picked at one of the pimples on his cheek. He did not seem pleased. "It must be a trick, though. A drug. No one could melt snow like this without drugs."

The crowd surrounding Danlo broke into tens of arguments. Most of the novices wanted to believe that he hadn't used drugs, though no one seemed to know what else could be the source of his heat.

Just then, Bardo the Just returned, wobbling on his skates. Despite the snow, his bulging forehead was dripping with sweat. His huge nose, which was shot with a webwork of tiny broken veins, glistened purple-black. He liked to drink beer at any time of the day; the novices knew this, and they tried to avoid him when he was drunk. "By God, what do any of you know about drugs!" he shouted as he heaved closer and wrapped his moist, meaty hand around the back of Danlo's neck. "He *is* hot," he pronounced. "But it can't be the result of a drug. When have the petitioners ever been tested by cold before, eh? Until the day before yesterday, I myself, Bardo the Just, didn't know what this year's test would be. How could this wild boy know? No, it's something else, something remarkable. Ah . . . strange. There are ancient disciplines—this Danlo the Wild has been taught things."

Pedar slung his toe pick against the ice, kicking up flowers of snow against Danlo's face. He asked, "What kind of things?"

Instantly Bardo pirouetted like a master ice dancer and cuffed Pedar's ear. He could turn cruel when he was drunk, cruel and sentimental. "What's wrong with you!" Bardo bellowed. "Kicking snow in this poor boy's face when he can't get off his mat! I told you to watch him, not torture him." Then he stroked his mustache and began talking to himself in a deep, melodious voice: "Ah, too bad, Bardo, my friend—why did you leave a novice to do your work?"

Pedar, stunned by the quickness and force of Bardo's blow, stood with his hand clapped over his ear. His face was full of hate as he cowered and glared down at Danlo.

The novices surrounding Bardo seemed to shrink back as if they too were afraid of being struck. One of Pedar's friends waved his hand at the almost empty Square and asked, "Please, Master Lal, how much longer can it go on? There are only a hundred of them left."

Bardo squinted his shiny brown eyes against the falling snow. He looked at Danlo and frowned. "Look at this poor, naked boy!" he exclaimed to the novices. "He's more patient than any of you!" Then he grunted and puffed as he bent low and cupped his hands over Danlo's ear. His breath was sour with beer, and he whispered, "Are you testing me, or am I testing you? I've never seen anyone as hard as you. Ah, that is, there's only been one other. Who *are* you, by God? No, no, do not answer, you may not speak. But tell me, Wild Boy—shake your head if the answer is no—if I let the test go on, you won't die and make me look like a barbarian, will you?"

Silently, Danlo smiled and shook his head.

"The test continues!" Bardo announced as he straightened up. "The test will be over when it's over."

And so Danlo and the hundred remaining petitioners waited through the long day. In the silence of the snowfall, in the whiteness of the buildings around the Square, it was hard to tell how much time had passed. Danlo knelt on his mat and watched sparkling snowflakes tumble through the air. He was afire with *lotsara* and with hope, but his body's tissues were burning too quickly. He was very thirsty. Quite a few of the petitioners had fallen deathly ill after eating mouthfuls of snow, but he knew better than to eat snow, even though his throat was hot and parched, even though his heart felt like a pool of lava surging against his breastbone. Soon he would collapse; soon would come crushing weakness, a stilling of eyelight, and finally oblivion. And then he would never journey beyond the stars to find *halla*; his only journey would be to the other side of day where the sea is white and cold and bare, and the ice of eternity goes on and on forever.

"Danlo, Danlo." He thought he heard Hanuman whispering to him, but in truth, Pedar and the other high novices were keeping too close a watch for anyone to risk whispering. And Hanuman was still sleeping beneath his double robes, beneath his mats and thick blanket of snow. How troubled the boy seemed, wincing and coughing in his sleep. Then, as Danlo looked on, Hanuman came gradually awake. He rose through his fever, murmuring, and he looked at Danlo. Danlo, Danlo, his eyes seemed to cry out, I owe you my life.

"Look," Pedar said as he pointed at Hanuman, "the sick boy is awake."

Bardo the Just and hundreds of chattering novices stood around making embarrassing comments as to Danlo's and Hanuman's courage, recounting the events of the day. And then Pedar snarled at Danlo, "It's unlikely that you'll pass the other tests even if you pass this one. But if you do, I hope you're assigned to my dormitory. It's called Perilous Hall, Wild Boy. Can you remember that name?"

Although this hazing was directed at Danlo, its effect on Hanuman was startling. Hanuman's face, already deathly white, grew cold and hard as if his skin were frozen. The only part of him that seemed alive was his eyes, which were burning with a pale fury. This fury frightened Danlo, for it seemed to come out of nowhere. Furious over Pedar's words, Hanuman tried to kick away the mats and sit up. But he was too weak to move. He lay staring at Danlo, helpless in his fury and his shame.

There, in the falling snow, Hanuman and Danlo waited together locked eye to eye; neither of them wanted to be the first to look away. While many people stood above them commenting on the unseasonable snowfall, a silent communication flowed between them, secrets that both of them knew they must never reveal. Danlo was aware of Hanuman's intense powers of concentration, his devotion to friendship and fate; they were both very aware of each other. Thus they waited all afternoon, and Danlo wanted to say, "Hanu, Hanu, you are as dangerous as Ayeye, the thallow." Then from a distance came the faint ringing of Resa's evening bells. The crowd around them stirred. Among the weary novices who had been patrolling Lavi Square since dawn, there were grumblings, quick arguments, a rippling wave of concern for Danlo and Hanuman, and for the others. Then Bardo the Just rubbed his eyes, shot Danlo a curious, admiring look, and he clapped his hands.

"Silence, it's time!" he said. He was speaking to the novices and to the crowd of onlookers; the miserable petitioners were as silent as they had been since the first morning of their competition. "Silence, it's time, by God! It's time that the Test of Patience comes to an end. You petitioners," he began, and then he shut his mouth abruptly. One of his novices, breathless from a quick trip through the Square, chose that moment to tell him something. Then Bardo went on, "You *seventy-two* petitioners have survived the first test. We welcome you to continue with the second test, which will begin five days hence. There are hot baths, coffee, and food waiting for you in the dormitories. The novices will escort you there. Congratulations—you may now leave your places and speak as you wish."

Instantly, there were shouts of relief; petitioners were arising from their mats shivering as they slapped blood back into their limbs and rushed to follow the novices inside.

"Danlo the Wild!" a novice in the crowd suddenly called out. "Someone get a fur for Danlo the Wild!"

Still on his mat, Danlo knocked snow from his disheveled hair and tried to stand. He could not. He no longer cared if Pedar and the others beheld his cut membrum. In truth, he could not stand because his joints were stiff and locked, shooting with pain. There was agony in his loins convulsing up his spine to his neck. As the snow and air found his exposed belly, as the fire of *lotsara* left him, he began shivering again. Even though someone threw a thick shagshay fur over his naked shoulders, he couldn't stop shivering. "Hanu, Hanu," he said as he staggered in a half crouch over to his friend. "Hanu, it's over."

Hanuman, of all the petitioners (except five unfortunate boys who were found dead), remained motionless on his mat. Indeed, many thought that he too had died, but Danlo could still see the life inside him. A novice arrived carrying a bulky shagshay fur, and Danlo helped him lay it over Hanuman's body.

"Danlo, are you all right?" Hanuman asked softly. He was breathing as rapidly as a snow hare, and he had stopped coughing. "I was afraid you were going to die."

After that the novices carried Hanuman away. Danlo was

left to fend off the congratulations of the curious crowd. Someone eased into his hand a mug of hot coffee, which he gulped down gratefully. He stood closely pressed by a hundred cheering strangers, surrounded yet alone with his thoughts.

And then Pedar came up to him; his pimply face was red and inflamed from the cold. "We'll take care of him," he said.

"What will you do . . . with my friend?" Danlo asked.

"Your *friend*?" Pedar asked. "Listen, Wild Boy, there's an old saying you should know: 'Save a person's life, make an enemy for life.' I don't think that boy will ever be your friend."

Danlo covered his eyes against the falling snow, and he wondered about Hanuman. As he began walking with the other novices toward the warmth of the waiting dormitories, he hoped that Pedar would be wrong.

C H A P T E R 7

PERILOUS HALL

The Universal Syntax—invented by Omar Narayama on Arcite twenty years before the founding of Neverness. The emergence of holism during the Fifth Mentality was fully realized in the development of the universal syntax. It is perhaps an accident of history that where the invention of science depended upon a mathematics as old as the civilizations of Babylonia and Ur, the universal syntax was discovered long after holism began to permeate and even supersede science. How human knowledge of the universe might have evolved had the reverse been the case is arguable, but without the development of the universal syntax, the full articulation of holism certainly would have been impossible.

Abstract of Main Line Information: Omar Narayama was a linguist in the Order of Scientists; ironically his life's work was to spell the demise of that ancient order and forever change man's approach to science. Narayama, like other scientists at the end of the Age of Simulation, had come to realize the limitations of computer modelings of the phenomena and laws of space-time. He sought a universalization of science—it was the Holy Grail of his times. A century earlier, the Fravashi language philosophies had profoundly influenced the intellectual climate of the Civilized Worlds. Narayama was a student of the Fravashi, and he began his career with a solution to the essential problem of formalistic cognition: what is it we see when we see? Narayama hypothesized that we see a bunch of glued-together sticks as a chair; we see a latticework of carbon atoms fixed into platinum as a diamond ring. It was with the formalization of the concept "as" that Narayama laid the foundations for the universal syntax. His life's work —and the work of those who followed him—was to uti-

173

lize the structures of language in order to model those aspects of reality too complex to be represented by a strictly science-oriented mathematics.

Branching Information Lines, more at Holism: *Omar Narayama, biography, History of Science; Causality; Causal Decoupling; Backward Causality and the Theory of Scrying; Arcite; History of the Order of Cetics; the Order of New Scientists; the Order of New Scientists —Schism and War; The Age of Simulation; the Fifth Mentality; the Fravashi Songlines; Fravashi Philosophy; Fravashi Theories of Language*

—Encyclopaedia Britannica, *1,754th Edition, Tenth Revised Standard Version*

During the days of his recuperation Danlo saw nothing of Hanuman li Tosh. By making inquiries of several high novices whom he befriended, he discovered that Hanuman had been taken to Borja's main hospice, there to be healed—if that was his fate— or to begin his journey to the other side of day. For Danlo this period of waiting before the next test was full of both pleasure and uncertainty. He worried about Hanuman; at times, when he fell back into the easy, familiar ways of childhood and forgot that he was a man (or almost a man), he worried about himself. But, in truth, it was not in Danlo's nature to worry overlong. Life is lived in the Now-moment, as the Alaloi say, and he took a joy in the simple and most immediate activities of life: in drinking hot mint teas, sleeping and eating, awakening every morning to coffee, bread, and hot baths, and before each morning was ended, sleeping some more. After his ordeal in the snow, his keenest joy was in simply being warm. He, like each of the other seventy petitioners, had been given a tiny private room in the Farsider's dormitory just west of Lavi Square. He spent whole days sitting in front of his room's fireplace. While spruce logs crackled on the grate and flames danced against blackened stones, he liked to turn his face to the fire, to bask naked in the rippling red waves of heat, and play his shakuhachi. At the end of each day he would eat a sumptuous meal of wild rice and almonds, snowberries in cream, egg flower soup, nut-cakes or other rich foods, and he would walk through the dormitory greeting his fellow petitioners. Sometimes various novices —boys and girls whom he did not know—would come to visit him in order to satisfy their curiosity. Once, on the third day following his ordeal, a tall, dour novice named Kiril Burian walked into Danlo's room and told him, "I saw what you did in the Square. How did you keep from freezing to death? Where is your home? If you get past the next tests, I hope you're assigned to my dormitory—Isabel Hall, it's called. You'd be welcomed there, even if you are an outsider."

Danlo found his instant fame and popularity strange. He didn't really understand popularity. He was familiar, of course, with prowess, veneration, and friendship—these were good Alaloi concepts. But the novices who sought his company did not really seem to want him as a friend, not at first, nor did they venerate what little wisdom he had acquired during his quest to find *halla*. His popularity, as far as he could see, stemmed from a single deed of friendship toward Hanuman and from a prowess of *lotsara* that all full men should possess. And how he hated the infectious nature of popularity! That people would wish to associate with him not for the qualities of his face—that is, for his self-awareness, character, and mind—but simply because they perceived a social utility in being seen with someone who was temporarily the center of attention, he found silly and perverse. He hated, too, the way the petitioners were maltreated and scorned. Petitioners—a very few of them—*could* become novices, but it seemed that since they had not attended the Order's elite schools, they would always be regarded as outsiders. This elitism and vanity of novices such as Pedar, he hated deeply. But because he regarded hatred as the vilest of emotions, a black, churning rent in the ocean of his being which might swallow him whole at any time, he did not allow himself to hate. Instead, as a discipline, he tried to make friends with as many novices as he could. In almost everyone, even in Pedar, he found some aspect of face, spirit, or *anima* that he could revere. Many years later, Hanuman li Tosh would say to him: "I've never known anyone who *liked* as many things as you do." Ironically, Danlo's unrestrained love of life wherever he found it was to win him many friends and bring him even greater popularity.

Early in the morning of the thirty-first day, Danlo was finally called to be tested. Unlike the Test of Patience, the next crucial tests were not public, and he underwent them alone. In a

175

cold stone room of the Akashic's Tower, a jolly master akashic named Hannah li Hua placed a heaume over his head and tested the physical structures of his brain. She tested for other things as well, but she refused to reveal the nature of these tests to Danlo. When she bade good-bye to him, she never told if he had done well or ill, but simply said, "I hope your petition is accepted, Danlo the Wild."

Over the next few days, Danlo came to know the Academy very well, for he crossed and recrossed its lovely grounds many times. Upplysa, with its basalt arches and narrow, winding pathways, was the largest of the Order's colleges. There, the master eschatologist, Kolenya Mor, tested his knowledge of holism and the universal syntax; there, too, he was summoned before Thomas Rane and Octavia of Darkmoon, who, as Old Father had warned would happen, tested him to see if he was a man of shih. His last test was with a famous pilot, an exemplar named the Sonderval. At Resa, the pilot's college, the Sonderval posed twelve mathematical theorems to Danlo and then invited him to attempt proofs or disproofs. Danlo was able to prove only five of the twelve theorems, and he therefore concluded that he had failed this very important test. When he asked the Sonderval if this was so, he was told, "The Master of Novices will inform you as to the results of your tests after the board convenes to decide your petition."

"The Master of Novices," Danlo said. "This Bardo the Just —he is a just man, yes?"

At this innocent question, the Sonderval smiled arrogantly, then said, "If you're accepted into the Order, then you'll learn about Bardo the Just."

Altogether, "Bardo the Just" had assembled a board of five prominent masters to examine the petitioners. As Danlo would learn, Bardo had chosen such an illustrious quintet to honor the petitioners. But it did not really require the skills and wisdom of famous masters to test petitioners. Bardo had inveigled his friends—Kolenya Mor, Octavia, and the others—to participate in the Festival of the Unfortunate Petitioners for selfish reasons. In truth, he had pleaded with them to do him this favor; he had done this because he wished to honor himself. Some years before, he had been passed over for the lordship of the pilots. Chanoth Chen Ciceron had been made Lord Pilot in his place— or so the envious Bardo complained to any of his friends who would listen. And Bardo, who thought of himself as the finest and most able of the pilots to have survived the infamous Pilot's

War thirteén years previously, had been made Master of Novices, a humble position with few possibilities for either power or glory. And so he liked to surround himself with the Order's most distinguished men and women, to share in their radiance, and all the while, secretly, he chafed and raged at the unfairness of life.

He was a vain man, yes, but ultimately his vanity (and his compassion) would accrue to Danlo's favor. After Danlo had finished his last test, he was summoned to the Novices' Sanctuary, a huge, forbidding building overlooking Borja's many dormitories. A novice met Danlo at the door of the Sanctuary and led Danlo to Bardo's formal chambers in the west wing. After Danlo knocked at the door, Bardo invited Danlo inside, into a room decorated with rich furniture and rare works of art. "Ah, it's the Wild Boy," Bardo said. "Danlo the Wild—are you really a nameless child, after all?"

Bardo led Danlo to one of the windows looking out over Borja. Almost at the foot of the window, set into the dark floor, were two rectangular stones all smooth and gray and slightly concave, as if a fine chisel had scooped out their centers. These were the famous kneeling stones of Borja. Bardo bade Danlo drop down on the kneeling stones, facing the window. He, himself, pulled up an immense, padded leather chair and positioned it at a right angle to Danlo, so that he could see the side of Danlo's face. While Danlo gazed out at the Tycho's Spire, which overwhelmed Borja's lesser buildings, Bardo studied his face and finally said, "By God, who *are* you?"

Although Bardo had warned Danlo not to turn his head, he had said nothing of his eyes, and so Danlo knelt there locked in thought, and his eyes flicked back and forth, straining to take in sights of the room. He could barely see Bardo, but directly ahead of him, Bardo's bearded profile and the shadow of his chair played against rich tapestries on the wall.

"You may speak when I've asked you a question."

Danlo touched the feather in his hair as he thought of how Old Father would answer the question of identity. Because he knew it was unseemly (and foolish) to vex his elders, he tried to restrain himself, but finally, he couldn't help saying, "Who are *you*, sir? Who is anybody?"

"Who am *I*?"

Danlo smiled slyly, then asked, "Have you ever seen me before?"

"No."

"Then how do you know it *is* me?"

There was a long pause full of Bardo's raspy breathing, and then he burst out, "Impolite boy! By God, how do I know it *is* you? Is this a Fravashi word game? You were a student of the Fravashi, weren't you?"

Danlo nodded his head while he looked out the window at the clouds in the sky.

"Well, listen, my funny boy: How do you dare play your impolite Fravashi games with me? Don't you know that I have to decide whether to make you a novice or not? Don't you know that—stop it now! Stop laughing, or I'll have to dismiss you immediately!" And then he was addressing himself again, mumbling wearily, "Ah, Bardo, Bardo, what have you done?"

Danlo couldn't help laughing because Bardo was a funny man, at once passionate and self-pitying, compassionate and slightly cruel. Finally, though, he restrained himself and said, "I am sorry, sir. It is just that laughter . . . is blessed, yes?"

While Bardo pulled at his beard, he cleared his throat and said, "The truth is, there *is* something familiar about you. Where are you from?"

"If I told you where I was from, you might not believe me."

"Test me, please; test my belief and tell me, who were your parents? On which world were you born?"

"I am not sure . . . I should tell you, sir."

"Ah, you think to keep secrets," Bardo said. "Well, at least you're not of Tria, nor have you had contact with the warrior-poets."

Danlo was cold in his robe and sandals, though not nearly so cold as he had been during his day and night in Lavi Square. The bare floor hurt his knees. He brushed his knuckles against the gray stone, which thousands of novices' knees had worn smooth. He thought the kneeling stones must be very old, though he couldn't know that along with all the other stones of the Sanctuary, they had been transported from Arcite at the founding of the Order long ago. "How do you know I am not from Tria?"

"Are you?"

"No," Danlo said, smiling, "I have never heard of Tria. What is Tria?"

From his side came Bardo's deep basso voice, "By God, why must you answer a question with a question! You should know something right away, Wild Boy. It's impolite for petitioners—or novices or even journeymen—to question their masters.

Unless they've first requested and been granted permission. Now, how is it you haven't heard of Tria? The merchant-pilots? Ah, you know nothing of the warrior-poets?"

Danlo looked out the window to the north. He saw the rows of fine, old granite buildings—the boys' dormitories—and the Academy's north wall just beyond them. "No, I have never heard of warrior-poets," he said truthfully.

"Ahhhh," Bardo said.

"May I ask you a question, sir?"

"Please, ask."

"How did you know I am not a warrior and a poet?"

"You mean, a *warrior-poet*. Warrior-poets are assassins who kill people for money and for religious reasons. And of course you're not one of them. You're too young—they all have a certain look. What I *know* is that you've never had contact with one. Master Hua told me this."

Danlo stared out the window to the south, at the girls' dormitories, which were arrayed in concentric circles, little white domes against the sparkling white of newly fallen snow. He had been afraid that when Master Hua examined his brain, she would discover everything about him. "She can see my mind, I think."

"Well, she can certainly *read* segments of your memory."

"Then she must have told you where I was born."

"Not true." Bardo's shadow moved as if he were pulling at his beard. On the wall in front of Danlo, darkening a tapestry of many nude dancing women, he could see a shadow hand against a huge shadow face. "Not at all true, Wild Boy. Master Hua is an akashic. She's been intimate with your memory. She must respect and guard confidences—the canons of our Order require this. I asked her certain questions about you. I was able to determine where you're *not* from. And that you're not a slel-mime of the warrior-poets, nor a Trian spy, nor an Architect of the Old Cybernetic Church or of any other religion, order, or cabal on the prescribed list."

"The prescribed list?"

"Is that a question, Wild Boy?"

Danlo pressed his knuckles against the floor to take some of the weight off his knees. He hated the custom of kneeling because he thought it unnatural and unseemly for a man to so defer to another. "I mean, may I ask you a question, sir?"

"Please ask."

"What is the prescribed list?"

Bardo belched and licked his lips. "It's the list of our enemies. The Order has survived for three thousand years, but not by admitting enemies into our halls."

"I am no one's enemy," Danlo said. He dropped his eyes down to the floor as he thought of what Pedar had said to him in Lavi Square. He wondered if his saving Hanuman's life could really cause two friends to become enemies. "I am . . . not even sure what you are talking about."

"How astonishingly . . . ah, that is to say, it's surprising that you could be so—"

"Ignorant, yes?"

Bardo belched again and coughed in embarrassment. "I didn't want to say the word. And don't interrupt me, please. Well, you *are* ignorant, aren't you? You're different from the other petitioners. And then there is the matter of your hair. Black and red—like that of Mallory Ringess. And your face, hard as flint—you've the Ringess nose, too. And your damn eyes. Ah, I don't really want to discuss your eyes. Please tell me, you've been sculpted, haven't you? It's a common enough practice lately. Mallory Ringess becomes a goddamned god, and so it's natural enough that people would want to sculpt their faces and hair color to look like him."

No one had ever remarked upon Danlo's resemblance to Mallory Ringess. Bardo's observation pleased Danlo and added weight to his theory of his true parentage, but he didn't want to explain this theory to Bardo, so he said, "This is how I was born. My hair is my hair, and my face . . . a man must grow into his face, yes?"

"Ahhh," Bardo said, "you may keep your secrets if you must, but *I* must inform you, it won't aid your petition."

Danlo stared out the window and said nothing.

"Well, then, perhaps you can tell me how you raised your metabolism so goddamned dramatically during your test? Your skin was as hot as a whore's breath! That's a cetic art—you've had cetic training, eh?"

"No, sir." Danlo pressed the point of his finger against his robe where it covered his navel and said, "There is a place in the belly . . . the life fire, indwelling, and if you can envision it as a flame, then—"

"Stop!" Bardo called out as he clapped his hands together. He pushed himself to his feet, which wasn't an easy thing to do considering his immense bulk and the lowness of the chair. He stood in front of Danlo and above him. His face was full of perplexity and wonder. "There's something strange about you. Who are you, by God? What you've just described—it sounds like the Alaloi practice of *lotsara*!"

It was as if Danlo had fallen through the ice into the sea, so quickly did he gasp for air and his muscles seize up. He knelt there looking up at Bardo the Just in amazement, and his belly muscles wouldn't stop quivering. How could this vain, ugly man know of *lotsara*? Had Hanuman betrayed him by telling of his origins and secret quest to find *halla*? Of course, had Danlo known more of the recent history of the Order, he would have heard the story of Bardo's journey to the Alaloi. But he never suspected that Bardo had accompanied Mallory Ringess on this disastrous journey. What he feared was that the akashic woman had read his deepest memories—either that, or somehow Bardo could read his mind. Didn't the men and women of the Unreal City possess many inexplicable powers? In truth, he didn't really believe that any human being could read another's mind without the aid of a *shaida* computer. (No matter how many times Danlo was to interface computers—and there would be many, many times—no matter how profound the experience, he would always think of computers as the most *shaida* of all mankind's inventions.) But, he mused, if Bardo really *could* see the thoughts behind his face, he had better be careful what he thought. And so, like a hunter passing into the open-waiting attitude of *auvania*, Danlo emptied his mind of everything other than immediate sensa: the sunlight streaming hot and low through the window; Bardo's sweetish, flowery scent overlaying the faint sourness of dried beer; and the slightly curved hollows of stone cupping his knees. His eyes, blue-black as twilight, focused on infinity, on the distant spires of the Old City shimmering in the west. There was a stillness in his eyes, a deep patience and clarity of vision.

"Danlo!"

"Yes?"

"Why this mystery?" Bardo huffed out. He grabbed his belly and bent over so that his face was nearly the same height as Danlo's. "I've seen eyes like yours before—tell me, my Wild Boy, why are you so quiet? What's behind your flawless eyes?"

Danlo was silent for a long time, and then he finally confided his fear that Bardo could see his thoughts.

"That's silly!" Bardo exclaimed. "Read your thoughts! By God, I can hardly read my own. Ah, *what* am I to do with you, Wild Boy?"

"I do not know," Danlo said, too truthfully.

"That wasn't a question."

"It wasn't? But, sir, it sounded like a question."

"It was a rhetorical question, a question not meant to be answered."

"Excuse me," Danlo said.

Bardo scratched his mustache and belched. He looked down at Danlo. "I know of *lotsara* because I've studied the Alaloi and their language—many in the City have. But how do *you* know? Ah, that is, how did you come to practice this art of the burning blood? Who taught you? Your Fravashi sponsor? No, no, that can't be—the Old Fathers of the Fravashi don't care about the body arts, do they?"

The late sun through the window limned Bardo's massive head. His rings of curly black hair were lustrous with refracted bronzes and golds. Because the dazzling light hurt Danlo's eyes, he put his hand to his forehead, squinted, and said, "Sir, you are a man of . . . rare sensibilities. Would I win your confidence by betraying another's?"

Bardo pulled at his thick lower lip. He smiled and said, "Well, you're really not so impolite after all. You've manners, strange manners, but manners nonetheless. I like that. I want you to call me 'Master Bardo.' *Bardo*—now that's a name with a certain euphony, don't you think?"

"No, Master Bardo." In truth, Danlo thought his name was ill-chosen, ominous, and somewhat absurd. It reminded him too much of the *barado,* which was the Alaloi word for the confusion a person's spirit undergoes just after death.

"No? Well, you needn't be so honest—aren't you afraid of insulting me?"

Danlo laughed and said, "No, Master Bardo."

"And now you laugh at me again. Ha, what have I done wrong that a petitioner isn't afraid of laughing at me?"

"Is that another rhetorical question?"

"By God, haven't I instructed you not to answer a question with a question?"

"Yes, Master Bardo. I . . . just wanted to say, you are a funny man, a kind, compassionate, funny man, and you make me laugh."

Bardo's face was flushed as if he'd been drinking beer, and he rubbed his huge snow apple of a nose. "Kind? Compassionate? Ah, well, perhaps I am," he admitted. "You've a talent for the truth. Everyone knows Bardo has a wit, but it wouldn't do for boys to laugh at him, do you understand? At *me*. Now, while you're being truthful, I must ask you the question you've been brought here for: Why do you wish to enter the Order? I ask all the petitioners this question. Your answer may determine whether you are made a novice—so consider what you say."

Danlo looked down and picked at the mortar of the loose, gray floor stone in front of him. From another part of the building, down the long corridor outside the room, came the sound of voices, creaking doors, and bells chiming. The Sanctuary, with its solemnity and air of hidden activities, reminded him of Old Father's house. "I came to Neverness to be a pilot," he began. "A pilot of a lightship. To journey to the center of the great circle of stars. I must find a way . . . to go over without actually dying, a way of looking at the universe, as from the other side. Or *inside*. Above time, beyond the starry night, I . . . I am not saying this well, am I? There is a Fravashi word, a splendid word: the asarya. You know it, yes? I have to *see* where the universe is in harmony and where it is not before I can affirm it. And I must affirm it, even where it is . . . cold and terrible. If I do not, I shall never become a full man. Never fully alive."

When he had finished telling Bardo that he had descryed signs he would be a pilot, that it was his fate, he sat back on his heels and winced at the sharp, tearing pain beneath his knee-caps.

"Ahhh." That was all Bardo said at first. He stood with his back to the window regarding Danlo for a long time. "Ah, that is quite an answer! A remarkable answer, even! Do you know what other petitioners typically reply when asked why they want to enter the Order?"

"No, Master Bardo."

"Well, they say things like 'I want to devote myself to study and increase the Order's knowledge.' Or—and this is the kind of thing which makes me want to slap their faces—they tell me: 'I want to serve mankind.' Liars! They give me these kinds of answers supposing that's what I want to hear, and all the time they're thinking that if I accept them into the Order, their careers are made. What they really want is a life of fame, power, and glory. As I, Bardo, of all men should know. But you, you're different, by God! You're not afraid of telling the naked, fantastic, dangerous truth. You want to become an asarya! I like that! I like you. Well, Wild Danlo, I shall help you where I can."

Danlo knelt down gripping his knees, and he asked, "Can you tell me if I . . . survived the tests?"

Bardo nodded his head. "It was close, but you acquitted yourself well enough. You've a curious deficiency in the universal syntax, but this was outweighed by your sense of shih. And your mathematics—"

"I am sorry, sir, but I was able to prove only five of the theorems."

"Well, that's two more theorems than anyone else was able to prove. You've a talent for mathematics, it seems. I like mathematical men."

"I have always . . . loved mathematics," Danlo said.

"Ah, very well, but will you please remedy your deficiency in the universal syntax? Otherwise, you'll make Bardo look like a fool."

"Why, sir?"

"Why?" Bardo smiled at him then, and with his thumb, he flicked a bead of sweat from his bulging forehead. "Because the board has recommended that you be admitted to the Order, and it's upon me to make the final decision. And I've decided to make you a novice—did I not just tell you that I'd help you?"

Without thought or hesitation, Danlo leapt to his feet, flung his arms wide, then jumped into the air. "Ahira, Ahira!" he cried out. Tears sprang to his eyes, and he was breathing so quickly that his fingers began to tingle. He forgot himself and his etiquette then, and he fell against Bardo as if he were his near-father, pressing his forehead to Bardo's chest while he tried to get his arms around his huge belly in close embrace.

"Easy now!" Bardo said as he gently peeled Danlo's hands from behind his back and pushed him away. He held him by the shoulder at arm's length. "Ah, easy there."

Danlo tried to catch his breath and gasped out, "O . . . blessed . . . Bardo!"

"No, no, *Master* Bardo," Bardo corrected. "Try to remember your manners."

"I am . . . sorry," Danlo said.

Out of sheer joy, Danlo had been dancing about like child, but suddenly he stood still and looked at Bardo. He was tall for his years, but his forehead was just level with Bardo's chest, and so he had to tilt his head back in order to engage Bardo eye to eye. "May I ask a question, sir?"

"Please, do."

"No one has been able to tell me about Hanuman li Tosh, and I have not been allowed out of the dormitory to visit him. Is he . . . well?"

184

With his fingers, Bardo smoothed his mustache and then laid his heavy hand on Danlo's shoulder. "Ah, yes, your friend," he said. "A beautiful boy—I've never seen anyone as beautiful, not even the exemplars of Kaveri Luz. Too bad, too bad. He has a cancer in his lungs. It's been controlled, but I'm not sure if he'll ever be really well."

"Then . . . he has not been tested?"

"Well, there was no need for further tests. Your friend was almost a graduate of an elite school. We knew the quality of his mind; it remained only to test his, ah . . . patience."

"Then he will be admitted, too?"

"He already has been. He's a novice now; he took his vows three days ago. I'm sure he's been assigned to one of the novices' dormitories."

Danlo stepped over to the window and pressed his head against the cold clary pane. He was happy for Hanuman, but once again he had been reminded how difficult it was for an outsider such as himself to enter the Order.

"Of course," Bardo continued, "I asked Hanuman his question, just as I asked you. About why he wanted to be a novice. Do you know what he told me? He said that he wanted power, fame, and glory! An honest boy! Of course, I *had* to admit him after that, didn't I? Ah, yes, but there's something about him that unsettles me. He's honest on the surface, but underneath, he keeps secrets. He's *too* ambitious, I think. Listen to me, I'm a keen judge of character, and I know. Be careful of this boy. I'm not sure he's a good choice for a friend."

A sudden gust of wind rattled the window, and Danlo stepped to the side, beneath the arching stone wall, in case the window shattered. He said, "But, Master Bardo, I have no choice, now. We can choose whom to make friends with, yes, but we cannot . . . *un*choose them, can we?"

Bardo pulled at his beard, seemingly lost in his memories. His voice rumbled out, "Ah, that's true. So very true. Well, be friends with him if you must. I'll even have the Head Novice assign you to his dormitory, if you'd like."

"Thank you, sir."

With a wave of his hand, Bardo motioned toward the door. "Now, please leave me. I've twenty other petitioners to interview today. I wish you well, Wild Danlo."

.   .   .   .   .

The next day Danlo began preparations for taking his vows. His old clothes, the jacket and trousers he had surrendered in the Ice Dome, were burned in a private ceremony. He was given new clothes: a formal white robe, three informal robes, undergarments, three kamelaikas, a wind jacket, and a parka made of cultured shagshay fur. And, of course, two pairs of ice skates and a pair of skis. All of this apparel was white, as was the wool cap he was required to wear on his head at all times. But before he could don the "Cap of Borja," as it was called, he had to have his head shaved. This posed something of a problem as Danlo placed great value on his long, flowing black hair. In fact, as an Alaloi man, he was not permitted to cut his hair—otherwise it would have been impossible for him to fasten and display Ahira's white tail feather in the proper manner. "All novices must shave their heads," Bardo said to Danlo. "Why are you so goddamned stubborn?" After a long, confusing discussion in which Danlo spoke of Ahira and the meaning of the feather he wore in his hair, Bardo decided that he was a remarkably superstitious boy who had adopted certain of the Alaloi's unfathomable, barbaric religious beliefs. And although Bardo himself eschewed a personal God or any formal notions as to how a man should relate to the godhead, he, as Master of Novices, was required to respect all of humanity's religions, even the most totalitarian and bizarre. He remembered that, twenty years ago, a Jewish novice had been permitted to wear a black skullcap called a yarmulke underneath the wool cap of Borja. True, many revered (or ridiculed) Judaism as the oldest of religions—Old Earth's ur-religion whose origins dated back at least four thousand years before the Swarming. But, Bardo reasoned, if exceptions in custom could be made for an archaic Jew, he could certainly arrange a compromise with a wild boy who believed that a stupid white bird could hold half of his soul. And so, in the end, a compromise was reached: Danlo submitted to a high novice who cut his hair and lathered the stubble with a rose-scented shaving soap. All of his scalp was shaved except for a round circle of hair at the back of his head. In the manner of the Chinese warlords of Old Earth, he wore a queue of black hair dangling halfway down his back. The queue was long and thick like the tail of a muskox; although some of the novices made jokes about it, Danlo was very proud to keep Ahira's shining feather bound to his hair.

A few days later Danlo finally took his vows. That year only twenty-eight petitioners were admitted to Borja. Seventeen girls and nine boys, all of them from obscure planets whose names were unfamiliar to Danlo, took their vows along with him and were assigned to the various dormitories. Danlo was delighted to be assigned to the same dormitory as was Hanuman, Penhalegon Hall, one of thirty-three boys' dormitories at the very northeastern corner of Borja. It was among the oldest of the Academy's buildings and was nicknamed Perilous Hall, with good reason. Over the millennia more than a few hapless boys had perished within its granite walls. Its interior was stark and austere, four stories of cut stone connected by a spiral of open, winding stairs. The stairs themselves were thin, fanlike slabs of basalt that had been transported from Arcite along with the other stones of the building; the stairs were chipped and worn, wickedly uneven and in many places canted off the horizontal at odd angles so that it was all too easy to catch the heel of one's foot and slip. Many boys had injured themselves tumbling down these stairs, or in a few cases had plummeted a hundred feet over the inner edge of the stairs' spiral, down the stairwell's central core to their deaths. It was an everlasting scandal that no banister or retaining wall had ever been built to prevent such accidents. But the founder of the Order, the infamous Horthy Hosthoh, had thought to train novices to mindfulness and care. And so, because the Order honored its traditions no matter how archaic or foolish, for three thousand years novices had carefully picked their way up and down these terrible stairs many times each day. It was something of a miracle that in all that time, only twenty or thirty boys had lost their lives in falls.

In truth, the fourth floor was the grandest of all the dormitory's floors, but it was also the most exhausting and dangerous to reach. Hence the newest of novices were made to trudge up to its heights, while the second-year novices occupied the next floor, and so on down to the first floor where the high novices resided. Like each of Perilous Hall's new novices, Danlo was assigned a bed on the dreaded topmost floor. One afternoon while the other boys were out taking their skating lessons, Danlo climbed the spiral stairs to find an open space of high ceiling arches and many windows set into the thick stone walls. In the main chamber, lined up against the windows in two long rows, there were twenty platform beds. Only one of them was unclaimed, and Danlo stowed his clothing and skates in the large wooden trunk he found at the foot of the bed. His shakuhachi went into the trunk, too, carefully wrapped in one of his informal robes. By rule, novices were allowed no possessions other than their clothing; by practice almost everyone kept one or two treasured items hidden in his trunk. After Danlo had made his bed, he lay atop white blankets and looked up. The twenty ceiling arches reminded him of a whale's skeleton, thick ribs of mortared stone spaced evenly down the length of the room. The arches supported a latticework of shatterwood roof beams, many of which were splintered and cracked. Danlo immediately liked the feeling of this chamber, especially the smells of old wood and sunlight streaming against woolen blankets. He liked the way sounds fell from ceiling to floor when he impulsively unwrapped and played his shakuhachi; perhaps because of its age, the vast chamber seemed to reverberate with memories and a quality of aliveness at odds with its cold austerity.

Later that morning, Danlo saw Hanuman li Tosh for the first time since their ordeal in Lavi Square. He came into the room with eighteen other chattering, raucous, boot-stomping boys. By good chance, he happened to have the bed next to Danlo's. He came over to Danlo and smiled nicely. "I haven't thanked you for saving my life," he said. "I was afraid I'd never see you again."

He stood shifting his weight from foot to foot next to Danlo's bed. His fingers were moving like spider's legs against one another; he seemed intensely kinetic and restless, as if he were unsure what his new friendship with Danlo would require of him. Danlo thought that he must be still sick inside, though probably no one noticed this but him. Indeed, Hanuman seemed much changed. Gone was his wracking cough, his fever, the deathly pallor of one who was ready to die. Gone, too, was the hair from his head; his shaved scalp was as white as an *alaya* shell. Like the other novices, he wore an informal robe with a casual grace, as if he had been born to the garments of the Order. Much of the delicateness seemed to have fallen away from his beautiful face, though with his head shaved, his cheekbones stood out more prominently, and his eyes appeared even more vivid and haunting than Danlo had remembered.

Shaida eyes, he thought for the thousandth time. And then he remembered that Hanuman was his friend, and he embraced him fiercely and cried out, "Hanu, Hanu, I am glad you are alive!"

Danlo's open, unrestrained joy obviously pleased Hanuman, although from the stiffness of Hanuman's body, Danlo immediately understood that he did not like to be touched. It was this way with most civilized people, as Danlo well knew, and so, even as he let go of Hanuman, he paid too little attention to the look of alarm on Hanuman's face.

The other novices gathered around their beds, then. They had witnessed Danlo's feat of *lotsara* in the Square, and they were eager to meet him.

And Hanuman was quite proud to make introductions. "Danlo," he said, "may I present Sherborn of Darkmoon?" And then there was a wariness in Hanuman's voice as he introduced a small boy with almond eyes and a quick, sardonic face. "And Madhava li Shing? Madhava's uncle was a master akashic, and his granduncle as well."

In turn, as Hanuman presented each of the novices, Danlo inclined his head and bowed in the proper manner. And the boys bowed to him, with too perfect a punctilio. Each of them was new to Borja, but each, like Hanuman, had studied in the elite schools of the Order. Each boy took extreme pride in being of this elite; by duty and by training no one was obviously impolite to Danlo. But as a group, they were at once disdainful of him as a lowly petitioner and envious of his instant fame. They kept a distance between themselves and Danlo, a physical distance of bare floor stones and a psychic distance of suspicious glances, awe, and a fragile, false superiority. No one wanted to exchange smiles with him or greet him eye to eye. He was popular, true, but his was the popularity of a strange new alien confined in fear and ignorance to a zoo. Only Hanuman accepted Danlo in friendship. He stood by Danlo's side, and he was unafraid to let the others know that he had nothing but contempt for their manner. It cut Danlo's heart, the way Hanuman stood apart from his peers, staring at them with his pale, icy eyes.

Because it was the beginning of the Academy's year, none of the novices had yet been assigned tutors, schedules, or duties. Danlo spent the rest of the afternoon in uneasy conversation with Madhava li Shing and others, fending off questions as to his origins. After an awkward supper in the first-floor dining room (all novices, high and low, took their meals together), Danlo and Hanuman raced up the stairs to the fourth floor where they played chess together. Hanuman had a fine, old chess set made on Yarkona. The black pieces were sculpted of shatterwood, while the white pieces were of ivory, and the set was valuable and quite rare. Hanuman's grandfather had given it to him when he was only eight years old; Hanuman had always treasured it, and it was one of the few things he had brought with him to

Neverness. When Hanuman set up the pieces for the first game, Danlo saw that the white god was missing. In its place, Hanuman had substituted a salt shaker, which was perfectly adequate for their games. But it troubled Danlo that the harmony of the set had been broken, and he was aggrieved to learn that the god had not been lost but stolen. As Hanuman explained—haltingly, choking on his anger—his father had never approved of the gift. To carve a chess piece as a god, his father claimed, symbolized the heresy that hakras (or humans) could become as true gods. It was a crime as well, pure blasphemy toward Ede the God, and on the night of Hanuman's eleventh birthday, his father had confiscated the white god as a lesson in piety. "My grandfather was a Worthy Architect, if not a Reader," Hanuman said. "He saw nothing wrong with giving me the set. But my father always had his own interpretation of doctrine. He was always so strict." After Hanuman had won three games in a row, Danlo returned to his bed to play his shakuhachi. Once, just after he had played a particularly sad passage, Hanuman shot a swift look at him. It lasted only an instant, this acid, apprehensive look, but Danlo immediately felt the deep understanding that flowed between them, as if they were the only ones in the room touched by his music.

Later that evening, in the bathing room just off the main chamber, an incident occurred that would further deepen the way Danlo and Hanuman saw each other. The boys were taking their nightly baths and shaving each other's heads; the room smelled of mildew, sweat, and fragrant shaving soaps. Due to the continual jets of hot water piped in from the geysers beneath the City, the air roiled with steam. The small, arched windows were misted over, and drops of water wormed their way down the wall tiles. Danlo was sitting cross-legged by the edge of the hot pool, gagging on lungfuls of steam, while next to him, Madhava li Shing drew a diamond-edged razor across Hanuman's scalp. Suddenly Madhava nicked Hanuman, and blood streamed from a cut on the side of his head. It was only a small wound, but Hanuman clapped his hand to it, and he gasped for air, and his eyes locked onto the black and white floor tiles as if he could discern a meaning to the pattern there that was lost on all the others.

"Excuse me," Madhava said. He moved over to one of the shaving basins, where he held the bloody razor beneath a spout of steaming water.

"It's not your fault," Hanuman finally said. "No one here has been taught how to shave another properly."

At this, Madhava stiffened up and said, "I'm sorry. I'll get some glue."

"Oh, no," Hanuman said. "*I'm* sorry. I'm sorry I let my ill mood get in the way of my tongue. Please, won't you finish shaving me?"

Hanuman went on to explain that he detested the daily routine of head shaving because it reminded him of one of the rituals of his own church. All the Worthy Architects of the Cybernetic Reformed Churches were required to shave their heads, a practice called "the little sacrifice." Ironically, he had fled his parents' religion for the supposed sanity of the Order, only to discover that he must daily sacrifice his hair not to Ede the God but to an arbitrary tradition whose beginnings no one remembered.

Just then, as Madhava began his work anew and Hanuman clenched his teeth at the razor scraping across his skull, Pedar Sadi Sanat and three other high novices stomped into the room. They were each bigger than any of the first-year novices, and they were dressed in kamelaikas as if they had just come in out of the cold. They lined up in front of the hot pool, posturing their bulky bodies to intimidate Hanuman and Danlo. It was bad chance, for Hanuman's mood, already turbid and dark, fell instantly black, and he exchanged quick looks with Danlo. Pedar, of course, noticed this look, which seemed to enrage him. "Stand up, won't you!" he called out. "Hanuman li Tosh and Danlo the Wild—we've come to greet you, so you could at least stand and greet us properly."

Together, almost as if their muscles were connected to a common nerve, Danlo and Hanuman stood up at the edge of the hot pool. Danlo was taller than Hanuman, and, with his tendons and muscles twisting like snakes along his limbs, much stronger-looking. In truth, Hanuman had yet to get his growth, and his body was small and undefined, more like a boy's than a man's. They were both naked and very aware of their nakedness.

"Welcome to Perilous Hall!" Pedar said. "We've been waiting for you."

Pedar apologized for missing the evening meal earlier; he cited his and his friends' exploits with four whores as reason for his absence from the supper table. Then he strode back and forth in front of Danlo and Hanuman, surveying their bodies. He glanced at his friends behind him, and shook his head. Of

the four high novices—indeed, of all the boys in the dormitory—
Pedar was the oldest, and his face was the most bepimpled. As
he picked at his face, his little eyes were pointed like pustules at
Danlo. There was a devoutness to cruelty in his eyes, a festering
diligence and resentment. Danlo remembered Pedar's taunts
during the ordeal in Lavi Square; he remembered Pedar kicking
ice in his face and how Master Bardo had cuffed him in punishment, and he suddenly realized that Hanuman (and he, as well)
had been assigned to Pedar's dormitory by something other than
chance.

"Well, it's the Boy of Ice," Pedar said. "Welcome, welcome! The Head Novice was reluctant to assign you here, but
we persuaded him that we'd be honored by the illustriousness of
your presence."

Again, Hanuman looked at Danlo, and Danlo didn't like
the way Hanuman's face emptied of all emotion.

Pedar stamped his boots against the wet tile. He snapped
his fingers at Danlo and said, "Can't you face me, Wild Boy?
Soon enough, it will be the Day of Submission, and then you'll
have to face me when I speak to you."

Danlo turned to face Pedar squarely, and Hanuman did
too. Behind them the hot pool gurgled and steamed, and Danlo
felt drops of water spraying up against his legs.

"Please go away," Hanuman said suddenly. His usually
clear voice sounded gray and dead. "When the Day of Submission comes, we'll submit. But now, please leave us alone."

At this, Pedar bent his neck and began knocking at the side
of his head as if he had water in his ear. To his friends he said,
"I'm not hearing properly. I thought one of these worms asked
me to leave."

"Yes, please leave," Danlo said. He blinked at the steam
irritating his eyes. Many of the boys, he saw, were wading in the
cold pool nearby. Sherborn of Darkmoon and Leander Morven
and others, were frozen like snow hares, watching them, listening.

"Look at you!" Pedar shouted. He pointed at Danlo's loins,
directing everyone's attention there. Despite himself, Danlo
looked down at the long scar on his thigh, where the silk belly
boar had once gored him; the scar glistened hard and white and
looked like a spear of ice pointing upward toward his membrum.
Everyone was now staring at his membrum, at the circumsized
bulb and at the round ocher and indigo scars decorating the
shaft. "What have you been doing to yourself, Wild Boy?"

192

Pedar asked. "Or did a whore bite off your foreskin and tattoo the meat?"

Hanuman obviously couldn't bear for Danlo to be insulted this way, for he clenched his fists and eased into the first attitude of his killing art.

But Pedar just laughed at him and snapped his fingers in the direction of Hanuman's membrum. "And look at *you*! You're just a little boy. Is that a noodle you have there or a worm? What do little boys do with their little worms? I wonder."

Now Hanuman was trembling all over, his hard little muscles dancing along his arms and thighs. His teeth were clenched, and his belly worked in and out as he struggled to breathe. Madhava li Shing, who had prudently edged away from the hot pool and was swishing his razor in a water basin ten feet away, looked at him and called out, "Be careful, Hanuman. It's immediate dismissal if you strike a high novice."

Danlo, standing next to Hanuman shoulder to shoulder, could almost feel the sick heat of adrenaline shooting through Hanuman's body. He brought his hand up to his mouth and whispered, "No, Hanu, no."

These words seemed to cool Hanuman's heart, for he relaxed his hands and slowly turned around so that his back was facing Pedar.

"If you ever strike me, it will mean more than your dismissal," Pedar said to him. "Look at me when I speak to you!"

But Hanuman just stared at the hot pool, and he would not turn his head.

"Damn you!" Pedar screamed. Very quickly, before Danlo realized what was happening, Pedar lashed out and cuffed Hanuman on the side of his head. The blow almost knocked Hanuman over. It opened up the cut on his scalp, and blood streamed down his temple and dripped from his earlobe.

"No!" Danlo said. It was only the second time in his life that he had seen one person strike another. He was afraid that Pedar might strike Hanuman again, so he moved between Pedar and Hanuman, and he said, "No."

Pedar, however, must have understood that he had gone too far. He began picking at his pimply face as if he were regretful of his loss of control, if not actually ashamed of his actions. He bowed to Danlo and said, "When the Day of Submission comes, what a choice I shall have: the Wild Boy or the Worm. I wonder—which one of you will submit to me? You may think about this during the next three tendays."

So saying, he nodded at his friends and led them from the room. The sound of their boots seemed to echo through the adjoining sleeping chamber long after they were gone.

While Madhava and the other boys began speaking in hushed tones of the Day of Submission, Danlo turned to see Hanuman still staring at the hot pool. He stood perfectly still, and his eyes were like perfect mirrors turned inward upon himself.

"Hanu, your blessed head—it is bleeding," Danlo said.

As they stood there breathing steam, drops of blood gathered at the tip of Hanuman's earlobe; they built into large red beads that splashed down against his shoulder and rolled across his pale chest.

"Hanu, Hanu, if you are afraid of—"

"Go away," Hanuman suddenly said. "Please go away."

"But your head is bleeding," Danlo repeated. As a child, he had been taught that wounds must be tended to promptly, and so he reached out to examine the cut on Hanuman's temple. But the instant that his fingers touched the bloodstained skin, Hanuman jumped as if he'd been touched with lightning.

"No!" Hanuman said. He jerked his head back and turned to face Danlo. "Leave me alone!"

Again, Danlo stretched out his hand to Hanuman, this time to touch his forehead, to touch away the anger that he had unwittingly aroused. It was a quintessential Alaloi gesture, an act of reconciliation and kindness, but it was the wrong thing to do. Suddenly, with a remarkable power for one so slight, Hanuman hammered the edge of his fist against Danlo's arm, knocking it away. A sharp pain shot up Danlo's forearm into his elbow; he could hardly move his arm, so deep was the shock of nerves compressed against bone. Something happened to Hanuman, then. In striking Danlo, it was as if he had unlocked a door to a room that should never have been opened. Again, he struck out at Danlo, with his feet and his knees and his fists. Danlo moved closer to him to fend off these blows, or to grab his wrists and shake him back to his senses. As Danlo grappled with Hanuman, hand to hand, hand to neck, he became aware of many things at once: the sound of falling water, boys gathering around him, gesticulating and shouting through a thick veil of steam, the soapy tiles slick beneath his feet, and, most of all, the terrible thing, the madness running wild in Hanuman's pale eyes. This madness seemed to come out of nowhere, like lava welling up from a rent in the ground. At first, Danlo thought that Hanuman had fallen into a blind rage, like that of a rabid dog slavering and snapping and slashing at anything that came his way; perhaps, Danlo told himself, Hanuman had mistaken him for Pedar, or mistaken his remembrance of the recent past for the reality of the present moment. And then he bumped foreheads with Hanuman, and they locked eyes together, and he knew that this was not so. In truth, he had somehow violated Hanuman's person in a way that Pedar had not. He didn't know, in his mind, what he had done to unleash such fury. But another part of him knew, and he knew it deeply, and even in his madness, Hanuman knew it, too. Again and agan, he struck Danlo, willfully, knowingly, as if he had freely accepted the part of himself that was pure energy and annihilation. Much later, when Danlo was able to remember events exactly, this image of Hanuman so clear-eyed and aware would haunt him. But now there was only fury, elbows and fists, drops of blood flung out into the steamy air. Hanuman's face was terrible with concentration as he kicked at Danlo and fell into the motions of his killing art. Hanuman punched him hard in the belly; he drove his knee into his exposed membrum and stones. There was a pain then, a quick, blinding agony that jumped along Danlo's spine and left him gasping for air. He doubled over, and as he fell, he kept a hold on Hanuman's neck and pulled him closer. They fell together, hard, down against the tiles edging the hot pool. Something—the tile or perhaps Hanuman's fist—struck Danlo's chin. His teeth cracked together, and he bit his tongue and tasted blood, and suddenly he was in the water holding Hanuman's head tightly against his chest. The water burned his skin and sloshed into his mouth as he panted in pain. He choked on the water, and he might have gone under, then, clutching at his groin and belly like a wounded beast. Even though the water was shallow, no higher than his belly, he might have breathed water and drowned. *Death is the left hand of life,* his body seemed to cry out, and with death close at hand, as he choked and thrashed in the burning water, he felt a great surge of life running strong as an ocean inside him. It was his *anima* deep within the cells of brain and blood, a pure will to life beyond the agony in his groin, beyond hatred, shock, or pain. In a way, fighting for life was a fusion of both terror and joy. He found his feet, suddenly. He gasped for air, and blood sprayed from his mouth. He was still holding Hanuman by the neck. And Hanuman was still fighting furiously, clawing at Danlo's throat and trying to hook his fingers into his eyes. Many times when he was younger, in the cave of his ancestors, Danlo had wrestled with other boys, but never like this, never with such wildness and abandon. Now he was as wild as any sea animal, and he felt the strength of his life flowing along his arms. He was stronger than Hanuman. With the water dragging heavy against their legs, neither of them could move freely, but Danlo was taller and much stronger. He got an arm up and wrestled behind Hanuman; he held him fast in a head lock with Hanuman's face inches above the churning water.

Life is the right hand of death—he thought someone was saying these words, but then he realized that it was Madhava or one of the other boys standing by the edge of the pool, shouting, "Let him go, you're killing him!"

He tightened his grip on the back of Hanuman's head. The scalp was slippery with hot water and blood, and he felt fine stubbles of hair that Madhava had missed shaving. By chance, his fingertips edged the bleeding gash along Hanuman's temple. Beneath his fingertips was bone and brain, and beneath everything, stiffening Hanuman's frail body like sheets of ice, fear. Hanuman's body was rigid with fear; he, too, was fighting to live, and Danlo could not quite force his face beneath the water. He knew he should kill Hanuman there and then, in the moment, with the passion for killing so urgent inside him. He was an Alaloi man (or half a man), and killing was a terrible necessity of life. But he could not kill him. In the water beneath him, blood from his bitten tongue spread out into hundreds of silken red strands, and strand to strand touched Hanuman's blood. He saw the deep correspondence that existed between them. In the surging waves beating against his chest, through the hot, churning water he felt a connectedness to Hanuman that could never be broken. *Tat tvam asi,* he thought, *that thou art.* All things were connected to all things, heart to heart and atom to atom, and in every part of Hanuman—in the pain of his twisting, thrashing body and in his frantic eyes—Danlo saw himself. He could not harm Hanuman without harming himself. *It is better to die oneself than kill.* He thought of Old Father's teaching of ahimsa then, and he knew that he could not kill him; he could not kill anything, ever again.

"Hanu, Hanu," he said, gasping, "be still!"

"No! Leave me alone!"

Danlo stood behind Hanuman with the boy's head clamped in his long hands. His tongue hurt on the side where he had bitten it, and it was hard for him to speak clearly. "Hanu, Hanu, *ti alashareth la shantih.* Be still! I am your friend, not your enemy!"

"Go away."

Again Danlo prayed, *"Ti alashareth la shantih,"* and he held his hand over Hanuman's mouth. After a while the madness went out of Hanuman, and he fell still. Danlo held him tightly, his chest pressing the rib bones of Hanuman's slender back; he felt this stillness as an unexpected letting go that passed from Hanuman's flesh into his own. Although Danlo could not know it, it was the first time since Hanuman's infancy that he had relaxed in the presence of another. Something passed between them then, a deep trust that neither of them would ever again harm the other.

"Why did you strike me?" Danlo whispered. "I am your friend, not your enemy."

Hanuman struggled to speak, and Danlo let his hand fall away from Hanuman's face, into the rolling water. Hot waves lapped at his fingers. From somewhere above him, through the steamy air, came the sound of feet slapping against wet tile and one of the boys shouting at them. "Hit him again!" someone cried out. "Hold his face under water until he drowns!"

"Be quiet!" Madhava li Shing said. "Be quiet, or the high novices will hear us and throw *us* in the pool."

But most of the boys were not calling for further violence. In truth, they seemed in awe of what they had just witnessed. They stared down at Danlo and Hanuman as if they were afraid for these two wild boys to emerge from the pool.

Danlo ignored their chatter and whispered in Hanuman's ear, "What is wrong?"

"Oh, no," Hanuman began, and his voice was lost to the sound of water running into the pool. "I'm sorry—are you hurt?"

Danlo let Hanuman go. While Madhava li Shing called for them to come out of the pool, they faced each other across the water. "I think . . . I bit my tongue," Danlo said.

"I'm sorry I hurt you." Hanuman laved some water over his bleeding scalp, then said, "But I thought you wanted to kill me."

"*Kill* you?"

"I should explain," Hanuman said. He looked down at the hot water for a moment. "I should explain, but I'm sorry, I can't talk here, with everyone listening. Can you wait until after everyone has gone to bed?"

Danlo reached back and pulled his queue of hair so it fell

over his shoulder across his chest. Ahira's tail feather, he saw, was somewhat torn and bedraggled; only the wax he had rubbed into it each day since his passage into manhood had kept it from ruin. "Yes," he said as he pressed his fingers against the feather's hard quill. "I can wait."

Later, after Madhava had glued Hanuman's scalp wound closed with a pungent-smelling collagen, after Borja's evening bells long since had rung and the cold flame globes had darkened and everyone was asleep, much later, Danlo and Hanuman stole from their beds and made their way to the center of the sleeping chamber. There the stairwell opened before them like a black hole in space. They crept down a few stairs, not so far as to emerge into the chamber below where the second-year novices slept, but far enough so that the thick stone floor above them would muffle their voices.

"I'm sorry I struck you," Hanuman murmured into the darkness. "I didn't mean to. It's just that I was so *mad,* and afraid. There's something about you. Your strength, your past, your courage, and—forgive me—your strangeness. You were going to touch my face, weren't you? My head. It's silly of me to be so bound by *my* past, but on Catava, no one ever touches anyone else, if they can help it. You must think this inhibition is odious. *I* do, when I think about it. I know I should overcome myself. I want to, I will. Oh, this is hard. It seems so indecent to talk about myself this way. So vainglorious. I think about myself too much, anyway. But I have to believe we have complete will over ourselves. If we're completely mindful. There's something about *me,* too, I know. And knowing it, I can control it. I'd *never* strike you again. Please. I'd rather die than hurt you."

Danlo listened to Hanuman's voice spilling like liquid silver out of the darkness. He could hear the truth in the words, as well as an immense sadness; he sensed that Hanuman was afraid to be alone with himself, and worse, he seemed to be always watching himself, as if he were standing guard against a murderer who slips through open windows during the night. If Danlo had been prudent, he might have accepted Hanuman's apology—only to flee into that frigidness of the soul that people betray when they wish to sever an awkward or dangerous friendship. But this Danlo could not do. Because of his experience with the Dreamers—or perhaps due to the terrible things he had seen when his tribe fell ill in their brains—he had an immense tolerance for madness. And so he smiled to himself as

Hanuman talked; he sat on the cold stone steps and listened as Hanuman told him things that no one else had ever known.

"I'm sorry I struck your face," Hanuman said at,last. "And the groin strike—are you all right?"

"Yes," Danlo said. He reached beneath his robe, down between his legs as if to reassure himself that he was still whole. "Now my stones have been hammered to match the cutting of my membrum."

"I'm sorry—I've wounded you."

Danlo was faintly nauseous due to his aching groin and the minty, collagenous odor of the glue wafting from Hanuman's head. On the dark stairs where they sat, the smells and sounds around them seemed very close. "Wounds heal," he said.

Hanuman was silent for a long time before whispering, " 'I love him whose soul is deep, even in being wounded, and who can perish of a small experience: thus he goes gladly over the world.' "

"You are quoting from your blessed book again, yes?"

"Some things are impossible to say otherwise."

"You can say anything to a friend," Danlo told him.

"*Are* we to be friends?"

"O blessed Hanu! We have *been* friends since the first day. Friendship is *halla,* like the circle of the world. It cannot be broken."

In the quiet of the stairwell where their whispers fell out into the open blackness, in friendship, they touched each other's forehead. For a long time they sat there talking about their lives and their fates. Because Danlo trusted Hanuman to keep secrets, he told him of his quest to affirm life wherever he found it. "Life," he confided, "is so strange, so splendid, so rare. To see it, quickening, life. This is what my Fravashi Old Father has taught: never killing or hurting any living thing, not even in one's thoughts. To affirm life this way, utterly, with all one's spirit—this must be a way to becoming an asarya, yes?"

They returned to the main chamber then, and Danlo lay awake listening to the wind outside and to the breathing of nineteen boys sleeping down the length of the room. Far into the night, in the bed next to his, Hanuman began tossing and murmuring in his sleep. He had fallen into one of his nightmares. "No, no, Father!" he called out. "No, no, no!"

Danlo kicked the blankets off himself and stepped over to Hanuman. The floor stones were icy against his bare feet, so he knelt on Hanuman's bed. Starlight silvered the windows above them and fell in faint streamers into the room. Hanuman's pale, delicate face was rigid with suffering. *With life,* Danlo thought, and in the Alaloi manner, he gently pressed his hand over the boy's mouth. "You must not wake the others!" he whispered. "Shhh, *mi alasharia la, shantih, shantih.* Go to sleep now, my brother, go to sleep."

THE DOCTRINE OF AHIMSA

They live in wisdom who see themselves in all, and all in them.

—from The Bhagavad Gita

In the uncertain first days of their novitiate that followed, Danlo and Hanuman became best of friends. As friends do, Danlo chose to blind himself to the worst of Hanuman's faults while cherishing those rare qualities that distinguished him from the other novices: his mindfulness, his intense will, and his loyalty. Hanuman, once he had accepted Danlo as a friend, proved astonishingly loyal. On the sunny glidderies of Borja, in the dormitories, or in Lavi Square where the people swarmed the ice after breakfast, Hanuman championed Danlo to the other novices. With charm, wit, and subtle intimidation (no one, after witnessing Hanuman's ferocity in the bathing room, wanted to provoke him to violence), he won a tentative acceptance for Danlo. It helped that Danlo was easy to like and that he liked to laugh at himself, even when the others pointed out his various peculiarities. Indeed, in many of his habits and daily devotions, Danlo gave the others much to laugh at. Each morning he arose with the sun, went outside into the frozen air, and bowed to the four points of the world. And each night, just before the cold flame globes were extinguished, he bent low, grunting as he lifted his bed and turned it perpendicular to Hanuman's bed. He did this so he could sleep with his head to the north; the other boys slept toward the windows oriented west to east, and Danlo knew (or believed) that such sleeping positions could lead to blood diseases, constipation, or even madness. Because he also believed it was harmful to hold his water, whenever he felt the need, he insisted on promptly pissing to the south, whether or not proper lavatory facilities were at hand. Once, a master horologe caught him outside behind the College of Lords drilling yellow holes in a gliddery's red ice, and his reputation for eccentricity was established. This reputation grew to almost mythic proportions when, one day before dinner, he forgot his promise to himself in the hot pool and ate the larvae of a fritillary butterfly. It was an easy enough mistake for him to make: after a long day of learning to use the tutelary computers in the library, he was talking with Madhava li Shing and some other novices outside that most massive of buildings. He was tired and hungry, and so, without really thinking, he had peeled open the bark of a shatterwood tree to find three fat fritillary larvae, each as thick as his thumb. Out of habit he had scooped these delicacies out of their burrow and popped them into his mouth before realizing that he had vowed never to harm another living creature. Since he had already killed them with his teeth and it would be a shame to waste a mouthful of good meat, he swallowed the larvae. He had eaten the young of the fritillary a thousand times during his boyhood; they tasted delicious, juicy and sweet, just as they should.

"You eat *worms*?" Madhava had asked him. His little face was screwed up with disgust and horror. And awe—he was awestruck that Danlo could eat living meat. He had come from one of the made-worlds of Enola Luz, where the only living things are human beings and the bacteria grown to feed them; he couldn't see the difference between an insect and a worm.

"No," Danlo said. "I mean to say, *yes,* I used to eat them, before I knew how terrible it is to kill, but today I was so hungry and I forgot. I . . . forgot." And then his voice fell low as he whispered a prayer for the larval fritillaries' spirits, *"Liliji, mi alasharia la shantih."*

But Madhava didn't understand, and to the horror of all present, he exclaimed, "Danlo the Wild eats worms!"

Ironically, this insect eating was to gain for Danlo a reputation as a man of peace. To Madhava—and to the other boys— Danlo was forced to confess what he had so far kept to himself: that he had made a vow of ahimsa. Many, of course, knew about the Fravashi and their doctrines; Sherborn of Darkmoon asked

Danlo outright if he had been a student of the Fravashi. Danlo, who did not like to lie, could not answer this question directly. Instead he talked about the nature of beliefs and belief systems in general. While admitting that he had adopted one of the Fravashi's crucial beliefs, he said that ahimsa was no mere doctrine, but rather a perception of the universe that had been interpreted and stated *as* a belief. "This perception is what matters," Danlo said. "The interconnectedness of all things. Ahimsa is *seeing* this connection. But sometimes . . . one forgets to see."

Soon after this, all the first-year novices were informed as to whom they would serve beginning on the sixty-fifth day, the dreaded Day of Submission. As Danlo had feared, it would be his "pleasure" to serve Pedar Sadi Sanat. Pedar, it was said, was on friendly terms with the Head Novice, who normally made such assignations; Pedar must have persuaded him that he was the novice most qualified to teach Danlo the ideals of obedience and submission. Surprisingly, however, Hanuman had been called to serve the Master of Novices himself, Bardo the Just. Such service was not without precedent, but it was unusual: first-year novices most often are required to serve the older novices, just as the second- and third-year novices serve journeymen; and high novices look after the needs of the masters. Many of the high novices escape servitude to an individual master by volunteering to work in cafés and bars throughout the City, but because of their age, this was not yet a path open to either Hanuman or Danlo. Hanuman had heard that Master Bardo was not an easy man to serve, and he wondered why he had been so honored. He didn't know—then—that Bardo liked beautiful boys, and more, that Bardo felt guilty for nearly causing Hanuman's death in Lavi Square and was moved to protect him from high novices such as Pedar. From the first, Danlo worried over Hanuman's assignation to Master Bardo, just as he worried over and hated the whole system of submission. Nothing Hanuman said could relieve Danlo of this hatred. After Hanuman wryly observed that all societies are based on reciprocity, on an exchange of duties, information, and favors, Danlo said, "A mother suckles her child, and a father must bring blood tea to the old grandfathers who have lost their teeth, but it is wrong for a man to serve another who is whole and strong. That is worse than parasitism; that is *shaida*."

As Danlo counted the days until the Day of Submission, he began his formal studies. In accord with Master Bardo's advice,

Danlo began to learn the universal syntax, and he soon found that his days were busy. In the early morning, after breakfast and his thought primaries were completed, he did his hardest work. He went to a notationist to study the three-dimensional mental symbols called ideoplasts. Late mornings were spent in memorization; there were twenty-three thousand basic ideoplasts, and he had to be able to visualize their shapes, colors, and configurations. He might have imprinted much of this knowledge, but after his experience in Drisana's shop, he had come to mistrust the unnatural act of imprinting, if not imprimaturs themselves. Then, too, imprinting had its dangers, not the least of which was the temptation to stive the brain full of too many data and facts. Indeed, the women and men of the Order disdain either memorizing or imprinting more than is needful; the ideal is to acquire a certain repertoire of basics before learning the skillful use of computers as extensional minds and memories. And so Danlo acquired this basic repertoire the long way, passing endless strings of ideoplasts before his mind's eye, burning the pretty symbols into his brain at a truly prodigious rate. After this grueling memory work came a quick meal of fruit, bread, and pulses, and then, for most of the afternoon until it was time to play hokkee or skate figures in the Ice Dome, he returned to the universal syntax, learning representation theory, formalization, modeling, and applications. Only during the evenings did he have time to talk and laugh with the other boys, to play chess with Hanuman, or to lie back on the rough white blankets of his bed and play the shakuhachi.

Besides the universal syntax, of course, the novices are required to learn a varied curriculum: history of the Order, Order etiquette, mathematics, science, history, skating, body yoga, languages, library arts, and the Fravashi thought exercises. And the cetic arts: hallning, zazen, meditation, fugue, and the interface with the cybernetic spaces. Toward the end of his Borja years, a novice will also study the fundamentals of the more important disciplines such as scrying, remembrancing, mechanics, and eschatology. These disciplines are studied intensely, and never are more than two of them pursued at a single time. Within these bounds, the novice is free to structure his own education. In fact, he—or she—is expected to follow the tree of knowledge down its many branchings, choosing the most fascinating arts and disciplines for special study. How well the novice chooses is a measure of his intellectual worth—and of his shih. Although each novice will have many tutors who offer advice and wisdom, ultimately, the novice alone is responsible for his education. At the end of his novitiate, when each novice is tested for admission to one of the colleges, he himself must bear the shame if he fails to become a journeyman and is dismissed from the Order.

Danlo's first tutor, as it happened, was the esteemed Master Jonath Haas, an old, old man with a warty face and a great mind and a passion for bestowing intellectual gifts upon his favorite students. Master Jonath was a classical holist of the school that had absorbed the old science, and like many of his fellow academicians, he had a love of theory and abstraction. It was his joy to compose models of the universe, to represent the incredibly complex processes of the cosmos with symbols of the universal syntax. There was great power, Master Jonath claimed, in such formal systems: the power of generalization and the discovery of universal patterns and metaphors. One day, on the fifty-first of false winter, over mugs of cinnamon coffee that he served Danlo in his little apartment near the Academy, he delivered one of his many lectures.

"And so you may think of holism as the formal study of interconnectedness—does that interest you, Young Danlo? I thought it might. Connections: what is language but an expression of connections? Relations? Metaphors? I am sitting *on* this chair. The sun pours down like *gold* on that peculiar feather you wear in your hair. It is impossible to map two coordinate spaces of different dimensions onto one another in a one-to-one and bicontinuous fashion. Map! Spaces! Dimensions! Fashion! What are the definitions of mathematics but metaphors? Torison spaces, embedding, paths and points—metaphors, all. Nature moves by metaphor. This is what mathematics is: a system of crystallized, highly refined metaphors. And more so with the universal syntax. What is the universal syntax if not a generalization of mathematics into a truly universal language? With mathematics, we may represent the distortions of the manifold or model the chaos of a cloud; with the universal syntax, we may relate the Dragon opening of chess to the use of color in the Scutari body change to the pattern of supernovas in the Vild. All *possible* relationships. All connections. The better models we make, the more connections revealed. How else but through holism to really see the overarching patterns of the universe?"

Danlo soon found that there was a great beauty in this ruling intellectual system of Civilized Worlds. Although he never forgot Old Father's warning that holism was the most seductive of all worldviews and systems precisely because it was the most universal, he devoured Master Jonath's lessons with a voraciousness toward knowing that pleased the old man. Every morning Danlo reported to Master Jonath's apartment at the appointed time, and together they studied the masterworks of the greatest holists such as Moriah Ede and Li Tao Cirlot. And every morning Master Jonath would assign Danlo the various exercises, problems, and compositions that are the bones of the holists' art.

Master Jonath, ever bemused and suspicious of the snowy owl's feather that Danlo sported, inevitably discovered Danlo's attachment to the Alaloi totem system. He seemed to know almost everything about this system, as he did about most everything else. As an exercise—a demonstration of holism's infinite subtlety—he suggested to Danlo that they begin a formal representation of the Alaloi system. It was his pride to demonstrate how holism could encompass any and all systems—even one so bizarre as that of primitive humans who anoint their newborn babies with menstrual blood out of the observation that this life-giving substance is permeated with the World-spirit in much the same way that a magnetic field surrounds a lodestone. And so, over the endless mugs of coffee greasy with sweet cream, they worked together encoding the two classes of animals, or the three aspects of the self, or the four elements of the world— blood, fire, ice, and wind—into the symbols of the universal syntax. (In the latter example, Master Jonath suggested selecting a quaternion often used to encode the four suits of the Japanese Tarot and the four circuits of the human brain—as well as the four Scutari sexes and the four movements of Beethoven's Last Symphony.) Danlo loved this difficult work, and he often wished that he could stop time for a year so that he might master the intricacies of holism, uninterrupted by other concerns.

But time—in the towers and apartments of the Academy, in the cold imperatives of civilization—moves in one direction only and is difficult to stop. Inevitably, the sixty-fifth of false winter arrived, the Day of Submission, and Danlo was forced to put aside his play with abstraction and symbol. After breakfast that day, all the new novices across Borja waited in their sleeping chambers as they exchanged bits of nervous conversation and doubts. Danlo was the first boy in Perilous Hall to be called down to the first floor where the high novices were waiting, lined up in front of their beds. They each bowed when Danlo came into their chamber. Pedar stepped forward, handed him a broom, and said, "Well, it's the Boy of Ice—welcome to Perilous Hall!"

Pedar Sadi Sanat stood red-eyed and irritable, picking at his face. Although Danlo didn't know it, Pedar was addicted to jook, a squalid drug whose effects include inflamed eyes and irritability—as well as bleeding gums, pimples, and even hallucinations. As people do, Pedar used it only to enhance his intelligence. It is known that the human brain, at puberty, releases a hormone that dissolves any unused synapses laid down during one's childhood. This enables adult human beings, with their adult, hardwired brains, to concentrate and apply the lessons they have learned earlier in life—but at the cost of flexibility and new insights. Jook, when snorted through the nostrils or dissolved in one's drink, inhibits the release of this hormone while stimulating new synaptic growth. It is said that jook can make a bright boy brighter; in delaying the onset of terminal adulthood, it can sometimes transform a dullard into a genius. There are always many who pursue this miracle, even though they sacrifice their sociability, their health, even their very sanity.

"Will you make my bed, Danlo the Wild, the Nameless Child?" Pedar scratched at his eyes and directed Danlo toward his rumpled, bloodstained sheets. "You may change my sheets every third day."

That morning Danlo did indeed make Pedar's bed, and in the mornings that followed he fetched his robes to and from the laundry, swept the floor around his bed, and sharpened his skates with a long, sparkling diamond file. The most onerous of his duties was the nightly shaving of Pedar's head. Each evening after supper he ran down the spiral stairway and reported to the first-floor bathing room; each evening he gagged on steam as he grasped the diamond-edged straight razor and drew it in short, deft strokes across Pedar's skull. A few times, Danlo considered how easy it would be to let the gleaming razor slip down Pedar's neck, to guide it across the great artery that pulsed in his throat. Such thoughts, however, were even more repulsive to Danlo than the reality of his servitude. *Never killing or hurting another, even in one's thoughts*—this was the spirit of ahimsa. Danlo tried ferociously to gentle his thoughts. In truth, he was not a violent man (or boy), and so each evening, in the Fravashi way, he tried to remake his consciousness into a mirror that would reflect the best parts of Pedar's spirit. He shaved Pedar's head until it was a gleaming white, with neither scrapes nor nicks to betray a lack of mindfulness and goodwill. Danlo was adept with cutting tools;

207

in fact, his instant skill with the razor angered Pedar. The high novices like to haze the newer boys, but to do so, they need to find an excuse. It was a tradition in Perilous Hall for a high novice to wait until his head was cut shaving—and given the inexperience most boys had with the barbaric, anachronistic straight razors, cuts were inevitable—before beginning this hazing. Danlo's natural nobility and his adamantine resolve not to hate seemed only to frustrate Pedar. Obviously, Pedar did not want to behold the better parts of himself, for he would not look at Danlo eye to eye or return his bow when the shaving was completed. In truth, Pedar reveled in his meanness. Some people are like that. Because he was cruel, vindictive, and blind to his own fundamental nobility, however stifled and sullied, one evening he ordered Danlo to do the unthinkable.

"You will shave my beard now," Pedar said. "Here, with this razor, and careful you don't cut me."

"You want me to shave your . . . *face*, O Excellent One?"

Pedar was sitting slumped on a stool in the first-floor bathing chamber. His hairless torso was flabby because he hated exercise; the skin across his chest was sallow from snorting too much jook, and he had large, loose nipples that looked like slices of raw liver. He pointed at the enameled shaving basin. Water hissed from old pipes in a continuous jet, which struck the half-filled basin and sent up a hot, soapy spray. In the steam, a cadre of Pedar's friends stood around in a circle, intimidating Danlo with their hard, naked bodies should he attempt to flee. Danlo himself was clothed in an informal robe. He was miserably hot and sweating inside his baggy woolens, and he repeated, "You want me to shave your face, O Excellent One?"

"I've tired of that title. You will begin calling me O Vastened One."

"But, O Vastened One," Danlo protested, "how can I shave your face without touching it?"

"Because, Wild Boy, I will give you permission to touch my face."

As he said this, his friends, who had been jeering at Danlo, fell silent and looked at one another in surprise.

Danlo did not want to shave Pedar's face. He had finally learned that on many of the Civilized Worlds, it was the worst of insults to touch another's face. And although he was coming to respect civilized customs, this was not his only reason for not wanting to touch him. "I might cut you," he said.

Indeed, it would have been impossible to shave Pedar's

scraggly beard without cutting him. His face was an angry red landscape of pimples, scabs, and irritated flesh. From temple to neck, volcanoes of infection rose up among the pockmarks and patchy scars. No area of his face (or on his chest and back) was free of abscess; it was impossible to find a smooth plane of skin to draw a razor across. And so, as Pedar stretched up his chin and glanced knowingly at his friends, Danlo tried to cut around the pimples. He used the razor's beveled tip to sever the downy hair follicles almost one by one. He worked as painstakingly as any Alaloi man carving a piece of ivory, but at last his fingers grew tired and shaking, and he let the razor slip. He cut open a huge red pimple on Pedar's throat. Blood and pus thick as yellow cream erupted and dribbled down Pedar's neck. Pedar gave a jerk, and Danlo cut him again, this time a long, nasty gash through skin and scar running along his windpipe. There was blood everywhere, blood running down Pedar's chest to spatter on the white stool, blood sticky between Danlo's knuckles and congealing along the razor's smooth diamond blade.

"You've cut me!" Pedar shouted.

Danlo swished the razor in the basin's soapy water, and almost instantly, flowers of red were sucked down the drain. Not knowing what else to do, he pressed the sleeve of his robe to Pedar's throat. "It is not a deep cut, but it is bad to let the blood run, and I—"

"You've cut me, goddammit!"

"I am sorry."

"Stupid Wild Boy."

"I am truly sorry."

Pedar jumped to his feet with his hand clamped to his neck. He glared at Danlo and shouted, "You're truly sorry *what*?"

"I am truly sorry . . . O Vastened One."

"The Wild Boy has forgotten his etiquette," Pedar said. He nodded to his six friends. They were each almost full men, and one of them, Arpiar Pogossian, with his blocky, cultivated muscles, was almost as large as Bardo the Just, who was the largest man Danlo had ever known. "Let's teach him the proper etiquette," Pedar said.

All at once, Pedar's friends fell on Danlo. They grabbed his arms and legs, throwing him to the floor. Danlo's ear smacked against the tile, and the pain of bruised cartilage made him angry. He struggled and thrashed like a shagshay bull being brought to the ice by wolves. He flailed out and kicked someone; someone shouted, "Why did you let go his leg?"

"He's damn strong!" Arpiar huffed out. "Too damn strong!"

Someone was groaning; as it happened, Danlo had kicked one of the boys' hands, breaking two fingers. Danlo could almost feel the sharp, grating pain of it in his own fingers. He was so ashamed of breaking ahimsa that his body fell slack and the other boys managed to pin him to the floor. Arpiar Pogossian was now kneeling on Danlo's thigh while the other boys each grasped one of his limbs.

"What's wrong with him?" Arpiar wanted to know. "Why is he just lying there?"

Pedar crouched above Danlo and said, "He was a student of a Fravashi Old Father. They say he's taken a vow of ahimsa."

A sad-faced, ironic boy—his name was Rafael Wu—stood off by himself and held up his mangled hand. "Ahimsa!" he shrieked out. "I think my fingers are broken!"

Danlo lay with his spine and joints pressed to the tile. On top of him, crushing his chest and belly, were four naked, sweating boys. It was hard for him to breathe, but he smelled the soap and sweat running off Pedar's glistening skin. Pedar knelt over him, looking at him upside down. From this perspective, his eyes seemed as darkly patterned as kawa shells, hard and scarcely human. Because Danlo was Pedar's personal servant—because it was against all tradition and rules—Pedar was not permitted to touch Danlo. But he had invented other ways to torment him. He had his fingers up against the gash in his neck. The bleeding had mostly stopped, but he squeezed up some blood which ran over the point of his chin and dripped down into Danlo's face.

"No!" Danlo suddenly shouted. "No!"

Pedar's fingers were working furiously across his inflamed, lacerated neck. By chance (or design), he squeezed a few pimples, which burst open, spraying pus and blood into Danlo's eyes. Danlo shut his eyes tightly. He shut his mouth so that none of Pedar's blood would get in. All of his life, long before he had vowed not to harm any living thing, he had known it was very bad to taste the blood of others, the worst kind of *shaida*. He wanted to cry out, "No, no, this blood will defile both our spirits!" but his mouth was tightly closed, and he could not speak.

Finally Pedar stood up and the other boys let Danlo go. Pedar seemed suddenly ashamed and confused. "Tomorrow evening," he muttered, "you'd better be more careful how you shave me."

Danlo fled up the spiral stairway, then. He fled into the

vast, cool familiarity of his dormitory chamber. Hanuman, who was practicing his killing art out on the floor, saw him covered in blood, and he froze with his fist pointed in the air. "Danlo, what happened?"

As Danlo hurried into the bathing chamber, he shook his head in despair. After stripping off his befouled robe and washing the diseased blood from his face, he returned to the main chamber. There he huddled beneath his bed's blankets and shivered with hatred. He hated Pedar Sadi Sanat. He hated him with a black, bitter passion. And more, he hated a system—a civilization, world, or universe—that could produce such a boy. This hatred poisoned his spirit. And the worst part of his hatred was his contempt for himself, or rather, his contempt for being weak enough to hate at all. Silently, at the vital moment, he had turned his sight away from ahimsa. He was far from the harmony of life that he sought, as far away as death was from life.

"Danlo, Danlo," he heard a voice say, "what happened to you?" It was Hanuman standing above him, shaking his shoulder as he called his name.

"I . . . broke my vow of ahimsa," Danlo said at last. He sat up and threw back the covers. Many of his fellow novices milled about the room, sharpening their skates for the next day. The sound of ridged files being drawn against steel whined through the air. As the boys prepared for bed, they stole glances at him, but he ignored them. "O blessed God . . . why did I break my vow?"

He told Hanuman everything, then. Hanuman stood there listening, biting at the calluses covering his knuckles. When he heard what Pedar had done to Danlo in the first-floor bathing room, his face fell fearful and secretive. He spoke no word of reassurance, but in his eyes was a shared outrage. In truth, Danlo was immediately afraid of what his friend's silent rage might lead to.

"I must suffer Pedar and his little tortures," Danlo said.

"I understand."

"If I continue to hate him or wish him harm, how will I ever learn ahimsa?"

Hanuman bit his knuckle and tore loose a piece of yellow callus, which he spat onto the floor. "I understand," he repeated.

"It must be hard for you, too," Danlo said. "To serve Master Bardo."

"It *is* hard," Hanuman said. A strange look came over him

then. "But it's possible to learn from such cruelty, isn't it? Someday, I'll have my revenge upon Bardo. As you will with Pedar."

Danlo reached beneath the blankets and brought out his bamboo flute. He held it lightly between his fingers and looked at Hanuman. "There is a saying I learned when I was young. *Silu harya, manse ri damya.* It means 'Children rage, men restrain themselves.' "

"Just so, Danlo. The ability to control oneself is everything."

"Yes," Danlo agreed. "But, Hanu, do we mean the same thing by this word 'control'?"

As false winter ended and the first snows of winter fell cold and deep, Danlo had many opportunities to practice control after some hundred days of Pedar's hazing had passed, Danlo had learned to restrain the worst of his hatred, and he began to understand the terrible patience and strength that ahimsa required of a man. Pedar never again defiled Danlo with his blood or other bodily substances, but he found more subtle ways to torment Danlo. In front of his friends, he ridiculed Danlo for wearing a bird's feather in his hair; he made Danlo polish his skates over and over until Danlo fell faint and sick from the smell of boot polish; he did everything possible to ruin Danlo's sleep. This was the cruelest part of his hazing, cruel in intent if not result. Every night after lights out, Pedar climbed the spiral stairs to Danlo's chamber. Since hazing was not officially permitted after the novices had gone to bed, he climbed quietly. And he climbed carefully, very carefully. Pedar had once slipped on the stairs as a first-year novice; he always placed his feet exactly in the center of the hard stone steps. Every night he would steal through the silent chamber where the youngest boys slept. He would rouse Danlo from his bed and lead him down the stairs to the first-floor meditation room. There he would make Danlo sing the traditional canticles of the Order or perform the strenuous postures of body yoga or—and this was his favorite torture—he would read aloud the beginning stanzas of some famous ancient poem and then make Danlo supply the concluding lines; if Danlo failed this test, he would have to perform a Sufi dance for the other boys or hop up and down on one foot until he fell writhing to the floor with leg cramps. As many nights passed, Danlo applied his phenomenal memory toward learning by heart hundreds of ancient poems, and then hundreds of hundreds. It soon became almost impossible for Pedar to surprise him with an unfamiliar poem, even such as the poems of Indra Sen and other obscure poets of the Third Dark Age. Danlo's feats of memory naturally infuriated Pedar. And so he devised a new game, which was to make Danlo recite as many poems as he could for as long as he could. Pedar loved poetry, and he loved it the more Danlo's voice grew hoarse from forcing out line after line of poems composed many thousands of years ago on Old Earth or some other abandoned world. Pedar, of course, sacrificed little of his own sleep listening to ancient poetry. When he grew tired and drowsy, he left the meditation room for his bed, only to be replaced by Arpiar Pogossian or one of the other high novices. In this way, working in shifts, Pedar's friends often made Danlo stay awake the whole night.

One morning after a particularly excruciating session of poetry recitations, Hanuman caught Danlo stumbling into bed and told him, "Oh, no, Danlo, look at you! There's nothing in tradition to allow Pedar to keep you awake like this. Why don't you go to Master Bardo and make a complaint? Or allow me to?"

Danlo glanced at Hanuman and yawned. He looked battered and gaunt, almost as if he'd had his nose broken. Dark half-moons bruised the skin beneath his eyes. The eyes themselves, however, were lively and seemed to hold a brightness at odds with his sleeplessness. *"Silu wanya, manse ri damya,"* he said. " 'Children complain, men restrain themselves.' "

"Do your Alaloi people have a saying for everything?"

"Yes," Danlo said, "they are natural philosophers."

"But you mustn't let Pedar ruin your sleep."

"But if I complain to Master Bardo, he might punish Pedar."

Hanuman grinned wickedly and said, "I hope Master Bardo takes him out into Lavi Square and slaps his face. There should be a public rebuke."

Danlo closed his eyes and shook his head. "Oh, Hanu, this is what must not happen! Nothing I say, nothing I do, not even in my thinking must I cause him harm."

"But you mustn't take this notion of ahimsa too far," Hanuman said. "Pedar is a pustule—why should you care if Master Bardo punishes him?"

"Pedar *is* a pustule," Danlo agreed, "but he is also something else."

"And what would that be?"

"Something splendid, something rare."

"But you *hate* him!"

"But I . . . must not hate him."

"Then I will hate him for you," Hanuman said. He touched Danlo's forehead to see if he had a fever, then continued, "Perhaps it's a noble exercise to restrain yourself from hating others. Perhaps. But you should keep your *will* to hate as sharp as a razor. Perhaps someday you'll give up ahimsa as an unworkable ethic—and then you'll need all your hate to protect yourself from Pedar or others like him."

During this time of hazing, which grew worse through winter into deep winter and was much more severe for Danlo than the other boys, three things saved him from physical and mental ruin. First, as luck would have it (and Danlo was always a lucky man), it was the season of holidays. Triolet, The Day of Remembrance, The Tycho's Day, Mourning Night, The Festival of the Broken Dolls—three days out of ten were given over to rest and celebration. Danlo was not required to serve Pedar on these days, nor did he have any other duties. He was free to curl up beneath his warm blankets and sleep as long as he liked. Second, Danlo had an unusual attitude toward sleep. He could do without sleep when he had to. Often, as a boy hunting seals with Haidar out on the sea ice, he had stood awake above a seal's hole, stomping his feet to keep them from freezing, waiting and waiting. Often he had waited more than a day for Nunki to rise up out of the sea and impale himself on his harpoon. Just as often, though, in deep winter when the west wind blew swift and deadly, he had huddled in his cave and slept continually for a day and a night. In truth, he had a rare ability for sleeping. And as a result of his experience with the autists, he was adept at descending into the cold, deep, healing waters of his dreams. More than once he dreamed of his other-self, the mysterious snowy owl. Ahira, with his orange eyes and shimmering white feathers, appeared to Danlo and told him that sleep was a rejoining with God and that he must seek this holy state whenever he could. And so, through the three nights and days of Triolet while the people of the City smoked toalache in celebration of the end of the War of Assassins, he slept in his bed, getting up only to relieve himself or to eat a little food. And when he finally awakened, clearheaded and fresh, he found Hanuman suffering the aftereffects of his first taste of toalache, and he said, "Sleep is bliss, yes? As long as I can return to sleep, how can Pedar harm me?"

The third thing that saved Danlo from ruin was Hanuman's growing love for him. Due to Hanuman's secretive nature, this love was not manifested openly, with words or the crude gestures of hand slapping favored by the other boys. But in a hundred ways Hanuman acknowledged the deep correspondence between them. With a quick exchange of glances or a slight, almost imperceptible head bow, he would indicate his love of Danlo's playfulness, his passion for life, his essential wildness. He admired the wild, dangerous side of Danlo's spirit, even though that wildness had nearly led to his drowning the day they had wrestled together in the hot pool. Many years later, when their friendship had grown beyond love into a profound and terrible understanding of each other, he would record in his universal computer: "I used to like watching Danlo skate—do I remember too clearly how he practically tore up the ice of Borja's glidderies? These bittersweet images so impossible to forget: the sunlight reflecting off his skate blades, his muscles bunching and flowing beneath his kamelaika. And his deep, quick eyes, the way he processed information: nuances of temperature, minutiae, a subtle change in the color, planarity, or texture of the ice that others couldn't see. He had such a reckless speed stroke, light and quick—I should say, 'lightning quick' —but there was always the power in his legs, the fluid, unpredictable power. Madhava li Shing used to say he was showing off, but no, he just loved skating too fast. It's strange, isn't it, how much of a man is revealed in the way he moves? Soul and selfness are the most elusive conceits, but from the first, I could see in Danlo's soul what always attracted (and repelled) me: his strength and verve. He was wilder than I, and beautiful in his wildness, like the strange white owl bird that he always emulated. And that always terrified me. Nothing is so terrifying as a man who possesses the innocence, the wildness and grace of an animal."

Above all, Hanuman admired Danlo's courage and will to endure in the face of Pedar's petty tortures. A man's will, he believed, the will to power over himself, was a singular, godlike quality. But will flows from life, and Hanuman well remembered how fragile life could be. And so, out of love and friendship, he secretly vowed to do what he must to preserve Danlo's life and keep him from harm.

One day, on the forty-ninth of deep winter, Pedar summoned Danlo to the meditation room and said, "I don't like your friend."

Danlo was kneeling on one of the room's wool mats, in the hated position of politeness. He stared at the lovely black and

215

red walls, appreciating the whorls and fine-grained texture of the jewood panels. The meditation room was full of silences and good smells, and he would have loved sitting in this ancient chamber but for the cruelties inflicted on him there. "Which friend, O Exalted One?"

"Hanuman li Tosh," Pedar spat out. "I don't like the way he looks at me."

"O Exalted One, how does he look at you?"

"I'm tired of that. Call me The Omniscient One."

"Yes, O Omniscient One."

"Your friend," Pedar said, "looks at me as one looks at a piece of ancient sculpture. Or worse, he looks at me as if I were a Scutari or some other loathsome alien. And worse yet, whenever I greet him on the stairs, he refuses to look at me at all."

"Perhaps, O Omniscient One, he cannot bear the sight of your pimply face."

As Danlo said this, Pedar blushed in rage, which caused the pimples across his cheeks and forehead to flare up red as blood. Danlo couldn't help smiling his rebellious, mocking smile that he had learned in Old Father's house. Ahimsa, as he understood it, required only that he never harm another's body or spirit. To inflict mind pain on another in order to provoke understanding was a Fravashi tradition that he cherished. In truth, he *liked* fighting Pedar with words. Deep in his belly he continued to hate Pedar. And deeper still, roaring like an ocean in the dark unknown part of himself—in truth, bred into his chromosomes —was an urge to destroy that which he hated.

"*What* did I hear you say?" Pedar screamed out. He balled his fist and made a move to strike Danlo's head. But he must have remembered that the penalty for such an act might be banishment from the Order, because he pulled his punch up short and smacked his fist into the palm of his hand.

"Your face," Danlo said, "as splendid as it is—"

"Never mind! Never mind, Wild Boy. Won't you ever learn your etiquette? Goddamn you! Tonight you'll think about etiquette while you're scraping slime off the tiles in the bathing room."

"O thank you!" Danlo said.

"Thank you *what*?"

"For yet another opportunity to practice restraint, thank you, O Pimpled One."

That night Danlo scraped the tiles of the first-floor bathing room, or rather, he scraped the black lines of bacteria growing *between* the tiles. Pedar provided neither scrub brush nor liquid solvents to digest the bacteria. Danlo had to use his long fingernails to scrape, dig, and ream. By the time morning came, he had cleaned between only two hundred of the room's 12,608 tiles. Most of his fingernails were splintered, broken down to the quick, and stained black with a sticky, evil-smelling filth.

"You'll report here every night until you are done," Pedar said as he examined Danlo's work. The morning sunlight, in faint filaments of silver, was diffusing through the frosted windowpanes high along the room's eastern wall. "Do you understand?"

And Danlo yawned, smiled, and then replied, "Yes, O Pimpled One, I do understand."

Later that morning, an exasperated Hanuman cried out, "He's given you an impossible task!"

Hanuman's outrage mirrored the feelings of the other first-year novices. Madhava li Shing was aghast when he heard of Danlo's "sentence," as he called it. He was a small boy, smaller even than Hanuman, but he had the arrogant, black, almond-shaped eyes and the sardonic superiority of Shing World's academician ruling class. "This is very much an injustice," he said in his calm, unperturbable manner. "Something must be done." Other boys—Adan Dur li Kadir, Javier Miro, and Sherborn of Darkmoon—agreed with him. Through the snowy days of winter, they had witnessed Danlo's fierce stubbornness, and most had come to respect him. Their initial suspicion had given way to admiration, sympathy, and, in quite a few of them, devotion. Danlo was a natural leader; there was something about him that compelled people to want to share his passions and his vision. Madhava would have gone to the Master of Novices in protest of Pedar's barbaric hazing, but Danlo enjoined him and his new friends to silence and secrecy.

Somehow, though, word of Danlo's struggle spread throughout Borja. Probably a high novice, one of Pedar's acquaintances or enemies on the first floor, talked too freely. Every boy and girl in the college, not only in Perilous Hall but those of Stone Row, The Hermitage, and other dormitories, learned that Pedar Sadi Sanat was testing Danlo's will to ahimsa. Some novices, of course, those from the more obscure Civilized Worlds, knew little of the Fravashi or their concept of ahimsa. (In fact, ahimsa is an ancient Sanskrit word and was a hallowed belief of Old Earth's Jain religion. The Jains wore gauze masks over their noses and mouths to keep from accidentally inhaling and killing the various flying insects that swarmed over the hotter regions of the Asian continent. Fravashi mores do not demand such strict reverence of life. For the Fravashi, the great wrong is the *intentional* harming of life's possibilities, without sufficient cause.) Most of the petitioners, however, appreciated the ideal of ahimsa, even if they thought it was unworkable as a rule to guide one's life. Hanuman was the first to observe ahimsa's irony. "Pedar," he said to Danlo one day, "has a pustule in place of a heart. You vow to harm no one, and he uses your compassion against you, to do you harm."

Inevitably, the story of Danlo's sufferings reached the Master of Novices. Bardo the Just immediately summoned Pedar to the Novices' Sanctuary. There, somewhere inside that fortress of stone and tradition, he chastised him. No records have been kept of Pedar's "interview" with Master Bardo, but soon a rumor circulated around the college that Pedar's punishment had been severe, private, and quite painful. Pedar was ordered to stop hazing Danlo. "By God!" someone heard Master Bardo bellowing through closed doors, "isn't life cruel enough without adding barbarism to the barbaric happenstance of birth? Ah, why didn't I see to it that Danlo served a worthy novice? I must have been drunk when I let the Head Novice make the assignations, too bad."

Pedar should have left Danlo alone after that, but he did not. Irrationally, he blamed Danlo for his humiliation in Master Bardo's chambers. He was indeed a cruel and vengeful boy, and worse, he was proud beyond all reason. Although his origins were the lowest of the low (both his parents were harijan who had come to Neverness in the mistaken belief that drugs such as jook or jambool and access to the cetics' infamous brain machines were free to all), he fancied that farther back along his genetic lines, the imprint of a ronin warrior-poet, neurologician, or an exemplar graced his chromosomes. How else to explain his surprising intelligence and the fact that he, a harijan boy, had won for himself a place at Borja? Would an exemplar allow a lesser breed of human being insult him? Would a warrior-poet, those most fearless of assassins, fear the outbursts of the bloated, bombastic Master of Novices? Out of respect for his pretend ancestors—one day he actually admitted this to Arpiar Pogossian—he planned to humiliate Danlo. He would respect the letter of Master Bardo's injunction against further hazing. But he would repay shame with shame and remind Danlo of his place and the proper respect due his superiors.

And so Pedar began collecting stories about Danlo. At night, after lights out, he crept up the shadowed stairs and crouched near the top, listening to whispers and murmurs of the younger boys talking bed to bed. In truth, he employed various means of spying on Danlo. He knew a journeyman horologe at Lara Sig who knew a courtesan whose friend was one of Old Father's students. There were many wild rumors about Danlo, and he tried to trace each one to its source. From the first day in Lavi Square, he had thought there was something mysterious about Danlo and his past, something dark, powerful, and profound. Because Pedar was a clever boy and expert at research (it was his ambition to become Lord Historian of the Order), he soon pieced together an explanation of this mystery.

On the sixty-fourth of deep winter, he confronted Danlo in Lavi Square. It was one of those blue cold, perfectly clear days in which the things of the world—the ice sculptures, the orange and red lichens etching the buildings, the individual needles of the yu trees—stand out almost too vividly. It was really too cold to be outside for very long, but the women and men (and children) of the City like to bask in the noonday sun no matter the season, and so, near the center of the Square a warming pavilion had been set up. Beneath a half dome of clary supported by wood pillars, scores of novices gathered to discuss the events of the day. Their white furs were open to the warm air gusting up from grates in the ice. They stood about kicking their skate blades against the grates as they looked for familiar faces in the stream of novices and masters passing through the Square. Every day after lunch, Danlo and a few of his friends from Perilous Hall would meet together beneath the pavilion with the other novices of Borja. Sixty-fourth day was a day much like any other —Danlo stood near the cooler air at the edge of the pavilion taking in the ring of steel against steel, skates click-clacking, and the fresh, hard smell of chiseled ice. Hanuman, Madhava li Shing, Sherborn of Darkmoon, and three girls who lived in The Hermitage surrounded him. He had just begun debating the paradoxes of causality with one of these girls, Rihana Brandreth Tal, when Hanuman pointed toward the corner of the Square and said, "Oh, no. Look, Danlo, it's the Pimple and his friends."

Two glidderies scissored the white ice, marking the Square from corner to corner with a giant red "X." Danlo looked along the line of Hanuman's rigid finger down one of the glidderies. He saw Pedar Sadi Sanat, Arpiar Pogossian, and Rafael Wu skating purposefully toward them. Pedar, in the lead, skated right up to the warming pavilion. Without pause or greeting, from the inner pocket of his furs he removed a stiff rectangular object—it was, in fact, a foto—and held it up in front of Danlo's face. "Is this man your father?" Pedar asked. He pitched his voice so that it carried through the pavilion out into the Square. "The man standing at the center of this foto—is he your father?"

"Look!" someone said. "It's a foto of Mallory Ringess."

Danlo drew in a breath of cold air as he wondered how Pedar had guessed his true lineage. He looked at the foto, at the swirl of colors which formed up beneath its clear outer skin. In the better fotos, of course, the millions of colored pixels sense which part of the foto a person is looking at and highlight and magnify this part. But because Danlo couldn't focus on any particular feature—he had never seen a foto before—the foto remained undefined. He could make out the greens and whites of what might have been a mountain; he beheld dark shapes, flesh-colored pigments, and a blue beyond blue. The foto held little jeweled specks of a deeper blueness than anything he had ever seen outside of his nighttime dreams. In truth, no object of the natural world, neither the eggshell of Ayeye, the thallow, nor even the midnight sky, was so deeply and perfectly blue.

"It's lovely!" he exclaimed. "What is it?"

Arpiar Pogossian came up behind Pedar and knocked his skates against one of the pillars to remove the ice shavings. To Danlo, he huffed out, "Remember your etiquette!"

Danlo favored him with a quick head bow, turned to Pedar, and repeated, "What is it, O Enlightened One?"

"It's a foto," Pedar said.

Danlo continued staring at the beautiful colors spread beneath the surface of the shiny rectangle before him. "And what is a foto, O Enlightened One?"

"It's a foto of Mallory Ringess's expedition to the Alaloi. Haven't you ever seen a foto?"

In Drisana's little shop, when Danlo had imprinted the Language of the Civilized Worlds, he had learned the word "foto." A foto, he remembered, was a two-dimensional array of images representing point for point—capturing in shape and color—the objects of the real world. In some ways, a foto was like a cave painting. Only a foto was more exact, more faithful to the surfaces and edges of reality, where the paintings of his ancestors revealed the truth and essence of Ayeye, Sabra, or Berura, the hooded seal, and the other animals of the world.

"Well?" Pedar said. He strained to hold the foto straight out without letting his arm tremble.

As Danlo studied the foto, he was aware of the novices chattering and pressing closer. He heard someone say, "Danlo the Wild doesn't know what a foto is!"

"Here, take it," Pedar said at last.

Danlo held the foto in his naked, gloveless hands. It had the heft and feel of a piece of bonewood. The four corners of the foto were sharp against his skin, and its surface was as glossy as *ilka-kweitling,* the young white ice.

"That *is* the Ringess!" Sherborn said as he nudged Danlo and jabbed his finger at the foto. "Mallory Ringess! And Bardo the Just, before he became Master of Novices. He looks so young!"

Pedar edged up very close to Danlo. He was so close that Danlo could see each of the large pores puncturing his cheeks and smell the metallic acridness of jook wafting off his breath. Pedar had been addicted to jook his whole life, ever since he was a fetus floating in his mother's jook-tainted womb. If Danlo had known of Pedar's bondage to jook, he might have pitied rather than hated him.

"Well?" Pedar said as he looked at Danlo eye to eye. "*Are* you the bastard son of Mallory Ringess?"

Again Danlo returned to looking at the foto. He tried to make sense of its pretty colors; he tried to see faces in the chaos of shape, shimmer, and shadow. He could see no faces. He wondered that Sherborn and others seemed to perceive the likeness of Bardo the Just near the edge of the foto. Danlo had keen eyes—he could pick out the ominous silhouette of a great white bear across nearly five miles of sea ice—and so he wondered why he could not begin to see what others could perceive so easily. Then he remembered a saying of Old Father's: "Seeing is an act of will accomplished by the brain." What was wrong with his will to vision, he wondered, that he could not see what was before him?

"Danlo!" This came from Hanuman who was standing by his side, looking back and forth between Pedar and the foto. "Danlo, give the foto back to him—you don't have to look at it."

At these words, Pedar shot Hanuman a hateful look, but he said nothing.

Danlo smiled and shook his head. He gazed at the foto, utterly entranced by what he was struggling to apprehend. The deep winter light—low streaks of silver off the polished ice—was dazzling, but it wasn't the sunlight which interfered with his vision. He dropped his head to the side and whispered, "Hanu, Hanu, it is not enough to see a thing just as it is, if I cannot make sense of what I see."

"You shouldn't blame yourself," Hanuman whispered. "It's a matter of the synapses linking up in the first year of life. As a child you never learned to abstract reality from these kind of images."

Beliefs are the eyelids of the mind, Danlo thought. And then he said, "But I am a man now. Should a child be able to see what a man cannot?"

Without taking his eyes from the foto, there on the ice of Lavi Square with the voices of fifty curious children humming in his ear, Danlo silently vowed that he would develop his sense of vision no matter the difficulty, no matter the terror (or shame) of what he might see.

"Don't pretend to ignorance, Wild Boy," Pedar said at last. Although he was the taller of the two, his posture was lax, and he slumped so that he stood face-to-face with Danlo. "Don't tell me you can't see the resemblance between yourself and the Ringess!"

From the middle of the crowd, Rihana Brandreth Tal's voice shrilled out, "It's true, Danlo has the Ringess hair—look at the strands of red in what's left of his beautiful hair." She was as small and quick as a sleekit, and one of her hands darted out and grasped Danlo's queue where it dangled beneath his cap. "Black and red—who has ever had hair like that?"

"And his eyes," someone said, "his face—it's sharp as a falcon's."

Arpiar Pogossian nudged Pedar and said, "The Wild Boy *does* have a lean and predatory look, doesn't he?"

"No, it's a *fierce* look," Rihana said. "He's fiercely beautiful, like his father—if it's really true that Mallory Ringess is his father. And that's why you've been hazing him, everyone knows. You're afraid of him or envious. Or both."

"He *is* the bastard child of the Ringess," Pedar said and he looked at Danlo. "Bastard child—do you want to hear the evidence?"

Hanuman held his palm out toward Pedar's chest. He said, "Please don't stand so close."

"First-year novices," Arpiar said as he pointed a white-gloved finger at Hanuman, "don't tell high novices what to do."

For a moment Danlo closed his eyes and let his belly pump in a stream of clear, cold air. Then he looked at Hanuman and said, "O Hanu, why can't I see it? *Is* there a man, the Mallory Ringess, in this foto?"

Hanuman cupped his hand over the back of Danlo's knuckles, and he pulled both hand and foto nearer in order to get a better look. "Of course it's the Ringess," he said. He traced his forefinger along the foto, picking out facial features. "This is his nose, and here, his hair—it's as black as a pilot's robe. Can you see it, falling over his forehead? And his lips, and his eyes—"

"I see him!" Danlo suddenly cried out. He had been looking deeply into memory and mystery when the veil of chaos was ripped away from the foto and the images embedded there suddenly "popped" into vision and made sense. There were three women in the foto, and three men each dressed in black robes. The man at the center was tall and sinewy; with his long, high nose and eyes of blue ice, he looked as fierce as a thallow. "He is splendid! He *does* look like me, yes?"

Danlo glanced up from the foto and exchanged a knowing look with Hanuman. Clearly the time had come for Danlo to confess that he had been adopted as a child into the Devaki tribe of the Alaloi. He could not imagine how Pedar had guessed this, though he was eager to hear his "evidence." And he could not imagine why he should be ashamed of such a father.

"Danlo the Wild," Pedar called out, addressing the novices assembled in the warming pavilion, "did *not* come to Neverness from an elite school, as you have. Nor did he come from any of the Civilized Worlds. I've been to the Hollow Fields and spoken to the Master of Ships; there's no record of his immigration. Therefore he must be a child of the City, as I am. But Danlo did not attend the elite school on Neverness—I should know. If he were a child of the City, why didn't he attend the elite school? Why? Why was he permitted to petition for special admittance to Borja if he'd been eligible to attend an elite school? What's the answer to this mystery? Please listen, I have a hypothesis."

And so Pedar strutted among the novices, and he delivered his theory as to Danlo's mysterious origins. Because he was an unsightly, unpopular boy, the other novices practically fell over each other trying to get out of his way. He glided here and there, ground his toe pick into the ice, spun about, and stroked his short jerky strokes, all the while waving his hands and gesticulating crudely. "Danlo the Wild has been heard speaking the

Alaloi language," he declared. "I believe he was raised among the Alaloi."

Pedar told them of the City's expedition to the Alaloi sixteen years previously, the quest to find the Elder Eddas embroidered within humanity's oldest DNA, that of the primitive Alaloi tribes. The expedition, he told them, had been a disaster. A scryer named Katharine had died in the cave of the Devaki. A spear had killed Bardo the Just (the City cryologists, of course, had later brought his frozen body back to life), and there had been a murder of a Devaki man. "The expedition," Pedar said, "lasted almost a year. In that time, is it or isn't it possible that Mallory Ringess fathered a child?"

"But Danlo doesn't look at all like an Alaloi," Rihana protested. She held a white linen to her tiny, runny nose, which was red and chafed due to constant rubbing. "If Mallory Ringess mated with a primitive woman—they're as hairy as apes, aren't they?—wouldn't Danlo bear half her chromosomes?"

Pedar picked at a pimple below his lip and said, "It's my hypothesis that Mallory Ringess had a child by Katharine the Scryer."

As he said this, Rihana and many of the novices fell silent and stared at Danlo. That his lineage had finally been proclaimed pleased Danlo, though he couldn't guess why everyone was staring at him so strangely.

"If Mallory Ringess and Katharine created a child together," Rihana finally said, "if Danlo is that child, why didn't they bring him home to the City? Why didn't the Ringess and the others bring him home?"

"Well, Katharine died and the Ringess abandoned the child —that's my hypothesis."

Danlo, who had listened in silence to this reconstruction of his personal history, suddenly touched the feather in his hair and whispered, "Oh, Ahira, Ahira, is it true?" Even as he spoke the words, he knew it must be true. Some part of him, deep in his chest where his *anima* cried out in pain, recognized a kinship with Katharine the Scryer and the man whom others called Mallory Ringess. Again Danlo looked at the foto flat in his hand, and it was like looking through a window of ice into the dark, churning waters of memory. The foto's shifting colors had captured the images of six people. Danlo had eyes only for these people; the sights, sounds, and smells of the world diminished into insignificance, as of an unreal city seen from very far away. While he studied the foto, remembering, a few journeymen eschatologists and masters had come up to the warming pavilion, but he ignored them. He ignored the chiming noon bells, the hushed explanations falling from lip to lip, and the white, icy glare hard in his eyes. The brain, he remembered, is like a fine, woven cloth, a tapestry of silken synapses which filter out noise in order to concentrate on vital information. He looked at the foto. There he recognized the huge, bearded bulk of Bardo the Just. He was surprised and amused to learn that Bardo had known his father. He learned the names of two of the women, Justine Ringess and Dama Moira Ringess. They were radiant, intelligent-looking women, aunt and mother, respectively, of the Ringess. The third woman was Katharine the Scryer, she who must be *his* mother, his blood mother. It hurt Danlo to look at her wise, beautiful, mutilated face. (Or rather, at the *image* of her face.) She had no eyes because she had blinded herself as a young woman. She had done this, at her initiation as a scryer, in order to see visions of the future. Everything about her face was a study of contrast and paradox: the shimmering black hair falling over her white cheeks and neck, the eye hollows black and mysterious beneath the white plane of her forehead, the passion and calmness stamped deeply into her lips. Danlo had seen his true mother only once before, and he had no clear memory of her face. But at last he understood the story of his birth, of how he had been born laughing. Katharine the Scryer was a woman who could laugh at any pain or presentiment of doom. And he, who was indeed her son as surely as day is the child of the night, must have inherited this loveliest of all her spirit's lovely qualities.

"*Mi pela lot-Mudda,*" Danlo whispered. "O blessed Mother of my blood, *shantih.*" Then he turned to Hanuman, tapped his finger against the foto, and asked, "Do you know who this man is?"

Hanuman, who was holding both of his arms out stiff as he tried to keep the people away, said, "That's Leopold Soli. He was the father of the Ringess."

Near the center of the foto, between Katharine and Mallory Ringess, stood a man who looked enough like the Ringess to be his brother. He, too, had eyes of ice smashed deeply into the bones of his sharp browridges and his long nose. He, too, bore the family fierceness and a silent, sad look that spoke of a too deep contemplation of life's meaning—or lack of meaning.

"*What* did you say his name is?" Danlo asked.

There was much shouting and shoving in the crowd around

225

Danlo. The air was thick with burning toalache and tobacco, body smells and curses. Someone spilled a mug of coffee over Hanuman's boots, and the dark brown liquid instantly dripped down and burned holes into the ice. "Leopold Soli," Hanuman repeated, "was Lord Pilot before Mallory Ringess deposed him." "It's known that Lord Soli was Mallory Ringess's father."

Pedar, whose boots were also dripping with splashed coffee, touched the foto and asked, "You've never heard of Leopold Soli?"

"Soli," Danlo said softly. "Yes, I knew a man by that name."

As he said this, the foto began to blur. The reds, whites, and blacks began to lose their distinctive hues, and they ran together. As Danlo watched, the faces and images set into the foto melted into each other and dissolved into a sea of muddy brown.

"Look!" Rihana said. "The foto is mutating. I wonder what the next scene will be?"

"It's a foto of the Alaloi expedition," Pedar explained. "The next scene is after Mallory Ringess and his family are sculpted. Watch this."

Danlo couldn't help watching the transmutations occurring beneath the foto's tough, clear, outer skin. Most of the other boys and girls knew the story of the expedition to the Alaloi, of how the Ringess family had been sculpted in their bodies and faces to look like Alaloi, but for Danlo the transmutation of civilized features into those of the rugged, primitive Alaloi was a revelation. The sculpting of a modern human being into a Neanderthal is no easy thing, and yet each of the six expedition members had undergone such a sculpting in order to win the acceptance of the Devaki tribe. Bones must be steened and thickened, muscles stimulated to grow, the browridges built up like rock overhangs around the eyes. New, thicker teeth must be implanted in the jaws. When the sculpting is done, the whole face will project at a greater angle outward from the skull. Some say the Alaloi are brutish-looking, with their hairy limbs and their overwhelming, open faces. Danlo, however, had always admired the primal beauty of his adoptive brothers and sisters, even before his brain had been imprinted with the word "primal." He loved the way his blood mother, Katharine, looked after she had been sculpted. Out of the colors and chaos of the foto, a beautiful woman took shape and emerged. She was tall and serene, and she wore a parka made of white shagshay fur. And she was blind no longer. Into her beautiful face, new eyes had been sculpted. Her eyes were blue beyond blue, eyes he had once seen in his dreams. In truth, he had first beheld the deep blueness of her eyes looking into the bathroom mirror in Old Father's house. Looking at himself. "But you have your mother's eyes," Three-Fingered Soli had said to him once on a cold night of death and despair. "*Yujena oyu*—eyes that see too deeply and too much."

Again, Danlo said a prayer for the mother he had never known, and then he looked at the foto's other images. To Hanuman he said, "Mallory Ringess—he looks splendid as an Alaloi, yes? I wonder what it would be like to become an Alaloi in body and face while keeping the spirit of a civilized man?"

He fell quiet and thoughtful for a moment, oblivious to the many novices discussing the scandal of his birth. And then he pointed at the foto and said to Hanuman, "I *know* this man. My father, the father of my blood—I have seen him once before. I have a memory, from when I was young—I was just learning to tie the laces of my boots. In Haidar's sled. My fingers were cold and it was hard to get the knot right, but Haidar said we had to travel and that I should keep my hands out of the wind or they would freeze and fall off. Haidar and Wemilo took me down to the sea on their sled to meet my blood father. He must have visited me, once. My father, the Ringess—even sculpted as an Alaloi, he has a fierce look to his face, yes?"

"You *are* his son, aren't you?" Hanuman said. He was now looking at Danlo intensely; there was envy, loyalty, and fear in his stare. "I should have known you were no common petitioner."

Danlo rubbed the side of his nose and said, "If Mallory Ringess is the son of Leopold Soli, then Soli must be my grandfather. *Mi ur-padda*. Three-Fingered Soli, my grandfather." He drew his fingernail along the foto until he came to the image of a man he had known almost all his life. A fierce, gaunt man who brooded too much—that was Leopold Soli. Three-Fingered Soli. When the foto had mutated, the image of Leopold Soli in his black pilot's robe had changed into Three-Fingered Soli, the strange Alaloi man who had cut his membrum and helped him pass into manhood on a deep winter night now long past. Obviously, Danlo concluded, not all of the expedition members had abandoned him at his birth. Obviously, Three-Fingered Soli must have remained among the Alaloi in order to watch over Danlo, to guide him through the dangers and pains of childhood.

There was now little doubt that Pedar had correctly guessed Danlo's origins. Words of the Alaloi language had spilled from his lips, and the lineaments of the Ringess (and Soli) chromosomes were written into his face for everyone to see.

"Well, Wild Boy?" Pedar said. He snatched the foto away from Danlo and waved it above his head. He nodded at the crowd of novices, most of whom were shouting, elbowing forward, and craning their necks to get a better look. "Well, *are* you the son of Mallory Ringess?"

Danlo tried to stand back, away from the many white-gloved hands grasping at the foto. "Yes," he said at last. "I am his son."

Pedar picked at his neck and smiled. There was a smugness in his smile and bloody pus staining the white leather of his glove. "Well, then, how can you stand here facing your fellow novices? Aren't you ashamed?"

"Why should I be ashamed?"

"You really don't know?"

"No."

Pedar addressed the novices, and there was a cruel, mocking tone to his voice, "Why should the Wild Boy be ashamed? Who will tell him?"

When the novices all suddenly fell silent and no one would speak, Pedar turned back to Danlo. "Why should you be ashamed? I'll tell you why—didn't you know that Katharine the Scryer was Mallory's sister?"

"No!"

Pedar smiled wickedly and pointed his finger at Danlo. "Your mother was Mallory Ringess's sister, and he swived her— he always put himself above morality and law, so it's said."

From the crowd surrounding them, a voice rose above the outraged murmuring. It was Rihana Brandreth Tal, and she too was outraged, not at the past indiscretions of Danlo's parents, but at Pedar's baiting Danlo. "You speak so crudely," she said.

"Well, it's a crude act, to swive one's sister." Pedar handed the foto to Arpiar Pogossian, who was standing nearby. Pedar made an "O" with his finger and thumb, and he pushed the forefinger of his other hand back and forth inside the circle, back and forth in the universal symbol (universal among human beings, that is) of copulation. "So very crude, isn't that true, Wild Boy?"

Danlo was aware that he should probably stand there silently, stand and face Pedar and listen to whatever taunts or

228

slurs he might hurl at him. But his knees and hips ached to move, and he could not remain standing.

Shaida is the man who lies with his sister, he remembered. *Shaida is the woman who—*

"Well, Wild Boy?"

There was an aching in Danlo's belly, in his throat, and in his eyes; at last he understood why the slow evil had come upon his tribe and killed all his brothers and sisters.

Shaida is the child born of shaida.

Suddenly, as a beast who has been brought to bay and wounded, he knew he had to flee. He flung his hand over his eyes, gasped for air, and pushed away from the warming pavilion. Blindly, he pushed aside several novices. He struck off onto the dazzling whiteness of Lavi Square. His skates struck the ice in a quick, violent staccato, flashing steel sending up sprays of ice powder. So quickly did he gain speed and so wild his stroking that he knocked into the shoulder of a journeyman pilot. He scarcely felt the jolt; he was only dimly aware of a blackness before him, the furry blackness of the journeyman recoiling from him, arms windmilling, falling to the ice. Danlo didn't pause to see if the journeyman was hurt. He shot down the gliddery into cold, hard air, and in moments he had left Lavi Square behind him.

MULTIPLICATION BY ZERO

O mighty Arjuna, even if you believe the Self to be subject to birth and death, you should not grieve. Death is inevitable for the living; birth is inevitable for the dead. Since these are unavoidable, you should not sorrow. Every creature is unmanifested at first and then attains manifestation. When its end has come, it once again becomes unmanifested. What is there to lament in this?

—Lord Krishna to Arjuna, before the battle of Kurukshetra

Without plan or destination Danlo skated east through the buildings of Borja. Just below the Hill of Sorrows, where the flat, frozen Academy grounds give way to the icefalls and lower slopes of the mountains, he came to a grove of trees renowned for its beauty. It was called the shih grove; it was a well-tended stand of 112 shih trees imported from Urradeth. On a stone bench beneath the silver trees, he sat playing his shakuhachi and looking for sign of Ahira in the deep winter sky.

I am that which should not be born, he thought.

A short while later there came the *click-clack* of skates against the grove's single gliddery. Danlo looked up to see Hanuman gliding toward his bench. "I *had* to follow you," he gasped out. "But you're too quick. I thought I'd lost you. And then I heard you playing your flute. Through the trees—the sound of it carries, you know."

"Yes, I know," Danlo said. And then he asked, "Is it true . . . what Pedar said? Were Katharine and Mallory Ringess truly brother and sister?"

Hanuman rested the toe of his boot on the bench. The wind and his exertions had brought his usually bone-white skin to a scarlet flush. He nodded his head. "Everyone knows they were."

"Then I am an abomination."

"Oh, Danlo."

"I am that which should not have come into life," he said.

Danlo looked off into the shadowed depths of the grove for a long time. The shih trees were truly unique, truly beautiful. Unlike shatterwood or yu trees, with their conical symmetry and pointed crowns, the limbs of each shih tree branched out from a main trunk without apparent pattern, dividing and redividing into thousands of sub-branches. And at the end of every twig, veined with silver and fluttering in the wind, were the shimmering leaves, ten thousand silver-green leaves seeking out the sun high above the ground. "Why?" he asked. "Why would the Ringess lie with his own sister?"

Hanuman shrugged his shoulders and said, "I don't know."

"Shaida eth shaida," Danlo said. And he thought, *Shaida is the man who touches his sister beneath the furs of night.*

"Danlo, you are—"

"No!" Danlo suddenly cried out. He was up on his skates, and he smacked the shakuhachi against his thigh four times in syncopation with each of the four terrible words he forced out: "I . . . am . . . *shaida* . . . too!"

"Danlo, you can't—"

"No, no, no, no!"

Without care or consideration of ahimsa, Danlo reached up to the lowest branch of the tree above the bench, and he plucked off a single leaf. He clenched his fist then, crushing the leaf. Silver sap as warm as blood ran beneath his fingers. It pained him, the sight of the tree's lifeblood spilled so carelessly, and he closed his eyes in order to weep for the dead leaf.

"Danlo, Danlo." He heard Hanuman's voice tighten with emotion and die off. And then he felt Hanuman's cold fingers against his forehead, and he opened his eyes. Hanuman quickly jerked his hand away. He was plainly embarrassed to be caught offering the simplest of kindnesses. (In truth, it was the first time he had initiated such a gesture since he was five years old, when his mother had told him he was too old to touch others in friendship.) Danlo and Hanuman looked at each other in silent understanding, and the only sound in the shih grove was the whoosh and murmur of the wind through the trees.

And then Hanuman quoted from *Man's Journey*: " 'I love all those who are as heavy raindrops, falling one by one out of the dark cloud that hangs over men: they herald the advent of lightning, and as heralds, they suffer and perish.' "

"I am the herald of death," Danlo said.

"What do you mean?"

"I am *shaida*, and that is why the *shaida* death came upon the Devaki."

Danlo sat back down on the bench. Even through the fur of his pants the stone's coldness stung his skin. He confided to Hanuman the secret he had never thought to tell anyone: of how the whole Devaki tribe had perished of a mysterious *shaida* fever.

"But it must have been a virus that killed your people," Hanuman said. "You didn't make this virus, Danlo."

"No, but my . . . coming into my tribe must have weakened them. It must have touched their spirits with *shaida*."

"Oh, no, that's silly," Hanuman said. "You mustn't think such thoughts."

"The truth is the truth."

With a long sigh, Hanuman shook his head and murmured, "I don't like to see you like this."

"I am sorry."

"*I'm* sorry about your people," Hanuman said. "But you have your life and your dream. Your fate."

Without warning, Danlo knelt down next to the gliddery. With his naked finger, which was still cracked and blackened from the labors Pedar had forced on him, he began drawing circles in the snow. And then he said, "O Hanu! How can I ever become an asarya, now? How can *I*? To see it, dancing, quickening, all life—how can I affirm anything if I cannot even say 'yes' to my own existence?"

"Danlo, you—"

"I was a fool to think I could be an asarya."

Hanuman looked at him and shook his head. "You—if you're a fool, you're a splendid fool. Perhaps you're even foolish enough to become an asarya."

"No, that is not possible, not now."

"But for our kind," Hanuman said, "all things are possible."

Danlo busied himself with drawing lines in his circles. The

snow crystals were gritty and cold beneath his fingernails. In truth, it was much too cold to be solving mathematical theorems in the snow. He finally abandoned his effort; he looked at Hanuman and asked, "Do you think we are so different from others?"

"You know that we are."

"But, Hanu, we are still *people*."

"There are people," Hanuman said, "and there are people."

"The blessed . . . people. All people are blessed."

"But few are chosen," Hanuman said. "All through history, there have always been a few people destined to be something more."

"More . . . than what?"

"More than they are. More than anybody is."

Danlo smiled at this and said, "I think you are a natural aristocrat."

"How not? It's only we, aristocrats in our souls, who can know what is possible."

"But what about the others?"

"Others are other. You mustn't think about them too much. All human society is a hierarchy. All life, this living pyramid. It's only natural that a few human beings should stand at the top."

"You mean, stand on top of others."

"I didn't make the universe," Hanuman said. "I just live in it."

Danlo knelt in the snow, listening to the wind fall off the Hill of Sorrows and the icy mountains above. "But it is hard to live . . . with the boots of others kicking at your face."

"Oh, yes, life is cruel," Hanuman said. "And to stand at the top, one has to be a little cruel. Cruel to others—and even crueler to oneself."

"Cruel? You? I?"

"Oh, yes. You'll see it, if you look hard enough."

"But, Hanu, *why*?"

"Because that's the only way for people such as you and I to become more. We look down at the others, beneath our boots. They seem so close—but there's a vast distance between us. Most of these people are quite content to bear us up. You might even say our weight is a comfort to them. All they see is our boots in their faces, and sometimes they think they hate that. But if we were to step off them only for a moment, what then? Then *they* would stand on the pyramid's apex. And the view of all the living flesh beneath would make them sick and dizzy, even mad. The greater the height, the greater the fall. That's why they're glad to leave the apex to our kind. And so this vast distance: the light-distances between the stars aren't greater than the distance between those who love their fate and those who fear it. Our kind are those who crave such distances. Because it creates in us a longing for the distances within our own souls. This is what we should live for, Danlo: the heightening of our sensibilities, the rarefying of our desire, the deepening of our purpose, the vastening of our selves. The power to overcome ourselves. To be more. Or rather, to *become* more. Who hasn't dreamed of such becoming? But who could think to distance himself from his lower parts without an act of cruelty?"

Just then a blast of cold air blew through the shih grove, rattling the tree leaves against each other. Danlo arose from the snow and looked up through the silvery canopy above him. The sky to the west, he saw, was no longer blue. A bank of ice clouds as gray as lead was moving across the sea, closing in toward the City. *Ilka-tetha,* he thought, the death clouds.

"I do not understand you," Danlo said. He turned to Hanuman, who was standing beneath a giant old tree. "You *like* people. And they like you. Yet you speak as if they have no value."

"I love people," Hanuman admitted. "I love animals, too."

"But people are not animals!"

Hanuman laughed harshly, then said, "In one sense—and this is the only sense that really matters—most people are nihilities. Think of Pedar. Think of his friends. They have zero chance of becoming anything greater. Trillions of people, trillions of Pedars—they fill the stars across the galaxy with copies of themselves and call this the fulfillment of man's destiny. But no, it's not. It's only multiplication by zero."

"But, Hanu, where would you be . . . without the people who made you?"

"Just so," Hanuman said. "The only purpose of lower people is to kneel down and form a pyramid so that the higher kind of man may stand above the clouds and complete a higher task. You mustn't think our kind are just some lucky accident of civilization. We're the only *reason* for civilization. We're its hope and meaning."

"Oh, Hanu!"

"It's hard, I know. To accept that people don't live their lives for themselves—this is hard. Because living as they do, they never really *live.*"

234

Like a shagshay bull, Danlo kicked at the crusty old snow. He said, "I know about slavery. About slaves—Master Jonath told me there used to be slaves on Summerworld."

"Do you think it's so despicable that the higher man should live off the lower? No, it's not. It's only natural. And necessary. We should acknowledge this. They give us their lives! They're an incomplete, diminished, sick, and broken people—we should accept their sacrifice gracefully. With gratitude. With compassion, even love."

For a moment Danlo covered his eyes and looked down at the snow. Then he said, "Since the Day of Submission . . . I have had a taste of what slavery is like."

"So have I," Hanuman said. "But this is good, not bad. Everyone should be a slave once in his life."

"How so?"

"Because this way, we know what it's like to feel the boots on our backs. Because ever after, when we come into ourselves, we'll have the ruthlessness to be masters."

Danlo stood leaning back against the trunk of a shih tree. His fingernails drummed the icy, broken bark; the sound they made was something like the *kap, kap, kap* of a mauli bird. "I shall never like Pedar," he said. "Or his friends. But . . . *we* are they. They are we. There is no real difference."

"Ahimsa," Hanuman said, and he shook his head. "A noble idea that will destroy you."

"No, it is just the opposite."

Hanuman shifted his boots atop the snow trying to keep warm. He said, "Our kind are animals, too, but we're also something more."

"As is Pedar."

"No, not really. The true juncture in evolution is not between the animals and man. It's between man and true human beings."

Because Hanuman's overweening arrogance deeply disturbed Danlo (and because he feared that there might be some truth to what he had said), he began wandering through the grove. There was one tree he particularly liked, a gnarled, lightning-scarred tree whose twisted limbs reminded him that even the life of plants was full of pain. He paced around and around this tree, making a circle. The snow overlaying the trees' roots was old and hard, and it crunched beneath his boots.

"All people," Danlo said, "are human beings."

"All?"

"Yes, all. Even the carked races. Even the humans some call aliens."

"No, Danlo. True human beings are rare. Rarer than you might think."

"What is a human being, then?"

Hanuman stood quietly in the snow, then said, "A seed."

"A . . . seed?"

"An acorn that is unafraid to destroy itself in growing into a tree."

"Then—"

" 'The true human being,' " Hanuman quoted, " 'is the meaning of the universe. He is a dancing star. He is the exploding singularity pregnant with infinite possibilities.' "

"I think the possibilities of all people are . . . infinite."

"I love you for your faith," Hanuman said. "But, in truth, I've known only two people who might possibly be human."

Danlo stopped suddenly and whirled around in the snow. Hanuman was looking at him intensely, as if they were the only two people who mattered in all the universe. "But I am a man just like any other," Danlo protested. "You and I—how are we so different from others?"

Hanuman bowed his head and replied, "In our consciousnesses, we are different. In our awareness of our deepest purpose. The way we see too much and too deeply."

"But, Hanu—"

"The way we feel pain."

The way we feel pain. Danlo took in a quick gasp of air and held it until his lungs burned with the urge to breathe. Then everything escaped from him at once, his exploding breath and his fundamental hatred of Hanuman's elitism. (And, most of all, his anguish at his own unique qualities and origins which separated him from all other peoples of Civilized Worlds.) "What do you know about pain?" he cried out.

"Not enough, it seems," Hanuman said. He was standing in front of Danlo with his arms folded across his chest, shivering. He was also smiling. There was something both wicked and profound in his smile. "But I know that human beings suffer as others do not. There's no help for it. To become greater one must be completely ruthless toward oneself. If the eye gives offense, it must be plucked out—do you understand? If something is hard to do, if it is hateful, even what others call evil— one must do that very thing precisely *because* it's hateful. One must hold a red-hot fire iron to the weaker parts of one's soul.

236

This continual mutilation of the self—this is pain inside pain without end."

Although Danlo nodded his head at Hanuman's words, he was not really listening. Usually he listened to others with all the concentration of an owl trying to detect sleekit scratchings beneath the snow, but now he was staring off into the darkening sky, remembering.

"Without *end*," Hanuman said. "The pain of self-overcoming is just the beginning. Then, for our kind, if we're strong enough, if our souls are great and deep—then comes the real pain. What's real pain, you ask? The power to choose what we will. *Having* to choose. This terrible freedom. These infinite possibilities. The taste for the infinite spoiled by the possibility of evolutionary failure. Real pain is knowing that you're going to die, all the while knowing that you don't *have* to die."

"But, Hanu, everything dies," Danlo said softly. He turned to face the scarred, old shih tree, and he pressed his forehead against it. When he looked up, he felt the zigzag mark where the tree's icy bark had cut into his skin.

Hanuman shook his head and continued, "But why die at all, Danlo? Mightn't there be a new phase of evolution? A new kind of being? Can't you understand? I'm trying to delineate an emergent quality of the brain. New synapses. New connections. A constellation of qualities and abilities, of new levels of existence. Consciousness heightened and exalted in itself, purified. This pure consciousness that we really are. That we struggle to be. For our kind, there's always the burning to be more. The eternal longing. And this is why true human beings feel more pain. Because we *are* more, but it's never quite enough—never. And we are aware of this neverness inside our souls. And aware of being aware. There is a feedback. Can you understand what this is like? Pain is magnified, infinitely. Each moment of time. Reality becomes almost too real. It blazes. All the universe afire with the possibilities of light, and madness, too. *Real* pain is the burning that never stops, the frenzy, the lightning."

Standing so long in the cold had exhausted Danlo so he leaned back against his tree. His fingers found the charred wound where a bolt of rare winter lightning had split the tree's bark. *Frenzy and lightning,* he thought. He stood there remembering the frenzied, frothing disease that had killed his people. The wind came up, then, carrying down the rich, ageless smell of the mountains. It was a smell of life and death. Danlo thought the best thing about the shih grove was the variety of its smells:

steamy sleekit droppings dotting the snow, ice, spindrift, crushed yu berries, and the pungence of hot sap when the wind occasionally tore the shih leaves from their branches. Somewhere, in the rising green forests above him, a pack of wolves must have killed a shagshay bull, or perhaps a doe. The wind was keen with blood scent, and it touched his nostrils with the faint, fermy smell of a shagshay's opened entrails. Most wolves, he remembered, liked to lick out the fermenting, vegetable contents of a shagshay's stomach before tearing into the liver.

"Danlo, have you heard anything I've said?"

In truth, Danlo was almost beyond listening. He had his hand up underneath his cap, rubbing his stubbly scalp as he recalled a certain custom of the Devaki tribe: a man, when he had unwittingly caused another injury, would make a blood offering to atone for the pain.

"Danlo?"

Anaslia, he remembered, was the Devaki word for the sharing of pain.

"Please, Danlo. Look at me."

But Danlo was now looking down, searching with his eyes for stones. Surrounding them was a circle of footprints broken through layers of snow. In a few places, his boots had exposed the ground. He dropped to the snow, and with his cold, stiff fingers he pried loose a roundish white stone and a chunk of granite. Quickly, precisely, he hammered the stone against the edge of the granite. A sharp piece of granite the size of a shih leaf flaked off. It was poor quality stone to cut with, but since he didn't have any flint or obsidian to make a proper knife, he shrugged his shoulders, grasped the flake between his fingers, and brought the point of it up against his forehead. He slashed himself from his stubbly hairline to his eyebrow. He cut deeply, diagonally across his forehead, down to the bone. He cut skin and veins, and his blood flowed over his eyebrows and fell in streams to the snow.

"What are you doing!" Hanuman cried out as he rushed through the snow and knelt at Danlo's side. "Oh, what have you done?"

Danlo tried to turn away from Hanuman. With rigid fingers he held open the wound, the better to let as much blood as possible touch the world. It would require many heartbeats of blood to atone for the deaths of Haidar, Chandra, and his nearbrothers. Of course, he knew it was impossible to share the death agony of a whole tribe of people—no one had that much blood inside. *Shaida is the man who brings death to his people.* No, he could never undo the Devaki's deaths; he could not even undo his own *shaida* life, for he knew it was not the right time to die. But he could give his blood to the dead. He could give them his pain. Across Danlo's bleeding forehead and behind his eyes was a whole universe of pain.

"Danlo, Danlo!" Hanuman began scooping up handfuls of snow and holding the frozen white mounds against Danlo's forehead to sop up the blood. There was too much blood, however, and the snow quickly turned to red slush in his hands. "Oh, God!" he repeated again and again. "Oh, God, my God!"

Danlo's head wound must have recalled terrible images of his own father's death—his murder—in the family reading room, because Hanuman was suddenly frantic with fear. "Danlo, Danlo," he said, "what have you done?" He fumbled with the zipper of his furs, pried the stone flake from Danlo's bloody fingers, and used it to hack a piece of cloth from his woolens. This cloth he bound around Danlo's head beneath the ruff of his blood-spattered cap.

"I was just giving blood to the dead," Danlo explained.

"Oh, no, not now!" Hanuman said. He grasped at Danlo's shoulder. "Come, quickly; we've got to get you to a cutter before you bleed to death!"

"Wait," Danlo said. Even though the pain above his eye was hot and intense, even though blood was soaking the makeshift bandage so quickly that it wouldn't freeze, he knew that scalp wounds were rarely as serious as they appeared. "Wait," he repeated, looking at Hanuman. "Your face—your blessed face!"

It is astonishing that the look on a person's face can change the universe. Or rather, what is *behind* that look. In the pull of Hanuman's elegant brow muscles, in the trembling of the too sensitive lips, there was something new, something Danlo had never expected to see. *Terrible beauty,* he thought. All across Hanuman's face were the terrible and beautiful marks of compassion. Of *anaslia. Anaslia* was the Devaki word for compassion; it meant, literally, "suffering with." And how Hanuman suffered! In truth, Danlo could not bear to look at him just then, with his silent, anguished face and his hooded eyes. There was something involuted and heartbreaking in his friend's compassion for him. Something twisted. Danlo lifted his head then, looking away, looking up at the black, infinite depths behind the blueness of the sky. He was suddenly afraid of something. Although he could not quite articulate this fear, could not bring it to mind as a concept made up of words, deep in his belly was an acid dread that he had awakened (or created) in Hanuman a twisted compassion far more terrible than beautiful.

"What are you looking at?" Hanuman asked. His eyes were watery with tears; they were like twin, pale mirrors quavering in the cold.

Anashaida—this is what Danlo's deepest self called to him; beware the twisted compassion that would change both their lives and perhaps the future of all living things.

"Danlo? Oh, God, my God, why won't the bleeding stop!"

Again Hanuman cut a cloth strip from his shirt and replaced Danlo's sodden red bandage.

"Push it against my head." Danlo grunted as he met Hanuman's eyes with his own. "Tightly—the pressure will stop the bleeding."

"Like this?" Hanuman asked as he pressed his palm to Danlo's forehead.

"Yes, that is good."

"It's still bleeding!" Hanuman called out. His furs were open to the wind; his woolens had been hacked into rags, and he was shivering violently. His teeth began to chatter, making a *tecka, tecka, tecka* sound. "My . . . God, I've never . . . seen so much . . . blood!"

He was standing close to Danlo, and his little hand was hard against Danlo's forehead. Danlo felt his carbon dioxide breath, in ragged hot jets, fall over his face. He said, "That is good. Thank you."

Hanuman relaxed his grip slowly before letting go altogether. He looked at his glove, now bloodstained and ruined. He made a fist and punched the air. "Why can't you apply this rule of ahimsa to yourself?" he said. And then, "Why did Pedar have to show you that silly foto?"

"It was not Pedar who killed the Devaki," Danlo said.

"No."

No—such a simple sentiment and declaration, and Danlo thought that he had never listened to a word uttered with so much contempt.

"Please," he said, "you must not blame Pedar. He is just—"

"He's a nihility," Hanuman said. "He tries to shame you because he can't bear his own shame. His weakness, his ignobility. He can't bear his suffering, either, as feeble as it is. And so he tries to share it with you."

"And you hate him for that."

"How should I not? Between his kind and ours, there's always been enmity and war."

"But the law of ahimsa requires—"

"Ahimsa!" Hanuman snapped. His face was white with fury. "That's no law for a human being!"

"But never killing—"

"*Listen,* Danlo, please: 'Do what thou wilt shall be the whole of the law.'"

"But . . . whose law?"

"Our law."

"O blessed Hanu!"

With his hand flung up to his forehead, Danlo turned to the west where the sun was lost behind the clouds. He covered his eyes then, trying to listen to what Hanuman was saying: "A few human beings prepared by evolution, each with unique abilities . . . your own father, Mallory Ringess . . . this ontogenesis of man into god, the genius to create a true self." Hanuman's smooth words of explanation barely penetrated the dome of sound enclosing Danlo. In the sky, somewhere, an ivory gull called to his mate. This *hrark-hrarking* cry frightened the teal eyes in their winter nests; the trees were full of fluttering wings and a nervous warbling that fell out into the air. A fresh, strong wind swooped down the mountain in a steady flow over the scree fields and glaciers; it rushed through the shih leaves, thousands of shih leaves vibrating like sheets of silver, almost ringing in the wind. Danlo submerged himself in these sounds, but finally, he couldn't ignore the brilliance of Hanuman's voice: ". . . the true self, discovering it, the true will to one's fate." These quick, clever words filled him with dread and made his blood jump along his veins. Hanuman, more than any person he had ever seen, had an urge to embrace the future, to love his fate no matter how tragic or terrible.

Ti-miura halla, he thought. *Follow your fate, follow your deepest will to life. Only, what if one's will led to the ruin of* other life?

They left the shih grove, then, skating below the icefalls and the great, looming ice sculptures of the Elf Gardens. Hanuman still wanted to escort Danlo to the college's infirmary, but Danlo did not want to explain the meaning of his gashed forehead, and so the two of them made their way along the Academy's easternmost gliddery to Perilous Hall. There, in the deserted fourth-floor bathing room, Hanuman glued shut the flaps of skin lying

241

ragged and open against Danlo's skull. But he applied the pungent shaving glue inexpertly: ever after, when Danlo's wound had healed, above his left eye he would bear a vivid scar shaped like the zigzag of a lightning bolt.

"Thank you," Danlo said when they were done. *"Shantih."* Since it was too late in the afternoon to resume their studies, Danlo sat on his bed playing his shakuhachi, brooding over the strange events of the day.

"Do you feel faint?" Hanuman asked as he pulled on his spare set of woolens and gloves. "Does it hurt very much?"

"It throbs," Danlo admitted. "But between heartbeats, there is no pain."

"Shall I bring you back an analgesic or narcotic?"

Danlo shook his head as he forced a laugh. The slight back and forth motion sent a pounding surge of pain into his skull. And then he asked, "Where are you going?"

"I have a few errands to make before dinner," Hanuman said.

That evening was the strangest Danlo had spent since taking up residence in Perilous Hall. After their daily games of hokkee and bump-and-skate, the other boys returned to the dormitory. A couple of them—Madhava li Shing and Sherborn of Darkmoon—tried to engage him in conversation. But when they saw the jagged wound on his forehead and beheld the private passion with which he played the shakuhachi, they left him alone. They went down to eat their dinners, where they were joined by Hanuman and the boys from the other three floors. Danlo went hungry that night. And so he was not present to witness the tenseness as Pedar and his friends sat down at one of the long dining tables to a meal of cultured meats, bread, fruit, and ice wine. He never saw, with his own eyes, the expression of guilt and mortification on Pedar's face when boys at every table began clinking their wineglasses together and speaking in awed, hushed tones of Danlo's lineage. While the others sipped their wine three floors below him, he remained sitting cross-legged on his bed, playing his bamboo flute, and he never suspected that Pedar's plan to humiliate him had gone awry. Indeed, the novices—and many of the journeymen and masters of the Academy as well—were enchanted with the idea of his being the bastard son of a god. In the cold, deserted sleeping chamber, he played his music alone, and with every breath taken and then released into his flute's cool ivory mouthpiece, he felt a hollowness inside him, a terrible doubt and presentiment of doom. He should have

242

paid close attention to these feelings. He was the son of Katharine the Scryer, after all, and he had inherited some his mother's sensitivity to the future. He should have seen the dark, chaotic images inside him as visions of moments soon to be. (Or as vivid omens that Ahira had put into his third eye behind his forehead). But he closed his eyes and played his shakuhachi, and in the flute's bottomless sound was a dread and estrangement that recalled only the tragedies of the past.

Later, long after the evening bells had rung and all the novices had returned, bathed and shaved, and were safe in their beds, Danlo slept fitfully. He had dreams. In truth, his sleep was with nightmare, a hellish time of twisting and turning between his hot sheets. His descent into the molten, bloodred sea of dreamspace was excruciating and endless. It seemed he would never wake up. And then there was a screaming. "Go away, go away!" Deep within the muscle-lock of nightmare, he thought that he, himself, must be screaming. Suddenly, with a terrible snap, he came to consciousness trembling and slick with sweat. There was total blackness around him, and the silence spread over the sleeping chamber was as deep and cold as ice.

But only for a moment.

"Light the flame globes!" someone shouted, and the lights came on. Hanuman, in the bed next to his, was sitting bolt upright, blinking, looking down the row of beds toward the center of the chamber. All the boys were now awake, and everyone had his head turned to the dark, open stairwell leading to the lower floors. From the stairwell came muffled cries and sounds of panic. "He looks like he fell!" a voice from the second floor echoed into the room. And then, other voices, a whole sea of frightened voices as the panic spread from floor to floor and the dormitory came awake: "He's dead, look at all the blood! He fell down the stairs! Look at him, he's dead!"

Danlo was the first to jump out of his bed and rush down the winding stairway; Hanuman and Madhava li Shing followed groggily behind him. As if a signal had been given, each floor emptied of boys wanting to see who had fallen down the infamous stairs of Perilous Hall.

"Send for a cutter!" someone called out.

"No, a cryologist. Freeze the body—maybe the cryologists can bring him back."

And then another voice answered him, "It's too late. He's beyond help—can't you see he's bashed out his brains?"

When Danlo reached the bottom of the stairs and pushed

his way through the gathering circle of high novices, he came
upon an incredible sight. There, in the center of the first floor's
main hall, crushed against the gray floor stones, was the body of
Pedar Sadi Sanat. He had apparently fallen headfirst down the
stairwell: His face had been smashed to the meat, and his skull
had come apart against the sharp edges of the two bottom steps.
Danlo wouldn't have recognized him if it hadn't been for the
boils and pimples on his broken neck. He stood over Pedar's
body and then tilted his head back. The stairway was a dark gray
ribbon of stone winding around and above him. And on almost
every step, there was a curious novice looking over the stairway's inner edge. In the light of the cold flame globes, their
skulls gleamed with greens and reds, a spiral of sixty rainbow
skulls staring down at him. The sight of the boys' horrified faces
disoriented Danlo and made him feel dizzy.

"How could he have fallen? He was always so careful on
the steps!" This came from Rafael Wu, the boy whose fingers
Danlo had kicked and broken during his torment in the first-
floor bathing room. Rafael, too, stood over Pedar's body. Next
to him was Arpiar Pogossian, who was yawning as he rubbed his
thick neck. They both looked at Danlo. "Did you push him,
Wild Boy?"

Danlo pressed his fist into the pit of his naked belly; across
the hall, the main door of the dormitory was ajar, banging
against the jamb with each gust of wind, and he stood there
naked and shivering in the draft. Unlike the other boys, all of
whom wore long, quilted sleeping robes, he always slept naked.
"Never killing or hurting another," he whispered, "not even in
one's thoughts."

"*What* did you say?" Rafael wanted to know.

Arpiar Pogossian shouldered Rafael aside and looked at
Danlo. "I don't think the Wild Boy pushed him. I was awake
when Pedar went up to the fourth floor. I heard what he
shouted, didn't anyone else? It was something like, 'Monsters,
they're all bloody, monsters go away!' Didn't anyone else hear
Pedar screaming about monsters?"

As it happened, at least four other boys had heard Pedar
screaming about monsters. The boys all began to talk at once, a
cacophony of voices shouting from floor to floor:

"He must have tripped."

"*Why* did he trip?"

"If you hallucinated a bloody monster in the middle of the
night, you'd trip, too."

244

"Who cares if he *did* trip? He shouldn't have been on the stairs after lights out."

"That's right!"

"He was on his way up to see Danlo."

"I'm glad he's dead."

"Quiet now—how would *you* like to fall on your thin head?"

Arpiar Pogossian shrugged his shoulders sadly and looked at Rafael. "I told him a hundred times he should purge himself of the jook."

While Arpiar and Rafael debated the hallucinogenic properties of jook and other drugs that Pedar had been fond of, Hanuman threaded his way down the steps. He came up to Danlo, and his face was as white as ice. He was carrying a sleeping robe, which Danlo pulled on and zipped closed. Everyone stood around, occasionally glancing at Pedar (or trying not to); no one wanted to touch the body. Many of the boys had never seen a dead person before, and no one seemed to know what to do.

Never killing, Danlo thought as he looked at Pedar. *It is better to die oneself than kill.*

He turned to Hanuman, half expecting him to be ill at the sight of so much blood. But Hanuman's face was empty of emotion and impossible to read.

Just then, the great wooden doors banged opened. Bardo the Just, accompanied by the novice who had gone to inform him of Pedar's accident, strolled into the hallway. Bardo's eyes were bleary and bloodshot, and a patina of snow sparkled atop his fur cape. He looked impatient, as if he had been disturbed from sex or sleep. With his massive black-gloved hand, he rubbed his eyes, rubbed his bulging forehead, and lastly, he rubbed the condensation droplets from his bulbous purple nose. "By God, one of my boys is dead!" he boomed. "Too bad."

Bardo walked slowly, measuredly through the hallway. High on the walls, halfway to the high, arched ceiling, the cold flame globes were all ablaze. Their light spilled out over a row of paintings, dreamy landscapes of Old Earth, Arcite, and Icefall. Spaced evenly between the paintings, every ten feet or so, were rosewood stands holding up the busts of famous pilots and academicians, all of whom had once been novices in Perilous Hall. "Tradition," Bardo's huge voice thundered, "tradition demands that I execute an inquest as to this poor boy's death. Who can tell me how he fell?"

245

For a short while—a very short while considering the gravity of the moment—he questioned Danlo, Hanuman, Arpiar, and various other boys. Some of them, those from the second and third floors, he sent immediately back to their beds. He strolled up and down the hallway, and at last, he knelt above Pedar. He looked up the stairwell, measuring angles and distances with his quick brown eyes. He noted the brain matter spread over steps and stones, and the blood. Pedar's head and torso were practically floating in a puddle of blood. A nervous boy named Timin Wang, in the first moments of confusion after Pedar had screamed, in the dark, had stepped in the blood and tracked it about the hall. Little bloody footprints led past the first-floor sleeping chamber to the bathing room where Timin had reportedly washed the blood from his feet. Bardo measured Timin's answers to his questions, just as he weighed and evaluated Madhava li Shing's assertion that both Danlo and Hanuman had been in bed at the time of the fall. He came to an immediate, official, (and quite mistaken) judgment as to the events of Pedar's death: sometime after dinner, on the sixty-fourth night of deep winter in the year 2947, Pedar had decided to apologize to Danlo for all the injustices he had inflicted upon him. He had come to this surprising decision because he could see that Danlo, no matter how he tried to hurt or defame him, was destined to become a popular boy, perhaps even a famous and powerful man. And, in truth, Danlo's toughness and faithfulness to ahimsa had changed Pedar. In the Fravashi manner, Danlo sought always to reflect the best parts of everyone he met, even his enemies. Pedar, in knowing Danlo, had finally seen himself as he might be: bright, devoted to truth rather than vengeance, magnanimous in defeat. And so Pedar vowed to make a public apology. As was his habit, after everyone had gone to sleep, he started up the steps to rouse Danlo from his bed. (Pedar, of course, could not wholly rid himself of cruelty merely by wishing it so. Pedar—this is what Arpiar Pogossian told Bardo the Just—wanted to frighten Danlo out of his sleep one last time only to surprise him with an apology and an offer of friendship. This is why he stole up the stairs like a slel necker in the night.) Somewhere near the top of the stairs, however, well above the third floor, he hallucinated his "bloody monsters." Most likely he slipped in panic and thus fell to his death.

"It's too bad," Bardo declared. "It's a pity, ironic and pitiful, but no one is to blame but Pedar himself."

"*Shantih,*" Danlo whispered. "*Mi alasharia la shantih.*" He

246

looked at Hanuman, who was still staring at Pedar. There was neither blame nor compassion in his friend's pale blue eyes. There was nothing but death.

"I think he hated himself," Hanuman said softly. "At least he won't have to suffer himself anymore."

Just then Bardo sighed and ambled over to Danlo. He bent his head low so that only Danlo would hear what he said. "I must speak with you soon, Danlo wi Soli Ringess. Perhaps tomorrow or the day after." He turned to look once again at the stairs of Perilous Hall and muttered, "Ah, too bad."

A couple of journeyman cutters arrived with a sled, then, and took Pedar's body away. Arpiar Pogossian and his friends brought out mops, buckets, and solvents that would disassemble and digest the bloodstains from the floor—this was one very personal piece of work they didn't intend to foist off onto the first-year novices. Bardo reminded everyone that there would be a requiem the following evening in the Sanctuary, and he sent them off to bed.

The rest of that night Danlo did not sleep. Beneath sheets and blankets as soft as snow, beneath the black, oppressive silence of the sleeping chamber, he lay awake repeating in his mind Master Bardo's words: "There is no one to blame but himself." But Danlo did blame. He, of all the novices, cutters, and masters, was sure he knew the genesis of Pedar's death.

Shaida is the way of the man who kills other men, he thought.

Once, on a night of despair much like this night, as he lay waiting in his bed for the slap of Pedar's boots against the stairs, he had envisioned him slipping and falling like a stone into the black, icy ocean. He had willed his death. It was the oldest and most basic of principles: the songs that one sings inside the heart correspond and resonate with the greater world outside. One single time, he had broken ahimsa, harmed Pedar in his thoughts, and now the boy was dead.

Shaida is the cry of the man who has lost his soul.

For a long time he wept silently into the dark, and he was glad that Hanuman was asleep and couldn't see the blankets quivering with each sob and spasm of his belly. Hanuman was sleeping, he thought, and so there would be no more sharing of agony that night. But after a long while, sometime near dawn, Hanuman began crying out in nightmare, "No, no, Father, please no!"

Danlo whispered, "Hanu, Hanu," and then he got out of

bed, leaned over Hanuman's sweating, stricken face, and covered his mouth. "*Shantih,* be quiet now, or you will wake the others."

He thought that Hanuman, too, must have suffered over Pedar's death. He stood barefoot in the dark drafty chamber, looking down at Hanuman. He listened as the wind howled outside the dormitory and gusts of air beat against the clary windows; their rattle almost drowned out Hanuman's muffled cries. He touched Hanuman's forehead; he felt the heat of his friend's skin and the burning of his own wounded forehead. And then, deep inside, he knew the truth. Hanuman suffered not for Pedar but for him. *Anashaida,* twisted love and compassion—this is what Danlo's deep self cried in the very center of his being.

"Shhh!" he said softly. He bowed his head, pressed his hand over Hanuman's lips, and whispered, "*Shantih,* my brother, go to sleep."

THE LIBRARY

What is language but a mirror of the natural world allowing us to define, discuss, and understand the events and relationships of the elements of the world? If mathematics is seen as a refinement of the natural languages— a crystallization of language's metaphors, concepts, and relationships into a symbol system of great logical precision—then what is mathematics if not the progressive polishing of this mirror? I would like to speculate as to the process and purpose of this polishing. I believe we must learn the infinite subtleties and the deepest logic of language. I believe we must become true speakers of the Word. When we have learned to speak of all possible connections between all things, then we may extend the metaphors of language into an infinite number of new relationships and forms. Only then will we be able to make a new mathematics. Only then will we create a perfect mirror in our words and thus make a grammar for all nature that will be truly universal.

—from the diary of Omar Narayama

According to the Order's canons, the body of Pedar Sadi Sanat should have been buried in an icy grave with the other deceased novices in Borja's main cemetery. But Pedar had family who lived in the shabbier districts of the Farsider's Quarter, and this family—his father, mother, uncles, cousins, nephews, and nieces —was harijan. They took his body away to be burned in one of their barbaric, secret ceremonies. They also lodged a formal petition demanding a deeper investigation of Pedar's death. As harijan, of course, they had no power to petition or make demands of any sort. Or rather, they had only one real power which was universally feared: they were wont to riot and mutilate themselves when ignored or treated unjustly. Occasionally at times of crisis, in public places such as the Great Circle outside the Hofgarten, harijan soak their robes in their holy sihu oil and set each other afire. They do this to bully and shame the lords of the Order into allowing them certain privileges. And so this melodramatic sect is despised as the lowest of humanity: poor, dreamy, displaced people who come to Neverness seeking the easy drug satoris or the simulated realities of the computer spaces. It was ironic that Bardo the Just, who regarded most men as his social, moral, and intellectual inferiors, had always had a strange sympathy for the harijan. Too, too ironically, as Bardo would say, Pedar's family blamed him for allowing Pedar to die. Because the harijan petition accused Bardo of malfeasance, he was kept busy defending his actions (or lack of action) to the College of Lords when they met to discuss the "harijan problem." He was very busy, too busy, in fact, to see Danlo during the cold, confused days following the tragedy in Perilous Hall.

"I've been to the Sanctuary five times," Danlo complained to Hanuman one night before sleeping. "Master Bardo is never there. How can he tell me the truth about my mother and father if he is never there?"

"You're the son of a man who became a god," Hanuman said. He was sitting on his bed with his chess pieces spread out across sixty-four white and black squares. He had taken on both sides and was playing a game with himself, against himself. He seemed intensely absorbed in this game. Since Pedar's death, he had been withdrawn, yet even more intensely alive than before in his secretive and anguished manner. "Your father is Mallory Ringess—what more is there to know?"

Danlo bowed his head as he remembered burying his adoptive brothers and sisters in the snow above the Devaki cave. "There is everything to know," he said.

"Are you thinking of your people, Danlo? The Devaki people?"

"Yes."

"You mustn't blame your father for what happened to them."

"I . . . do not want to blame him."

250

"Nor should you blame yourself for what happened to Pedar."

Danlo looked up suddenly and said, "You know me too well, I think."

"It was his fate to fall," Hanuman said. "It was just an accident."

"But the harijan do not believe it was an accident."

"The harijan are free to believe what they want."

"I have heard," Danlo said, "that some of the lords also do not believe it was an accident."

From the corner of the board, Hanuman picked up the salt shaker that substituted for the chess set's missing white god; he slid it over one square, making his move. He appeared relaxed and nonchalant, almost uncaring. "It's true," he said. "The Lords Jurasek and Ciceron are calling for an akashic's inquest."

"The akashics, with their computers—they can look into any part of one's mind, yes?"

"Perhaps," Hanuman said.

"Then Lord Ciceron might order us before the akashic courts. To see if any of us might know why Pedar died."

"But you mustn't worry about this," Hanuman said. "Bardo has promised that he won't allow any novice to submit to the akashic courts."

"I . . . think I know why Pedar died," Danlo said. He looked at Hanuman for a long time, and then bent his head as he rubbed above his eyes.

Just then Hanuman finished his chess game, and he tipped over the salt shaker in token of defeat. It clacked against the wooden board, and tiny cubes of salt spilled out of it and bounced across the black and white squares. He stared at these hundreds of salt crystals, then asked softly, "And why did he die?"

In a quiet voice that would not carry through the dormitory and alarm the other novices, in broken streams of words heavy with memory and shame, Danlo told of how he had broken ahimsa and willed Pedar's death. When he was finished speaking, he picked up the salt shaker and began using its heavy bottom to grind bits of salt into white dust.

"But you must never regret what you *willed*," Hanuman said. "Or what you thought. A man's thoughts are his own."

He went on to assure Danlo that there were no mind crimes in Neverness, unless, of course, one belonged to one of the Cybernetic Churches. "You must know that in the Church's cleans-

ing ceremony, akashic computers are used. To read one'
thoughts, even the most secret parts of the soul. But there ar
always ways to evade such computers."

"What . . . ways?"

"Ways," Hanuman said, and his eyes fell clouded and
opaque as the salt dust covering his chessboard. "It's said tha
the cetics know ways to control any computer. The ways of the
cetics, the mind yogas that they teach their students."

"But we will never be cetics," Danlo said.

"Whatever we will be or not, you mustn't worry about a
akashic inquest. There's really no reason to worry."

Danlo kept grinding grains of salt with the blunt bottom o
the shaker. He nodded his head but said nothing.

"Just now, it is Bardo who must worry, not us," Hanuma
said. "It's silly, but certain lords are blaming him for Pedar'
death. The harijan blame him, too."

"But why?"

"For allowing the Head Novice to assign you to submit t
Pedar. For allowing the emnity between you and Pedar to pro
ceed so far. And, of course, for allowing Pedar to climb the
stairs every night to our room."

"I am sorry . . . that I have brought Bardo so much trou
ble."

"Oh, no," Hanuman said. "It is Bardo who always bring
himself trouble. Just as Bardo, being Bardo, will always find
way out."

"But what if the Lords' College rebukes him? What i
someone else is made Master of Novices?"

"What if some star near Neverness explodes into a super
nova tomorrow and kills us all?" Hanuman said. "You might a
well worry about the harijan hiring assassins to avenge Pedar'
death."

Danlo looked up suddenly and asked, "Do you worry abou
this, Hanu?"

For a while Hanuman looked down at his chessboard, the
laughed awkwardly. "I think you know *me* too well," he said.

"But the harijan don't hire *assassins*!"

"Once a time, it's said, a hundred years ago, they assassi
nated the Lord Librarian. When she forbade the harijan to us
any of the Order's libraries."

"I had heard . . . that it was the Timekeeper who ordere
the Lord Hinda's death. And then blamed this crime on th
harijan."

"Perhaps," Hanuman said.

"But even if the harijan *wanted* to assassinate somebody, they are too poor to afford an assassin. They do not have any money."

"Perhaps," Hanuman said again. He bent his head down and pursed his lips as he blew the salt powder off his chessboard. Then with quick motions of his little hands, he began setting the pieces on their squares in preparation for a new game. "The truth is, I can't believe the harijan would assassinate Bardo—or anyone else. Now, would you care for a game before lights out, or do you intend to worry all night about these poor harijan? I'm sure Pedar's family won't ruin their sleep worrying about you or me."

But even as Danlo and Hanuman played their game of chess on the fourth floor of Perilous Hall—and for many days previously—the family of Pedar Sadi Sanat *had* taken note of their names. With friends and far relatives, they had talked about the novices Danlo wi Soli Ringess and Hanuman li Tosh, and so in decrepit rooms and apartments in the Farsider's Quarter of the City, these two names came to be passed among many harijan who had no real interest in Pedar's death. But people can always find a way to enhance their self-interest out of others' misfortunes, and so Danlo's and Hanuman's names were eventually passed along to wormrunners and seekers of information who usually have few dealings with the harijan sect. Although these few hundred harijan could not have foreseen the results of their waggling tongues, it was this name passing that led directly to the terrible incident—and to Danlo's terrible discovery—that occurred ten days later at the Academy's main library.

For Danlo, his visit to the library on the eighty-first of deep winter was no everyday event. Or rather, his reason for using the library was unusual and connected to what he had learned from Pedar in Lavi Square: he wanted to learn more about the galaxy's gods; specifically, he wanted to know if his father's ontogenesis from man into god was *halla* or *shaida*. Hanuman's reasons for accompanying Danlo that day were perhaps as deep, but he made a secret of his true purpose, and he would not reveal whatever mysterious information it was that he sought. As on other days, early in the afternoon, they skated over to the library, which lies between Borja and the dark, densely arrayed buildings of the academician's college, Lara Sig. The library itself is the darkest of structures. From its eastern entrance, where

253

the sparkling red glidderies from different parts of the Acade
converge, it looms as an almost featureless wall of gray-blac
basalt. In truth, it is an ugly thing, with its square-cut angles an
exact rectilinearity. There are five floors to the library, but onl
the top floor of the west wing is graced with windows. The effec
of this monolithic blackness is to make one feel small, to dimir
ish one's vanity and conceit; it reminds human beings that the
precious intellects are as nothing before the acquired wisdom c
the ages. The novices, journeymen, and masters passing beneat
the massive doorway cannot forget that they must serve the va:
edifice of Knowledge and, someday, if they are brilliant enougl
add to it brick by brick. Although the doors—two massive, rec
angular slabs of basalt hung in perfect balance—almost alway
stand open, the library is a forbidding place to approach and on
does not enter it easily. Eighty-one steps lead from the ice of th
main gliddery to the doorway. The steps, too, are all of basalt,
dense, dreary stone that can turn quite slippery when wet. Fc
thousands of years, the lower steps have been carved with gra
fiti: parallel wavy lines, circles, pictographs, the interlocking tr
angles of the Solomon's Seal, and other symbols. The man
curlicues and grooves provide good traction for wet boots, bu
they had not been placed there so that academicians could clim
more safely.

Most of the symbols, in fact, are harijan signs. Throughou
Neverness; across all the cities of the Civilized Worlds, th
harijan sect has affixed its various signs to libraries, restaurant
hospices, shops, and even private houses. There are hundreds c
these signs, and they denote the kinds of information vital t
any itinerant harijan: use of brain machines free and un
restricted; a good place for a meal, coffee, and conversatio
tortrix in use, beware!; free drugs available in exchange for ser
vices; and so on. If one is familiar with the signs, it is possible t
stand facing the eighty-one steps and decipher the history of th
relations between the Order and the harijan. The oldest sigr
mark the lowest steps; three thousand years of snow and ic
(and the tread of leather boots) have worn them nearly smootl
Information free to all!—this is a typical invitation of the earlies
and most blurred of chiselings. As one proceeds up the step:
the signs become more and more distinct, and progressivel
more chary of the possibilities to be found in the Order's mai
library. Many of the middling-old signs, which date from th
time of the War of Assassins, warn that the library's informatio
pools are heavily censored, or restricted to guests of the Orde

On the highest steps cut with the most recent graffiti, the meaning is plain: *Guarded information pools! Outsiders forbidden!*

At the top of the steps, between two huge pillars holding up the library's frontispiece, Danlo and Hanuman bowed to the seven librarians lined up in their formal indigo robes. One of them, a remarkably ugly woman, stopped them before they could approach the great doors. Her name was Lillith Volu. Danlo had met her and the other journeyman librarians earlier in winter. Lillith glared at them with strabismic eyes, which were of an ocher color and fairly popping out of her head. Like the stone gargoyles set atop the famous Jacarandan temple walls, she glared at everyone who tried to pass by her.

"Please give me your names," Lillith said. Her voice grunted deeply, as if she were a silk belly sow in rut. And she had a sow's nose: huge, hairy nostrils which she could open or close at will. Danlo could scarcely believe her claim that the peoples out near Primula Luz had once bred for such facial deformations according to the dictates of a religious code long since forgotten.

"But, Lillith, you know me, yes?"

Danlo, with his fine memory, found it only natural that Lillith should remember him after a single meeting some 180 days earlier. In fact, he hadn't seen her since then. During his previous visits to the library, various other journeymen on duty had subjected him to these hated formalities. Of course, Lillith *did* recognize his voice and face, but only because a remembrancer had trained her to identify all of the Academy's novices by sight.

"Please give me your names," she said again in her brusque, insolent manner.

On the steps behind Danlo and Hanuman, a group of people were queued up, waiting for them to speak. There was a red-faced master horologe, impatient and severe in his red robes, a haikuist who had the haggard, disoriented look of someone who had recently experienced too much computer simulation, and three high novices fresh from a game of hokkee in the Ice Dome. Danlo smelled their clean, salty sweat; they stood on the cold steps chatting, jumping up and down, and blowing puffs of steam as they looked back and forth between Hanuman and him.

"I'm Hanuman li Tosh," Hanuman said as he stepped ahead of Danlo.

"Very well, then—you may pass," Lillith said.

Danlo smiled at Lillith before saying, "And I am Danlo. Everyone calls me . . . Danlo the Wild."

Lillith smoothed her robe over her squat, lumpy torso and said, "Danlo wi Soli Ringess—this is your full name, isn't it?"

At the base of the nearest pillar, sheet ice was frozen to the rounded stone fillets. Danlo kicked at the ice. A piece cracked off and went skittering down the steps. "Yes," he said. He was embarrassed that everyone seemed to have heard the news about his lineage. "Danlo . . . wi Soli Ringess."

"You will please state your proper name each time before you are admitted," Lillith said. "Is this agreeable to you?"

"Yes," Danlo said.

"Then you may pass."

Lillith's formality and seriousness amused Danlo as much as it irked him, and so again he smiled at her, then bowed just a little too deeply. He turned and followed Hanuman through the great doorway into the library's main hallway. This was a huge room of polished stone, stale air, and semidarkness. Despite the circle of cold flame globes suspended above the central fountain (or perhaps because of their flickering bronze and cobalt lights), it was hard to make out the robe colors of the professionals hurrying to and fro. Danlo could not tell the eschatologists, with their blue robes, from the librarians. Still following Hanuman, he stepped past archaic scrolls and manuscripts preserved in airless clary crypts; they made their way toward the far wall, where the west wing gave out into the hallway. There they found three master librarians sitting on benches inside their little alcove. Danlo knew they must be librarians because they all looked up at them with a pallid, helpful look, as if their only purpose in life were to attend young novices.

Again Danlo gave his name, his full name, and asked if he and Hanuman could be assigned a couple of cells. One of the librarians told them to wait a moment, and they waited. The librarian's bald head and gaunt, pale features gave him the appearance of a living skull; he rubbed the back of his shiny head and went over to the table at the center of the alcove. Quickly he studied a map of the library's west wing. The 532 cells of the huge novice's wing were represented as rectangles of colored, inlaid woods. Little white figurines—intricately carved pieces of onyx the size of a child's finger—occupied all the rectangles. The librarian continued to rub at the prominent bone beneath his scalp, and as he rubbed and pursed his lips, a new librarian appeared out of the west wing's darkness. The new librarian entered the alcove, checked the map, and removed two of the figurines from the table. "If the young novices require cells, 212 and 213 are free," he said.

The first librarian took the figurines from the other librarian's hand and put one back on the number 213 rectangle while the other figurine he placed on number 212. He drummed his fingers against his skull and studied Hanuman's face. Then he turned to Danlo and asked, "Are you both first-year novices? Then you'll require a guide today, won't you? Is it agreeable that you share a guide today?"

During Danlo's previous visits to the library, he had never minded such sharing, though he knew very well that Hanuman preferred having a guide all to himself. (In truth, Hanuman would have been happiest having no guide at all.) Hanuman never liked sharing anyone's attentions, but all first-year novices were encouraged to visit the library in pairs, the better to husband the library's scarce supply of librarians. This was a relatively new rule for the novices; it had been in effect only since 2934, during the Pilot's War when 110 master librarians had defected from the Order to join the Encyclopaedists of the great library on Ksandaria. In the thirteen years since that time, the librarians of Neverness—the better ones—had been forced whenever they could to take novices to their cells two at a time.

"Is this agreeable to you?" the librarian repeated.

Danlo noticed Hanuman staring at the three idle librarians who remained on their bench. Clearly, they were keeping themselves in reserve for those favored high novices who might require a private guide.

"It is agreeable," Hanuman said at last.

"Yes," Danlo said. "We have come here together before."

"Very well," the librarian said, "then please follow me."

He led Danlo and Hanuman into the west wing, up a flight of chipped and very worn stairs, and then down branching stone corridors almost devoid of light. The brightest object Danlo could see was the master librarian's skull, nodding up and down as he shuffled along. The air was warm, and it stank of mold, moisture, and thirty centuries of sweating bodies. One by one, they passed doors of dark, rotting wood. There were many doors. At last they came to the door of the 212th cell, or rather, the door leading to that cell's gowning room.

"Here we are," the master librarian said as he opened the door for Danlo. He walked on a dozen paces into the darkness

257

until he came to the door of the 213th cell, which he opened and invited Hanuman to enter. Then he turned and walked back to the auricle room built between both Danlo's and Hanuman's cells. Before he entered it he said, "My name is Baran Smith. I wish you both a fruitful journey."

Hanuman stepped down the dank corridor, turned and bowed to Master Baran Smith. Then he looked at Danlo and smiled. It was a strange, nervous smile, like that of a child about to enter a room of his parents' house that has been forbidden to him. With a quick head bow toward Danlo, he went inside his cell and pulled the door shut behind him.

As Danlo had done on other days, he entered his cell's steamy, semidark gowning room; he shut the door and performed the customary ritual: he pulled off his boots, disrobed, hung his clothes on the wall hooks, filled the hot pool with water, and bathed. The room was so tiny and cramped that by stretching out his arms like a bird, he could touch either wall. When he was done, he stood dripping water and sweat. He faced the black cell opening at the end of the room. He touched Ahira's feather, to give himself courage. He touched the scar above his eye. Quietly, he recited the librarians' mantra: " 'Every act of knowing brings forth a world.' " And then he whispered, *"Shantih,"* and he stepped into the cell.

Almost immediately the cell sealed itself behind him. The cell was even tinier than the gowning room; it consisted of nothing more than a low tank of water surrounded by a ceiling and walls of deep purple neurologics. These neurologics were a crystalline latticework of proteins, the living circuitry of the cell's tutelary computer. *The cell is a computer,* Danlo reminded himself. In a way, entering the novice's cell was like entering into the heart of a computer, or rather, like squeezing inside the artery of a computer's brain. As he moved about the cell, he was very careful not to touch the neurologics, much as one is careful not to touch another's eyeball. He eased himself into the tank and lay back. The water was as warm as blood. The water was dense and heavy with dissolved mineral salts, hundreds of pounds of carbonates and sulfates, which increased its buoyancy. As the room grew dark, he floated easily on the water's surface, bobbing up and down like a piece of driftwood on a tropical sea. Soon the tank's wavelets stilled, and there was no motion at all. The blackness encompassing him was as total as deep space. There was neither sound, nor heat, nor cold, nor any other sensation to stimulate his nerves. The warm water touched every part of him except his face; it dissolved his sense of gravity and his sense of being a discrete organism cut off from his environment. In truth, he hadn't any feeling for the separateness of his skin and could scarcely tell where the membranes of his body ended and where the dark salty water began. This dissolution of his physical self into the computer's innards was at once soothing and profoundly terrifying. Twelve times before he had lain thus, with his belly trembling beneath the water, waiting for the computer to fire his quiescent nerves with information.

In the beginning, at the moment of creation when the energies of eternity burst forth into time, the whole of the universe was immanent in a single point. The universe was infinitely hot, infinitely compact, and pregnant with infinite possibilities.

Suddenly, inside Danlo's head, there was light. Or rather, there was the perception of light, the shapes and textures of shimmering images, the blues, golds, and reds by which light is known as light. As the tutelary computer—the vibrating neurologics surrounding him—came awake to the touch of his thoughts, it scanned his brain for chemical and electrical events; to use the akashic's terminology, it began to "read" his mind. And in turn, the computer directly excited the horizontal, bipolar, and anacrine cells inside the retinas of his wide-open eyes. These cells began to process information, the images and symbols flowing out of the computer. And then other cells began to fire, the ganglion cells whose very long axons formed the optic nerve leading up into his brain.

I am the eye with which the universe beholds itself and knows itself divine—he suddenly remembered Hanuman saying this, once, just as he remembered that the eye's retinal cells are the most efficient and highly evolved of all neurons. Indeed, the retina is really an extension of the brain tunneling through the tissues and bone of the eye sockets, reaching out to the world of light. The retina is the seeing part of the eye, the knowing part; without the coding of light into exquisitely timed, varying voltages, it would be impossible to see.

There are many ways of thinking about the evolution of the universe. Most of the Order's eschatologists teach a fusion of the old science's strong anthropic principle and the theology of the cybernetic religions. The universe is regarded as God, an evolving being trying to create new information and complete its self-organization. Historically, this is known as a Socinian universe, a universe that is trying to wake up and behold itself in order to attain perfection.

Without eyes—or without the photocells and webwork of neurons lining the back of the eyes—it would be impossible to receive and interpret the light of the universe. And yet he knew there were other ways of seeing. A pilot, it was said, could interface his ship's computer even if he were as eyeless and blind as a scryer. While Danlo floated in the warm water and faced the cybernetic space of the tutelary computer, he couldn't help wondering what terrors he must endure if ever he became a pilot. Someday, he thought, he would be sealed inside the pit of his own lightship, and it would be very like floating in a saltwater tank. Only, the ship computer would infuse images directly into his visual cortex, directly into the neurons at the back of his brain. *Seeing is an act of will accomplished by the brain,* he remembered. What would it be like to see the splendid stars as a pilot sees, melded directly into the information flows of a lightship's computer?

"You'll have to wait until you become a pilot to know this," Master Jonath had told him some days before. "Total interface between computer and brain is too profound for a novice to experience properly. And safely."

As Danlo entered into the most apprehensible of all the cybernetic spaces—into that universe of knowledge the cetics call "shih space"—he wondered how any interface could be more total. The tutelary computer read the stream of his questing, chaotic thoughts and infused him with images, sounds, and other sensa. The computer touched his optic nerve, touched the auditory nerve leading from his inner ear into his brain. It touched the nerves of his nose, mouth, throat, and heart, all the nerves of his body. In this way, he saw the first spinning galaxies form and coalesce out of creation's brilliant light; through his skin burned the gamma and the beta and other radiations of a hundred billion stars; he felt the hot lava seas of Old Earth heave and flow and harden, and then fracture suddenly, only to melt again and be reabsorbed in itself, over and over for an aeon until vast floating continents formed, islands of primal basalt that trembled beneath his bare feet and vibrated up through his bones into his skull; he tasted salt water in his mouth and listened to the long, dark roar of the first oceans, the ageless oceans out of which had emerged the first living things; he smelled life: it was a rich scent of chlorophyll and blood, strong, vital, and urgent; following the marvelous smell of life as it drifted, branched out, and spread over the black soil, all across Old Earth and a million other worlds much like Earth, he sought to understand the evolution of the bacteria and protists, the fungi, plants, animals, and all the alien kingdoms of life. Always, life was a reaching out into diversity and strangeness, into new forms of organization. He felt this life all about him, and inside, pulsing, touching, tasting, eating, dividing, and redividing; he felt himself as green-veined leaf breathing cool, sweet carbon dioxide and cell by cell growing outward and up to taste the sun, and as a volvox, a hollow sphere of cells rotating like a tiny world inside a water droplet, and as an ancient calymene, and as a jewfish, and as snowworm writhing in the belly of a bird, and as a man, and suddenly the possibilities of evolution were too many and the sea of life's infinite sensations overwhelmed him.

—Danlo wi Soli Ringess?

He watched the many clades of life divide and branch out into their ancient lineages, and he was aware, dimly, of a voice calling out to him. He slowly realized it was the voice—or thoughts—of the master librarian. In the auricle room next to him, on the other side of the wall of neurologics, Master Baran Smith was monitoring his journey through shih space. (As he was also helping Hanuman with his journey.) Because they both shared parts of the same cybernetic space, Danlo could read quite a few of Master Smith's thoughts.

—Danlo wi Soli Ringess?

—Yes?

—Please face away from sight/sound/smell for a moment. You're too deep into simulation.

—Like this? If I do not reach out . . . with a *will* to see, then the images will fade out and die, yes?

—Use your sense of tapas to restrain yourself; you know the way.

Of course, after only twelve brief, initiatory journeys into shih space, it would have been impossible for Danlo to have mastered tapas, or the other cybernetic senses. To face and cross the landscape of the computer's information flows, one needs the mental disciplines that the cetics have developed and evolved into the cybernetic senses. Although shih, the sense that "tastes," feels, and organizes varying concentrations of information, is the highest of these, there are others. There is plexure and iconic vision, simulation, syntaxis, and tempo. Tapas is really more of a mental discipline than a sense; indeed, it is the ability to control—to restrain—the simulation of seeing, hearing, and smelling. First-year novices always have trouble learning tapas, which is why a master librarian must be present to guide their first journeys into shih space.

—Do not depend too heavily on simulation, Young Danlo.

—But, to see/hear/smell, to . . . *simulate* the history of the gods—it is more immediate to experience the field of knowledge than to kithe it.

—It's more immediate, but it takes much longer. And it exhausts the mind.

—I . . . did not mean to say it was merely more immediate. It is *necessary,* to experience, or not . . . to know—I am not saying this clearly, am I? Or thinking it. What I mean is, it is vital to distinguish simulation from true living, yes?

Although it was dangerous to dwell very long in a simulated reality, Danlo felt strangely attracted to the unreal thought-scapes that the computer painted with its electrons. To experience information constructs *as* blue waters, or as flowing lava rivers, or as mountains of rock and ice, to experience a simulated world *as if* he were a bird soaring above shatterwood forests, which, in their finely re-created black branches and shimmering green-gray needles, seemed almost real—this was as spellbinding as it was terrifying. In truth, he mistrusted and hated computer simulation. His deepest fear was that he might confuse unreality with reality, whatever "reality" truly was. *Reality is truth,* he thought. *The truth of the universe.* And so, ironically, because he had a passion for truth, he made himself journey through the false worlds and surrealities of simulation as deeply he could. He did this to test himself. He bared his nerves to the computer's sly touch because he had a passion to master this most basic of the cybernetic senses.

As he floated in the warm water and felt the cold wind of a computer-created landscape ice his eyes, he tried to explain this to the master librarian. But he did not explain himself well. The electronic telepathy of shih space was a poor way to communicate emotions because one could not see another's face or mannerisms, could not look deeply into another's true self.

—You're young still, and you'll have many years to learn simulation. But now you should face your syntactic sense and kithe the history that you're seeking. This is most efficient for simple information searches.

—But what I am looking for is not simple.

—What is it you want from today's journey, then?

—I am not sure. There must be a purpose . . . to the evolution of gods. All evolution. The way the ecologies spring forth from a god's ontogenesis, the sprung ecologies, like . . . the Golden Ring, a pattern and purpose.

—This is teleological thinking, Young Novice.

—But I . . . must know more about the gods. Their evolution. Mallory Ringess, my father—he became a god, yes? I must know *why*.

Danlo knew that the Order academicians were fairly divided over the manner in which life's evolution should be viewed. Many of the mechanics, for instance, eschewed and reviled teleology. Those who honored the ancient scientific philosophy regarded life as the result of uncountable, random chemical and quantum events; for them, all of history was a pushing process, the micro-events of the past determining and pushing life into an unknown, arbitrary (and meaningless) future. While Danlo appreciated the stark beauty of determinism and chance, he found that this philosophy gave a distorted vision of reality, or rather a narrow vision. This vision did not fundamentally lie, but it was much like examining the colors of a painting molecule by molecule in order to perceive its symmetry or the artist's intention. There were other ways of seeing, and teleology was one of these. For Danlo, as for any good scryer or holist, the future was as real as the present moment; when he closed his eyes or looked up into the starry night, he saw intimations of a something infinite and splendid pulling him into its heart. Or pulling him with its bloody talons and beak into its belly—the wild, atavistic part of Danlo still saw the universe as an infinitely vast silver thallow just beginning to wake up and devour all living things.

—But teleology is like a lens . . . that reveals history's direction, yes?

Master Smith's response to this question—his directed thoughts—should have been nearly instantaneous, so Danlo was surprised at the silence inside his head. But then he remembered that the librarian was also guiding Hanuman's journey, so he waited patiently for Master Smith to reenter the shared space of their computer.

—Danlo wi Soli Ringess? You wonder about teleology? This is true; there are many epistemological systems you might choose, Young Novice.

—The Fravashi call the ability to see knowledge as through different lenses, that is, through different epistemological systems, to enter and hold different worldviews . . . they call this "plexure."

—The Honored Fravashi misuse the word. They've broadened it to fit certain concepts of their philosophy.

—But plexure is . . . a splendid way of seeing, yes?

—Properly, plexure is one of the cybernetic senses. You're here today, Young Novice, to attend to these primary senses.

—Such as syntaxis?

—You'll never become a pilot unless you master it.

—But the symbols, the word storm.

—Is it that you have trouble visualizing the ideoplasts?

—No, sir, it is just the opposite. I visualize them . . . too intensely. Even when I am faced away from the computer, I can still see them. They burn in my mind.

For many moments, Danlo held his breath as he let his head fall back into the waters of the tank. He floated in liquid darkness and silence. When his brain's throbbing need for oxygen grew unbearable, he breached the surface, gasped for air, and tasted mineral salts in his mouth. The sound of his deep breathing echoed off the neurologics close all around him. He faced the computer's shih space then, calling up his sense of syntaxis in order to see his way through the word storm building up inside his mind. When he closed his eyes, he saw fields of glittering, three-dimensional symbols, the jewellike ideoplasts of the universal syntax. His mind's eye beheld and kithed the ideoplast for the concept "as," which appeared in the form of a pentacle, or rather a wispy, five-pointed starfish frozen with the rigidity and crystalline perfection of blue topaz. This connected to the double diamond bars of the "god" ideoplast, and to others. Each ideoplast, like the characters of the ancient Chinese script, was designed as a unique, graphic (and beautiful) expression of the most complex or simple of things and ideas, and there were many, many ideoplasts. Danlo, in his study of the universal syntax, had memorized some fifty thousand of them. The notationists say their number is potentially infinite, and this must be so, for reality itself may be sliced up, viewed, symbolized, and reassembled into concepts of infinitely refined nuance and profundity. Ideoplasts are sometimes referred to as the "words" of the universal syntax, but in fact, they can also represent the sounds of spoken language, or ideas, or axioms, definitions, formalizations, logics, or even entire models of the universe.

—Young Novice, you must kithe now, or else you'll become lost in the word storm.

Kithing, the deciphering and understanding of the ideoplasts—the reading of symbols—is the most elementary part of syntaxis, but it is not an easily learned art. Inside Danlo's visual field, the computer placed arrays of brilliant mental symbols, artful orderings of the many teachings and concepts relating to the godhead. He studied the relationships between the ideoplasts; like diamonds and emeralds set into a Fravashi tapestry, there was an implicate pattern and meaning revealed in the way they linked together. He kithed the ideoplasts one by one, and as a wholeness which revealed startling juxtapositions of alien and ancient philosophies. In kithing the almost organic correspondences among the ideoplasts, the way in which the placement of each one influenced the placement and meaning of any other, he saw beautiful ideas and truths that otherwise might have been impossible to apprehend.

The computationists of the first cybernetic religions viewed the universe as a computer. Every bit of material reality was treated as a component of this universal computer. Every event in spacetime therefore was seen to be the result of the universe computing the consequences of nature's laws, which the computationists called algorithms. According to the oldest cybernetic theologies, twenty billion years ago, at the moment of creation, the universe was programmed with these algorithms to run until it reached its halt state and the answer to some great question was finally decided.

Because the arrays of ideoplasts were now forming up too quickly for him to easily kithe, Danlo faced away from the computer's word storm. He wanted to think alone and in silence. All around his naked skin was blackness, warm waters, and real air heavy with salt and moisture, but inside his mind he could still see too many of the ideoplasts. He had been born with his mother's "memory of pictures," a vivid, eidetic memory which often caused him as much consternation and confusion as it did joy. In his memory field, where the colors of each image were as pure and clear as the silvery greenness of a shih leaf, one ideoplast in particular stood out. This ideoplast derived from one of the great formulas of the Upanishads, and it symbolized the mystical equation between one's deepest self and the supreme godhead underlying all of reality. It appeared as a tear-shaped diamond drop suspended in the center of a sphere of ten thousand other similar drops, each one shimmering violet or red or deep blue, each one reflecting the light of all the others. He could not rid his inner sight of this beautiful ideoplast, nor could he forget the many other ideoplasts placed in correspondence with it. Or rather, he could forget only with utmost difficulty. He had to use a trick of the remembrancers, to conjure up in his mind a vast snowfield onto which he dropped the ideoplasts, one by one, until they had all vanished through layers of fluffy white *soreesh* snow. Only then could he efface his memory. Only then could he find the quiet place where his thoughts ran deeper than the flow of mere symbols or words.

—The reality behind all things, the deep reality that some say is unknowable, and ineffable . . . if there is a deeper reality, a *will* beneath the reality of natural laws, snow and ice, the blessed natural world, how could I ever know what it is?

For many moments of real time, the objective time that the horologes sometimes call outtime, Danlo floated in his tank pondering the cybernetic theologies. He decided that if the universe really *were* an infinite computer, then it would be impossible to ever know deep reality, for the same reason that the information flows of a simple computer could never "know" the architect who had designed and written the programs. There was no way for a human being or any other part of the universe to get outside that universe, to see reality (or the "God" who had created that reality) as it really was. Because he craved knowledge of the true nature of God, he decided to learn everything he could about this strange cybernetic theology that had influenced so many peoples across the Milky Way galaxy and so much of man's history.

—Nikolos Daru Ede, the first Architect of the Cybernetic Universal Church, as . . . the first god. The first human being to become a god, if he was a god, or *is,* still, then where is his freedom . . . to be and become, since he is still, like everything else within our universe, a being of matter and energy programmed by the god outside . . . by the *real* God's universal algorithm, yes?

Again, he faced the tutelary computer, letting the stream of his turbulent, half-formed thoughts flow freely. He waited a long time for the master librarian's voice to speak inside his inner ear.

—Do you understand this question, Master Smith?

He waited and waited, but the tutelary computer had fallen into silence.

—Master Smith, I do not mean to interrupt but . . . is Hanuman all right? He is looking for something that he should not, yes? He sometimes becomes too absorbed . . . in the possibilities of computers.

Danlo waited in his hot pool of water, and still there was only silence and darkness. After he had waited almost longer than he could bear, he became aware of Master Smith's chiding thoughts.

—Danlo wi Soli Ringess, you must not ask about your friend or his journey. On pain of your forbiddance to the library, you must not ask this.

Librarians, Danlo suddenly recalled, on pain of banishment from the Order (or sometimes even death) may not reveal anything to anyone about journeys that they have guided.

—I am sorry, sir, but when you did not answer my question . . .

—To get a precise answer to your questions, Young Novice, it's best to form your questions precisely. Don't the grammarians teach that the whole art of the universal syntax is in precisely asking the right questions?

Danlo agreed that this was so, and he began thinking precisely in order to pose his questions. In the cybernetic visual space, which was as clear as a blue sky and seemed to open in all directions just behind his eyes, he conjured up various ideoplasts. One by one, their intricate, crystalline shapes appeared as out of nothingness. He stacked the ideoplasts together into an array. Or, to use the precise terminology of the cetics, he pleached the ideoplasts, weaving together ideas and ancient paradoxes, much as a Fravashi Father weaves golden threads into a tapestry. "To pleach" is the verb form of the art and sense known as plexure; literally, it means "to weave together simplex thoughts in order to reveal complex truths." Deep in plexure, with care and precision, he applied the rules of the universal syntax to pleach the ideoplasts into a unique question array. For the hundredth time since beginning his novitiate, he marveled at the power and beauty of the universal syntax. He began to see it as a profound language that he might use to ask questions, not only of the tutelary computer, but of the universe itself. The syntax rules, he knew, derived from the logic and relationships of natural language; as language encoded concepts into words, the universal syntax was an organic language symbolizing and interrelating the knowledge of all the arts, particularly the art of mathematics. In fact, mathematics could be regarded as a highly abstract, formal language which was merely a part of the universal syntax. Or—and this, he had learned, was one of the many disagreements dividing the cantors and the grammarians—it was possible to argue that the universal syntax was really just a branch on the infinite tree of mathematics. In both arts, ideoplasts were pleached into arrays, whether to make discoveries about natural law, or to create beautiful new philosophies, or elegant mathematical theorems—for Danlo, what did it matter which art contained which, so long as he mastered plexure and learned to speak the secret language of the universe?

—It is hard to formalize . . . concepts about gods or God, yes? About the universe? There is always the problem of self-reference. Russell's paradox, the paradoxes.

—Danlo? Young Novice, can you understand me? Please face away from your sense of plexure, for a moment.

—Like this? Shall I face into telepathy?

—That's good.

—It is hard for a human being . . . for me, to think about God.

—But you have indeed formalized this difficulty, haven't you?

—Do you mean the expression "By none but a god shall a god be worshiped"?

—That is correct. The expression is implicate in your question array. Did you know that you have rediscovered a saying of the ancient Sanskrit: *Nadero devam arcayer*?

—No, I did not know that, sir.

—And your formalization of the scholastics' attempted reconciliation of human free will and God's providence is as precise as it could be.

—Thank you.

—However, your relating this reconciliation with the modern cybernetic Doctrine of the Halting is not precise. The correspondences are weak and unsupported by historical fact.

—But, haven't I shown that . . . there is no universal algorithm for deciding whether or not a computer will reach its halt state?

—Your proof of this is elegant, Young Novice. Perhaps even brilliant. However, you've only reestablished what was known millennia ago.

—But if God, the cyberneticists' conception of a god, or a first cause, outside this universe, if this god programmed the universe to get an answer . . . to some almost impossible question, then there is no way to know what this answer will be. If there *is* an answer, or solution, it would be impossible to know it without letting the universe-as-computer run until it has reached its halt state and . . .

268

—Please continue.

—And therefore Ede-as-God . . . could not really *be* God, or could not be proclaimed as becoming God, since the future . . . since the universe is creating the future moment by moment in the only way it can be created. Or known. There is no way to foresee Ede's destiny. Or the destiny of anyone. And therefore the reconciliation of free will and determinism must . . . have a correspondence with the Doctrine of the Halting.

—Of course, that is so. But you'll never find the correct correspondences unless you kithe the history of the Cybernetic Universal Church.

—And which part of this history shall I kithe?

—That is for you to discover, Young Novice.

—But I . . .

—You must kithe now, Young Danlo. Please excuse me while you kithe.

This time, when Danlo returned to the word storm, he kithed the arrays of ideoplasts more quickly and with a clearer mental vision. He struggled to illuminate the sometimes dark and subtle relationship between the Cybernetic Universal Church's doctrines and the history of the Civilized Worlds. Information appeared before him in arrays of ideoplasts, and then in arrays of arrays. Concerning Nikolos Daru Ede and the founding of the Church there was more information than he ever had imagined, glittering, vast, frozen seas of information. *Information is not knowledge,* he told himself. *And knowledge is not wisdom.* Even though he knew this saying of the librarians was certainly true, in the word storm building inside him, he found both knowledge and wisdom aplenty. The work and wisdom of five hundred generations of the best human (and Fravashi) minds was crystallized into the ideoplasts; as he kithed discoveries, facts, and concepts tested and retested over the millennia, he felt himself touching these minds. He called into play the most generalized of the cybernetic senses, his sense of shih. Shih was the aesthetics of knowledge, or more precisely, the relationship between wisdom and knowledge. In many ways, shih was both a sense and a sensibility, the sense of realness, beauty, and truth which guided him among the mountains and flowing glaciers of information. This information was built up of many layers linked together, interconnected and crosslinked in subtle ways. There was a fractal, intricate quality to this information; kithing it was almost like following the icy points of a

269

snowflake as they divided and redivided out from its dazzling center. It was possible to view the information arrays as beautiful wholes that synthesized the conclusions of various philosophical systems, or to examine the meaning of each frozen point, or the many branching sub-points: crystallized knowledge within crystals within yet smaller crystals. Each layer was structured with the same complexity as the next layer, lower or higher. Delving deeply through the information layers for a specific fact and then reascending quickly to perceive certain historical trends and patterns left him dizzy in his mind. Without shih to help him appreciate the elegance of these patterns and facts—and to help him choose which pathways through the richly textured knowledge were worth pursuing and which were not—the arrays of ideoplasts would soon have overwhelmed him.

According to the Doctrine of the Halting, the universe will reach its halt state when and only when Ede-as-God has absorbed and become co-extensive with that universe. Those who believe that it is impossible to foreknow the universe's halt state must also believe that Ede is not destined to become God, that he must face the same evolutionary pressures as any other organism or god. These unbelievers are said to be guilty of the Evolution Heresy.

For many moments of computer time, Danlo learned about the religion known as Edeism. Here is a part of what he learned: that almost three thousand years ago, on the planet of Alumit, there had lived a simple computer architect named Nikolos Daru Ede. That is, Ede was simple in the sense that the whole of his life was given over to a single idea: it was his dream to make computers that would illuminate, vasten, and preserve human consciousness. In other ways Ede was a complex man, at once a master architect and a rebel against all architect ethics, a pragmatist and a mystic, a plagiarist of ancient writings and an author capable of creating such brilliant literature as *Man's Journey* and *Universals*. Above all, he was both a man of acts and a dreamer, and toward the end of his long, turbulent life (it is a matter of historical fact that he lived 213 years) he succeeded where all other architects of his time had failed. He designed and created a computer, a work of art and genius which he called his eternal computer. And more, he discovered a way to copy and preserve human consciousness into this computer, supposedly without disfiguring that consciousness. And then, while he was still keen of mind and healthy in his body, he defied the Third Law of Civilization. He—this is what his followers have believed and preached for three millennia—this extraordinary, visionary, defiant man bade his journeymen architects farewell and carked his consciousness into his computer. The process of scanning and downloading the information in his brain destroyed it; a few faithless scoffers said that Ede had merely found an ingenious way toward suicide, but most others testified that the memories and algorithms comprising his very essence had been exactly duplicated in his eternal computer. Ede had been vastened, they said, made into something much vaster than a mere man. From this singular, tremendous event, the religion of Edeism sprang forth almost overnight. Ede's faithful student, the architect Kostos Olorun, proclaimed that the ancient prophecies and the purpose of man's evolution had at last been fulfilled: man had created God, or rather, had downloaded his essence into a computer destined to become as one with the universal godhead. Over the next few years, Ede's eternal computer—Ede himself, as God—rapidly continued his ontogenesis toward the infinite. Many times, Ede copied and recopied his expanding consciousness into a succession of larger and more sophisticated computers which he himself designed and assembled, and then into whole arrays of robots and computers of various functions. (Where Ede-as-man had been a master of computational origami, Ede the God perfected this art of interconnecting and "folding" together many computer units so that they functioned as an integrated whole.) One day, it came time for Ede to leave Alumit and go out into the universe. He ascended to heaven, into the deep space above the planet that could no longer be his home. Using his power as a god, with the help of tiny, self-replicating robots the size of a bacterium, he disassembled asteroids, comets, and other heavenly debris into their elements; he used these elements to fabricate new circuitry and neurologics. He feasted on the elements of material reality, and he grew. According to the Doctrine of the Halting, which Kostos Olorun hastily formulated to prevent other architects from following his path, Ede the God was destined to grow until he had absorbed the entire universe.

And so Ede faced the universe, and he was vastened, and he saw that the face of God was his own. Then the would-be gods, who are the hakra devils of the darkest depths of space, from the farthest reaches of time, saw what Ede had done, and they were jealous.

Danlo, floating in his tank and faced into the dark tapestry of the tutelary computer's neurologics, began thinking of the details of his father's own ontogenesis. Mallory Ringess, he remembered, had never wholly abandoned his human flesh; he had begun his journey into godhood in a very different way than had Ede. But as the Fravashi say, all paths lead toward the same place.

And they turned their eyes godward in jealousy and lust for the infinite lights, but in their countenances God read hubris, and he struck them blind. For here is the oldest of teachings, here is wisdom: No god is there but God; God is one, and there can only be one God.

There could only be one god, and as Danlo learned, in the Cybernetic Universal Church that formed around the creed of Edeism, there could be only a single architect—or *Architect*—blessed with the power to talk with him. Kostos Olorun, a vain and cunning man possessed of great energy, was the first of these Architects; he named himself God's Architect because Ede himself had supposedly entrusted him with his eternal computer, the very one into which he had first carked his godly soul. As God's Architect, Kostos Olorun was guardian of this holy computer, and more, it was said that only he of all Worthy Architects could interface it; only he could read out Ede's instructions to mankind or receive the new revelations commonly known as algorithms. This supreme vanity of Olorun's became reified in the Doctrine of Singularity: that henceforth and for all time, Ede's power over man would be embodied in the singular person of God's Architect. Over the next fifteen hundred years, there were sixty-three of these God's Architects. Many of them were gifted individuals who led an expansion of the Church unequaled in zeal since the rise of Islam or Holism on Old Earth. And so Edeism spread across the galaxy, riding the crest of the Swarming's third wave. It might well have become the universal religion of humanity, but in the year 1536 since Ede's vastening, a schism almost ruined the Church. The Elder Architect, Olaf Harsha, who was guided by a heartfelt (and heretical) ambition to directly face and speak with Ede the God, led a majority of Architects to rebel against the Doctrine of Singularity. Thus began the War of the Faces, which grew to be the greatest war ever fought by human beings and lasted for over two hundred years.

The atrocities committed by Architects against Architects became more numerous and savage as the war continued. With victory almost certain, the Elders of the Reformed Church inevitably turned this war inward and began a purge of their own members, those millions of Architects suspected of various here-

sies or impure thoughts toward the Church. It was at this time that the Cleansing Ceremony became a weapon used to disfigure the brains of anyone who dared to think of dissent. There is evidence that a few Elders even hired warrior-poets to assassinate their enemies. Almost certainly, the rule of the warrior-poets to kill all hakras sprang from a secret pact made between the warrior-poets and the Elders of the Church.

As Danlo learned about the War of the Faces, he squirmed and shifted in his tank. The water suddenly felt too hot, too thick with dissolved mineral salts. He remembered too well what Hanuman had said to him in the shih grove the afternoon before Pedar's death. For an Architect to voice a desire to be more than a mere man was the worst of sins, and so the Elders of Hanuman's church would certainly have regarded him as both heretic and hakra, that is, if they had ever been able to read his innermost thoughts. In another age, the warrior-poets might have pursued him across the stars and slain him. Danlo was very glad that they lived in gentler times, though he could never understand the attitude of his friends who believed that such wars were now unthinkable. His father, after all, had led pilots to war against their fellow pilots, and if this kind of tragedy could occur within the Order, then anything was possible. He thought about his father for a long time as he brooded over the nature of war within the universe.

—A man becomes a god . . . and then there is war, yes? An ecology of organized murder. Who knows what ecologies will spring forth from my father's apotheosis?

—It would be foolish to blame Nikolos Daru Ede for the War of the Faces, Young Novice. Or to blame Mallory Ringess for the problems our Order now faces. The Ringess was the greatest human being our Order has ever produced, and it is not upon us to judge him or blame him.

Danlo, alone inside his cell, separated from the librarian by a wall of purple neurologics and a lifetime of different experiences, couldn't help smiling at Master Smith's admiration of his father. Since entering the Order, he had found that there were two types of academicians: those who reviled the Ringess name and those who practically worshiped his father as a god. Clearly, Master Smith belonged to this second category.

—I do not want to blame anyone. I just need to see . . . the interconnectness between act and actuality. Like a spider's web, the way everyone's fates are spun together. The web of *halla*. Or *shaida*: pull any strand, and the entire web quivers.

273

When my father became a god, he pulled at this web, and I think the universe has yet to stop its quivering.

This thought gave birth to other thoughts that competed to occupy Danlo's mind. One thought, as dark and ominous as a death cloud rolling across the sea, soon blocked out all the others: In his kithing the history of the War of the Faces, he had perhaps overlooked something vital to his life and the lives of everyone he had known. He interfaced the word storm, then, looking for this elusive fact or idea. As a snowy owl scans an icefield for a hare's bounding white form, he used his sense of shih to single out a particular event occurring near the end of the War of the Faces: a scarce one hundred years after the Architects of the Reformed Churches had defeated what they called the Old Church, their missionaries first reached Yarkona, and a terrible plague spread wildly across the Civilized Worlds.

The lower estimates place the numbers killed at 49 billion people. On some planets, such as Yarkona and Simoom, the death rate was as high as ninety-six percent. Because the plague struck down whole populations simultaneously, many died of neglect rather than from the outright effects of the plague virus. With no one to care for the victims or replace the fluids that ran from their bodies, the immediate cause of death was often dehydration.

Even though Danlo was enwombed in water, he could now feel himself sweating, salt water bursting from his pores and merging with the dark waters all around him. Ever since coming to Neverness, he had known that civilized people blamed certain diseases on the worms, protozoa, bacteria, and viruses that swam through each person's tissues and blood. Privately, deep in the cavern of his most secret thoughts, he had both evaded and ridiculed this notion; he had supposed that the civilized dread of disease was nothing more than a wild fear of the life living inside everyone. Now he was not so sure. When he wondered how a simple virus could kill a full man many billion times its own size, the computer engaged his sense of simulation with a sudden flood of images. He "saw" a single plague virus tumbling among the salt ions, water molecules, amino acids, lipids, and sugars suffusing a neuron cluster of a living brain. The virus was a splendid, symmetrical, terrible thing, a tiny jewel of protein encasing dark coils of DNA. It floated among the intricate, branching neurons and finally attached itself to one of them. It fit into the neuron's membrane as a knife blade slides into a sheath. There the virus DNA passed deep into the neuron's

274

center, into the nucleus of human DNA evolved for billions of years from the simplest of elements.

It is known that the Architects of the Old Church, with the help of the warrior-poets, designed the plague virus from a common retro-virus. After immunizing themselves, they used this bio-weapon against the schismatic Architects. But the virus proved unstable, and by chance, it mutated into a radical DNA structure infecting all Architects and all human beings indiscriminately.

Althought the structure of the plague DNA was truly new, the retro-virus from which it had been wrought was older than mankind. Human retro-viruses, he discovered, were essentially little pieces of ancient DNA that had broken off from human chromosomes and were trying to return home. In the neurons of a human brain (or especially in liver or sex cells), the plague DNA found a perfect home; possessing the same chemical "memory" as did a retro-virus, it stitched itself into a neuron's DNA, masquerading *as* human DNA, hiding. Sometimes it might hide for many years before taking over the neuron's own chemical machinery to reproduce itself. And then something astonishing and terrible would happen. As Danlo watched the computer-generated simulation inside his mind, he saw the infected neuron swell with new life until it burst, and thousands of newly made viruses swarmed into the brain's tissues. These viruses infected new neurons, which died the same way, in turn infecting others, again and again in a chain of explosive reproduction until whole segments of the brain had been killed. The death and rupturing of millions of neurons inevitably caused the brain sac to fill up with fluids until it crushed against the inside of the skull.

The plague sufferer, within one day following the breakout of the disease, manifested the following afflictions: fever, vomiting, diarrhea, accompanied with the hallmark "lightning bolt" headache. Then came convulsions, lockjaw, bleeding from the ears, and inevitably—

—No!

The computer placed a picture in Danlo's visual field, a many-hued simulation of an Architect man dying of the plague. But Danlo had no need to view the plague's terrible colors: the white foam that frothed from pale lips; the crusts of red-black blood; the blackened eye hollows, and the eyes themselves, gray as lead, lightless in death. He suddenly knew that he had seen death from the plague before. *Shaida is the death that takes a whole people to the other side of day,* he thought. Haidar and Chandra and Wemilo and eighty-five others of the Devaki tribe had died of the great plague—of this he was suddenly certain. How they had died of an ancient and extinct virus, though, he had no idea.

The plague virus is not extinct. By the end of the War of the Faces, it had infected virtually all human beings of the Civilized Worlds. The survivors carried the virus within their chromosomes and passed it to their descendants. The virus has become embroidered within the human genome as a passive, if parasitical, segment of DNA. Suppressor genes inhibit the virus DNA, in most people keeping it quiescent and inactive. Only in those few societies isolated from history's convulsions are there to be found human beings possessing little or no inheritance of these suppressor genes. Such human beings are susceptible to contact with and infection by—

"No!"

In an instant of electrified muscles, frothing water, and breath exploding hot and hurtful from his lips, Danlo rose up in his tank. The submerged tiles were hard and slippery against his feet; dark waves of displaced water churned and slapped against his belly. Because he had broken interface with the tutelary computer, he could see nothing at all, neither with his mind nor with his eyes, which burned with liquid salts and ached every time his heart beat. "No!" he cried out again, an angry sound born deep in his throat. The sound filled the blackness of the cell all around him. It struck the living, inner walls of the computer, echoed for a moment, then died. In the dank air, the cloying protein smell of the neurologics mingled with the acridness of his sweat.

"*Shaida* is the man who kills other men," he whispered.

But no one heard him recite this line from the Devaki Song of Life. The tutelary computers of the library are sensitive to the subtlest of human thoughts, but when one is faced away and speaks only the language of voiced words, the sound waves fall off neurologics that are as deaf as stone.

"Father, Father, what have you done?"

But no one answered him; the only sound was his breath streaming through his throat and water tumbling off his naked body into the warm pool below him.

"Master Smith!" he said aloud. "You say that we should not blame my father. But . . . he led an expedition to the Devaki people!"

276

He realized, then, that no matter how loud he shouted, neither Master Smith nor anyone else could hear him. The walls of neurologics were perfect insulators of sound, and the interior of a tutelary computer could be the quietest place in the universe. Because he wished to bring Master Smith to a keener appreciation of the tragedies (and crimes) of the life of Mallory Ringess, he sank back down into the waters of his tank, and he reached out with his mind. He interfaced the tutelary computer, immediately engaging his sense of electronic telepathy.

—Master Smith? You admire my father because he sought the secret of the universe. He thought the Elder Eddas . . . was coded into the Alaloi DNA. The highest gods carked this secret into the oldest DNA, yes? My father thought that the Alaloi DNA was different from that of civilized peoples. Splendid and blessed, in this way.

He waited for Master Smith to respond, but the telepathic space that they shared was as quiet as still water. He supposed that Master Smith must be guiding Hanuman's search, or perhaps he was angry at Danlo for having broken interface so suddenly moments before. Many times, Danlo had been warned against the dangers of too abruptly breaking interface.

—Therefore my father journeyed to the Alaloi. To the blessed Devaki. And their DNA *was* different. It . . . is. They lived on Kweitkel for five thousand years—the War of the Faces never touched them, the plague. O blessed God! They were so innocent, so untouched, so rare.

He waited for Master Smith to defend the actions of Mallory Ringess, to deny that Mallory Ringess should have known that the Alaloi peoples bear no immunity to the plague. He waited for Master Smith to condemn Mallory Ringess for the crime of carelessness in not realizing that he—and all civilized humans—were carriers of a murderous plague.

—My father was a murderer!

His father, he knew, had once lain with the women of the Devaki. He had shared his seed with them. It was murder to knowingly infect others with such *shaida* DNA. His father must have known that someday—whether in fourteen years or in fourteen generations—the virus infecting the Devaki would come to life, and that would be the end of the Devaki.

—My father must have known this, yes? But he did not care. Why should a god care if he murders men or women?

Why should a god care if he murdered many tribes of people? Danlo remembered that Haidar and others of his tribe,

277

when he was younger, every winter when the sea froze, had visited the Olorun, Sanura, and Patwin tribes of the Alaloi. And over the years, the men of these tribes most certainly had visited many other tribes far west of Kweitkel. The plague virus had murdered the Devaki, and even as he floated in his tank and wondered why Master Smith would not answer him, the virus was secretly murdering his cousins of the Patwin tribe. Soon, someday, perhaps after next deep winter, if he did nothing to restore the *halla* nature of the world, the virus would murder all 212 tribes of the Alaloi, and his people would be no more.

—A man lusts to become a god . . . and then there is murder. Murder upon murder upon murder. Why is the world of men nothing but murder?

After a long while of waiting for Master Smith to answer him, Danlo began to worry. It occurred to him that the reason for Master Smith's silence was that Hanuman's journey was not going well. Perhaps, he thought, Hanuman had become lost in the word storm and could not find his way out of shih space. Perhaps he was so absorbed in cybernetic samadhi or one of the other states of computer consciousness that he had no will to return to himself. Or perhaps Hanuman had tried to penetrate the library's secret pools of information only to be struck senseless by the computer's guardian programs. It had happened to other novices before. Perhaps Hanuman lay in his tank, eyes closed and mind dead, breathing warm, heavy salt water.

—Master Smith, please! Is Hanuman all right?

Master Smith had told Danlo that he should not inquire about the journeys of other novices, but now he was too worried to mind such prohibitions. He should have waited patiently in his cell, then. He should have delved back into the computer's lovely information flows and waited for the touch of Master Smith's thoughts, but he had no desire for more information. He might have lain back and floated in his tank, waiting for hours or moments or days, waiting endlessly as Haidar and Three-Fingered Soli and the other men of the Devaki tribe had once taught him to wait. After a long time of waiting, however, he began to smell something faint and far off; although he could not quite identify this smell, muddied as it was with the rankness of the neurologics and salt water, it disturbed him. The smell was almost fruity, and it had a sharp, effervescent quality that penetrated his nostrils deep into his brain. This ominous smell set loose a flood of emotions and memories, and he was suddenly afraid.

278

Hanuman has not been the same since Pedar died, he thought. *Oh, Hanu, Hanu, why haven't you been yourself?*

When Danlo could bear waiting no longer, he fairly leapt out of his tank and rushed out of the cell as it opened before him. He passed into the gowning room where he worked his clothes and boots over his wet skin. He opened the door to the corridor beyond. Steam billowed out into the corridor, and suddenly the smell that had worried him was much stronger than before. He knew that he should recognize this smell. He should dread and loathe it as the smell of death, though it bothered him that he could not remember why.

Death upon death upon death.

As quickly as he could, he ran down the corridor until he reached the door to the librarian's auricle room. With his knuckles he knocked on this dark, rotten door. "Excuse me, please, Master Smith—can you tell me if Hanuman is all right?"

He waited a moment, then knocked again, pounding and pounding against the door with his fist until he realized that Master Smith would not answer him. Up and down the dimly lit corridor, the sound of him hammering away at the shatterwood door reverberated from bare wall stones. But the auricle rooms and cells themselves were built to damp all exterior sounds, and no matter how desperate his pounding or shouting, neither Master Smith nor any other librarian or novice would ever hear him.

Kana oil is the smell of death, he suddenly remembered. *The warrior-poets wear kana oil perfumes.*

With this dreadful thought, he cast aside all rules and etiquette, and he pulled the door open. Now the smell of kana oil was thick and intense. It rushed like electricity into his brain, and his throat clutched up, and he gasped for breath. In the auricle room, there was another smell, too, rich and quick and running with life. As a child, he had smelled this thrilling smell many times before. It was the smell of blood—the smell of death. On a small white futon at the rear of the auricle room, Master Baran Smith sat politely with his hands folded across his lap. Danlo had almost expected to see him floating in a pool of water, but then he remembered that the master librarians do not need such aids in order to interface the tutelary computers. Master Smith, he saw, was fairly floating in a pool of blood. The floor of the cell glistened with blood, and the futon was no longer white but now almost pure red. There were drops of bright blood sprayed against the auricle room's neurologics, and blood dripping down the curves of Master Smith's shiny bald head. It had been four years since Danlo had seen so much blood, when Haidar had speared a shagshay ewe against the clean new snow and used his knife to cut her throat. Danlo stepped closer to Master Smith, the better to see more clearly. Master Smith was not really sitting at all, but rather slumped back against the wall neurologics. His eyes were open and his face was twisted in surprise as if someone had caught him in deep interface unable to see or hear or move. Someone must have opened the door unbidden, even as Danlo had; he must have rushed upon Master Smith and cut open his throat.

Murder upon murder upon murder.

Although it seemed that room's redness and the reek of kana oil would go on and on forever, all this seeing and smelling and remembering of Danlo's lasted only a moment. When he saw that Master Smith was dead beyond hope, he turned and ran from the room.

Warrior-poets murder because they love to murder.

Toward the door of Hanuman's cell he ran, and he moved so quickly that his wet queue of hair whipped about violently, flinging drops of water into the air. He wanted to tell Hanuman that the ontogenesis of man into god was dangerous beyond belief and fraught with *shaida*. He wanted to tell Hanuman other things, too, and he was very afraid that there would never again be time for such telling. There was a warrior-poet loose in the library—of this he was sure. He was sure, too, that the warrior-poet had killed the librarian only as a preliminary and that his masters had really sent him to murder Hanuman.

CHAPTER 11

THE MOMENT OF THE POSSIBLE

How do I prepare for death?
Learn how to live.
How do I learn to live?
Prepare for death.

—saying of the warrior-poets

When Danlo entered Hanuman's cell, he found it empty. Much water had been splashed out of the cell's tank; this water had overflowed into the cell's gowning room and now lay gathered in shallow puddles across the uneven floor tiles. Hanuman's clothes—his kamelaika, undersilks, and furs—still hung from the wall hooks. His boots were neatly stowed on the rack beneath them. Danlo quickly looked about for blood-sign, but he saw nothing to indicate that Hanuman was dead or dying. Only the strong and terrible smell of kana oil pointed toward the warrior-poet as the cause of the cell's emptiness.

The warrior-poets are like spiders—they like to take and bind their victims before killing them.

In truth, the warrior-poets liked to torture their victims, and Danlo thought about this as he tore from the cell and turned into the corridor. He might have gone for help, then. He might have turned toward the right and passed back through the corridor the way that he had come, into the soft lights and safeness of the library's main hallway. He might have scrambled frantically to find a librarian or anyone else, to give the alarm and cry out

281

that Master Smith had been murdered by a warrior-poet. He might have given way to panic (or prudence), but he began remembering many things about the warrior-poets, and so when he stepped out into the corridor, he turned toward his left. He turned into the darkness of the long corridor. He rushed deeper into the library, and the smell of kana oil grew denser and sickening, like that of wolverine musk sprayed into the air. The corridor was empty, nothing but moist wall stones and the numbered doors of the novices' cells. As he ran farther into the corridor, the numbers grew higher. There were many doors and many novices enwombed safely within their cells, lying blindly and deafly as bodies in a prayership. They would not know that a warrior-poet had recently passed their way; they would never suspect that one of their fellow novices was soon to be murdered.

Hanu, Hanu.

Somewhere in this almost endless corridor, beneath one of the flame globes that had burned out years ago, he came across a black cloak flung against the floor stones. He picked it up and smelled it; the coarse wool reeked of kana oil. Sewn to the inside of this noxious garment were rows of little leather pockets. In each pocket, there was a feathered dart no bigger than his finger. At random, he slipped one of these darts free of its pocket. He held the dart up to the faint light diffusing down the corridor. The tip of the dart was a steel needle enameled with some dark, hard substance as red as dried blood. He pulled other darts free. Each dart was tipped with a different colored poison, chocolate or puce or violet. The warrior-poets, it was said, carried many drugs and poisons to play tunes of agony upon the human body as a musician does a gosharp.

Oh, Hanu, Hanu.

Almost without thinking, Danlo grabbed up a handful of darts and continued his wild dash down the corridor. Soon he saw a faint light ahead of him where the corridor ended and a little-used stairwell led to the library's other floors. He drew closer to the stairwell, and his boots pounded against the floor stones, and he gasped at quick lungfuls of air. There were two people in the stairwell, as he could now plainly see. One of them, bound fast to the stairs' heavy railing, was Hanuman li Tosh. And the other was a warrior-poet wearing a beautiful rainbow kamelaika. He had the beautiful and dangerous look of a tiger, and he held a long killing knife against Hanuman's pale throat.

282

"Please don't come any closer," the warrior-poet said, and his voice spilled out like honey into the corridor.

Something in this marvelous voice compelled Danlo to obey, and so, some twenty yards from the stairwell, he stopped. He stood frozen with indecision, trying to get back his breath.

"No, Danlo—the drug, the pain, you mustn't!" This came from Hanuman who was pulling and thrashing against his bonds. Many circles of glittering kasja fiber wound over his arms and chest and looped around two balustrades of the iron railing behind him. Each movement must have caused him considerable pain, for the kasja fibers cut at his skin, which was raw and bloody below his shoulders and along the curve of his lower ribs. The warrior-poets, Danlo remembered, sometimes refer to the kasja fibers as acid wire because the touch of these protein filaments against the flesh is like acid opening up a wound.

"No, Danlo—no!"

Beneath the acid wire imprisoning him, Hanuman was naked. The warrior-poet must have pulled him from his tank and forced him at knife point to walk through the corridor. And Hanuman must have fought fiercely with all the skill of his killing art: the warrior-poet's neck was scratched and bleeding as if Hanuman had tried to claw open the arteries of his throat. Clearly, he had succeeded in yanking off the warrior-poet's cloak, but this had hardly impeded the poet, for he must have caught Hanuman in a headlock or some other hold and dragged him into the stairwell. And Hanuman was still fighting, only now he warred against himself, against his urge to scream and whimper and plea for Danlo to somehow help him.

"No, Danlo, please!"

Even though the light in the empty stairwell was quite strong, it was hard for Danlo to tell if the moisture beading up on Hanuman's face was water remaining from his cell's tank or sweat. In truth, Hanuman's face glistened, and it shone with light, and with fear, with hatred, and with other deep emotions impossible to guess at. His eyes were wide open as he stared up at the warrior-poet; his eyes never left the warrior-poet's eyes, except once, when he peered out into the corridor to look at Danlo.

"Please, go away! Run, Danlo, run!"

"Yes," the warrior-poet said, "please run away. Go and fetch the librarians or their robots. By the time you do, I'll be done with Hanuman."

"Danlo, please, no!"

Still standing close to Hanuman, the warrior-poet smiled politely and bowed. He pointed his knife at Danlo, saying, "You must be Danlo wi Soli Ringess. The son of the Ringess whom everyone is talking about. I had thought you would remain in your cell a little longer, but meeting you is an honor, under any circumstances. I'm Marek of Qallar. I've come to Neverness to meet you and your friend."

Danlo looked into the stairwell, at the long flight of worn basalt steps that led to the higher floors above Hanuman and the warrior-poet. A part of him hoped that a group of librarians or perhaps journeymen pilots, at any moment, might appear upon these stairs and swarm the warrior-poet. Another part of him however, whispered that no number of men or women or robots would be quick enough to save Hanuman before the warrior-poet plunged the knife into his throat. Most likely nothing could save Hanuman now, and therefore Danlo should flee back down the corridor lest the warrior-poet take his life, too.

"If you wish to remain," Marek said to Danlo, "you've only to wait a moment or so. I've already asked Hanuman his poem."

The warrior-poets, Danlo recalled, sometimes honored their victims by reciting part of a poem. If their victims could supply the last lines and complete the poem, they were set free. If they could not, then . . .

"Alas, your friend is no student of poetry," Marek said. "And so now it's time I gave him the drug."

So saying, with blinding speed, the warrior-poet removed a silver needle-dart from a pocket of his kamelaika and stabbed it into the side of Hanuman's neck. Instantly, Hanuman screamed out and began writhing inside his cocoon of acid wire. Instantly too, Danlo began to move toward the stairwell, but the warrior-poet held out his knife and shook his head.

"Please don't move," Marek said. He kissed the yellow ring that encircled the little finger of his left hand, and then he kissed the violet ring on his right hand. He grasped Hanuman's head between his hands, leaned over, and gently kissed his forehead. "The drug won't kill him. It will only bring him to the moment of the possible."

Again, Hanuman screamed, a high, hideous sound like that of a sleekit caught in a snow tiger's claws. Danlo ached to jump forward and help him, but he could not move. It was as if he himself had been caught and immobilized by one of the warrior-poet's paralytic drugs. Danlo watched as Hanuman's face twisted in anguish. Then Hanuman bit his tongue, and his musles jumped beneath his sweat-streaked skin as if touched with n electric current. His eyes were rigid and locked open as he ried out, "No, the light—no, no!" The warrior-poet, Danlo hought, must have inoculated him with ekkana, a drug that endered the body responsive to the faintest of sensa. For Hanu-nan, the photons of the flame globes above him would be like lrops of molten gold poured through the dark opening at the enter of the eye. The neurons of his retina would sizzle and hiss t the searing touch of light. The ekkana, in its excitation of the ervous system, was like an acid that dissolved the myelin coat-ng of every nerve, leaving each nerve fiber open to the world's ruel kiss, and to the interior electrochemical storms and meta-olic signals that rage through the body. Soon, in moments, Ianuman's entire universe would be a blazing tapestry of erves, these endless filaments of fire that branch off and fray nto ever tinier fibers, winding like acid wire through every or-;an and tissue, touching every cell and imprisoning the flesh nside the terrible pain of its own being. And yet, astonishingly, aradoxically, this torture was meant to free Hanuman from imself. The waking brain acts as an eyelid to consciousness; its unction is to shut out the blinding shimmer of all things, inside nd out, lest one lose sight of the everyday world of needs and langers and fears. But the ekkana drug—one of the more ele-;ant trans-psychedelics—opens the eyes. It opens the brain to ight reflected from all possible surfaces, from rocks and wind-orn leaves and the frozen sea, from broken souls and from iightmares and from corpses spread out upon fields of snow. To tand naked and wide-eyed before this blazing light is to open)neself to all the pain in the universe. Then comes the moment)f infinite vulnerability. This is the moment of the possible, vhen one feels the pain of all things reflected and magnified nside oneself and accepts it utterly, without fear. In this mo-nent before death, beyond death—in the pain beyond pain—here is an utter awakening to the fact that one is infinitely more han one's own body and self. In this one soaring, marvelous noment, if one is strong enough to drink in the terrible fire of ife, all things become possible.

"Danlo, please!"

If one is strong enough to overcome oneself—this is what he warrior-poets believe—then there is a golden moment as :ternal as the heaven of the Kristian sects or that ineffable state hat the Architects call cybernetic samadhi. But if one is weak or earful or damaged in the soul, then there is only hell.

"Please—the warrior-poet!"

Again, Hanuman turned his head in Danlo's direction, but it was as if he were looking into a wall of flames. Hanuman shook his head back and forth as if blinded; he ground his teeth and cursed and cried out to Danlo. And all the while Danlo stood in the gloomy corridor amid the smells of steam, neurologics, mildew, kana oil, and sweat. He looked back and forth between Hanuman and the warrior-poet, and he did not know what to do.

"Let him go!" Danlo finally said. "No one can bear this kind of pain!"

The warrior-poet brought his killing knife up to his lips and kissed it. "We shall see," he said.

"Not . . . Hanuman."

"Your friend is stronger than you could know. Can you read faces, Danlo wi Soli Ringess? Look at him—he's almost ready for the knife!"

Danlo gripped the warrior-poet's darts in his hand as he stared at Hanuman's face. All he could see there was agony, terror, and death.

"Please let him go," Danlo said. Soon, perhaps after Danlo's racing heart beat ten more times, the warrior-poet would push the point of his killing knife through the center of Hanuman's eye. He would push it back and back, slowly twisting the knife up the optic nerve into the brain. In this way, he would try to bring Hanuman to his greatest agony, and thus to his greatest possibility for freedom.

"The ekkana drug," Danlo said. "There must be . . . an antidote. Please give him the antidote."

The warrior-poet smiled at Danlo and said, "You must know there is no antidote. And even if I were to free your friend, traces of the holy drug would always remain in his body. The ekkana never completely metabolizes. Even after many years—or lifetimes."

"Let him go, then. So that he will have the rest of his life . . . to come to his moment of the possible."

The warrior-poet smiled at this, a wide and lovely smile that spoke of his approval of Danlo's mindfulness in the face of death—even if that death was to be Hanuman's and not his own. "You know things about us warrior-poets," he said.

"Some . . . things."

"Then you must know that we've been well paid for the life of Hanuman li Tosh. For his *life*—do you understand?"

"Whatever you have been paid, we will pay you more. I, we . . . the Order."

"And what would you pay for your friend's life, Young Danlo?"

"A . . . billion City disks." Danlo, who had never even seen a City disk, much less appreciated its value, named the first figure that came to him.

"A *billion* City disks? Do you have such a sum? Does your entire Order?"

"A million, then," Danlo said. "A hundred—we will pay whatever must be paid."

"That's a generous offer," the warrior-poet said with a smile. "But I'm afraid it's too late for Hanuman's life to be bought with money."

"But someone has paid you!"

"Of course," the warrior-poet said. He used his knife to point at Hanuman's rigid, eye-locked face. "And this is the payment."

"The Architects! On Catava, the Architects of Hanuman's church—they solicited his murder, yes? Because they consider him a blasphemer. A . . . hakra."

"In truth, they have only excoriated him as a potential god."

"But not . . . condemned him?"

"Not for that reason."

"For what reason, then?"

The warrior-poet laughed softly. "For someone who is himself close to his moment, you ask many questions."

"I ask you . . . not to kill him."

"Others have asked that, too."

"Who?"

"His mother, of course. She wanted him brought back to Catava to be cleansed of the worst of his programs. But his uncles pleaded for a more final fate."

Danlo closed his eyes for a moment and shook his head. Then he took a step toward the warrior-poet. "Let him go," he said. "Please let him go."

"One moment, please, if you will." The warrior-poet touched Hanuman's forehead, then looked into his eyes. "In a moment he'll be free."

At this, Hanuman suddenly shouted, "No!" He banged his head back into the railing behind him with such force that the stairwell rang with the sound of humming iron. "Please, Danlo, the warrior-poet—kill him!"

"Hanu, Hanu!"

"Kill him, now! Kill him, kill him!"

Danlo stared at the warrior-poet as he held a fistful of darts down by his side. The warrior-poets were the ancient enemies of his Order. The warrior-poets had once made the virus that killed his found-father and his mother and all the Devaki people. And *this* warrior-poet, Marek of Qallar, with his long, shimmering needle of a knife, was about to kill Hanuman, too.

"Be careful of the darts," the warrior-poet said. "Careful you don't prick yourself."

Moving with mindfulness and great care, Danlo took four of the darts into his left hand. Between the fingers of his right hand he grasped the red-tipped dart.

"The green dart gives one unconsciousness for an hour or so," the warrior-poet said. "And the one that looks like it has been dipped in chocolate—this robs one of the power of speech, forever."

Danlo drew his arm back behind his head, sighting on the warrior-poet's throat.

"The blue dart carries a truth drug."

With a rising of his belly, Danlo began to take in a breath of air, the way he once did before spearing a snow tiger or casting a stone at a hare.

"The dart that you hold in your hand kills instantly—it paralyzes the nerves of the heart. It's a quick death, Young Danlo, but truly ignoble."

As Danlo stared at the place on the warrior-poet's throat where the great brain artery pulsed along the windpipe, he wondered if he could kill him. Once, two years ago, at nearly twice the distance, he had cast his spear and precisely pierced the heart place behind the shoulder of a charging silk belly boar. But warrior-poets were not animals; it was said that they had mastered the art of slowtime, that lightning state of the body-mind where the firing of one's nerves accelerates so that time slows down and each event of the exterior universe seems to occur more slowly. No matter how precisely or quickly Danlo cast his dart, for the warrior-poet it would appear almost as a feather floating in the air, or if he were very adept, as a furfly falling through a jar of honey. Most likely he would snatch the dart from the air and cast it back at Danlo. And even supposing this were a day for miracles and Danlo could possibly kill him, he didn't know if he *could* kill him. The warrior-poet seemed so happy holding his knife above Hanuman's eye; he seemed fearless and fey and utterly alive.

"Please, throw it now!" Hanuman screamed. "Don't be afraid—kill me now! Kill me, kill me!"

Of course, Danlo's cast might miss the warrior-poet altogether and strike Hanuman, and this was reason enough for not throwing the dart. But there were deeper reasons for not killing the warrior-poet. There was the smile upon his lips and the calmness spread over him like a magic cloak and the impossible awareness lighting up his eyes.

The eyes are the windows of the universe, Danlo remembered.

In truth, the warrior-poet had impossible eyes, a violet so deep and dark they were almost blue-black, the color of his own. They were a predator's eyes, eyes that would feed on the faces and fears of other men. As Danlo lost himself in these marvelous eyes, he could not decide whether the warrior-poet was mad or utterly sane. In a way, of course, he was completely mad because his death-loving doctrines were a complete unbalancing of life. Certainly he was *shaida* in his madness, but so willfully and utterly *shaida* that he almost made this concept into something beautiful. Danlo thought that he had rarely seen anyone so beautiful, and never anyone so alive. The muscles of the warrior-poet's neck and naked forearms were like writhing snakes; his hair was a halo of black curls, and his skin was like living gold. *He is like an angel of death,* Danlo thought. The warrior-poet's face and form radiated a terrible beauty as if he belonged to a higher order of being where terror and beauty smiled at each other and joined hands. And yet despite his joy of living so intense a death-in-life, there was something about him infinitely tragic and sad. The warrior-poet—like every child of the highly bred races—was one of evolution's myriad experiments and pathways that had attained a kind of perfection but would go no further.

He is almost a human being, Danlo thought. *A true human being.*

The warrior-poet looked down at the gleaming steel that he held above Hanuman's eye, and Danlo saw that the distance between a man such as the warrior-poet and one who was truly human was as narrow as the edge of a knife. As narrow, yes, yet as great as the distance from Neverness to the edge of the universe.

He is a murderer of men. Shaida is the way of the man who kills other men.

The infinite pain that the warrior-poets worshiped was like a whirlpool that sucked them down into the dark froth of madness and murder. The warrior-poets were the supreme murderers of mankind. They liked to think of themselves as bonsai masters using their terrible knives to prune dangerous or diseased individuals like so many twigs—all so that the greater tree of life might remain vital and strong. They were supreme in this art of bringing death. The universe, they believed, would always require such agents of death.

But I am not a murderer, Danlo thought. His arm, which he held back behind his head, trembled to release the dart. *I am not he.*

Although Danlo had a strange sympathy for madness, he could not countenance the need to murder, especially not in himself. His way, he thought, must always be the opposite of murder. He must be a bringer of life, even though his ideals and actions cost him his own blessed life.

Never killing or hurting another; it is better to die oneself than kill.

And this was the deepest reason of all why he could not kill the warrior-poet: because killing led to wanton killing and unbalanced all of life, and was thus *shaida*; because such killing was a negation and saying "no" to life's infinite possibilities; because killing one such as the warrior-poet eliminated the possibility that he might be healed of his madness and thus be transformed into something truly marvelous.

"Warrior-poet!" Danlo finally shouted. He relaxed the fingers of his left hand and let the darts drop to the floor. Then he turned, whipped his right arm forward, and threw the red-tipped dart so that it sailed through the air of the corridor and ticked into the door of the 264th cell. "Let Hanuman go!"

At the sound of Danlo's voice, Hanuman shook his head. "No, please kill me. Danlo, please."

"I'm sorry, Young Danlo," the warrior-poet said. His eyes were violet streaks of light reflected from the polished blade of his knife. "But the moment must always come."

"Then take me in his place," Danlo said.

"No, no!"

"Take me, and I will live his moment."

The warrior-poet, who had begun lowering the knife

toward Hanuman's eye, suddenly froze. "What are you saying? Do you know what you ask?"

Danlo knew very well what he was asking. He remembered a tradition of the warrior-poets: that if someone such as himself offered to take another's place in seeking the moment of the possible, the warrior-poet who held the killing knife must consider his request.

"Take me," Danlo repeated. "Not Hanuman."

The warrior-poet stared at Danlo, then bowed his head in respect for Danlo's obvious love for his friend. "Your offer is noble," he said. "But nobility is not enough."

Danlo stood with his hands open toward the warrior-poet. He saw that the warrior-poet was reading the curve of his lips, searching in his face and eyes for some crucial thing.

"Your offer is brave, too, but bravery is not enough."

Danlo let his face fall free and open, like that of a sleeping child. He remembered, then, that the warrior-poets only rarely honored such requests.

"Are you so ready to die, then?" the warrior-poet asked.

For a long moment Danlo stared at the warrior-poet's killing knife, and he did not know if he was ready to die. Certainly he had no wish to die, nor was he sure if this was the right time to die. In truth, death beneath the warrior-poet's knife, even though an excruciating possibility, was far from inevitable. Even if the warrior-poet should allow him to take Hanuman's place, there would be no instant execution. First, with acid wire or some drug, the warrior-poet would immobilize him. And then he would ask Danlo his poem. If Danlo could complete this poem, the warrior-poet must set him free.

"Even the readiness to die is not enough," the warrior-poet said. "Not quite enough."

All this time the warrior-poet had been staring out into the corridor, and he was staring still, and his eyes never stopped searching Danlo's eyes for that rare quality of being he hoped to find there.

"I must ask your friend if he is willing for you to take his place," the warrior-poet said. He looked down at Hanuman and asked, "Is this agreeable to you?"

"No!" Hanuman screamed. He lunged against the wire binding him, and he spat blood at the warrior-poet. And then there was a moment of quiet as his body fell still and he looked at Danlo. He looked at him for a long time (or perhaps it was only a moment), and then, to the warrior-poet he said, "No, I won't agree—kill me if you must, not him."

The warrior-poet nodded his head gravely. He turned to Danlo and said, "He does not agree that you should take his place. He has said 'no,' so shouldn't we abide by his wish?"

"No! He does not know what he wishes or wants!"

"Of course, if he *had* let you take his place, I would have had to kill him instantly, to repay such cowardice."

"And so you ask a question that leads to this . . . paradox?"

"We warrior-poets love paradox."

"But why ask him anything if you intend to kill him?"

"I didn't say I intend to kill him."

"But—"

"He has given us his answer, made his wishes known. Now it's upon us to decide what to do."

"Let him go, and you may ask me your poem."

"I *would* like to recite a poem for you," the warrior-poet said. "But are you ready to hear it?"

"Yes," Danlo said. But as soon as this word pushed apart his lips and flew out into the air, he was afraid that the warrior-poet would refuse to say his poem. For a moment he regretted throwing away the dart. He hated waiting helplessly for the warrior-poet to decide his and Hanuman's fate. And then he remembered something that Old Father had once said about the nature of ahimsa. Ahimsa, according to the Fravashi, need not be merely a passive refusal to harm other things. For some people, sometime, there was a rare power to ahimsa, and this power came from the will to affirm all other life as identical to one's own. The will to affirm death: if he asserted no preference for his life above that of others, then he would never defend his life at the cost of another's death. And therefore, in the violent and bloody universe into which he had been born, *he* must soon die. Today, tomorrow, a moment hence—he would cast his life away as if it were an uneaten bloodfruit, still ripe and sweet with juice. When his time came, he would make this affirmation forcefully and fiercely, as he would have thrown the dart at the warrior-poet. But until then he would live freely, without fear.

The power of ahimsa is not just the readiness to die, he thought. *It is the willingness to live. To live utterly without fear— this is a fearsome thing.*

"Yes," Danlo said again, "I am ready . . . to hear your poem." He took a step toward the warrior-poet, and then another. The warrior-poet's knife shifted slightly, and Danlo saw streaks of blue-black light, the fearsome reflection of his own face. The warrior-poet moved the knife slowly away from Hanuman's eye. He looked at Danlo. He smiled, slowly, knowingly. Danlo took another step forward, and his foot seemed to hang in the air forever. Now the smell of kana oil was overpowering. It brought to him the memory of his passage into manhood when he had lain beneath the stars and learned to go beyond pain and death. It brought to him, too, an awareness of the warrior-poet's childhood. He could see this timeless time as streaks of violet lighting up the warrior-poet's eyes. In the golden glow of the warrior-poet's face, he could see the little child who sensed the terribly unconscious closeness of death. It was the whole of the warrior-poet's art to bring this deep knowledge into full consciousness. The warrior-poet smiled at Danlo, and he touched his lips to his violet ring, and as he accomplished these movements against the heavy pull of space and time, he sent waves of air molecules flowing out into the corridor. Danlo's nostrils were open to this air, open to the smell of kana oil that pierced his nerves and stabbed into his brain. He stepped closer to the warrior-poet, and he could not take his eyes off the warrior-poet's knife. Soon, perhaps, if he failed to complete the poem, the knife would stab through his eye into his brain. In a blindingly quick moment of time, his life would be done. Done, yes, but not destroyed. He could never cast his life away in the sense of wasting it, for life could never be unmade or destroyed. When the sharp, cold knife broke through the bone at the back of his eye, his blood would flow out of him like a river. It would spray over the wall stones and the steps and the iron railing; it would redden the warrior-poet's black hair and touch his beautiful eyes with the sting of iron and salt; it would fall over Hanuman's face like drops of morning light, and when Hanuman opened his mouth to scream his final "no!" it would touch Hanuman's tongue and flow down his throat, into his belly, into the onstreaming life and tissues of his body. His blood would flow as endless and deep as an ocean, touching everything, nourishing everything, making everything more alive. He would live in everything, forever, just as the wild smell of kana oil and the marvelous colors of the warrior-poet's robe and Hanuman's beautiful, broken soul lived now and forever in him.

"Come here!" the warrior-poet said to Danlo. He was smiling at him, looking at him in gladness as if he had found a younger brother who has been lost. "It *is* enough—you are ready to hear the poem, I think."

With ten quick steps, Danlo rushed into the stairwell. He came over and stood next to Hanuman. He touched Hanuman's bloody hand and his glistening forehead. He touched the cool strands of acid wire encircling him. He looked at the warrior-poet, who was standing so close that he could have touched him too. "Please cut him free," Danlo said. "You have agreed to ask me the poem—so please free him."

The warrior-poet stepped so close to Danlo that it seemed he was drowning in the smell of kana oil. The warrior-poet lightly ran the tip of his knife down the cocoon of acid wire over Hanuman's chest; this made a metallic, zippering sound, but the acid wire remained whole and unmarked. "The kasja fibers are hard to cut," the warrior-poet said. "And even if I could cut him loose, I would not. If I did, he would try to kill me. Or kill himself."

Hanuman was shaking now, his whole body shivering with rage and pain. His pale eyes were locked open, and they fixed on Danlo. It was hard for Danlo to tell if Hanuman could understand what was being said.

"But if I . . . fail to answer the poem," Danlo said, "then you will free him, yes?"

"In a way," the warrior-poet said. "I have a drug that will make him sleep—he'll wake up in three days, and he'll remain alive, if he wants to."

"Then give him this drug."

"Not yet. He must be awake to witness the moment of the one who takes his place."

"But—"

"If you answer the poem, you may give him this drug. There is the purple needle-dart that you dropped in the corridor, do you remember?"

"I remember," Danlo said. Then he nodded to the warrior and told him, "Please ask me the poem now."

The warrior-poet examined the tone of Hanuman's eyes and he said, "It is too bad. Your friend has passed his moment. Now we shall never know what might have been possible—for him."

"Ask me the poem—before it is too late."

The warrior-poet nodded his head and reached into the side pocket of his kamelaika. He removed a needle tipped in pink. "Please stand with your back to the railing, next to your friend."

Danlo moved over next to Hanuman so that they stood side by side. He felt the hardness of the iron railing press against his spine. Behind him, below him, the stairs disappeared into the lower levels of the library. In the depths of the stairwell, he heard the dark, underground sounds of hissing steam and water gurgling through unseen pipes. "You will not bind me with . . . the acid wire?"

"No," the warrior-poet said. He stood in front of Danlo, eye to eye. Danlo felt the warrior-poet's breath fall over his face; it smelled sweet, like oranges and honey. "I've no more wire."

"Then why not let me stand free, without drugs?"

In his left hand, the warrior-poet held his paralytic needle near the side of Danlo's neck; in his right hand, he gripped the killing knife. "If I recite the poem and you fail to complete it, you might wish to run away."

"I will not . . . run away."

"You might wish to struggle, to avoid the ekkana drug." The warrior-poet looked at Hanuman and bowed his head. "You've seen how the ekkana licks the soul with tongues of fire."

"Truly, I *have* seen this," Danlo said. "But is it not possible . . . for one to reach the moment of the possible without the ekkana?"

The warrior-poet turned to study Danlo's face for a long time, and then he smiled. "Perhaps it *is* possible," he said. "We shall see."

Danlo felt Hanuman's shoulder pressing against him. He reached down by his side where he found Hanuman's hand all hot and slippery with blood. He held Hanuman's hand tightly, and he said, "Tell me your poem, then."

Now the warrior-poet moved in close to Danlo so that their chests almost touched; he pressed the needle against Danlo's throat and held the killing knife above Danlo's eye. "Do you like poetry, Young Danlo? Do you know many poems?"

At this question, Hanuman came to life. He screamed and then laughed hideously; his hand squeezed Danlo's twice in secret code as if to remind him of all the nights that Danlo had spent memorizing Pedar's ancient poetry.

"I know . . . some poems," Danlo said. He neglected to mention that during the last half year, he had memorized some twelve thousand poems.

295

"Few people care about poetry anymore," the warrior-poet said. "But once a time, poetry was the soul of civilization."

"My . . . father liked poetry," Danlo told him, not knowing what to say.

"This is known. The Ringess once said that poems are the dreams of the universe crystallized in words."

"And the poets . . . are the part of the universe that dreams?"

"True," the warrior-poet said. "Though sadly, the dreams often destroy the dreamer. The price of perfect words paid with broken lives."

Despite the extreme peril of his situation, Danlo smiled. He thought that the greatest paradox of the warrior-poets was that they used poems as well as knives in trying to reach the moment of the possible.

"I shall now recite the first four lines of a poem," the warrior-poet said. "An old, old poem—are you ready to hear this poem, Danlo wi Soli Ringess?"

Danlo felt Hanuman's fingers suddenly clasp his hand as if he were struggling to hold on to a rock on the face of a cliff. "Yes," Danlo said. "Say your poem, then."

The warrior-poet nodded again. His lips were only inches from Danlo's face, and in a clear, strong voice he said:

> *"Sweet infancy!*
> *O heavenly fire! O sacred light!*
> *How fair and bright!*
> *How great am I . . ."*

Danlo, upon hearing these sixteen perfect words, looked off into the flame globes that filled the stairwell with such a beautiful light. This dazzling light fell over the warrior-poet's face and touched every stone and streak of mortar with colors of cobalt, lavender, and rose. Because everything he could see was so beautiful and perfect with light, he touched eyes with the warrior-poet and began to smile.

"Did you hear me, Young Danlo? I shall say the poem again—listen to the words.

> *"Sweet infancy!*
> *O heavenly fire! O sacred light!*
> *How fair and bright!*
> *How great am I . . ."*

The words that the warrior-poet spoke were like a lovely, golden music in Danlo's ear. He did not need to listen to these words a second time. His memory of the poems he had learned by heart was complete. He had known instantly, upon the first line of the warrior-poet's first recitation, that the poem was unknown to him.

"What is the last line?" the warrior-poet asked. He pushed the point of his knife a half inch closer to Danlo's eye. "Do you know the words?"

Danlo felt Hanuman's hard little hand trembling in his own, and he turned to look at him.

"Say it, Danlo," Hanuman forced out. "Say it now."

Hanuman's face, too, he saw, was very beautiful, and it shone with all the colors of hope. Hanuman was sure he must know this poem. At that moment Hanuman was sure that Danlo must have known every poem in the universe.

"Please say it!"

Danlo tightened his grip on Hanuman's hand and drew in a long, deep breath. And then he said:

> *"Sweet infancy!*
> *O heavenly fire! O sacred light!*
> *How fair and bright!*
> *How great am I . . ."*

With a shake of his head, Danlo's voice faded off to infinity. He had hoped that he was wrong, that somewhere in his memory, like a diamond hidden among mountains of lesser jewels, he might find this poem. He had hoped that one perfect word might lead to another, and thus in saying the poem's beginning he might remember the last line. But how could he remember what he had never known?

"I shall say the poem a third time," the warrior-poet told him. "The third recitation must be the last. If you can't complete the poem, you must prepare yourself for your moment.

> *"Sweet infancy!*
> *O heavenly fire! O sacred light!*
> *How fair and bright!*
> *How great am I . . .*

"Well, Danlo wi Soli Ringess?"

Down by his side, Danlo felt Hanuman's long fingernails

cutting into the palm of his hand. Little drops of blood ran from the gap between their hands, and it was impossible to tell whether this blood was Hanuman's or his own.

"Danlo, Danlo."

He heard Hanuman whispering his name, and he saw that Hanuman's eyes were moist with the madness of pain.

"Please," Hanuman whispered.

The warrior-poet was very close to Danlo; he was very aware of the smell of kana oil and the warrior-poet's bittersweet breath. Danlo's whole world, at that moment, was composed of Hanuman's deep-throated moans, the sound of his own deep breathing, the silvery glint of needle and knife. His mind was empty of words, as empty as the blackness between the stars. There was nothing in his mind. And yet there was everything. There was light from the flame globes, brilliant streams of light reflected from polished basalt in lovely polarized waves. There was something wild and strange about light. It was as if the million million photons carried memories of distant stars and other times. He knew that somehow everything must be coded into light: hopes and words and the universe's deepest dreams. With this thought, the curtain of light falling over him (and over Hanuman and the warrior-poet, too) was torn away to reveal something impossible to look at, impossible to turn away from. There was a light beyond light, behind and beneath light. This marvelous light was made of a thousand strange new colors almost impossible to behold. And in each color there was a whole world of space and memory and time. *A whole world.* He sensed that just behind his eyes, spinning in the depths of his blood, there were worlds inside worlds. There was a deepness, a strangeness about himself that astonished him. There was something strange about his memory, as if there was more inside him than he had ever known. He should have remembered himself. There was something utterly crucial to his life (and perhaps to the lives of others) that he should have remembered. Now, and every moment of his life, like a child standing by the ocean's shore, he was always on the threshold of remembering, but always this great memory eluded him. He was haunted by a sense of missing time, a terrible suspicion that he had forgotten great segments of his life. And most terrible of all was the certainty that these memories lay just beneath the surface of his soul, waiting, onstreaming, like the shimmering ocean beneath a layer of ice and snow.

I have forgotten what I have forgotten.

In the strange light of the stairwell, the warrior-poet looked at him, and a terrible smile touched his lips. He touched the blade of his killing knife with his beautiful finger. And then suddenly, like an iceberg rising up out of a starlit sea, a word appeared in Danlo's mind. Almost instantly there were other words, six splendid, perfect words. The words were strange but somehow completely familiar to him, as if long ago he had composed them himself. Or rather, as if he were composing them now in completion of a poem, as if these six simple words were the only words that had ever been or could ever be.

Whom the whole world . . .

"Danlo wi Soli Ringess!" the warrior-poet whispered. "Are you ready for your moment?"

Danlo inclined his head slightly, but before the warrior-poet could touch him with the knife, he fixed the warrior-poet's eyes and said:

> *"Sweet infancy!*
> *O heavenly fire! O sacred light!*
> *How fair and bright!*
> *How great am I,*
> *Whom the whole world doth magnify."*

"Yes!" Hanuman cried out as he crushed Danlo's hand against his leg. "Yes—the poem, the poem!"

Through the count of five heartbeats, Danlo watched the warrior-poet's eyes fall through the colors of astonishment, elation, awe, and dread. There was an immense sadness about him as he lifted the needle away from Danlo's neck and lowered his knife. He told Danlo, "You have said the poem perfectly. By the rules of my order, in a mòment, you will be free to go."

The warrior-poet stepped backward a few paces, all the while regarding both Hanuman and Danlo. He looked down at their bloody hands locked together. He slipped the needle back into his pocket, but he kept his hold on the knife. From the corridor behind him came the faint creaking of doors and muffled voices; he paid no attention to these sounds, instead concentrating on the strangled words that Hanuman was struggling to say: "Why . . . should . . . he . . . free . . . us?"

"Because I must," the warrior-poet said.

"But . . . you . . . contracted . . . to . . . kill . . . me!"

"We did, and so you might suppose most people would be

299

reluctant to make contracts with us poets for this reason. But the truth is, it has been a long time since we allowed a friend to take a friend's place. A *long* time. The last time was 212 years ago, at the temple on Jacaranda, before the Valerian Gates. And of the few who have asked to seek the moment of the possible, in all the time of my order, not one has ever completed the poem— until today."

The warrior-poet looked long and deep at Danlo, who should have been exultant (and mystified) at his completion of the poem. But now Hanuman was coughing against his pain, coughing and struggling to breathe.

"May I retrieve the dart?" Danlo asked. "So that he can . . . sleep?"

"In a moment," the warrior-poet said. "There is still one more thing that Hanuman must witness, if we are to obey the ancient forms."

"What . . . thing?"

A harsh smile split the warrior-poet's face. "A life has been paid for—haven't I told you this earlier?"

"Yes," Danlo said, confused. "Hanuman's uncles have paid you to put a knife into his brain."

"No, that is not true. You misunderstand the nature of our contract. His uncles wanted Hanuman safely killed, from a distance. With poisons or viruses. An inexpensive death, an ignoble death without honor."

"I still do not understand."

"We've been searching for Hanuman this past year. We suspected that he had journeyed to Neverness, and then our informants confirmed this. They told us that the harijan were outraged over the death of the boy called Pedar. The names of Danlo wi Soli Ringess and Hanuman li Tosh were associated with this death."

"And so the harijan also contracted to have Hanuman . . . murdered?"

"Of course not. Warrior-poets would not accept contracts from harijan. Our only contract was with the Architects."

"Then—"

"When we learned of Hanuman's involvement with Pedar's death, we saw that there might be cause to alter the contract. And so I was sent to Neverness."

"But Hanuman had nothing to do with Pedar's death!"

At this, the warrior-poet pointed his knife at Hanuman and

shook his head. "In truth, I suspected from the first that he had *everything* to do with Pedar's unfortunate fall."

"No! What are you saying?" Danlo held Hanuman's hand tightly and turned to look at him. But, for the moment, Hanuman's face was pale and empty, and his gaze was turned inward upon his own pain.

"I *suspected* that Hanuman killed Pedar, but of course I couldn't know until I saw his face. And that is the first reason why I bribed that ugly librarian to let me enter this ugly building. So that I could get close enough to Hanuman to read his face."

"But Hanuman . . . could not have killed Pedar!"

"But he *did* kill him," the warrior-poet said. "He murdered him. Look at your friend's face! He hears our words, he understands. Have you learned anything of the cetics' art? The way each face always tells the truth? Read the tells, Young Danlo. No, not just the mouth, the way he bites his lip. Look at his eyes, the pattern of the pupils, dilating, then narrowing at each utterance of the word 'murder.' He murdered Pedar. Probably with some drug that made him slip on the stairs. He murdered Pedar to save your life. He murdered out of love for you. He had the *will* to murder in a noble cause—this I suspected when I interviewed the harijan elders. This I discovered when I bound him with acid wire and asked him if he had the courage to be a murderer. With his eyes he said 'yes!' A rare and noble being, this Hanuman li Tosh. And therefore worthy of a rare and noble death. The true death—it's a pity that he may never live his moment of the possible, once you've set him free."

"Hanuman is *not* a murderer!" Danlo shouted. "You are the murderer! You, with your contracts and your needles—your murdering knife!"

The warrior-poet did not dispute the last of Danlo's accusations, but only looked down at the long knife that he held lightly between his fingers.

"My contract," he said softly.

At that moment, from behind the warrior-poet, the sound of voices floated through the corridor and into the stairwell. The warrior-poet turned, momentarily looking back over his shoulder. Danlo followed his gaze, looking into the darkness past the rows of cells to see a bald librarian and a white-robed novice walking their way. The librarian was an old man who moved in fits and jerks; his head was tilted close to the novice as if they

301

had just finished a journey through shih space but the librarian still thought it seemly to monitor the novice's conversation. Something—perhaps it was Hanuman's moaning—caused the librarian to stop abruptly and jerk his head erect. He looked through the steam and the uneven light into the stairwell directly ahead of him. At the sight of a warrior-poet brandishing his killing knife, he clapped his hands to his face and cried out, "Oh, no!" Then he grabbed the novice's arm, turned, and ran in the opposite direction toward the main body of the library. The sound of their footsteps echoed through the corridor for a moment, and then died.

"Now the librarians or their robots will come," the warrior-poet said to Danlo. "I haven't very long to fulfill my contract."

"What do you mean?" Danlo quickly asked.

"A life has been paid for. The next few moments won't satisfy the Architects, but a contract is a contract."

So saying, he stood with his feet slightly apart and stared straight ahead at Danlo. Then he turned the point of his knife toward his own face and smiled to himself.

"No . . . do not!" Danlo said.

He started to move toward the warrior-poet, but then the warrior-poet plucked a violet killing needle from his robe and said, "Please don't come any closer. Only one life has been paid for today, not two. Your moment may come sooner than you know."

"My moment?"

In the warrior-poet's left hand, he kept the needle pointed at Danlo; in his right, he aimed the knife toward the center of his beautiful eye. "I've said that the first reason I entered the library today was to behold your friend's glorious face. This is true. But there was another reason—we poets always love multiple missions. After I was through with Hanuman, I would have come for you next, Danlo wi Soli Ringess. Not to kill, at least not this time. To see. To see for myself who you really are. Because there is a new rule for us warrior-poets, a new rule that is old: we must find and kill all potential gods. Your father brought us to this, did you know? Your father, Mallory Ringess, *the* Ringess—I was sent to Neverness to determine if you were the son of the father."

In truth, in that moment of blood and beauty and terror, Danlo did not quite know who he really was. He was a stranger to himself, and his life was a mystery as deep and inexplicable as his sudden memory of the poem.

"His father . . ." Hanuman began, but he could not finish his sentence. His hand wrenched at Danlo's, and his face twisted, and it was almost possible to see the waves of agony ripping through his body.

Never taking his eyes from Danlo, the warrior-poet said, "For you, there *is* a possibility. You will be who you will be. *You* will choose, Danlo wi Soli Ringess. Someday, you must choose. And when you do, we poets will be waiting."

From the main body of the library, down the dark, dingy corridor past tens of soundproofed cells, there came the faintest murmur of voices, rolling metal wheels, and many footsteps.

"It's time," the warrior-poet said. For the count of three of Danlo's heartbeats, the warrior-poet looked at his knife. His entire awareness seemed to narrow and become one with this glittering, murderous weapon. "It's strange. I've lived my whole life for this moment. But now that it's come, I find I'm not ready to die."

"Then . . . do not die," Danlo said. "Live."

Everything about Danlo—his love of ahimsa, his marvelous will, his deep, vivid eyes—was urging the warrior-poet into life. But there is an identity of opposites, and irony is the law of the universe. As Danlo stared at the warrior-poet, a sense of kinship and a terrible joy passed between them. At last the warrior-poet smiled at Danlo and said, "Thank you—*now* I'm ready."

"But I did not want—"

"*This* is my last poem," the warrior-poet said. "My death poem—I give this to you in remembrance. Please do not forget it."

Quickly, for five journeyman librarians armed with lasers were making their way down the corridor behind the cover of an armored, rolling tutelary robot, the warrior-poet looked at Hanuman and Danlo, then said:

> *"Two friends*
> *Joined left hand and right,*
> *My death—my life."*

The warrior-poet tilted his head back, facing the light of the flame globes. At the same time he raised both hands up and together almost as if he were praying to the heavens somewhere beyond the enclosing stones of the library. His straight arms came to a point above him, like the spire of a cathedral. And clasped between his hands was his killing knife, this gleaming needle of steel. For an endless moment of time, he gazed upon the knife's infinitely fine point. Then, with terrible force, he plunged it straight down through his eye. His aim was precise and true, and the knife drove home through bone and cortex down into his brain stem. He died almost instantly, died with the knife's ivory handle sticking out from his forehead as if it were a horn of some mythical beast; he died falling, and falling slowly and forever to the stairwell's floor he died, even as Danlo fell forward in a desperate surge to save his life. But Danlo was too late. The warrior-poet fell to the floor with an explosive outrush of breath and the possibility of infinite pain upon his lips. It surprised Danlo that there was so little blood.

"His moment, oh, his moment—oh, oh, oh, oh!" This came from Hanuman, who was laughing and crying and howling in pain, all at once.

After that the robot came and used a laser to cut Hanuman free. One of the journeymen discovered Master Baran Smith dead in his cell; he went to call for three litters, for Master Smith and for the warrior-poet, and for Hanuman who had collapsed in Danlo's arms. While the oldest of the journeymen—an angry little woman named Kalere Chu—went to retrieve Hanuman's clothes from his cell, Danlo let the other journeymen hold the still-naked Hanuman away from the stairwell's icy floor stones. Danlo went out into the corridor, then; it took him only a moment to find the warrior-poet's dart, which had skittered across the floor and come to rest near a heating grate. He returned to Hanuman's side, and before the journeymen could stop him, he stabbed it into the muscle bunching up on the side of Hanuman's neck. As the warrior-poet had said, the drug gave Hanuman almost immediate unconsciousness.

"What are you doing?" one of the journeymen asked him. This was a large, frightened man scarcely more than twenty years old. He was sweating and swallowing continually, as if he were chewing on some unpalatable root that made him sick. He rudely chastised Danlo and pushed him away. "Do you want to kill him?"

Danlo stood alone resting his bloody hand against the stairwell's cold railing, and he watched Hanuman's tortured eyes finally close into sleep and forgetfulness. "Go to sleep, my brother," he whispered. Then he looked down at the warrior-poet who was sleeping his final sleep, who had died the true death. He knew that he would never forget the warrior-poet's last poem. And he would never forget the terrible thing that the warrior-poet had said, that Hanuman li Tosh was a murderer of men.

THE MASTER OF
NOVICES

A wearer of the two rings must always carry two weapons: a knife to cut away the lies of the body and a poem to lay bare the truth of the mind.

—maxim of Nils Ordando, founder of the Order of
Warrior-Poets

During the days that followed, as the warrior-poet had promised, the ekkana drug poisoning Hanuman did not leave his body. Because Hanuman would have to bear the acid touch of the ekkana for all his life, he was taken to the cetics' tower, there to learn techniques for blocking nerve signals and controlling his mind pain. Although Danlo was not allowed to visit Hanuman, a master cetic named Javier Hake kept him apprised as to Hanuman's condition. Hanuman, as the master cetic told Danlo, should rejoice that he was still alive, for of the few persons known to have survived a warrior-poet's knife, even fewer had been able to live with the ekkana burning through their veins. Hanuman's mind and his power of will clearly impressed the master cetic, which was not an easy thing to accomplish since the cetics are usually as imperturbable as stone.

One morning at breakfast—while Hanuman practiced aduhkha and other healing attitudes with the cetics, while Danlo worried over Hanuman and tried to remember all the events leading up to their meeting with the warrior-poet—Danlo finally received an invitation to visit Master Bardo's private chambers.

ndeed, it was more of a summons than an invitation, and so, after gulping down his coffee and fetching his warmest fur, Danlo dashed out into the cold, gray air. The night's snowfall had whitened the buildings of Borja, and it was snowing still: tiny, irregular, broken flakes that he knew as *raishay*. By the time he had reached the Novices' Sanctuary, his cap, his furs, and his long black queue were covered with *raishay* snow. So cold were the Sanctuary's long stone hallways that the snow remained unmelted as he pulled off his mittens and banged the steel knocker on the door of Bardo's apartment. And then the door suddenly opened to waves of heat that washed his eyes and turned the powdery snow to water.

"Ah, Danlo, the warrior-poet didn't touch you, I see. By God, don't just stand there letting in all cold air—come inside and sit with me!" Bardo stood in the doorway, and with a sweep of his massive arm, he invited Danlo inside. "I like my rooms warm, perhaps warmer than you're used to. Let me take your furs before you faint."

Indeed, Bardo's fire room was too warm, and Danlo instantly began to sweat. At either end of the room, stone fireplaces were heaped with fatwood, which popped and crackled with orange flames. Bardo wore only a single, thin robe over his mountainous body. The robe was black, as a pilot's robe must be, but it was made of the finest Japanese silk and embroidered with platinum and gold strands. Around his fingers he wore jeweled rings, and around his neck seven silver chains. Bardo's chambers were full of such finery: a shatterwood dining table and outrageously expensive chairs carved on Urradeth; Fravashi tondos and tapestries hanging from the walls; a piano, gosharp, and synthesizer; and a chess table inlaid with obsidian and white opal squares. Atop several low tables, growing inside stone pots, were tiny bonsai trees thousands of years old. Each tree, with its diminutive needles and twisting branches, was exquisite. A succession of owners, supposedly going back to the ancients on Old Earth, had cultivated the trees and passed them on to their heirs or had sold them at market. Danlo thought it strange that full men should spend lifetimes painstakingly binding and pruning the limbs of plants in order to stunt their growth; he marveled at the care and art (and time) necessary to shape them. If he had known anything about money, its scarcity and value, he would have been astonished that the seven trees had cost Master Bardo more than three thousand City disks each.

"Are you an aficionado of bonsai?" Bardo asked.

"No, sir."

"Well, I'm not either, anymore. I once had twelve other trees, but they died. Perhaps I'm not watering them properly."

Danlo reached out and stuck his finger inside one of the pots, down into the sticky black soil. There was too much water around the trees' roots, he thought; the trees were surely being killed with water.

"On the Day of Submission, Hanuman asked me if he could take care of the trees," Bardo said. "There's something about bonsai that fascinates him, I think. Ah, well, perhaps when he leaves the cetics' tower. And I hope that is soon. I don't trust the damn cetics—who does? The way they look at you as if they'd like to cark your goddamned mind. The sooner Hanuman is free from their spider's web of yogas and mind games, the gladder I shall be."

Bardo wrapped his hand around Danlo's shoulder and fairly pulled him across the room. "Please, sit here," he said, indicating the beautiful sealskin couch opposite the fireplace. He, himself, with a sigh and a smile, eased down into an immense, padded chair that he had imported from Summerworld years ago. Although it was early morning, he had already been drinking his favorite drug: a half-empty mug of black beer sat on the chair's armrest. He leaned forward in the chair, elbows on his thighs, and the firelight reflected ruby from his shiny black beard. "We have to talk, you and I."

Danlo looked into Bardo's large brown eyes, which were bright and full of cunning, and he nodded his head. "Master Bardo, may I ask a question?"

"Please, do. And henceforth, when we're alone, you may ask your questions without first asking my permission."

"Master Bardo, what happened in the library—"

"Call me Bardo, if you please. Just Bardo. This is how your father knew me."

"My father—"

"Your father," Bardo said, again interrupting, "was Mallory Ringess. There, I acknowledge it. I knew it the first time I saw you. In Lavi Square, during your test, naked as a whore and freezing to death. You, with your wild face—everything about you, the wild manner and style of the Ringess. I thought perhaps he'd visited a courtesan once, and you were the result. I never guessed you were Katharine's child, too. I should have seen it."

Here he sighed and paused to tap a massive finger against his

308

ugly, bulging forehead. "Well, I *did* see it, with my eyes, but my stupid brain denied the truth."

"You were my father's best friend, yes?"

Bardo looked at Danlo and rubbed the huge, platelike muscles over his heart. He began to speak slowly, as if to himself, and there was bitterness in his voice. "Can one be *friends* with such a man? A man destined to become a god?"

"But you joined him on his expedition to the Devaki!" Danlo said. His mouth was dry and there was a swelling pain in his throat. "My father . . . and my mother."

"We all followed the Ringess out to that damned frozen island, it's true. To Kweitkel. We lived among the Devaki tribe for most of a year."

"The Devaki," Danlo said quietly, almost whispering. He stared down at the gleaming wooden floor tiles. "The blessed Devaki."

"Ah," Bardo said in a deep basso voice that rumbled across the room. He took a long drink of his beer. "Ah, you've heard the story of your birth, have you? From Pedar, the afternoon before he fell down the stairwell? The poor boy. Pedar showed you a foto of the expedition, isn't that so? I suppose you'll want to know the truth about your father, about our expedition. Well, it's too sad to say, but your father with his wildness and his lust made enemies among the Devaki. Your father, and your mother —your whole damn family with their murderous hearts and incestuous ways. Of course they made enemies. Ah, *we* made enemies. I, too. Yes, I admit my part in this madness. The truth is, I was more than Mallory's friend—he loved me like a brother! Once, long ago it seems, and then the damn expedition. Your father killed a Devaki man, Liam was his name, and *his* brother killed me, pushed his damn spear through my heart! And yes we made enemies, but we also made friends, and that's the hell of it, I *liked* the Devaki, and they liked me. The women, of course, Mentina and Nori and Tasarla, with their fat, long thighs, but the men, too. Haidar and Wemilo were my friends. And Choclo, especially Choclo. It's too bad, Little Fellow, that you were abandoned, but at least there was Soli to watch over you. Your grandfather, as you must know. Soli the Silent—what can you tell me about Leopold Soli, is he well?"

Danlo watched Bardo suck down the last of his beer, and he forced out, "Soli is dead."

"Dead! The great Lord Pilot, dead at last? How did he die?"

"At my passage into manhood, he ate the liver of a jew fish . . . and it poisoned him."

"That's too bad," Bardo said. With his fat red tongue, he licked beer foam from the inside of his mug. "But tell me, Little Fellow, why did Soli eat the liver? Where was Haidar—why didn't Haidar help you with your passage?"

"Haidar is dead, too."

"Oh, that's too bad—I liked Haidar."

"They are all dead."

"What?"

"Everyone is dead, Bardo. The blessed Devaki tribe."

"Dead, did you say? All of them? Choclo, too?"

"Yes."

"Dead of what?"

"A disease."

"By God!" Bardo roared as he hammered the beer mug against his chair. "They were the strongest people I've ever known! How can they all be dead?"

Shaking his head, muttering to himself, Bardo rose to his feet, and he grabbed up a pitcher of beer resting on the ledge beneath the icy windows. He poured foamy black beer into his mug, took a sip, then looked at Danlo as he licked beer from his mustache.

"A plague killed them," Danlo said. "A virus that men made." He touched the scar above his eye then, and he told Bardo what he had learned in the library about the Architects of the Cybernetic Universal Church and the plague they had created.

"Oh, too bad," Bardo said. Drops of sweat broke out across his fleshy face and tumbled down into his beard. "Too bad."

"My father infected the Devaki with this virus."

"A filthy bio-weapon!" Bardo said. He gazed out the window, up at the snowy sky. He began speaking in a low, private voice, as if he were alone in the room. "Oh, no, this is very, very bad! The worst thing I've ever heard. By God! We're all plague carriers, then? *I* am, too. Why didn't the splicers warn us that the Devaki carried no immunity? Why didn't I consider the danger? Why else was I given this fine brain, if not to consider such possibilities? And why not you, Mallory, my friend? Ah, but you were always so *reckless*. Wild and reckless—it was your god damned fate."

Bardo's eyes were now rigid and glistening. A liquid lens of tears had formed up, making his bright eyes seem even brighter.

310

intensifying the look of sadness there. With his moist red lips, liquid eyes, sweat, and belly sloshing full of beer, he seemed a most watery man. Waves of emotion flowed across his huge face: guilt, compassion, self-pity, and love, whether love only for the passion of loving, or love of others, it was difficult to know. Danlo thought that such a man would too easily feel the world's cold: at winter's first breath, he would freeze as hard as *galilka* ice and then crack into a thousand pieces.

"All the Alaloi tribes, I think, have been infected," Danlo said. He pressed his thumbs against his own eyes and felt the wetness there. He was reminded that like all men he too was made mostly of water.

"Ah, perhaps they *are* infected," Bardo said. "But we mustn't suppose they're doomed. No, that would be too, too finally bad—I can't suppose that, can I?"

"But the *shaida* virus kills everyone it touches! Everyone . . . who is innocent, everyone without an immunity."

"Well, there might be a way to provide your Alaloi with an immunity."

"Truly?"

After taking another pull at his beer, Bardo patted his rumbling belly and said, "I know little of splicing, of course. I'm a pilot. But why couldn't the suppressor genes that protect you and me and every civilized person—why couldn't this DNA be spliced into the Alaloi chromosomes?"

"Is that possible?" Danlo asked.

"By God, I hope so! It seems a simple thing. Even if we have to ferry every last Alaloi to the City splicers."

At this, Danlo rubbed his forehead in sudden worry. He thought of everything that had happened to him since coming to Neverness, and he said, "Bringing the Alaloi to the Unreal City . . . this might destroy them as a people."

"Would you rather see them all bleeding their brains out through their ears?"

Danlo looked into the fireplace, and he held his eyes open against the heat. In the dark red flames of memory, he saw the death fires burning in the Devaki cave the night that his tribe had died. "No," he said.

"Well, I suppose they could be returned to the wild once we've cured them of this stupid plague."

"But there are two hundred tribes!"

"So many? It will be difficult, then, won't it? The covenants will have to be suspended. Again."

"What . . . covenants?"

Bardo belched and smiled, and he took a sip of beer. "The Alaloi were the first people to find this planet. When the Order moved from Arcite three thousand years ago and found it occupied by bands of wild men, well, we made a covenant with them. Haven't you studied our history? We're confined to this island, to Neverness. The rest of the planet belongs to the Alaloi. Contact with them is forbidden."

"But my father . . . came to the Devaki tribe, yes?"

"Ah, that's true. But, of course, he'd petitioned the Timekeeper to suspend the covenants."

Danlo touched the white feather bound to his hair and said, "The covenants were suspended, once, and now the Devaki are dead."

"I'm sorry, Danlo."

"And you think the covenants should be suspended . . . again?"

"It's the only way. Now the Timekeeper is dead, we'll have to petition the College of Lords."

"Do you think they would grant such a petition?"

Bardo rose from his chair and stood above Danlo. He wiped the sweat from his cheek, belched, and said, "By God, they'll have to! We must undo what we've done. *I* must, you see. I, Bardo—I have friends among the lords. They'll listen to me. If there's a way to cure the Alaloi, we'll find it. I promise you this, Little Fellow."

Danlo looked up at Bardo and smiled. It is understandable that Bardo did not tell him that his influence over the Lords' College was more in the realm of wishfulness than reality. In truth, now that the death of Pedar Sadi Sanat had led directly to a warrior-poet infiltrating the library (or so some of Bardo's enemies believed), many lords were calling for Bardo to resign as Master of Novices. It is easy to forgive Bardo his misdirection and little lies. In staring too long at Danlo's dark, deep-set eyes so grave and full of hope, Bardo obviously lied out of compassion rather than pride, and who can blame him for this?

"I never guessed our little library would be such a dangerous place for novices," Bardo said. "First, you discover the source of this murderous virus, and then the warrior-poet. It was too bad for that poor librarian—what was his name? Master Smith. He's the first Orderman killed this way since that insane warrior-poet ripped through the Danladi Tower and nearly assassinated Leopold Soli fourteen years ago. It's a bad sign that the warrior-poets are active again, too bad, so very bad."

Bardo's flowery body stench and his beery breath were so overpowering that Danlo stopped his breathing for a moment. Then he said, "I am afraid for Hanuman."

"Do you fear that another warrior-poet will try to kill him? That's unlikely, now. By the laws of the poets' order, once a contract has been fulfilled, there can be no more killing. Of course, usually there is no one left alive to kill—it's unbelievable that Hanuman survived the poet. And you as well. You're as brave as your father. And twice as reckless—be careful else you'll give the gossips too much to talk about, you know."

Danlo smiled in embarrassment, then stood up and looked out the window.

"The puzzle here"—Bardo's voice boomed in his ear—"is why anyone would contract with the poets to kill Hanuman. Not only why but who?"

"You . . . do not know?"

"Do you?"

Because Danlo did not wish to discuss what had occurred in the stairwell of the library, he turned to Bardo and asked, "How could I know?"

"By God, you *still* answer my questions with more questions! Is this a trait bred into the goddamned Ringess chromosomes?"

"I am sorry."

"As Master of Novices, I must ask you certain things. The College of Lords has charged me with this duty. Of course, it's unlikely you would know what must be known, but it's possible that the poet might have said some small thing that might be of help in solving this puzzle. Few people know this—this is something your father once told me—but the poets like to talk to their victims before they kill them."

"I . . . do not want to remember what the warrior-poet said." Danlo looked down at his boots, which were now dry from the heat of the fire.

"No? You can't remember? Ah, how strange!"

"I was afraid . . . for Hanuman's life."

"But you weren't afraid for your own."

Danlo lifted his head up and looked at Bardo, but he said nothing.

"You weren't too afraid to remember the poet's goddamned poem!"

313

"How do you know . . . I remembered it?"

Bardo's cheeks puffed out for a moment, then he clapped his hands together. "How do I *know*? I shall tell you how. Do you think I haven't been to see Hanuman? Well I have. He couldn't tell me much, he could barely speak. But he remembered how you tricked the warrior-poet, how you took his place beneath the poet's knife. He admires your courage, as do I. And even more I admire your cunning. You use ahimsa as a weapon to make the poet let you recite the poem, and now the poet is dead. What irony! You defeated a warrior-poet, by God! Like your father—you must know that your father once defeated a warrior-poet, too."

Because Danlo did not want Bardo to see his eyes just then, he covered them with his hand and dropped his head. "I did not know . . . that the warrior-poet would use his knife against himself."

"Well, he did. You'd ruined his mission, and it was the only way he could fulfill his contract with the goddamned Architects."

At this, Danlo dropped his hand away from his forehead and looked up.

"Ah, this interests you, does it? Of course, it must have been the Architects who hired the warrior-poet. *Not* the harijan, as some of the stupider lords believe. Of course it's true that the harijan blame both you and Hanuman for Pedar's death. You, because of your devotion to ahimsa. You resisted his barbarities, did you not? And you did so in a way that shamed him and made him all too aware of his baseness. You antagonized him willfully, did you not? Ah, the angslan, this Fravashi game of inflicting holy pain. It's a sweet, sweet irony, but you tortured Pedar's soul more than he ever tortured you. And so you goaded him into climbing the stairs after lights out—it was almost inevitable that Pedar would drink too much wine one night and fall to his death. Or so the harijan say."

Danlo stared down at his hands for the count of twenty heartbeats. And then he asked, "But why blame Hanuman, too?"

"Well, Hanuman is your closest friend, isn't he? It's known that he antagonized Pedar whenever he had the chance."

"Then some of the lords must think that the harijan contracted with the warrior-poets . . . to murder *both* Hanuman and me?"

"Ah, and so they do. But there is a flaw in their thinking.

Much more than either you or Hanuman, the harijan blame *me* for Pedar's death. If they had hired a warrior-poet, it would have been *I* who would have had to face the goddamned knife."

This thought must have unnerved Bardo, for he suddenly rubbed his neck, belched, and lifted up his mug, and then, in three huge gulps, he drained it of beer.

"So, it must have been the Architects," Bardo said. "Since the day that Hanuman took his vows, I've known that he fled Catava before coming to Neverness. He told me that there had been trouble, that his family had made enemies with the Architect Elders. His father, apparently, died under mysterious circumstances. I suspect assassination—these bloody-minded Architects are always killing each other. I don't know *why* they would pursue Hanuman so far, so relentlessly. What could he have done? Ah, well, it doesn't matter what he's done. Our Order is as old and rotten as Lord Ciceron's stinking teeth, but it's one of our virtues that we still protect our own. Hanuman could have sold his DNA to a slel necker or even have murdered his father—it wouldn't matter once he'd crossed the Academy gates and taken his vows."

Although Bardo had spoken this last thought carelessly without innuendo or hidden meaning, Danlo held his breath as if a sudden cold wind had blasted his face. He dreaded hearing of any connection, however inadvertent, between Hanuman and the idea of murder.

"I . . . do not know why the warrior-poet was sent to Neverness," Danlo said. Indeed, the warrior-poet had never told him the true reason why the Architects had contracted to kill Hanuman. Although Danlo burned to know what this reason could be, he did not want Bardo to know of his concern. "But the warrior-poet said a thing . . . that I remember. He said there was a new rule for the warrior-poets. A new rule that is an old rule. He said the warrior-poets must kill all potential gods."

"Ah, ahhhh—aha!" Bardo rumbled. "The poet said this to you, did he? Is it true what he said? And if it is true, why should he tell *you*?"

"He asked me . . . if I was the son of my father."

"Ahhhhhh! I can't tell how this interests me. The warrior-poets had good cause to follow the career of your father. He began something, your father did. A man, a god—he pushed against the universe, and so the warrior-poets feel the heavens shake, and they fear the stars must fall. Is this why they must kill all potential gods? And what do they *mean* by this word 'potential'? Surely they can't mean they would kill all the hakras of the Cybernetic Churches—the heretics arise among the Architects like maggots out of a corpse. There must be millions of them. Surely the poet would have killed Hanuman for a reason other than his little heresies. Is there something about Hanuman I've missed? Could the poets think that Hanuman Li Tosh would try to follow your father's path? That he *could* follow it? Ah, what a thought—I can't tell you how this makes me think!''

So saying, Bardo began pacing about while he stroked his beard and muttered a series of soft, rumbling sounds. Danlo stood before the flames of the fireplace, and he too began to brood about his thoughts and his memories. He remembered perfectly what the warrior-poet had said about Hanuman murdering Pedar. And he remembered that the path of his father had been one of hubris and murder: Mallory Ringess once murdered a man called Liam, and a warrior-poet, and three pilots during the Pilot's War, and finally, fatefully, he had murdered the entire tribe of the Devaki.

"Listen," Bardo finally said to him. "It wouldn't do for us to repeat mere hypotheses as to why the warrior-poet was sent to find Hanuman. Do you understand? Perhaps it would be best if you didn't tell anyone about this 'new rule' of the warrior-poets.''

"I . . . do not want to tell anyone."

"Good. Perhaps we shall never know why the warrior-poet was sent. But here's another hypothesis: Perhaps there was no contract with the Architects, after all. Perhaps the poet came to Neverness because his masters on Qallar commanded him to do so. Perhaps the poet had calculated the events in the library to a nicety—he might have predicted that you would leave your cell and find him about to murder Hanuman. This bloody torture as a test—of *you*. Could this whole assassination merely have been staged as a test of *your* potential? Ah, Danlo, Little Fellow—*are* you the son of your goddamned father?''

With this thought Bardo looked deeply into Danlo's eyes, so deep that it seemed he was no longer looking at Danlo but at a reflection of himself.

"Ah, ah, ahhh—is it possible?" Bardo continued. "Why haven't I thought this thought before? Have I blinded myself or merely been a coward? Is it possible? Is it possible that we're all as children of your father's murderous heart, his mad, marvelous soul? By God, who *are* you? Who am I? Who is anyone? Is it possible that others might follow your father's way? I've wonlered about this every moment of every day for thirteen years. The question is, Why didn't I *know* that I wondered? Ah, but now I know—and I know that I know, by God!"

Bardo laughed his deep-bellied laugh as if he were immensely pleased with the universe and all the things it contained, not excluding himself. Then he suddenly clapped his hands and said to Danlo, "Although it's always a pleasure to talk with you, there's another reason I invited you here today. It's time I gave you what's yours."

He ambled over to the fire room's central table and kicked aside a priceless chair blocking his way. On the table sat a box inlaid with little pearl triangles and squares of shatterwood. He picked up the box, carried it over to Danlo, and dropped it into his hands.

"It is lovely," Danlo said. The box was cool and hard to the touch. He looked up at Bardo and smiled. "Thank you."

"No, no, you misunderstand," Bardo huffed out quickly. "The *box* is mine—I paid a hundred maunds for it on Urradeth! What's *inside* belonged to your father. And mother. Open it, now, what are you waiting for?"

Danlo did as he was told. The lid swung open smoothly on gold hinges, and he immediately smelled the mustiness of old leather. Inside were two books, each as thick as a snow block, and a clear stone that looked like quartz. And other things. He ran his fingers along the inside walls of the box, which were furry with black velvet. Because the box's interior was deep and dark, it was difficult to determine all its contents.

"Well?" Bardo said.

Danlo stepped over to a priceless tea table and set the box down. He lifted out one of the books, opened it, and flipped through the dry, weathered pages. His eyes were wide open as he said, "I have *seen* this before! I have touched it . . . with my fingers, once, long ago."

"What! How is that possible?"

Outside the window snow covered the glidderies and fields of Borja, and Danlo was reminded of another snowfield he had crossed long ago. The memory was faint, perhaps only a memory of a memory: once, just after his naming at his third birthday, he and Soli had sledded away from Kweitkel's shore to find an *ikalu*, a little hut of snow, flung up from the frozen sea. He had entered the hut alone. There, he had discovered the very book that he now held in his hands. Someone had taken the book away from him—he could still feel his anger at being dis-

317

possessed of it. And that was all he remembered. He, whos
memory of his life was usually so clear, could bring to mind onl
these inchoate images and emotions. Because he thought i
shameful and strange that his memory should so mysteriousl
fail him, he decided to say nothing more about it.

"Do you know what that is?" Bardo asked.

"Yes," Danlo said. "It is a book. Old Father had man
books in his house. He . . . taught me to read."

"You can *read*? Ah, I confess that I've never learned thes
barbaric arts. I wonder why the Fravashi bother."

"But it is so simple!" Danlo said. "Much simpler tha
learning to kithe ideoplasts."

"Indeed?"

"Truly . . . Bardo. Shall I teach you to read? It is a blesse
art."

"Now? Here?" Bardo's nose was as purple as a ripe blood
fruit, and he had a strange, faraway look about his eyes. He wa
a man who fell through moods as easily as he might chang
clothes to go outside on a snowy afternoon. "Perhaps som
other time—if I'm to help you with your Alaloi problem, I've
busy day ahead of me."

Danlo opened the book to its title page, and as he did sc
the leather spine crackled and creaked. Aloud, he read, *"A Re
quiem for Homo Sapiens."*

"That was the Timekeeper's book," Bardo said. "A cynic
history of the human race. Your father inherited it from him—c
stole it, perhaps."

After turning a couple of yellow pages, Danlo came to
passage that interested him:

> "Homo Sapiens as a mystery of evolution: It is both
> mysterious and miraculous that roughly the same intel-
> ligence *necessary* to flake a barbed spearpoint is *suffi-
> cient* to discover the theorems of mathematics. In a
> different universe, it might have been otherwise.
> And so human beings would have been spared the
> tragedy of existing half as ape and half as god."

He read these words to Bardo, who stood above him puf
ing out his fat cheeks.

"Ah, but the Timekeeper was a cynical man, wasn't he
Read this book at your own peril, Little Fellow."

With a smile on his lips, Danlo bowed his head, the

318

reached into the box to remove the other book. Its cover was of ancient brown leather embellished with gold scrollwork around the border. In many places, the gold had chipped or worn off.

"A collection of poems, as you see," Bardo said. "The Timekeeper once gave it to your father. As a *present*—we can be sure of that, at least."

Danlo read through the first few poems of the book and said, "I cannot understand these words. The way the letters are put together, the sounds . . . make no sense."

"Well, most of the poems are ancient," Bardo said. "Written in dead languages. Your father loved poetry—all poetry—as other men love women."

"I shall have to learn these dead languages, then, to read this book."

"If you wish. I, myself, have never had the patience."

"Thank you for giving me these books, Bardo."

"*I* have given you nothing." Bardo stood next to the window, licking the rim of his beer mug as he looked out into the snow. "I've merely held them in trust for your father, should he ever return. Now they're yours. The truth is, I'm glad to be rid of the responsibility."

Danlo watched him sadly swigging his beer, and he thought that the huge man was not really glad at all. "Thank you, anyway," he said.

"Ah, well, I've been keeping more than books. The ring, of course. And the ball. Take it out of the box, Little Fellow."

From the box Danlo removed a clear crystal ball. It was slightly larger than his fist and heavy as a stone. Indeed, it was the most perfect of stones, a scryer's sphere made of diamond without impurity or flaw.

"Oh, I think this is a blessed stone," Danlo said. "*Imakla,* like a thallow's eye."

"It belonged to your mother," Bardo said. "These spheres —the scryers make them."

"My mother . . . was a scryer, yes?"

"She was one of the finest scryers there's ever been."

Danlo held the diamond sphere up toward the window. Its polished surface was brilliant with refracted colors; as he turned it between his hands, quick bronze and violet lights sparkled like tiny fireflies caught in ice. He looked through the clarity of diamond, deep toward the sphere's center. There, all color dissolved into a shimmering whiteness that dazzled his eyes. "I have never seen anything . . . so splendid or rare," he said.

"All scryers," Bardo said, "when they take their vows—they're given these spheres. After Katharine died, your father kept it instead of returning it to the Lord Scryer, as he should have."

Because Danlo had smeared the diamond with his skin oils, he breathed over the cool stone to condense a layer of mist and then rubbed his sleeve around its surface until it shone cleanly. "Bardo," he suddenly asked, "do you know how my mother died?"

With a toss of his head and a few hard gulps, Bardo finished the last of his beer. He used a silk handkerchief to wipe his lips, and he said, "Ah, Little Fellow, she died in the Devaki cave, too bad. Giving birth to you—it was a hard birth, you see, and she lost too much blood."

Danlo was looking at Bardo as he said this. He saw the blood drain from his huge face, watched his eyes fall hard and shiny as diamonds. He knew then (or thought he knew) that this sad, passionate man could not be telling him the full truth.

"Here," Bardo said, too quickly, "take the ring, and we'll be done."

Again, Danlo reached into the box. He found the ring nestled against thick velvet, and he grasped it tightly.

"Let's see it, now," Bardo said.

Danlo withdrew his arm and opened his fist. There, in the center of his palm was a ring of black diamond. It was a pilot's ring, he knew, spun diamond stived with a unique configuration of impurities, an atomic signature written in iridium and iron that would distinguish it from all other rings. He slipped it over his little finger, but it was slightly too big.

"Your father's ring, by God! You'd better not be seen wearing it, or the other pilots will rip your finger off."

"But someday I'll be a pilot, yes?"

"We can only hope so."

"Can I wear the ring then?"

"*This* ring? No, no, Little Fellow, even if you grow into it, you may not wear it. Each pilot must have his own ring—you'll be given yours when you take your pilot's vows."

With a grunt and a sigh, Bardo pulled off one of his silver chains and eased it over Danlo's head. "But you may keep it on your person," he said. "Put the ring on the chain around your neck. There, clasp the chain like so, and keep it beneath your robes where no one will see it."

"You are a generous man," Danlo said as he tucked the

ring down into his kamelaika. The ring was cold, and he felt it pressing the skin over his breastbone. "Thank you."

"You're welcome."

"My father entrusted this ring to you before he left Neverness?"

"He did, and it was the saddest moment of my life."

"*Where* is my father, do you know?"

Bardo rubbed his eyes and sighed. "All I know is what everyone knows: Mallory Ringess left the City six years ago. Out to the stars. There's evidence that he disappeared with his ship into the nebula of the Solid State Entity. He'd prophesied once that he would join with that goddamned goddess, but I never really believed him. And now he's gone."

For a long time Danlo stared into the fire as he held his fist pressing the ring over his heart. And then he asked, "Bardo, *what* is he? Do you know what my blessed father is?"

"He's a god!" Bardo suddenly called out. "A goddamned god."

"But what does it mean . . . to be a god?"

"Only a god would know."

"Then—"

"Your father," Bardo interrupted, "was the first to remembrance the Elder Eddas. And perhaps the only one to remembrance them deeply. He looked inside himself and found the secret of life—the secrets of the gods. I believe he's found the secret of immortality. Great power, these powers of mind that the gods must love above all things."

While listening carefully, Danlo never let his eyes fall away from the fire, and he said, "To be a god must be . . . nothing but pain."

"Eh? Why do you think that?"

"I . . . do not know."

"Well, certainly your father has paid a heavy price for his godhood. He's carked his goddamned brain! Two-thirds of it has been replaced by neurologics, by these bio-computers that the Agathanians made for him when they brought him back from his death."

"But part of him is still human, yes?"

"Perhaps."

"And this human part, the man that he still is—does he exist in his body? *Of* his body? Is he a being of blood and bone, just as you or I?"

"Ah," Bardo said, "the crucial question. But the truth is, I don't know."

"But if his brain is still partly human," Danlo insisted, "if his heart beats as a man's heart, then he must exist . . . somewhere. Somewhere in spacetime."

"Perhaps."

"Then, does he still dwell in the *Immanent Carnation*? Around which star does his lightship circle?"

"How should *I* know, by God!"

"But you were his best friend!"

"I believe," Bardo said as he moved back over to the window, "I believe that he's been lost into the Entity. Absorbed, in his mind, if not body."

"My father . . . has gone over, then?"

"Not really. Ah, there's been a kind of marriage. It's a mystical notion, and I detest mysticism, but I'm coming to believe it's true."

"Why?"

Bardo rapped his rings against the windowpane and pointed up at the sky. "How else can one explain the timely appearance of the Golden Ring? I believe that it's the child of your father's mind. And of the Entity's."

Danlo looked out the window, then, and he saw that the snow had stopped. The sky was like a sodden gray blanket, heavy and too low. He thought of the Golden Ring growing like a second atmosphere far above the clouds. He vowed that if ever he became a pilot, he would journey there to see what kind of creatures and new life that his father had designed. He unzipped his kamelaika, touched the ring Bardo had given him, then asked, "Do you think the Golden Ring will shield the animals of the world from the Vild's radiation? Truly?"

"That was your father's plan—he always had a plan."

"Then the life of this world . . . will continue to live?"

"By God, I hope so, since I'm still alive on this god-frozen place!"

"Then my father has slain a people . . . and saved a world."

"Well, he was always a man of irony, your father."

Danlo pressed his knuckles against his forehead and softly recited, " '*Halla* is the way of the man who cherishes the world.' "

"Eh? *Halla*?"

"I should leave now," Danlo said. He stood up and

squeezed the diamond sphere in his hand. He was sweating, and his eyes hurt from staring too long at the sky. He thought of his father, who had once murdered Liam of the Devaki tribe and many others, and he whispered, "*Shaida* is the way of the man who kills other men."

Bardo, whose hearing had always been acute, shook his head at these words. He said, "You shouldn't judge him, Little Fellow. Even when he was a man, he wasn't like other men."

"Truly?"

"No, he was fated to become a god. I see that now." Bardo reached down to grab the empty pitcher of beer from the windowsill. He was smiling to himself now, and his moist brown eyes seemed full of memories and dreams. "I wonder what it's like to become a god?"

With his free hand, Danlo touched Bardo's sweaty forehead, and then scooped up the two old books sitting atop the tea table. He worked them up beneath his arm, and said, again, "I should leave."

"Wait! You've too much to carry—you should have at least one arm free, else you'll fall and split your face on the ice." Bardo picked up his jeweled box and handed it to Danlo. "Put the books in here. The ball, too. And keep the box, if you please."

"Thank you," Danlo said.

"Where are you going in such a hurry?"

"To the cetics' tower," Danlo said. "Perhaps Master Javier will allow me to visit Hanuman today. There is a question . . . that I must ask him."

"Ah, well, I'll send for you in a few days, then. The College of Lords will have to give us a decision about the Alaloi, and I want you to be there."

Danlo pulled his furs on and bowed. "Thank you, Bardo," he said.

He left the Sanctuary, then, and as he struck out across the slick glidderies of Borja to ask Hanuman a simple question, he was very careful not to drop the box that the Master of Novices had given him.

IN THE COLLEGE OF THE LORDS

I am not interested in things getting better; what I want is more: more human beings, more dreams, more history, more consciousness, more suffering, more joy, more disease, more agony, more rapture, more evolution, more life.

—*from the* Meditations *of Jin Zenimura*

It did not take very long for Bardo to provoke a decision from the Lords' College concerning the plight of the Alaloi people. While Hanuman remained sequestered with the cetics (during which time the master cetic still refused to let Danlo visit him), Bardo petitioned the Lords' College on behalf of Danlo and all 212 tribes of the Alaloi. As it happened, the lords were eager to dispose of this troublesome petition, just as they were fairly frantic to clear up the harijan problem and the mystery of why a warrior-poet would try to assassinate a mere novice. In truth, many of the lords were eager to dispose of Bardo altogether. These enemies of Bardo, serious men and women thrice his age, dismissed Bardo as merely a young pilot of braggadocio and bombast. Some said he was too careless (and brutal) to be Master of Novices. Nassar wi Jons, the Lord Imprimatur, had decried his sloppy inquest of Pedar's murder; quite a few others blamed him for instigating the cruel competition in which too many petitioners had died in Lavi Square. As Bardo discovered in the days after he had given Danlo his father's ring, few lords seemed worried over the fate of the Alaloi tribes. And no one wanted to suspend the covenants at a time when the whole Order was overwhelmed with more cosmic concerns.

"By God, they're fools!" Bardo said to Danlo one night when he paid a visit to Perilous Hall. "Cowards and fools—they think only of the doomed, man-cursed stars!"

He went on to admit his fear that the College of Lords might not give their petition the deep consideration it deserved. The lords of the Order, he said, were too eager to return to their debate concerning whether a second mission should be sent to the Vild.

"There's even talk of establishing a second academy within the Vild," Bardo said. "A fissioning of the Order, a legal schism to extend our power. And to prevent the Cybernetic Universal Church from exploding more goddamn stars. *Talk* is what it is, the old lords love to talk, to blather on and on. Did you know that they've been talking about this question for six years, since the First Vild Mission returned in failure? Listen to what I say, Little Fellow: You'll have grown into your manhood and taken your pilot's vows before the lords ever stop talking and act. Ah, why did your father abandon us to be run by a barbaric council? It's beyond understanding! When your father was Lord of the Order—and the Timekeeper before him!—things were *accomplished.*"

It is a sad truth that rule by council is the most inefficient and corruptible means of government. At the time Bardo petitioned to suspend the covenants, the College of Lords was a testament to the evolution of both inefficiency and corruption. Six years previously, after Mallory Ringess so unexpectedly had left the City, the lords of Neverness had been empowered to decide the Order's future. For as long as anyone could remember, the imperious, fierce, old Timekeeper had ruled the Order, and then, for a brief moment in history, so had Mallory Ringess. And so the lords had grown weary and fearful of rule by a single lord, and so they had decided that there would never be another Timekeeper or single Lord of the Order. During the year of 2942, the College of Lords—the 121 lords of the various disciplines—had tried to rule by consensus. It was a noble experiment in democracy, an attempt to reform the Order's most venerable institutions, but it had failed. Of course it had failed. The very nature of the Order, its soul and name, implies an *ordering* of each individual's passions, conceits, and dreams. Those who give themselves to the quest to discover the universe's ineffable truths, if they take vows and join with others who share a calling, must find their place within a hierarchy organized around a singular vision. If they do not, there will be chaos; in time, they will discover a hundred or a thousand individual truths that will destroy all order, pulling apart human-made structures as surely as a flock of hungry gulls dismantles a whale's corpse. So, there must be a unifying vision, and vision is the glory of a single living organism, whether woman or man, or an animal finding its way across the icefields of the world.

In truth, a council of human beings has less vision than a snowworm burrowed into a drift. The lords of the Order, in the first year of their ascendency, found themselves squabbling endlessly over rules of order, protocol, religious and political definitions, and over creationism or cybernetic gnosticism or other ideologies. The old lords never agreed about anything, or rather, the only consensus they reached was that consensus democracy could not work. And so they had reorganized. Thereafter, the College would decide all important questions by a vote of two-thirds majority; they appointed four of the most prominent lords to set agenda, to make administrative decisions, and to break deadlocks when the vote in the College was tied. These four lords—they called themselves the Tetrad—had gradually gained power. On the third day of midwinter spring in the year 2944 since the founding of Neverness, the Tetrad proposed a new canon giving themselves the authority to decide which matters were important enough to submit to the College, and to "dispose" of those that were not. Most lords, to their everlasting shame, were glad to be relieved of the petty decisions that consumed so much of their time, and they had voted to instate this canon. In the three and a half years since then, the Tetrad had deemed few matters worthy of the other lords' trouble. (The debate over the second mission to the Vild was almost the single issue the College kept to itself.) In effect, the four lords of the Tetrad had become the real rulers of the Order. Although Bardo despised the entire College of Lords as blind fools, he reserved the most acid part of his anger for the Tetrad.

"They call themselves the Tetrad," Bardo said. "*I* call them the Four Barbarians, all of them. *Especially* Chanoth Chen Ciceron. He told me the Tetrad had no power to suspend the covenants. And that's a damn lie, the Tetrad does what it damn pleases. Lord Ciceron said that only the entire Lords' College could suspend the covenants—and then he told me that the Tetrad would not burden the College with a request to make such a decision at this time! By God, these old lords gall me! They don't like to listen. Ah, but I finally gained the Lord Akashic's ear, otherwise it would too bad for us, and worse for the poor Alaloi. Nikolos the Elder—he used to be your father's friend, and mine. His powers have spoiled him, too bad, but at least he still honors friendship. He persuaded Lords Ciceron, Pall, and Vasquez to put the question to the College. They're convening on the seventy-fourth, the entire College of Lords, and so we'll have our answer then."

On the morning of the convocation, Danlo donned his uncomfortable formal clothing. The formal robe, cut all of a piece, was roomy enough below the waist, where the pantaloons billowed out to allow his legs free play for skating. But, because his body had thickened with muscle since his first days at Borja, the fine white wool pulled too tightly across his chest and shoulders. In fact, the robe was so tight that he had to ask for Madhava li Shing's help in working the zipper closed up his back.

"May I touch you?" Madhava asked in his sarcastic but friendly way. "May I touch the only novice in the history of the Order who has defeated a warrior-poet?"

Danlo smiled sadly as he put on the tight wool jacket, his cap, gloves, and fur cloak that completed his attire. He fastened the steel chains holding his cloak in place, and he said, somewhat mysteriously, "I . . . defeated no one. In the end, the warrior-poet had his triumph."

He met Bardo beneath the cold flame globes lining the steps of that square, white building called the College of Lords. The air was frigid and harsh with little sounds: ice being chipped away from stone steps, skate blades ringing, and the faraway music of children's voices. Although the clocks of the City had marked the beginning of a new day, by Danlo's reckoning it was still night. It was late in the darkest of seasons, and the deep winter sun would not rise for hours. Below them, thirty yards to the north, the shih grove's 112 trees glittered silver under the intense starlight.

"Ah, Danlo, there you are!" Bardo called out. "Listen, there's something I should warn you about. A few nights ago, I drank too much beer, as I sometimes do. There is the slightest possibility that I *might* have told the story of you defeating the warrior-poet to certain persons of low character who can't keep secrets. Perhaps they told their friends. You should prepare yourself for questions—I think there'll be many gossips who'll want to know how you remembered that goddamned poem. Ah, why is it my fate to always be making legends of *other* people?"

Danlo smiled at him and said, "Thank you for warning me."

Bardo snorted and stamped his huge boots against the white granite steps. "By God, Little Fellow, it's cold! Let's go inside and drink coffee while we wait—likely the lords will keep us waiting all day before they blather their way to a decision."

Bardo was dressed brilliantly, in black sable and gold, but his furs stank of spilled beer. His breath was yeasty with alcoholic vapors, his eyes bleary and red as if he'd been drinking all night. Up the steps he plodded, and at every fourth or fifth step, he let loose a resounding belch. Twice he farted, loudly. Danlo, who was beginning to wonder how this huge buffoon of a man could help save the Alaloi people when he couldn't even save himself from stupefaction, followed close behind. He was afraid that Bardo momentarily would stumble and break open his head. Bardo, though, was used to drinking great quantities of his beer drug, and he kept his feet. In his great, booming voice he called out for the College doors to be opened, and the doors were opened. A novice dressed in formal robes met them at the top of the steps. He bowed to Bardo, nodded at Danlo, and he led them through the doorway, down a long drafty hall, and into an anteroom off the main council chamber. There they found a blue pot of coffee and two blue mugs set out atop a plain wooden table. There was no other furniture, nor rugs, nor decoration of any sort in the plain, cold room.

"By God, this is an insult!" Bardo huffed out. He poured coffee into the mugs and, with an unsteady hand, held one of them out to Danlo. "I should call for chairs—do they expect us to sit on stone? Or keep us standing all day?"

As it happened, the lords did not keep them waiting all day; although it might have been better if they had. If Bardo's bodily tissues had been allowed more time to metabolize the beer poisoning his brain, he might have knelt before the Lords' College with clear eyes and tight lips, and the future of the Order and Neverness might have unfolded in a very different way. *If*— the subtlest of all words. As the scryers teach, though, ifness is an illusion. Or rather, it is our belief in pure chance that is illusory. According to the ancient metaphor, the events of one's life, each of the billion billion "ifs" and moments of possibility are like water molecules tumbling along a river. However chaotic the little whorls and eddies may seem, the river itself flows in only one direction, toward the sea. As with life: whatever has happened *will* have happened, the scryers say. And so, in the deepest sense, Bardo chose his own future and drew it forth roaring into reality by the force of his will alone.

Before either of them had finished their first coffee, the novice returned and said, "It's time; the College will decide your petition now. Master Pilot, Wild Danlo, if you please, come with me."

The novice crossed the room and slid open the rear door. Danlo followed him and Bardo out into the main council chamber. All at once, as when stepping from a cave into the open, Danlo was overwhelmed by new sensations: there was light everywhere, streaming in cold colors from the flame globes, filling the huge chamber with reflected reds and blues and golds. The circular walls were polished white granite; high above him, where the chaotic noises of the room bounced around and fell through the open spaces, a great clary dome let in the starlight. There was a coldness in the air, emanating in waves off the black floor stones, and Danlo thought of the chamber as a very inhuman place, even though many people were waiting for him there. The lords of the Order—there were 110 gathered there that day—sat behind tables of glistening jewood. The crescent-shaped tables were arrayed in concentric half circles around the far side of the chamber; four or five lords shared each table. As Danlo made his way nearer, the eyes of each lord fell upon him. He heard many voices, the muffled rush of a hundred breaths, and there was a gradual silence. The novice invited Bardo and him to kneel on a square Fravashi carpet in the chamber's very center. The lords were close all around him, close enough that he could see their black or brown or blue eyes staring down from their stern faces. Many of the lords were ancient, some of them with their second or third remade bodies. He smelled the sickly sweet decay of oldness and the pungent hormone perfumes concocted to neutralize and mask the stench. The jewood tables reeked of lemon oil polish. So powerful were these smells —and Bardo's beery aroma and his own acrid sweat—that he scarcely heard the novice announce them: "My lords, the Master Pilot and Master of Novices, Pesheval Lal, called Bardo, and the novice, Danlo wi Soli Ringess."

At the center table, directly in front of Danlo and aligned facing the chamber's great double doors, sat the four lords known as the Tetrad. One of them, a tall, thin, delicate man with cropped hair and black teeth, looked straight at Danlo. He was

Chanoth Chen Ciceron, the Lord Pilot, and he said: "Danlo wi Soli Ringess, we are pleased you could join us today. Even though Master Lal has approached us on your behalf, since you are in fact the primary petitioner, the College will direct its remarks to yourself. Is this agreeable to you, Young Novice?"

Danlo looked at Lord Ciceron's soft face, and he thought of what Bardo had said about him: that here was a man, the oldest of all the pilots, who lied out of habit as easily as a boy squashes flies, who was often devious without being clever, voluble but rarely speaking what others thought of as the truth.

He was also, for all his years, an impatient man. When Danlo did not respond immediately, he repeated, "Young Novice, is this agreeable to you?"

"Yes," Danlo finally said.

"Excellent."

"Well, Lord Pilot," Bardo's voice boomed out, "it's not agreeable to me! What am I, a lump of stone to bounce your words off? The Alaloi have been infected by a filthy virus; I'm *involved* in their fate, by God!"

He knelt there sweating and glowering at Chanoth Chen Ciceron. He did not explain that he, Bardo the Bull, who was famous as a rakehell and swiver of women, had infected many of the young Alaloi women with his semen, if not with the plague virus itself.

Lord Ciceron turned and nodded to the other lords of the Tetrad. On his right sat the Lord Ecologist, Mariam Erendira Vasquez, and Nikolos the Elder. Nikolos was a plump, quiet man whose natural tendency toward timidity was balanced, in times of crisis, by a staunchness and a steely will to action. He was famous for helping to organize the schism that had led to the Pilot's War and the Timekeeper's downfall thirteen years previously. Of the four lords of the Tetrad, he was the most respected, the most well liked. And Audric Pall, the Lord Cetic, sitting at Lord Ciceron's left, was the most feared. Lord Pall suffered from the rare genetic malady of albinoism; his skin and hair were the color of bleached bone, and his eyes were pink, as if the irises had been smeared with a mixture of milk and blood. He was very old. Now that the Timekeeper was dead, he claimed to be the oldest person in the City. He exchanged glances with Lord Ciceron and made an intricate sign with his gnarled fingers. Lord Pall never uttered a word. He was well known for communicating only in signs, or in the secret facial language of the cetics. Some said that he had been born a mute;

others—and these were mostly his students—held that he merely had lost the habit of speaking and his vocal cords had withered from neglect and nonuse. Danlo knelt on the carpet and stared up at this horrible old man; he thought Lord Pall must be possessed of sublime and corrupt inner powers, truly a man of *shaida*: cynical, jaded, brilliant, and barely human.

Lord Ciceron rapped his pilot's ring against the table and spoke to Bardo. "Lord Pall reminds us, Master Pilot, that much as we all desire to be enlightened by your opinions, you may not speak here unless a question is directed at you. Is this agreeable to you?"

"As agreeable as drinking piss," Bardo muttered.

"*What* did I hear you say?"

Danlo, kneeling straight-spined on his carpet, looked back and forth between Lord Ciceron and Bardo. He knew that there had been enmity between the two men even before they had taken opposite sides in the Pilot's War. During Bardo's journeyman years at Resa, Lord Ciceron had been the harshest and cruelest of all Bardo's tutors. Then, too, Lord Ciceron's elevation to the lordship of the pilots still obviously rankled Bardo—everyone knew that he had coveted that highest of ranks for himself and resented everything about Chanoth Chen Ciceron. Bardo's cheeks were puffed out, his face flushed purple from his drinking too much beer. He glared at Lord Ciceron, then called out, "How should *I* know what you heard me say?"

This belligerence of Bardo's did not make a good impression on the Tetrad, nor on the rest of the lords. They sat at their tables, shaking their heads and whispering to one another. Kolenya Mor, the Lord Eschatologist, and Jonath Parsons, Rodrigo Diaz, Mahivira Netis, and Burgos Harsha, with his serious, glass-pocked face—the greatest lords of the Order admonished Bardo with their disapproving countenances. They looked down at Danlo as if they pitied anyone whose fate was interwoven with such a rude man.

"Master Pilot," Chanoth Chen Ciceron said to Bardo, "is it wise to insult those from whom you beg such extraordinary favors?"

Bardo turned to Danlo and laid his heavy arm across his shoulders. He tilted his head until it touched Danlo's. All the lords, as Danlo was keenly aware, were watching the two of them. Although he could scarcely breathe and he wanted to push Bardo away, he held himself rigid, in the posture of formal politeness. And then he heard Bardo whisper, "Piss on him! Ah, but this Lord Ciceron is a man of lies and pretensions: he pretends that our actions, our words or demeanor, can still sway the College. Well, look at their faces, Little Fellow! You don't have to be a cetic to see that the old bones have already made their decision, too bad."

Danlo looked up at the lords, resplendent in their formal robes of amber, indigo, gray, and a hundred other colors. Their faces, he saw, were indeed hard with resolve and decision.

"Master Pilot, you may not speak to the boy—is this understood? If you can't restrain yourself, you'll be removed from this convocation."

At this, Bardo let loose a belch and glowered at Lord Ciceron, but for the moment he kept his silence.

"And now," Chanoth Chen Ciceron said, "we invite Lord Vasquez to address the petitioners."

Sitting next to Lord Ciceron, the fourth lord of the Tetrad, Mariam Erendira Vasquez, smoothed out the folds of her viridian robe. She had a square, cheerful face and a reputation for clear thinking and pragmatism. She smiled at Danlo, and he liked her immediately, even though her first words discouraged him: "Danlo wi Soli Ringess, we are sorry to say that your petition to the Lords' College to suspend the eighth covenant has been made with false assumptions and false hopes. Before we vote your petition, yes or no, we must explicate the nature of this falsity."

In her clear, cold voice, Lord Vasquez spoke of the War of the Faces and of the plague virus that the Architects of the Old Cybernetic Church—with the help of the warrior-poets—had designed to murder their enemies. She kneaded her small, square hands together and half turned in her chair, addressing the lords of the College, as well as Danlo. She described the way in which the virus DNA had embroidered itself into its victims' chromosomes, becoming, inevitably, a part of every civilized person's genetic inheritance. "The virus can be thought of as a genetic disease that has remained dormant in most human beings for nearly a thousand years. And now, unfortunately, the tribes of pseudo-primitives known as the Alaloi most probably have been infected with the plague virus. A virus which, in them, is nondormant. This is a disaster for these people because this is a disease that has no cure."

A disease that has no cure—Danlo silently repeated this phrase to himself, and his fists were clenched, and his collar was suddenly too tight against his throat. Listening to the Lord Ecologist speak of the Alaloi's certain death concentrated and intensified his awareness: he heard the wind driving ice particles against the dome, while nearer to him Bardo grunted in anger and Chanoth Chen Ciceron sucked at his blackened teeth and sighed. Many of the lords were sighing; many of them were facing Danlo, eye to eye, and their eyes were hard with pity. All around him, the cracked granite walls and pillars bespoke the rigidity of an Order which, across the millennia, had made too many hard decisions. Lord Vasquez's clear voice echoed off the walls: "A disease that has no cure." Danlo closed his eyes then, and he remembered one of the hardest sayings of his tribe: *Tianasa daivam*—love your fate. For the first time he reflected how strange it was that the word *anasa,* as the Alaloi used it, could mean either to love or to suffer.

"Danlo wi Soli Ringess."

Danlo opened his eyes and looked up, aware that Lord Vasquez was addressing him. "Yes?" he said.

"Do you understand that a cure for this disease has never been found?"

"I understand . . . but I do not *understand.*"

"How may I enlighten you?"

"The imprimaturs," Danlo said, "ages ago, they sequenced the entire human genome, yes?"

"This is true, Young Novice."

"Then why isn't it possible to identify and cut out the virus segments of DNA? And if each . . . civilized person has inherited genes that suppress this DNA, why can't these genes be spliced into the Alaloi people?"

Lord Vasquez twisted the wool of her bright green robe between her hands and said, "You speak as if engineering were a simple thing. It's not—it's hideously complex. You must understand that in general there is no one-to-one mapping of a gene with a specific structure or function within the organism."

"In truth?"

"Consider," Lord Vasquez said, "an imago used in the planning and construction of a building. Each point of light, each stone, archway, or spire that you can see looking at the hologram or simulation, each of these images represents, in a one-to-one manner, the exact structure to be expressed in the completed building. But DNA is not like a building imago."

Danlo waited a few moments for her to continue, then asked, "What is it like?"

"It's more like a recipe for baking a cake. A set of instructions, Young Novice. Millions of simultaneous instructions. If the DNA code—the instructions—is expressed in the proper manner, an organism is constructed. *Do* you understand? So few people do. So many think it's an easy thing to engineer for an extra thumb or purple eyes. But it's hideously difficult. Could you bake a cake in the shape of a cathedral merely by adding extra flour or deleting eggs from the batter while raising the heat of the oven? No, of course not, and sometimes it's impossible to engineer one's genetic inheritance in the desired manner."

Lord Vasquez went on to explicate the complexity of the plague virus. It was theorized, she said, that the virus DNA had stitched itself into at least five of the twenty-three human chromosomes, in certain loci actually replacing exons, the working genes vital to life. The virus was a duplicitous kind of DNA: at times, when suppressor genes kept parts of it turned off, it coded for the production of proteins necessary for all bodily metabolism. At other times, it produced—reproduced—the viral elements that had killed the Devaki tribe. Cutting the virus out of the genome likely would kill anyone so engineered, that is, assuming the virus DNA could be identified and edited. In fact, it could not be. In fact, there was much about the function and interactions of the three billion nucleotides of the human genome that remained unknown. It was unknown, for instance, exactly which genes suppressed the virus. The imprimaturs theorized that certain of the genome's introns—the so-called nonsense genes separating the exons—might code for vital functions. These fossil genes, after lying dormant and useless for thousands (or even millions) of years, sometimes could come suddenly alive and suppress the viral genes. No one knew what quickened these suppressor genes. The environment in which they either thrived or failed was one of chaos, the chemicals of life that existed in a delicate, dynamic imbalance.

"Consider the human organism as an ecology," Mariam Endira Vasquez, the Lord Ecologist, said to Danlo. "Consider what happens to an ecosystem when its predators are destroyed —disaster. Similarly, it's often impossible to cut out unwanted genes without harming the organism."

Danlo touched the white feather in his hair. Although he immediately saw Lord Vasquez's point, he said stubbornly, "But predators do not slay all of their prey animals, else they would then starve. The plague virus is a disease . . . that will slay all the Alaloi."

"But not all human beings."

"You have already made your decision, then." Danlo looked up at the lords of Neverness sitting above him. Their faces were stony and hard, much like the countenances carved into the statues of the Order's most famous lords that stood in a grim circle around the walls of the chamber. "Have you ever *seen* anyone die . . . of the slow evil?" he asked.

Lord Vasquez evaded his question, saying, "It's a disaster for your Alaloi, but it is not an arbitrary disaster. It's well known that the ancestors of the Alaloi carked their chromosomes. No doubt they engineered out certain unwanted introns. It's possible they cut out segments of the suppressor DNA by mistake. Certainly they altered the ecology of their bodies—and doomed themselves to die of this plague."

Danlo held his fingers against the scar on his forehead. "*Mi pela lalashu,* the . . . blessed people, doomed."

"It's what comes of degrading or editing a cell's information," Lord Vasquez said.

"*Shantih,*" Danlo whispered.

"The Order's splicers," Lord Vasquez said, "were not able to cure the disease at the time of the plague a thousand years ago. Nor since then. Nor the engineers of Urradeth. Even the Agathanians, according to our librarians, have pronounced it incurable. Can you understand this?"

"Yes," Danlo said. And then, after considering that the Agathanians, in their mastery of biological engineering, were like gods, he intoned, "*Ti-anasa daivam.*"

Lord Vasquez forced a smile and asked, "What does this mean?"

"It means 'Suffer your fate.' You must love what you suffer."

"I'm sorry, Young Novice," Lord Vasquez said in her kindly, if officious, way. "But there can be only one fate for your Alaloi. Can you accept this?"

"No."

"We know it's difficult, Young Novice."

Danlo was aware of Bardo breathing heavily next to him, staring at him, obviously intent on his every word. "It is true we must love our fate," Danlo said. "Only . . . no one knows his fate until his life is lived."

"The scryers would dispute this belief."

"Fate," Danlo said softly. And then, "A disease that has no cure. But . . . how can we *know* this?"

Just then Lord Pall flashed Danlo a keen look and turned to

Lord Nikolos. His ancient fingers began writhing like worms. Perhaps only a third or a fourth of the other lords understood the cetics' sign language. Those who did not watched Lord Pall's precise motions with looks of annoyance and boredom coloring their faces.

"Lord Pall," Nikolos said, interpreting for the Lord Cetic, "would remind our young novice that, of course, we can't absolutely know of the impossibility of a cure for this disease."

And then Lord Ciceron added in his silky, insincere voice, "We can, however, calculate the cost of the Order of a quest for a cure. We can weigh the benefits and chances of success—which are almost nil—against this cost."

"Calculate!" a great voice suddenly boomed out. Bardo pounded his fist against his knee and glared at Lord Ciceron. "Costs! Benefits! What are we, barbaric merchants who put a price on even the most priceless of things?"

"Be silent!" Lord Ciceron ordered. "I shall not tell you this again."

"Ah," Bardo said. He looked down at the pilot's ring glistening darkly against his finger. He fell into silence then, a silence as dark and fearsome as deep space.

Lord Ciceron turned away from Bardo and looked at the other lords. He said, "The cost to the Order in calling such a quest would be very great. We should consider this as we vote."

So saying, Lord Ciceron called for the College of Lords to decide Danlo's petition. Danlo was not surprised to see that only three lords raised their hands in favor of trying to cure the plague virus. All the others voted "no."

"We're sorry our decision must be thus," Lord Ciceron said to Danlo. "But perhaps your Alaloi will still survive. It may be many years—or, we sincerely pray, never—before this unpredictable virus explodes into its active state."

"Ah," Bardo whispered to himself, "ah, *do* you really care?"

Lord Ciceron took no notice of Bardo, but instead smiled weakly in Danlo's direction. "And now there is one more matter to dispose of before you are dismissed. We all know that there are questions that the Master of Novices should have asked concerning the death of the novice Pedar Sadi Sanat. We would like to ask you these questions now, Young Novice. If your answers are satisfactory, it may be that we won't have to call for an akashic's inquest. Is this agreeable to you?"

Danlo looked quickly at Bardo, then said, "Yes . . . it is agreeable."

"Very well," Lord Ciceron said. He dropped his voice and turned to consult with the three other lords of the Tetrad for a moment. "Then I shall ask you the first questions."

While Lord Ciceron cleared his throat to ask his questions, Lord Pall turned his head to look at Danlo. He stared at Danlo intensely, and Danlo remembered that the cetics supposedly could read the truth or falsity of a man's utterances in the way he said his words. He remembered, too, that during one endless, unforgettable moment in the library the warrior-poet had claimed to read the truth from Hanuman's tortured face.

"I must ask the young novice," Lord Ciceron said, "if Hanuman li Tosh ever threatened the novice Pedar's life?"

Danlo closed his eyes for a moment, then said, "No."

"Did you ever threaten to kill Pedar?"

"No."

"Did *you* kill Pedar?"

As Danlo drew in a breath of air, he could almost feel Lord Pall's eyes burning like lasers into his face. All the lords of the College of Lords, he saw, were looking at him, too.

"Did you cause Pedar Sadi Sanat to fall from the stairs?" Lord Ciceron repeated.

"I . . . may have," Danlo said.

From a hundred of the lords, almost at once, there was a lowing sound and a low hiss of voices, men and women shaking their heads. Next to Danlo, still kneeling on their carpet, Bardo looked at him in disbelief.

"Please tell us how you killed him."

"I . . . imagined him dead."

"What?"

"With the eye of my mind," Danlo said, "I saw him dead upon the stairs."

Lord Ciceron waved his hand in annoyance. "But did you push Pedar? Did you serve him any food or drink that day? Did you dissolve any drug in his wine?"

"No."

"Did you *physically* cause him to fall from the stairs?"

"I wished him harm. I wished him to die. I . . . willed this to happen."

"And that is *all*?"

"Isn't that enough?"

Lord Ciceron traded glances with Lord Pall. Danlo saw

Lord Pall lift his index finger, slightly. Lord Ciceron sucked at his blackened teeth and said, "Anyone who had to submit to a boy such as Pedar might have imagined his death. We do not blame you for thinking what you thought. We can see that you are not to blame for what happened to Pedar."

"Ah," Bardo muttered softly, "this is really enough."

Apparently Lord Ciceron did not hear him say this, for he pointed his skinny finger at Danlo and continued, "At least, we cannot blame you for *causing* his death directly. But is it possible that someone else might have caused his death on your behalf? Are you listening, Young Novice? Is it possible that Hanuman li Tosh killed Pedar?"

"No," Danlo said. "I cannot believe . . . that he did."

And then Danlo looked up at the starlit dome above him, and he became aware of a deeper thought: *I will not believe this of Hanuman.*

"But what is it that you *know,* Young Novice? Do you know if he killed Pedar?"

Danlo was silent for a moment, and then he said, "No."

"But do you know if Hanuman li Tosh was in his bed when—"

"By God, this is too much!" Bardo suddenly cried out. He struggled to his feet, and his face was full of blood and rage. He shook his huge fist at Lord Ciceron. "Too goddamned much! You've asked him enough questions—isn't it enough you've condemned his people to die? What's wrong with you? You're the filthy murderer, not he!"

"Be silent!" Lord Ciceron ordered. He pointed a long finger at Bardo. "Kneel down, Pilot!"

"*You* be silent," Bardo said, "or I'll slap your face until your lips swell shut."

"*What* did you say?"

"Your face, be silent."

"My face!"

Bardo stood drunkenly on his massive legs and bellowed, "You have the face of a barbaric merchant-pilot, not of a pilot of the Order!"

"I'm the *Lord* Pilot of the Order, and you've taken a vow of obedience!"

"By God, *I* should have been Lord Pilot, not you! Then I'd be reminding you that it's a pilot's duty and glory to seek impossible things, even such as a cure for this damned virus."

"If you don't kneel immediately—"

"And I'd remind you that a Lord Pilot is to be an exemplar and teacher of novices, not their inquisitor."

Lord Ciceron's hand and finger were now trembling, whether from fear or anger, Danlo couldn't tell. His smooth old voice, then, grew calm and full of deceit; it seemed he was trying to provoke Bardo to some disastrous action. "But I'm the Lord Pilot, after all, and you are Master of Novices. I believe that the elevation—or the debasement—of the Master of Novices can fairly be called an administrative decision, and lies thus well within the duties of the Tetrad." He bowed to the other three lords sitting at his table and smiled.

"Ah, but Mallory Ringess, before he left Neverness, made *me,* Bardo, Master of Novices. The Ringess, himself, did this."

"And we four lords," Chanoth Chen Ciceron said, "may unmake the more foolish of his elevations. Your friend betrayed you when he raised you to a position beyond your abilities. And then betrayed the Order by leaving the City and leaving you to brutalize the novices."

"By God, I think I *will* slap your face!"

Bardo made a move toward Lord Ciceron, but just then Danlo, still kneeling rigidly, reached out and grabbed Bardo's wrist. He clenched his fingers as he would around a spear shaft, feeling the power of the great, swollen muscles running along Bardo's forearm. Although Danlo was very strong, with hands hardened by a lifetime of work outside in the cold, he was not quite a fully grown man, and he could feel that Bardo easily could have broken away. Something in his grip, however, must have restrained Bardo. He looked down at Danlo, belched, and then smiled. "Please let go," he said softly.

It must have been clear to most of the lords that Bardo, purple-faced and bellowing like a muskox, posed an immediate physical threat to their persons. One of them, the Lord Imprimatur, sent the novice to summon the roving journeymen who policed the Academy. Other lords—and Chanoth Chen Ciceron was one of these—shrank back in their chairs and tried not to look Bardo eye to eye. In truth, it was the duty of all lords present to rise up and swarm Bardo, to subdue, restrain, and chastise him for breaking his vow of obedience. This was the way of the Order. All of the lords, in their time as journeymen, had enforced the Order's canons and codes. It remained their duty to do so, but many of the lords were old, and it had been many years since they had touched another human being in violence. Only Lord Vasquez and Lord Nikolos, of the Tetrad, arose from their chairs to discipline Bardo. Rodrigo Diaz and a few other lords joined them, but all the others remained at their places.

"Wait," Chanoth Chen Ciceron said. He had finally gathered up his courage. He stood and pushed his way to the front of the lords as they advanced on Bardo.

"Ah, piss on you," Bardo muttered.

"*You* are no longer Master of Novices!" Lord Ciceron shouted.

"Piss on you!" Bardo roared out. And then he did an astonishing thing, unprecedented in all the Order's astonishing three-thousand-year history. He pulled loose from Danlo and opened the zipper at the front of his pantaloons. He removed his membrum. It was a huge tube of flesh, truly the longest and thickest membrum Danlo had ever seen attached to the loins of a human being. It was half-engorged and purple, like the membrum of a shagshay bull. In his huge fingers Bardo held this astonishing-looking appendage as he began to piss on the floor. Then he aimed the dark yellow stream at Chanoth Chen Ciceron and laughed as the Lord Pilot jumped back, nearly tripping over his own legs. Bardo whipped the stream of his piss back and forth in zigzags, keeping the other lords at bay, and for a long time he continued to laugh his deep-bellied laugh. That night he had drunk much beer and was as full of water as an ocean. Danlo marveled at the huge man's capaciousness. He watched as Bardo's piss flowed in rivulets over the black floor tiles and began discoloring the Fravashi carpet. The piss was deep amber, almost orange, and it stank of sugars and goatroot. Even though Danlo saw it would only be a matter of moments—or ounces—before the piss soaked through the carpet beneath his knees, he remained kneeling politely.

"Stand back now!" Bardo called out to the lords. "Stay away!"

Despite the utter ludicrousness of the moment—perhaps because of its absurdity—Danlo couldn't help thinking of how his near-brothers and near-sisters of the Devaki had lost their bladder tone and tightness in the time before death. His eyes burned with tears, and he watched Bardo waggle his membrum back and forth, and suddenly he was laughing, simultaneously laughing and weeping at the fundamental absurdity of life.

"By God, I'm almost done!" Bardo said. "Stand back, there's no need any longer for you to chastise me, I'm done, do you understand? Done with you barbarians and old fools, done with the Order."

His words fell like thunder through the chamber. For a moment nobody moved. Then Bardo, neglecting to shake himself dry, zipped up the pantaloons of his robe and pulled the great black ring off his end finger. He held up his pilot's ring for everyone to see. "With this ring, eighteen years ago, I took my pilot's vows. I now abjure them. Piss on the Order! Piss on all of you!"

So saying, he drew back his arm, and with terrific force hurled the ring against a nearby pillar. The ring, made of diamond and stived with a unique signature of flaws, shattered. The sound of it breaking into pieces was terrible to hear. Danlo stared at the diamond shards glittering darkly against the black floor; he had always thought that the splendid pilots' rings were unbreakable.

"Farewell." Bardo smiled at Danlo, reached down, and laid his hand atop his head. Then he bowed to the lords, turned, and, with surprising grace considering his huge mass and drunken state, sashayed across the chamber and out the double doors.

Soon after this, Chanoth Chen Ciceron restored the convocation to order. He called for novices to clean up Bardo's strong-smelling emission. A new carpet was brought for Danlo to kneel on, and the stunned lords returned to their seats. And then, for a brief time, they continued to question Danlo. They asked him if he had ever heard Hanuman blaspheme against the god of the Architects, Nikolos Daru Ede; they asked him about Hanuman's reasons for coming to Neverness, and in slightly awestruck voices, they asked him why (and how) he had taken Hanuman's place as a would-be sufferer of the warrior-poet's tortures. When he was done speaking, the lords conferred among themselves. Danlo knelt on his carpet listening as Lord Kutikoff proposed banishing all warrior-poets from the City, or at least forbidding any more of them to immigrate. Then Lord Vasquez observed that they should be glad that Bardo had abandoned the Order; his self-banishment, she said, should satisfy the harijan elders and put an end to the problems created when Pedar had taken his unfortunate—and accidental—fall. And as for Hanuman li Tosh, the lords absolved him of all blame.

"We are sorry," Lord Ciceron said to Danlo. "We are sorry that the cold light of suspicion fell upon you and Hanuman. But obviously, Pedar's fall was as it seemed—a tragic accident. Obviously, neither you nor Hanuman are murderers. You are both fine young novices, and your courage in facing the warrior-poet was outstanding. We shall be happy to welcome you as pilots when the day comes that you take your vows."

So ended the "harijan problem" and the minor concerns of the lords of Neverness. Danlo was dismissed then, and he left the Lords' College the same way he had entered it. When he moved out into the frigid morning air, he immediately saw Bardo leaning against a cold flame column at the bottom of the steps. Although the Academy buildings were golden in the day's first light, the flame globes were still afire, bathing Bardo in soft colors. His face shone with indigo, violet, and puce; his hand was thrown over his eye, and the band of skin around his finger, where his pilot's ring used to be, gleamed like phosphorescent ivory. As Danlo descended the steps, he heard the huge, sad man addressing himself: "Ah, Bardo, what have you done? It's over now, it *is* done, too bad."

"Are you all right?" Danlo called out. At the sound of his voice, Bardo started and looked up at him. "Bardo, Bardo—I am sorry."

"Little Fellow, *I'm* sorry, I've failed you. But did you see the faces of those old lords? They won't forget this day, not even if they live three more lifetimes."

"I will not forget . . . either," Danlo said, and he drew up close to Bardo.

"Nor I. The last day of Bardo's life in which he tasted beer."

"What?"

"I, Bardo—after today, I'll never drink beer again, I promise you, Little Fellow. When I'm old, I'll look back on this day and say, 'Here lies the great divide of my life.' Before, Bardo was weak, a coward and a drunkard. And afterward—ever after, I promise—a man of purpose, truth, and fate."

"But what will you do?"

"What will I *do*? What will I *not* do. I will do something extreme. Something outrageous which will one day be called great. Ah, Little Fellow, as I look into your flawless eyes, even as I stand here blathering away, an idea is coming into this great, fat brain of mine. I will do something which will make all the lords of the Order wake up and say, 'We should have seen Bardo for what he truly is and listened to him when we had the chance.' "

"Will you leave Neverness?"

"Perhaps. Perhaps not. Let us not discuss what *I* will do. The question of the moment is, What will *you* do?"

Danlo looked off into the shih grove below him. In the morning wind, the pretty silver trees were rippling like water. "I should leave the Order, too," he said.

"No, no, that is precisely what you must *not* do."

"Why not?"

"You must become a pilot. Your father, before you, was a pilot, and you must be, too."

"Why?"

"Because there will be a second mission to the Vild. Someday. It will take five or ten years to organize, but there will be a mission. Ah, a great mission to the Architects of the Old Church. It was the goddamned Architects who created the plague, and it's said they know of a cure."

The sky above Danlo was a blue-black dome, but in the east, where the sun was now rising, the ridge lines of the mountains glowed a deep crimson. He whispered a silent prayer to the sun, and then asked, "Truly? A cure . . . how do you know this?"

Bardo belched, let out a huff of steam, and then thrust his hands beneath his armpits to keep them warm. He said, "Once, when I was a young pilot, when the Timekeeper called *his* quest, I journeyed to Ksandaria. It's a dull, unenlightened place, devoid of skilled women, good food or beer, but the Ksandarian encyclopaedists keep the best library in the Civilized Worlds. And I penetrated it! Deep, deep, Little Fellow, deep into their inner sanctum where they keep their forbidden pools of knowledge. By happenstance—by pure good luck, as I admit—I learned almost everything there is to know about ancient religions and secret orders. And cults, sects, and bizarre theologies. Ah, you wouldn't believe the lunacies people believe. So many, so many. And while I admit that I have my failings, a poor memory is not an affliction I suffer. And the things I remember! I remember kithing a secret deposition made by a man named Sharanth Li Chu who was an underling of Edmond Jaspari. You've heard of Jaspari, this so-called God's Architect of the Cybernetic Universal Church? The high priest of the goddamned Architects. Well, as I was saying, Li Chu deposed that Edmond Jaspari ordered the engineering of the plague virus. This was in 1750, Neverness time, during the second year of the War of the Faces. The Old Church was losing the war, and the

Architects were desperate. And so they solicited the warrior-poets to create the god-cursed virus. But it mutated, of course, and nearly obliterated the Old Church—along with three quarters of humanity. Everyone knows this. It was Li Chu's claim, however, that Jaspari's engineers designed an inhibiting drug that could keep the virus dormant. The drug—if one believes Li Chu—was given to every surviving Architect. It enabled them to live, even though few of them would have inherited the so-called suppressor genes that protect the rest of us. Think of the Architects of the Old Church as a population as genetically distinct—and vulnerable—as the Alaloi. It's probable that they still must use this drug, to this day."

As Bardo's basso voice died into the deeper sounds of the morning, Danlo did a curious thing. With his wrists together, fingers closed and pointing downward, he raised his arms toward the sky. He bowed his head to the sun. Then, having completed this most basic of daily Alaloi rituals, he jumped up three steps, smiled, and jumped down again. And then back up. "But, Bardo, if you knew . . . this history, why didn't you tell the lords?"

"There are three reasons," Bardo said. "Firstly, it will be at least five years before the Vild mission is organized, another five before the first pilots return to Neverness. The Alaloi—I am loath to have to say this—could well be dead before then. Secondly, the Order, as I conceive it, as I *used* to conceive it, when I cared, the Order shouldn't have to go begging the barbaric Architects for a cure to this disease when it's possible our splicers could duplicate Jaspari's inhibiting drug. And thirdly, well . . ."

"Yes?"

"The third reason I kept this from the stupid lords is that they wouldn't have believed me. *I*, who have told untruths only once or twice in my life. Chanoth Chen Ciceron in his slippery way would have called me a liar. And then what would be left for me to do? Murder? Could I have killed him, as I should have done in the war when I had the chance? No, no, that's impossible, I couldn't even slap his barbaric old face, too bad."

For a long time Bardo talked to Danlo, persuading him that if he wanted to help the Alaloi, he should become a pilot, and hence be selected for the second mission to the Vild. "It will be your best chance," Bardo said. "The Order, I think, will divide in two, and the best pilots will go to the Vild. Maybe I'll build a lightship and go, too."

Danlo kicked at the icy steps and said, "I am sorry . . . I have caused you much sorrow."

"*You?* No, no, it's not your fault. I was finished as Master of Novices before we ever entered the Lords' College. Lord Ciceron has been waiting years for this chance."

"I am sorry," Danlo said.

"Well, I'm sorry, too. Who will watch over my girls and boys now? You and Hanuman—especially Hanuman. He hasn't been himself since Pedar's accident."

"No."

"Ah, he's too damn sensitive. I think he can't bear the thought of death—anyone's death, even such a miserable boy as Pedar."

"I think you are right," Danlo said.

"And now this barbarous affair with the warrior-poet. Too bad."

"He still suffers . . . because of the ekkana drug, yes?"

Bardo nodded his head. "Please take care of him while I'm gone, Danlo. He has a hundred admirers, but I think you and I are the only ones who understand him."

"I will always . . . be his friend."

"Ah, nothing's harder than true friendship, as I should know." Bardo spread out his cloak and rubbed his hands together. "Don't give up hope, Little Fellow. These are strange times—anything can happen. Do you still have the ring I gave you?"

Danlo held his hand over his chest and nodded his head.

"Good. Please keep this ring in case your father returns. Someday he'll return, by God. Someday."

Bardo embraced Danlo, and he made ready to leave. He patted his belly, belched, then said, "Well, then, I'm off to the cafés. I'm going to drink twenty glasses of beer and become gloriously drunk—it's a glorious day, don't you think?"

"But . . . Bardo," Danlo said. "I thought you just abjured drinking beer."

"*Did* I? No, no, I did not. I said that after this *day,* I'd drink no more beer. Well, the day's not over yet, is it? By God, it's hardly begun!"

So saying, he bowed deeply to Danlo and then ambled down to the gliddery and snapped in his skate blades. The sight of Bardo fumbling about drunkenly might have moved Danlo to despair, but strangely, at that moment, he felt nothing but hope.

"Good-bye, Bardo!" he shouted.

He watched Bardo disappear down the street, and then he turned toward Perilous Hall where the other boys would be waiting for the news of what had occurred in the College of the Lords.

C H A P T E R   1 4

A GAME OF HOKKEE

The man of knowledge must not only love his enemies;
he must also be able to hate his friends.

                      —Friedrich the Hammer

Danlo spent much of the next few days wandering around the Academy grounds, lost in an ice fog of brooding and deep reflection. He did no work. He restrained his impulse to go to the library, to enter the cybernetic spaces in search of some certain knowledge, or episteme, which might help him think more clearly about the Alaloi's fate. Nor did he visit his tutor, nor take meals with his friends. One bright, cold afternoon, however, on the seventy-seventh, he remembered that his hallmates were scheduled to skate against the first-year novices of Stone Row in a game of hokkee. And so he returned to Perilous Hall, donned a kamelaika, snapped his hokkee blades into his boots, grabbed his mallet, and he hurried across Borja to the Ice Dome.

In truth, it was not a good day for hokkee. The news of Bardo's abjuration had stunned most of the other boys, and they seemed more interested in talking about this scandal than in slapping a hard wooden puck across 150 yards of ice. It was now certain that Bardo would be leaving the City, perhaps for good. Madhava li Shing and Sherborn of Darkmoon—and others—pestered Danlo with questions concerning Bardo's plans. And then, just before the first chukkar of the game, Hanuman li Tosh appeared at the far end of the huge arena. He made his way between the empty sled courts and the five ice fields laid out in perfect, white rectangles at the Dome's center. He skated up to

Danlo and to his hallmates, whom he had not seen in many days. Only half an hour earlier, the cetics had finally let him leave their tower, and he had come straightaway to the Ice Dome. Hanuman loved playing hokkee, Danlo remembered, almost as much as he loved the precise movements of his killing art.

"Hello, Madhava; hello, Lorenzo; hello, Ivar; hello, Alesar." Hanuman greeted the boys of Perilous Hall, and they swarmed around him, bowing and congratulating him on his miraculous escape from death in the library. Then Hanuman broke free and came up to Danlo, who was standing alone near the edge of the field. He looked at him for a long moment before saying, "Hello, Danlo—it's good to see that you're well."

"And you, Hanu—are *you* well? Is there still much pain?"

Hanuman laughed softly, strangely, and he said, "Didn't you once tell me that pain is the awareness of life?"

"Yes, but that was before I had seen . . . what the ekkana drug can do."

"Well, pain is always pain," Hanuman said. "But there are ways to control it."

"I have heard . . . that many people have died from the ekkana."

"But as you can see, I'm still alive. I owe you my life. Again." He said this clearly, coldly, but then, seeing the hurt he was causing Danlo, he forced a smile and told him, "You always amaze me. You faced the poet of your own will—not even my mother would have done what you did."

Danlo touched the scar above his eye and said, "Everyone speaks of this as if I had a choice."

"But you did. You might have run away."

"You know . . . that I could not run away."

"Oh, yes, I *do* know," Hanuman said. He looked at Danlo and tried to smile, but something was obviously disturbing him. "It's a miracle that you remembered the poem. There was a moment—I thought you *wouldn't* remember it, but you did. Didn't you? Of course you did. With your impossible memory that I shall never fathom, you remembered the poem. Which is why the poet put the knife in his eye and we're still alive to talk about it."

While the twenty novices from Stone Row at last filed into the Dome and took their places on the opposite side of the field, Hanuman and Danlo stood talking about what had occurred in the library, and after when the College of Lords had denied

Danlo's petition. They spoke together easily, but there was a distance between them which had not been there before. Danlo wanted to know more about the healing arts of the cetics, but Hanuman was reluctant to reveal what had happened during the days that he had spent in their cold, isolated tower. Danlo asked him other questions as well, little questions concerning the sharpness of Hanuman's skate blades or their strategy for the day's game. Because of Hanuman's secret suffering and his coolness, however, Danlo avoided the deeper questions that he might have asked. In truth, there was only one question that he wanted to ask, but as friends often do, he found himself talking about everything other than this one crucial thing.

Then one of the novices from Stone Row called for the game to begin. Much to Danlo's dismay, Hanuman used the excitement of the game—the flashing steel, the fear and frenzy of young bodies tearing across the ice—as a kind of shield against Danlo's concerns. Little by little, Hanuman fell reticent, and then silent altogether. Through five chukkars of skating, he kept this awkward, hurtful silence, and he kept himself apart from Danlo. Although he played his usual lightning-fast game and he wielded his black shatterwood mallet with both mindfulness and savagery, he seemed to care little about winning. And all the while, in his aloof posture and in his pale eyes, in the way he looked at Danlo (or looked away from him), his manner was full of anguish and despair.

"Why are you . . . so inward today?" Danlo finally asked as they rested before the sixth and final chukkar. They were sitting together near the end of a long shiny bench, which had been painted blue earlier that season. Some of their hallmates, at the opposite end of the bench, sat slumped over their knees. Others stood about gasping for breath, or spitting blood, or talking, or fingering crude signs at the Stone Row novices across the ice field seventy yards away. Through the fog steaming off the ice, Danlo could see the opposing team, twenty loud-faced boys, each of them kicking their boots against their red bench and holding erect two fingers. This was a sign—depending on how interpreted—that either there was some doubt as to Danlo's hallmates having been born of real wombs in the natural manner, or that they were losing by two goals. Certainly, Danlo thought, they were losing by two goals. His own skating, for most of the game, had been distracted, erratic, mechanical. He and Hanuman usually scored most of Perilous Hall's goals, but between them that afternoon there had been no *halla*, no interplay of thought and act. Hanuman was as cold as the white ice of the polo field, while Danlo was haunted by the memory of murder and death.

"In some ways you're more inward than I," Hanuman said.

"That may be true . . . but neither of us was meant for inwardness."

Hanuman looked up and squinted at the light streaming through the Dome's thousands of triangular windowpanes. "How do you know what I was meant for?"

"Ever since Pedar fell down the steps," Danlo said, evading his question, "you have fallen in on yourself. Why? You hated him . . . almost as much as I did."

Hanuman, still staring up at the dome, closed his eyes and winced, as if in pain. He said, "Because he's dead. Isn't that enough? How do you think *you* seem now that you've discovered the fate of the Alaloi tribes?"

"But they are my people!"

"I'm sorry, Danlo. Perhaps a cure for the plague will be found. Perhaps you'll even find it. But even if you do, we're all dead, aren't we? Eventually. All people, living their lives so quickly—and why?"

Here Hanuman looked at Danlo and quoted one of the passages in the *Book of God* which Nikolos Daru Ede had plagiarized from an ancient body of mystic writings, the False Bhagavad Gita: " 'The world of the living burns the flesh, and all creatures rush to their destruction like moths into a flame.' "

"You think about death too much," Danlo said.

"I?"

"There is no cure for it. Death is a disease . . . that has no cure."

"The Cybernetic Churches," Hanuman said, "teach otherwise."

Danlo touched Ahira's feather and said, "Even if it were possible, I would not want myself, my soul—my *purusha*—carked into a computer."

"But there are other ways. There is the path godward that your father chose. Bardo used to talk about this all the time. Once he said that anyone who was willing to suffer as the Ringess did could become a god."

"Bardo . . . liked to talk to you, yes?"

"Especially when he was drunk. He took an interest in my career—he always insisted I should become a pilot."

"You will be the most blessed of pilots," Danlo said.

"Do you think so? I'm not so sure. Yesterday the Lord Cetic invited me to have tea with him in the tower. He suggested I should apply to Lara Sig and learn the cetic arts."

"The Lord Cetic!"

"You seem surprised."

"But you must not become a cetic!"

"And why mustn't I?"

"Because . . . cetics are too inward," Danlo explained.

"Once again we're arguing in circles."

"Cetics are . . . too withdrawn from life," Danlo said. Due to a collision with someone's mallet during the fourth chukkar, his chin was cut, slightly; he wiped the blood away with the sleeve of his kamelaika, which left a long red streak against the clean wool. "Cetics," he said, "seek the truth about consciousness, yes, and I understand this attracts many novices. Samadhi and fugue and simultaneity, all the states of computer consciousness. But you cannot know . . . about *real* consciousness by facing a computer."

It was almost time for the sixth chukkar, and Danlo's hallmates were busy sharpening their skates and wrapping their mallets with black tape, not because their blades were really dull or the shatterwood shafts needed reinforcing, but because this was a game-ending ritual almost as old as Perlious Hall itself. The air whined with the sound of diamond files cutting across steel, and Hanuman raised his voice, saying, "But there's more to the cetic arts than facing a computer."

Someone handed Danlo a role of sticky black tape, and he used his strong white teeth to bite off a piece. He said, "There is mastery, yes? Mastery over the mind; mastery over *others'* minds."

"There are dangers, I know," Hanuman said. "Which is why, of all the Order, the cetic vows are the strictest. 'Cetic ethics,' and all that."

"But the cetics are hermetics," Danlo said, supplying a saying commonly bandied about the Academy. "They are mystics who keep secrets . . . about the mastery of consciousness."

"But this is part of their ethics. Most people, if shown the secrets of their consciousness—they're like children playing with hydrogen bombs."

"Hanu, Hanu, this is just what I am afraid of."

"You're afraid of *me*?"

"I am afraid *for* you."

Hanuman finished taping his mallet and said, "Is that true?"

"Have you *seen* the master cetics?" Danlo asked. "Have you looked at their *faces*? The old ones? I have . . . three days ago, in the Lords' College. The Lord Cetic. Lord Pall. He is like the others. He is corrupt and horrible, too conscious . . . of himself. He is mad, I think, barely human. Do not become a cetic, Hanu."

"Most cetics live too long," Hanuman said. "Probably it's my fate to die young—but even if I don't, I'll never grow old like that."

Danlo looked at his best friend and said softly, "But there are other reasons for not becoming . . . Why do you think Lord Pall wants you to apply to the cetics?"

"Well, the cetics and pilots are always competing for the best novices. I'm sure the Lord Cetic will invite you to tea before the year's end, too."

"But I could never become a cetic!" Danlo said.

"No?"

"No." Danlo ejected the blades from his boots and ran his thumbnail across the edges. With a file that Madhava tossed to him, he began sharpening them. "Before I entered the Academy I was . . . involved with the Returnists. And the autists. These sects and religions—the cetics. This makes for a dangerous combination, yes?"

"Which is why cetics are forbidden any kind of religiosity."

"Then you have no interest in the new religions?"

"No, none."

Danlo looked down at the ice around the bench. In its milky smoothness, he caught sight of Hanuman's reflection. Something about this ghostlike image, so delicate and pale, hinted at a secret passion. It was as if the ice, in distorting the clean lines of Hanuman's face, were acting as a lens to a deeper, truer self. There was an intensity and devoutness in his friend's pale blue eyes; for the first time, he could see that Hanuman burned with an intense religiousness. Never mind the boy's scorn of the Cybernetic Universal Church, the hatred and ridicule of his parents' faith which had informed his childhood; never mind that he had often referred to Edeism as the "slave religion." The real problem, Danlo thought, was that Edeism and other religions, for one such as Hanuman, were not really religious enough.

"It is known that the cetics, some of them, practice almost

continual interface with their computers," Danlo said. He looked up from the ice at Hanuman, and continued speaking in a clear, pained voice, "In violation of the canons . . . and the law of Civilization. You have heard this, yes?"

"If one believes the rumors, there's a grade of cybershamans called neurosingers who misuse their computers—I think this is true."

"And they seek interface . . . with the godspace, yes?"

"Perhaps they do, Danlo. Who knows what the neurosingers seek?"

"But what do *you* seek?"

"I don't really know."

Danlo, glimpsing the light that came into Hanuman's eyes as he said this, thought that he knew precisely what he sought. "Have you decided to become a cetic, then?"

"Possibly," Hanuman said.

"But we were to be pilots together!"

"You'll be the pilot—it's what you were born for."

"But to journey to the stars—"

"I'm sorry but these last days, I've lost any desire to see the stars."

"But a *cetic*? No, that would be so wrong . . . for you."

"How do you know what's wrong?"

"I can see it. Anybody could."

"You can see it," Hanuman said, and he rammed a diamond file back and forth across his skate blade. "You're a scryer, then, and you can see it."

"Why are you so angry?" Danlo asked.

"You think I'm angry?"

"Truly, you are angry, your face—"

"Why should you always have to tell the truth? To try to *see* it? Can't you ever lie, a little?"

"I do not want to see you . . . become a cetic."

"Perhaps it's my fate," Hanuman said.

"Your fate?"

"I should love my fate—isn't this what you like to say?"

"But you cannot *know* your fate!" Danlo said.

"Well, I know I've decided to become a cetic. Just now— thank you for helping me decide."

"No, you must not become a cetic."

"I shall, however, become one. I'm sorry."

"But, Hanu, *why*?"

They sat staring at each other as they had done on the day

of their meeting, in Lavi Square; neither of them wanted to be the first to break eyelock. Then Madhava li Shing called out that it was time to play the sixth chukkar, and Danlo and Hanuman —and the eighteen other boys from Perilous Hall—skated out onto the polo field. With much chatter, grinding skates, and scurfed-up patches of ice, they took their places behind their goal line. Up ice, at the field's exact center, someone had placed the polo puck inside a small violet circle. All faces were now turned toward this puck, Danlo's and his hallmates', and, behind their own goal line, the tense faces of the Stone Row novices at the field's upper end. The boys fell quiet, their hands gripping the shafts of their mallets. From other parts of the Dome, from the sled courts and figure rings, came the slicing softness of steel over ice; but when Madhava gave the signal for the face-off, these little sounds were obliterated by the moment's tumult: mallets being slapped against the ice, whoops of exhilaration and relief, clacking skates, and breath exploding from the lips of the boys all around Danlo. The two teams raced together, up ice and down, toward the puck at the center of the field. Danlo and Hanuman, who were the fastest of the Perilous Hall novices, were the first to reach it. Almost immediately, however, three Stone Row skaters blocked them, and as the teams came crashing together, there was a flurry of mallets, skates flailing, shouts, and boys crying out in pain. Danlo managed to break out of the melee, using his mallet blade to smoothly guide the puck up ice. And then he passed the puck to Hanuman. The strategy of the Perilous Hall novices called for him to skate as right point while Hanuman took the left point. Because they had been unable to coordinate their attack, however, for most of the game Madhava (who was stroking desperately ten yards behind Danlo), Alesar Roth, and others had taken on the brunt of the offense. But now a curious thing happened. Ahead of Danlo, to his left, Hanuman was trying to break free from a swarm of Stone Row skaters. Danlo became aware of him, not just with his eyes, but with a finer, truer organ of perception, as if his sense of life were seeking out across the ice to find his friend's secret fire. And Hanuman, who burned bright as any star, was seeking him; Danlo could feel it in Hanuman's flashing eyes, and in the angle of his neck, and in the pattern of his furious mallet work, and in the way his own heart beat to the rhythm of their pounding skates. Something—perhaps their anger at each other or their fear (and love) of fate—had renewed the connectedness between them. They skated together up ice, and all the while, an invisible cord grew between them, a numinous tissue of kinship connecting them belly to belly, and mind to mind. In the brilliance of this bond there was a mutual anticipation of act and movement, intimations of the future as it unraveled moment by moment. The ice flowed beneath Danlo like a gleaming sheet of satin, and through it he felt Hanuman's skate blades striking, left foot and right, gliding and striking. The beat of the steel rang out as separate and distinct from all the other sounds around him: the mallets clacking together, the groans, gasps of breath, and Madhava's faraway, singsong voice calling out instructions to his hallmates. Just then Hanuman found an opening. Danlo found it at the same instant, even before Hanuman's mallet flicked out and slapped the puck through. The puck, a circle of red jewood much dinged and scarred, shot directly at Danlo, who whipped down his mallet blade to intercept it. Two novices wearing the flowery seal of Stone Row on their kamelaikas immediately bore down upon him. Danlo pulled sharply to his left even as Hanuman pulled away from the skaters swarming him. Danlo passed him the puck. As he accelerated up ice, a sudden wind chilled his face, cutting his eyes, and there was a reddish blur as Hanuman passed the puck back to him. Together, almost in lock-step, they raced toward the Stone Row goal box, passing the puck back and forth, like a corpuscle of blood, back and forth. Among the Stone Row novices they dodged and darted, and their sense of space and time was uncanny. "Hanu, Hanu!" Danlo cried out in his mind as he passed the puck again. Hanuman reached his mallet out, slowing the puck, and then, with a lightning stroke, he fired it across fifteen yards of ice into the goal box. It was the first of the goals they would make during the chukkar.

"Luck!" one of the Stone Row novices called out as he banged his mallet against the ice in frustration. He was a good-looking boy with reddish-black skin and a look of pride coloring his face. "That was a lucky shot."

One of his hallmates held up his middle finger—knuckle side facing outward—at Hanuman. "We're still winning by one goal," he reminded him.

Sherborn of Darkmoon, who was leaning against his mallet, sweating and panting for breath, held up his own middle finger. He said, "One more goal is all we need to tie the score." Again, at the Stone Row novices circling about, he thrust his finger into the air. "And one more goal after that, you lose the game."

The novices each returned to their goal lines, then. The

proud boy from Stone Row—his name was Lais Motega Mohammad—called the signal for the chukkar's second face-off. Again the boys rushed together pell-mell, converging on the puck as carrion birds over a corpse. There was a frantic melee. The violence of scything mallets, boots, and elbows flowed around Danlo, who pursued the puck with glee and abandon. He had no care for himself. Of all the boys he was the quickest and toughest, the most wild. This wildness, many times during the past season, had caused him to injure the other boys. And many times, he'd considered giving up the game altogether. Once, after he'd caught a Lavi Hall boy in the face with his mallet, breaking the jaw and knocking out four bloody, splintered teeth, he despaired of ever wholly honoring his vow of ahimsa. But he reasoned that ahimsa, as Old Father taught the doctrine, required that he never harm anyone *intentionally*. In truth, he hated harming others, and he never did so if he could help it; it was only his recklessness and love of intense motion that caused the novices (even those from his own hall) to fear the boy they called Danlo the Wild.

As for himself, however, he had no fear. He sustained injuries frequently, and in the first moments of the melee, Lais Mohammad scraped the end of his mallet across Danlo's eye. The pain of it burned like fire; his eye immediately blurred with tears. But he was used to pain and never minded it as much as the civilized boys did. *Pain is the awareness of life*—this saying was as near to him as the throbbing of his own heart, which he could feel pounding up behind his eye. It was his way to become his pain, to let it wash through him like the burning of ice water. Half-blinded in pain, in the middle of a sea of flashing mallets and skates, he found the puck and touched it along with his mallet. All around him was the press of hard bodies, ice grinding, and cries of anger. He entered into this violent stream of chaos roiling across the polo field. He let it sweep him along. This was his genius and his strength, to become himself a part of the chaos rather than resisting it or trying to control it. He, who had spent his childhood in ice and wind, called upon his animal senses to feel his way across the field, and he skated with a rare and vital grace.

Suddenly he heard Hanuman cry out, "Danlo!" In the tangle of limbs near him, an opening appeared. He knocked the puck through, and Hanuman took it with his mallet, and then the opening closed, as the sea closes in around a stone. The melee's flow shifted away from Danlo, moving in a swarm of bodies across the field. It engulfed Hanuman. Danlo saw him skating at the center of ten or twelve boys, trying to break free.

"Pass the puck!" Madhava shrilled out. "Pass it now!"

"Hanu, Hanu!" Danlo said as he pushed his skates against the ice and ducked between two boys from Stone Row. He felt the secret cord between Hanuman and him tighten, pulling him back into the melee. There was a moment, he saw, when Hanuman might have passed him the puck. "Hanu, Hanu," he whispered, but Hanuman was intent on defending the puck from the Stone Row novices' darting mallets. He was very good at defense. Where some feared Danlo for his wildness, the novices of Borja's dormitories were terrified of Hanuman because he skated with a fury and a will to harm others. This was the logic of his life, his tragedy and fate. With his malice and his mallet (or with his fists and murderous aura when unarmed), he sought always to keep a space about himself, an impenetrable sphere of violence whose center was himself. Thus he protected himself— and the puck—from others, but in doing so he cut himself off from the stream of the game as it flowed around him.

From across twenty yards of ice, Danlo watched him pass the puck to Madhava and then artfully slice his mallet into the kneecap of a Stone Row novice who had gotten too close. Hanuman made it seem an accident, as if he couldn't check the force of his stroke. The Stone Row novice fell to the ice then, grabbing at his knee, screaming, shaking his head from side to side as his eyes streamed tears. And on Hanuman's face there was a terrible look, a mask of fear that Danlo had glimpsed at their first meeting. Danlo was perhaps the only one to see it. While some of the novices skated over and crowded around the screaming boy, Danlo stared at Hanuman's face. With his eyes, and with a deeper sense of seeing for which he as yet had no name, he became aware of the essential paradox of Hanuman's existence: Hanuman was truly afraid of others, of the hard icy otherness of all things outside his person and self. This fear compelled him to cut himself off from life, as a protection, and yet it was this very act of severance that made him feel vulnerable and alone. And so he feared, and so he hated, hated and harmed any who threatened him.

When Lais Mohammad drew himself up and pointed his mallet at him, accusing him of cruelty and cowardice, Hanuman immediately used his own mallet to knock it away. The force of the blow deflected the mallet into the cheek of one of Lais Mohammad's hallmates, a small boy with the eyes of a terrified shagshay ewe. He bleated out in pain, and he flailed his mallet back and forth in front of his face, striking Sherborn of Darkmoon in the jowls around his neck. All at once, like a tidal wave spreading out over the sea, the violence overwhelmed the boys of Perilous Hall and Stone Row, and they flew at each other with mallets and kicking boots and spit whipping out of their mouths as they shouted and cursed and screamed. Danlo stroked over and pushed his way into the brawl. He used his arms to ward off blows, but he was careful not to skive any of the fallen boys with his skate blades nor to deliver blows of his own, even when striking out would have been the simplest way of defending himself. The cord between him and Hanuman was now so tight it seemed he could feel his friend's heart beating inside his own chest. He came up close to Hanuman, almost close enough to touch him. Then someone whacked Danlo's ear; a sour-faced boy whose name he didn't know rammed the knob of his mallet into his solar plexus. As Danlo pulled his elbows in toward his belly, gasping for breath, he saw Hanuman strike the boy's temple. The boy dropped to the ice as if his legs had been chopped away. Perhaps he was dead, Danlo thought; the blow might have killed anyone. And Hanuman was angry enough to kill, Danlo could see it in his cold, mad eyes, in the way he singled out his victims and attacked them, with mallet and skate blades and a will to annihilation. No one, of choice, would have stood before him, but the crush of skaters was too thick for anyone to flee. Just then Hanuman, with his uncanny sense of space, found Lais Mohammad working his way behind him. He whirled about and brought his mallet up. Mallet clacked against mallet as the two boys tried to club each other. Lais Mohammad swung his mallet blade at Hanuman's nose; no doubt he wanted to shatter his bones, to ruin his fine, delicate face. He swung his mallet, and Hanuman blocked it, and his eyes were pale with death.

"Hanu, Hanu!" Danlo cried out and he threw himself across the ice. To the boys struggling nearby, if any looked his way, Hanuman's face must have seemed only a mask of fury, for he attacked Lais Mohammad with lightning strokes, high and low, exulting in the exercise of his killing art. But Danlo could see that his friend's face, for all the hatred there, was really frozen with fear. In fear, Hanuman drove his mallet against Lais Mohammed's mallet, again and again, hacking as if he were desperate to fell a tree, knocking and beating down until the wood splintered suddenly and his mallet thwacked into his enemy's chest. And with every stroke of his mallet, he winced as if in pain, as if meting out such violence mutilated his deepest self and caused him agony. It was *this* agony that he feared. Above all things he feared the will to power over himself, even as he loved it and called it his fate. Danlo came up between Lais Mohammad and Hanuman, then, and he could feel the fear in the center of his friend's belly, rippling along the cord connecting them. Danlo wrenched the mallet from Hanuman's hands. And Lais Mohammad threw down his broken mallet with a skidding clatter of wood, and grabbed another from one of his hallmates and rained blows against Danlo's back, cursing as he tried to get at Hanuman. Danlo fell against Hanuman and bore him down, almost straight backward, down with a grunt and a slap against the hard, misty ice. He covered him with his body. Lais Mohammad's mallet cracked against Danlo's spine, and the sudden, jumping agony of bruised nerves and bone recalled the wounding of the deeper tissues of Hanuman's soul. *Pain is the awareness of life,* Danlo remembered. In a single, enduring moment of pain he became aware of the most fundamental thing about Hanuman's life: his best friend, this pale fury with whom he would be bonded until death, was by nature a compassionate and gentle boy. But he had mutilated his own nature. Or rather he had tried to sear away and annihilate this gentleness, much as one might murder an unwanted baby by plunging it into a pool of lava. He did this with a will, *because* he was possessed of a bold and furious will, a will to overcome himself and be greater. And it was Danlo who had excited the will to power in him, who had quickened it and made it stronger. This is why he loved Danlo. He loved Danlo's wildness, his vitality and grace, and, above all, his fearlessness of life. And yet he hated these very qualities because he himself lacked them.

All this Danlo saw in an instant, as he lay against Hanuman belly to belly shielding him from Lais Mohammad's busy mallet. And all the time Hanuman kicked out beneath him trying to heave Danlo off, right leg and left, the staccato of his skate blades against the ice exploding showers of snow and glittering chips, and sending through its crystalline layers secret tremors of rage and helplessness and hate. *Hatred is the left hand of love,* Danlo remembered, and with this thought the whole course of their future came to him in a wave of sudden inevitability, although it would be years before he could articulate this vision or see it clearly.

"Danlo, get off me!" Hanuman screamed.

One of the Stone Row novices had come up behind Lais Mohammad and was holding him, keeping him away from Danlo. Slowly, Danlo stood up and faced Lais Mohammad. He said, "I am sorry."

"Get back!" Lais Mohammad shouted at Danlo. He was trying to break free from the boy holding him. He twisted and grunted and raised his mallet.

Now Hanuman, too, was on his feet, shaking and furiously searching the ice for his mallet. But Danlo looked at him and said, "Hanu, no!"

For a moment Hanuman froze, staring at Danlo. "Hanu, Hanu," Danlo whispered. Lais Mohammad, too, looked at Danlo, and then a gradual calm fell over the novices on the polo field. Danlo's faithfulness to ahimsa—and his obvious love for his friend (even one so feared as Hanuman li Tosh)—shamed and gentled the boys of Stone Row and Perilous Hall. Many of them threw down their mallets. From other parts of the Ice Dome came novices, journeymen, and even four master akashics red-faced and breathless from their game of skemmer on the sled courts. One of these, Paloma the Elder, an old woman with a young face and middling-old body, chided the boys for falling into violence. She dismissed their respective protestations of innocence and accusations of culpability, saying in a fussy old voice, "In violence, there's no beginning and no end, and you're all to blame." She saw to it that the injured were cared for, their torn muscles rubbed with quickly absorbent enzymes, their lacerations glued shut. A few of the boys had broken bones or fractured teeth; Paloma sent these off to the cutter for surgery and implanting. As it happened, the boy whom Hanuman had clubbed in the head was not dead at all but merely concussed. He bravely called for the game to continue. The boys returned to their benches then, to take a rest before finishing the chukkar.

"Are you badly hurt?" Hanuman asked Danlo as they stood near their hallmates' blue bench. The fury had gone out of him, and he reached out to touch Danlo's sleeve. "Do you need ice? Let's see your back, get your kamelaika off."

When Danlo unzipped his kamelaika and pulled down the shirt, a fire burned along his back: It felt as if someone were using a hot knife to flay the flesh away from his muscles. He hunched his shoulders over, resting his elbows on his knees. In the middle of his spine, at least one of the vertebrae hurt with a quick piercing pain every time he drew in a breath. His back was a welter of broken skin, livid patches, and streaks upraised against ivory that would soon run to the blue and black of deep bruises. He could not see these bruises, but he felt them seaming him from buttocks to neck.

"You *do* need ice," Hanuman said. The other boys were passing around a steel pail; inside it, thirty-one icicles clanged and sloshed about. Hanuman took an icicle—a cylinder of water frozen around a wooden stick—and he rubbed it up and down over Danlo's back. "Oh, Danlo," he said, "your vow of ahimsa will get you killed one day."

"But I had to come between you!" Danlo said, and then he ground his teeth together as Hanuman rubbed in a foul-smelling ointment. "He might have murdered you or . . . you might have murdered him."

"Do you really think I have that much courage?" Hanuman asked.

Hanuman finished a task that obviously distressed him—Danlo knew that he always dreaded having to view or touch any sort of wound—and he glided over a few feet to the violet line marking the edge of the polo field. With his skate blade, he kicked at the ice, reaming and grinding the toe point into the hole he made. His head was bowed, but his eyes were full of light.

"Hanu, please," Danlo said, coming over to him. "There is a thing I must ask you."

Hanuman looked up in both calmness and dread, but he said nothing.

"In the library, just before the warrior-poet killed himself, he said a thing." Danlo touched the sleeve of Hanuman's kamelaika and told him, "I cannot forget . . . what the poet said about Pedar."

"And what did he say?"

"You do not remember?"

Hanuman hesitated only a moment before answering, "No, I can't remember."

"The poet said that you . . . murdered Pedar."

"Murdered him? Do you really think I murdered him?"

"I . . . do not want to think that you did."

"But how could I have murdered him?"

"I do not know."

Hanuman looked straight into Danlo's eyes, and then he did an astonishing thing. He reached down and grasped Danlo's hand as he had done in the library, and he squeezed with all his strength, so powerfully and urgently that bones of Danlo's hand hurt with a sharp, almost breaking pain. Hanuman brought his lips up close to Danlo's ear and whispered, "The warrior-poet was wrong. Or perhaps he lied. No one murdered Pedar but himself."

"In truth?"

"I promise you, Danlo."

As they clasped hands, Hanuman held himself still and tried to smile. There was a vast comfort and sincerity in this smile, but there was something else, too. Beneath the surface of finely controlled muscles and easy emotions, like a boil deep within the flesh, Hanuman's face was full of torment. He might have cried out in agony at any moment if his need for self-control were not so great.

"I think that the cetics did not heal you, not . . . wholly," Danlo said. "It is not just the ekkana drug, is it? I think it must be something . . . other."

Hanuman broke away from him and ground his skate blade against the ice. "You're too truthful—I've said that before. You're too earnest, too curious, too . . . too many things. You don't care about yourself, do you? Your *self.* I don't have that kind of courage—who does? The wildness, Danlo. When we first met, and I saw it in you, in both of us, I thought I had the courage for it. I don't. It will kill me, unless I kill it first. Do you understand?"

"Yes," Danlo said. His body ached with a spreading stiffness, and he suddenly felt cold. He closed his eyes, remembering when he had first come to love the danger and the wildness of his life; it had been during the cold night that he and Soli had buried the Devaki people. Then, after a moment of prayer and remembrance, to Hanuman, he whispered, "No, I don't want to understand."

Hanuman looked at him and quietly said, "I don't have your *grace.* The way you accept everything, even your own wildness."

"But I do not accept . . . everything. This is the problem with life, for human beings. For *us,* Hanu, don't you see? To say 'yes.' *This* would be true courage. But I cannot, not yet, be an asarya. Everywhere I look, at Bardo, at the blessed people, even at you—everything I see shouts 'No!' "

"But you're still determined to be a pilot?"

"Bardo thinks this is my best hope for saving the people."

"The Alaloi?"

"Yes, the blessed people."

"But that isn't the only reason you want to become a pilot, is it?"

"No."

"You told me once that you wanted to find the center of the universe."

Danlo looked off into the depths of the Ice Dome. All around him were the sounds of sleds rocketing across their courts and water vapor hugging the ice like a wet gray fur. He crossed his arms over his chest and said, "I used to think of the world, of the universe . . . as a great circle. The great circle of *halla*. Sometimes I still believe that I might journey to the center of this circle."

"To see the universe just as it is?"

"Yes," Danlo said. "The world, as most people see it, the way they live life . . . it is false, a deception, a lie."

With his skate blade Hanuman began chopping at the mound of snow he had dug up. He said, "And that's why I'll become a cetic. I have to uncover the center of myself. To see if it's a lie."

"And then?"

"And then war," Hanuman said. "I'm at war with myself, and I need to know if I'm capable of *this* kind of murder."

That was all he said to Danlo then. He might have admitted more, much more, but he was good at keeping secrets, sometimes even from himself. It is probable that he wanted to tell Danlo the full truth about his decision to become a cetic. But truth, as the Fravashi say, is multiple and complex; finding the truth is like uncovering the most perfect grain of a beach's billions of glittering sands. In truth, Hanuman never understood that marvelous quality he called wildness. Wildness is that urge, trait, sense, and part of the will that recognizes one's deep self in all the elements of creation and feels the fiery signature of the universe written deep inside oneself. True wildness kills. It pulls one into consciousness of all things, deeper into life, and thus into death, for death is the left hand of life and is always as close as the next heartbeat. There are quick deaths accomplished by climbers of mountains falling from the heights, or by lost pilots seeking the impossible whose lightships fall into the centers of blue giant stars; there is the slow death of the alcohol addict, the whoremonger's diseased life and death, the autist's sad death of dreams, and the mad death of neurosingers who cannot face away from the cybernetic heaven of their computers. There is the timeless, recurring death of the Alaloi hunter far out on the sea ice, out in the great loneliness, who listens to the Song of Life and enters into that mystical land called the *altjiranga mitjina*. And then there is the hardest death of all. To feel the fire for the infinite inside and let it burn, to die each moment and each moment be reborn from the ashes of that holy inner fire, to create oneself anew in the image of one's deepest passions and vision—this is the death and life of a man who would become a god.

All Hanuman's instincts pulled him toward this fate. Only, he lacked the courage for his best possibilities; he feared his own essential wildness. And so he clung furiously to his sense of himself, to his identity, to his ideals, emotions, and awareness, to all the parts of his being that Danlo would have called merely "face," but which Hanuman revered as precious and immutable, and would not suffer to come to harm. Other qualities he sacrificed without mercy or shame. Because he thought himself fated for the hardest of paths, he willfully—and tragically—annihilated precisely those passions that would have made him truly great. He, born a sensitive and gentle manchild, had tried to make himself the hardest of men. He, blessed with a rare will to life and compassion for others, had twisted his love for Danlo into hatred of his tormenter, and so he had made himself murder the novice Pedar Sadi Sanat. The warrior-poet had not lied, after all; Hanuman had truly executed this murder. He had done this deed not with the imaginings of his mind's eye, but with his hands and his will and his hateful heart.

And so on the evening after Danlo had slashed his forehead in the shih grove, after Hanuman had repaired this dreadful wound, he had gone into the Farsider's Quarter, down to the Street of Smugglers. With the last of the money he had brought to Neverness, he had purchased a dreammaker. A dreammaker: a shiny black device the size of a child's heart. An array of neurologics and chips of etched diamond programmed to produce a certain image field. Dreammakers were toys for adults jaded with the everyday world; dreammakers were also pedagogic tools of the cetics, who used them to test their students' ability to distinguish the simulated from the real. Hanuman had found a different use for his dreammaker. While the other boys were asleep, he had hidden the dreammaker beneath his covers. He had lain in wait for Pedar to pay his nightly visit. And then, just as Pedar crested the stairs, when he had a clear line of sight, Hanuman had aimed the dreammaker carefully. Certain images were infused directly into Pedar's visual cortex at the back of his head. Images of Scutari mothers eating their firstborn children. Dark, writhing, bloody aliens that Hanuman created to frighten Pedar and make him fall. To kill him—Hanuman did not like to lie to himself about his own deepest purposes. He murdered to save Danlo from further torment and shame. And he murdered because the very act of murder had always been hateful to him. And most of all, he murdered because he needed to sear away the secret weakness of his soul. *This* was the real reason he would become a cetic. He would use the sublime and powerful cetic arts to continue the fiery work of remaking himself. At the center of his soul, where the pain was the most urgent, he might find the source of his own suffering and burn it away, utterly. All this he longed to tell Danlo, but he was afraid he would be misunderstood.

And then Madhava li Shing led their thirteen remaining hallmates onto the ice of the polo field, and the moment was lost.

"Danlo, are you coming?"

Danlo stood at the field's edge, watching Hanuman force his way to the center of his hallmates as they skated together in a swarm. *Oh, Hanu, Hanu!* he thought. *What have you done?* The light streaming down through the dome fell over Hanuman so that his face reflected the colors of white and gold. Because Hanuman's face was so terrible to behold, just then, Danlo looked down at the ice. He looked away from the truth, much as one might look away from a beautiful but doomed star for fear that it might explode. He was aware of his heart beating, strongly, quickly, pushing him moment by moment into a future that he could never quite know. And then, from deep inside himself, there came a whisper like that of the wind through a grove of shatterwood trees. He heard himself answer the dread question that he had asked, but this one time in his life he did not listen.

"Danlo, are you coming?" Hanuman called out again.

"Yes," Danlo said. And then he skated out onto the ice to finish the game of hokkee.

PART 3

THE WAY OF RINGESS

THE RETURN OF A PILOT

All of history is man's attempt to find his proper relationship to God.

—Horthy Hosthoh, *from* A Requiem for Homo Sapiens

To a young man, even a student of the most fabulous and powerful school on the Civilized Worlds, the times during which he comes to maturity always seem normal no matter how extraordinary, how turbulent with change they really are. Imminent change and danger act as drugs upon the human brain, or rather, as rich foods that nourish the urge toward more life. And how easily one becomes used to such nourishment. Those who survive the signal events of history—the wars, plagues, alien contacts, vastenings, speciations, and religious awakenings—develop a taste for ferment and evolution next to which all the moments of "normal" existence will seem dull, flat, meaningless. Indeed, viewed from a godly coign of vantage, across more than two million years, nothing about humankind's astonishing journey from the grassy velds of Afarique to the galaxy's cold, numinous stars can be seen as normal.

If the career of Danlo wi Soli Ringess was truly remarkable, truly pregnant with wild moments, tragedy, historic decisions, and acts, it is nevertheless also true that he rarely thought of himself as a remarkable man, nor did he regard the universe into which he had been born as a hostile or an essentially tragic

369

place. It was a hard place, certainly, full of capriciously exploding supernovas, terrible gods, and new ecologies of life. A universe out of balance. The world around him was steeped in vice, injustice, lies, slelled diseases, all the manifestations of human evil. All the worlds around the stars were tainted with *shaida,* perhaps flawed to their fiery, molten cores. Possibly there was no help for the universe's evil; possibly he (along with all of humanity) might find a way to restore the primeval balance of life and bring all things into that state of correctness and natural order that he called *halla.* But not even a *halla* universe, he knew, could ever be peaceful. Like a winter storm, the universe would always roar with violence, chaos, and change. It was this essential chaos of his times that he had come to relish. It never occurred to him—as it did to Hanuman li Tosh—that the universe might be transformed in fundamental and horrible new ways.

There is not a great deal to tell of Danlo's passage from Borja and his early years as a journeyman at the Pilot's College, Resa. He was a brilliant student, though brilliant in a natural, offhand manner that never aroused his fellow journeymen's envy or ire. Mathematics, fugue, fenestration, and hallning—the disciplines that he learned to become a full pilot required much of his time but did not mark him deeply, at least, not until the end of this exciting period. To be sure, he had to master the interface with his ship computer, and in doing so, he became enraptured with the different states of cybernetic consciousness. All journeymen pilots must suffer through this love-addiction with their computers. Danlo quickly became an aficionado and adept of that marvelous state known as samadhi vastening. Unlike the first and lowest samadhi state—that of savikalpa samadhi—in the vastening through the computer, there is no awareness of one's mind as distinct from the computer's lightning number flows. The sense of oneself dissolves, as of electrons rushing and spreading out through the microscopic filaments of a computer's neurologics. There is an experience of oneness, a unity with the cybernetic space of the manifold. Time nearly stops. In entering the onstreaming realm of pure mathematics, a pilot has a giddy and joyous sense of thinking faster, making connections, of being a vaster mind. This intense depersonalization and vastening of the self is a marvel to some, a nightmare to a few, and a peril to all who face their computers deeply. Many are the pilots who have been lost into the number storm's cold and terrible beauty. Pilots die in a thousand ways, and the foremost of these deaths is into their computers. Although Danlo did not design the computer that was the brain and soul of his lightship, he soon learned to meld his mind with it totally and comfortably—but never *too* comfortably.

His ship itself—a beautiful sweep of spun diamond that he named *The Snowy Owl*—he did design and make, with the help of a cadre of tinkers, architects, programmers, and robots. He took his ship out into space to the nearby planets, Ninsun and Silvaplana, and then into that brilliant, eternal mathematical space that lies beyond and beneath the space of the visible universe. It was Danlo's talent and strength not only to survive his first tentative entries into the manifold, but to gain from these journeys knowledge that he might apply to his own peculiar problems, and to the basic problem of great civilization spread out all around him, above the icy streets and glittering towers of Neverness, and out across the stars.

And what did he learn during these years as a journeyman pilot? He learned no startling new truths about his world, but rather refined his way of seeing it. This was a continuation of a quest for vision that had begun early in his childhood, only to intensify during his stay in Old Father's house and his entrance into the Order. It was his admitted purpose to "see the universe just as it is." To behold it, clearly, deeply, and truly, and to say "yes" to all he could see. Ironically, though, the more keen his vision grew and the more adept he became in seeing into the wasting soul of humanity, the more he was tempted to say "no." As he grew into a full and free manhood, he became ever more critical of civilized people and their strange beliefs, cultures, and institutions. He donned the black racing kamelaika of a journeyman pilot, and he skated alone down forbidden City streets, roaming the dim glidderies of the Farsider's Quarter, making friends in all classes and sects of people wherever he went. And almost always, in almost everyone, he found something wanting. (Though, because he was a compassionate man who still honored the Fravashi ideal, he took care never to reflect or remind others of this want; even in the lowliest of wormrunners, he always found qualities he could like, or even love, and thus he was always loved in return.) He would go among the harijan, whores, exemplars, autists, and arhats, looking in their hurried eyes for the light of consciousness. All too often—especially in the lords of the Order—the light was sickly and fragile, like an oilstone's naked flame wavering about in the wind. Watching the way people watched each other, always judging or desiring or dismissing, always in fear of themselves, he came to realize that the basic fault of everyday human consciousness was that it was cut off from the rest of the universe. All human beings in all places had suffered the pain and loneliness of living as separate beings, but over the millennia, this pain had deepened to a racial agony. As humankind had evolved from bands of primitive fruit gatherers to sophisticates dwelling in a star-flung civilization, the split between the self and the other parts of creation had grown as vast as the great emptiness between the galaxies. Human beings, he learned, had sought to heal or overcome this split in different ways. Some became nature mystics and lost themselves in their rapture with earth, wind, and sky; some used drugs; some dreamed deep and lucid dreams; some disciplined themselves to be mystics of the computer: the neurosinger grade of the cetics, some of the cyber-shamans, his fellow pilots of the Order of Mystic Mathematicians, and others. The men and women of a few sects, such as the astriers, ignored the deeper problems of existence. They did this by spawning large broods of children. Sometimes one woman, over her hundred-year fertility, would give birth once every year. Astriers wholly surrendered themselves to the animal activities of life: the getting of food, water, clothing, money, jewelry, and often dreammakers and other devices with which to dull the brain and soul. Other human beings had denied the fault of their consciousnesses; many—during the Age of Science—had even gloried in the separation of man from nature, subject from object, fact from meaning, mind from matter. But the most universal human method of bridging the Void has always been the invention of religion. It was Danlo's fate to become a student of religions, as well as of mathematics; during his first and second year at Resa, he spent many moments trying to understand the fundamental passion that lay at the core of all religions: the urge of the self to embrace the universe's cold, mysterious otherness.

If animistic totem systems, alien philosophies, holism, the Creed of Chance, and the beliefs of various disciplines as different as cantorian mathematics and scrying are all seen as springing from this fundamental urge, then it is fair to say that Danlo experienced forty religions by the time he was twenty years old. At least forty religions. Much has already been said of his initiation into the Alaloi dreamtime, of the *altjiranga mitjina,* the Old Ones, and the Song of Life. Since coming to Neverness, he had absorbed a good deal of the Fravashi language philosophy, flirted with tychism, and learned something of the autists' dream system of reconstructing reality. He won friends among the scryers and inveigled them to teach him the secret doctrine of the sarvam asti. He dabbled with the ancient kabbalah and number mysticism. In order to understand Hanuman's hatred of Edeism, he sought out various sects of the Cybernetic Universal Church which were still prominent on Neverness: the Architects of the Universal God, the Church of Ede, and the Cybernetic Pilgrims of the Manifold. Once or twice, he even participated in their rituals, including the ecstatic facing ceremony. This exotic and arcane experience of Danlo's—Hanuman cynically referred to it as religious gourmandizing—was a necessary phase in his life's journey to become both visionary and asarya. Entering into the passion and beliefs of any particular religion was like viewing reality through a crystal lens. Always, like a child's prism held up to one's eye, the lens of ritual and belief distorted reality and colored it in strange (and sometimes beautiful) ways. But in each religion, cult, or faith, Danlo hoped to find a universal center, a jewel of truth as pure and clear as a diamond. It was his task and destiny, as he conceived it, to grasp each religion he could find, to apprehend the world through its beliefs, and with the hammerstone of his will to shatter the lens. Only then might the diamond center be revealed; only then could he see things clearly. And someday he might look at the universe through his own eyes only, free of even diamond lenses, free to behold the infinite stellar fires and humanity's burning pain through the consciousness of his deepest self.

"Seeking freedom through religion," Hanuman said to Danlo one day after they had passed on from Borja and become journeymen, "is like trying to understand aliens by offering oneself as a Scutari's dinner."

Indeed, the whole of Danlo's life journey was perilous, like crossing over a narrow, icy bridge. It is hard to see one's way through the ice fog of different belief systems. He who seeks easily gets lost. Or falls. Of all the religions he encountered, the most treacherous and difficult from which to break free was the Order's omnipresent holism. Of course, most masters of the Order would have denied that holism was anything like a religion. They would have pointed out that becoming a novice in the Order required no profession of faith, no theology, no adherence to doctrine or sacred beliefs. And at first glance, this was true. Thus it was all the more difficult for Danlo to swing the hammer of his insight and smash this subtle, evanescent lens. Holism lay at the very soul of his civilization; people took the holistic worldview for granted and did not question its beliefs, any more than they thought about the air they breathed. Few remembered the origins of holism; few realized (or cared) that humanity had once conceived the universe in a very different way.

"Holism," Master Jonath once said to Danlo, "defines the Sixth Mentality of man. Some call it the Last Mentality—how could there be a more evolved way of modeling reality, can you tell me?"

Historically, holism had been a break from the reductionist methods of science. Holism—some call it the "second science" —is a way of viewing the universe as a web of interactions and relationships. Whole systems—and the universe can be seen as an overarching system of systems—have properties beyond those of their parts. All things are, in some sense, alive, or a part of a living system; the real world of mind and matter, body and consciousness, cannot be understood by reducing it to pieces and parts. "Matter is mind"—this is perhaps the holists' quintessential belief. The founding theories of holism had tried to explain how mind emerges from the material universe, how the consciousness of all things is interconnected.

The first science, of course, had failed utterly to do this. The first science had resigned human beings to acting as objective observers of a mechanistic and meaningless universe. A dead universe. The human mind, according to the determinists, was merely the by-product of brain chemistry. Chemical laws, the way the elements combine and interact, were formulated as complete and immutable truths. The elements themselves were seen as indivisible lumps of matter, devoid of consciousness, untouched and unaffected by the very consciousnesses seeking to understand how living minds can be assembled from dead matter. The logical conclusion of these assumptions and conceptions was that people are like chemical robots possessing no free will. No wonder the human race, during the Holocaust Century, had fallen into insanity and despair.

Holism had been an attempt to restore life to this universe and to reconnect human beings with it. To heal the split between self and other. But ultimately, over the centuries, holism too had failed. Over the three thousand years since the founding of Neverness, the professionals and academicians of the Order had mostly forgotten that holism should be a merging of theory and personal experience. They dwelled too deeply in abstraction and theory. The new theories that had given birth to holism—quantum mechanics, batesonian epistemology, general systems theory, cybernetics, and information theory—had grown into elaborate, intricate systems representing reality with the language and symbols of the Universal Syntax. From the very beginning of holism, some viewed this reality as a cybernetic reality. Nature was seen as a network of programmable entities exchanging information, life as an information flow that terminated when the flow was cut off. The computer became a model for the mind and a metaphor of the universe. Indeed, the most dogmatic of the cybernetic holists regarded the universe *as* an actual computer, the mind *as* a set of programs run by this computer, or by its component units. Using Omar Narayama's Universal Syntax, the holists of the Order constructed a formal system, or science, that treated the individual mind as sub-programs of a universal algorithm. It was a brilliant, but ultimately alienating way of conceiving the universe. Alienating because it resolved the self/other split in form only.

For example, the holists have canonized the infamous bell theorem of ancient quantum mechanics. They exalt the sublime properties of light, teaching that each photon in a pair of photons will instantly "remember" the polarity of its mate no matter how far in spacetime the two are separated. Matter is memory, the holists say. They teach that each person's body-mind is wholly connected, electron to electron, to the whole fabric of the universe. Each quantum event, each of the trillions of times reality's particles interact with each other every instant, is like a note that rings and resonates throughout the great bell of creation. And the sound of the ringing propagates instantaneously, everywhere at once, interconnecting all things. This is a truth of our universe. It is a mystical truth, that reality at its deepest level is an undivided wholeness. It has been formalized and canonized, and taught to the swarms of humanity searching for a fundamental unity. Only, human beings have learned it as a theory and a doctrine, not as an experience. A true holism should embrace not only the theory of living systems, but also the reality of the belly, of wind, hunger, and snowworms roasting over a fire on a cold winter night. A man or woman (or child), to be fully human, should always marvel at the mystery of life. We each should be able to face the universe and drink in the stream of photons shimmering across the light-distances, to listen to the ringing of the farthest galaxies, to feel the electrons of each hemoglobin molecule spinning and vibrating deep inside the blood. No one should ever feel cut off from the ocean of mind and memory surging all around; no one should ever stare up at the icy stars and feel abandoned or alone. It was partly the fault of holism that a whole civilization had suffered the abandonment of its finest senses, ten thousand trillion islands of consciousness born into the pain and promise of neverness, awaiting death with glassy eyes and murmured abstractions upon their lips, always fearing life, always longing for a deeper and truer experience of living.

And yet there have always been those who are little interested in the tenets of holism (or science, or any ism), those who have turned inward to listen to the exquisite rhythms of mind and blood. Holism, some say, is a failed mysticism, a mysticism without a heart, and so the ancient quest for a tao, or way of life, continues. Throughout all of history, dating back past Old Earth's ur-civilizations to the primitive shamans of the forests and deserts, seekers of this way have carried on an unbroken, hidden tradition, an evolutionary journey deeper into life. These remarkable women and men are the founts of energy that each society of humankind calls upon when its vitality has weakened and dimmed. The Order itself has always depended upon its seekers of the ineffable and the immanent: the secret grades of cyber-shamans, a few maverick pilots, the yogin branch among the cetics, of course, and the best of the scryers and remembrancers. This is ironic, perhaps even tragic. For this brilliant minority has always sought to transform the Order, while the Order—the old orthodox masters and lords with their cold hearts and stony faces—has appropriated its finest discoveries, sucked the life out of the most vital knowledge, and reworked its remains into the theories and formal systems of holism. The Order, grown rigid and ossified as old bone, in many ways has exacerbated the basic fault of human consciousness. The people of the Civilized Worlds have always looked to the Order for truth, and too often, they have been given instead the symbols of the universal syntax, artificial intelligence, computer simulations of reality, form over essence, formalizations of the infinite in exchange for life.

And thus the great stellar civilization of Danlo's time, after three thousand years, had grown as worn and brittle as old glass. All around him, in Neverness and in a million other lesser cities, were men and women who lived too long and became strangers to their bodies, who feared the organic, who dwelt too long in dreams, or in their computers' tantalizing surrealities, or in cold libraries of stone. And yet everywhere, in the pretty streets and cafés, he saw people who longed for something more, even if they were unaware of their desire. All human beings desire deep in themselves to feel the life fire quickening along their blood, to be awakened to this ancient and holy burning inside others. Civilized human beings, Danlo thought in his more cynical moments, were like trillions of lumps of dead matter awaiting an intense light to ignite them. Inevitably, some remarkable and brilliant man (or woman) would return from the drears of space with starlight in his hand and fire in his eyes, and then the burning would jump from lip to lip and brow to brow as human beings came alive to their possibilities. Then there would be chaos. Then humanity would fuse together and explode across the stars, either into true awakening, or into something else, perhaps some horrible mechanism for destruction the shape of which Danlo could only glimpse. That he had been born into such times and might live to see this explosion never surprised him. But he never guessed the initial flash would originate from an astonishing source so close to him, or that he would be caught up in its fervor from almost the very beginning.

On the twelfth of false winter in the year 2953 since the founding of Neverness, a deep ship fell out into the nearspace above the City. Its name was the *Ring of Glory,* and it was owned by a renegade pilot of the Order, Pesheval Sarojin Vishnu-Shiva Lal, whom everyone knew as Bardo. For three days and nights, ferries rocketed up through the atmosphere. Their thunder and fire split the air above the Hollow Fields, making a fine show for the inevitable swarms of people who lined the pads and runs while awaiting a deep ship's arrival. One by one, the ferries glided planetward, fetching the contents of the deep ship's holds. Bardo had brought back with him riches and many, many things, the pelf of a hundred worlds: gosharps and sihu oil, furniture, bonsai plants, sacred jewelry from Vesper, blacking oil, tondos, paintings, and Darghinni sculpture, many kinds of sense boxes including dreammakers and other exotic toys, and Yarkona diamonds, and Darkmoon rubies, emeralds, opals, firestones, and pearls from the ocean floors of New Earth, Fravashi carpets, of course, and drugs such as jook, jambool, toalache, beer, and skotch. How he had acquired this vast wealth in only five years was the talk of the City. Some said that he had broken his vow of poverty as long ago as his novitiate, that he had inherited a part of his family's estates (he was born a prince of Summerworld) and had kept money in secret. He had parlayed this minor fortune, some of his old friends said,

377

into a very great one. Others were not so kind. His enemies among the lords and masters accused him of trafficking in women, or running outlawed technology. A few—the Lord Pilot Chanoth Chen Ciceron was one of these—hinted that he had betrayed the Order. "It's always tempting for a pilot to sell his skills to the merchant-pilots of Tria," he was heard to say. "Or to teach the way of our mathematics, which we must always keep secret."

There was some truth to these rumors, but only some. In truth, Bardo *had* traded secrets for money, but not the secrets of the Order. Years ago, on his infamous journey to Ksandaria, he had penetrated the forbidden knowledge pools of the great library, and he had illicitly copied much information. This information—topological mappings of lost worlds, outlawed technology, historical facts that might be used to discredit the doctrines of major religions, and antique music, fantasies, and tone poems of incalculable value—he had stored in a firestone that he kept always on his person, usually on a silver chain about his neck. Except for this single firestone, he was a poor man, for he had long since spent the remnants of his family fortune. After abjuring his vows and being stripped of his lightship, he sold all his other possessions for eight thousand City disks. He used this money to buy a passage on a prayership bound for Vesper, Larondissement, and Tria. On Tria, at first, he was taken for just another wormrunner with a firestone to sell. He was treated poorly. But when the merchant-princes and merchant-pilots discovered that he was Bardo, a former master pilot of the Order, they feted him. They provided him a low estate, women, the finest of drugs, musics, and foods. They offered him a high estate and the title of merchant-king, if only he would join them and teach them the Order's ineffable art of mathematics. It would be wrong to suppose that Bardo wasn't tempted by this offer. He was very tempted. He wouldn't have been the first pilot to defect to Tria, but he would have been the greatest pilot, the only master pilot to ever so betray the Order. In the end, he declined to become a merchant-king, not because he loved the Order, but because he was possessed of a larger vision and purpose. And so he sold the Trians his firestone and all the information it contained. He bought a vast, silvery deep ship. And he left Tria without regret, entering into the twisted space of the manifold that lies beneath the stars. He fenestered from window to window as he journeyed through the fallaways into the heart of the Civilized Worlds.

"All of history is humanity's attempt to increase its wealth," Bardo once said, and the next few years of his life were to prove the poignancy of this saying. To chronicle the exact sequence of Bardo's journeys from star to star and his acquisition of wealth would be pointless. He visited many worlds, buying and selling many things. He was a brilliant and cunning man with a talent for trade, and his inherent laziness had evaporated before the blaze of his purpose. He prospered. He enjoyed an exponential increase of wealth. A large part of his fortune he gained in a triangular trade among the worlds of Simoom, Yarkona, and Catava. The trade worked like this: On Simoom he would fill the holds of his ship with thousands of astrier families. These were all Architects of one kind or another; at that time, the Simoom hierocracy was persecuting all the Cybernetic Churches, and any Architect who could afford a passage was fleeing to Yarkona and other open worlds. The richest Architects paid Bardo fabulous amounts of money for their passages. They did this because Bardo was a master of the pilot's art and his *Ring of Glory* could make the run between Simoom and Yarkona with fewer falls and much more quickly than any deep ship of the Trian merchants. With every arrival of families desperate to establish themselves, the price of property on Yarkona increased, hence the Architects' panic to reach that rich planet before the next wave of refugees drove the prices up still further. Then, too, the Architects could never be sure when Yarkona would close its cities to them and they would be isolated on Simoom, perhaps to suffer pogroms and genocide. On Yarkona, Bardo would unload this human cargo. He would relax in the most luxurious of brothels, eating spiced, fiery foods and losing himself in the silky clasp of the Yarkonan women while he awaited the yearly opening of the Yarkonan gem market. On the first hour of the market, he would use the Architects' passage money to buy up the best of the bluestar diamonds and firestones. He always outbid his competitors. He would load the gems onto the *Ring of Glory,* collect a few thousand pilgrims, and make the long journey to Catava. Again, because he had once been a pilot of the Order, one of the finest there had ever been, he made this long journey in only a few falls. He was always the first of the gem merchants to arrive each year. Catava, of course, is the seat of the Cybernetic Reformed Churches; it is the only place on the Civilized Worlds to fabricate the priceless Edic lights that grace the altar of every Cybernetic Church across the galaxy. And the Edic lights, according to the revised version of Nikolos Daru Ede's *Principles of Cybernetic Architecture,* must always be made of true Yarkonan firestones. The Catavan Architects can never get enough good firestones, and so Bardo always sold these jeweled, living computers at enormous profit. After which he would fill his ship with facing computers, and with cleansing and vastening computers. "Catava makes the holiest computers," as the saying goes.

He would then complete the third segment of his journey. On Simoom he would sell these holy computers to the many Cybernetic Churches there. The manufacture of computers on that austere world, naturally, has always been illegal, but the Architects must have computers for their ceremonies. And so Bardo paid huge bribes to his Simoom agents and the wormrunners who smuggled his wares; he emptied his holds, added to his fortune, and began anew selling passages to refugees bound for Yarkona. Five times he made this triangular journey. When he returned to Neverness, he was perhaps the richest man in the City. He astonished everyone by buying a famous house in the Old City and announcing that he would spend the rest of his days (and fortune) pursuing a deeper way of life.

On the sixty-ninth of false winter, after remodeling his house and installing it with many beautiful things, he opened his doors to the artistic elite, the seekers, outsiders, and brightest malcontents in the City. Each night, beginning at dusk, Bardo held a joyance, a feast of life, a quickening of all the senses that was supposed to be a celebration and remembrance of the secret of life. "Mallory Ringess sacrificed himself seeking the Elder Eddas," Bardo was fond of telling everyone as he served them rare foods, wine, and pipes glowing with toalache. "The Elder Eddas, the secrets of the gods—it's inside each of us, coiled like trillions of sacred snakes into our very cells, coded into our goddamned chromosomes. To try to remember the secret of life—that's the way of the Ringess."

Bardo's parties quickly became very popular; he gathered around himself a circle of spelists, courtesans, neurosingers, and old friends. And others: most nights his rooms overflowed with ronin warrior-poets, wormrunners, hibakusha, and many uninvited guests. These seekers of the earthy and very effable delights of his house quickly became a nuisance, and Bardo had to begin issuing invitations to his joyances. Only those bearing a steel card engraved with the hologram of two interlinked rings— a black diamond ring and a ring of gold—were admitted through his outer doors. Throughout the City, a card to Bardo's house became a much coveted thing. By the end of false winter, even many of the Order's professionals and academicians had grown curious about Bardo's strange and exciting celebrations, and they schemed to acquire an invitation, often badgering Bardo or one of his circle until a card was forthcoming. But not everyone was so lucky; a desperate few demeaned themselves buying the much-traded cards that the wormrunners sold on open market outside the Hofgarten, or they bribed other masters to surrender theirs. So when, on the eighty-eighth of false winter, a messenger arrived at one of Resa's dormitories bearing a gleaming steel card for Danlo wi Soli Ringess, his fellow journeymen and master pilots were envious indeed.

"May you be enlightened tonight," a sarcastic young pilot named Orah Bey said to Danlo as he stopped him on the well-tended ice of Resa Commons. Danlo was eager to see Bardo again, and he impatiently slid his racing blades back and forth across the ice as he listened to Orah lecture him. "This will likely be your only journey to Bardo's house—if the lords don't issue an injunction against attending his parties, I'll be much surprised."

As it happened, that very same morning, Hanuman li Tosh had also received an invitation. When Danlo discovered this during lunch (the two of them had remained friends and frequently took meals together) he arranged to accompany Hanuman to Bardo's joyance. At sunset they met outside the Academy's west gate, whose scorched, steel doors always stood open to the lights of the City. Hanuman was waiting near the door, beneath the granite blocks of the Wounded Wall, and he greeted Danlo as he always did, with a smile and a quick head bow. "Hello, Danlo," he said.

"Hanu, Hanu, are you ready?" Danlo said. "This is a splendid night."

It was an evening of songbirds and sweet smells, the kind of restless evening that drives the citizens of Neverness out into the streets seeking uncertain delights. Thousands of fritillaries, their wings violet and blue with the season's colors, fluttered among the snow dahlia and other flowers that lined the Wounded Wall. The glidderies of the Old City shone with melted water, here and there gathered into shallow puddles, or spread out like a silvery lens over the crimson ice. It would be hours yet before the air fell to freezing and the streets glazed over. Despite the warmth, however, Hanuman was dressed in a formal cetic's robe, with a thick fur stola draped around his shoulders. His clothes were of a cetic's orange madder, a hideous color for any human being to wear. In truth, Hanuman, with his pale eyes and pale yellow hair, looked ghastly all swaddled up in orange. His milk-white skin had a sickly, translucent cast to it, like that of a paper lampshade inadequately covering the inner fire that kept him living. He stood coughing into his gloved hands, catching and coughing at the cancers in his lungs that he had been unable to cure himself of. Although he had attained his full growth—he and Danlo were both twenty-one years old—he was still slight of stature, and still too thin.

"Let's skate down the Serpentine," Danlo said. "The most beautiful women promenade there this time of night."

The contrast Danlo made with Hanuman was striking. He, too, was lean, but his was the leanness of an animal of the wild who loves wind and sky and movement, who takes nothing more from the world than is needed to live. Over the past five years he had grown even stronger and quite tall; he had grown the beard of a full Alaloi man, and his black hair, long and wild as tundra weed, rippled about his neck and shoulders. He still kept Ahira's white feather fastened in his hair. Gone was the white cap of Borja, and gone too was his deference to rules and the expectations of others. He wore a black racing kamelaika tight around his body and limbs. It was a garment one might choose for a game of hokkee or bump-and-skate, but hardly appropriate for a party attended by Neverness's illuminati. When Hanuman chided him for his indecorous attire, he smiled and said nothing. He flung himself down the Old City streets, and he moved as lightly as a seabird skating along cold currents of air.

They picked their way among the crowds of the Serpentine, that longest of slidderies that sinuously twists throughout the entire City, from the Elf Gardens to West Beach. Once or twice they paused to admire the beautiful women. These were mostly young astriers whose families forced them to promenade in fetching fur gowns or kimonos, in the hope of soliciting marriage contracts from the wealthy astrier men who swarm the upper segments of the Serpentine each night.

"They are each . . . so lovely," Danlo said. He caught the eye of a woman on the far side of the sliddery. She was dressed in a kimono of Japanese green, and her arms were laced through the arms of two other women who were probably her sisters. Although astriers shun others outside their sect, especially pilots of the Order forbidden by their vows to marry, when Danlo smiled at her, she bowed her head coyly and smiled back at him.

"Your love of women will be your death," Hanuman said.

"But, Hanu, you have said that about other things, and here I am, still alive."

"And alive you'll always be—until you're not."

Danlo drank in the sensations of the street: the lowing voices, the swish of expensive fabrics brushing him as the swarms of humanity passed by, the polished boots and gleaming skates, the smells of wet ice and rare perfumes and sweat. He turned to Hanuman and said, "I have already admitted that Bardo is a dangerous man. Dangerous . . . to me, at least. Must we dwell on those dangers?"

"Why shouldn't we? Since you love any kind of danger."

Danlo rubbed the livid, lightning-shaped scar above his eye and smiled. "I think Bardo is attempting something new. Truly. To attempt to remember the Elder Eddas—this is a noble thing, yes? The Order should be leading the way in recovering and delineating this knowledge. The remembrancers should be. Instead, there is talk of imposing an injunction against Bardo's joyances."

"Do you expect the Order to encourage the conceits of a new cult?"

"A cult?" Danlo said as he brushed back the hair from his forehead. "But Bardo has denied he has any religious aspirations."

"And the louder he denies it," Hanuman said, "the more surely he condemns himself."

"Sometimes I think that civilized people . . . *need* a new religion. They are so unhappy. So dead inside, so lost."

"I'll never understand your passion for religions."

"That is because your sole religious experience has been with Edeism."

"Which is all the experience I desire."

"And here I stand," Danlo said, and he laughed softly, "both tychist and holist, and Architect, and Sufi, and Zenbuddhist, and a Fravashi adept, and perhaps even . . . a would-be Alaloi shaman. I must vex you, sometimes."

Hanuman led Danlo into a vacant warming pavilion at the edge of the street where they might have a space of privacy. He said, "You do vex me. Which is why you're my friend."

"If Bardo has truly found a way to remember the Elder Eddas," Danlo said, "this is not religion. It is experience."

"Oh, there's no doubt that Bardo and his circle have remembered *something*. But the Elder Eddas? Do you really believe a race of aliens—or gods—encoded their secrets into human chromosomes?"

"Why not?" Danlo said, and he smiled.

"I thought you didn't like to *believe* anything. Don't your Fravashi teach that 'beliefs are the eyelids of the mind'? That one should put aside all beliefs?"

"Yes," Danlo said, still smiling, "including the belief that one should put aside all beliefs."

"You amaze me," Hanuman coughed out as he shook his head back and forth. "Amaze me. Can I conclude that you will therefore embrace this *experience* of Ringism that Bardo claims to offer everyone?"

Danlo now was laughing openly, and laid his hand on Hanuman's shoulder. His black leather glove sank into the orange fur of Hanuman's stola. "Yes, I will embrace it. But only for a while. Perhaps only for tonight."

For a moment Hanuman smiled at Danlo, but then his face fell tight and secretive. "I'm afraid that Bardo will want to use you," he said.

"Oh, but Bardo uses everyone. He would not be Bardo if he didn't."

"But you're the son of Mallory Ringess. Your very presence validates his joyances, you should know."

"That is true," Danlo said. "And I accept that. But can you accept that Bardo . . . might want to use *you*?"

"As a cetic? Because I've become a cetic?"

"Yes."

"Well," Hanuman said, "we cetics have our skills, and we aren't as corruptible as you might think. Perhaps a little cetic neurologic might keep Bardo from gulling his followers. It might keep them sane."

"I cannot forget . . . that Bardo never wanted you to become a cetic."

Hanuman coughed suddenly and then looked over his shoulder at the diners sitting at the edge of the street. Two of them were master eschatologists, bright-eyed and fat as seals, but they seemed aware only of their wine and plates of cultured meats. "That's true, he didn't, but you don't have to inform the whole world."

"I am sorry," Danlo said.

"I must pose a dilemma for him," Hanuman said. "He'll be dying to make use of me at the same time he's afraid to. Like

384

beer, Danlo. To him, I must be as dangerous as his dreaded beer."

"But surely he knows other cetics."

"You should know," Hanuman said in a low voice, "Lord Pall has issued an injunction, for the cetics only. He's forbidden us to attend Bardo's joyances."

"Then you are in violation of your lord's orders, yes?"

"Yes and no," Hanuman said. His eyes seemed to cloud over like old, opaque glass, and Danlo remembered how he had always hated his friend's hellish eyes. "Lord Pall must be an exemplar of our ethics," Hanuman continued, "and so, obviously, he's had to forbid us contact with Bardo's cult. But secretly—and you mustn't tell anyone this—secretly he requires information as to what Bardo is doing."

"Why? Has he become a seeker of the Elder Eddas? Lord Pall?"

"Lord Pall," Hanuman said, "is a complicated man."

"It is said that he wants to dissolve the Tetrad. That he would like to be Lord of the Order."

"Perhaps."

"Are you his spy, then?"

"Danlo!"

"I am sorry. May my tongue freeze to my teeth—I did not mean to insult you."

"You're forgiven," Hanuman said.

Just then a group of journeyman horologes in bright red robes clacked down the sliddery in front of the warming pavilion. They skated tightly together in a pack, bumping shoulders, laughing lewdly, intent upon themselves. Their lips were purple from smoked toalache and their faces were set with eagerness and guilt (and fear), as if they were on their way to spend the night in one of the alien brothels in the Farsider's Quarter. Danlo gave them a quick head bow, but they didn't notice him. Then he turned to Hanuman, and at the same instant, upon the same breath of air, in unison they each exclaimed the word "Whoremongers!" They laughed together for a while. It was a game they liked to play, this discernment of others' secrets, motivations, and plans. Hanuman had taught him the cetic's art of reading faces, and he had become adept at interpreting the tightened muscles, the eye movements, the stress patterns of the vocal chords—all the tells that betray workings of one's mind. In fact, Danlo's sensitivity to faces was so great that he could sometimes read even Hanuman's exquisitely controlled face.

"I think," Danlo said, "that you yourself are a seeker . . . of the Elder Eddas. Is this true?"

Hanuman gazed at Danlo, and his eyes were like old blue ice; his face was like a frozen and featureless seascape. All emotions, Danlo remembered, were embedded in the body's muscle fibers; all one's thoughts were coded in the firing of the nerves, the electrochemical signals with which the nerves touch the muscles into rigidity. The way Hanuman held his eyes unblinking bespoke a deep disdain of many things, and yet prefigured a passion for power over himself and his love of fate.

"It *is* true!" Danlo said. "But not . . . *wholly* true, I do not think. Since you do not believe in the blessed Eddas, it must be that you are taken with the search for them. The search for the sake of seeking, itself, yes?"

Hanuman laughed softly and said, "Can't I keep any secrets from you? I should never have taught you figuration and reading, you know. That was a violation of my ethics."

"But then I would never know . . . what you truly think about things. You have been so inward these last years."

" 'As silent as a cetic,' " Hanuman said, quoting the old saying.

"As silent, yes," Danlo said. "And as troubled, as . . . otherworldly."

"Well, let me dwell in your world for a moment," Hanuman said. He coughed into his orange-gloved hand then, and with a ferocious force for a man so slight, he snapped his wrist and sent a glob of cancerous phlegm splattering against the wet orange ice. "Certainly I'd like to learn the *technique* of remembering the Eddas. The remembrancers' techniques. It's said that Bardo has won over a master remembrancer who's giving away his professional secrets like a madman casting pearls before swine."

Danlo looked boldly into Hanuman's eyes and asked, "And you want to gather up a few of these pearls and bring them back to your tower?"

"Well, as long as I'm to be the Lord Cetic's spy, I should receive *some* sort of payment, don't you think?"

As the street filled with yet more people flashing past on promenade, and the smells of roasting coffee, kurmash, garlic, and sweatmeats wafted out of the cafés, they talked briefly of the ancient rivalry between the cetics and the remembrancers. Hanuman, who had studied more history than had Danlo, told him how the cetics, five thousand years previously on Simoom, had once been their own order. And the remembrancers had been a branch within the cetics, as devoted to understanding the secrets of consciousness as any neurologician, cyber-shaman, or yogin. But when the cetics had merged with the holists of Arcite and the Order of Mystic Mathematicians was born, the remembrancers had insisted on reorganizing themselves as a separate profession—as did the scryers. Long before the move to Neverness, the remembrancers had kept the secrets of their art from the cetics, whom they regarded either as stultified by the ancient, orthodox mental arts or corrupted by their use of computers. And the cetics had guarded *their* secrets from everybody. Even from their best friends.

"I have always wondered what you do in your tower," Danlo said. "Everyone wonders about the Cetics' Tower. It is said that you use akashic computers . . . to recover lost memories, is this true?"

Hanuman allowed a smile to break across his delicate lips, and now his face was truly silent, truly impossible to read. Danlo rarely discussed with him the arts of their respective disciplines. He knew, of course, that Hanuman had elected to become a cyber-shaman; and so his best friend certainly had mastered electronic telepathy, gestalt, fenestration, and the other states of computer consciousness. Hanuman's eyes were always fragile with the hollow, haunted look of someone who has experienced too much computer interface, who has journeyed deep into his computers' shih space, or into thoughtspace, memory space, or meta space, perhaps even into the mythical godspace that the cyber-shamans were said to seek with an almost religious devotion. In truth, Danlo was afraid that Hanuman's essential religiousness had been transfigured into his love of computers. Perhaps, Danlo thought, he would soon be initiated into the secret grades of the cyber-shamans; perhaps Hanuman's masters would implant biochips in his brain, and he would face his computers continually, and thus become an outlawed neurosinger.

"Let's discuss computers some other time," Hanuman said. "If we don't start for the joyance soon, we'll be the last to arrive."

They turned off the Serpentine then, skating down narrow glidderies closed to all sled traffic. They cut across a district of cafés, imprinting shops, libraries, and fine old apartment buildings wrought of black and pink granite. Rich émigrés and the professionals of the Order, mostly, lived in these apartments, each of which had its own private multrum and fireplace. The air was sweet with the smell of woodsmoke and flowers. Everywhere Danlo looked, there were flowers: snow dahlia and sapphire blossoms and fireflowers of crimson and gold. Each apartment's outer windowsills were hung with flower planters, and the explosion of colors drew Danlo's sight outward and up to the sky.

The blessed Ring is growing, he thought as he gazed at the heavens. In places, the sky above Neverness was tinged with a pale golden fire, a growing cloud of gases and new life that only the brightest of stars could burn through. Five times, he remembered, he had journeyed to the stars he could not see. And he had never discussed these journeys with Hanuman. He had never talked about the torison spaces that twist like black worms through the manifold, nor the beautiful mathematics of the Great Theorem, nor his dread at being lost in an infinite loop, nor his joy at passing through the number storm and entering into dreamtime. (The computer-generated dreamtime of the pilots, that is.) He had never told Hanuman a secret that the pilots had discovered: as the Golden Ring grew and spread outward into the near space above their planet, it was somehow distorting that very space. Some kind of life within the Ring, perhaps some vast and marvelous god evolved from one of the myriad kinds of newly created organisms, was twisting the superluminal fabric from which the manifold is woven. Making it knottier, more complex. And it was tearing rents in the manifold, creating new windows that pilots map their lightships through when they fall from star to star, or from point to point in the neighborhood of a star. Someday, perhaps even the great thickspace near Neverness's yellow sun might curl onto itself. The thickspace—an infinite density of point-sources where pathways from every star in the galaxy converge—might be lost into a hideous complexity of knots impossible for pilots to map. And then Neverness would no longer be the topological nexus of the galaxy. The City of Light would be cut off from the stars, and that was a secret Danlo must not tell anyone, not even his best friend.

"Look," Hanuman called out. He and Danlo had just crossed the Old City Glissade and had turned onto a purple street lined with yu trees and grand old houses. He stretched out an orange-gloved hand and pointed. "Bardo's house. Hideous, isn't it?"

"Hideous," Danlo agreed. "But splendid, too."

The house stood on the east side of the gliddery, and it was much the largest on the block. Three thousand years earlier, the

Order had built the main body of the house along classic lines of laser-cut granite, long clary windows, and beautifully grained woods: jewood and Japanese cherry and shatterwood beams rubbed with scented waxes. As with the other nearby houses, various ambassadors had lived there until the Order moved all such farsiders to the Street of Embassies. And then, during Ricardo Lavi's lordship, the north and south wings of the house had been added to provide rooms for journeymen unable to find dormitory space within the Academy's walls. This was at the beginning of the Order's Golden Age when women and men from the Civilized Worlds were coming to Neverness in swarms. It was a time of enthusiasms, caprice, and reckless technologies. The wings of Bardo's house had, in fact, been grown organically. Tiny robots the size of bacteria had assembled its structures atom by atom, bit by bit, a seamless pattern of diamond and crewel and organic stone. Viewed from the street, the house looked something like a huge, fantastic insect: the main body of natural stone, gray and solid, and the organic stone wings stived with bits of color, with filaments and streaks of cinnabar, orchid-pink, and amethyst. The two wings swept upward and out, north and south for fifty yards along the street, and they seemed as lacy and delicate as feather ice, almost impossibly delicate, as if the aretes and arches and points might crumble beneath any sudden wind. But they were strong enough, as all works of organic stone are. Originally, 256 windowpanes of spun diamond had graced the rooms of either wing. Only a few of these panes remained, however, the rest having been sold off over the centuries or stolen. As Danlo stood gazing at the splendid octagonal windows, the way the low evening light fell upon the diamond sheets and broke into showers of color, he found himself wishing that the Order hadn't abolished all assembler technology. Only a few houses in the Old City—those built between the years 620 and 694—displayed this kind of stonework, and that was too bad.

"I never thought Bardo would return," Hanuman said.

"I always . . . hoped he would."

"Do you have your invitation?"

"Yes, right here." Danlo held the steel invitation in the palm of his hand, and he flashed it at Hanuman.

"Please promise me," Hanuman said, "that you'll think carefully before embracing any of the joys of Bardo's house."

"Only if you will promise to forget you are a cetic for tonight and enjoy yourself."

"Oh, very well," Hanuman said. "I promise."

"Then so do I."

"Then let's go inside. There's supposed to be a gatekeeper to take our invitations."

So saying, they skated off the street and up the walkway to Bardo's new house.

THE WAY OF THE SERPENT

*This brings us to the Yoga concept of the Kundalini or
the snake as an image of inner strength. Kundalini is
represented symbolically as a snake coiled up upon itself in the form of a ring (kundala), in that subtle part of
the organism corresponding to the lower extremity of
the spinal column; this, at any rate, is the case with ordinary man. But, as a result of exercises directed towards
his spiritualization—Hatha Yoga, for instance—the
snake uncoils and stretches up through wheels corresponding to the various plexuses of the body until it
reaches the area of the forehead corresponding to the
third eye of Shiva. It is then, according to Hindu belief,
that man recovers his sense of the eternal.*

—*from* A Dictionary of Symbols, *by*
Juan Eduardo Cirlot

Around the grounds of Bardo's house was a metal fence, a cruel
construction of iron spears set upright into a stone border.
Danlo had heard a rumor that Bardo sometimes kept an inner
light fence around his house; but since the possession of lasers
was reason for banishment from the City, he thought the rumor
must be untrue. The gate of the fence was open, and Danlo and
Hanuman stopped to hand their invitations to the gatekeeper, a
bouncy little man with happy eyes and the aggressively ragged

look of an autist. He said, "You're late, honored journeymen, but welcome, welcome—the remembrance will soon begin."

They bowed and continued up the walkway, past intricate ice sculptures, shih trees, and lawns of snowblooms. Despite the gatekeeper's words, Danlo skated slowly and easily, enjoying the fall of evening. The air smelled of flowers and had a quality of lightness that aroused in him feelings both of anticipation and dread. The sounds of laughter, clinking glasses, and strange musics spilled out around him. Attached to the front of the house, where the shatterwood doors of the entranceway opened to the outside, was a large veranda, or rather a stone and mortar warming pavilion packed with people. Danlo and Hanuman ejected their skate blades and pushed into the throng. They bowed to various masters of the Order, and to hibakusha, and to spelists, and even to the merchant-princes in their gem-studded jackets. Everywhere Danlo looked, he saw people drinking ice wine or skotch or jambool, or smoking toalache. All kinds of people: wormrunners and harijan, poets and phantasts, and even two beautiful courtesans who were highly placed in the Society of Courtesans. It seemed that Bardo had invited a third of the City to his joyance, but it was not so. Other than Hanuman, there were no cetics to be seen; there were few astriers and very few Architects. One might have thought that scryers would attend any celebration of memory—these eyeless prophets sometimes call their visions "memories of the future"—but Bardo mistrusted scryers and kept them away.

Because it was almost too noisy to talk, Danlo lightly touched the sleeve of Hanuman's robe to draw his attention. Using the cetic hand language that Hanuman had taught him, he signed: *Let's find Bardo and wish him well.*

They went into the house, following a stream of people through the entrance hall and into a large, richly decorated sun room. Bardo had returned from his journeys with the finest of gosharps, Yarkona furniture, Darghinni sculptures, tondos and paintings and crewel work. And Fravashi carpets, of course, and too many sense boxes. Danlo was surprised that mantelets, fones, sulki grids, and other kinds of forbidden technology were so openly displayed, hanging from the walls or sitting atop shiny lacquered tables. But then, Bardo was an open, expansive man who liked to flaunt his way of living, however excessive or careless. It amused Danlo to see twenty-three bonsai trees lined up in front of the sun room's diamond windows. The leaves of the trees looked sickly and yellowish-green, as if Bardo were still giving them too much water.

Hanuman caught Danlo's eye and said, "I've heard that sometimes Bardo doesn't greet his guests until just before the midnight remembrance."

"Then perhaps we should take our supper," Danlo said. "Have you eaten?"

"I'm not hungry," Hanuman said.

"Will you excuse me, then? I cannot bear the smells of all these foods."

Danlo, who was always hungry and always ate enough for three men, wandered off to see what delicacies he might discover. At the far end of the room, a long table had been set with stacks of clary plates, chopsticks, wine goblets, and many platters of food. There were pepper nuts, curried vegetables, cheeses, grilled tombu, mounds of glittering red salmon roe, and cultured meats. And baldo nuts, sliced snow apples, bloodfruit in cream, breads, and a dozen kinds of fairy food. Danlo squeezed between a shivering autist and a beautiful, black-skinned woman whom he recognized as the diva, Nirvelli. He helped himself to a plate of steaming kurmash. He stood there gobbling these exquisitely hot nut grains as he looked about the room. Nirvelli wasn't the only famous person there. He saw Zohra Bey, and Moriah Li Chen, and Thomas Sonderval, *the* Sonderval, raimented in a rather dandyish robe—which he had probably designed himself—and in his vast and brilliant arrogance. Danlo was wondering if he should introduce himself to this pilot of pilots when something caused him to look back across the room. There, standing next to Hanuman, wearing the silk pajamas of a courtesan, was the most beautiful woman that he had ever seen.

"Losharu shona!" Danlo whispered to himself. *"Losharu halla!"*

He stared at her, much too openly, and his eyes burned because he could not blink them, and his heart pounded with the thrill of shooting adrenaline. For much too long he remained frozen there, like an animal of the forest watching another. He forgot that he was holding a plate of kurmash in his hand. He let the plate tilt, and little yellow-brown kernels rolled off, fell, and bounced against the marble floor. His hunger—the empty, contracting hunger in his belly for food—was suddenly gone. The loveliness of this young courtesan struck like a lightning bolt to his core and burned him inside. He loved, all in a moment,

393

everything about her: the graceful way she moved her hands when she talked; her easy, natural smile; and, above all, her pure animal vitality. She was tall and voluptuous, and smoothly muscled like an ice dancer. Her face was unique and memorable, though he was dimly aware that no single feature seemed to go very well with any other. Her lips were a shade too red, too full, too sensuous against the creaminess of her skin. She had a long, imperious nose set between high cheekbones, and thick blond hair, and japanesque eyes, intelligent and lively, as dark and liquid as coffee. Her entire face stood out prominently, almost prognathously, an atavism that hinted of something deeply primitive in her. Danlo found this primitive quality instantly compelling. A part of him wondered if he would later see her in a different light, but now other parts were burning with a need far beyond wonder. His chest was hot and tight, and his eyes were afire with the sight of her, and his hands ached to touch her splendid face.

Halla is the woman who shines like the sun, he thought.

She looked at him then. She turned her head and looked past all the bright, chattering people standing between them. She looked straight at him, boldly and openly. Their eyes met and locked together, and there was a shock of instant recognition, as if they had known each other for a billion years. Danlo felt himself falling into her eyes, and the world about him narrowed, intensified, and stopped altogether. He knew he had never seen her before, yet his eyes burned with this electric and ancient connection. His lips burned, and his fingers, and his blood; everything about him was afire with a sudden knowingness that swept his breath away and astonished him.

"Excuse me," he said when he had finally recovered his voice. Next to him stood a thin, amused-looking woman dressed in a gaudy silver gown. He had spilled his kurmash over her silver slippers. Without taking his eyes away from his lovely courtesan, he mumbled, "Excuse me, would you mind holding my plate . . . for a moment?"

He pushed the plate into the woman's hands, bowed perfunctorily, and walked off. He fairly flew across the room. He came right up to Hanuman and the courtesan, and all the while his eyes never left hers.

Hanuman smiled at him, but he scarcely noticed. He scarcely heard Hanuman say, "Danlo, may I present Tamara Ten Ashtoreth? Tamara, this is the friend I was telling you about, Danlo wi Soli Ringess."

Danlo bowed to her, and then he forgot all his manners. He reached out and grasped her hand, which was gloved in blue silk. He held her hand gently, and he immediately wished he could pull off his black leather gloves, the better to touch her long fingers with his own. "You are beautiful!" he gasped out. "I have never seen anyone . . . so beautiful."

This outburst caused Tamara to smile, a wide and lovely smile that broke over her face like the sun. She was much too accomplished and poised to return his compliment, in words, but her eyes were full of light and laughter, and an openness that said: You are very beautiful, too.

"Is this your first joyance?" Danlo asked.

"I've attended two others," Tamara said. Her voice was clear and strong and lovely to hear. "Bardo has invited courtesans to each of his joyances. Everyone says he's trying to convert our Society."

Danlo let go of her hands and said, "Could it be that Bardo just likes to surround himself with beautiful women?"

"I'm sure he must have many reasons for what he does," Tamara said. "But he's *your* friend, isn't he? I'm sure you must know his intentions."

"No, I have not seen him for five years. People change, don't they?"

"Everyone is calling Bardo a religious man," Tamara said. There was a wariness and irony in her voice. "I do think he's a charismatic man. He has a very great passion, which has impressed us all. But a passion for what? He *seems* devoted to remembrancing the Elder Eddas. He *seems* involved with unfolding the racial memories. I've only recently met him—has he always displayed such a passion for the possibilities of his memory and his mind?"

"The Bardo that *I* knew," Danlo said, and he was suddenly laughing, "had a passion for other parts of himself. Other . . . possibilities, yes?"

"I think I know what you mean," Tamara said. She, too, began to laugh. They stood there facing each other, looking into each other's eyes, and laughing.

Here Hanuman coughed and cleared his throat as he shot Danlo a cold look. It was he who had engaged Tamara in conversation, a significant feat considering that she was a courtesan and he only a journeyman cetic; he coughed and looked askance at Danlo's instant infatuation. He said, "It should be obvious that Bardo is trying to convert the courtesans. If I wanted to influence the Order to accept a new religion, that's what I would do."

"I'm sure you overestimate our importance," Tamara said.

"Do I?"

"Our Society has never had a formal connection to the Order."

"Which is why your influence has been so pervasive."

Tamara smiled, and then, in her lovely musical voice, she said, "But our purpose, as everyone knows, is pleasure, not politics. I detest politics."

"Many voluptuaries say that," Hanuman coughed out. "And then, when they're older—well, you know what the masters say, don't you?"

"No, I don't think I do."

"They say this: 'Find a paramour, lose your soul.'"

Again, Tamara laughed, and she smiled at Hanuman. "You're a cynical man, I think. I've been taught that our Society was founded precisely to *keep* men from losing their souls."

The Society of Courtesans, in fact, had been founded in the year 1018 as an investment cooperative designed to protect the fortunes of a few dozen women who were extraordinarily skilled in their arts of ecstasy. And to protect their lives. When the newly formed Society of Courtesans began buying property in the Farsider's Quarter and conducting the finances of their art themselves, they had severed all connection with their procurers and pimps. In revenge, these violent, cruel, and parasitical men had beaten them, and sometimes even tortured them with nerve knives that caused their beautiful bodies to convulse and spasm. More than one courtesan had died this way. And so the first courtesans pooled their money to hire assassins. The assassins exterminated the procurers, of course, and then betrayed the very women who had hired them. They demanded three quarters of the Society's yearly profits—or else they would assassinate the courtesans one by one. This tribute was a far greater bite of their wealth than their procurers had ever taken, and the courtesans decided not to pay it. Instead, they sent their most accomplished diva—her name was Natasha Urit—to the planet Qallar.

There, Natasha made an infamous pact with the warrior-poets. In exchange for the warrior-poets' murderous services, the courtesans promised to consider the strange religion of Qallar and, if possible, to help subvert the masters and lords of the Order. This was a time when the warrior-poets were proselytizing all across the Civilized Worlds, as well as murdering for the sheer joy of living closer to death and life. The warrior-poets desired to bring all peoples to an intenser experience of life, especially the Order academicians, who valued only their vast knowledge and their minds. Natasha Urit promised to introduce young courtesans to the men of the Order, that they might ply their art and open the academicians' hearts to new realms of experience. Pleasure was their key to this opening, and over two millennia, the courtesans had learned all there was to know about pleasure.

Long after the warrior-poets had murdered every assassin in Neverness, long after their proselytizing zeal had faded and they dissolved their pact with the courtesans, the courtesans kept alive the flame of the warrior-poets' teachings. And they maintained a special relationship with the Order. Over time, the Society grew and evolved, but they continued to train their novices in the arts of tantra, sex dancing, music, maithuna, and bodywork. And their novices, century after century, matured and ripened into voluptuaries who enraptured any young Orderman who could afford one. And the voluptuaries grew old, and they returned their bodies to youth, and they became the paramours of masters and old lords who had learned to love them. The Order had long forbidden pilots and other professionals to marry, and so in place of wives, they took paramours into their arms. Some of these paramours even bore children, illegitimately, illegally. Some of the most famous lords acquired money and kept their families in secret splendor. They listened too well to the counsel of their paramours, and they lost their independence, if not their souls. But the best of the courtesans, whether paramour, diva, or voluptuary, continued to practice their art for only the highest of reasons.

"If our Society *really* wanted to influence the Order," Tamara said, and she smiled at Hanuman, "we'd train men to please your women. Almost half your professionals are women."

"That's true," Hanuman said, "but seven of ten lords are men."

Danlo brushed the hair away from his eyes and looked at Tamara. He almost had to shout to make himself heard above the music and the many ringing voices. "Could you really do that—train men to please women?"

In answer, Tamara laughed softly and nodded her head.

"I should think that's the secret of their art," Hanuman

397

said. "What better way to enrapture a man than by exciting his vanity?"

"I'm afraid you don't really understand," Tamara said.

For a while Hanuman and Tamara bantered with each other like two novices slapping a hokkee puck back and forth. Hanuman stared at her uneasily, his eyes hooded yet intense. He affected the manner of a young journeyman who couldn't afford a courtesan's arts: he seemed full of awe, resentment, guilt, and ill-concealed desire. But he was partly playing at these emotions, as cetics often do. Most likely he was trying to manipulate Tamara in subtle ways, perhaps to crack her dazzling surface charm in order to show the love-blind Dànlo a facet of her he might otherwise not have seen.

But Tamara was as imperturbable as a diamond, and despite Hanuman's manipulations and veiled attacks, she continued to smile and sparkle. "When you've become a full cetic," she told Hanuman, "I'm sure you'll find a courtesan who will teach you the greatest of all pleasures."

"Do I dare ask what that would be?"

"I think you already know," Tamara said.

Hanuman let loose a hollow laugh, and then said, "Yes, I'm a cetic, and I'm supposed to discern such things."

There was a long silence, which Danlo broke by asking, "And what is the greatest of all pleasures?"

"The giving of pleasure, of course," Tamara said. She looked at Danlo, then at Hanuman. "Though some men have always found their greatest pleasure in the giving of pain."

These words obviously caught Hanuman unprepared. His face fell crimson, for a moment, and he seemed outraged, hurt, shamed. It was a rare thing for him to betray such emotion. "You should know, Danlo, that courtesans are very skilled with their tongues. They've much to teach—even a cetic could learn from them."

"You're very gracious," Tamara said. "Thank you."

"However there's so much to learn, and so few nights in which to learn it," Hanuman said. He bowed to Tamara and smiled his frozen cetic's smile. "And on this night we've come to learn remembrancing, Danlo and I. We should excuse ourselves and pay our respects to Bardo."

Again, he bowed, deeply, a shade too deeply for the occasion. He turned to Danlo and said, "I wonder if he's grown fatter these last five years?"

Danlo knew he should make his good-byes and find Bardo,

but something in Tamara's dark, lustrous eyes seized his muscles and held him motionless.

"Danlo?"

Hanuman's soft, too-restrained voice fell among the hundred other voices in the room, and Danlo scarcely noticed that he had spoken.

"Are you coming?"

"Not yet," Danlo finally said. "Why don't you tell Bardo I am waiting to wish him well. I shall find you . . . later."

His eyes were still fixed on Tamara's, so he did not see the look of fury that burned across Hanuman's face. It never occurred to him, then, that Hanuman might instantly have loved Tamara, even as he loved her. In truth, he never suspected that Hanuman was capable of such a purely self-consuming emotion.

After Hanuman had sulked out of the room, Danlo shook his head, and to Tamara he admitted, "Sometimes he likes to hurt people, truly. But I cannot see why he would want to hurt you."

Someone nudged Danlo from behind, causing him to step closer to Tamara. The long room was now quite full of people. The air was hot and steamy from the heat of a hundred bodies. Many were smoking triya seeds in little wooden pipes. The *pop-pip-pop* of the tiny seeds was everywhere, and plumes of purplish smoke unfolded like satin gauze and veiled over the room's three chandeliers. This smoke stung Danlo's eyes, and breathing it exhilarated him. He looked at Tamara, standing beneath Bardo's glass chandelier. The thousands of glass pendants were incandescent with electricity, of all things. Electric light spilled down over Tamara's head and covered her in soft violet tones. Danlo thought she looked like a statue of the goddesses they sculpt on Gemina. Then she moved closer to him, and her dancer's muscles played beneath her violet-blue pajamas, and Danlo was very aware that she was a living creature of flesh and blood and sweet, hot breath.

"Sometimes I think the courtesans and cetics are too much alike," Tamara said. "We're both too aware of the power of words."

Danlo was now so close to her that he could feel the moisture in her breath; he could talk without raising his voice. "I have heard that courtesans are accomplished in the art of conversation."

"Conversation is the third greatest pleasure," Tamara said.

"I have . . . never spoken with a courtesan before."

Tamara smiled at him and said, "And I've never known anyone like you before."

"But you know . . . *about* me, yes?"

"Hanuman told me how you came to Neverness. That you had to eat *dogs* to stay alive. I think he's a little in awe of you."

"Did he tell you how I was born? *Where* I was born?"

"I've heard the stories," Tamara said. "It can't be easy being the son of Mallory Ringess."

"Oh, that is not so hard," Danlo said. "This is what is hard: living in a city where people can worship a man who has become a god."

"I think the people in all cities are very much the same."

"All civilized people, yes. But other peoples have . . . other ways."

She looked at him in instant understanding and asked, "Are you speaking of the Alaloi people?"

"Yes."

"But could you ever return to the Alaloi tribes? To their way of life?"

Danlo rubbed his forehead and touched the feather in his hair. "I have never told anyone, but I have often dreamed of going back."

"Because the Alaloi live more simply than we do?"

"No, it is not that. At least, it is not just the simplicity. All my life, it seems, I have been looking for a kind of beauty that I call *halla. Halla*, it is . . . the harmony of all life. The way all things are connected, the web, the way each thing becomes purely itself only in relation to all other things. Once or twice when I was a child, on quiet nights when the stars came out . . . I have a memory of this kind of beauty."

Tamara touched his hand then; she reached down between them where her pajamas nearly touched the kamelaika covering his thigh, and she wrapped her long fingers around his. "I listened to a recording of one of the Alaloi dialects a few years ago," she said. "I thought it was a beautiful language."

"Are you a student of languages?"

"I think I've imprinted fourteen languages and learned three others the long way."

Tamara, like many courtesans, preferred to converse with her clients in their milk tongues, and she did so whenever she could. Those familiar with their talents sometimes refer to courtesans—usually with snide double meaning—as linguists.

400

"Do you remember much of . . . the Alaloi language?" Danlo asked.

"No, but I love to hear it spoken."

Danlo squeezed Tamara's fingers. She was standing quite close to him, almost eye to eye. He drank in the clean smell of her hair, and he looked at her and said, *"Halla los li devani kicharara li pelafi nis ni manse."*

"But what does that mean?"

"It means 'Halla is the woman who lights the blessed fire inside a man.' "

Tamara laughed in open delight and beamed a smile at him. "You're a beautiful man, and I like talking with you. But it's well that you didn't say that when your friend was here. He's very jealous of you, I think."

"Hanuman . . . jealous?"

Tamara nodded her head and sighed. "I think he was about to propose a contract when you interrupted us."

"But he is a journeyman—does your society make contracts with journeymen?"

"No, my *society* doesn't. But some journeymen—I hope I'm not insulting anyone—despite their vows, some young men keep money. Some courtesans make secret contracts with them."

"They do this to enrich themselves, yes?"

"To enrich themselves at our society's expense. Of course, these courtesans are punished when they're found out, but it still happens."

"I do not know how Hanuman could have gotten money," Danlo said.

"It doesn't really matter," Tamara said. "I'm afraid I would have had to disappoint him, money or not."

"A woman as beautiful as you . . . must make many contracts."

"My society has appointed me contracts the next fifteen nights."

Danlo pulled his hands away from hers and carelessly ungloved himself. He stuck his gloves in his pants pocket. Then he reached out and gently grasped her hands, and he stripped off her tight silk gloves. Around the middle finger of her left hand, she wore a gold ring cast in the form of a snake biting its tail, but he scarcely noticed this. He touched her long naked fingers, and the sudden shock of skin pressing hot skin delighted him. He looked at her, and he said, quite boldly, "But you have made no contracts for tonight?"

"No," she said, "not for tonight." She wove her fingers between his and smiled.

"I have never had . . . any money," Danlo said.

"Is that what you've thought to give me?"

"Money is just a symbol, yes?" Danlo said. "It is meaningless as a gift. If I could give you anything . . . it would be a pearl, to wear around your neck. Have you ever seen a pearl of the palpulve oysters? They are splendid and rare."

"Oh, Danlo, you shouldn't promise what's impossible."

"But what can I give you?"

In answer Tamara pulled his hands close to her body so that they brushed the lower part of her belly. "You're so beautiful," she said. "I've never made a contract with a man just for the sake of beauty."

He laughed then, easily and gladly, as he sometimes did when he was overwhelmed with pure delight. His laughter, falling out in the middle of a room where tens of people were smoking psychedelic triya seeds and also laughing, might have gone unnoticed, but then Tamara was laughing, too, and their obvious passion for each other attracted many stares. At that moment, however, Danlo had no care for anyone other than Tamara. They locked eyes together, and it was as if they were the only truly alive people in the room, possibly in the universe. There came a sudden knowing of each other's minds and hearts: they both thought it was intensely funny that they could stand there in open sight of many others, touching hands and falling into love. This knowingness was intensely real, more real even than the musky smell of Tamara's perfume or his own acrid sweat. It drew him into a brilliant and wild future that he could see forming even as he looked into her lovely eyes.

"We should be alone together," he said.

"I think that would be best," she said. She stroked the palms of his hands and pulled at his fingers. "I keep a house up near North Beach—we could go there."

"That is too far. It would take too long to get there."

She laughed and then said, "But where else could we go?"

"I have heard that there are thirty sleeping chambers in this house." He swept his arms out and smiled. "This time of night, they cannot all be taken."

"You propose we begin our contract, *here*? Now?"

"Yes, why not?"

"That would be rash," she said. "There's no way to make preparations."

Danlo winced, inwardly, at the word "preparations." Many times since entering Borja, he had seduced the Order's young women; many times, the more adventurous akashics or holists or scryers or even other pilots had seduced him. And each time, before their love play, these lovely women had diligently made their preparations. Each of them had worn a pessary, artificial tissues that lined the vagina and protected against pregnancy and disease. How he loathed the gelid, alienating feel of these tissues! But civilized women feared contagion almost as much as death, and so they did what they could to quarantine their bodies and safeguard themselves. Indeed, many women and men renounced swiving altogether in favor of other forms of sex. Journeymen of all professions were supposed to satisfy themselves with masturbation or simulation. Although Danlo was quite aware of civilized customs, he disdained both these alternatives as *shaida* acts that could only lead him to false ecstasy. Both acts required the infusion of the brain with images— whether the false images of pure fantasy or the totally compelling images and sensa of a computer-generated surreality, it did not matter. Danlo craved real copulation as much as he craved life, and he sought such love play whenever he could.

"Let's be rash, then," he said to Tamara.

"Are you so eager to be the father of a child?"

"Is that to be the result of our contract?"

"Do you want it to be?" she asked.

Danlo touched her long hair, then said, "I had heard that courtesans have an awareness of their fertility. That they can *control* their own fertility, yes?"

"Some of us master these skills, that's true."

"Then you must know if tonight . . . is a dangerous time for you."

"Oh, it's dangerous," she said. "It's always dangerous, isn't it?"

"But *how* dangerous?"

"Shall I calculate the probabilities for you?" she asked. She smiled, and it was obvious this whole conversation amused her. "There's only a very slight chance we'd conceive a child together tonight."

"If we did," he said, "I could quit the Order and we could make a marriage contract together."

At this, she laughed for a long time before saying, "You shouldn't promise what you're not ready to do."

"But I might want to marry you anyway—I promised myself this the instant I saw you."

"You have a sweet tongue," she said, "but let's not speak of marriage right now."

"Should we speak of love?"

"No, that would be even worse."

"Then let's not speak at all," he said. "Let's be rash . . . together."

He touched her forehead, and his fingers knew an instant and intense thrill. He touched her eyes, her cheek, her long neck, and then the primal urge of life toward more life caught them both, as in a firestorm, and she said, "All right."

Hand in hand, they made their way from the room. They squeezed past many women: a harijan poet whose old, gnarly face he vaguely recognized; the fat wife of a merchant-prince; a thin toalache addict with her burned-out but intelligent eyes. Danlo was so enraptured, he found something to love in each of them. All women were beautiful, he thought, and he told himself that he could make a marriage with almost anyone, if he were ever free to marry. He told himself this even as he walked through brilliant rooms full of brilliant people, deeper into Bardo's house. They passed into a great hall of high arches and long windows, and then up a flight of stairs into the north wing. Here the skylights were clear diamond panes and the walls glittering sweeps of organic stone. Guest rooms lined both sides of the corridor; the doors of each room—slabs of plain jewood polished with lemon wax—were closed. Danlo chose a door at random, glanced at Tamara, and then wrapped his knuckles across the gleaming, resonant wood. The sound of his knocking seemed very loud and cracked out along the corridor. When there was no answer, he opened the door. He saw immediately that someone had used the room that night: the windows were open, and in the fireplace, the embers of a dying fire glowed and hissed. The room smelled of lemons and triya seeds and the essence of snow dahlia blowing in from Bardo's lawn, good smells that drew him quickly inside. He was smiling and laughing and pulling at Tamara's arm, and then he kicked the door closed, and there were other wonderful smells: that of woodsmoke and fresh new furs and the thickness of Tamara's hair. He liked everything about the room, although it was so dark at first that he could see little of it. There were the lovely diamond windows, of course, and clothes chests inlaid with rare woods. Low, lacquered tables were set out with pipes and little bowls of

404

triya seeds, and with decanters of wine, and boxes of black toalache, and with half a dozen other drugs that might be snuffed or smoked or drunk. Near the fireplace was a huge futon covered with shagshay furs. He stood over this futon, looking for Tamara's eyes in the darkness. He was still holding her hand, and he pulled her closer so that he could see her face.

"Let's breathe together," she said.

She kissed him then, touched his lips with hers. He had never kissed a woman before; the Alaloi do not practice this art, nor do most of the civilized peoples. He found the play of mouth against mouth and quick slipping tongues to be strange but very exciting. In truth, the unexpected pleasure of it shocked him and left him breathless. She pressed up close to him, and their bodies molded together. Her silk pajamas rubbed against his kamelaika. The friction of silk against wool rubbed off surface electrons from the molecules of either fabric and electrified their garments. When he unzipped her pajamas and pulled them off her, faint crackles of blue and green electricity ran along the silken folds, then died into the room's darkness. There was some difficulty getting his kamelaika off, not because of the little shocks of static electricity that tickled his hands, but because it was very tight and his muscles were swollen with blood. At last, however, they were naked together, kissing and clutching each other with abandon. She ran her fingers along his membrum, and she gasped in surprise as she touched the hard little scars that had been cut there during his passage into manhood. They stood there for a long time as they stroked and rubbed against each other. Then she pulled him down atop her, and they sank into the furs covering the futon. They swived each other furiously, pushing and panting and sweating and moaning in delight. She was in her first youth, only a couple of years older than he, and she was as strong and wild as any animal. His hands were beneath her, and he felt the muscles bunching along her back and buttocks, her anus a hard ring of muscle coiled like a snake. Because she wore no pessary, the deep clutching of her vulva around him was direct and intense, a silky, heavenly slickness that drew him on and on. They moved together, in rhythm and rapture, and he couldn't tell where his body ended and hers began. It was as if the cells of his body loved the cells of hers, or rather, remembered them from some ecstatic union long ago and were at last returning home. She gasped and wrapped her hands around his back and pulled him deep into an exploding joy, deeper into the supreme risk of life. There was a moment of total surrender and dying to himself, as if he were only an atom of consciousness completing some universal plan. And then he suddenly cried out and shuddered, and there was true union, a true returning. They cried out together in their ecstasy, and he wanted to go on and on forever, but the pleasure of passion had grown into agony and he had to stop.

They lay there awhile, panting and joined to each other in exhaustion. Then the air streaming in the window chilled the sweat on their bodies and drove them beneath the furs. He asked her if she would like a fire, and she said "yes," and so he got up and threw some logs on the glowing embers and poked about until the fireplace was full of crackling orange flames. Soon it was too hot for the furs, and they kicked them off. They held each other and lay naked before the fire. They talked about little things, such as the fine weather the City was enjoying and the excellence of the foods that Bardo served. And then their conversation grew more serious. Danlo told her of his reasons for coming to Neverness; he tried to explain why he had become friends with Hanuman li Tosh. But he was really better at listening than talking, and most of the time he gazed at Tamara and nodded his head attentively while she spoke of her stultified childhood as an astrier and her later initiation into the courtesan arts. As he discovered, she had a brilliant mind. In fact, she might have entered the Order and become a cetic or a remembrancer, but her parents, as good astriers and Architects, had denied her a formal education. And so, while still quite young, she had left her home and applied to the Society of Courtesans. She had become an accomplished voluptuary; indeed, many said she was destined to become a diva. She had applied her mind and the intelligence of all her senses toward one end: the awakening of herself and others to a greater intensity of life. It soon became clear, from her manner and the way she looked at Danlo, that what she loved most about him was his wildness (or rashness) and his own burning love of life.

"You're still hot," she said as she touched his face. She rubbed his chest, and then ran her fingers through the black hair of his belly and pubes until she touched the little white pearl of liquid beading up on the tip of his membrum. She touched the naked bulb, softly, and the many scars running along the shaft. She rested her head on his chest, staring down at him as she fingered the round, shiny, blue and red scars. "It must have hurt to have had these affixed," she said.

Danlo thought of the night he had lain on his back beneath

the stars while Three-Fingered Soli cut him, and he said, "Yes . . . it hurt."

"Do all the Alaloi decorate themselves this way?"

"Only the men."

"How strange," she said. "Do they think it will stimulate the women and give them more pleasure?"

"No, that is not the reason."

"Then why do they do it?"

Danlo stroked her hair and said, "I do not mean to be secretive, but I . . . cannot tell you. That is, I *may* not." In truth, the twenty-ninth verse of the Song of Life told of the cutting of a man's membrum, and he was forbidden to reveal this knowledge to anyone. Although a part of him had long since cast off his childhood beliefs, a deeper part whispered for him to keep his silence.

"Do they think to desensitize themselves?" she asked.

"What do you mean?"

"I've known a few men, mostly wormrunners—they have themselves circumcised. The skin of the bulb then dries out, which lessens the intensity of sensation. Or so they think."

Danlo clenched his jaws, then said, "But why would anyone want to be cut . . . for that reason?"

"Because they hope to prolong love play. To give the woman time to reach her ecstasy, too."

"But such cutting does not prolong anything," Danlo said. "I have been cut, as you can see—all Alaloi men have. Everyone knows that men most often reach their ecstasy before women."

"And leave us unsatisfied?"

Danlo watched the firelight dance over her naked limbs, and he traced his fingers over her hip. "When we are still boys, we are taught how to touch women to their ecstasy. If I had reached my moment before you . . . I would not have left you unsatisfied."

She smiled and kissed his navel, and she said, "There are different intensities of satisfaction."

"That may be true," he said, "but the universe is made the way it is, yes? Men are made the way they are. All male animals. Have you ever seen a shagshay bull mount an ewe?"

"No, I really haven't."

"The entire copulation lasts less than ten seconds," he said. "Ten . . . thrusts, a little bellowing, and the bull is done. Would you change all that is natural?"

"Would you?" she asked. She looked at him and smiled, almost as if she could read his thoughts. And then they both broke into laughter.

"I have often thought about this problem," he said. "Why should the passions of a man and a woman be so out of joint? And if we are both of us natural children of a . . . natural nature, isn't this proof that the whole universe is *shaida*?"

"Is *shaida* the opposite of *halla*?"

"Not precisely. *Shaida* is . . . the left hand of *halla*."

"I see. You want to do only what's natural." She sat up, spine straight with her feet beneath her. She folded her left hand over his right hand and squeezed it.

After a while he asked, "Do you think a man should try to forestall his ecstasy to match a woman's?"

She touched the scar running across his forehead. She smiled and said, "Some men find that in forestalling their ecstasy, they make it more intense. And then ecstasy is multiplied by ecstasy—the possibilities between woman and man are said to be infinite."

"I do not know how it could be any more intense," he said.

"I can't always match my passion with the quickness of yours," she said. "And I wouldn't want to, even if I could."

"But how is it possible to forestall such a force? When one's moment comes . . . it is like stopping a star from exploding."

"Shall I show you how?"

"Could you do that?"

"It would be my pleasure," she said.

Again, she kissed his mouth, kissed his eyes, kissed his body from his neck to his knees. And he kissed her. They spent a long time, kissing and caressing, and then he moved to lie atop her as before. But she pushed her hands against his chest and eased him onto his back. She knelt over him, clenching his dense chest hair in her fists as she settled atop him and slipped back and forth. She did this not as an ecstasy-forestalling technique, but because she was a courtesan obeying her Society's rule of the alternation (and equality) of sexual positions. In fact, it would have been easier for her to apply these techniques with him atop her, but Tamara was not one to break rules merely for the sake of expediency. She moved back and forth, faster and faster, sliding and pressing down against him with her loins. Danlo ached to thrust freely inside her, to control the pace of their copulation. He was sweating now and breathing quickly, and every part of him felt swollen and overfull. He was dying to reach his moment and be done, he was very close, and then suddenly she reached down behind her and touched his stones, and pressed her fingers down into the taut skin below them. She showed him the pressure points to forestall his ecstasy. She showed him how to breathe, and she cooled his surging blood and his blind desire. Two times she did this, and each time she allowed his passion to build to a greater intensity than he had ever known before. At last, after a long while, she took pity on him. Her fingers found other places on his body that urged him straight into ecstasy. It began as a quickening of energy that seemed to coil around the base of his spine, or rather, uncoil, rapidly, filling his loins with a rare and marvelous power. She, too, was full of this power, he could see it flashing in her lustrous eyes. They looked at each other, and something vast and vital passed back and forth between them, eye to eye, hand to hand, cell to cell. Then she closed her eyes and started rocking back and forth in frenzy, still pressing him with her knees and her vulva and her artful fingers. He was young and full of seed, and the soft clasp of her body was squeezing the liquid life out of him. He was now too full of life; it burned like a river of fire inside him, inside his belly, up to his heart, then behind his eyes. For a moment, while he could still see, he looked up at her as she threw back her head and gasped for air. Her eyes were tightly closed, her face a mask of rapture glowing in the light of the fire. And then he closed his eyes, too, and the pressure in his loins grew so intense that he cried out and clawed the muscles along her thighs. There was a wild rush of energy, as of lightning shooting along his spine from his hips to his head. In this moment of pure, blinding joy he felt something marvelous completed between them. He emptied himself into her in quick pulses of life, over and over until she fell gasping against him and kissed his neck and pressed the side of his head with hers. He lay there in utter exhaustion, with her collapsed atop him, and he was utterly empty. And yet he was as full as he had ever been, aware of all that was going on around him. He heard voices from the deep parts of Bardo's house and the wind against clear diamond panes; he was aware of fireflowers opening in Bardo's garden, and the pungence of triya seeds, and the sweet smell of sex. Tamara's breath rushed in his ear, and her heart beat next to his, and he was aware that he had never felt so strong, so whole, so utterly alive.

After a while they rolled onto their sides. Gradually they passed back into a normal, waking consciousness, and then into a conversational consciousness. Tamara ran her fingers through his hair and touched his white feather. She said, "I've never known anyone like you before."

"And I have never known . . . *anything* before," he said. "There is so much to know, isn't there?"

She nodded her head and laughed. "Some men practice with courtesans for years before the serpent strikes them."

"The . . . serpent?"

"Did you know we call our art 'the Way of the Serpent'?"

He grasped her hand and touched the ring coiled around her middle finger. It was made in the form of a thick-bodied snake, whose eyes were two tiny rubies set into gold. The snake's mouth opened onto its tail, as if it were about to swallow itself. This continuity of golden fang to golden flesh made a perfect golden circle.

"I noticed that you wear the ring of Ouroboros," he said. "This is an ancient symbol, yes?"

"Then you *do* know about the serpent?"

"Not really. That is, I have studied the religions and have learned the meaning of their symbols. A few symbols. Ouroboros, the serpent who swallows its own tail—this is a symbol of nature itself, yes? The immortality of all things. The way life lives off of life, consumes itself, yet continues. The great circle of life and consciousness, continually shedding death like an old skin and being born anew."

Tamara looked back and forth between her ring and his eyes, and she said, "I think I like your interpretation better than the one I was taught. It's simpler, more profound."

Danlo bowed his head and smiled. "This symbol means something different to you, yes?"

"Have you ever heard of the serpent called Kundalini?"

"No, I am not familiar with that name."

"But you've heard of the tantric yoga?"

Shaking his head back and forth, he said, "We are taught many yogas, of course. But not the tantric yoga."

"Tantra is the ancient name for this yoga," she said. "It's the yoga of sex and energy, the life energies. Many of its techniques have been incorporated into the other yogas."

"And the courtesans are masters of this yoga?"

"Not precisely," she said. "We have our art—it's been evolving for a long time. Our practices differ, in many ways, from the tantra. Our theories are different."

"Is the Kundalini a theory or symbol, then?"

"Both," she said. "In the ancient theory, the Kundalini energy lies coiled around the base of the spine like a great serpent. Various techniques are used to—"

"I felt something like that!" Danlo said all at once. "At the base of my spine—only it was more like a twisted bolt of lightning than a serpent."

"It *is* like lightning, once it's teased out of its sleep," she said. "Once the serpent energy is awakened, it uncoils, straightens, and strikes the body like lightning. It pierces the spinal cord and rushes upward through the chakras. Behind the navel, there's a chakra, and the heart chakra, and—"

"These are the energy centers, yes?"

"How did you know?"

He sat up and stared at the fire. He thought of his test and trial in Lavi Square when the heat of *lotsara* had flared up just behind his navel and had saved him from freezing to death. He told Tamara about this, and then said, "The Alaloi have their theories, too."

"I would have thought your people were too busy just living life to worry about awakening their chakras."

"Is that what the Kundalini does? Is that what courtesans do?"

She laughed and continued, "I was telling you about the ancient theory. In this theory, the Kundalini energy burns its way up each of the seven chakras. Ideally, it burns through them —sometimes the pathway is blocked, of course, by old wounds to the body or mind, and the energy is trapped."

"Like light in a bottle of stone?"

She nodded her head. "If you like."

"There is no flow," he said. "No release, no . . . connection."

"For most people, this is the way it is," she said. "But in a few people, the Kundalini burns through the chakras one by one. At last it bursts through the thousand-petaled lotus at the crown of the head."

He was sitting cross-legged with his back to the fire, listening and thinking. She came around behind him then and pressed her hand against his tailbone where it rested in the soft furs. She traced her fingers in sinuous waves up the naked skin over his spine, then across the nape of his neck to the top of his head. Her fingers danced through his thick hair and sent shivers of pleasure across his scalp.

"And then?"

"Then there *is* a connection," she said. "The Kundalini shoots into the sky, and the ancient connection between mind and the heavens is completed."

He turned his head and kissed the inside of her arm. "And this is the old theory?"

"A very old theory," she admitted.

"Then the courtesans have abandoned it?"

"Most have, of course. Though we still retain the Kundalini as a symbol of the life energies. The Kundalini, once it's awakened, enters every nerve in the body, every cell. And then it wakes up the cells."

Quickly, in her serious, dulcet voice, Tamara told him a little of the courtesans' theory of the Kundalini. She explained that each cell of the body has its own consciousness, a cellular consciousness of electron transport chains and protein synthesis and DNA. When the cells were completely awakened to the secrets locked inside them, segments of DNA that had never been active before—this DNA was sometimes called the "sleeping god"—would turn on and come alive to its true purpose. And then humankind would truly evolve. It would be a willed evolution, a conscious journey into a new symmetry of body and mind that few dared dream of. And then someday, perhaps farwhen, perhaps tomorrow, man and woman would come together to give birth to the first truly human being.

"This is a splendid theory," Danlo said. "But is it true?"

"No one really knows what causes the DNA to turn on, or to evolve," she said. "Some of your eschatologists postulate form fields or super genes. These theories are almost as old as the tantra. I've heard that a few masters still teach the random mutation of the genome as the driving force of evolution, if you can believe that. The best theory, I think, comes out of the Rian school. You've heard of Cipriana Ria?"

"No, who was he?"

"*She,*" Tamara said. "She was the Lord Eschatologist a hundred years ago. She postulated a consciousness field isomorphic to the genetic fields the biologists claimed to have discovered. Of course, this is all still theory. Your Order has been trying to understand the nature of consciousness and matter for five thousand years."

She went on to discuss the different schools of eschatology, bringing in theories from other disciplines—such as the cetics' theory of the circular reduction of consciousness—to support her arguments. "Of course, everything that's known about mat-

412

ter and consciousness will have to be rethought in light of your father's discovery."

"Do you mean the Elder Eddas?"

She nodded her head. "It's said that your father discovered a mathematics of consciousness."

"And this mathematics, this consciousness . . . is locked up in memory?"

"The memory of the cells," she said. "If we could wake our cells up, we could recover these memories."

"Is this why the courtesans are so interested in Bardo's remembrances?"

"Some of us are," she said.

"And you?"

She met his eyes and looked at him a long time before saying, "I want to wake the body up. The self, the whole bodymind. If this awakening involves the cellular memories, then I've a passionate interest in remembrancing."

"You seem to know a great deal . . . about a great many things," Danlo said. "You might have been a holist. I did not know the courtesans were so erudite."

Tamara combed her long blond hair with her fingers and beamed in obvious pleasure with his compliment. As he could see, she loved praise as some people loved chocolate candy. She was quite vain, in an open, unself-conscious way. And she was quite proud, not of her physical beauty, which she took for granted, but of her accomplishments in the courtesan arts, and most of all proud of her memory and mind. Many courtesans learn smatterings of the various Order disciplines so that they might converse intelligently with the lords and masters about important subjects, but few had learned so deeply or well as Tamara Ten Ashtoreth.

"I never knew a pilot could have such a talent for ecstasy," she said.

He laughed and said, "Neither did I."

"It's rare for the Kundalini to be awakened so easily, with so little art."

"You call what happened tonight . . . a 'little art'?"

She knelt in front of him, and she seemed both happy and amused. "We haven't even touched the first things of the art," she said. "We haven't listened to each other's heartbeat, or synchronized our breathing, or—"

"Let's breathe together," he said. He took her hand, which was cold from the night air pouring in through the window. His

413

hands, too, were now cold, as was his face and the whole front of his body. But his back was still hot; he sat with his back near the fire, and the heat of it still burned up his spine.

"It's late," she said. She had an excellent time sense, much better than his. "It must be near midnight."

"Then we have three hours till dawn. Let's breathe together till the first light comes."

"I thought you came here to attend the remembrance ceremony."

"No," he said, "I came here to meet you. I just did not know it till now."

"O beautiful man," she said, "there will be other nights."

"But what of your contracts?"

"Contracts can be broken," she said.

"Truly?"

She laughed and then kissed his hands. "When we join the Society, we don't surrender our free will."

He sat there for a few moments looking at her. At last he said, "Shall we go down to the remembrance together, then?"

"I'd like that."

"I suppose I should wish Bardo well," he said. "And thank him for the use of this room."

They put their clothes on slowly, leisurely, as if time were a crushing weight that might exist for other people, but not for them. Then they kissed each other's lips and laughed together, and they went out to rejoin the party.

THE WAY OF THE CETIC

People were also waxen mechanical toys, part of a mechanical toy process and were made of candy. People were an utter absurdity as they went about their rituals, which I contained completely and knew to be absurd in their circularity, unconstructiveness, and superstitiousness. But they went about their rituals with a sense of absolute self-righteousness, hilarious zombies who failed to recognize me as the one who beneficently supported their existence.

—from the cetics' archives, source unknown

Danlo and Tamara returned to the sun room as they had come, walking through the house and holding hands. The room was now overflowing with Bardo's guests; the air was even thicker than before, a cloud of purplish-gray smoke that choked Danlo and irritated his eyes. It was very noisy. A cruel-looking wormrunner with jeweled eyes was sadistically banging away on the strings of a gosharp, and it seemed everyone was trying to talk above everyone else. Twice people bumped into Danlo and nearly spilled their goblets of wine. Despite the unpleasantness of the room, the people's mood was one of camaraderie and celebration. Danlo pulled at Tamara's hand as he stepped over the legs of a woman collapsed into stupor, who obviously had been celebrating with too much devotion. He turned his head right and left, looking among the sea of faces for Bardo.

"Danlo!" a voice boomed out. "Tamara Ten Ashtoreth, come over here!"

In the center of the room, surrounded by eight or nine women, stood Bardo with a plate of pepper nuts in his hand and tears running from his huge brown eyes. Since giving up beer, he had become addicted to eating hot foods which burned his mouth and made his eyes glisten with water. He was even huger than Danlo had remembered, and he seemed vaster, inside, bubbling with energy as if his belly, throat, and lips were a fleshy tube channeling the plasma of the stars. His rolling, basso voice riveted the attention of those around him. And when he spoke, he moved his hands and fingers in a lovely dance of signs which reinforced his words. Danlo glanced at Bardo's fat hands, at his bearded face and gaudy robe. The huge man wore a jeweled ring on each of his fingers, and his rainbow robe was studded with emeralds, rubies, and opals. Around his neck, openly, he wore a brilliant Yarkonan firestone. Such ostentation might have diminished a lesser human being, but Bardo's truest self was as opulent as any jewel, and so his outer style served only to magnify this inner self, to deepen his pride and make him seem even larger.

Bardo set his plate atop a table laden with lacquer ware, and he threw his arms around Danlo. "Little Fellow!" he called out as he thumped Danlo's back. "Little Fellow, by God, you're not so little anymore!"

Indeed, he and Danlo were almost of the same height, though Bardo carried enough muscle and fat to make two men. Danlo looked at him eye to eye, and then he was smiling, embracing Bardo without restraint as the Alaloi men do, as if they were brothers of the same tribe.

"You look well," Danlo said at last.

"Ah, but I *am* well. I've never been so well—sometimes I think it's impossible to be more well, but I try, as you'll see."

He turned to Tamara and bowed as deeply as his belly would allow. "I'm honored that the most beautiful of the courtesans could attend another joyance," he said. He grinned at her with an easy and obvious gladness, and with a hint of lust as well. "I've, ah, heard that you've already made Danlo's acquaintance."

Just then there was a flash of orange behind Bardo, and Hanuman stepped into view. He sipped from a tumbler of water as he looked back and forth between Danlo and Tamara. He seemed relaxed and nonchalant, but he kept looking at them as if he were drinking in information that only a cetic could make use of.

"Hanuman li Tosh!" Bardo said. "I didn't see you standing there—why didn't you announce yourself sooner?"

Hanuman bowed to him and smiled. "Hello, Bardo" was all he said.

"As silent as a cetic, I see. Ah, but you've done well for yourself, too. I'd hoped you'd become a pilot, but the cetic's robe suits you, Young Hanuman. Did you know there's talk among your masters that you're destined to be Lord Cetic someday?"

Hanuman flashed Bardo a quick, piercing look that spoke of an old tension and an instant understanding between the two of them. Danlo watched the way Hanuman bowed his head very slightly, the way his eyes hooded over and his breath quickened. He saw the faintest lineaments of the subtle and sinister relationship existing between Hanuman and Bardo. But he could not, then and there, descry any deeper pattern to this relationship; he could only listen as Hanuman enunciated each of his words with great precision and clarity: "But I'm not even a full cetic yet, much less a master. Of all the professions, we take the longest to train masters. You should know, there's never been a journeyman who has proceeded up the grades to master cetic in less than fifteen years."

"Well, fifteen years *is* a long time," Bardo said. He swept his arm out and nodded to the many people standing about. "Especially during these times. Fifteen years ago, Mallory Ringess was still a man, and I was just a drunken fool."

As he spoke, a tiny woman with red eyes and purple-black skin the same color as Bardo's edged her way to his side and said, "You were *never* a fool. Would Mallory Ringess have chosen you as a friend if you were a fool?"

"Ah," Bardo said, "may I present my cousin, the Princess Surya Surata Lal of Summerworld? These are my friends. Firstly, Tamara Ten Ashtoreth, voluptuary in the Society of Courtesans."

Surya bowed to Tamara, quickly and coldly, as if she disapproved of her title and way of life. Tamara returned her bow and smiled nicely, and her natural grace and graciousness seemed only to irritate Surya and cause her to turn away.

"And may I present Hanuman li Tosh and Danlo wi Soli Ringess—they've been inseparable since their novitiate."

Upon the pronouncement of this name, all the people in the

immediate area of the room looked at Danlo. A horologe in her bright red robe, a merchant-prince sipping from a tumbler of skotch, a dreamy-eyed autist, a harijan boy carrying plates of sizzling food from the kitchen—they all paused to examine Danlo, to bow politely and stand attentively as if they were waiting for him to say something of moment. But Danlo could think of nothing to say. He was too aware of the smells of curry and capsicum burning in his nostrils, too aware of his own acrid sweat. Tamara pressed close to him, and the marvelous, thick smell of sex was like a drug waking up all his senses. He heard someone across the room whisper: "He's the son of Mallory Ringess!" From other parts of the house came waves of distracting sounds: the melodies of the improvisatori plucking at gosharps and making up verses, the irritating hum of mantra musicians, and three hundred voices buzzing and braying and hissing at him. He was suddenly aware that everyone was aware of him. Or rather, they were aware of him only as the son of his father. And thus they truly could not see him, as man or human being, and this lack of mindfulness and vision on their behalf shamed him. It was a shame he would feel burning up his throat every time he entered Bardo's house.

Surya bowed to Danlo and said, "I'm honored to make your acquaintance. My cousin tells me you hope to leave Neverness soon. You're to be a pilot, like the Ringess, and you hope to be chosen to make the journey to the Vild, do I remember correctly?"

"Yes, that is true," Danlo said. He glanced at Tamara, whose face fell sad with disappointment. This sudden look wounded him. He had meant to tell her of his plan to join the Vild mission, but in the excitement of their evening together, he had forgotten.

"It's a pity that the Order is training pilots for this mission," Surya said. "The Order can't really stop the stars from exploding, do you think? No, of course not. It would be better if the Order trained remembrancers instead of pilots."

She had a sharp, presumptuous way of speaking that amused and annoyed Danlo. As she looked him over, she rubbed at her eyes, which were bloodshot from smoking the potent bhang they grow on Summerworld. She was addicted to bhang, although she would never admit it, citing instead allergies to Icefall's strange flora as the cause of her red eyes. Danlo thought that she was an ambitious woman who would too easily lie, and he immediately mistrusted her.

4 l 8

"There must be a way . . . to keep the blessed stars from dying," Danlo said softly. "If the stars die, we shall die, too. The animals, the birds, even the iceblooms and snowworms—everything will die."

"Oh, Young Danlo, you should have more faith in life," Surya said.

"Life," Danlo said, "it is blessed, truly . . . but fragile. Nothing is so blessed and fragile."

With a tiny, clawlike hand, Surya caressed the sleeve of her blue kimono, and said, "But what of the Golden Ring? Your father created it to shield your planet from the Vild's radiation. All life, didn't you know? Soon all the Civilized Worlds will see such rings growing around them. Mallory Ringess, himself, spoke of these things before he left Neverness. Isn't that so, Bardo?"

Bardo patted his rumbling belly and touched the shoulder of a rather fat woman standing off behind him. She looked at him with dark, fawning eyes, as if she were only waiting to fetch a tumbler of toalache or another plate of food. "Ah," Bardo said, "the Ringess never stated this *explicitly*. But that was the intention of what he told me on the beach before he left, certainly."

Danlo gazed out the window, thinking of the galaxy's vast light-distances, the cold and almost endless spaces filled with photons, neutrinos, and gamma rays. Nearly twenty years before, when he was still a baby in his milk-stained furs, a star in the Abelian Group had exploded into a supernova. With each breath that he had taken since then, this star's killing radiation had expanded outward through deep space half a million miles. Even as he listened to a hundred murmuring voices and watched Surya Surata Lal's face fall cold with smugness and sanctimony, the supernova's wavefront was only forty thousand billion miles from Neverness, and soon, in only eight more years, it would fall over the City of Pain in a lightshower of death. Or of life. Perhaps, he thought, the Golden Ring would absorb this deadly light, shielding Neverness and continuing to grow across the heavens.

"Who knows what the Golden Ring truly is?" Danlo half whispered. "What it will be?"

"Don't you believe what your own father said?" Surya asked him.

Here Hanuman, who was standing across from Danlo, let out a rare burst of laughter. And then, in his clear cetic's voice—

an intensely ironic voice—he said, "Well, you should know that Danlo doesn't like to *believe* anything. You might say he's the world's greatest believer in unbelief."

Everyone laughed at this little joke, even Tamara, who eyed Hanuman as if he were a beautiful but venomous snake that one had to handle with great care.

Bardo reached out a massive hand and rumpled Danlo's hair. His voice rolled out, "Beliefs are the eyelids of the mind, isn't that so?"

"The mind has many eyelids," Danlo said. After Bardo was done mauling his head, Danlo touched Ahira's white feather to make sure that it was still fastened to his hair. And then he looked at Hanuman in reproof as if to say: What is wrong with you tonight?

After a brief silence, Surya asked him, "Were you a student of the Fravashi? Bardo invited a Fravashi Old Father to our joyance but he refused to come."

"In fact," Bardo said as he rubbed his belly, "I invited *your* Old Father, the one who taught you when you came to Neverness. By God, I wish these Fravashi had real names! Ah, I wanted to demonstrate to an Honored Fravashi the power of our remembrancing techniques, but he turned me down, too bad."

"Why?" Danlo asked.

"He gave me the silliest of excuses. He said that he couldn't enter my house, that the Fravashi have a superstition against entering buildings taller than one story."

Danlo laughed and said, "But this is true!"

"Really?"

"They believe that dwelling in large buildings will cause them to sicken and die," Danlo said.

"Doesn't it ever disturb you," Surya asked Danlo, "that a race of superstitious old aliens still have a power in your City? In your Order?"

Bardo suddenly rolled his eyes and let loose a sigh. "You see, Danlo, my cousin believes that alien thoughtways are, ah, *inappropriate* for humans."

"The Fravashi," Surya said, "supposedly teach methods for freeing the individual from all systems of belief. All systems of thought, even their own—I understand this goal. What could be more seductive than total freedom?"

"Ah," Bardo said to Danlo, "have I told you that my cousin is a great champion of freedom? No? Did you know that she freed the slaves on Summerworld? Of course that was before the rebellion. Before our family fell and was banished. But Surya Surata Lal is still remembered, I'm sure."

In truth, Surya Lal had been a princess of Summerworld, and she had spent her maturity fighting for the freedom of enslaved peoples and robots, just as she had spent part of her youth campaigning for the rights of dolls, those strange information ecologies that exist in computer space and are said to be alive. She was a woman who loved freedom and embraced the great movements of her time, a formidable woman now devoted to her cousin and the movement that soon would be called the Way of Ringess.

Danlo ran his fingers through his hair. "All peoples think they love freedom," he said.

"Of course," Surya said. "But real freedom, for a human being, lies in discovering *human* possibilities."

"Human possibilities," Danlo repeated softly. He closed his eyes, vividly remembering Tamara's very human face during the moment she had cried out in her ecstasy. It had been a moment of complete freedom, and yet, paradoxically, of complete surrender to the forces of life. "Who knows what is possible?" he asked.

He hadn't really expected an answer to this rhetorical question, so he was amused when Surya said, "Your father gave his life to bring back the secret of human possibilities. The ways we might transcend our limitations. Our stupidity, our baseness, even our human bodies. *Especially* our bodies and brains— you're smiling at me, Danlo wi Soli Ringess, but that's because you're still young and beautiful. I don't think you can imagine what it's like to grow so old that you can't be brought back to youth, anymore. Old in the *brain*. Old and rotten and ugly."

As they spoke, a circle of people crowded around them, pressing them closer together. He felt Tamara moving up against him, intertwining her fingers in his. Surya was pushed over against Bardo's great belly, and Danlo was so close to her that he smelled sihu oil and the sweet smokiness of bhang clinging to her silk kimono. Directly across from him stood Hanuman, watching and listening. Danlo read cynicism on his pale face. He saw Hanuman lift a finger to point at Surya; no one else saw this subtle, almost imperceptible movement, just as no one else understood his hand language as he signed to Danlo: *This is an ugly woman. It's as I've always said: Beauty is only skin deep but ugliness penetrates to the bone.*

421

Danlo shook his head as if to reproach Hanuman for being so cruel. He turned to Surya and took note of the lines about her tiny red eyes, at the corners of her wormhole of a mouth. He didn't need the cetics' art to read the fear there. Although she was only middling old and might last another three hundred years before her final old age, it was obvious that decrepitude and death terrified her. Not even wailing, jittery Old Irisha, during the days his tribe had gone over, had been so dehumanized by fear. "There is something about civilized people that I have always wondered at," Danlo said. "The longer they live, the more they are afraid of dying."

"Ah, but dying isn't so hard," Bardo said as he rubbed his chest. Once, when he was a young man, he had taken an Alaloi spear through the chest and had died his first death. He had been frozen and thawed and healed, only to face death once again when his lightship had disappeared into the fiery heart of star. A goddess called Kalinda had resurrected him, or so he liked to tell everyone, and ever since he had waxed philosophical about all such vital matters. "What's death but a brief moment of peace before the pieces of ourselves are reassembled and we're condemned to live again?" Bardo said. "It's living that vexes the soul. Living fully and well."

At this, Surya tightened her lips as if she had too often endured Bardo's musings. Then she scowled at Danlo and said, "*Everyone* is afraid of dying. Human beings are in bondage to the fear of death."

"That's very true," Hanuman said. "You're a perceptive woman."

Surya, quite obviously, didn't perceive any irony in this simple utterance, for she favored Hanuman with a smile and her face brightened. "I've heard that the cetics claim all emotions flow from fear."

"That's almost true," Hanuman said. "The propagation of life is the fundamental algorithm of life. Is the urge to propagate really the same as the fear of death? Let's suppose it is. All emotions, then, if treated as caused responses programmed into an organism, are in some way designed to preserve life so that it may propagate itself."

"I've heard that cetics can read the emotions off people's faces."

"It's one of our arts," Hanuman said. "One of the most ancient."

In fact, as Hanuman had once told Danlo, the cetics trace

the genesis of face reading at least as far back as the work of the ancient portrait artists, Titian, Duret, and the Leonardo, whose ideal was that the portrait of a person should be the mirror of the soul.

"I've also heard that cetics can read thoughts," Surya said, "but I've never really believed it."

"Sometimes we can do something like reading thoughts."

"But thoughts aren't programmed into us like emotions," she said.

"Aren't they?"

Here Bardo rubbed his hands together, and to Surya he said, "Did you know that Mallory Ringess learned something of the cetics' powers? He could look at you and tell you what you were thinking, by God. He could lay your soul bare, and that's why people were afraid of him. And more, he could look at a stranger and tell what he was about to do and say before he said and did it."

"Can *you* tell these things?" Surya asked Hanuman.

Hanuman bowed his head and looked at her. "Sometimes I can read the tells," he said. "But this is a trivial use of the art. It's really rather silly, don't you think?"

"Could you do it *now*?" she asked. She was obviously enchanted with this notion of face reading, and enchanted with Hanuman as well. She suddenly held up a small, bony finger and pointed across the room. "There, do you see the tall man in the brown robe?"

"The historian? The one who's bald?"

"I suppose he's an historian," Surya said. "I really haven't had the opportunity to learn which academicians wear which colors. Can you tell me what he's thinking?"

Hanuman stood very straight as he looked across the room. His intensity of concentration caused Surya and the others to look at him, instead of the historian. Despite Hanuman's words making little of the face-reading art, he secretly relished exhibiting his talents.

"He's thinking of danger," he said. "He's thinking that Bardo's house is full of dangerous people, and now, it's in his eyes, the extension of slight danger to life-threatening peril—people always do this—he's thinking of fleeing the City. And now, the guilt at his own cowardice. He would *like* to believe that the Golden Ring will shield the City from the Vild's radiation. But he's a cynical man, and half a coward, even though he would describe himself as a prudent man, a 'man for all time,' or some other such conceit. He's an historian—he pays attention to the emigration figures. But he's also aware that twice as many people are swarming *into* Neverness as are leaving her, and he can't quite understand it. He's really a bit befuddled. Which is why he's attending this joyance. He has questions of universal moment, or so he thinks. He's looking for answers. The greater the doubt, the greater the need for faith. Faith—what is this emotion but a desperate attempt to escape from mind-burning fear?"

Surya nodded her head, obviously amazed by Hanuman's performance. And then Danlo, who was also looking toward the historian with a certain concentration of senses, broke into laughter. It began as a slight flutter in his belly and then spread out so quickly that he was shaking and laughing like a young man giddy from his first taste of magic mushrooms.

"By God, is there a joke here?" Bardo wanted to know.

"No, not . . . a joke," Danlo said, after he had caught his breath.

"What then?"

Danlo closed his eyes for a moment, listening. His sense of hearing had been quickened by a lifetime of identifying the smallest sounds of the world. Tonight, this sense was extraordinarily keen. He could hear, very faintly, the historian talking about the Way of Ringess and other religions. Even though they stood across the room from each other, he could pick out the historian's high voice and frightened words from the words of all those around him. He opened his eyes then, and he said to Hanuman, "I think the historian has just been discussing the very things you have revealed to us."

"Are you saying he's been cheating?" Bardo asked.

"I have heard that the cetics can read lips," Danlo said, and he smiled at Hanuman. "This is part of your art, yes?"

"Of course it is. The lips are part of the face, are they not? What better way to read a face?"

"Then you *have* been cheating?" Surya asked. "I didn't think it was possible to read someone's thoughts."

Again, Hanuman bowed to her, and he then looked her up and down, and his eyes were shiny and hard. He said, "It's impossible to cheat if there aren't any rules to cheat against. However. Do you see the woman slumped over against the far wall?"

Surya turned to look at a woman standing alone in front of one of Bardo's wall paintings. Danlo and the others looked at her, too. She was dressed in a distinctive cowl jacket, complete

424

with the baggy hood and braided strings, the kind the aphasics wear.

"She's an aphasic," Hanuman said. "Do you know about the aphasics, Princess Lal? The sect is probably unique to Neverness. They have voices, but no language. They can hear words but they can't understand them. They disfigure the brains of their children to destroy the language centers. Don't looked so shocked—they're not the monsters most people think. They do what they do because they think words interfere with the direct apprehension of reality. And distort reality. Which is why I've chosen her. She can't have spoken to anyone because she can't speak. She's come here tonight in the hope that you illuminati, those who have been touched by Mallory Ringess, will have found a way of communicating directly, heart to heart, without words. But she's disappointed. She's lonely. She's bored. She's been unable to connect with anyone here. She's thinking—people can think, you should know, even when the words have been stolen from their minds—she's thinking of leaving the party."

"I'm not convinced," Surya said. "If I had known about these poor aphasics, just looking at her, I might have guessed everything you've said."

Hanuman flashed Surya a dangerous look, then continued, "When I move my finger like this, the aphasic will leave the room." He waited a moment and then raised his finger slightly. As if a signal had been given, as if an invisible string connected the aphasic with Hanuman's gloved finger, she jerked herself erect and turned her back on Bardo's guests. With a heavy, shuffling gait, she walked out of the room.

"By God, how did you know? How did you do that?" Bardo asked.

"I'm beginning to be convinced," Surya said. "But are you certain you're not still cheating? This aphasic isn't an acquaintance of yours, is she?"

In answer, Hanuman smiled his secretive smile. Then he singled out various men and women across the room. "Do you see the old phantast with the huge Adam's apple? When I signal, he will cough." And Hanuman lifted his finger, and the phantast did indeed cough, and so it went, around the room, Hanuman pointing at people and descrying the moment they would cough, rub their eyes, laugh, dance, frown, speak, or drink from their goblets of wine. He would lift his finger, and people would move in the appointed ways, as if he were a doll master pulling at their heartstrings. It was an eerie, almost sinister demonstration of the cetics' art. It convinced Surya that Hanuman was a man of rare power, but she wasn't quite ready to admit that he could have any power over her.

"These people," she said, "they don't suspect you're watching them. It's hard to believe you could read the face of someone who has composed herself."

"Such as yourself, Princess?"

"What am I thinking, right now?" she asked. Her face tightened up like a piece of dried bloodfruit. She was almost squinting with the effort of keeping her face empty. "Can you tell me?"

"No, Hanu, don't," Danlo said softly. He looked at Hanuman and shook his head. He hated this game of Hanuman's; he hated everything about treating human beings as robots whose very lives were programmed into them. Most of all he hated what he saw in Hanuman, the pride and the sudden fury flashing in his eyes.

"Should I be silent merely because my best friend so implores me?" Hanuman asked. He stepped forward so that Danlo, Tamara, Bardo, and Surya surrounded him. Clearly, he relished being at the center of things, just as he exulted in the practice of his powers. He looked at Surya and said, "Or should I be silent because my ethics discourage reading someone's thoughts to her face? Should I be silent at all? Isn't there a time for rashness and truth? I believe that Danlo would admit there is. Tamara, too. Let me be rash, then. Let me be truthful. No, Danlo, please don't look at me that way—this is a rare chance for you to find out what others are thinking of you. To see yourself just as others do. Oh, I know you've no care for yourself. Which is why everyone loves you. And is afraid of you. It's your wildness, your childlike qualities: you're too absorbed in the things of the world to worry about yourself. But others worry. The Princess Lal—she worries. She'd like to believe in this silly art of reading faces because she'd like to read *you*. She's been thinking about you ever since Bardo announced your name. You disturb her. Your very name offends her."

He turned from Danlo to Surya with an intensity of motion, whirling about as if he were executing a movement from his killing art. His face was as hard and sharp as a knife, and he said to her, "Everyone calls him Danlo the Wild. You're wondering, Princess, if he's really as wild as his name. I assure you that he is. He's even wilder than you'd want to imagine. Where will all this wildness lead, you ask yourself. Is he truly the son of his father? *Danlo wi Soli Ringess*—I've said that his name offends you, but not which name. I'll say it now: Danlo is *a* Ringess, if not *the* Ringess. Does the universe need another? Or is one Ringess one too many? You doubt. You're full of doubts. Do you know about instantaneity? Stopping time? Stop! In this instant, stop your thoughts and fix them, as if they were ants in amber. That's the way. Your face, if only you could see it now, now that you truly believe. You're thinking of Mallory Ringess and all the things he wrought. The Golden Ring. You wonder how this specific thought, this golden image, could be written across your face. And another thought, which you dread more than death: Am I making you think these things? Am I? *Are* thoughts programmed into us, or are we masters of our will? Please, don't turn your eyes away! If you do, you'll only wonder if that's what I wanted you to do. You wonder about human freedom. You're agonizing over this right now. What is possible for human beings? Mallory Ringess gave his life to discover his own possibilities. Who is so fearless? Is Danlo, whom we all love like we love the sunlight, made of the same substance as the father? You pray that he is not; you fear that he is. Fear is the quintessence of the soul. It shapes all that we do. If Danlo is truly fearless and wild, then what might *he* do? More precisely, what might he *not* do? Where will his wildness lead? You wonder this. Your thoughts are turning in circles. Turning and turning. Let me break the circle, then, and leave you with a new thought: Who of us can match this wildness of Danlo's? And why should we want to?"

Hanuman ceased speaking and stood very still. He stared at Surya. It seemed that he was only waiting to lash out with his tongue again.

"Here, now, that's enough," Bardo said. He moved over by Hanuman's side and laid his arm across his shoulders. He stood over him like a mountain, and his voice boomed out: " 'Debate a cetic, hate a cetic.' "

But Surya did not hate Hanuman, for all that he had said to her. She was enchanted with him. She, whose soul he had laid bare with his sensitive eyes and cutting tongue, looked at him as if he were a god, or rather, a superhuman man in personal contact with the realm of the godly. Her face fell from astonishment to adulation to embarrassment at having her thoughts uncovered. In an effort to hide her embarrassment, she turned to Danlo and began to lie.

"I wasn't really thinking about you at all," Surya said. Her face was now an ugly reddish-black mask of misdirection and untruth. "I don't know why your friend would say such things. The whole time, I was thinking about the recipe for curried chicken that my mother taught me. I've always loved curry dishes—I suppose this was cheating, to hold my thoughts this way."

Danlo rubbed the scar above his eye, looked at Tamara, and then smiled. Although it took a great deal to embarrass him, Hanuman's strange soliloquy might have succeeded in doing just that if he hadn't been in love and overflowing with a marvelous sense of aliveness. He was embarrassed for Surya, however, even if he wished that she had remained on Summerworld with her curry dishes and her slaves. He bowed to her and said, "As Hanuman has reminded us, there is no cheating in a game . . . that has no rules."

Hanuman gazed at him then, with his compelling cetic's eyes. But Danlo was the one person that he could never stare down, and he finally broke eyelock and looked away.

Surya rubbed her neck and sighed. She seemed mollified by Danlo's last statement. "I must tell you," she said, "I've nothing against your name. You can't help the accident of your birth."

"We each have our own fate," Danlo said.

"And we each have free will. Your father taught that ultimately, fate and free will are the same thing."

"You seem to be a woman of . . . unusual will," he said.

Surya's face came aglow and she smiled at him for the first time. Despite her thin lips and coffee-stained teeth, she had a beautiful smile. He saw that this difficult woman, but for her dishonesty and fear, might have attained a shibui beauty so rare among the people of the City.

"You're not afraid," she said, "of being kind to a difficult woman who hasn't been very kind to you. Perhaps you really are fearless."

"No one is fearless," he said.

"Hanuman was right about that, at least," she said. "We're all afflicted with fear—it's the human condition. But there's a way out, didn't you know?"

"If you mean my father—"

"When the Ringess was still a man," she said in a rush of breath, interrupting him, "he suffered from the great fear, just as everybody does. But he found a way out of suffering, a way to free himself."

Bardo, who was obviously glad that the conversation had turned back upon matters more closely allied with his purpose, suddenly smacked his fist into his open hand. His rings clicked together, and his voice rang out, "By God, that's the way of Ringess, to face the universe *as* a god and never look back in fear!"

"It's the way of Ringess," Surya said, "to find freedom from suffering."

"Yes, the Ringess pointed the way toward real freedom," Bardo said. His great voice dominated the room, and everyone looked at him. It was suddenly very quiet. He seemed delighted, and relieved, to be once again at the center of an attentive audience. "And the only real freedom is the freedom of a god."

There was a moment of silence and then someone called out, "And anyone can become a god."

"Or *God*," another person said.

"Give me a couple sips of kalla and I'll see God."

"Give me three sips of kalla and I'll *be* God."

"But it's never that easy," a plump woman standing near Bardo said. She wore the blue robe of an eschatologist, and her name was Kolenya Mor, Lord Mor, the Order's Lord Eschatologist. "At least, the remembrances are never so easy for me. Why does it have to be so hard?"

Bardo nodded his head and he rubbed his hands together vigorously. He looked about the room to fix the eyes of his various guests, and in his huge voice he laughed out, "It *is* hard, that's true, and this brings us again to our work. Or, I should say, to our joy. By God, everyone knows Bardo is the laziest man in the City, so if I can drink kalla and remembrance the Eddas, anyone can. Ah, it's past time. I invite any of you who haven't had a remembrance for ten days to come with us into the music room. Tonight we have a young cetic with us, and his friend, Danlo wi Soli Ringess. The son of *the* Ringess, who may become a god someday, too."

Again, many people in the circle around Bardo bowed to Danlo, and he felt a heat wave of shame burning his eyes. He noticed Hanuman smiling at him both in mockery and compassion, and perhaps with an intimation of challenge, too.

As Bardo and the others began moving toward the door of the room, Tamara pulled at Danlo's hand and took him aside. Even though courtesans love to talk, she had mostly kept her silence during Danlo's discussion with Surya and Hanuman. But now she said, "I think you should be careful of Hanuman li Tosh."

"I am always careful of him," Danlo said. "Friends should always take . . . careful awareness of each other, yes?"

"Please be careful in the remembrance."

"Is remembrancing so dangerous?"

"Oh, it's dangerous enough," Tamara said. "The kalla drug itself is dangerous, but I think the greatest danger is attempting a remembrance when your soul is on fire. Don't let Hanuman poison you with his doubts. Or his despair."

"Tonight," he said, "I am as far from despair as I have ever been."

"I can't go into the remembrance with you," she said. "It's only been five days since my last one."

"And you are not ready for another?"

"I'm not sure," she said. "But even if I were, Bardo believes the kalla should be taken as a sacrament. One doesn't partake of sacraments every day."

"No, but perhaps they should," Danlo said.

"I'm sorry."

Danlo drew her hands up to his lips and kissed them. It was a shocking thing for him to do, in open sight of others. "Then we should say good night, now," he said.

"If you like, we could meet again in a few days."

"Why such a long time?"

"After your remembrance, you'll want to be alone."

"I can't imagine wanting to be alone."

"Danlo, please be . . ."

"Yes?"

As people streamed by them, almost brushing their garments and trying not to notice their adoration of each other, Danlo touched her forehead, looking for her thoughts in the darkness of her eyes.

"Please be careful of yourself," she said.

She kissed his lips then, and said good-bye to him. He left the room stepping so lightly he could scarcely feel his feet, and all the time he never stopped wondering about what she had said.

C H A P T E R 1 8

KALLA

Drink! for you know not whence you came, nor why;
Drink! for you know not why you go, nor where.
        —*from* The Rubaiyat of Omar Khayyam

Danlo followed a group of Bardo's admirers out of the sun room's north door. A river of silk and flesh swept him down a brilliantly lit hallway. He was aware, dimly, that most of the guests were being left behind. He heard many grumbles and moans and little arguments, tens of voices protesting Bardo's restrictiveness. Most thought that they should be allowed a re-membrance at least as frequently as every three days; a few reckless characters—such as Jonathan Hur—called for a daily remembrance, or even a moment-to-moment, continual remem-brancing of the Elder Eddas. But Bardo was clearly in control of events and master of his house, and so he allowed only a tenth of his guests to follow him into the north wing. Including Hanu-man, who walked by Bardo's side, there were thirty-eight of them, and their excited, buzzing voices made for a good deal of noise. Danlo found it strange the way this noise seemed to melt into the glittering walls and vanish abruptly. Everything about this hallway of organic stone was strange: the odd angles or absence of any angles at all, the luminescence of billions of tiny light cells embedded within the walls, the sudden silences that enclosed them and followed them as they moved deeper into the house. Danlo had an uneasy feeling that he was moving down-ward, though he could plainly see from the pitch of the floor that he was not. After he had walked on a way, past guest rooms filled with rare furniture and flowers, Bardo dropped back through his procession of followers and threw his arm around Danlo's shoulders. "In a way," he said, "it's too bad this house was ever sold."

As they strolled together he talked of little things, avoiding any mention of Hanuman's performance. He told Danlo something of the house's history. He explained that the Order had owned the house for two thousand years, but after the War of the Faces, with the Order in decline and nearly ruined, the College of Lords had found themselves suddenly impoverished. Consequently, various properties across the City had been sold off, including Bardo's house. It had since been owned by exemplars, by harijan trying to establish an unofficial embassy on Neverness, again by exemplars, and then by a wealthy family of astriers who had lived there for almost four hundred years while awaiting a fresh planet to colonize. Most recently a merchant-prince had owned the house, though he never occupied it and was very glad to sell it to Bardo.

"It's too bad for the Order," Bardo said. "But their loss is my gain, or, I should say, the good luck of those wishing to explore the possibilities your father discovered. Heretofore, the Order has made it difficult for true seekers, such as myself, too bad."

"Perhaps the Order will come to support your work," Danlo said.

"No, Little Fellow, that's unlikely, now." Bardo tilted his head closer to Danlo's, and he dropped his voice low and deep. Danlo noticed immediately that the familiar aroma of beer was gone from his breath. "Shall I tell you a thing about the remembrancers? It's a sad truth, but only a few of them have been able to fully remembrance the Eddas. And *they* have all but left the Order to live with me and train memory guides."

"But what about the other remembrancers?" Danlo asked.

"They took a vote and a third of them decided that the Elder Eddas do not really exist, that your father was a liar. That he wanted to excite people to a belief in the ineffable. He did this only to revitalize our Order, they say. Ah, *your* Order, now, that is. Another third regard the Eddas as false memories, or myths, or universal archetypes, confabulations of eternal truths created by our goddamned brains."

"And the other third?"

"They're undecided," Bardo said. "The Order, as a whole, is undecided about the secrets your father brought back to them. Barbarians, all of them. Ah, well, *most* of them. The truth is,

432

they're more concerned with this mission to the Vild. Obsessed with it. Everyone who's got any talent or vision is campaigning to be included in the second Order, when it splits off, as it inevitably will."

Bardo paused to squeeze Danlo's shoulder and shoot him a pointed look. They were standing in the middle of the hallway outside the music room. As the others ducked through the music room's circular doorway one by one and took their places inside, Bardo said, "I understand why you'll have to go to the Vild, Little Fellow. When I was younger, I would have gone, too. These are apocalyptic times, by God, but there's a lot to worry about other than exploding stars."

"You must know what I worry about," Danlo said.

"The Alaloi? It's been five years—you haven't forgotten about their, ah, predicament?"

"Forgotten!"

"Ah, no, I can see you remember very well. Perhaps too well. Well—I hope you find a cure for the plague virus, if you journey to the Vild."

Danlo touched the lightning scar on his forehead, and he pressed his finger down until there was a pressure against the bone. He said, "And I hope you find the Eddas."

"Well," Bardo said, "Kolenya Mor was right, for most people the Elder Eddas *are* hard to remember, too bad."

"Have *you* remembered them?"

"Ah, but you've always asked the hard questions, haven't you, Little Fellow?"

Danlo bowed his head and smiled. "Do I?" he asked.

"In truth, I've remembered *something,*" Bardo said. He tapped at his massive head and then looked through the doorway of the music room. "Something marvelous. Why else would I have gone to all the trouble and expense of buying this goddamned house if I hadn't remembranced something we might as well call the Elder Eddas?"

"Some might say . . . can I be truthful, Bardo?"

"Must you? Ah, of course you must—it's the curse of your family."

"Some might say that you had a taste for power. Or glory. Or even . . . women."

"Women? Well, it's true, women are always attracted to men such as I. Like moths to a flame. So, I enjoy beautiful women, who wouldn't? But I've a taste for other things, too. A

433

taste for the miraculous, to put it plainly. Life is complicated, isn't it? Hideously complicated, as your father used to say."

"And you are a complicated man," Danlo said.

"A deep man," Bardo agreed, "a passionate man."

"And men of passion . . . must do passionate things, yes?"

"How well you understand!"

Danlo smiled at Bardo and inclined his head. As if a signal had been given, they both began to laugh. Again, Bardo embraced him and smacked his hand against Danlo's back and said, "By God, it's good to see you again!"

"I am glad you have come back," Danlo said.

Bardo continued laughing without restraint, and he held his knuckles up to his watery eyes. By chance, a teardrop touched one of his rings, a platinum band implanted with a pink and blue opal. With the tip of his finger, he smeared the salt water around the opal's sparkling surface, and he said, "I've always had a fondness for jewels, though I confess I always disliked the pilots' rings. Black is such a dreary color, no color at all to make diamond. Ah, I've wanted to ask you about the ring—do you still have your father's ring?"

From the neck of his kamelaika, Danlo withdrew the silver chain that Bardo had given him five years earlier. Fastened to the end of the chain was a black diamond ring.

"Ah," Bardo said, "aha, there it is." So saying, he plunged his hand into a pocket in his robe and removed one of his steel invitation cards. "Do you see it, Danlo?"

Danlo looked at the card in Bardo's hand. A hologram of two interlocked rings, gold and black, jumped out from the steel and seemed to spin as Danlo examined it. The hologram of the black ring, obviously, was an imago of his diamond pilot's ring.

"People need their symbols, you see," Bardo said.

Danlo read a strain of longing and sadness in Bardo's weepy eyes, and he said, "Shall I return the ring to you? If you would rather keep it . . . it is just a simple pilot's ring, yes?"

For a moment Bardo hesitated as he stared at the ring that Danlo held between his fingers. Then he sighed and said, "No, no, *you* keep the ring. But keep it safely—I wouldn't like to see it lost."

Danlo tucked the ring back down his kamelaika. He peered into the music room and saw that everyone had taken their seats. He said, "They are waiting for us."

Again, Bardo laughed, and said, "And that's not all that's waiting there."

"What do you mean?"

"I mean, the Elder Eddas—if you can find them. Confusion and complexity. Hideous complexity, by God."

"I am glad you invited me tonight," Danlo said. "But I had hoped to find . . . other things."

"You'll find what you'll find. But be careful, Little Fellow. Most often, people find what they *want* to find."

"Have you ever known me not to be careful?" Danlo asked.

"Don't make jokes," Bardo said. "Be careful of yourself. And be careful of Hanuman. I don't like what he did just now, this face-reading trickery, what he said about you. Ah, the *way* he said it. He's fallen crueler, these last five years."

They went into the music room then. The others had seated themselves on futons in front of a low wooden stage. From time to time, on concert nights, musicians would set their gosharps and pianos on this stage and play music for Bardo's guests, but now it was being used for other purposes. It had been laid out with various objects that might attract the eye or excite the senses. Someone had nearly covered it with vases of flowers. There were golden candelabra and long, tapering candles. At the stage's center stood a high table holding up a golden urn and a gleaming blue bowl. And behind the table, half hidden by snow dahlias and drooping nitsa blossoms, was an instrument or robot of a kind that Danlo had never seen before. It was a glittering thing of quartz tubes and valves and gurgling chemicals and neurologics. As Danlo sat cross-legged on the futon that Hanuman had reserved for him, he nodded his head at this bizarre instrument and asked, "What is *that*?"

"An odor synthesizer," Hanuman said coldly. "The remembrancers use them."

They had the position of honor at the center of the front row; on Danlo's left was Surya Surata Lal, who was sitting on her heels in a tense and formal manner. Next to her sprawled Kolenya Mor, plump and nervous inside her billowing blue robes, and all across the front row, and in the rows behind them, curving around the stage, were women and men shifting and settling into their futons, waiting for the remembrance to begin. For Danlo, who had participated in many rituals in many churches, there was something familiar about the music room. And yet there was something strange, too. There were too many people for intimacy, he thought, but too few to feed each other's fires and create a true religious passion. The windowless room was too dark, too quiet, too full of private hopes and expectations. From somewhere behind him came the sound of dripping water. He smelled wet stone and moss, the rich reek of freshly cut earth. Then Bardo glided into the room, followed by a handsome and noble-looking man wearing the silver robe of a remembrancer.

"Friends and colleagues, fellow seekers," Bardo said as he promenaded back and forth in front of the stage, "may I present the master remembrancer, Thomas Rane? He and I will guide tonight's remembrance."

Thomas Rane stood almost on top of Danlo, and he bowed deeply. He had a fine head of black hair which had run to silver around his temples; he was a proud man, Danlo thought, and slightly arrogant, but also a man whose eyes were bright and sad with a deep understanding of human beings. He stepped up to the stage and began to light the candles. There were three candelabra, thirty-three candles to light, and Danlo couldn't help thinking that his father had been thirty-three years old when he had supposedly ascended to heaven.

Just then Bardo sat down at the edge of the stage, and he steepled his fingers beneath his chin as he rested his elbows atop his huge belly. He leaned toward Hanuman and Danlo. "Everyone asks me how the Ringess became a god. *Did* he become a god? they ask. A real god? How is it possible for a human being to become a god, eh?"

"Perhaps it is not possible," Danlo said. He was suddenly aware that Surya, and others, were looking at him as if they regretted his invitation to the remembrance.

"Oh?" Bardo said. "Please explain yourself."

"The Cybernetic Churches," Danlo said, "teach that human beings may not become gods. *Can* not. Except for Nikolos Daru Ede. They say Ede carked his selfness into a computer and became the only true god but . . . none may follow his path."

Bardo stroked his beard and nodded his head before calling out, "Are there any Architects here tonight? Do any of you accept the basic doctrines of Edeism? No? Ah, that's just as well, else what I'm about to say might get me assassinated."

Upon the utterance of this word, Danlo and Hanuman exchanged a quick, meaningful look. It had been five years since the deaths of Pedar Sadi Sanat and the warrior-poet who had been sent to assassinate Hanuman. In all that time, neither of

436

them had discussed this tragedy, nor had a day passed in which the memory of it had left their minds.

Hanuman turned to Bardo and laughed harshly. He said, "I was born into a Cybernetic Church—you should know, you've already said enough for an elder to order your assassination."

"Well, let me say more, then." Bardo smiled as he held up two fat fingers. "The Architects are wrong in at least two ways. You can't become a god by carking your goddamned soul into a computer. But there's a way that you *can* become a god, anyone. And that's the way of the Ringess."

Someone behind Danlo, a skeptical old hibakusha who had lived too long, asked, "How are you defining this concept of godhood?"

"I'm not here to *define* anything," Bardo said. "I didn't invite you here tonight to argue theology. As I've stated, again and again until my lips are numb, it's not our task to correct the doctrines of Edeism, as false and pernicious as they are, nor are we here to start a new religion. By God, hasn't humanity had its bellyful of religions? No, we're here, together, to remembrance the Elder Eddas. A simple but deep experience, this remembrancing. The great secret. It's inside each of us, coded into our goddamned chromosomes, a way toward immortality. A way to develop new senses. A way that the body and brain can continue to grow, vaster, toward the infinite things. That's the way of Mallory Ringess. I was his friend, and I know. Someday—this is a promise he made to me—someday he'll return to Neverness, and then you'll see what it's like to be a god and follow the Way of Ringess."

He looked across the stage at Thomas Rane, whose face glowed with the light of thirty-three flickering candles. "Master Rane will introduce you to a few, ah, simple techniques," Bardo said. "And then we'll begin our remembrance."

Thomas Rane walked across the stage and sat down by Bardo's side. He had a sensitive, serious face, and when he spoke, it was with a grave and serious voice. "There are sixty-four attitudes to remembrancing," he said. "Although it will be impossible for you to learn all these attitudes tonight, I will say something about each of them."

He proceeded, then, to deliver a serious and fascinating exposition of the remembrancer's art. He quickly dispensed with the more basic attitudes such as association memory, imaging, sequencing, and logic memory. These attitudes are fundamental to many professions, and he didn't want to bore his audience. As

437

the room filled with the whisperlike sounds of a Fravashi song drug, he talked about mnemonics, mythopoesis, and gestalt. He talked for a long while. It was obvious, from the way he spoke, that he had a reverence for his art. Danlo thought he was a reverent man, at least in the surface calmness of his face and in his cool gray eyes. "We believe that the Elder Eddas are coded into our chromosomes," he said. "It's possible to use the recurrence attitude as a doorway to DNA memory. We've developed a simplified technique to accomplish this."

Kolenya Mor, squirming about on her futon, looked up at him and said, "A *difficult* technique."

"Difficult for some people, at first," Surya Surata Lal said.

"It's difficult, I admit," Thomas Rane said. "But the memories are always there. All the memories of one's life. And the other memories, too. Memory can be occulted but never destroyed. Can you remember this?"

"I will try," Kolenya said wryly.

"Just so," Thomas Rane replied. "Then let's remember down the DNA."

He stood up and joined Bardo by the table at the center of the stage. He gave Bardo a slight head bow.

"Let's remember down the DNA," Bardo said in his melodious voice, and the people in the room picked up this saying as if it were a chant, repeating, "Let's remember down the DNA." The music room had been made to reflect and deepen sounds, and the sound of thirty-eight human voices, for a few moments, drowned out the quieter Fravashi song drug. Then Bardo clapped his hands, once. The room filled with a Japanese tone poem, which seemed to float in the air like a strand of pearls. The lovely, murmuring music instantly brought Danlo back to the time in Old Father's house when he had learned to play the shakuhachi and he had entered into the dreamtime of his people. He sat there on his futon, remembering other musics of his childhood: Haidar's skin-covered drum beating to the howl of the west wind; his found-mother singing lullabies over the light of the oilstones; the sacred chant of the Song of Life that he had learned only incompletely. Music surrounded him and beat inside his chest. He stared up past Hanuman, looking for the source of this music. The walls, he saw, were sheets of vibrating organic crystals. But the music seemed not to emanate from the walls, nor from any other point in space or time; rather it sounded everywhere at once, as if each air particle carried whole tones and progressions of tones. He dwelled in this music for a

438

long time, remembering. He could not have said how long he listened, for it seemed that the whole of the tone poem was bound up inside each silvery note, and each note was beautiful, deep, and eternal.

"Let's remember," a deep voice called out. Danlo looked up at the stage to see Bardo bending over the table. The huge man reached forward and grasped the handles of a golden urn. Then Thomas Rane moved forward and picked up the blue bowl from the table. He held it in his open hands, waiting. Into the bowl Bardo poured a clear liquid that looked like water. But it was not water; it was kalla, the remembrancers' drug. The remembrancers had spent five thousand years developing it from such sources as the sacred mushrooms of Old Earth, alien plants, and synthetics modeled after the information molecules that are grown inside the cybernetic spaces. Drinking kalla, the remembrancers say, is like clearing a window of frost in order to see another world, the forgotten realms of experience buried beneath the snowdrifts of memory.

"Let's form a circle," Bardo said. Thomas Rane handed the bowl of kalla back to him, and he stepped off the stage. Danlo stood up, and Hanuman, and then everyone in the room was standing, making a circle over and around the futons. Thomas Rane and Bardo made their way to the circle's center. "This is kalla," Bardo said as he held the blue bowl up for everyone to see. He caught Danlo's eye and began to chuckle. "Take one sip, and flee God. Two sips to see God. Three sips and you'll *be* God."

So saying he lifted the bowl to his mouth and drank the kalla. He wiped his lips on the back of his hand. "Please, take *two* sips," he warned. "No more, no less."

He passed the bowl to Thomas Rane, who took two quick sips before passing it on to Surya. She received the bowl into her hands as if it were made of eggshell and might break at the slightest touch. Her little red eyes were lit up like wood coals, and she held the bowl's blue edge up to her little lips. In this way, passing from lip to lip and hand to hand, the bowl made its way around the circle. By chance, Hanuman was the next to last person to drink the kalla. He held the bowl in his cupped hands as he turned to his left and looked at Danlo, who was standing close to him.

"Drink!" Bardo said. "It's not poison, you know. Drink and let's be done."

Hanuman's fingers slid up around the side of the bowl. He

performed this subtle movement so that only Danlo could see it, the three orange-gloved fingers held against the gleaming blue porcelain. It was a signal, Danlo realized, a challenge. There was challenge in the stiffness of Hanuman's body, in the way he threw his chin back and took three large swallows of the kalla. Danlo watched his neck tense up three times, just as he watched the hard knot of his Adam's apple jumping up and down in his throat as if it were an animal trying to escape a trap. And all the while, Hanuman's hellish eyes never left his own; he gazed at Danlo in a silent challenge that might have said: You're bold enough when playing hokkee and risking all kinds of physical death, but can you face the wilderness of perils that devours the mind?

With a sly smile, he passed the bowl to Danlo, who was the last to drink from it. Danlo touched his tongue to the kalla and took a long, deep drink, and then another. It tasted both cool and bitter. Because he was in a wild mood, out of his devotion to wildness, he took a third sip. In truth, he drank much more than a sip; three times altogether he did this, and there was no way to tell how much of the kalla drug he swallowed. When he was done he looked at Hanuman, who was standing close, shoulder to shoulder, and watching him in his intense but anguished way. *How he hates this blessed drug,* Danlo thought. *How he hates this ceremony.* He looked around the circle, then, and he was amazed that thirty-seven civilized people could suffer such a shared and intimate touching of their lips to the bitter kalla.

"Sit down, now," Bardo called out. Among the futons he strutted as if the kalla were rocket fuel powering his limbs. He was almost dancing with the energy of something beyond himself. He moaned and laughed and shook his head. His eyes rolled right and left, his great, soulful, brown eyes. Then he threw his hand up to his forehead; he closed his eyes and said, "Ah, mmmm, yes, there it is. Do you see it? All of you sit down before you fall down, the memories will soon begin. We'll guide you through the layers. Begin with your first childhood memory. You may use the imaging attitude, or olfaction, if you'd like, to bring it to mind."

Everyone returned to their futons, then. Danlo sat down too hard, and he felt the shaft of his shakuhachi gouge into his thigh. Always, he kept the bamboo flute shoved down into the long pocket of his pants, where most people stow their skate blades after leaving the ice. He slid the shakuhachi out of his pocket. He pressed its ivory mouthpiece to his lips. Many times since Old Father had given him this gift, he had used its intense, piercing sound to send him into reveries. But he made no music that night, for Hanuman was next to him, watching, and he knew well how his friend hated the breathy cry of the shakuhachi. There was really no need for such music, he thought, nor even the lost music of the Handel which Bardo had brought back from his journeys and now reverberated throughout the room. Already, inside him, the memories were forming up, great waves of memory that rushed through his mind and broke upon the lens of his inner eye. He beheld these memories, and he listened to them, to the sounds. His heart was a beating organ of sound that pumped a rich blood music into all the cells of his body. The skin of his face burned, and his fingers dripped sweat into the holes of the shakuhachi's bone-yellow shaft. He felt wild and wary and full of wonder, all at the same time. Had he wanted to stop the tide of memory, he could not have, nor could he understand why anyone would ever wish to do so. He could not understand how Bardo and Thomas Rane kept their feet as they walked about the room, here whispering helpful words into a woman's ear, there touching a man's closed eyelids, or the arteries of someone's throat, or placing hand upon rising belly to help with the breathing and to quell the fear of the inner world, the lost world of experience and remembrance. Perhaps, Danlo thought, one became immune to kalla after consuming it many times; or perhaps Bardo and his master remembrancer had merely faked the drinking of it, and were as free from memory as lumps of stone.

"We're all children inside," Bardo said. His voice sounded distant, as if it were falling off the rocks of a sea cliff far away. And yet the words were close to Danlo, like hot breath in his ear. "We're all children now, folded up into babe, into fetus and embryo and egg, back into our goddamned DNA. Find the way you're folded, and you'll find the Elder Eddas."

Danlo closed his eyes, and he immediately smelled milk, rich mother's milk all warm and slippery and sweet. He guessed that the smell was wafting out of the synthesizer, but he could not be sure. In the music room the air was hung with pungent smells of no particular direction, or rather, smells that pointed in thirty-eight private, individual directions, straight through the nostril and deep into the brain's smell center. And there, inside Danlo, as inside all nonengineered human beings, the olfactory nerve fibers connected synapse to synapse with the hippocampus and the almond-shaped amygdala, those ancient brain struc-

441

tures that mediate the neurochemical storms of memory. "We use smells to evoke the early memories," Thomas Rane had said. Danlo remembered him saying this, and he smelled milk, and the memories that came then were so vivid and real it seemed that he was an infant again, suckling and swallowing, his nose pressed up against his found-mother's swollen breast. Even as he sucked air through his nose and drank in his mother's warm, seal-oil smell, he knew he was deep into the recurrence attitude of remembrancing; in truth, he was not really remembering at all, but rather reliving the moments of his life.

"There are many levels of memory," he heard Thomas Rane say, "and deepest of all is recurrence."

I am two years old, Danlo thought, and he opened his eyes.

In most people the earliest memories are like pieces of ice floating in a twilight sea: fragmented, disconnected, and hard to perceive. With difficulty these fragments can be reconstructed into a semblance of past events, but this reconstruction always wavers like a sea mirage and does not satisfy. Danlo had been born with the rare "memory of pictures," an eidetic memory which imprinted the color and detail of objects seen, and then, at will, brought these perfect images before the mind's eye. He had always been able to see things more clearly than others, to remember, but even he had never guessed that the images of recurrence could be so intensely real.

I am always two years old.

In truth, the eidetics' attitude is like a key unlocking the door of recurrence, an opening into sights and sounds that cannot be destroyed. Danlo opened himself to reliving the moments of his life, and he saw with all his senses. There was light, then, the soft yellow light of oilstones filling up a cave. The light was everywhere, and it touched everything. The cave's curving rock walls and his busy little hands and his mother's face were suddenly blazing with light. He was curled up naked in his mother's lap, deep in soft white furs and the warm smells of his mother's body. Sitting close by the oilstones were other people, his near-brothers and near-sisters, Rosalehe and Yoshi and Arri, and he could see them clearly, their faces, their brilliant brown eyes and each of the thousands of hair follicles erupting from their sunburnt skin. They spoke liquid, musical words that he could barely comprehend, but that *he,* Danlo wi Soli Ringess, in the timelessness of his remembrance, recognized all too clearly: "*Ali, pela Ali, losa li pelasa i hallasa Ayeye.* Yes, God was truly a blessed and beautiful silver thallow, but Danlo could see, even

442

with his two-year-old eyes, that God was also something other. Moments earlier, on the far side of the cave, his brother Choclo had finished painting a picture of God. Everyone was looking at it. God's painted feathers blazed silver against black stone. God's wings were outstretched to beat the air, and in his great black talons, he clutched a moon, one of the six silver moons that circled the planet. And God's eyes were black and fierce, and God was dying to hook his beak into the moon, to tear it into pieces and devour it. Gazing at this brilliant painting made Danlo's eyes lock with fear. The fear rippled in waves through his body down into his scrotum. He could feel perfectly what it would be like when the great thallow's beak ripped open his belly. He grasped his hands over his navel, then, and he screamed, and the sound of his own voice was as high and wild as a thallow's, and that was the most frightening thing of all, this terrible scream. There, in his mother's lap, he was sobbing in terror, in hatred, in pain. There, too, his awestruck mother bent over him, touching him. She touched his hands, his belly, the skin above his throbbing heart; she touched the tears away from his face. This image he saw and felt with all the cells of his body. He marveled at the way image connected to emotion, to the feeling of intense love his mother's voice and fingers called up in him. He had long forgotten this love, the warm and liquid pleasure of it deep in his blood. But now he lived the child inside him again, and his delight was pure and timeless. He was connected not memory to event, but rather joy to joy, and lip to lip, connected directly with the spacetime of a singular moment as his mother kissed his mouth, his forehead, his burning eyes. That was the wonder of recurrence, he thought, the way this intense reliving of himself connected him with the source of his life and being. And at the center of his deep self was just pure laughter. He had always known this, but now he felt his belly opening to waves of laughter. His brothers and sisters gathered in close, standing over him as they dug their fishy-smelling fingers into his ribs and belly, tickling him out of his terror. *Laughter is the holiest state and brings one closest to God*—he remembered this saying as he convulsed in laughter and kicked about on his mother's lap. There, in the music room, he lay back upon his futon convulsing in remembrance, and the swells of love and laughter overwhelmed him.

I will always be two years old.

He heard a voice whispering this, and he recognized it as a truth. He had a clear and compelling sense that all the events of his life (and, perhaps, of the universe) were eternal and folded up in each present moment of time. He could almost see the folding. He listened to the sound of his laughter and followed it backward into himself, into all the selves he had ever been. This was a classic remembrancing technique. Making this journey was something like a snake swallowing its tail, or like a child trying to crawl back into the bloody womb of time. And in the deepness of experience and life, there was always terror. Always, each seeker of remembrance reached a moment of supreme terror. This moment, like a sharpened wooden stake buried in a snow trap, might be embedded within any layer of memory, but it was always there. As Danlo relived the laughter of his infancy, he thought he had escaped the worst of terrors, but it was not so. He was only stepping nearer and nearer to it. He suddenly sensed it beneath him, hidden by the thin and icy crusts of memory. It was essential, he had been told, to relive the moment of his birth, but he suddenly knew that this was impossible.

"No!" he heard himself shout. He lay writhing on his futon, with fists clenched and muscles cramping as he convulsed in terror. "No . . . I cannot!"

Almost immediately, Thomas Rane was kneeling over him, massaging his knotted limbs. Danlo could feel the pressure of his long, skillful hands and hear his voice, but he could not see him because his eyes were shut much too tightly to open.

"Danlo wi Soli Ringess," Thomas Rane said, "you're fleeing yourself."

"Take one sip of kalla and flee God," Danlo whispered. "But I took . . . more than one sip."

"Very well, but the drug cannot take you where you will not go."

"It should be so easy," Danlo said. "They say I was born laughing. The laughter should carry me back to the first moment, yes?"

"It's always hard to remember your birth."

"It is so close. I can almost see it. Almost *be* . . . there, the blessed moment."

"You must force yourself, Young Pilot."

"No, I cannot. If I was born laughing, truly, the holiest consciousness . . . Once I've returned, I could never leave it again, don't you see?"

Thomas Rane touched Danlo's eyelids, then, and with difficulty he opened his eyes. He turned his head. Next to him, on his blue futon, Hanuman lay still as a corpse. All around the music room were women and men lying straight and still, frozen into the position of remembrance.

"Ah, what's wrong?" This came from Bardo, who stepped across the room lightly and carefully. He, too, knelt by Danlo's futon, and his eyes were like bottomless brown pools.

"He's reached the fleeing stage," Thomas Rane said. His face was grave and impassive, as if he thought that a master remembrancer should always wear such a face.

"And what is he fleeing?"

"His birth. He's been told—and he believes—that he was born laughing."

"Ah," Bardo said. "Ahhh."

"We must take him through it."

"Must we?"

"He's told us enough," Thomas Rane said. "We might be able to use word keys, now."

"Words?"

"To force him back to the image storm."

"But is that wise? By God, look at him! He's gone back faster than any of the others."

"Who remembrances faster, remembrances farther," Thomas Rane said.

"Well, let him go straight back, then, as far as he can. He can remembrance his birth some other time."

Danlo looked straight into Bardo's eyes, and he saw that he too was deep in remembrance. Although he thought it was impossible that Bardo could have witnessed his birth, he sensed that the huge man was reliving the images of it, even as he smiled sadly and looked Danlo eye to eye. Friends who drank kalla together sometimes claimed they shared an almost telepathic remembrance. Danlo lost himself in Bardo's deep eyes, and he wondered if Bardo could be pulling lost images out of his mind.

"Go back if you can, Little Fellow," Bardo said.

"If we circumvent the proper sequencing," Thomas Rane said, "he may remembrance the Eddas imperfectly."

"Well, by God, has anyone but Mallory Ringess ever remembranced them perfectly?"

Thomas Rane smiled, then removed a blue vial from the pocket of his robe. He held it so Danlo could see it.

"Am I to have more kalla, sir?"

"No," Thomas Rane said, "this isn't kalla. It's water. Just plain seawater. Please open your mouth."

Danlo lay back with his mouth open as Thomas Rane opened the vial and used its dropper to let a little water fall onto his tongue. Instantly the essence of pure salt burst through his mouth.

"It tastes saltier than the sea," Danlo murmured. "Almost like blood."

"Smell and taste are almost the same sense," Thomas Rane said. "Taste the ocean, inside; this is what it was like before you were born."

"To live, I die," Danlo whispered.

"No, don't speak. Taste what's in your mouth, the ocean. You were never born. Never born, endless as the ocean—how can you die?"

I am never born, Danlo thought. *I am not I.*

He closed his eyes and lay back as he crossed his arms over his chest. As he rolled onto his side, he drew his knees up over his belly. He slept for a long time. He was two hundred days old, and he slept and dreamed frequently: dark, rhythmic, peaceful dreams. When he awoke, at last, his mouth was thick with warm salt water, the ageless taste of the sea. He was floating in a lightless sea inside his mother's womb. In truth, the idea of lightlessness had no meaning, for he had never seen light, nor could he imagine that he might someday develop a sense of vision. There was only darkness, an undifferentiated darkness as black and seamless as deep space. It absorbed him so totally that he was unaware of it. But he could hear sounds: the gas gurgling and squeaking through his mother's bowels, the muscles pulsing in peristaltic waves, his mother's heart booming everywhere in the water around him. His own heart beat more quickly, and he could hear that, too, just as he could feel the river of nourishment streaming in through his belly. Along a slippery, coiled tube, blood flowed into him and quickened him; he was conscious of very little, but even now, a never-born manchild floating in a vast ocean, he had a burning sense of his own life. And yet, paradoxically, he had no life of his own for he was wholly connected to the deepest tissues of his mother's body. Near him, across the layers of the placenta, he felt the womb arteries pulsing with blood. It was a magical and numinous thing, this ancient connection of blood. It seized him and pulled at him, just as he seized the nutrients from his mother's body. *I am not I,* he remembered. He was all water and fat and urgent cells organizing

446

themselves into something new; he was muscle and memory and skin, and yet he could not quite tell where the boundaries of his flesh gave way to the long, dark roar of his mother's womb. He swallowed amniotic water and he breathed it into his lungs, and he sensed that he had no boundaries. Like a drop of water melting into the sea, even as his blood interchanged carbon dioxide and oxygen with the blood of his mother, he felt himself growing ever vaster, ever fuller, surging outward into infinite possibilities.

I am infinite memory.

He fell deep into recurrence, and he relived all the shapes of himself since the moment he had been conceived. Each cell of his body was woven with the memory of its origins, and all of his cells—blood, belly, and brain—remembered their genesis within himself. He was a curled-up knot of urgent possibilities no larger than a baldo nut; he was a quivering ball of cells, dividing and redividing, furiously organizing themselves into liver, stomach, and heart; he was a single cell, a fertilized egg, a union of sex cells made inside both mother and father. He would always be that cell, and he suddenly knew that he was a completion, a union in ecstasy, a miracle of trillions upon trillions of chemical events connecting back to the moment of life's creation. *All living things are conscious,* he remembered. He was nothing but consciousness, the life consciousness of a single cell. Inside him was violence of metabolism, mitochondria ripping hydrogen atoms off glucose molecules, enzymes exploding through plasma, but inside, too, was a peacefulness more perfect than anything he had ever known. *I am that I am.* He was hunger, simple and pure, an overwhelming urge to eat and grow. And, at the same moment, he lived in the silent joy of floating down an endless tube, floating and touching and tasting the sugars which sweetened the waters all around him. For the first and perhaps last time in his life, he was a perfect harmony of being and becoming. To seize the free-floating molecules of alanine and trytophan and other amino acids and to feel them diffuse through his membranes was to know *halla,* and something more, to feel quickening inside himself a perfect and terrible will to life. He marveled at this will, this love, this complete affirmation of living. It would be many days yet before he developed throat, mouth, and lips, but if he had been able to give voice to all that he knew, the only words he could have spoken were: "Yes, I will." *That,* he remembered, was what the consciousness of a zygote was like, what it would always be like.

All things are in consciousness; the memory of all things is in all things.

He might have been content, for a very long time, to remain himself as this single cell. But as he consumed sugars, amino acids, and rich lipid molecules, he felt himself swelling, growing vaster, becoming ready to divide in two. He feared this division, and yet he longed for it, for he could never experience all the beauties of human life as this single, swollen cell. He was too full of himself, and this was a kind of pain tearing apart his deepest membranes. There, at the center of his self, inside his nucleus, was an awareness of pain and the memory of life. He felt it twisting and uncoiling, this long, ageless molecule of memory. His DNA was the most alive and holy part of him. It was always in motion, bending, twisting, and vibrating, a billion times each second. It rang inside him like a bell announcing the miracle of creation. And now the ringing was loud and unmistakable, and the sound of it shivered outward in waves through his cytoplasm. And now the almost infinitely long strand of DNA was unfurling, splitting like a zipper down the middle, replicating, creating more life. In the DNA's endless string of codons, as they opened up, was the secret of life.

The secret of life is more life.

DNA was designed to make more of itself and to arrange amino acids into proteins, into the very stuff of life. All the cells that he might become, through birth and boyhood, down to his final old age, would bear the signature of this DNA. And they would bear something else, too. Part of his chromosomes, where the DNA was ancient and usually silent, coded for the assembly of unique and rare proteins.

Memory is chemistry; chemistry is memory.

He was twenty-one years old, and he would always be twenty-one years old, and the memory molecules flooded the deepest parts of his brain. He tried to visualize these molecules, the proteins bent and folded into patterns of hideous complexity. Could memory, he wondered, truly be coded into chains of valine, cysteine, and aspartic acid? Was his brain simply reading the memories coded there? Or were these molecules only chemical keys fitting into his neurons, unlocking the great remembrances that would always exist inside him?

Memory is memory is memory is . . .

In truth, no one had ever understood the mystery of memory. The remembrancers, for five thousand years, had theorized that memory is like water locked up in ice, or like information coded in bits inside a computer, or like a hologram. It was said that a race of gods, the Ieldra, long ago had tampered with the human genome and had carked all their knowledge into man's most ancient DNA. All their memories: the Elder Eddas were said to be nothing other than pure memory, but no one knew what they truly were or how it was that a woman or man could remember them.

Memory *is*.

A black hole spinning stars and stars and stars swallowing light out of blackness in blackness velvet bellywomb annihilating creating jewels of light and stars and planets preserved glittering bluewhite light spacetime distortions and gravity light locked in matter is light is light is light light light light.

The great memories came, then, and Danlo lay still as he let them wash through him. The Elder Eddas welled up inside him like an onstreaming of pure consciousness, or rather, a single, vast, eternal memory, as pure as the ocean. And yet, like the ocean in a storm, the Eddas were murky and multiple, great waves of memory swelling and breaking and re-forming for a moment, only to burst into spray and fall back into the ocean's wild waters. The Elder Eddas were like drops of water, infinite in number, sparkling bits of knowledge, forbidden technologies and new logics, philosophies beyond counting, mathematics, languages, and theories of the universe. The Elder Eddas were memories of religious movements, of the genesis of stars, and of strange alien yearnings, and of the love (and fear) that all life has for other life. The dreams and agonies of ancient civilizations were written there, and the memories of the gods. He relived the death of a galaxy out beyond the Ursa Major Cloud of galaxies, and he watched the stars of the Rossette Nebula being born. To remembrance the Eddas was to walk across alien landscapes, worlds of ocher and violet dust spinning in light of a red giant stars. And worlds of fire, worlds of ice, worlds constructed inside godlike computers, perfect crystalline worlds built up of endless strata of pure information. Much of the Elder Eddas was a memory of one race's journey godward. The secret of immortality was a part of this memory, deep and dark as an underwater cavern. Another part was a design for new senses, an extension of the esthetic and philosophical senses that Danlo knew as plexure, fugue, and shih. Without these senses, it would be impossible to apprehend the universe, in all its strange and infinite beauty. A god must have a sublime sense of beauty, and so, encoded within the Eddas were a thousand concepts of beauty, as variegated and vivid as a painter's colors. Deep in the deepest of memory storms, Danlo tried to imagine what wonders the universe might unfold, but he could not see with a god's senses, not yet. And thus he could not truly understand. He could not understand the Ieldra's mathematics of the continuum, the paradoxicality of time and no-time, which were stranger than ever he had dreamed. Nor could he grasp the calculus of systems, the connectedness theorems, the way in which all life and all ecological systems everywhere were related to one another. In truth, the Elder Eddas were hideously complex, a boiling chaos of memories, and he understood only a portion of them. He was a man ravished with thirst, like a seal hunter stranded on an ice floe, contenting himself with a few of sips of snowmelt while the great ocean of truth roared all around him.

At the center of the galaxy was a black hole, spinning . . .

He sank into the softness of his futon as he tried to understand his memories. The Elder Eddas came into his mind in the form of voices, musics, images, and brilliant dramas. Much of this memory a part of him automatically encoded into words, or into the symbols of the universal syntax, or even into mathematics. This was a way toward grasping the ungraspable, a highly formal and abstract way. But gradually, as he descended deeper into the memories inside him, he became aware of another way. His nascent sense of iconicity—the ability to see equations, theorems, information, or ideas as vivid icons—gradually quickened. He remembered very well that there was a great black hole spinning at the center of the galaxy, where the stars were thick and brilliant as diamond clusters around a ring. He remembered almost perfectly the mathematics of black holes. He remembered so intensely and vividly that he began to understand gravity not through symbols or the elegant mathematical ideas encoded as symbols, but rather as something like a grave and heavy "face" that was completely familiar to him. This transformation of idea into image was eerie and frightening. He marveled at the way Schwarzschild geodesics flowed into cheekplanes, the spinors transfigured themselves as eyebrows, and the tensor fields spread out and grew into the forehead of this blazing, inner face. He saw the naked singularities as brilliant black eyes staring out at him and drinking in whole galaxies of light. But most compelling of all was the way the Lavi Curve became as one with the face's mouth, the smiling mouth, the blessed and terrible mouth whose lips were turned upward in mysterious laughter. The image of this face was as real to him as the memory of the cave into which he had been born. He could see its blackness opening up into the blackness of night, could feel its intense gravity pulling at his cells and hear the echoes of the universe inside. The memories that came to him, then, consisted of a billion such faces graven with the expression of all possible knowledge. Some of these faces he had to struggle to see. Some were more like archetypes or ancestral dreams than faces, and these he knew as deeply as his own scarred countenance which stared back at him whenever he looked into a mirror. But most of the iconic faces were utterly alien, and they flickered inside him at an impossible speed. This flickering caused the faces to merge together so that it seemed a single, dynamic face was weeping and singing and dancing, continually evolving toward some unknown shape. This, he thought, was the unfinished face of the universe, all clear-eyed and fierce and shimmering with a terrible beauty.

What is the color of the night? What was your face before you were born?

Once, when he was a young novice, he had tried to identify a picture of his family in the seemingly chaotic colors and shapes of a simple foto. Through the sheer force of his will he had succeeded. But now he had to apprehend an endless sequence of thoughtscapes, idea complexes, and alien sensibilities, to view and understand these memories through a sense that he did not yet fully possess. This heightened vision and new consciousness nearly overwhelmed him. In truth, it was infinitely more difficult to make sense of the Elder Eddas than the faces of a foto.

At the center of the galaxy was a great black hole, spinning around and around a point of singular and infinite density. The black hole was like a belly—or like a womb—of infinite blackness. Its intense gravity had pulled many stars down toward its center, pulled them apart into letptons and photons, annihilating them. And yet paradoxically, in the black hole's tremendous time distortions, each star was perfectly preserved, ten thousand glittering jewels flung against an event horizon of black velvet. Each star was an exploding mass of two billion trillion trillion grams of matter; locked in matter was energy and light. The black hole was an organ for the creation of infinite streams of light. Someday, at the still point of the black hole's center where all was eternity and silence, a whole universe of light would burst forth into time. That was the true secret of the gods, the way light created more and ever more brilliant light.

But the most brilliant of human beings could understand this secret only imperfectly, and most men and women hardly at all. For many long and harrowing moments, as a hunter trying to break free of a *sarsara*'s blinding snows, Danlo approached the threshold of a new way of seeing. Guiding him on this journey, above all other things, were his wildness and his will. He had an intense will to seeing, a will to live new experiences and new worldviews. He was quite ready to abandon all that he knew, including himself, in order to behold the Elder Eddas. And so he made difficult associations and startling connections between impossible ideas and phenomena, and he remembered things that few other human beings had ever remembered. He almost understood the connection of matter to memory, could almost see it, the way memory is locked up inside matter's terrible symmetry. He could almost see the dazzling, undifferentiated oneness of the universe as it eternally differentiated itself, falling into time, willing and becoming and evolving. And thus he almost understood the important thing about gods, which is that they must continually create, or die. They must create themselves. All gods, especially the Ieldra, regard creation as the supreme work of art. And so every moment they create themselves from the stuff of the universe, and create the universe in their marvelous, eternal memories.

Oh God oh God oh God . . .

God is memory, Danlo thought, and he realized a truth about the Ieldra, that race of gods who had carked their memories inside human beings and carked their consciousnesses into the black hole at the center of the galaxy. The taste of the Elder Eddas was salt on his tongue, and the sound of the universe was a great wave swelling up inside him. For a moment he knew all there was to know. Then the memories built to a wild white roar; they crested and broke, crushing him under an infinite weight of remembrance. He could neither see, nor hear, nor feel, nor breathe, nor even think. He was aware of himself as made up of a billion billion memories that shimmered like drops of light and dissolved into an ocean of memory, the cool, clear, single memory that lies deep inside all things. He might have died to this one memory and spent an eternity absorbed in it. But he recalled, then, that there was place where memories are continually created out of hunger and passion and pain, a whole universe of life, and he suddenly knew he had to return there, to tell Bardo and Hanuman about the remembrance of the gods.

"Oh God, oh God, oh God!" he heard someone call out.

In stages, like a turtle pulling himself from the ocean's shallows up across a beach's frozen sands, he returned to the music room. He opened his eyes and sat up. He touched the feather in his hair, the scar above his eye, the sharp ivory mouthpiece of his flute. Although it was very late and the thirty-three candles had burned low, everything seemed ablaze with light. And everything—the shatterwood floor tiles, the flowers, the golden urn of kalla—all the material objects within his sight called up memories. Memory was written into all things, and he could not help seeing the connections, in the grain of his shakuhachi, and in the lines of Hanuman's pale, blood-flecked lips, and in his own long hands, which were hard and weathered and burned brown from the bright false winter sun. He might have fallen back into remembrance then, but Bardo was kneeling beside him, squeezing the back of his neck. Flecks of compassion danced in Bardo's eyes, and he said, "Ah, Little Fellow, go slowly, now, and don't speak too soon."

But Danlo had to tell him what he had remembranced, the essence of the Eddas, and he gasped out, "Bardo, Bardo . . . *oni tlo justoth*!"

"What did you say? It sounds like the gibberish that the Fravashi teach."

Danlo recognized the words that flowed from his mouth as ancient Moksha, and he wondered why (and how) he had translated the Elder Eddas into such a language. Old Father, after all, had never taught him *ancient* Moksha. Then he thought for a moment and whispered, "Listen, Bardo, this is important: Nothing is lost."

"Ah, perhaps, but what do you mean?"

"The memory of all things . . . is in all things. The mathematics of memory, the infinities and the paradoxes are just—"

Bardo nodded his head and announced, a little too prematurely, "You've had a clear memory of the Eddas, eh? It's rare when anyone has a clear memory."

A red-faced man sitting near them overheard this exchange and repeated it to a harijan woman. Danlo heard him say: "He's had a clear memory," and then others began talking, passing information back and forth. Almost everyone had returned to waking consciousness. Around the room women and men were sitting in ones and twos, staring off at the crystalline walls, or listening to the lovely, floating music of the Debussy, or talking together about their remembrances. All Danlo's senses were afire, and he became aware of ten different tracks of conversa-

453

tion, all at once. The experience of remembrancing had terrified and confused many people, but even these were caught up in a group excitement. The spirit of the moment was one of exaltation and profound accomplishment, and it hung in the air like an intoxicating drug. Many believed that they were the initiators of a new direction in humanity's evolution. Many sensed the species' possibilities within themselves, and whether this was delusion or revelation was impossible to tell. Danlo listened to the people in the music room, and this is what he heard.

". . . inevitability is the only way to describe . . ."

". . . the feeling of total peacefulness must be the whole . . ."

". . . for me it was like a fire burning up my brain and . . ."

". . . how can anyone describe information coded into light? . . ."

". . . I don't think I understood anything, my experience was . . ."

". . . a dream, the Elder Eddas are a dream, and we're not really . . ."

". . . gods is what we might become, of course, and Mallory Ringess . . ."

". . . if the Eddas are instructions for becoming gods, then . . ."

". . . after that I became a ball of light pulsing *out* of . . ."

". . . the energy densities would have to be nearly infinite . . ."

". . . and expanding or else it would just collapse into . . ."

". . . a black hole at the center of the galaxy which I fell down . . ."

". . . was so intense, the fetal stage, I had to return but . . ."

". . . once the DNA transcription begins, no one could remembrance . . ."

". . . the Ieldra coded all of it into the DNA, the memories of . . ."

". . . infinite possibilities, but only a god could . . ."

". . . remembrance too long and it's like being drunk with fire . . ."

". . . into madness if you stay in the memory space too long . . ."

454

". . . look, even the son of the Ringess has returned, and he's . . ."

". . . Danlo wi Soli Ringess, they said his name was . . ."

". . . wild, both of them, but only the cetic remains and he's as . . ."

". . . a god, listen, if he's calling for *God*, he's lost in . . ."

". . . the great remembrances, as rare as lightning striking twice . . ."

". . . the same place we were all trying to find but they've seen . . ."

". . . God, oh God, oh God . . ."

Danlo looked over to see Hanuman rocking from side to side on his futon, lying back and rocking as he moved his thin lips. It was Hanuman, he realized, who had been crying out in his remembrance, calling for God. His eyes were closed so tightly that he seemed to be squinting; sweat beads rolled down his cheeks, leaving streaks of water against his white skin. Danlo leaned over to him and placed his hand over his friend's mouth. Hanuman's lips were hard and hot. "Shhh, *mi mokashu la, shantih, shantih*," Danlo said. "Wake up, now, my brother, and be at peace."

But Hanuman was locked into remembrance, and Bardo edged over, then. He reached down to pull Danlo's hand away from Hanuman's mouth. "There, careful you don't smother him," he said. "You won't bring him back by words, too bad."

Thomas Rane came over, and Surya Surata Lal, and others. They stood in a circle over Danlo and Hanuman. They looked down at them, and their eyes were full of candlelight and awe.

"Who remembrances deepest, remembrances longest," Kolenya Mor said.

"Well, Danlo has had a clear memory, and deep," Bardo said.

"It's plain that the journeymen, both of them, remembranced *too* deeply," Surya said. "We've got to control these experiences before someone dies of them."

"Quiet now," Thomas Rane said. His face was calm, and the silver fibers of his robe gleamed. "No one has ever died from remembrancing."

Surya's little face tightened up and she said, "I think the young cetic drank too much kalla. Well, he was warned."

455

"Take three sips of kalla and be God," someone said.

"We should have controls," Surya huffed out. "I've said that before."

"I've never seen anyone remembrance *this* deeply," Kolenya Mor said. There was amazement in her voice. "What must it be like?"

Thomas Rane knelt down next to Danlo and began working on Hanuman's face muscles. But the massage did little good, for Hanuman continued to cry out, and his words grew more even pained and ominous: "*Everything* is God, I am God, my God, my God . . ."

"Of course, it's not just the kalla, it's his own memories that are eating him up," Surya said, and she shot Danlo a quick, sour look, as if to ask him why his friend should suffer such deep memories.

Hanuman's hands were locked together over his navel, and Danlo covered them with his own hand. He looked up a ring of concerned faces, and a truth of the Elder Eddas came to him. *We are all food for God,* he remembered. *We are all—*

"So the young cetic is God now," Surya said to Bardo. "Well, we've all been tempted to think that, haven't we?"

"Ah," Bardo said. "No one should ever interpret another's experience."

"But Mallory Ringess didn't become a god by remembrancing the Elder Eddas," Surya said. "Not *just* by remembrancing them."

Danlo felt for the pulse in Hanuman's wrist, and he found it, fast and quick like a bird's, rising up in fluttering waves against his fingertips. Hanuman was still drowning in a wave of memory, he thought, and he shut his eyes and let his own memories run through him.

The universe is a womb for the genesis of gods.

"We should try to bring the Ringess into our hearts," Surya said. "We should let his compassion guide us. Remembrancing the great knowledge means nothing without the compassion to understand it. Mallory Ringess struggled his whole life to find compassion, and we must find a way to love and honor him for that, or we'll never follow his way."

Nadero devam arcayer, Danlo remembered. *By none but a god . . .*

While the room echoed with the soothing music of flutes and gosharps, Danlo opened his eyes to smile at Surya Lal. He took a deep breath of air, and then said, "By none but a god shall a god be worshipped."

"No one has said anything about worship," Surya told him.

"But you speak of my father . . . and there is worship in each of your words. He was just a man. Now he is a god, it is said. We may become gods, truly, but for a man or woman to worship anything, that is the greatest sin."

"Is it a sin to follow the way that the Ringess showed humanity?"

"But there are many ways," Danlo said. "As many ways as there are human beings."

"We only know one way of becoming gods, Young Pilot."

"But would you rather become a god . . . or God?"

Surya glanced at Bardo, and she said, "As my cousin has repeatedly emphasized, we're not here to start a religion. I don't know anything about *God.* I do know about one man's immortality. The development of great powers, growth without end. The Ringess spoke about this often, the possibilities of humankind."

Infinite possibilities.

Danlo still held his hand over Hanuman's hands, and he felt his friend's belly rise and fall with every breath. The rhythm of it carried him back into remembrance, and as he stared at the bloody flecks on Hanuman's lips, he thought about *infinite possibilities.* With difficulty he spoke, half to Surya, half to himself: "It is possible to develop . . . a new way of seeing. Possible for anyone, man or god. I did not know this earlier today, but I know it now. That is, I have always known it, but tonight, in the Eddas . . . this new sense. Call it yugen, that is the best word for it I know. Yugen is . . . a way of seeing behind surfaces, pine needles or ice or words, the fragility even of the universe. Everything is so fragile, our eyes, our breath, our mathematics, our stars. Yet tough as diamond, eternal. The paradoxes. You cannot see anything unless you can see how it is not a *thing.* Yugen is seeing the connectedness of all things. The folding through time, past into present, thereness into nowness. Matter is memory, and DNA, and life, and in everyone it is all folded up, the memories of the future. To see it, waiting ten billion years to be born, the possibilities of evolution—you cannot even begin to imagine the possibilities."

For a while, Danlo sat cross-legged and talked about the Elder Eddas, or rather, told Surya and the others about his experience of them. It was hard for him to describe the indescribable, but quite a few people in the room had remembranced the Eddas themselves, however shallowly, and they seemed to understand much of what he said. At last Bardo stood up and rested his hand atop Danlo's head. He looked down at Hanuman, and then addressed the people gathered around him. Their faces were written with excitement and expectancy. "Danlo wi Soli Ringess has had a great remembrance," Bardo said. "That's clear, isn't it? Perhaps his friend has, too. Few of us have remembranced so deeply as the young cetic."

Just then Hanuman began to speak again, and his words were cold knives ripping open the veils of time. For an instant, Danlo saw the future fall open in a cascade of images, and the vision of it cut him with dread and despair. "I am God," Hanuman murmured, "I am God, my God, I'm one, I'm *the* one, my God, my God." And then, after a space of silence, he cried out, "No, no, no, no!"

Danlo let go of Hanuman. He stood up, cupped his hands, and whispered in Bardo's ear, "What shall we *do*?"

"Ah, Little Fellow, it will be all right," Bardo said softly. And then, so that the others could hear him, in his most reassuring voice, he said, "The young cetic is not the first to become lost in the memories. I, myself, and Thomas Rane, and the other guides—we've all journeyed deeply. But there are always ways back, techniques the remembrancers can apply, at need. We'll take the young cetic to the Well, now. While we're bringing him back, please remain here and review your memories. It's been a night of great remembrance, by God!"

So saying, he squatted down and lifted Hanuman up against his belly. Bardo was endlessly strong and had no trouble carrying him. Danlo thought Hanuman looked as small as a young boy in his arms, small and fragile and sick with memories.

"Thomas Rane!" Bardo called out. "If you will, please accompany us."

Thomas Rane and Bardo bowed their heads toward the urn of kalla on the stage, and they bowed to the circle of people still standing around Danlo. They bore Hanuman away to the Well, which was a room of dark tanks and healing waters in the deepest part of the house. Everyone returned to their futons, then. Because the music room was now too quiet, Danlo put his shakuhachi to his lips and began to play the long, deep notes of a song Old Father had taught him, and the memories consumed him.

We are all food for God.

He knew this as part of a true remembrance, but whether or not it was a great one, he could not yet say. He looked up at the stage, at the urn gleaming golden against the black lacquer table. The next time he was called to a rite of remembrance, he promised himself he would again take three sips of kalla.

DOLLS

*Every time consciousness contemplates itself, it must fall
into an infinite regress. At the end of this spiral into
neverness is God—or Hell. Hell was created when God
gave human beings the power to behold themselves, just
as they are.*

—*from* A Requiem for Homo Sapiens,
by Horthy Hosthoh

It was two full days before Danlo saw Hanuman again. As
Tamara had foretold, after the night of the joyance Danlo found
himself craving solitude, and he avoided talking to people. He
spent most of each day and night skating the streets, or drinking
chocolate alone in cafés, or sitting on the cold rocks of North
Beach, watching the waves roll in from the ocean and burst
against the icy shore. Although he was exhausted, he could not
sleep, nor did he really wish to. The memory of the Elder Eddas
was too sharp in his mind, and he remained in a wild, open state
all this time. He remembranced frequently. As the aftershocks
of an earthquake unsettle a city, the great memories trembled
inside him and only gradually died away. He contemplated these
memories, trying to find a way to interpret them to himself.
Finally, on the evening of the ninetieth, he returned to Bardo's
house. The gatekeeper admitted him to the nightly festivities,
even though he had no invitation. After greeting various guests
(Bardo was obviously quite proud of Danlo's accomplishment
and wanted to introduce him to all his friends), he excused himself. He made his way into the north wing. There, in a luxurious
room smelling of Fravashi carpets, scent sculptures, and freshly

cut flowers, he found Hanuman recuperating from his remembrance.

"Hanu, Hanu," he said.

Hanuman sat in an immense chair upholstered with seal leather. He had positioned it directly in front of the blazing fireplace. He was entirely naked, without even an undergown covering him. He, too, looked as if he had not slept since the remembrance. His fine hair was a tangle of greasy blond clumps, here pressed and matted, and in other places irregularly parted to reveal his white scalp. When he turned to face Danlo, he seemed not to see him. His eyes, usually so colorless and cold, were like pools of pale blue fire. He appeared to be gazing into himself, through himself into a place of utter darkness and pain. Danlo thought that he had the haunted, unhappy look of a man who had been brought back to his youth once too often. A stranger, meeting him for the first time, might have guessed he was a thousand years old.

"I'm glad you've come," Hanuman said.

Danlo noticed, then, that Hanuman was holding a black crystal sphere the size of a thallow egg. He cupped it in his left hand for a moment, then he squeezed it and let it roll into his other hand. It looked much like a satori stone which the aficionados of zanshin use to strengthen their hands.

"Are you well?" Danlo finally asked.

"As you see," Hanuman said.

"Have you been able to remove yourself from . . . the memories?" Danlo stood beside Hanuman's chair, and he pressed his fingertips against Hanuman's forehead. His skin was oily and hot; the whole of his body seemed twisted with an intense inner fire.

"Perhaps it would be wisest," Hanuman said, "if we didn't talk about the remembrance."

"I was afraid . . . the kalla had taken you too deep."

"*Kalla,*" Hanuman said. There was bitterness and despair in the way he spoke the word. "Take three sips and be God. I wonder, of all the things we've been told, could there be a greater lie?"

"I think kalla is a blessed drug."

"And perhaps it is—for you."

Danlo slowly rubbed his eyes. "Surya Lal has said that the kalla nearly poisoned you. That three sips is too much, a poison for human beings."

"Kalla is a window," Hanuman said. "Nothing more. It's

looking through the window too long that burns the eyes and poisons the soul."

"Everyone is saying you have had a great remembrance."

Hanuman was silent for a moment, and then in his secretive way, he said, "I've seen what I've seen; I've remembered what I've remembered."

"Have you seen . . . the interconnectedness of the ecologies? Did you understand the rules for embedding, the way each quark, each cell, each organism, even the gods, building on each other, the ecologies spreading out across—"

"I've seen too much, Danlo."

"Truly? Is it possible to see too much?"

"I've seen too clearly."

"The One memory," Danlo said, "to see it, shimmering, the way memory is connected to matter, to our minds, to ourselves. I have spent the last two days trying to see it, to keep the memory clear."

Hanuman smiled quickly, then said, "I'm glad your remembrance was so exalted. I've never seen you so happy."

"I have never really seen before . . . so many possibilities."

While Hanuman listened, Danlo talked about evolution and the possibilities of life within the universe. He spoke of human beings, of their freedom to grow into godhood, or to remain gloriously human, to *become* truly human for the first time. As Danlo conceived it (a vision shaped by his remembrance of the Elder Eddas) true humanity was neither a tragedy nor a doom to flee from, but rather, a marvelous, golden, never-before-realized possibility that each person might someday create. He spoke for a long time, trying to elicit some comment or response from Hanuman. But Hanuman just sat in his leather chair squeezing his black sphere, and he was as silent and mysterious as a cetic.

And then he looked straight at Danlo and said, "No." He pronounced this single word with great authority, and then, like a tortoise pulling back into his shell, he returned to his silence.

"No? What do you mean?"

With a great force, Hanuman pushed himself out of his chair. He paced quickly back and forth across the carpets in front of the fireplace. The muscles along his pallid thighs quivered like the strings of a gosharp; his whole body shook with the tremors of exhaustion. Danlo thought that he might have been pacing thus for most of two days. Hanuman took no care for his nakedness, or rather, he flaunted it as if he wanted the world to view him just as he was. For a moment he paused in front of the fireplace and held his arms outspread to warm himself. The light of the fire licked across his hard shiny body, red flame tongues against white skin, then he turned and stepped closer to Danlo. It seemed that he was stepping *out* of the fire, like some ancient piece of metalwork come to life. Danlo could see that he was a changed man, that the blaze of his remembrance at last must have fused together his will and his sense of fate. Hanuman's face and his artful body and his newly forged awareness of himself—everything about him shone with a terrible beauty. And yet, for all his seeming vitality and the brilliance of his eyes, there was a darkness about him, inside him, as if a great part of his soul had cracked and broken. He smiled at Danlo, sadly, knowingly, and he said, "No, for the universe, and therefore for human beings, there is only one possibility."

He told Danlo a part of his remembrance, then. It was the only time he ever spoke of this experience to anybody. But his single revelation—his remembrance of the Elder Eddas—would soon make him famous and would cause Danlo the greatest of anguish.

"There is war in heaven," Hanuman said. He stood close to Danlo with his arms crossed over his chest. "The gods throughout this galaxy, and in every galaxy, the gods are at war. There are many gods. So many, even from the alien races. You can't guess how many. Your father is one, you should know. That is, he *was* one—who knows if he's still alive? They're killing each other. They've been killing each other for a million years. *This* is the ecology I've seen: survival of the fiercest and the vastest. And, of course, Ede the God was *not* the first, as the Architects teach. Not nearly the first. You say human beings can evolve into gods, but that's not enough. It's never been sufficient. There are three requisites for growth without bound, and only three: the will to remake oneself, the genius to survive, and the strength to suffer."

He proceeded to expand upon a specific part of his remembrance: he told Danlo of a great battle that two gods had fought out near the edge of the Sagittarius arm of the galaxy. Beyond the 18th Deva Cluster, where the stars grow thin as a handful of snow cast into the wind, sixty thousand years previously, some god of war had destroyed another. The corpse of this unknown god—Hanuman said it was the size of a small planet—circled a red giant star. In a low, steady voice, he divulged the fixed points of this star. This was knowledge only a pilot could have. It was of a rarefied, purely mathematical nature, and either Hanuman had learned it from a pilot of the Order, or he had indeed remembered it as a part of the Elder Eddas. Since pilots were forbidden to betray such knowledge to outsiders (and since any pilot fortunate enough to have discovered a dead god would surely have made his name in announcing this discovery), Danlo concluded that Hanuman was telling the truth. Truth was written across Hanuman's tormented face: the truth of a man who has beheld a force too terrible ever to forget.

"For here is the oldest of teachings," Hanuman said as he smiled at Danlo. He rarely quoted from the *Book of God* anymore; in fact, he did so only in moments of distress. " 'Here is wisdom: No god is there but God; God is one, and there can be only one God.' "

He said no more of his remembrance of the Elder Eddas. He never spoke of the One memory, as others did, nor did he ever hint that he had been enlightened. But everyone who encountered him during the days that followed was to comment on the way his whole being seemed to glow. Danlo, himself, had seen this the moment he had entered the room. And now he stood face-to-face with Hanuman, looking for the source of the light, trying to understand the change that had come over him. He decided that "enlightenment" was a poor word for the descent into the darkest parts of oneself. He thought of Hanuman's great remembrance as a bedarkening, a kind of negative enlightenment that had led him only deeper into pride and love of his fate. He might have described Hanuman, with his burning eyes and broken soul, as being utterly awakened, but that was not quite right, either.

He is the opposite of awakened, Danlo suddenly realized.

In truth, the opposite of awakening is not sleep, but rather the coming into full consciousness of the great "No." Danlo could see that Hanuman was too aware of life's ultimate negation and was suffering a vast unhappiness behind his smiles and his silence. He knew then that Hanuman would never have the strength for such suffering. If he were not healed of his basic fault, as he fell farther into neverness and the pursuit of personal godhood, the weakest part of him, like a crack in the sea ice under a hot sun, would open up and destroy him.

"In eight more days," Danlo said, "we shall be invited to another joyance."

"Perhaps," Hanuman said.

"The kalla is a wild drug, I think," Danlo said. "Wild like the sea. It is always easy to become lost. But you could learn . . . to go wherever you will."

"You're the pilot, not I."

"But you are a cetic!"

"A cetic," Hanuman agreed, and he stared off into the air. "Cetics are masters of consciousness, yes?"

Hanuman glanced down at the sphere in his hand. "Are we?" he asked.

"Kalla is a blessed drug. A doorway . . . to the deepest consciousness."

"You really think so, don't you?"

"I have seen it. Truly. I have *been* . . . this consciousness. Only for a moment, and never perfectly—but I have only tasted the kalla one time."

Hanuman stared straight at Danlo then, and his words poured out of him like molten rock bubbling from a rent in the earth: "You've *seen* it. I shouldn't dispute your vision, should I? You know what you know. However, I wish you could see, just one time, what *I've* seen. But that's an impossibility, I know. It's silly of me to wish such a thing. You have your blessed consciousness—never the fear of annihilation, never panic, never hatred, never pure retching despair."

For a while Danlo stood staring at Hanuman, trying to quell the despair forming up hard inside his throat. Then he swallowed and said, "But, Hanu, to remember yourself, the Elder Eddas, to become conscious of the One memory—everything is there, yes? All occurrences, all light, all time, all possibilities."

"You'd like to believe that. But in fact, this consciousness, this God memory of yours is like a trap. Think of it as a lava pool covered with a crust of rock. Step carelessly, take your three sips of kalla, and then you break the crust and fall through. And then there's drowning, burning, annihilation, nothingness."

"No, it is just the opposite," Danlo said. "To remember yourself is to become whole again. To become completely yourself, your deep self, then there is joy. Just pure joy."

"No, memory is pure fire."

"No, memory is just—"

"Danlo, listen to me!" Hanuman's belly quivered as every muscle in his body seemed to jump and come alive at once. He seemed intensely alive, Danlo thought. Curiously, for the first time since they had become friends, he was not coughing. Yet he was far from being well. He was sick with a strange and horrible disease that moment by moment was consuming him. He fairly jumped over to the flower table beside his bed and reached out his finger. Earlier that day, one of Bardo's underlings had placed a vase of sunflowers there. Seven sunflowers pulled ominously at their thin green stems. Each one was a perfect hemisphere of hundreds of orange-gold petals exploding outward toward the eye. Hanuman stabbed his finger into the center of one of the sunflowers, and he said, "Look at these glorious flowers! Do you see what I see? Not the alienness, not even the beauty, but the burning. They burn my eyes. I look at them, straining to find the sun in this ugly little room without windows, and my eyes are on fire. I can see the leaves, the individual cells, the molecules of chlorophyll burning for the sun. The memory of the sun—everything remembers. Do you think the stem cells don't remember being cut away from the stem this morning? Do you think they don't convulse at the pain of the knife? Do you think they don't burn to be rejoined with the main body of the sunflower plant? Yes, they convulse; yes, they remember; yes, they burn. Everything burns. The leather in that ugly chair in which I've sat for two days burns with memory of every hurt and every pain the seal felt during her life. The air passing my lips as I say these words: it burns. I breathe, and in each lungful of air, I inhale a molecule from the dying breath of every animal and bird that's ever lived on this planet. The remembrancers are right, you should know. The memory of everything is in everything. And it's all burning, and it never stops. *This* is what memory is. *This* is what I am. And no, I'm not telling you this because I desire your compassion. That's the last thing I'd wish of you. But you've always said you wanted to see things as they are. If that's really true, then open your eyes and look."

Danlo touched the scar above his eye, and he stared at the sunflowers bursting golden out of their black stone vase. Then he looked at Hanuman. There stood his best friend, burdened, unhappy, doomed, trembling with unutterable pain, yet in his own way exalted. He had his own burning vision, his own unique connection with the forces of the universe. *He has the look of a prophet,* Danlo thought. Hanuman walked over to the fire and stood there, wild-eyed and fey, as if he, and he alone, had been called to accomplish some great task. Upon his sad, beautiful face was written the conviction that all the forces of evolution since time's beginning were converging upon him, that the very future of humanity depended upon his will, his genius, his strength.

"Do you remember the day in the shih grove?" Danlo asked. "You said then that the animals and the plants, and people . . . do not feel true pain."

"I remember," Hanuman said. "I was wrong, and I was right. Their pain is real. They suffer—everything does. But next to the pain of the gods, it's nothing."

"Pain is pain," Danlo said. "And you are still a man."

"That's mostly true. Do you suppose, however, that the cells in my brain can't foreknow what it's like to grow without bound? They know, they remember. Inside my brain, there's a burning more brilliant than any fire. It's beyond all color, beyond even light, and it goes on and on and on."

"There is a way to make the burning stop," Danlo said.

"No, Danlo, not in this universe."

So saying, Hanuman went over near the fireplace where there stood a table. He beckoned Danlo closer, the better to view the table. It was a low, square, ancient-looking table, the kind of table one might sit at with a friend in enjoyment of coffee and conversation. As Danlo could see, the tabletop was wrought of some translucent substance such as clary or glass. It was cold and smooth to the touch. It had a dead, grayish look to it, and Danlo could not imagine why anyone would wish to make such an ugly thing.

"The whole universe is on fire," Hanuman said. He held the cold, black sphere motionless above the table. "Haven't you ever wondered what makes the universe the way it is?"

Just then, the tabletop came alive with light. Blue dots and clusters of red, amoebalike structures flashed beneath the glass. Danlo realized that these colorful arrays were likely being generated by liquid crystals inside the table.

"What kind of computer is this?" he asked.

"Properly, it's not a computer at all," Hanuman said as he rolled the black sphere from hand to hand. "It's just a display table."

"And what is it displaying?"

Hanuman squeezed the black sphere and looked at it for a while. "Dolls," he finally said. "It's displaying dolls. Haven't you ever seen the dolls before?"

"I have heard of . . . artificial life," Danlo said. "These are information structures, yes? It is said that computers can bring information to life."

"In a way, information *is* life," Hanuman said. "And the computer is the universe in which it lives."

"Which computer?"

"*This* computer," Hanuman said.

Here, he held the black sphere before the firelight, and he stared at it as if he were an astronomer peering into the very heart of the universe. He explained that the sphere was a special kind of computer that the cetics make. It was fifteen cubic inches of crystalline neurologics of the same kind used in the creation of firestones; as with any good firestone, it generated an almost infinitely dense information field. He called it his "universal computer," and he told Danlo that it supported entire information ecologies of life.

"The table will display this life," he said. "Shall I show you a picture of what's occurring inside this computer?"

The tabletop was now a smooth plane glittering with bits of light. There were millions of these light bits, which winked on and off in a blizzard of colors: crimson, sapphire, violet, and green. And magenta, rose, flame red, indigo, and aquamarine, and a hundred other colors. Each light bit represented a certain configuration of information stored inside the universal computer. The light bits—or rather the information they represented—were like artificial atoms, each of which was programmed with unique properties. These fundamental information structures existed in the cybernetic space that the cetics call the *alam al-mithral*. This is the space in which images are real, the space halfway between the real world and the Platonic world of ideals. On Old Earth, a thousand years before the first computers, Avicenni the Wise had posited a realm of existence midway between matter and spirit. For millennia, the cetics had applied all their ingenuity to creating such a realm; it was the claim of the cyber-shamans that they had succeeded. Many cyber-shamans possessed black spheres like Hanuman's. Many cyber-shamans had created and programmed their own unique information atoms in order to evolve life made of pure information.

"This is the tenth universe I've designed," Hanuman said. "It's the best, most fascinating thing I've ever done, this creating of universes."

In fact, he had not created his universe as a finished piece, as one might sculpt a block of diamond or weave a tapestry. Rather, he had created information atoms and rules by which these atoms interacted with their environment, and with each

468

other. This was all that he had done. Other professionals, of course, experimented with artificial life in different ways. Some ecologists liked to shape their universes as they evolved, continually adding new programs and editing out various kinds of informational life. But the cyber-shamans disdained this personal interference as inelegant and lacking in profundity. In this tenth universe of Hanuman's, he had created exactly 187 information configurations and had programmed 23 laws specifying the ways they might combine with each other. He had done this five hours previously. And then he had let the universal computer run. As he held the black sphere up to his forehead in contemplation of what was occurring inside, it was running still.

"But why this game?" Danlo asked. "Why play games . . . now?"

"Do you think this is a *game*?"

"You are making models of the universe, yes? Models of different universes . . . that might reveal the possibilities of our own."

"I already know about *this* universe, Danlo."

"But evolution—"

"The only evolution that matters anymore," Hanuman said, "is that which we might control."

"Such as the evolution of the dolls?"

"Of course," Hanuman said. "Shall I arrange a display of their evolution?"

"If you would like."

Danlo clasped his hands behind his back as he stared down at the tabletop. Now the cloud of colored lights was not quite so chaotic. In various places beneath the glass, with a quickness almost impossible to apprehend, points of vermillion light swirled around green light bits, and tiny aquamarine light bursts interpenetrated those of crimson. In this way, the 187 colors of light combined to form thousands of different kinds of information molecules, and then thousands of thousands. The glass sparkled with brilliant new patterns of information almost geometric in their perfection. The patterns vibrated and organized themselves and rotated against each other as they combined to make ever more complex patterns; or they absorbed each other and grew, or sometimes, they annihilated each other in showers of gold and purple light. And then other information molecules would feed on this light, and all this feeding and growing and making of new patterns happened so quickly that Danlo dared not blink his eyes, lest he lose sight of the overarching pattern that was beginning to emerge.

"*Loshisha shona,*" Danlo whispered. "These lights are beautiful."

The lights were indeed beautiful, beautiful with an evolving order that emerged from chaos. No one could predict what this order might be. It was impossible, even in theory, to foreknow what forms might evolve within the *alam al-mithral* space of Hanuman's computer.

"This program has been running for five hours. The molecules you see evolved within the first five nanoseconds."

"Then the current state of the program is far beyond this, yes?"

"Far beyond."

"How long will you let the program run? What kind of doll . . . are you trying to create?"

Hanuman tapped his fingernail against his temple. He said, "I've created nine other universes, but I've never let one run to its halt state. It's inelegant to seek some sort of solution to life or some final, perfect form of life."

"I understand," Danlo said. He looked up and nodded, and he wondered if Hanuman was telling himself the truth.

"It's the dynamics of artificial life that are beautiful," Hanuman said. "*Making* the information atoms and the universal laws so perfectly that everything occurring in the universe is without flaw or taint of ugliness. I've never been able to tolerate ugliness."

Danlo bowed his head then, and he looked down to see the information molecules combining into long chains, the chains knitting themselves into gleaming membranes. After a while, these membranes had grown and folded into globules that looked something like organic cells. Only they were not creations of protein, lipids, or RNA; they were only of light, or information coded into light. Each information cell was a tiny jewel glittering with ten million points of light. He watched the cells collect together into a cluster that vibrated with an astonishing brilliance of colors, and he looked over to see Hanuman watching, too.

"What's beautiful," Danlo said, "is that a creator can be astonished by his own creations."

For a while, as the evening deepened and the fire burnt low in the fireplace, Hanuman showed Danlo how his creations had evolved into dolls. To recapitulate five hours of evolution in a

470

few moments, he speeded up the table display. Danlo watched as the cells clumped together and exchanged gleaming bits of information and combined into new forms; he watched the evolution of simple informational organisms that Hanuman had jokingly named infosoria. From these jewellike arrays of information evolved new kingdoms of artificial life. Hanuman had classified this life into emerging phyla, and into entirely new classes and orders that had never existed within any cybernetic space. The tabletop, a few square feet of brilliant geometric patterns and flashing glass, could display only the tiniest fraction of this evolution. Even so, the display was a riot of colors that exploded outward and radiated into ten thousand species of artificial life. Many times each second, species mutated and claded off into new species; sometimes these species would remain stable for a moment or two and would fill whole sections of the tabletop with a uniformity of life that Hanuman called a synusia. But always there was movement and mutation and information exchange; there were always new forms and the violence of broken information arrays. A series of ecological communities followed one another so quickly that Danlo could scarcely hold their patterns within his mind. These seres, as they were called, were ever more complex and ever more beautiful. The last sere, which had evolved within the universal computer only an hour earlier, was full of lovely shapes that seemed made of silver light. In the way they grouped together and changed direction without warning, they seemed much like a school of fish. At times, they would nudge each other as they vied for space; or they would vibrate and send out waves of information molecules, and when they did this, they resembled nothing so much as a herd of bellowing, silvery seals. Hanuman called them dolls, and he said that soon they would become as intelligent as human beings.

"As you'll see," Hanuman said, "they have a complex social organization. They build something like cities—you could call them information arcologies. Most importantly they make weapons, and they make war. What more ominous sign of intelligence should we desire?"

Danlo kept his eyes on the tabletop, and he asked, "But what does it mean . . . to call these dolls intelligent? They are just arrays of information ordered by programs. Each information bit . . . has no choice in how it interacts with others. Each cell and cell cluster. And each organism is built up of these information bits, yes? Each organism, each doll, everything they

471

do—it is all determined by the programs you made. How can they have will? Or mind? How can such creatures truly be alive?"

"You ask such obvious questions," Hanuman said. "The deeper question is, How is it that *we* seem conscious of our will? Why is it that *we* seem to be alive?"

"But, Hanu . . . we *are* alive."

"Are we really?"

"Yes!"

"Aren't we made of atoms of matter? Bits of carbon and oxygen that combine according to universal laws? Aren't these laws programmed into the very fabric of our universe? And if this is so, if each neuron in your wild, brilliant brain fires solely according to the laws of chemistry, then why should you think that you have any will at all?"

"But our will," Danlo said, "our *consciousness* cannot be reduced . . . to the firing of neurons. And the mind of our cells cannot be reduced to chemistry. Mind cannot be understood by a reduction to matter—to the interactions of smaller and smaller pieces of matter. There is no smallest piece of matter, I think. If matter is infinitely reducible, then it is not really reducible at all. Not reducible in any way that could explain consciousness."

Hanuman gazed at the black sphere resting in his hands, and he asked, "But what is consciousness, Danlo?"

Danlo was quiet for a moment, and then he said, "Consciousness is not anything. Not any *thing*. Consciousness . . . *is*. It is just what it is, nothing more."

"But what is matter?"

High above Danlo, stretched between the angles of the ceiling and the wall in the room's corner, there was a spider's web, as large and intricate as any he had ever seen. In the light of the fire, the web was all shimmering gold, and he wondered how a simple spider could know how to weave such a glorious thing. He relived a part of his great remembrance, then. He stared at the spider's web, and this afterimage of the Elder Eddas burned inside him: *Matter is memory.* Matter, he knew, was not bits of smaller, lifeless bits, but rather the ordered flow of something he could think of only as mindstuff. *Matter is mind,* he remembered, and he told Hanuman this as he stared up at the lovely web that some unseen spider had made.

"But what is mind?" Hanuman asked. "Once again, our argument is turning in circles."

Danlo smiled and said, "But how should it not? Isn't the

contemplation of consciousness . . . like a snake swallowing its own tail?"

They stood there talking about the cetics' theory of the circular reduction of consciousness. In this reduction, the human mind is supposedly explainable by neural analysis, and neural analysis by brain chemistry. And brain chemistry is reducible to simple chemistry, which in turn, ultimately, can be reduced to pure quantum mechanics. For millennia, quantum mechanics has been a precise description of the interactions of the smallest pieces of observable matter, but it has never been an explanation of how—and why—these pieces come to be. To this day, some mechanics continue the attempt to explain matter in terms of itself, but most have given up this quest as hopeless. (The mechanics of Neverness, of course, have reduced all physics to pure mathematics. It is as if they seek to hone their equations until they are sharp and perfect as swords, thence to pierce the veils of Platonic space in the hope that all conceivable particles will spill out into creation like golden eggs from a sac. In this cosmic conceit, they are closer to the truth than they could ever know.) It was the cetics, in the time of Jonath Chu, who proposed the radical notion of explaining matter in terms of consciousness, rather than consciousness as an emergent property of the more highly organized forms of matter. Pure consciousness, according to Lord Chu, was the very stuff of reality. It underlay all matter, all energy, all spacetime. It was always moving, yet always still, as formless and eternal as water yet containing the possibilities of all things. Lord Chu had invented a physics of consciousness; he had attempted to explain, mathematically, how pure consciousness differentiates itself into all the particles and parts of the universe. Ultimately, the infamous Chu Wave Theory was proved inadequate and inconsistent, but Jonath Chu had almost succeeded in closing the circle of the reduction of human consciousness to the pure, universal consciousness that is only itself, and nothing more.

"I think you have your own theory of consciousness," Danlo said.

"Every cetic has a theory."

"Yes, but I have heard that you made improvements on the Wave Theory . . . as a part of your masterwork."

"Who told you this?"

Danlo shrugged his shoulders and said, "I have many friends, Hanu. They cannot help talking about what you have done."

473

"What *have* I done?" Hanuman wondered aloud. He began pacing back and forth. "I've simply abandoned this notion of consciousness. What can we say about pure consciousness? It's not this, it's not that, it stirs, it stirs not, it's undefinable, unmeasurable, paradoxical. In a sense it can't be said even to exist."

"But you exist. We exist. We know . . . that we exist."

"Perhaps."

"In the Elder Eddas, it is all there, the One memory . . . which is identical in each of us. The way consciousness becomes—"

"I've had a different remembrance of the Elder Eddas, you should know."

"But at the deepest level, where all differences disappear, where memory is universal—"

"We each create our own universe, Danlo."

Danlo touched the feather in his hair, then looked at the black sphere that Hanuman was holding. "I think you love your own universe too well."

"Should I love this world any better? This tangibility of stone and substance rushing to destruction? All the ugliness of a world that rots or decays or falls apart? No, I can't love it. There's so much pain. Even wickedness. You've seen the hibakusha children—the way they live. The way they die. You say that pain is the awareness of life. But, no, pain mocks life. Life, in this ugly flesh we're trapped in: it's all affliction and torment. A burning without end. And what is it that burns? Do *we* burn? What are we, really? We're pure flame, and flame burns, it's true, but it doesn't burn *itself*. There's a flame inside my flesh—call it pattern or program or soul, it doesn't matter. *I* am not matter. I can't tell you how I loathe any connection to this flawed, pinkish material that never stops burning." Here, he paused to grasp the skin on the back of his beautifully made hand, and then he shook it so violently that his knuckle bones fairly rattled. "How should I love these common elements of blood and bone that keep my true self imprisoned? You say that matter is mind, but no, matter is misery. Matter is all mutability and disintegration. So long as we're bound to matter, we fall into decay atom by atom, or fall quickly to disease, but we all finally fall. And then there's only death and annihilation. Extinction. The memory of every fine feeling we've ever had or friends whom we've loved—all erased. Which is why I must find a way to free the fire from the flesh. It's only human to desire escape.

We all desire this. Let's never forget that you've had your blessed remembrance."

After Hanuman had finished this little speech, Danlo bowed his head in remembrance of the disease that had swept all the Devaki tribe into death. He touched the lightning scar above his eye, then said, "Truly, everyone wants to escape suffering. But, Hanu, your world of dolls, this new passion of yours . . . this is an escape *from* material reality. Remembrancing is escaping *into* material reality."

"I don't see the difference."

"But, there is all the difference in the world. It is the difference between what is real . . . and what is not."

Hanuman's face fell cold, and he asked, rhetorically, "Should a cetic listen to a pilot circumscribe the nature of reality?"

"That was not my intention," Danlo said. He tapped the glass tabletop glowing with the light of Hanuman's dolls. "I only wanted to distinguish between real life . . . and a simulation of life."

"I see. A *pilot* wishes to make this distinction."

"Life cannot be made . . . from bits of information."

"No, that's precisely wrong," Hanuman said. "Information is the most real thing there is. The essence of everything is pure information."

Like a zanshin master preparing to defend the space near him, Hanuman placed his feet precisely on the wooden floor tiles. He seemed preternaturally relaxed, yet wary. He stood in the orange glow of the dying fire. He told Danlo something of his contribution to the cetics' theory of the circular reduction of consciousness. He admitted that he knew nothing of consciousness but nearly everything about mind. All mind, he said (and all matter, too), could be seen as a precise ordering of information. This was especially true of life, of the logical form that underlay all life. He claimed that the logical form of any living thing could be separated from the elements of material reality. Aliveness, he said, our sense of selfness and existence as minded beings resided only in this logical form and not in matter. Our minds were nothing but pure and elegant patterns that could be encoded as programs, thence to be preserved in the cybernetic spaces of a computer.

Hanuman's sudden reversion to the philosophy of cybernetic gnosticism—the belief that matter was evil and that mind or soul could be redeemed from flesh and saved forever in some

475

cybernetic paradise—bewildered and disturbed Danlo. From the moment they had set out for Bardo's party, he'd thought that he had understood a part of Hanuman's attraction to Ringism: it was pure heresy against the fundamental doctrines of the Cybernetic Universal Church. Hanuman loved playing the heretic as he loved playing chess. It was his delight to mock the sanctimonies of the church into which he had been born. He had hated everything about Edeism, especially the easy machine ecstasies that were an Architect's reward for cleansing negative programs from one's brain. He had hated this corrupt old religion, and so it was his intention to play the prophet of one that was new. And so he stood there clutching a precisely machined ball of neurologics between his hands, and he seemed hollow-eyed and haunted by his own words. Danlo wondered if Hanuman truly believed that mind could be encoded as a computer program. He did not want to think that Hanuman might be as insincere as a wormrunner selling a dead firestone. As they faced each other in front of the room's darkening fireplace and he listened to Hanuman talk about dolls and the perfecting of all life, he was dazzled by the darkness of Hanuman's words. He could see only the faintest shadow of what would be obvious to historians a thousand years hence: that Hanuman's genius, as man and cetic, would be to infuse Ringism with cybernetic gnosticism and the ecstatic use of the computer, thus causing an explosive and universal religion to be born.

While staring at the beautiful dolls that Hanuman had made, Danlo ran his finger along the feather in his hair. Except for the zippering sound of his fingernail against the feather's barbs, the room was very quiet. At last, he stepped nearer to Hanuman and told him, "You have fallen crueler, the older you have become. Cruel toward yourself."

"Perhaps," Hanuman said. "Although it's cruel of you to remind me, if this is so."

"I am . . . sorry," Danlo said. He bowed his head, ashamed at having spoken too freely.

"If I'm cruel, I'm no crueler than this ugly world I was born into."

"The world is the world. The universe—"

"The universe is running to ruin," Hanuman said. "If you wish to envision the future of the universe, think of the Vild. Ten thousand light-years of ruined stars and dead planets. Dust, decay. Think of this when you look out the window at night."

Danlo pressed his fingers to his forehead, then said, "But,

Hanu, haven't you ever stood on the ocean just before the moons come up? When the world is all ice and starlight? Why is everything so *beautiful*?"

"Is it? How many times have I heard you decry this world as *shaida*?"

"It is true, the world is full of *shaida.*"

"Then why seek so blindly to affirm it?"

"You think I am blind . . . to the world?"

"Your aspiration of becoming an asarya—this is a blind man's quest."

"But there must be a way to go beyond *shaida*. To live, even if the living is lethal."

"Live?" Hanuman cried out, and he pointed at the scar above Danlo's eye. He thumped his chest with both hands, then held his palms upward in exasperation. "Do you call this living?"

"This is the only life we will ever have."

"A blind man's philosophy."

"This is the only life we *could* ever have," Danlo said. "Of all the trillions of times the universe has called living things into life, you could have been born . . . only when you were born."

"But why should anyone have to be born at all?"

"I do not know," Danlo said. "But despite the *shaida,* there is something marvelous in the way the universe—"

"No, *our* universe is flawed," Hanuman said. He rubbed his red eyes. "Horribly and irredeemably flawed. Everywhere we look: disease, delusion, despair. Everywhere, all the elements of this creation, the immutable laws of nature. Who created these elements? Who wrote these laws? God? It's silly to believe in God, even sillier to ignore his handiwork. If there was ever a God, he must have been drunk when he created this abomination. No, I'm being too kind. Let's look at the universe just as it is. What is this infinite stellar machine that grinds us until we bleed and die? It's nothing more than a computer made of common matter, programmed by universal laws. The universe is computing the consequences of these laws. Why? So that we might live in marvel? No. No, no, no. The universe was programmed to arrive at the answer to some great question. The Programmer must have his question answered. What question? you wonder. It's a silly question, really, a cruel question better asked by a mathematician or a merchant: How much? *That* is the only question the universe asks, and every time a child dies of radiation burns or a man grows so old and feeble-brained he forgets his wife's name, her very face, the nearer the universe is to an answer. How much, Danlo? How much suffering and ugliness can a man behold before he falls mad? Before he falls upon the crowds outside the Hofgarten with foaming teeth or lasers or knives? How much insanity can a civilization hold before it blows up the stars? God wants to know. Make no mistake, God is completely cruel, and this universe he's created is hell. God wants to know how much hell we can bear, because the hellfire that consumes *Him* is infinite and unbearable, and it never stops. God tortures the creatures of his hand in the hope we'll join him in suffering, and thus ease the loneliness of his pain."

At these words, Danlo rubbed his eyes and walked over to the sunflowers. He studied them awhile, then looked at Hanuman and said, "And so you sit alone in this room and play with dolls? Why, Hanu?"

Hanuman was still holding his black sphere, and he turned it around and around between his hands. He said, "If I could build a computer large enough, if I could write programs with enough subtlety and elegance, then I believe it would be possible to evolve a perfect metalife. A life without war, without death, without bitterness, suffering, or even pain."

"Truly? You believe this is truly possible?"

Hanuman smiled, then said softly, "It must be."

He spoke with such sincerity and rare openness that Danlo could not bear looking at him. Danlo's head was beginning to ache, and his eyes burned, and he could not bear to meet the look of terrible hope on Hanuman's face. And so he stared off at the logs glowing red in the fireplace. After a long while he said, "But what about *you*?"

"You mustn't concern yourself."

"Even if you achieve . . . what you wish to achieve, what about yourself? The fire, the light, inside—it will still be there, yes?"

"Perhaps."

"But, Hanu, there is a way to make the burning stop."

"No, you don't understand."

"In the remembrances—"

"No, no."

"The blessed kalla . . . it is like an ocean that will quench all burning."

"Oh, Danlo—no, no, no, no."

"The One memory—we have only begun to see it."

"In so many ways, you're still so *blind*."

478

There was bitterness in the way that Hanuman said this, and something more, and Danlo felt as if a serpent had spat venom into his eyes. His eyes began to sting and water, and he threw his hand across his forehead. "That may be so," he said. "But a friend would not say that to his friend, not in that way."

"A friend wouldn't push his friend into the ocean, either."

"Not even if he were mad with fire?"

Hanuman's head snapped toward Danlo, and he said, "We always argue in circles, don't we? Leave me alone now. Go back to your whore. Go drink your kalla and swim in your oneness and your memories—I don't care."

Never, since the day they had almost killed each other in the hot pool of Perilous Hall, had there been such ill will between them. Danlo stared at Hanuman, and all he could think to say was "Will you attend any more joyances?"

In silence, Hanuman returned his stare, as if to reply: Will you?

"You have no interest in the Way, then?" Danlo asked.

He thought that Hanuman would not answer this question, either, but after a few moments of contemplation, he said, "Oh, no, I've complete interest in the Way of Ringess. Sometime we might discuss this. But not now. Please leave me alone—I can't talk anymore."

After a long, awkward silence, Danlo said good-bye. He watched as Hanuman went over to the fireplace and heaped three new logs onto the grate. In moments the fire was blazing again, red-orange flames fairly leaping out into the room. Hanuman stood close to the fire. He turned away from Danlo, turned toward the glittering black sphere that he still held in his hands. Danlo left him there, standing completely naked, completely absorbed in staring into the flames reflected in the surface of his universal computer. Danlo left him alone with his dolls, and he was too full of grief to foresee that they both would become deeply involved with the Way of Ringess, and soon.

A CONVERSATION

Who, having eyes, can see the unseeable?
Who, having hands, can touch the untouchable?
Who, having ears, can hear the unhearable?
Who, having lips, can say what cannot be said?

—from the Meditations of Jin Zenimura

It is an historic truth that new religions always grow in ways that their founders do not foresee. Religions, to survive, must make accommodations with the larger political and ecological structures that nurture them; they must organize themselves around a body of doctrine, law, and ritual, an immortal and sanctified body that its adherents may not violate with their personal revelations of the infinite; above all else, cults that would become universal religions must control and channel humanity's spiritual energies, for if they do not, they will make deadly enemies of world emperors, lords, and the architects of other religions—either that, or passion will consume them from within. This control is always a delicate matter, and it always, ultimately, fails. Most cults let the godfire flow too freely and so burn themselves out in a few years; like supernovas, they shine brilliantly even as they explode apart into a confusion of disillusionments, ecstatic visions, megalomanias, and ruined lives. Some cults, from their very beginning, damp the most natural and numinous of human passions; they substitute theories of the universe for the experience of God, and thus become philosophies or sciences rather than true religions.

Only rarely do religions such as Edeism arise and flourish and infect the swarms of humanity with their faith. But it is the fate of all religions, as of all things, to grow old. Doctrines meant to guide individuals to the deepest truths of the universe become walls of words separating society from society, men from women, and cutting people off from the holiest part of themselves. Vision becomes degraded into creed; faith degenerates into belief; zeal and piety replace ecstasy and the mystic union with the godhead. In time, the heart of each religion grows hard and dies. And so seekers of the godly will always turn to new prophets and new ways, never realizing that, ultimately, all religions separate man from God.

Danlo, of course, in his quest to discover why the universe had fallen into *shaida*, had long been aware of religion's essential irony. But until his involvement with the religion of Ringism, as it came to be called, he had always played at religiousness; he had moved from church to church and ritual to ritual as easily as his skates could carry him throughout the different quarters of the City. Never had any doctrine or reading of canon law prevented him from beholding a religion's pure and numinous core. And then, one night in early winter, while the first of the season's snows caught Neverness in a cloud of fractured crystals and whiteness, he attended a second party at Bardo's house. He went alone. Hanuman remained in Bardo's guest room, sequestered and still recuperating from his great remembrance (and still playing with his dolls), while Tamara Ten Ashtoreth, who loved Bardo's joyances almost as much as she loved love play, had a prior engagement that evening. And so once again, Danlo entered the music room and listened to rare musics and smelled ancient smells, but this time he found himself cut off from the deepest experience of the Elder Eddas. The drug called kalla had been his window to great remembrance, and he had vowed to take three sips of it again upon his next journey into himself. But when he stood in the circle of seekers and awaited the passing of the blue bowl, he was forbidden to drink from it freely.

"We've had to make changes in our ceremony," Bardo told everyone. He stood inside the circle with Thomas Rane, who bore the bowl of kalla as if it were a great weight in his hands. Bardo nodded at him, then looked directly at Danlo. He said, "As my cousin, Surya Lal, has observed, kalla is too potent a drug to swig down like beer. Therefore, we've made changes."

He held in his hand a small silver jigger, similar to the kind bartenders use to measure liquid toalache into their patrons' cups. Similar but not the same: he had ordered it made in a jewelry shop on the Street of Diamonds. It was an ornate piece of work. Constellations of tiny white diamonds encrusted its surface, while inside, thin golden bands demarcated the various levels to which it might be filled. Counting the topmost band, which ran in a golden circle around the jigger's rim, there were three levels. While Thomas Rane held the bowl of kalla steady, Bardo dipped the jigger into the clear liquid, and he was careful to fill it only two-thirds full.

- "This is an exact measure of what two sips should be," he said. "Take two sips, and see God."

He approached Surya Lal, and she knelt before him and opened her little mouth as if she were a bird. He poured the kalla onto her tongue. She swallowed in a quick convulsion of jaw and throat, and honored him with a head bow. And then he moved on to the next seeker of remembrance and administered a second jigger of the holy liquid, and so on, one by one to all the kneeling people around the circle.

"Journey far and journey deep," Bardo said.

And once again Danlo remembranced the Elder Eddas, farther and deeper than almost anyone else, but not as deeply as he would have liked. Although he was the pride and wonder of Bardo's circle, his growing fame meant little to him. He was a young journeyman, full of wild dreams and willfulness, and he had a journeyman's hatred of kneeling before others.

"The changes you have made in the ceremony are unseemly," he said to Bardo a few nights later. He had arranged to meet with Bardo in his observatory atop his house's centermost tower. The room was little more than a circular stone floor encased in clary dome. It was a cold room, but it was quiet and private, and on clear evenings, it afforded a fine view of the lights of the Old City. "Kalla is a blessed drug," Danlo said. "We should not have to go begging on our knees for a couple of sips of it."

He argued that all men and women should be able to partake of kalla according to their need and inspiration, a sentiment which was felt by quite a few of Bardo's followers. This sentiment flowed like a dark undercurrent at each of the joyances. Ringists of all backgrounds resented having to wait ten days between tastes of kalla; the most radical formed a clique, or fellowship, to trade stories of their remembrances and to persuade Bardo to place an urn of kalla in his front hallway so that anyone entering his house could dip their hands and lips into it. They disdained the patronage of memory guides, even that of

482

master remembrancers such as Thomas Rane. They believed that each individual must approach the great memories individually, without help, guidelines, or interference from others. To control the journey into the self, they believed, was to inhibit discovery; it was like setting out across the snowdrifts and crevasses of the moonlit sea ice with one's legs tied together, or like standing beneath the night's strange new stars with a veil of others' suggestions thrown over one's eyes. Only those with the courage to plunge alone into the unknown, it was said, could ever hope to remember themselves. Only those with the self-taught insight and skill to navigate the roaring universe inside them would ever truly behold the Elder Eddas.

"Even supposing I agreed with you, as one man talking to another, there are other considerations," Bardo admitted to Danlo. "As the owner of this house, and, ah, as *initiator* of these joyances, I have responsibilities. By God, you can't imagine the responsibilities! Do you have any idea how much food my four hundred guests eat each night? How much wine and toalache they suck down? Ah, Bardo is a rich man, you say, but have you ever counted the cost of smuggling kalla into the city? Yes, *smuggling,* I said. Don't look so surprised, Little Fellow—where did you suppose your 'blessed drug' comes from? We can't just squeeze it like bloodfruit juice into a cup, you know."

"I had thought . . . that the remembrancers make the kalla," Danlo said.

Without warning, Bardo smacked his fist into his open hand. The sound of flesh against flesh was overloud and echoed about the room. "Well, it's true, they do make it—on Simoom. You're aware that the remembrancers were once a branch of the cetics, before both disciplines merged with the Order? And did you know the cetics established themselves on Simoom largely because plants grow there unlike any others in the known universe? No? Well, the remembrancers have maintained their druggery there, all these millennia. Each year they ship a *small* quantity of kalla to the remembrancers throughout the Civilized Worlds. And to Neverness. And all of it goes straight to the remembrancers' tower. Of course, when Thomas Rane and his students agreed to help me with the joyances, they brought their personal stocks of kalla with them. But that lasted less than a tenday, too bad. Fortunately, I'd had the foresight to woo a master on Simoom—the master pharmacologist for all the remembrancers. He loves money more than his devotion to his vows. You might say I suborned him—I've had to pay *enormous* bribes, just so I could load a few barrels of kalla into one of my deep ships. And *that,* Little Fellow, is the source of your god-damned drug."

"But why can't you synthesize the kalla, here, in the City?"

Bardo's face fell sad, like a clown's, and he said, "Some secrets the remembrancers keep very well, even from themselves. Even that treacherous pharmacologist has *some* scruples. I can't find anyone who knows how to make the kalla, too bad. Not even Thomas Rane knows, and he knows almost everything. Then, too, of course, it's a violation of the covenants for anyone to synthesize chemicals inside the City."

"If all this is true," Danlo said, "then should you be telling me these things?"

"Why not? Are you a spy for the Lord Cetic and his underlings?"

"No," Danlo said. He touched the sleeve of his kamelaika; he ran his fingertips back and forth over the tight black wool, and he remembered that Bardo had once worn a similar garment. "No, I am not a spy, but I am still a journeyman pilot . . . of the Order."

"Yes, the Order. Well, God damn the Order."

Danlo stood with his forehead just beneath the dome, where waves of cold air rippled and touched his breath into steam. He peered out at the City, eastward, in the direction of the Academy. But the curving clary panes were dusted with fresh new snow, and he could see almost nothing.

"I felt as you did, once," Danlo said. "Do you remember? But you persuaded me to remain in the Order."

"I did? Ah, I *did,* too bad."

"I am not sorry . . . that I have become a pilot," Danlo said. "The dreamtime, the number storm, the stars—I have learned so much."

Bardo rocked back and forth on his slippered feet, and he let loose a long, deep sigh. "Ahhh, but you could learn more in my music room than you'll ever find out in the galaxy's wastelands. *I* should know. You've a talent for remembrancing, anyone can see that. Why do you think I've issued you an open invitation to my parties?"

"I had thought it was because . . . we were friends."

"By God, we *are* friends! Though I admit I must be two-thirds a madman for making friends with another Ringess."

"Is it a condition of our friendship that I keep secret . . . the secrets of your house?"

"And what if it were?"

Bardo stood staring at Danlo, and his eyes were dark pools full of sadness, belligerence, and devotion. Danlo stared back at him a long time before saying, "Then I would keep your secrets."

"You would?"

"Yes," Danlo said. He nodded his head slowly as a memory suddenly came to him: an Alaloi man, upon pain of death, may not reveal to any uninitiated male (or woman) the secrets of the Song of Life. Full men, he knew, could be silent as the sky when needful. He held his eyes steady, and he said, "I would rather die than tell anyone your secrets."

"You *would*? Well, you're too damn noble—I've said that before. In truth, we've nothing to conceal. It's been obvious where we must be getting our kalla from. I expect the Lord Remembrancer, if not the Lord Cetic, will soon expose our pharmacologist and debase him. Just as well we've stockpiled enough kalla to last a couple of years—unless you and your friends go after it like dogs lapping up puddle water."

Danlo smiled at him and said, "Take three sips of kalla and be God."

"You should be thankful you're allowed any kalla at all. That may not last."

"What do you mean?" Danlo quickly asked.

"I mean, the lords of the Order can keep young journey-men—or anyone else—from dabbling with forbidden drugs."

"Forbid the use of kalla?" Danlo half shouted. "But how could they do that? If they forbade it, there would be war, I think."

Of all the horrors of civilization, Danlo thought it most horrible the way civilized people sought always to control the bodies and minds of others. This age-old struggle for control had led to untold bloody wars. He had studied enough history to know of the drug wars fought on Old Earth, and on many of the Civilized Worlds. Billions of people had died in these wars. He had thought that human beings long ago, a millennium before the Swarming's second wave began, had established the right to alter their consciousnesses at will. Danlo, himself, had always regarded this as a fundamental and inalienable human right, but now Bardo hinted that this was not so.

"Ah, war," Bardo said as he looked out the window. "Some wars will have to be fought again and again, till the last woman gives birth to the last poor babe."

"Even the drug wars?"

"Listen, Little Fellow, anyone with enough power can make anything unlawful. Or worse—unobtainable."

"But forbidding the drinking of kalla . . . that would violate the covenants," Danlo said.

"So? Do you think the covenants have never been suspended before?"

"I know . . . that they have."

"In truth," Bardo said, "the lords needn't forbid kalla to keep people from the Way. They've only to discourage anyone of the Order to associate with myself, or to enter my house. Or they can deny immigration to seekers of the Eddas—keep them from ever entering the City. Or they can spread rumors that kalla poisons the brain cells. Or—I admit this is utter paranoia—they could secretly release poisoned kalla to the populace to discourage the drinking of it. Or, if we force them to extremes, they could even hire warrior-poets to assassinate our leaders."

"And therefore you would appease the lords of the Order?"

"Appease them! By God, I'd like to forget them, if I could, the whole rotting Order. But I can't, too bad."

Danlo brushed the long hair away from his eyes and said, "But mightn't it be possible . . . to help the lords remembrance the Elder Eddas?"

"To suborn the whole Order, eh?" Bardo laughed out. "Well, I'd suborn the whole damn universe, if I could. The Elder Eddas are the key to everything, these goddamned memories. The memories of the future that a few of us have seen, a new way of living for our bloody kind. Ah, listen to me, I'm my own best propagandist! But the truth is the truth. The Way of Ringess is not just some cult designed to bring Bardo women, money, and power, I promise you. Not *just*. It's *the* way, or, I should say, lest I appear a fanatic, it's the best damn way that humankind has ever found to fulfill its destiny."

"And you believe . . . that our destiny is to be as gods? Truly?"

"Do I *believe* it!" Bardo roared out. "I've *seen* it, with my own eyes, your father, who became a goddamned god even as I watched."

The universe is a womb for the genesis of gods, Danlo remembered.

He looked deep into Bardo's eyes, then said, "Take three sips of kalla and—"

"Your father," Bardo interrupted, "remembranced the Eddas more clearly than anyone, and he never in his life tasted kalla."

"I have often wondered . . . what my father remembered. What he *saw*."

Bardo clasped his hands behind his back and he began strolling around the room. His steps were heavy and ponderous; he dragged his feet across the floor, obviously not caring that the rough stones were shredding his pretty silk slippers. "Well, if he descryed the future, as I believe he did, he would have seen that kalla is a dangerous drug."

"I think it is a blessed drug."

"Our enemies," Bardo said, "are already questioning how *any* drug could induce such an exalted experience as the remembrance of the Elder Eddas."

"But why should they doubt this?"

"Well, it's the old problem of chemicals and consciousness. Ah, matter and spirit. Everyone knows deep remembrance to be a *spiritual* experience. It's a mystery how the juice of a few goddamned plants could bring anyone closer to God."

Danlo smiled at this and said, "But there is no mystery, Bardo. A harpist plucks the strings of her gosharp and plays the rhapsodies of Ayondela. A simple gosharp, this instrument made of kasja wire and shatterwood . . . makes the sweetest music. A man takes three sips of kalla, and he touches off the release of neurotransmitters, acetylcholine and tryptamine and serotonin. Is the music of the mind any less sweet for being made with . . . these blessed molecules?"

"Has Thomas Rane taught you the chemistry of this drug? Then you'll know how *dangerous* it really is."

"But danger," Danlo said, "is just the left hand of exaltation."

"There speaks Danlo the Wild," Bardo said, and he sighed. "You've had your three sips of kalla and your exaltation. Others have had, ah, *other* experiences."

"Do you mean Hanuman?"

"For a while, Little Fellow, I was afraid he'd fallen mad."

"And you?"

Bardo puffed out his cheeks, then said, "Did you think I'm too much a coward to have taken three sips? Well, I've done exactly that. On six different nights. And each one was a journey into heaven and hell, a sort of divine madness. I remembered myself, I think, but I wasn't really myself, I *was* my memories, or

487

became them, in a hellish sort of way, but more than that, I . . . ah, dammit, Little Fellow! Who can talk about these things?"

Danlo looked at Bardo and smiled. "But if we do not talk about the Elder Eddas, who will?"

"No doubt skeptics who've never remembranced them will blather on and on, explicating in detail our drugged delusions."

"We will have to tell people the truth, then."

"And how do we do that?"

"By using the truest words we can find," Danlo said.

"What words?"

"*These* words," Danlo said. He closed his eyes and let his fingers touch the feather in his hair. "We should say that the stars and rocks and dreams of men and women . . . the memory of all and everything is contained in the Elder Eddas. The Eddas are full as a cup overflowing with water, yet empty like the Void, infinitely empty, more empty than the nothingness out beyond the Southern Wall of galaxies. There will always be . . . a space for more memory. These things we have seen: that memory is always being created and always destroyed, and that it is eternal, too, preserved like pearls floating in an urn of blacking oil. And everything is memory, yes? The universe is like an ocean roaring with memory. I *am* the Elder Eddas, and that is my truth, and you are, too, and that is your truth, and people forget this almost the moment they see it as it is. It is *hard* to remembrance the Eddas. The deepest part. It shines through everything, the light that blinds. It is like a dance of starlight, an endless photon stream, always moving, always beautiful, impossible to really see. And the colors, shimmering, dissolving into each other, the infinite points of silver and violet and living gold —all the colors, and no colors that I have ever seen before, or imagined seeing. And *behind* the colors and the motion, there is a total stillness, a silence more real than rocks or wind or the ice of the sea. It is just pure memory. *I* am that silence, truly, and nothing else. As you are, and everything *is*."

Danlo ceased speaking, and he stepped over to the western quadrant of the room. There, in front of him, the dome was free of snow; through this transparent section of clary he saw the hotel district lit up with rows of cold flame globes, thousands of distinct points sparkling in their colors among the millions of lights of the City. He pressed his forehead against the dome, and the clary was so cold it hurt his skin. For a long while he stood there motionless, looking out at the lovely, quiet lights.

"Danlo?"

"Yes?"

Bardo came over to him and laid his hand across his shoulder. With much mmming and ahhhing, he cleared his throat. When he finally spoke, his voice was almost a whisper. "What you've just said—would you really tell people that?"

"Yes, why not?"

"Well, your words, pretty as they are, contradict each other. You say the Eddas are empty and full, silent and roaring like the goddamned sea, all at the same time. Motionless yet always moving—aren't you afraid people will laugh at you?"

Danlo smiled and said, "I would not want to keep anyone from laughing . . . if that is what he wants to do."

"But can't we just say that this, ah, experience of the Eddas is beyond words? Shouldn't we just admit that it's ineffable and be done with it?"

"But it is not ineffable," Danlo said.

"Well, I think it is, Little Fellow."

"You have had your three sips of kalla," Danlo said. "Does my account of my journey strike you as being untrue?"

Bardo's face filled with blood then, and it was hard to tell whether he was angry, embarrassed, or frustrated. "No, not *untrue*," he said. "But, worse: absurd. We can't go around proclaiming that the deepest experience a man or woman can have is paradoxical."

"But the deepest parts of the Elder Eddas *are* paradoxical," Danlo said.

"But we can't *say* that, can we?"

"We can say . . . whatever we have to say."

"But what about logic, then?" Bardo roared out. "We live in a world of goddamned logic, don't we?"

"Yes, of course . . . that is true."

"Well? Would you throw away the rules of logic like a madman casting pearls down a multrum?"

Danlo smiled at this earthy image, and he said, "The world, as we normally see it—as we speak of it—it is all multiple, yes? All the buildings of the City, the individual people, their possessions and plans, everything they do—every *thing* or act must be distinguishable from all others. What is logic, if not the rules keeping all objects and events distinct? A bird is a bird, we think, and thus it cannot be a man. A man either exists . . . or he does not exist, but not both, simultaneously. And we exclude any middle possibility, and we live by this law. And rightly so. If we did not, we could never properly speak of things, or say that one event causes another. Or even that there occurred separate events. The blessed laws of logic . . . define what we mean by multiplicity."

Bardo, who had devoted half his lifetime to the study of mathematics and logic, suddenly belched, releasing vapors of garlic and goatroot into the air. He belched once more, and he said, "I've never thought about the matter in quite that way before. I suppose you're about to conclude that logic cannot be applied to the experience of the Eddas because of the, ah, unity of memory?"

Danlo nodded his head and smiled. "The words I have spoken . . . I have tried to consider them, to polish them like a mirror. I believe they reflect the experience of remembrance truly, as much as words can reflect *any* experience. But remembrance itself is beyond logic. In the deepest part of the Eddas, there are no distinctions between things. In the way the universe remembers them. The memory of all things is in all things—the remembrancers say this. I have seen . . . that this is true. There is a oneness of all memory, yes? A blessed oneness."   "And so you intend to skate up and down the streets blithely speaking in paradoxes about this—ah, I can scarcely force my lips to make these goddamned mystical words—this *oneness*?"

"As you have said," Danlo reminded him, "the truth is the truth."

"And if you go telling it everywhere, we'll have every hibakusha and seeker in the City knocking at my doors for an invitation to a joyance."

"But . . . isn't that what you want?"

"Ah, is that *indeed* what Bardo wants?" Bardo asked himself as he glanced down at the floor. The huge man's lips cracked with the beginning of a smile, and Danlo immediately knew that Bardo, all along, had been plotting the radical expansion of Ringism. Danlo smiled, too, and then they were smiling at each other in sudden understanding.

"Of course," Bardo said, "even true words can only draw people to the Way. We'll still have to show them the truth."

"It would be better . . . if they showed themselves."

"Take two sips of kalla and see God," Bardo said. "We'll have to teach the people how to see."

"No, Bardo. One teaches oneself to see."

"Well, we have to control these goddamned remembrances, don't we?"

490

"If you control it . . . then you will destroy it, the great memory."

"I'm sorry, we've no choice but to ration the kalla."

"Let the people drink the kalla as they will."

"No, it's too dangerous."

"Living is dangerous, too," Danlo said. "Would you ration out and control the moments of your life?"

"Again, there speaks Danlo the Wild."

Danlo ran his finger along the hard, cold scar above his eye, and he said, "All of us, every time we drink the kalla, we are all plunged into the same blessed sea. Some will swim where others drown."

"And if you continue gulping kalla as if it were water," Bardo said, "eventually you'll drown, too. Even you."

"That is possible."

"Well, I can't allow you to go plunging yourself into madness, can I?"

We are all food for God, Danlo remembered. Somewhere inside his ears the Elder Eddas roared, and he knew that this great memory might someday consume him; it might digest the tissues of his soul so totally there would be neither escape nor recrystallization into that image he knew as himself. But that moment, he thought, if it ever came, lay far in the future. Now was the time for boldness and journeys into the dark currents of the self. It was his faith that will and wisdom would always guide him back to the world of living things.

"But, Bardo, when I spoke of drowning . . . this was only a metaphor. It is always possible to lose yourself in the sea of memory. But then, there will always be another journey, yes?"

"Perhaps this is true—for the remembrancers," Bardo said. "But they discipline themselves for years before drinking the kalla. Why do you think they restrict it so?"

"But Thomas Rane has said—"

Bardo suddenly stamped his foot against the floor stones and laughed out, "Thomas Rane! By God, he's as wild at heart as you. But even he must know that if we go spraying our kalla into the mouths of humanity, then some poor people will be lost in a very unmetaphorical insanity and die very real deaths."

Danlo looked down at his empty hands and said, "To live, I die."

"Still speaking in your goddamned metaphors, eh? Well, listen, Little Fellow, I can't let you lose yourself in the kalla."

"Please do not worry about me."

"Well, I have to," Bardo said. "Because of who you are. You may not like it, but you're an exemplar, now. As is Hanuman. Both of you—the lords of the Order are watching what we do, and we can't have our best young Ringists annihilating themselves with kalla, can we?"

Danlo slipped his shakuhachi out of his pocket and held it cupped in his fingers. "If we are forbidden to drink deeply of the kalla," he said, "how can you think we will remembrance the deepest part of the Eddas?"

"Ah, the Eddas," Bardo said as he rubbed his eyes. "I must confess a thing to you. *I*, for myself, don't care if I ever remembrance them again. There, I've said it. In truth, no one *needs* to remembrance the Eddas so deeply. At least, not more than once. The goddamned paradoxes. The Way of Ringess can't be just for a few prophets and prodigies. I've a responsibility to the *spirit* of Ringism, to anyone who wants to follow the Way. Even those who'd drown in the Eddas, if we let them. The goddamned Elder Eddas—yes, I admit there's truth there, the truth of how we can become gods. And *that's* the way of Ringess. The only way. The great memories can lead us toward that truth, but it's madness to become lost in them."

Out of respect for Bardo's thinking and his passion, Danlo bowed his head. He put the flute to his lips, then, and began to play a song that he had spent the last few days composing.

"Am I wrong then? Do you think I'm wrong?"

Danlo looked at Bardo, and he felt all his gladness for the huge man concentrating in his eyes. He said nothing and continued to play.

"By God, is it wrong to protect our friends? I'm *afraid* for you, Little Fellow."

An intensely melodic music spilled out around Danlo, but the acoustics of the room were dead and only accentuated his shakuhachi's shrillness. The sound of it was high and harsh and cold, and he listened as it broke in waves against the snow-covered dome. It suddenly came to him that Bardo was right, that he must renounce the drinking of large dosages of kalla. In truth, he must renounce kalla altogether, but not because of the danger of madness. For him, if not for all seekers of remembrance, there were other dangers more insidious and subtle. Kalla was truly a blessed drug, truly a window to the world within. As with all windows to deep reality, however, he thought that the kalla might actually limit his experience of the Elder

Eddas; it might stain or blur his vision in a vital way, thus keeping him from the deepest apprehension of the One memory.

After he had finished his song, Danlo slid his flute back into his pocket. He said, "Do not be afraid, Bardo. I . . . will drink no more kalla."

"What!" Bardo stood next to him, and his eyes were wide open with puzzlement. "What did you say?"

"The kalla," Danlo said, "its very blessedness . . . is a force that I must not come to rely on."

"And so you'd renounce it?"

"Yes."

"Completely?"

"Yes."

"How can you stand there, after all that's been said, and tell me with a smile on your goddamned face that you'll give up kalla so easily?"

Danlo held his hand up to his mouth, then said, "Not . . . easily." As he scratched the thick beard covering his chin and neck, he explained to Bardo his reasons for renouncing kalla.

"Ahhh," Bardo said, "are you certain that you're not merely angry with me? I'm afraid my restricting the kalla has made you bitter."

Danlo laughed and shook his head. "I am not angry with you."

"But you'll have no more remembrances!"

"I did not say that."

"But you won't be able to share the kalla at the ceremonies, will you?"

"That is true," Danlo admitted. "But there are other paths . . . toward the great memories. If I am still welcome in your house, I would like to ask Master Rane to teach me the remembrancing attitudes."

"But there are sixty-four attitudes!" Bardo roared out. "Most people spend a lifetime learning them."

"Perhaps I will have a short life and learn them quickly."

"Some people *never* learn them," Bardo said, obviously not amused by Danlo's little joke. "But even supposing that you're a prodigy, or even a prophet, and that you accomplish all that you dream of, by natural means, what then? You can't spend the rest of your life absorbed into a goddamned memory."

For a little while they discussed the art of remembrancing, and then Danlo said, "You look to the Eddas for clues and directions toward personal godhood. That is your way, and perhaps it is a true and splendid way. But I think that my way is . . . something other."

"Ah, do I dare ask what this way might be?"

"I am not sure," Danlo said. "But someday, if I remembrance deeply enough, then I shall know."

"Well, then," Bardo said as he rubbed his hands together, "I wish you well. And I wish I could remain here chatting with you, but someone must guide tonight's remembrance, eh?"

So saying he ambled off toward the stairway, but just before he went down to the party below, he pirouetted and said, "Oh, Little Fellow, *of course* you're always welcome in my house."

Danlo stood there alone then, and he stared out through the curving windows at the streets of the Old City. Snow was falling now, and off toward the east-west sliddery, the ice and the trees and the houses were covered with a new layer of *soreesh* snow. The quiet and the whiteness recalled the forests of his childhood, where he had first caught a glimpse of the rare white thallow. It had been a long time since he had thought of Ahira, and longer still since he had prayed to his other-self. He did not like to think that he continued to see the world through the symbols of a primitive totem system, but in truth, whenever he was most troubled and walked alone through a grove of trees or through the deserted City cemeteries, a part of him always listened for Ahira's wild cry. He listened for it now, and strangely, even though he was encased in a dome of synthetic glass and cut off from the night, he heard a bird scream out in his killing ecstasy. The scream was inside him, he suddenly realized; it was only a memory of Ahira digging his talons into a sleekit's neck. And then a deeper memory came, a truth of the Elder Eddas: *That thou art.* The thallow's cry shrilled out and filled the universe inside him, and he remembered, *I am that sound.*

He knew then that his way toward the godhead, if such a way really existed, would be both marvelous and terrible. He stood there pressing his forehead against the cold clary dome, and he gladly would have told Bardo this—or Hanuman—but no one was there to listen.

THE ART OF ODORI

Once, when he was a young man, thirteen years before his Completion, The Perfect One became drunk on wine and gambled away his family estates on a single throw of dice. And Sarojin Garuda, who was his brother and chief disciple, said to him, "You have thrown away our lives, for now we shall have neither money to spend, food to eat, nor a roof over us to keep us dry when the rains come."

And The Perfect One replied, "All life is a gamble into the unknown. Now the sky must be our roof, and we must spend our lives Perfecting ourselves. And when we are Complete, we shall never be hungry again."

"Do you mean," Sarojin Garuda asked, "that we shall nourish our souls with the wind and sun, and that the union with the Whole will fill us with joy?"

And The Perfect One, who is also called The Laughing Monk, replied, "Of course, but I also mean that when we achieve Completion, our followers will give us their bread, their clothes, their very lives."

"But how will you attract followers when it is discovered that you were so foolish as to drink wine and gamble away our estates?"

And The Perfect One replied, "As you will see, the people love no one so much as a perfect sinner who repents and becomes a perfect saint."

"Then you are ready to repent and give up all vice?" Sarojin Garuda asked.

And The Perfect One laughed and replied, "No, not yet."

After that The Perfect One went down to the South Lands, and he seduced the daughters of the vintners and drank their wine, and he danced the forbidden dances, and he ate the magic mushrooms that grew in the for-

ests. He wandered for thirteen years before coming to the Holy City. There, at the Pool of Eternity, he renounced the world and achieved Completion, and all that he had prophesied came to pass.

Many years later, The Perfect One acquired palaces for each of the six seasons, and he filled them with priceless sculptures and fine wines; he took for himself 313 concubines and fathered four times as many children; he began to dance and eat mushrooms and throw dice again. Sarojin Garuda came to him and said, "Once again you've fallen into vice."

And The Perfect One replied, "In Completion all distinctions are as One, and there is neither vice nor virtue. The advantage of being Perfected is that one can see this clearly."

"But the people," Sarojin Garuda said, after considering this, "are far from Perfection and do not see what you see."

And The Perfect One replied, "And that is why they love me as they do. They know that a Perfect One is beyond the good or evil of the world, and thus nothing can touch him."

Then The Perfect One began to laugh, and in listening to this holy laughter, the mind of Sarojin Garuda was freed of all doubt and imperfection, and he finally achieved what he had been seeking all his life. They both laughed together for a very long time, and they died very old, very rich, and very Complete.

—from The Life of The Perfect One

During the early days of winter, as Danlo studied the remembrancing attitudes under Master Thomas Rane or spent long, lascivious hours with Tamara in front of a blazing wood fire learning a very different art, he kept his promise to renounce kalla. But his single, great remembrance could be neither renounced nor forgotten. Bardo had warned him that he (and Hanuman, too) would become an exemplar for others, and so he did: ironically, the radical Ringists, those who would drink kalla freely, regarded Danlo as something of a hero, and they sought to emulate his wildness and his deed, if not his renunciation. This clique, though never large, included Ringists who were close to Bardo, such as the diva, Nirvelli, and Dario Chu. And at least two of Thomas Rane's memory guides fell into the secret worship of kalla. The brothers Jonathan and Benjamin Hur (of the infamous Darkmoon Hurs) embezzled a large quantity of kalla from Bardo's storeroom, and they let it flow in rivers among their friends and confederates. Unknown to Bardo, they held secret remembrances in various apartments throughout the City, and sometimes, when they were feeling especially bold, within the very rooms of Bardo's house. Jonathan Hur, himself, spent much time alone in the Well, floating in a saltwater pool as the kalla rushed through him in cold, lucent streams and carried him down into the deep memories. He contrived it so that his friends were allowed free use of the Well. And then, in secret, he served them kalla and abandoned them, each to his own wisdom, will, and vision. It was the glory and conceit of these radical Ringists that at any moment one of their number should always occupy a tank in the Well. When one of their fellowship was finished journeying through the world inside, another would drink three sips of kalla and take her place, and in this way, working in shifts, they sought to remembrance the Elder Eddas continuously. This wild and clandestine worship might have gone on for a long time, but inevitably, the weight of antichance fell against them. A wormrunner named Isas Nikitovich managed to drown himself in one of the tanks, and worse (from Bardo's very selfish point of view), a brilliant journeyman akashic swallowed at least fifteen sips of kalla and did not return from her journey. Or rather, she returned in madness, emptier in the eye than any autist. When Bardo heard the news that one of his favorite lovers had been disfigured in the mind, he wept, then flew into a rage and smashed nine priceless Agathanian alaya shells before Surya Lal calmed him. He was heard to shout out, "By God, if I can't trust my guides with the goddamned kalla, who can I trust?"

This remark was to prove most ominous. It heralded the great changes about to take place within the Way of Ringess. The cult, at this time, was splitting into three factions, none of which trusted the others completely. There was Jonathan Hur's kalla fellowship, of course, and also the main body of Ringists, the seekers who were glad to attend the ceremonies of remembrance and receive their two sips of kalla. They were less interested in the Elder Eddas, as an experience of its own, than in discovering how they each might grow into godhood. The third faction was an offshoot from this main body. From the very beginning quite a few Ringists were unable to remembrance the Eddas—either that or they could not make sense of their memories. In truth, they were too stupid or lazy to learn the techniques of remembrancing, and above all, they were too afraid. They avoided or renounced the drinking of kalla, not because they sought a clearer way of seeing things but because the journey into themselves terrified them. They were drawn to Ringism for the most basic of reasons: they sensed that Bardo and his inner circle had discovered a way toward something vast and important, something beyond their individual concerns, and they desperately wanted to be a part of this movement. If they could not know the light dance of pure remembrance, in themselves, then at least the satisfaction of intense religiousness could still be theirs. Bardo's house, day and night, seemed aglow with intensity and a sense of possibilities. It was enough for some people to bask in the golden radiance of luminaries such as Danlo, or the beautiful and accomplished Nirvelli, or even Thomas Rane, for it is always easier to stand beneath the light of another than to shine with one's own. Many spoke of new directions in evolution, of the infinite possibilities of the human race, but few were willing to make even the slightest of changes in themselves. They dreamed of transforming their bodies and minds into something new, something vast and marvelous, but they lacked the courage to create their own fate. They thought they wanted to become as gods, and some of them wanted to *want* a path toward the godly, but they were as insincere as rich astriers who profess compassion for the poor, and all the while hoard diamonds and firestones and other precious jewels.

And so they gave up kalla and substituted excitement as their drug; they mistook zeal for true ecstasy; they satisfied their longings for transcendence with promises and hopes, even as they neglected the dangerous work of going over themselves. In this way, they betrayed themselves, and they fomented revolution instead of the evolution of humankind. They were a nervous and desperate people, all too eager to believe that the Golden Ring would protect them from the fury of the Vild, or that if they tried to follow the way of a man who had become a god, a little of his divinity might cling to their grasping hands. These were the failed and false seekers, and other Ringists derisively referred to them as "godlings" or "godchildren." In the early days of winter in the year 2953 since the founding of Neverness, this faction of godchildren still composed only a tenth of the membership of Bardo's cult.

"But everyday there are more of them," Thomas Rane confided to Danlo one night after he had helped him through the forty-first attitude of remembrancing. He had been meeting with Danlo almost every evening after dinner—on those evenings when Danlo couldn't contrive to visit Tamara—and he was very proud to be tutoring him in his art. Though he rarely favored Danlo with words of praise, it was his way to praise him indirectly, negatively, through denigrating the efforts and skills of others. "Remembrancing is the most treacherous of the arts: at first it's all roses, roses, roses, and soon enough thorns, thorns, thorns. People give up too easily. And some people never learn the discipline of the self. Unfortunately, I'm afraid these are the very people Bardo will attract, if he tries to expand this little cult of ours. We've already given our kalla to the City's most brilliant —who's left? Now, shall we return to dereism, or would you rather proceed to the mythopoesis attitude?"

To be sure, none of the three factions was ever a discrete group, completely separated from the others. Many of the kalla fellowship sought personal godhood as well as remembrance of the One memory. Many seekers would burn for transcendence like stars in the night, only to stumble out of bed one morning red-eyed, discouraged, doubting, full of coldness toward themselves and their deepest dreams. A few of these might rekindle their passion for a while, but most would look for easier ways of annihilating the longing inside them. And it was never easy to tell when a seeker had left her path to become a godchild of Ringism who blindly followed another's way. Many there were who accused others of falsity and faithlessness, even as they gouged out their inner eyes and knelt raptly while Danlo or Bardo spoke of the wonders of the Elder Eddas. Bardo's house became something of an arena where Ringists of all factions vied with one another for spiritual superiority. Or rather, his brilliantly decorated rooms were like sets of a stage: at any time of day, men and women would sally down the glittering hallways, seeking each other out. They would pose and smile and beam at one another; they worked their faces into the silliest and most simple of configurations as they tried to emote an aura of enlightenment. They acted as they imagined godlings should act, and subtly, slowly, they tried to shape each other into this idealized image of the perfect Ringist. People were always seeking to fix another's eyes, always looking deep into the eyelight as if to ask: Have *you* remembranced the Elder Eddas? Or, more pointedly, Are *you* becoming a god? And no one was a more fervent devotee of this game than Surya Surata Lal. She played it with Danlo and Hanuman and Tamara, and she played it with the brothers Hur, and she played it with any new Ringist who came into Bardo's house; in truth, she very probably played it staring into a mirror at herself.

"She has no real talent for remembrancing," Thomas Rane confided to Danlo. "And that is a pity because she tries very hard. Too hard, I think."

In some respects, Surya Lal was typical of those who went back and forth between being seekers and mere followers of the Way. Although she was never lazy and she possessed an outward courage and intelligence that fooled even her friends (it was true that she'd risked her life trying to free the Summerworld slaves), when it came time to find the way into herself, she would blink her red little eyes and purse her little lips, and she would fall stubborn, as dull and stolid as a muskox. She had little imagination. She curried the good opinion of others, and so she began pretending that her remembrances were deeper and more profound than they really were. Because she clinged to the prettiness of her own self-image, try though she might, she always balked at applying to herself the insights of her best memories. She was afraid of personal change, and of wildness, and she was jealous of those who had no such fear. From the very beginning, she resented Danlo's ability to delve into the heart of the Elder Eddas. She wrongly saw this ability as springing from kalla, hence her disapproval of that marvelous drug.

One night, after the kalla ceremony, she was heard to say, "No one can know if Danlo's first remembrance was a great one or just a descent into illusion. I'm beginning to mistrust this kalla. It's far too dangerous to give to the inexperienced."

As the days grew shorter and the weather colder, she began to mistrust the very act of remembrancing. She was envious of Thomas Rane and Danlo, and if the truth be told, even of Hanuman li Tosh. Since she, herself, lacked the skill to explore the great memories, she could never teach others the remembrancing art, never become a guide and an authority in Bardo's nascent church. Thus she sought to control the remembrancing ceremony, and ultimately to undo it altogether. After the drowning of Isas Nikitovitch, she argued against giving kalla to new Ringists. It was her idea to substitute plain seawater for the kalla at the nightly ceremonies. She implored Bardo to make this change. And Bardo, for his own reasons, heeded her strident words. Beginning on the evening of the forty-eighth of winter, those bearing their first invitation to Bardo's house were given water as a symbol and sacrament, while more experienced Ringists received their two sips of kalla doled out from Bardo's diamond-studded jigger. It might be thought that this corruption of the ceremony would have alienated many people, but ironically, it had the opposite effect. Would-be godlings could now flock to Bardo's house without fearing that they would be required to accomplish anything so arduous or risky as self-remembrance. Indeed, more than a few longtime Ringists, who were sick of the kalla, were only too glad to sip water in its place. As for the new converts burning for a taste of the holy drug (approximately one third fell into this category) they could always hope to be admitted to the elect of Bardo's new religion. They could do this by attending at least thirty-three remembrancing ceremonies, by professing a faith that human beings could become as gods if only they would follow the example of Mallory Ringess, and most importantly by surrendering at least a tenth of their worldly wealth and income to the Way.

"We need money," Bardo confessed one night. In his tea room, he had called together those closest to him. Surya Surata Lal and Thomas Rane were of this inner circle, of course, as were Kolenya Mor, Nirvelli, Hanuman, and Danlo. The brothers Hur, after the Nikitovitch incident, had fallen from favor, and so they were not invited to sit at Bardo's exquisite tea table to drink the rare teas and thick Summerworld coffees that Bardo served in little white cups. "There's now a twenty-day wait for invitations to the remembrances—we can't fit all the seekers who want to attend one into this house. Therefore, we need to buy a property that will accommodate everyone. A couple of blocks off Danladi Square, there's an abandoned building I'd like to consider acquiring. A grand building, a glorious building. But it's hideously expensive. As my cousin has pointed out, the only way to finance such an acquisition would be for the new Ringists to pay for it."

Now, Bardo had organized his cult as most religions have been organized since the beginning of civilization: he was lord, high priest, and guru of the followers of the Way, and he ruled on all church matters with absolute authority. He had no real need to consult others. But he was always a reasonable, congenial man who loved good drink and the interplay of friendly argument. He invited comment, and so he couldn't have been surprised when Thomas Rane said, "There are already too many godchildren. Too many new Ringists. We should cull the best of these and discourage the others. The Way needs *fewer* seekers, not more."

"I strongly disagree," Surya said as she tapped her teacup. "We've a duty to teach the Way of Ringess across the Civilized Worlds. And possibly beyond—wherever human beings are still human."

Danlo, who had never really understood the getting and spending of money, looked at Bardo and said, "If you require new Ringists to pay money in order to attend the ceremonies, then this is . . . tantamount to selling the kalla, yes?"

"Ah, but this is the wrong way to view the situation," Bardo said. "We—any who call themselves Ringists—are simply buying a building. We'll own it in common, each Ringist holding shares according to his or her contribution to the Way."

"But what of those who have no money to contribute?" Danlo asked.

"Well," Bardo said, "they won't be able to hold any property in condominium, will they?"

"But you will allow them to attend the ceremonies?"

"Of course," Bardo said. "The Way of Ringess is open to everyone."

"Even autists?"

"Even autists, Little Fellow."

"But what of the Order, then? The novices and journeymen, most of the academicians . . . what of their vows of poverty?"

"Ah, but that is a delicate matter," Bardo said, and he slurped down a cup of his sweet, black coffee and ate a cookie. "From all new Ringists we'll require a tenth of all property and income. At least. But a tenth of nothing is still nothing, eh? Those who are truly poor will pay nothing."

As Bardo and Danlo argued finances for a while, it became clear that Bardo considered few of the Order to be truly poor. He pointed out that journeymen and novices, who don't even own their own clothes, often come from wealthy families. "It's been my experience that everyone likes a little money pressing his palms, and almost everyone hoards a little. Or they can acquire it, or create it."

"I have never even *seen* a City disk," Danlo said. "Much less held one in my hand."

"Well, that's because of the way you grew up. But even Danlo the Wild could get money, if there was a great enough need."

"I do not think so," Danlo said. In truth, he thought the invention and use of money was *shaida,* one of civilization's worst perversions, and he could not imagine ever wanting any.

"If you had to, you could sell yourself on Strawberry Street." This came from Hanuman li Tosh, who had been sitting quietly at the end of the table. He was referring, of course, to the male brothels down in the worst part of the Farsider's Quarter. Although he hadn't touched his coffee, his eyes, his hand motions, his entire body and being seemed electric with alterness, as if he had just drunk nine cups of coffee. He looked at Danlo, and his face radiated awareness of the cruelty in his words. This rare cruelty caused Danlo to stare at Hanuman in disbelief and despair. Everyone at the table must have sensed the hurt flowing between them. "I'm sorry, now I've wounded you," Hanuman said. He spoke as if he and Danlo were the only two people at the table. "I really didn't mean to."

Bardo—and most of the others—suddenly seemed very intent on eating their cookies and drinking their teas. Nobody spoke.

"No one should *have* to sell herself for money," Nirvelli finally said in her beautiful, dulcet voice. She was wearing white pajamas, and the contrast against her black skin was striking. "Is the Way of Ringess about money, or is it about joy? Pleasure can be bought and sold, as I well know, but joy is beyond price."

"This talk of money demeans us," Thomas Rane put in, and his face was hard with disapproval.

"Money is just money," Surya said. "And we have to decide how to accept money from those of the Order able to contribute." Here she gave Danlo a swift, chiding look, then continued, "The young pilot is correct that most of the Order have taken vows of poverty. Therefore, they can't own property, not even in condominium."

Bardo swished some coffee inside his mouth before swallowing. He belched, waved his hand as if to shoo away a furfly, then said, a little too carelessly, "But this problem of ownership is really a nonproblem. All Ordermen who can't own property *can* make a donation to established Ringists. Even if they must make this donation in secret. Property can then be held in trust for them by these Ringists. This should satisfy the Order's god-damned canons."

If it was Surya Lal who first suggested squeezing money from the new Ringists, and Bardo who schemed to legally implement such a tithe, then Hanuman li Tosh must be credited with attracting the flood of converts that would soon swell Bardo's church. Just as he must be blamed for the ultimate corrupting of the Way. But to give a full account of his remarkable transformation and his rise to religious authority, it is necessary first to say more of his quest to understand the universal nature of suffering.

"Those who follow that part of themselves which is great are great men; those who follow that part of themselves which is little are little men"—thus spoke the great Lao Tzu millennia before Hanuman was born. He might have been foretelling Hanuman's astonishing career, for Hanuman's whole life was a tragic blending of the little and the great. At first, however, to the followers of the Way, only the great part was obvious. He was very young to become a leader of a great religious movement. Some thought that he was too young, but others pointed out that the Emperor Aleksandar had been as young when he tried to conquer Old Earth, and that Jin Zenimura had been only two years older when he repudiated the Order of the Warrior-Poets and founded Zanshin. As it happened, Hanuman's youth was a sword that cut two ways, both of which aided his rise: his admirers cited his age and accomplishments as proof of his genius, while his detractors dismissed him as merely a vain young man full of pretensions and impossible ideals and didn't take him seriously until it was too late.

Danlo was perhaps the only one to descry Hanuman's true potential. Once, after an empty remembrancing ceremony in which they both sipped only salt water, Danlo found Hanuman alone with the ferns and the waterfall in Bardo's meditation room, and he said, "The most dangerous kind of idealist . . . is one who has the power to make his ideals real."

"And you think I have *ideals*?" Hanuman laughed out.

"Truly, since the night of your great remembrance, you have envisioned *something*. A fate and way for human beings. I can almost see it. You never talk about it, but in the silence, in the shadow of your thoughts . . . this fate."

"I believe in free will, you should know."

"Why can't we talk anymore?" Danlo asked.

"I talk all the time. You never listen."

504

"But the others . . . they listen, yes? The godchildren. For them, your words are like quicksilver, and you speak and speak, and more and more people knock at Bardo's gates to listen."

How is it that a few rare people can compel the attention of others? Why should any one person, or whole swarms of people, stand in a driving snow, entranced, while they listen to another's words and feel the pounding of his passion and drink in the fire of his eyes? If it is true that Hanuman li Tosh was born with the gift of tongues, then it is equally true that all his studies and his life's experience contributed toward developing this gift. He was a cetic. No one should ever forget that he was of the Order's oldest discipline, a way of mastery reaching far back to the deserts and forests of Old Earth. To be exact, he was a cyber-shaman, and at the age of twenty-one, he had nearly mastered the different states of computer consciousness. This mastery would be of critical importance to the Order, to Neverness, to all the worlds on which human beings live and call themselves civilized. But for all his skill at interfacing the cybernetic spaces, he had not ignored the other cetic branches. From the yogin, he had learned meditation, psychedelics, the body arts, rhapsody, chanting, and inner theater. And from the neurologicians: configuration, face dancing, ritual analysis, mythopoeisis, charisma, and outer theater. All the cetic branches had incorporated the Fravashi language philosophies, and Hanuman became adept at using word drugs to soothe others' suspicions. He learned to analyze belief systems and to design specific word keys that would free his listeners from their conceptual prisons. And, as Danlo soon discovered, to his horror, Hanuman began creating in those around him wholly new mental prisons that bound them to Hanuman's words, to his vision, to his burning sense of his own fate.

Ultimately, though, it was his great remembrance that bestowed upon him the mantle of prophet. He had said that the death of a god was recorded in the Elder Eddas. At first many ridiculed this remembrance. The pilots, especially, called his memory a drugged delusion: six hundred years earlier, Dario the Bold had mapped all the stars and planets of the 18th Deva Cluster, and no such god, alive or dead, had been discovered. Hanuman's prediction—or memory—might have been quickly forgotten if the Lord Pilot had not spoken so vociferously against kalla and the remembrancing ceremonies. Chanoth Chen Ciceron, one day at the Lords' College, cited Hanuman's remembrance as an example of the kind of danger that Bardo's cult posed the Order. "We must forbid all novices and journey-men contact with Bardo's cult," he told the assembled lords. "Otherwise, we'll see the minds of our brightest youths destroyed."

Now, Lord Ciceron had many enemies, not the least of whom was the maverick pilot known as the Sonderval. The Sonderval had fought side by side with Bardo in the Pilot's War against Leopold Soli and Lord Ciceron. Because the Sonderval despised Lord Ciceron and hoped to humiliate him (and because he was one of the most arrogant human beings ever born), on a whim he decided to journey to the 18th Deva Cluster. In his lightship, the *Cardinal Virtue,* he required only three days to reach the Cluster. He had the fixed points of the red giant star that Hanuman had divulged to Danlo. He was perhaps the finest pilot in the City, perhaps the only one able to use the Continuum Hypothesis, the Great Theorem of the pilots, as it should be used. He journeyed across the stars of the galaxy from Neverness to the Deva Cluster in a single fall. It took him fifteen days to locate the corpse of the dead god. It was as big as a moon and had a glittering diamond skin ten miles thick; its brain was composed of neurologics of a kind the eschatologists had never seen before. As Hanuman had predicted, it orbited a red giant star which the Sonderval immediately named Hanuman's Glory. And indeed, this discovery did bring Hanuman sudden glory. It brought glory and credibility to the Way of Ringess. Upon the Sonderval's return to Neverness, within half a day, the news that a god had truly died had spread across the City.

"This will prove the power of remembrancing," Thomas Rane said to Danlo. "Now everyone will come to me and demand I show them the way to the Elder Eddas."

But Thomas Rane, who understood so much about remembrance and the individual human mind, was quite ignorant of mass religious fervor. Most of the would-be converts to Ringism that winter did not come to Bardo's house to be guided by Thomas Rane. They came to behold such phenomenons as Bardo and Danlo wi Soli Ringess, and most of all, they came because they were curious about Hanuman's great remembrance. They wanted to be close to him, to hear his voice, to touch the silken sleeve of his robe as they stood drinking ice wine with him or eating spicy little meats in Bardo's sun room. Although Hanuman never spoke of kalla, never again delivered another prophecy, his very silence created about him an air of mystery and power. He would listen attentively as strange women and men confessed their dreams to him, and all the while, he would look into their eyes and hidden fears as if peering into the very heart of the Elder Eddas. Almost everyone remarked upon his compassion, his rare and unique understanding of others' pain. He, himself, burned with memories; his face shone with the awareness of a terrible and primeval force buried deep within. People sensed this about him. Such awareness cannot be created at will, nor can it be faked using the techniques of charisma or outer theater. It is as real and compelling as an electric storm at night; it's like the smell of ozone in the air after a lightning bolt has struck. People swarmed Hanuman li Tosh because he was connected to the deepest of forces, and through him they felt the pulse-beat of a universe that was more poignant and intense than they had ever known, and infinitely more real.

Soon after his great remembrance, after he had recuperated and begun counseling Ringists at Bardo's parties, he set out to strengthen this dark connection. Because he wanted to understand everything about pain and suffering, he began to cultivate for himself a secret life. Unknown to his fellow cetics or to Danlo, he began climbing the icy cliffs of Mt. Attakel, where they loomed like a gleaming white wall above the Elf Gardens. He would don a heated kamelaika, pull on a pair of friction boots, and force his way up the crumbly, rotten rock faces. He always climbed alone, without the aid of a rope or net. Many times he suffered frostbite of fingers and face, and twice he lost toes, which had to be regenerated in secret at the cloning shop. Many times he was close to the pain and terror of falling. But alone, he could only know *his* terror and *his* pain, and so he turned to other pursuits. He sought out and entered zanshin tournaments. He fought with fists and elbows and feet until both he and his partners were broken and bloody. He fought bravely, never betraying the slightest tension or anxiety, and he earned many points for demonstrating a perfectly relaxed and alert posture in the face of maiming, and, rarely, even brain disfiguration and death. Other passions of his were less dangerous, though no less cruel. At night he would journey deep into the Farsider's Quarter and purchase otherworldly delights from the alien Friends of Man. He solicited male whores, and he mistreated them, not because it gave him pleasure but because it brought them pain. In truth, the act of coupling with alien females and graceless, sculpted young men sickened him, and he did so only to discover how much sickness he could endure. This descent into darkness went on all during the deep, dry snows of winter, even as he delivered little sermons about the virtue of gods to Bardo's guests, and once, when Bardo was ill from eating too many chocolate cookies, conducted the nightly ceremony himself in Bardo's music room. It was only by chance (or perhaps it was fate) that Danlo discovered his friend's secret life.

One evening, after Danlo had spent the day studying the mathematics of the manifold, he was out in the Old City looking for a café in which to take his evening meal. He was very hungry; he had become lost in the intricacies and elegance of the Great Theorem, and he hadn't eaten anything since the previous night. He was contemplating a rich dinner of kurmash, peas, and saffron rice when he espied Hanuman ahead of him, weaving his way among the skaters filling the street. Hanuman was dressed out of color, in a formal kamelaika and a gleaming brown fur; he might have been mistaken for a rich pilgrim or a farsider. Danlo thought to call to him, to ask him if he wanted to share a grand bowl of kurmash, but Hanuman's dress and secretive manner bade him keep his distance. He decided, out of sheer caprice, to follow him. For two blocks he kept a good distance between them, watching Hanuman stroke his distinctive and skilled strokes. And then Hanuman turned onto the Serpentine, and the crowds of people thickened up. The snowplows had heaped glittering white drifts to the sides of the street, closing the slow lanes. Skaters were all forced onto a ribbon of ice between this wall of snow and the sleds rocketing down the center of the street. Danlo had to stay close behind Hanuman lest he lose him. Self-important men and women in expensive furs jostled him, blocked his way, and shot him anxious looks as he darted among them. The skating was quite treacherous. A fresh layer of snow covered the street and muffled the hard striking sound of Danlo's skates. He couldn't see his skate blades cutting the ice, couldn't make out the divots, rills, and bumps that one usually avoids. With difficulty he followed Hanuman down the Serpentine where it curves west into the Farsider's Quarter.

At the edge of the Diamond District, Hanuman turned off onto a lesser gliddery. Snow completely obscured the redness of the ice, and at first Danlo did not realize that they were making their way up Strawberry Street. Then he noticed the brothels lining the street on both sides: cold stone row houses without lights or windows. The street was dark and peopled with worm-runners, wealthy men, and middling-old women, avid and nervous in their hooded furs. Outside the brothel doors were

508

beautiful boys and young men wearing tight silk kamelaikas; among them stood dangerous-looking procurers who rudely whistled at the passersby. Danlo had a strong sense that he was in a place he shouldn't be, that many eyes were watching him, appraising him, wondering what a young pilot should be seeking in such a district. He himself wondered that Hanuman could make his way down the street with so great an ease, as if the smells of incense, perfume, and burning jambool were quite familiar to him. It amused and alarmed him to think that Hanuman might have a taste for young men. He expected that Hanuman would stop momentarily before one of the brothels' luridly carved doors, but then Hanuman suddenly turned down a dark alley and vanished.

Now very much alarmed, Danlo followed him down the icy gap between two brothels, which were built so close together that two men could not have squeezed between them shoulder to shoulder. He was very near the district's edge. In front of him, gleaming out of the darkness, was a snowy embankment separating the line of brothels from crumbling old buildings that might have been flung up three thousand years earlier. He thought these ugly buildings must be restaurants, for the air smelled of baked breads and pastries, cheese and cilka, garlic and meats roasting over an open fire. Strawberry Street runs near the Bell District, so-called because its network of streets, as seen from the air, takes on the shape of a great purple bell. It seemed that Hanuman was skating toward the Bell and intended somehow to enter it.

For a moment Danlo did not understand how this could be so. Strawberry Street is a red gliddery, whereas all the streets in the Bell except the main one are of purple. In Neverness, red glidderies connect only with the major orange slidderies, or with each other; the purple glidderies intersect green glissades. Red streets never flow into those that are purple. Thus the City is something of a topological nightmare, and travel between the districts is often circuitous and difficult. Long ago, the Time-keeper had ordered the City built this way. He had wanted to isolate the various sects and alien races should it ever be necessary to close off the streets in case of rebellion or war. From almost the very beginning, however, the people had undermined his plan. In many places throughout the City, the harijan and other peoples had built illegal white streets connecting the red and purple glidderies, and thus connecting the City's many districts.

When Danlo reached the end of the alley, in back of the brothels vibrating with strange musics and muffled cries, he surmised that he had discovered one of these illegal streets, for the alley did not dead-end as it should have. Rather, it cut through the embankment, through a black tunnel hung with hollow sounds, and it gave out onto a narrow walkway of ice leading into the Bell. He cheerfully followed Hanuman onto this walkway, then down a well-lit purple gliddery lined with apartments and various shops. He saw him enter a windowless restaurant, a dingy old building of flaking sandstone that it would have been easy to ignore. Danlo stood across the street leaning on his knees, watching the restaurant door, and wondering what he should do.

For a long while he waited, wearing grooves in the ice as he slid his skate blades back and forth. It was very cold, the kind of cold that Danlo once would have called *haradu*. It had begun snowing again. Millions of delicate snowflakes danced violet and rose in the light of the flame globes. The smells of delicious foods floated all around him. He remembered then that he had planned to meet Tamara later that night. He would need to eat very soon, to fortify himself for that meeting. At last he decided to join Hanuman inside the restaurant, even though he could see it was a private one and he had no money. Since coming to Neverness, he had eaten only in free restaurants, and he was quite ignorant of the etiquette of exchanging money for food.

Upon opening the outer doors, in a foyer full of coat closets, alien artifacts, and jets of hot air, he was immediately greeted by a jaded-looking hostess wearing a red kimono. She took his furs from him and asked if he required a fry table.

"I am not sure," Danlo said. "I had thought to meet . . . a friend."

"Would your friend already have arrived?"

"Oh, yes, I am sure he is here."

"Can you tell me his name?"

Danlo, who still retained his Alaloi inhibition against the telling of true names, said, "Most likely he would not have given his name."

"But is he an aficionado or a newcomer?"

"I would think . . . that he has not been here more than once or twice."

After waiting a moment and looking askance at Danlo's worn racing kamelaika, his beard, and his wild hair with the feather in it, she said, "Could you *describe* him, please?"

510

"Well, he has a splendid face, perhaps too intense, but sensitive, and his eyes truly—"

"What does he *look* like?" the hostess snapped out.

Danlo quickly bowed his head in anger and shame, and then he told the hostess what Hanuman looked like.

"You mean the Worthy Hiroshi li Tal of Simoom," the hostess said. "He's one of our most discriminating aficionados. If you'll follow me, I'll show you to his table."

The hostess opened the inner doors, and without pausing to let Danlo go first, she led him into a lavishly decorated and intimate room. The lights were turned down low, so at first Danlo could see little, just the polished jewood walls, forks and knives of gleaming steel, and the dark faces of the aficionados sitting at their tables. As if dazzled by too many sensa, he moved through a wall of little sounds and odors: sizzling meats and conversational tidbits, woodsmoke and scorched oil and icevine burning thick and sweet. Everything about the room nauseated and repelled him, and yet, he felt strangely drawn into its depths, by hunger, by curiosity, and by another need for which he had no name.

"We have a nice table for you," the hostess said. "May you enjoy your meal."

They had walked toward the rear wall, then up a couple of steps to a slightly higher level where five private tables overlooked the rest of the room. Hanuman sat in a padded leather chair with his back to the wall, and he said, "Hello, Danlo, I was wondering when you'd come in."

Danlo looked at him in amazement and said, "You knew I was following you?"

"Cetics are supposed to know such things, aren't they?"

"I wanted to see . . . where you were going," Danlo said with a smile.

"Well, here I am," Hanuman said. "Here we are. If you'd like, would you please join me?"

Danlo sat beside him and worked the gloves off his hands. In front of him was the strangest table he had ever seen: it was built in the shape of an octagon, and the half of it nearest him was of black shatterwood, while the far half was sunken and surfaced with gold. A shallow gutter ran along the edge of this golden half. He was about to comment on this unique table when a waiter brought them a plate of slivered kona nuts in pepper sauce.

"Have you eaten?" Hanuman asked. "I've already ordered,

mostly meat dishes, but there will be more than enough other food to share. You should know, that's the way here, for everyone seated at the same table to share."

Danlo picked up a pair of bone chopsticks and maneuvered a few nut slivers into his mouth. The dish was very hot, very sweet, very good.

"How did you get the money to eat here?" Danlo asked. "And look at you—your clothes! And why are you using the name of a Simoom Architect? You despise Architects, yes?"

He waited for Hanuman to illuminate these mysteries, but Hanuman just sat there, sipping from a goblet of red wine, staring at him.

"Perhaps you should leave," Hanuman finally said.

The words were like drops of hot wax in Danlo's ears; he shook his head slowly back and forth, unable to understand why Hanuman would say such a thing.

"Perhaps it would be best if you go."

"But, Hanu, is this what you truly want?" Danlo asked. "Why did you invite me to sit down, then?"

After taking another sip of wine, Hanuman picked up his knife and dragged the sharp edge of it lightly back and forth across his palm. He seemed puzzled, self-absorbed, aggrieved. A scryer might have said he was full of remorse for events that had not yet occurred. Danlo wondered why he would frequent such a hole-in-the-ice restaurant, with its strange little tables and wealthy patrons stealing furtive glances at each other. Close all around was a faint odor of bruised flowers and burning blood, as well as an air of anticipation that sickened Danlo and made him want to flee. He might have said his good-byes, then, but Hanuman suddenly smiled and told him, "No, stay; I've decided you should. I'd thought to spare your sensibilities, but that's silly of me. Please stay."

Hanuman picked up a crystal bottle and asked Danlo if he would be taking alcohol that evening. Danlo nodded his head "yes." As he watched a stream of ruby wine flow into his goblet, he became aware of a subtle change in the room. The buzz of voices had died to a few scattered whispers. Just below them, off to the side, was a wood and gold table at which sat two pairs of men and women. One of the men was a sullen-looking worm-runner; he was accompanied by an elegantly dressed common whore, who, except for her tattooed lips and red-rimmed eyes, might have passed as an ambassador's wife. The other man and woman each had brilliant green eyes too large for their delicate faces. They were obviously engineered farsiders from some noncivilized world, and it was hard to understand how they should be sharing a table with a criminal and a whore. All the patrons in the room were now looking at this table, or rather, their stares were fixed on a small, efficient man standing at the edge of the table's golden half. This was one of the restaurant's chefs. He was swaddled completely in white cottons; he wore a white turban and white slippers and white cotton gloves; each article of clothing was spattered with dark red stains. From a steel cart next to the table he removed a bowl of oil. He quickly dribbled out this oil in zigzag lines over the table's golden surface. He then used a broad brush to spread the oil evenly.

"Gold heats the most perfectly of all the metals," Hanuman explained. "Which is why the tables are wrought of a gold alloy."

It was now obvious that the chef was about to cook a meal for the aficionados. Danlo could not tell how the tabletop was heated—probably by plasma or jets of burning hydrogen—but in very little time the sheet of oil began to blister and smoke. The chef reached his hand into a basket on one of the cart's lower shelves. He grasped a fat, struggling female sleekit by the neck. The sleekit's body, from snout to tail, was a quivering pink and white mass which everywhere oozed blood; moments earlier, in the kitchen, the chef's assistants had flayed the skin off it. The chef held it up so that everyone could appreciate its size and sex. In his other hand he held a metallic device that looked like a nutcracker. He used it to quickly break each of the sleekit's legs. These four wrenching motions were accomplished so suddenly that Danlo scarcely could believe it. He sat frozen to his chair, holding his breath, watching. The sleekit had remained curiously silent at the breaking of its legs, but when the chef heaved it onto the table, it let out a terrible whistling cry, the way sleekits do when they are mortally wounded. The sleekit tried to spring off the hot tabletop, and then tried to run, but its legs were quite useless and could get no purchase on the popping oil. All it could do was to flop about in panic as it sizzled and whistled and cried.

"No!" Danlo whispered. "No, no, no."

"This method causes the animal to release great amounts of adrenaline before it's killed," Hanuman explained. He sipped his wine and then smiled sadly. "Some say this makes the meat more pungent. Certainly it's fresher, this way. Now let's see if the sleekit is pregnant, or not."

The chef had his knives out now, and he touched them to the sleekit, whose sad, black eyes still burned with life. Then, with startling efficiency, the chef plied his knives, slashing and sawing and slicing, and the sleekit suddenly lay in pieces that cooked in the hot oil and in its own blood. There was much blood, most of which ran over the golden cooking surface and into the gutters before draining down a dark hole at the table's corner. Some of the blood, though, the chef used to baste the liver and sweetbreads and the other cuts of meat. He stirred in a decoction of the juice of snow dahlia and other flowers, and in this way he made a delicious sauce. While the meat simmered, he discarded the bones and intestines and other offal. Danlo was glad to see that no baby sleekits spilled out of the severed uterus, though clearly, some of the aficionados were disappointed. When the chef's dish was finally finished, he served it up on delicate white plates. He garnished the steaming sleekit pieces with sliced oranges and fresh mint. Then he bowed to the aficionados and began wiping his knives with soft white cloth.

"An elegant dish," Hanuman said. "Though I should tell you, I've never really liked the way sleekit tastes."

Danlo heard Hanuman's voice hissing out of the darkness, but he could not look at him. He was sweating now, struggling to breathe, and both his palms were pressed to his forehead. He sat utterly still, fascinated and stunned by what he had just seen.

"You . . . were right," he said when he finally caught his breath. "I should not have stayed."

"But then you'd never have experienced the art of odori," Hanuman said. "Didn't you tell me once that a human being can never have enough experience?"

"But the killing of a sleekit this way . . . this is *shaida*." He stared at the candlelights hanging from the ceiling, and he remembered: *Shaida is he who cuts meat from a living animal.*

"I should have thought that you'd be gratified that some civilized people spurn cultured meats in favor of the real thing."

Danlo watched the aficionados eating their dinner, and then for the first time in years, he said a prayer for the spirit of a slain animal: *"Pela Churiyanima,"* he whispered, *"mi alasharia la shantih, o shantih L'Ali."*

"Of course, it's cruel," Hanuman said, "but all killing is cruel."

· Danlo looked at him and said, "It is wrong to kill."

"But your Alaloi kill animals, don't they? I should have thought you'd be used to the sight of killing."

514

"A hunter never kills . . . just for the pleasure of it," Danlo said. "An Alaloi man kills to live, only because there is no other way."

"Have you ever seen a cat play with a mouse?" Hanuman asked.

"I have never seen a mouse, but I know about the snow tigers," Danlo admitted.

Hanuman glanced over at the kitchen doors for a moment, then said, "You're sworn to ahimsa, Danlo, and I admire your devotion. I honor it, even though I think it's slightly silly. But you yourself admit that killing is a necessary part of life. If that's so, why shouldn't we enjoy it? Why shouldn't we praise the act and savor everything about it?"

Danlo was about to answer him when another chef, a big woman with meaty hands and a tight, grim face, emerged from the kitchen. She pushed a steel-drawered cart right up to their table. Danlo wanted to rise up and flee then, but everyone in the restaurant seemed to be watching him. While the chef grunted and panted and bent low to ignite the burners beneath the table, Danlo told himself that this art of frying live animals was just another of civilization's decadences. The right side of him called out for him to run away as fast as he could, but his left side whispered that he should stay and learn from this decadence. Like a seabird caught in the ocean's ice, he was frozen into inaction. He watched the chef smear an orange-colored oil across the golden fry table. He realized that civilized people, in their comfortable cafés and effortless getting of clothing, warmth, and luxury, in the isolation of their professions, in their acquisition of knowledge or money, in their easy entertainments, were so benumbed and cut off from life that they could see neither the world's horror nor its beauty. The various drugs and art forms so common in the City were ways toward a forced and artificial appreciation of beauty; the abomination occurring before his eyes was an attempt of a jaded people to experience —safely—sheer horror. Danlo hated people for needing such stimulations. He was horrified to discover that after seven years in Neverness, a part of himself had grown too used to accepting their ways. In truth, at that moment, the right side of him despised the left, even as his belly churned and tightened at the smell of burning oil. He watched the chef open a steel drawer packed with fresh snow. When she removed a snowworm as long as his forearm and held it up for him to see, he pressed his fist into the center of his belly. For the first time, he glimpsed a part of Hanuman's vision of their world: that all people crave suffering as instinctually and fiercely as they do joy.

"This is *shaida*," Danlo said. He leaned his head closer to Hanuman's, and he whispered, "Tell her we have changed our minds."

"Have we?" Hanuman said.

"Please tell her to stop."

The table surface was now quite hot, and the chef held the snowworm over it. The worm kept trying to coil onto itself; it was only with difficulty that the chef managed to pull it straight.

"No, do not!" Danlo suddenly shouted. "Don't you know that Aulii . . . has a rare sensitivity to heat?"

But the chef did not listen to Danlo. He wasn't the first newcomer to fall squeamish and lose his taste for his meal. The restaurant's chefs had instructions to heed only the aficionado's commands, and since Hanuman said nothing, the chef dropped the worm onto the table.

"No!"

There was a sudden sizzling sound, and in front of Danlo, the worm bounced about and writhed in the hot grease. It tried to coil, but the proteins in its segments were shortening up, congealing, cooking. Using the dull edge of her knife, the chef rolled it back and forth across the frying surface. And it never stopped writhing, and inside Danlo, his intestines and stomach and esophagus writhed and burned with bitter acids. His eyes burned with tears, and his throat burned, and he coughed and he said, "Do not let it die this way! Aulii's nerves are buried . . . so deep."

He was too choked up with hatred to say more about the snowworm's anatomy. He wanted to tell the chef that most animals, when they burn to death, suffer pain only a short while because the nerves most sensitive to heat are concentrated in the skin and are quickly destroyed. He wanted to tell Hanuman, and every aficionado in the restaurant, that the snowworm's consciousness was different from that of other animals. A snowworm's awareness of cold and heat—of everything—was spread throughout every tissue and cell of its body. A snowworm was fantastically sensitive to heat. It would take a long time to die, writhing on the griddle, and each moment of burning would last forever.

"Kill it now," Danlo pleaded. "Please, now."

But the chef only smiled at him with her tight, thin lips, and she poured an amber liquid over the length of the worm. The liquid—it was probably cognac or some other spirit of alcohol—hissed and steamed. The chef used a little hand light to ignite the liquid, and now the worm writhed inside a shroud of hot blue flames.

"Tell her to kill it," Danlo said. He looked fiercely into Hanuman's eyes for a moment, then back at the worm.

"I can't do that," Hanuman said.

"Tell her!"

"But that would be pointless. In a few seconds she'll slice the worm into segments, and it will be over."

"Not . . . *over*," Danlo gasped out. "You cannot kill a worm that way. Each segment . . . has its own life. The chef can slice Aulii onto your plate, but the parts will still be alive."

"That's the way this dish is eaten," Hanuman said. There was no emotion in his voice and nothing in his eyes except the reflection of a worm writhing through blue flames.

"But first the worm must be killed!"

"I'm sure the chef doesn't know how."

"It must be killed!" Danlo repeated.

"Then perhaps you should kill it."

"I cannot," Danlo said. "You know I cannot."

"No, that would be an ignoble act," Hanuman said. "Out of compassion for all living things, you've sworn never to harm anything, not even a dying snowworm."

For what seemed a long time Danlo could not move. Then he looked at the snowworm again, and his heart was suddenly on fire. He fairly leapt out of his chair, leaned far over the table, and he plunged his hands through the blue alcohol flames. He grabbed the snowworm. As quickly as he could, he squeezed one end of it between his forefinger and thumb, and then, in the Alaloi way, he ran his fingers up and down the worm, squeezing deeply, popping the nerve tube segment by segment. When he was done, he dropped the worm in front of Hanuman. He stood holding his burned, greasy hands open in the air. "What is wrong with you!" he shouted at Hanuman.

And Hanuman just smiled at him; he looked at the worm and said, "Now you understand."

And Danlo did understand, and the understanding was a pain burning inside him more urgently than any pain he had ever known. He fell deep into hatred then, hatred for Hanuman and the bewildered aficionados, hatred for himself. His face was like a burning mask of skin smothering and blinding him. He leaned forward and grasped the edge of the table. It was wrought of dense black wood and gold, and it was shockingly heavy, but with a single convulsion of muscles and popping spine, Danlo straightened up and threw the table over. It crashed to the floor. Wine goblets and plates and the table's flower vase shattered, and shards of porcelain sprayed out into the dark room. Without pause or thought, Danlo sprang over to another table where a chef was frying some prawns, and he threw that table down, too. And then he found a stew table where a lobster was boiling inside a great clary kettle, and over it went, and he didn't hear the screams of the aficionados splashed with boiling water, couldn't see their outraged faces. Two of the chefs tried to block his way and subdue him, but he knocked them aside and ran from the room. He barely had enough sense to grab his furs before rushing into the snowstorm that blew through the streets outside.

When he had lost himself in the dark, twisting glidderies of the Bell, at last he stopped and gasped out, "Oh, Hanu, Hanu, why did I break my vow?"

He looked into a streetlight, and there, tongued in the pretty, colored flames he saw an image of Hanuman's face smiling at him. A part of him, on his right side, expected to see Hanuman rushing from the restaurant to make his apologies. But the left half of him whispered that he would never come. He stood on a nameless street listening for the sound of skate blades against ice. He felt the snow breaking and melting against his face, and he waited a long time in silence before setting out toward the Old City. He had to find a café before it grew too late; he was now very cold, very weary, and very, very hungry.

THE FIRE SERMON

Then The Awakened One, having dwelt in Uruvela as long as he wished, proceeded on his wanderings in the direction of Gaya Head, accompanied by a great congregation of priests, a thousand in number, who had all of them aforetime been monks with matted hair. And there in Gaya, on Gaya Head, The Awakened One dwelt with the thousand priests.

And there The Awakened One addressed the priests:

"All things, O priests, are on fire. And what, O priests, are all these things which are on fire?"

"The eye, O priests, is on fire; forms are on fire; eye-consciousness is on fire; impressions received by the eye are on fire; and whatever sensation, pleasant, or indifferent, originates in dependence on impressions received by the eye, that too is on fire."

— *from The Teachings of The Awakened One*

On the second day of deep winter, Bardo completed negotiations on a cathedral in the Old City. It was indeed a glorious building of sweeping arches and ancient stone. A sect of Kristians, during the lordship of Jemmu Flowtow, had built it near the Academy in the hope of attracting young novices to the worship of a god-man they called the Messiah. But Kristianity was a decrepit, tottering, and sickly religion; its ancient doctrines and rituals had as little vitality as a toothless old man who has long since undergone his last return to youth. The Kristians could not establish themselves on Neverness, and so they had sold their beautiful church and abandoned the City. Various investors and owners, for thirteen centuries, had kept it in good repair. Bardo acquired it from a group of Architects known as the Universal Church of Ede. They, too, had abandoned Neverness, and quite recently, not because their religion was dying but because they feared that the light from the Vild would soon destroy the City. In fact, since they had owned the cathedral a scant twenty years and had never made use of it, they were desperate to sell it. And so Bardo paid much less money for it than it was worth. To celebrate this mercantile victory—and to prepare for the anniversary of Mallory Ringess's supposed ascension to godhood—he declared a holiday. On the nineteenth of deep winter, at the Ring of Fire, the Way of Ringess would hold a mass joyance, the greatest gathering and party the City had ever seen.

All Are Welcome! This was the message recorded on the invitation disks that Bardo's followers distributed throughout the four quarters of the City. Although no one knew how many people might attend an outdoor joyance in the deeps of winter, Bardo had chosen the largest of the City's ice rings to accommodate the hoped-for crowds. Naturally, when Lord Ciceron learned that thousands of the religiously curious would be swarming the ice ring nearest the Academy, he was irate. But there was little he could do. Each of the City ice rings was, by canon law, a commons; while the Order's zambonis maintained every street and ring in the City (except the illegal ones), keeping the ice clear and smooth, the lords of the Order could not forbid the people to gather upon them. Of course, they could forbid all Ordermen to attend the joyance, but Lord Ciceron perceived that such a forbiddance might be disobeyed, and so he wisely restrained the lords of the Tetrad from issuing a formal injunction.

In many ways, however, he made it known that the Order disapproved of the joyance: he refused to lend Bardo's church any of the Order's movable warming pavilions; for fifteen days preceding the event, he kept the zambonis away from the Ring of Fire and its surrounding streets so that the ice throughout the entire district would run to seed and become nearly impassable; he peevishly announced that all the Order's restaurants and multrums near the ice ring would be closed. It must have galled him that Bardo thwarted each of these measures and turned adversity to his advantage.

The nineteenth of deep winter dawned clear and bitterly

cold. The sky was a perfect blue-black circle hung in silence over the Ring of Fire. The ring itself—a circle of ice a quarter mile in diameter—shone like a red mirror with the light of the sun rising over the mountains. Around the rim of the ice ring were many warming pavilions, great open tents of scarlet silk that flapped and rippled in the wind. Bardo's followers had worked through the night erecting the pavilions, which Bardo had paid for with money collected from new Ringists, just as he had paid for the kiosks and food pavilions that dotted the ice ring. He had hired chefs from the City's best restaurants; from the vendors in the Farsider's Quarter, he had bought vast quantities of food and drink. As the morning warmed and the first people ventured into the ring, the smells of roasting sweetmeats and bread spread out from kiosk to kiosk. And jambalaya and hot curries and fairy foods were available for those wishing to gorge, and a hundred other dishes, and with each hour, more people gathered together eating their steaming delicacies and drinking coffee and chocolate and hot ale. By noon there were three thousand people there.

Then, from a wooden stage built near the ring's southern rim, musicians began to play, and the sound of gosharps and booming drums could be heard across the City. People began swarming the streets leading to the ring. Since the ice of these glidderies was rotten and in places packed with snow, they had to eject their skate blades and make their way by boot toward the joyance. Bardo eased their impatience by having hundreds of new Ringists go among them with billies full of beer and wine. He distributed other drugs as well. Freely, from his own stores, he gave away dried triya seeds and teonancatl mushrooms; he provided little silk bags full of tobacco, toalache, and bhang, and other plants that might be smoked. To walk up the Serpentine, where it curved around the nothern rim of the ring, was to move slowly through clouds of blue smoke, to see a hundred pipes glowing red and orange, and to hear millions of the little triya seeds popping as they burned and released psychedelic vapors into the air. People everywhere were laughing and singing, and they buoyed each other along in unbroken streams. Most of them, by the time they entered the ice ring, were slightly drunk from this smoke. And there they gathered shoulder to shoulder before the stage as the music of the mantra musicians vibrated through their bellies and up their spines. There were rich astriers dressed in chukkas and capes; and ill-clad autists with their bare, frozen feet; and wormrunners, aphasics, warrior-poets, nimspinners, and arhats; and many, many academicians bedraped in their bright-colored furs. Almost half the Ordermen in Neverness were there, and they stood easily among the hibakusha and the harijan and the other peoples of the City. Throughout the afternoon they gathered, a great rippling swarm of humanity (and even a few curious Darghinni and Fravashi) who never stopped eating and singing and smoking and spinning and dancing.

"By God, there must be eighty thousand people here!" Bardo said. He stood in the opening of a huge warming pavilion at the rear of the stage. The mantra musicians had ceased playing, and the stage was empty, which allowed a clear line of sight out over the ice ring. He gazed at the sea of people swaying and waiting below him, and he started to laugh. "Perhaps as many as ninety thousand—ah, this will be a night to remember!"

At his right side stood Danlo, and on his left, Hanuman li Tosh. Since the night in the restaurant, they had not spoken to each other; now there was a wall between them of little politenesses, formalities, and anxious silence. Danlo, too, looked out over the manswarm, counting. It was almost dark, but he could still see the people's black and white and brown faces shining before him. At any moment, at various points across the ice ring, little orange lights would flare quickly before dying. They looked like hundreds of fireflies winking on and off. But it was only the flames from matches striking, he realized; in a crowd so vast, there would always be a few people lighting their pipes.

"I count . . . ninety-six thousand people," Danlo said. He had to shout against the roar of voices filling the ice ring. "And forty-nine aliens."

Bardo ahhhed and hmmmed, and he stroked his beard and seemed very pleased. In his black furgown and cape, which were trimmed out in gold, he was an impressive figure of a man. All the Ringists in the warming pavilion—Surya Lal and Thomas Rane and the inner circle, as well as many godchildren serving hot drinks and making important errands—looked to him to orchestrate the evening's events. He smiled at Hanuman, belched, then said, "So many people—who's ever faced so many before?"

Hanuman was brazenly dressed in his formal cetic's robe; atop his head was an orange satin toque. He hated wearing hats of any sort, even on cold, windy nights. He wore it only for camouflage. Beneath the floppy toque was a headgear of another kind: a common cetic's heaume, a chromium cap of neurologics that gleamed from his brows across his head to the back of his neck. Or rather, it would have gleamed had he dared to take his hat off.

"There are 96,391 people here," he said. His eyes were wide open, but blind with the intensity of computer interface. The cetic's heaume generated an intense field, suffusing his brain with information. "And even as we speak, more are arriving."

"It's time we started the testaments," Bardo said. "Before it falls too cold."

Now Hanuman's eyes began to clear, and he scrutinized the people below them. It was obvious to Danlo that he had faced away from his computer, for the moment, and was now seeing with the eyes of a cetic.

"I should think we might open them more," Hanuman said.

"With more music?" Bardo's voice boomed out.

Hanuman nodded his head. "However I'd dispense with the improvisatori altogether and reschedule the song masters for a later time. Now it would be best to call up the concertists. They should play no more than a quarter hour."

"And then the testaments?"

"And then the testaments," Hanuman said. "But there should be no more than five of them."

"Including my own?" Bardo asked. He frowned and stamped his boots up and down on the wood with such vigor that the whole stage vibrated and shook.

"Your testament," Hanuman said, "will be incorporated as part of the kalla ceremony. There should be five others."

"Danlo's testament, of course," Bardo said after smiling at Danlo. He held up a huge finger gloved in gold leather. "And my cousin's. And we mustn't overlook Thomas Rane. And I suppose we should also include Jonathan Hur."

Hanuman shook his head. "I would alternate the sexes. Thomas Rane should speak first, and then Surya, followed by Danlo. And then we should let Nirvelli give her testament. Have you heard it yet? She has an elegant style, a powerful voice—as many of the courtesans do."

"I wish that Tamara could have spoken," Bardo said. "But she told me that she had an engagement tonight, too bad."

Just then, Danlo and Hanuman exchanged glances. They both knew that Tamara had declined to attend the joyance because she disliked Hanuman.

"Someday we'll persuade Tamara to share her remembrances," Hanuman said. "But tonight, Nirvelli will have to speak for the courtesans."

"You'll go last?" Bardo asked.

"That would be best."

"By God, I wish we could just follow the original schedule."

Hanuman smiled and said, "When we composed the schedule, we did so knowing we'd likely have to change it."

Bardo frowned again, and it was obvious that he was uneasy with allowing Hanuman to help orchestrate the joyance. In truth, Hanuman was the real architect of all that occurred that evening. It was he who had suggested giving away drugs to the people; he had arranged the Fravashi chants, the tone poems and body musics that would open the manswarm to their words. He was a master of nada yoga, the yoga of sound, and he had carefully placed the sulki grids that filled the ice ring with symphonies and drumsongs and whispers, with mystic tones that worked upon the body and brain. He had ordered the lasers and the dishlike moon lights and had overseen their installation around the ring's circumference. He had interfaced all this machinery with a master computer hidden under the stage, and then he himself had interfaced this computer in order to control things. As a cetic, he was sensitive to the slightest changes in people's consciousness, and he could read their mood as easily as an Alaloi hunter identifies bear tracks in the snow. He could change this mood and consciousness. This manipulation of masses of people was an unforgivable violation of his cetic ethics. Danlo hated this skill of Hanuman's, even as he was fascinated by it. He watched Hanuman smiling sweetly at Bardo, and he suddenly knew that Hanuman was planning to betray him.

"I'm worried," Bardo said to Hanuman. He puffed out his fat cheeks and let a lungful of steamy breath escape into the air. "I'm worried that you'll compromise yourself. There are other cetics out there. Surely they'll discern your hand in all this."

"Perhaps," Hanuman said.

"Well, you'll be banished from the Order."

"Is that the worst fate that might befall me?"

"Are you ready to leave the Order, then?"

"Should I give my allegiance to the Order?" Hanuman asked. "Or to the Way of Ringess?"

"By God, I hope you don't blame me for forcing you to such a decision!"

"But I haven't been forced to do anything," Hanuman said.

"You know it's my hope," Bardo said, "that no one should have to make this choice."

"And it's not an ignoble hope. I share it, too. Tonight's joyance should bring the Order and the Way closer together."

"Either that or it will ruin us," Bardo said.

"No," Hanuman reassured him, "there's no chance of that."

"Well, ruin or no, I'd hope that the people would never forget the Way of Ringess."

"After tonight, they won't forget," Hanuman said.

He turned his head to let his eyes meet Danlo's. His face, Danlo saw, was cold and white and set with anticipation.

Then Hanuman smiled and said, "A hundred thousand people, and none of them will forget what they hear and see tonight."

They went back into the warming pavilion while nine concertists in heated clothing took the stage. The concertists stood in a half circle facing the dark swarm of people below them, and they fingered the keys of their pralltrillers. A long, low, thunderous music vibrated the ice ring. It was terrible to hear. It emptied the mind of all thought and set the hearts of thousands booming up through their brains. The trance concerto continued for exactly a quarter of an hour. Then the concertists put down their instruments and left the stage.

It had been agreed that the speakers that evening might talk about any aspect of Ringism, so long as they spoke from their hearts and kept their testaments short. Thomas Rane, sleek and serious in his silver furs, was the first to take the stage. As at any joyance, he delivered an account of the remembrancing art, and he speculated upon the nature of the Elder Eddas. He slighted the dangers of kalla while extolling its virtues. Surya Surata Lal quickly followed him. From the warming pavilion, Danlo watched her walk out almost to the edge of the stage. The tiny woman coolly faced the people spread out over the ice below her, and she talked of the essence of humanness, and of her love and hate for her all too human body. She spoke with a brutal honesty. All people, she said, lived their entire lives in bondage to hunger, pain, and lust. And above all to the fear of death. But there was a way to transcend the body and achieve immortality. This was the Way of Ringess: to sacrifice body and self in order to grow into godhood. All people, she said, should open their hearts to Mallory Ringess's tremendous and miraculous sacrifice; all people must die to themselves if they would

525

truly live; all people must take the image of Mallory Ringess inside themselves, and cherish it as a revelation of what they might become.

When she was finished, it was Danlo's turn. He walked out across the creaking stage, out to where he could feel the roar of a hundred thousand voices engulf him. Foolishly, he wore only his racing kamelaika and a pair of black gloves. The wind whipped through his hair, and he heard someone down in front of him shout out, "It's Danlo the Wild!" In truth, he was unaware of how wild he looked; his senses and mind were concentrated upon what lay before him: the dark air gushing over him in cold waves that shocked him down to the bone; the hundred thousand pairs of eyes burning to meet his eyes; the words that spilled from his lips and were carried outward to each point within the ice ring, and far beyond. As he had told Bardo in his observatory, he had considered these words well. He had polished them as clearly as words could be polished. He spoke with a rare devotion to truth, though if anyone had asked him, he probably would have said that he spoke too freely, with much more playfulness and passion than a civilized man should betray. When he had finished telling of his great remembrance of the Elder Eddas, he was sweating despite the cold. Sweating and shivering and smiling as the people stamped their boots and cheered him. This cheering grew to a roar that vibrated his groin and shocked his lungs and drove burning needles of pain inside his ears. He had never heard such an exhilarating and terrible sound before; he had never imagined human beings could make such a sound.

"You spoke well," Bardo said to him when he returned to the warming pavilion.

Danlo nodded to him and then grabbed up his parka, fur hat, and a wind mask. He wanted to listen to the remaining testaments as one of the people, and so he silently bowed to Bardo and to Thomas Rane, and he left the warming pavilion. He ran down the steps at the rear of the stage. He walked along the rim of the ice ring, into the edge of the manswarm. With a black wind mask covering his face, no one recognized him as the man who had just spoken to them of remembrance and the One memory. Slowly, brushing fur to fur past hundreds of people, he made his way toward the center of the ring. All about him were the smells of bubbling cheeses, sweetmeats, and bread mingled with the thrilling aroma of toalache. And everywhere, the triya seeds burning and popping, and the pungent skin greases worn against the cold, and the vapors of hot beer. Everyone seemed excited. A few nimspinners, in their heated silks, danced about ecstatically, but most people stood in their places, shifting from boot to boot atop the packed, squeaking snow. They stood facing the southern segment of the ring. Danlo could not help thinking that no important ceremony should be made facing south. One hundred thousand people faced the wrong way as they chatted and conferred with each other, and craned their necks toward the stage. Danlo was taller than most of them, and he could clearly see Nirvelli as she stretched her arms wide like a bird and spoke of the joy of remembrancing the Elder Eddas. She was a lithe and beautiful woman with skin as black as space, and she spoke of joy as a force that could transform each individual, and whole civilizations, and someday, farwhen, perhaps the entire universe. Her words fell out of the night like pearls into blacking oil; they floated in the air, these indestructible words that seemed to have neither source nor direction. Danlo gazed at the stage, at Nirvelli's distant figure, and the sound of her voice spilled out behind him, below him, and all around.

Everything is alive with joy, just sheer joy; creating joy is the purpose of the universe.

When it was Hanuman's turn to speak the people near Danlo, and all over the ice ring, fell silent. They could not have known what was to come. Yet, they must have had some presentiment of a great event, for when Hanuman took the stage, every mouth was still and every eye rigid. Danlo, too, watched in fascination as Hanuman stepped out to the stage's very edge. In his flapping orange robes and intense manner, from a hundred yards away, he seemed like single flame alone against the dark horizon. And then he threw back his head and lifted his face to the heavens; he held his hands above him, and his voice blazed out: "He is watching us, now, at this moment, as we stand beneath the stars he knew so well."

Danlo had wondered if Hanuman would recount his great remembrance, and it soon became clear that he would speak of nothing else, but only indirectly. His voice fell over Danlo like a silvery, three-dimensional net of sound. The twenty-three great, gleaming sulki grids around the ring convolved echoes, reverberations, and acoustic cues, rolling these components together to produce a perfect holophonic sound. Danlo perceived Hanuman's words as if Hanuman were standing close by, whispering them in his ear. Or shouting them at his heart. That is the nature of this abused technology, to make it impossible to distinguish

527

simulated sounds and images from events occurring in the real world. Each person in the ice ring that night experienced Hanuman's words in a similiar manner. And almost each of them experienced his words uniquely. Around the ring, mounted unobtrusively, were hundreds of computer eyes that fixed on the people's faces and read them as they smiled and gesticulated and moved about. The emotions and mindsets of a hundred thousand people, moment by moment, were sorted and coded into information. Hanuman had smuggled in a cetic computer that made use of this information; he had been the sole architect of a hideously complex program that tailored his words according to the configuration of each person's face. Or rather, it colored his voice and intonation and stress syllables, and coded these sounds into the sulki grids so that each person was touched in a unique way. Thus everyone heard the same sermon, yet for everyone it was slightly different. This was a triumph of the cetic art. Danlo marveled that Hanuman could manipulate so many people in so many different ways. (Just as it appalled him that Hanuman would do such a thing.) He stood behind a fat wormrunner listening as Hanuman spoke of the suffering and evil of the world, and he wondered what murmurs and lamentations those around him were hearing. He stepped closer to the stage, the better to listen, but Hanuman's dreadful voice surrounded and followed him like a cloud of buzzing flies, and did not change: "And what is the first thing that Mallory Ringess would see when he looks at us? He would see, and he does see, that each of us is suffering; each of us burns with the pain of pure being."

It occurred to Danlo that with the leather wind mask covering his face, the computer eyes could not read him, and therefore Hanuman's computer could not find the specific sound keys to manipulate his mood. Perhaps he, of all the maskless people around him, was the only one to hear Hanuman's silver voice just as it really was.

"All things are on fire," Hanuman said, and his voice sizzled in the air. "Atoms are on fire, and electrons, and nuclei stripped to plasma are on fire. The rocks in the mountains are on fire. The air is on fire, and the ice of the sea, and the stars, all the stars in all the galaxies across the sky are on fire. The Vild stars are exploding into fire one by one. And with what are these things on fire? They burn with the fire of pure being; they are afire with pure consciousness, the primeval urge to be, to organize into forms, to interconnect with other forms, to evolve."

528

Danlo closed his eyes, the better to hear Hanuman's voice more clearly. It was a marvelous voice, a powerful voice cut with the inflections of thousands of other voices from other times and other places. In this one beautiful voice, he heard the joy and menace of the warrior-poet, as well as dreamy tones of an autist. There was the nobility and command and cruelty of Old Earth's war kings, the whining and the solemnity of the priest, the sing-song grandeur of a rabbi saying kaddish for the dead. And further back, to the forests and steppes of Urasia, in Hanuman's pulsating vocal chords, he heard the chanting and the drumbeat of the shaman. Every wisdom, artifice, and discovery of philosophy seemed to flow into Hanuman's voice and strengthen it, charging it with an electric energy. There was infinite subtlety in his words, the refinements of century upon century of man communicating his visions to others. Yet, despite all the evolution and art of the cetics, in the deepest part of Hanuman's voice there vibrated a singular, primeval sound. It was the howl of an animal crying out in hunger or pain or sheer longing at the sight of the winter moon. It broke from Hanuman's throat as it must have broken upon grassy veld of Afarique a million years ago. All of history was only an elaboration upon this single howl. Danlo listened as Hanuman spoke on and on, and the howl intensified and deepened and wound back upon itself until it drew out high and insistent, like the repetitive sob of a child crying for his mother. This cry was buried in each of Hanuman's words; perhaps it was buried in the chests and cells and atoms of a hundred thousand people standing in the snow, and in all women and men who had ever lived, or who ever *would* live, across all the galaxies' stars and worlds. This long, dark, endless cry from Hanuman's heart was terrible to hear, and the sound of it burned like fire in Danlo's ears.

"All the living things of the world are on fire," Hanuman said. "The trees on the hillsides are on fire, and the bacteria which are too small to see, and the snowworms, and the sleekits, and the shagshay lambs crying for their mothers' milk. The tigers in the forests at night—they burn so brightly it wounds the eyes. You, who listen to these words tonight, are on fire. *I* am on fire. And with what are we all on fire? We burn with the fire of pure being; we are afire with pure consciousness, the primeval urge to be, to organize ourselves into new forms, to interconnect with other forms, to evolve. We burn with the fire of passion for life, and with pain, with fear, with birth, old age, and death. With hatred, misery, sorrow, lamentation, and suffering are we on fire. What is humankind but a knot of flames burning with nostalgia for the infinite? We burn with the urge to overcome ourselves and with the terror of failing to evolve. We are afire with our possibilities, with what we might become. With dread, with longing, with despair are we on fire."

Here Hanuman dropped his hands to his sides and paused to take a breath of air. And then he raised his hands again; he held them out toward the ice ring as if beckoning, as if conjuring some force that only he could see. Danlo could not help staring at him; all around the ring, everyone was staring, stamping their boots, breathing out their steamy breaths, and coughing at the cold air. Then Hanuman's flowing robes burst into flames, and all at once the people across the ring let out a great cry. Hanuman's robes burned as if soaked with sihu oil; smokeless orange flames shot up and writhed about his body and limbs, completely enveloping him. Danlo watched to see him gasp in pain, to see his skin blacken and burst open in running red cracks. But, of course, no such thing happened. Hanuman held his hands out and smiled sadly—Danlo had exceptional eyes, and from a hundred yards away he could see this smile of twisted compassion break across his face. Hanuman remained untouched by the flames because there were no flames, just light made and shaped by the sulki grids into the image of flames. It was only an illusion, a simulation of fire, though hardly less compelling for not being real.

"All things are on fire," Hanuman said, "and we are each of us on fire, and everything tells us this is so. Our eyes are on fire; whatever we see is on fire; eye-consciousness is on fire; images received by the eye are on fire; and whatever sensation or thought these images engender inside us, that too is on fire."

Suddenly, at many points across the ring, many people seemed to ignite into sheets of crimson fire. Flame tongues licked the panicked face of an autist near Danlo, and passed to a horologe, whose red robe was suddenly a shroud of fire burning around him. Danlo counted a hundred of these human torches before he gave up and concentrated on what Hanuman was saying.

"And with what are our eyes on fire? With the fire of passion for life, and with pain, with fear, with birth, old age, and death. With hatred, misery, sorrow, lamentation, and suffering. The whole of our being burns to behold our possibilities, and what we might become. With dread, with longing, with terror, with despair are we on fire."

Now many thousands of people were ablaze with illusory flames. Many screamed in alarm; for a moment it seemed possible there might be a riot and a stampede. But then scores of harijan and nimspinners flung their arms above their heads and danced about ecstatically, and the mood of the manswarm segued from near panic to mass fervor. In any large gathering of people, there is always the intoxification of the swarm, the surrendering of the individual's personality to group consciousness. The people near Danlo ached to be part of this consciousness; they longed to *create* this consciousness, this higher identity, this incendiary religious frenzy. And so they touched each other's garments, and they watched each other as they clapped their hands and smiled and swayed back and forth upon the hard-packed snow, and their hundred thousand voices sang out as a single voice, a long, dark roar that split the night like winter thunder. They let their separate selves burn away like so many thousands of matches, annihilating themselves in an all-consuming transcendence. The ice ring was full of this fire that Hanuman had made. And full of the other fire as well. Between Danlo and the stage where Hanuman stood was a roiling wall of chrome-red fire. Had it been a real fire of hot, glowing gases, no one could have seen through it. But the fire was only of light and evanescence, and everywhere Danlo looked, he saw men and women dancing or shaking or staring up at Hanuman. Their eyes burned with dread and longing and terror, but their faces were now blazing with an emotion that was the opposite of despair.

Hanuman held his flaming hands out toward Danlo and the other people, and he motioned for silence. "It is said that there is a way to be freed from this burning. If our eyes are afire, we should cover them with damp cloths. If our ears burn, we should stop them with wax. We should conceive an aversion for images, and sounds, and smells, and tastes, and information, and for all things that might touch our body or that we might touch. It is said that we must renounce sensations, and whatever thoughts or ideas these sensations engender in our minds. We must conceive an aversion to mind consciousness, and to the mind itself. For all the things of the world we must conceive an aversion lest we become attached to them and to our burning for them. It is said that in this renunciation we may become divested of passion, and by the absence of passion we become free, and thus we become aware that we are free, and then there is nothing in life that can cause us to suffer and burn."

As he said this, the flames flowing around him seemed to take on a hotter, bluer color. He moved about the stage in an intensely kinetic manner, gesturing and twisting and beckoning as if a real fire were burning him, from without and within. At times he would stand perfectly still, posing as one possessed by a vast energy. And then he would move again and give voice to his passions, and everything about him was alive, compelling, and fey.

"It is said that you should renounce all things in order to quench the fire in yourselves, but this is the way of a vegetable or a buddha or a stone, not a human being. A true human being burns to be more, and as long as you burn, you belong to life. *This* is also said: You must consume yourself in your own flame; how could you wish to become new unless you had first become ashes? This is what I've remembered and what I've felt and what I've seen: Whoever would shine brightest must endure burning. For a true human being, there is no other way."

Across the ice ring, fairy flames of cobalt and blue jumped from garment to garment, from person to person. Then the flames at last reached Danlo, and he too seemed to catch fire. Flames leapt from his furs, from his eyes, from his wild hair and crackled along his white feather. Almost all the people in the ice ring were now burning with this single, deep blue fire.

Each man and woman is a star.

These words were very close to Danlo, as near as the arteries throbbing in his ears. His whole body was aflame with brilliant blue fire. He held up his blazing hands before his eyes, and he marveled that the fire had no heat to it and could not really touch him. Despite the flames, the air surrounding him was still frigid, and his fingertips and toes burned not with fire, but with bitter cold.

"Each man and woman is a star!" Hanuman called out. The flames falling over him suddenly billowed out in a ball of cobalt fire and light. "Starfire is the hottest fire, the pure fire, the refining fire that would burn away the weakest and most ignoble parts of ourselves. Whoever would give light must endure burning. We must burn for a higher organization of our beings, burn for more and deeper consciousness, burn for more life. We must each consume ourselves in our own flames. Only then will a vaster self be born who is a master of fire. Only then will the burning for the infinite lights be understood. Only then can a true human being become himself. Only then can a god let birth, old age, and death burn away and be no more.

532

"I must speak to you of the god within each of us. This god is lord of fire and light. This god *is* fire and light, and is nothing but fire and light. Each of us is this god. Each man and woman is a star that burns on and on with infinite possibilities. I must speak tonight of becoming this star, this eternal and infinite flame. Only by becoming fire will you ever be free from burning. Only by becoming fire will you become free of pain, free of fear, free of hatred, sorrow, lamentation, suffering, and despair. This is the way of the gods. This is the way of the Ringess, to burn with the fire of a new being, to shine with a new consciousness as bright as all the stars, as vast and perfect and indestructible as all the universe. This is the way of Mallory Ringess, who watches over all the people in the City where he was once as human as you and I."

When Hanuman had finished speaking, he stood with his hands held out over the people's heads, as in a formal blessing, then he swept his arms up toward the sky. He was at once exhausted and exultant, panting and sweating and shivering in the cold. He burned and twisted inside of a sphere of blue fire that filled the whole of the ice ring. The kiosks were on fire, and the food tables, and the mugs of foamy black beer, and the toalache pipes, and the multrum stalls, and the warming pavilions, and the ice beneath the people's boots—all and everything blazed with bluish flames. The air itself was on fire. And then this fireball exploded upward into the night. Hanuman looked up, and Danlo, and all at once a hundred thousand heads snapped back upon their necks. Flames of violet and indigo shot high above the ice ring. A column of fire swelled and blazed and streamed from ice to sky. Flames of crimson, copper, and orchid-pink leapt from man to woman and fed the vast fiery column pushing its way upward above them. All at once, the people near Danlo gasped and cried out with a single, great, bellowing voice. Danlo, too, was caught up in the brilliance of the moment, swept up with topaz flames, connected to this spectacular event despite all his doubts. He hadn't known that Hanuman had programmed his computers to generate such a compelling illusion; he had never guessed such a thing was possible. He held his hand shielding his eyes as he looked up. The flame column was now a quarter mile wide and seemed almost as high as the peaks of the mountains. Blazing streamers of orange and green and iron-red—and every other color—disappeared into the sky. It seemed that there was no limit to this upward rush of fire, that it might burn hotter and brighter and ignite all the atmosphere.

But there was indeed a limit. The sulki grids, which Bardo had leased from a renegade phantast, could cast their illusions only so far. Ten thousand feet above the City the flames died into the night, a limit to this sophisticated technology that Hanuman li Tosh apparently could not accept. As all would soon see, he sought to manufacture an even greater illusion, or rather a mass illumination that no one would ever forget. Suddenly the flames went out. There was only darkness in the sky. To Danlo's eyes, and to a hundred thousand pairs of eyes dazzled by fire, the people and the bright pavilions and all the other features of the ice ring were suddenly lost in a sea of vibrating blackness. And then there was light, again, an instant surge of blinding lights that stabbed into Danlo's brain and made him fling his arm over his face. Around the rim of the ice ring, the moonlights had come on. Hanuman had ordered this so, and the moonlights and the lasers beamed great rivers of light up over the ice ring and high above the City. The hundreds of incandescent beams touched and wove together in a luminous dome that filled the sky. Photons burned through the air and were scattered and reflected by tiny ice crystals high in the atmosphere. *Through* the atmosphere, above all ice and air. The moonlights blazed up fifty miles above the planet and illuminated the microorganisms and ionized gases of the Golden Ring. A shower of light fell across the sky; it framed the ice ring and much of heavens above the City, this shimmering, golden cathedral of light.

Hanu, Hanu, why have you betrayed yourself?

Danlo stood gazing upward at the splendid lights as he wondered about everything that Hanuman had said and done. In truth, Hanuman had betrayed Bardo and the Way of Ringess, for they had planned to loom the moonlights only at the end of the joyance, when Bardo led the kalla ceremony.

Only by becoming fire will you ever be free from burning.

Danlo was suddenly very aware of his hot breath stifling him beneath his wind mask, so he pulled the sodden piece of leather away from his face. No one noticed him, or recognized him as the son of Mallory Ringess. The eyes of all around him were held up toward the lights in the sky. Thousands of boots crunched against snow; the air was broken with moans and coughs and muffled cries. A gasp deeper than the wind rushed from ten thousand lips all at once and blew across the ice ring. How many people, Danlo wondered, would believe what Hanuman had told them? How many would look up at the golden sky and open themselves to what Hanuman had said was the truth?

Each man and woman is a star.

There was a man, standing near Danlo, a itinerant cantor of the Order dressed all in gray. His face was as thin as cut ice, and it bore the tired and wary look of one who has seen all there is to see. The collar of his traveling robe was embroidered with the blazons of many planets: Yarkona, Solsken, Alumit, Arcite, and other places where he had taught his art of pure mathematics. Clearly, he was a gypsy scholar who had never attained his mastership; like all his kind, he was doomed to wander the planets of the Civilized Worlds, teaching at the Order's elite schools and dreaming of the day when he might return to Neverness. And at last he had returned, not in triumph as a master, but as a pilgrim on sabbatical seeking the holy city of his youth. At first sight, he seemed still a youth, with his creamy, unlined skin and his aching awareness of his muscular pose. But he was far from being young, as Danlo could clearly see. His eyes glowed bright purple with the light of luminescent bacteria colonies implanted in his irises. This was a look fashionable a hundred years ago, but now considered quite gauche. This poor, outworn man's flesh had recently been restored, his bulky new muscles regrown under the pull of artificially induced gravities. He was clumsy and uneasy in his new body, and everything about his posture bespoke old habits, hardened reflexes, the armoring of body and mind built up over two lifetimes of suffering. That he suffered, anyone might have noticed. He suffered from his bitterness and disappointment with life. He was afire with every kind of sorrow, lamentation, and despair. His was the agony lost love and broken dreams and hatred of all the hurts and inanities of all the worlds he had known. And yet, even this empty eggshell of a man stood beneath the lights that Hanuman made, and his face came alive with a golden radiance. He was far too proud to fall into exaltation, and yet the lights in the sky touched him and quickened his whole being, and perhaps caused him to wonder if all the secrets and possibilities of the universe might still be within his grasp.

Each man and woman is a star.

If a cynical, old Orderman could look up at the sky and burn to become something new, then what of all the others? Everywhere Danlo looked, the faces of the manswarm were bright with wonder and hope: one hundred thousand faces afire with longing, with the overwhelming need to be released from their suffering. Hanuman had told them that if only they endured the holy fire long enough, they might be freed from burning. They might become pure fire and light, and be free to create their own possibilities.

Each man and woman is a star.

Danlo pushed closer to the stage, past musty hats and the smells of perfume, sweat, and excitement. He squeezed by awestruck women staring at the sky. He, himself, had eyes only for Hanuman, and he sought him out where he stood at the edge of the stage. Hanuman, though, was still frozen like a statue with his arms raised and his head thrown back. His eyes were closed and his face twisted as if he had fallen into a deep ecstasy. Or deeper into the fire that can never be quenched.

"Hanu, Hanu," Danlo whispered, "why couldn't you tell them the truth?"

Each man and woman is a star.

In truth, all things burned with a unique life, and just as human beings suffered more than did the snowworms or stones, the pain of the gods was infinitely greater than any man or woman could ever know. The whole universe burned with pain, from the Pavo Indus to the Ursa Major Cloud of galaxies. No god, however brilliant or vast, could ever escape this pain, and Danlo wanted to tell Hanuman this. He wanted to tell Hanuman, and tell everyone, that, yes, they could become gods, if this was their genius, if this was their fate, but only the cool and timeless depths of Elder Eddas could ever heal them of their suffering. But he no longer had the stage, and his moment for speaking the truth was past.

After a while, Hanuman opened his eyes and smiled as the people let loose a tremendous cheer. The whole ice ring shook with the sound of it. Hanuman returned to the warming pavilion, then. The moonlights were still gleaming when a furious Bardo stamped across the stage and gave his testament, and then guided the dazzled swarms through a mass (and false) kalla ceremony. Cadres of newer Ringists, acting as guides, distributed jiggers of seawater in the thousands. (It should be noted that Jonathan Hur went among the people in secret, passing out slip tubes of real kalla to anyone who sought the Elder Eddas. The kalla fellowship—and many, many others—soon gathered near the stage and lost themselves in true remembrance.) This salty water was drunk, ritually, mechanically. It was affirmed that Mallory Ringess became a real god and would one day return to Neverness. It was revealed that he had given humankind the secrets of the Elder Eddas in order to guide all the race into godhood. It was repeated that human beings could become as gods if, and only if, they would follow the Way of the Ringess. Next to the marvels that Hanuman had wrought, the ceremony seemed hollow and meaningless. The people sipped their water and made their professions of faith, and all the while they stood beneath the golden sky, and their eyes glowed with the heavenly lights, and wonder was written across their faces.

When the ceremony was finally finished, they began talking among themselves, in whispers and hoarse voices and relieved laughter, tens of thousands of sudden little conversations. Many were skeptical of all they had seen during the joyance; many regretted losing their time and freezing their faces in such a cold, windy place. They left the ice ring quickly. But of all who remained to be with each other and drink hot beer that night, it was agreed that the joyance was a great success, that Hanuman li Tosh was a very great man, and, most importantly, that each of the thousands of women and men spread out over the ice ring did indeed burn with the fire of the stars.

THE PEARL

My womb is memory; in that I place the seed.
Thus all created things are born. Everything
born, Arjuna, comes from the womb of
memory, and I am the seed-giving father.

—from The Bhagavad Gita

Looking backward at the turbid flow of history, or looking forward into the evolution of human and artificial life within the galaxy, Hanuman's Fire Sermon can be seen as a signal event. It was the moment when the religion of Ringism announced itself to the universe. Its effect upon the Order was immediate and profound: in the early days of deep winter in the year 2953, many professionals and academicians began attending joyances inside the cathedral that Bardo had bought. Many embraced what would come to be called the three pillars of Ringism: that Mallory Ringess became a real god and would one day return to Neverness; that he had given humanity the secrets of the Elder Eddas in order to guide all the race into godhood; and that human beings could become as gods if, and only if, they would follow the Way of the Ringess. Quite a few prominent masters and lords—Kolenya Mor, Hugh wi Siri Sarkisian, Jonath Parsons, Daru Penhallegon, and others—entered the nave of the cathedral and knelt on the cold stone floor as they made their professions of faith, along with hundreds of new godlings from across the City. Just thirty years previously, during the lordship of the Timekeeper, the Order never would have tolerated this kind of religiosity among its members. To keep order within the stone buildings of the Academy, lords and masters would have been debased, journeymen chastised, and novices forbidden to take vows. But the Timekeeper was nineteen years dead, and a war had been fought among the pilots; now there was devisiveness within the College of Lords. No one really ruled the Order. The four lords of the Tetrad, as a whole, never gained the kind of total power that the Timekeeper had wielded. And they never really functioned as a whole. Chanoth Chen Ciceron railed against Ringism and Ringists while the quiet-spoken Nikolos the Elder advised restraint. Mariam Erendira Vasquez, perhaps guilty at having denied Danlo's petition to save the Alaloi, was quite taken by the stories of his great remembrance. Quite openly, she championed the exploration of the Elder Eddas, if only by using the traditional techniques of the remembrancers, and not through Thomas Rane's kalla ceremonies. And as for the mysterious Lord Pall, no one could tell whether he wanted to destroy the new religion or merely subvert it.

On the thirty-fourth of deep winter, at an open convocation of the Lords' College, Chanoth Chen Ciceron scolded Lord Pall for allowing the most brilliant of his journeyman cetics to fall into collusion with the demagogue-prophet of a new religion. "The Lord Pall must explain to us why Hanuman li Tosh hasn't been chastised for violating his ethics. The Lord Pall must explain why Hanuman li Tosh has been allowed contact with the renegade pilot known as The Bardo."

But, of course, Lord Pall did not have to explain anything, especially not to Chanoth Chen Ciceron, whom he must have regarded as the most obnoxious of his rivals for power. Lord Pall rubbed his pinkish, albino eyes and stood to address the lords. In his cetic's hand language, he made swift little signs that his translator interpreted to mean: "The Lord Ciceron's talents are much too elevated to waste concerning himself with a journeyman cetic. I shall deal with Hanuman li Tosh as he must be dealt with. It's true that all religions are dangerous, but we shouldn't think that we can't control this little religion of Bardo's. We shouldn't worry that we'll let the Way of Ringess, whatever that is, polarize our eternal Order."

But the Way of Ringess had already begun to polarize the Order. Or rather, its radical expansion was the final cause among many historical causes dividing the Order in two. Already, at the time Danlo had come to Neverness, hundreds of professionals had volunteered for the Vild mission because they hated the work of religions and their gods: they regarded the Vild, the light-years of exploded stars and ruined space, as the tragic work of a religious group who worshiped a god called Ede. They were sick of religiosity in all its forms, just as they were sick of the Order's omnipresent and stifling holism. They wanted to flee Neverness on a mission of freedom and deliverance, and now that their fellow Ordermen in Upplysa and Lara Sig and the other colleges were worshiping Mallory Ringess as a god, their desire to flee this madness became both a panic and a crusade. Others, those who had drunk kalla or listened to Hanuman's sermon, saw Ringism as a fresh and fiery wind that might blow away centuries of stale thoughtways and dogmas, those outworn ways of viewing the universe that, like a mechanic's equations chiseled into stone, had long been reified into the Order's most venerable institutions. They told each other that this brilliant stellar wind would breathe new life into their fellows and into their City. Although they must have worried that Ringism's growing fervor might sweep them away like so many cinders into the night, they reasoned that if only they could be a part of Ringism from its very beginning, then they might control this explosive movement. They were the elite of an elite Order, and they thought to control the malcontents and madmen who always swarm to the light of a new religion. That Hanuman li Tosh was one of this elite was their hope and pride. They listened too well to his clever words, and they didn't foresee that their adulation of him would eventually ruin the Order.

Of course, most of those who lionized Hanuman were not of the Order. They were hibakusha or harijan or autists from the poorest streets of the City. They were arhats and infolaters and princesses: Surya Surata Lal, after Hanuman's sermon, began calling him The Agni, which means "The Burning One" or "Lord of Fire," and other devoted Ringists addressed him in that manner, too. His popularity waxed so quickly that it amazed everyone, especially Bardo, who was very jealous of Hanuman's rising star. He was more than jealous; he was wounded and wroth with Hanuman for betraying him at the great joyance. "By God I'll never invite him to another joyance!" a swollen-faced Bardo said to Danlo a few days later. "I'll banish him from our goddamned church!" He might have done just that, but for all his bluster, he found Hanuman much too valuable to cast aside like a bloodfruit that had been sucked dry. Thousands of godlings flocked to Bardo's newly opened cathedral, and Bardo was sober enough—if outraged—to perceive that they came to listen to Hanuman and not to him.

Most of those who followed the Way hoped to gain some-

540

thing for themselves, whether godhood, enlightenment, mass communion, or remembrance. A few people, however, became Ringists solely because they wanted to give of their talents and themselves. Tamara Ten Ashtoreth was one of these few. It was her conceit to infuse the Way of Ringess with the ancient secrets of the Tantra that she knew so well. She clearly saw, after the night that Hanuman delivered his Fire Sermon, that the religion of Ringism was like a sacred, golden tree that might grow in any one of several different directions. As Hanuman had prophesied, it might indeed grow toward the fire of the stars, out into the universe's infinite lights. Tamara also saw that this tree of humanity would be made up of millions of people in their all-too-human bodies. She believed—this was her heart's great passion—that human bodies must be nourished as often as possible with the elixir of pure sexual energy, or else they would never come truly alive. And so her purity of heart impelled her to give herself to the Way of Ringess. However, as Danlo discovered during the coldest days of deep winter, she was a complex woman who had many reasons for doing the things that she did.

It was Danlo's pleasure to spend as many evenings and nights with Tamara as he could. These nights were always too few. Usually, in fulfillment of her professional duties, Tamara would sally out on a bitterly cold night to keep her appointments with other men (or women), quite often with the most prominent lords and masters of the Order. Danlo might have been jealous of this time lost to him, but he was not by nature a jealous man. Then, too, his early experience among the Devaki had trained him away from jealousy. The Devaki—all the Alaloi —are the most promiscuous and tolerant of peoples, at least until they make their marriages. Danlo still believed that it was unseemly for an unmarried man to be jealous of an unmarried woman.

Therefore, on those nights Tamara kept free, he would visit her at her house in the Pilot's Quarter, and he was always glad for the marvelous gifts that she gave him. He loved being alone with her in her house, which stood on a quiet street on the cliffs above North Beach. It was a small chalet of stone and naked shatterwood floors, quite austere—not at all the kind of house he would have imagined a courtesan would keep. But Tamara always met her appointments down in the Farsider's Quarter, where her Society maintained the grandest of the City's pleasure domes. Because she never invited men to her house, she had no need to please anyone but herself, and what pleased her was not dark luxuries or rich furnishings but open windows and flowering plants and floors of rare inlaid woods that she liked to dance upon, barefooted, in the style of the best Sufi dancers. Indeed, she liked to go about her house bare of any clothing at all. She could do this without fear of tantalizing her neighbors because the houses on either side of hers were kept by pilots who had been off exploring the Vild for as long as she had lived there. In her meditation room, on plain cotton cushions, she would sit naked in front of the sliding windows, looking out at the sea cliffs and the frozen waters of Neverness Sound far below. To accommodate her need for nakedness, she usually kept her house rather warm. On those nights Danlo came to visit, it was always more than warm. Tamara's fire room had two fireplaces, one on either side of the room, and she would set logs blazing in both of them before inviting Danlo to lie with her on a shagshay fur on the middle of the floor. There, in the light of the fires, she would take him through the positions of her sexual yoga. Quite often, they would begin with him sitting cross-legged on the fur in the Tortoise or Lotus position while she sat astride him. They would breathe together as they joined, muscles straining, skin gleaming, and sweating, always sweating in salty, pungent rivers that ran down the hollows of their backs. As she had told him, more than once, it was important to raise the body's heat so that he sweated freely.

One night, after a session of particularly fierce love play, Danlo lay back against the furs to catch his breath. His hair was a sodden mass of black clumps stuck to his dripping face and neck. "I am dying . . . of the heat," he said. "Couldn't we open a window?"

"Are we done?" Tamara sat near him, looking down at him, and streams of sweat ran between her wide, heavy breasts and flowed down her belly into her navel. The golden hair between her legs was thick with moisture, and her whole body glistened like cream. She used her fingers to comb her long, wet hair away from her face while she evened her breathing, then she smiled at him and said, "If we're done, why don't we go into the tea room and take our refreshments?"

They dried themselves with towels then and put on kimonos of black silk. They went into the tea room, which adjoined the meditation room. It was much cooler there. Danlo always liked the feel of the tea room, with its rosewood beams, paper walls, and clean, good smells. It was starkly decorated, but Tamara was an aficionado of beautiful things, and the few objects to be seen impressed him with their beauty: the porcelain tea service set out on a low table; a shatterwood *doffala* sculpture of a bear that had been carved by a man of one of the Alaloi tribes; and, arrayed atop the sill of the sliding windows, seven oiled stones that she had found on the beach. He sat between the table and the window, and he turned to admire these stones. The window was cracked open, letting in streams of cold sea air. Below him, below the cliffs he sometimes liked to climb, was the Starnbergersee, frozen and quiet with the cold of deep winter.

"Would you like tea or coffee?" Tamara asked.

"Tea, please. Peppermint, if you have any."

Tamara went into her kitchen to prepare their little meal. Hers was one of the few houses in the City to have a kitchen. Most people considered taking meals alone in one's own house to be a barbaric, most unsocial act, but she was a courtesan, after all, and she found it difficult to dine in public restaurants. After a while, she reentered the tea room carrying a tray laden with a teapot, silver knives and spoons, a small bowl of honey, and a larger bowl, full of bloodfruits and tangerines. She set the tray on the table and sat across from Danlo. She poured the steaming, golden tea into their little blue cups, and she served him with the precise and graceful movements that the courtesans are taught when they first learn their art.

Danlo took a sip of the scalding tea while his eyes followed her long, lovely hands. "I love watching you," he said. "The way you move."

She smiled at this compliment the way she always did, then she used her long fingernail to slice open the skin of a tangerine. She peeled it with exquisite care, in a most peculiar manner: she pulled the skin away from the meat in a single, long, twisting strip, around and around the tangerine from north pole to south. When she was done, she gave it to Danlo, who held the ends of the spiral strip between his fingers and played with it, pulling up and down, letting the peel uncoil and then coil again as if it were a bouncy orange spring. He marveled at the care she took in accomplishing little things. He loved the way she poured tea into the exact center of the cup, the way she *meditated* on the golden stream as it arched out of the teapot. Everything seemed to delight her. She seemed intensely interested in spoons or teacups, or in the clear articulation of her words as she searched his face and spoke to him. She paid attention to everything that happened around her, and she paid attention to him as no one

543

had ever done. This was her grace and her gift, to pay attention. The whole of her art was to know people intimately and help them awaken into joy. She wanted to be the bearer of joy, to spread it among the people she knew, just as she used a silver knife to spread honey over each of the tangerine sections before putting them into Danlo's mouth. It was her deep desire to let her awareness spread out and encompass every rock and snow-flake in the world, to take joy in everything, and in every act, whether it be the washing of dishes or polishing stones or joining with Danlo in slow, sweaty ecstasy. "Ecstasy lies in details," she told him one night. It was her pride to bring him to a greater ecstasy of life, and so she ate tangerines with him and talked about little things, and she listened as only a courtesan can.

"I love watching the way *you* move," she said to him as she tore apart two sections of a tangerine. "The fluidness—it must come from growing up in the wild. Civilized men move like they're made of metal."

"Have you taught many men . . . how to move?"

"I've tried," she said. "But the men of your Order are so stiff and brittle."

"I cannot believe you have not had your successes."

She bowed her head and smiled in false modesty. "No one is unteachable," she said.

Danlo wiped a drop of tangerine juice from his lip and said, "You like teaching people things, yes?"

"Some people," she admitted.

"I have wondered . . . if it is your intention to teach your art to the Ringists."

"Do you think I should?"

Danlo ate another section of tangerine, then took a sip of tea. The cold-hot mint tea brought out the fruit's acidness and quite succeeded in waking up the taste buds along his tongue. "I have wondered why you take such an interest in the Way. I have wondered why any of us have. You want to wake people up—you have said that before. The cells of our bodies, to wake them up so that we can live . . . as true human beings. But this does not accord very well with the third pillar, does it?"

Tamara took a bite of tangerine and smiled. "Which is the third pillar? I keep forgetting."

" 'That human beings can become as gods if, and only if, they will follow the Way of the Ringess,' " he quoted.

"But don't you think we should become fully human before we go off becoming gods?"

"Does it matter . . . what I think?"

"It matters very much."

"Then I think that you should teach your art to Ringists," he said. "You were born to teach these things, yes?"

She nodded her head, then she picked up a bloodfruit and examined it as if it were a diamond and she were looking for the perfect way to cut it. "Even when I was a little girl," she said, "I wanted to be a courtesan. Of course, so many do, and so many are turned away, but I always had a *sense* that this was my calling, that I'd be very unhappy if I were turned away, too."

Danlo smiled at her and said, "But how could they have turned you away? You are the most beautiful person I have ever known."

For a while she laughed easily with a rich, musical laughter. Then her face fell serious and she said, "You know it's thoughtless of you to flatter me as you do. I've always been much too vain."

In truth, she *was* quite vain, and she hated being so, even though she tried to accept this part of herself in a graceful and natural manner, as she did everything else.

"You are what you are," he said.

"And you're not completely glad that I do what I do, are you?"

"It limits certain possibilities between us," he admitted.

"Are you speaking of marriage again?"

He nodded his head. "Marriage, yes, but not just that. The making of a family . . . a true union."

"Is that so important to you?"

"In the end, it is everything," he said. He turned and pressed his forehead to the cold window before saying, "Ever since I came to the City, I have lived . . . for myself. *My* quests, *my* misfortunes, *my* dreams. This is the civilized way. So many here do the same. Even the professionals and pilots. We are supposed to give ourselves to the Order, yes? We *crave* this giving. To sacrifice a part of our lives for a greater life . . . as part of something greater than ourselves. Everyone knows this. This is the ideal, but few achieve it, I think. The Order is dead—everyone is saying this—and so we turn to the Way to fill the hollowness. But it cannot be filled by crowding elbow to elbow into a cathedral. Or by kneeling together while Bardo gives us a taste of seawater. At least, *I* cannot . . . fill myself this way. I would be glad to leave the City forever, if it were not for you. What we could make together. Call it marriage or union, it does

545

not matter. It would be something splendid. Blessed. It is what we were meant for. I see that now. I was blind for so long. When my tribe died . . . I died. A part of me. But now—I never dreamed that anyone like you existed. Now, these nights here, I am alive again. For the first time in a long time, I think I am truly sane."

He finished talking, and he slid open the window to let in some fresh air. The night was cold and clear; far below, the frozen waves of the Sound sparkled in the starlight. And beyond the Sound, the mountains rose up and loomed upon the horizon like dark, ancient gods.

Tamara came over to him and knelt by his side. Despite the serious lines of her face, her eyes were sparkling. She touched his hand with her fingers, and she said, "You're a beautiful man and you always speak so beautifully. But is it fair to speak of marriage when you're forbidden to marry?"

He turned his head and looked at her. "I am still a journeyman—I have not taken my pilot's vows."

"But you will soon, won't you? They'll forbid you to marry, and then you'll be chosen for the Vild mission, and we'll have to say farewell because you'll be gone forever."

"Not . . . forever."

"Would you return to Neverness?"

"As soon as I could. As soon as I find a cure for the plague. *If* there is a cure."

"I understand—you have to complete your quest."

He shrugged his shoulders, a habit he had acquired only since his admission to Resa. "You could call it a quest, if you would like."

"You'll complete your quest, and heal your Alaloi, of course. And then? What would we have become? I've heard the stories of women who wait for pilots to return."

"Do you mean the problem of the time distortions?" he asked.

"I've heard of pilots that age three years to their paramour's thirty."

"Those are einsteinian distortions," he said. "Sometimes, they are offset by the distortions of the manifold."

She looked at him and said, "Slowtime and dreamtime speed up body and brain, isn't that true? They speed up the interior time, the *intime*."

He smiled and squeezed her hand. "I keep forgetting that you know . . . almost everything."

"Not everything," she said. "I wouldn't know how to be married to a pilot. I don't think I'd know how to be married to anyone."

She spoke of many things, then, that she had been reluctant to reveal. They drank tea and ate bloodfruits, and she told him about her dreams and her secrets and her fears, especially the fear that all courtesans have: that of growing older more quickly than other people do. Because courtesans bring themselves back their youths after only twenty years of aging, and because they can only make themselves young again three or four times, they must face their final old age much sooner than others. She feared growing old, and she feared losing her beauty, but more than anything else, she was afraid of what she might have become if the Society had not accepted her as a novice twelve years previously. "If I hadn't left home I would have died," she told him. "I would have grown up to become like my mother, and that would have killed my soul. I'd be dead inside, just like everyone else."

That night, after she had shut the window and stripped off her kimono so that she could sit more comfortably, she told him about her extraordinary family. She had come from a large astrier family who had settled more or less permanently in Neverness. Of course, all astrier families are large, and hers was in no way distinguished because of its size: she was the tenth of thirty-two children, most of whom still lived with her parents in a huge house in the Farsider's Quarter. Although it was unlikely that her family would ever achieve the ideal of a hundred children, her mother was still quite fertile, and she continued to give birth year after year. On five different occasions, she had borne twins, and once, quadruplets. Tamara suspected that her mother was really quite sick of breeding babies (as she put it, "the way furflies breed little white maggots"), but she was an Ashtoreth, an old and proud family who traced their line of descent, mother and daughter, back more than a thousand years to Alexandra Evangelina Ashtoreth. Alexandra was perhaps the most famous mother in history: half of her children had converted to the new religion of Edeism and established the Ashtoreth name, while the other half had carked their DNA and had claded off into the alien race known as the Hulda. The Hulda had disappeared into obscure parts of the galaxy, while the Ashtoreth family, in their millions, had gone on to populate planets. And cities: one of Tamara's ancestors had immigrated to Neverness and established her family there. Many Ashtoreths, over the centuries, had since left the City but many remained. Just south of the Winter Ring, where the Serpentine winds toward South Beach, the houses and apartments were overflowing with Ashtoreths. In fact, this district is known as the Ashtoreth District, and Tamara could count some ninety thousand cousins, nieces, and great-grandaunts who bore her name. The Ashtoreths were not the only astriers in the City, but they were exemplars of their religion, and they upheld their traditions in the strictist manner. Tamara's mother—her name was Victoria One Ashtoreth—in many ways was the quintessential astrier matron: imperious, practical, materialistic, deceitful, and intensely critical. She was fiercely loving, too, and self-sacrificing, patient, proud, and terribly vain. Tamara's greatest fear in life was that she would grow to become like her mother. And she nearly had. When she was eleven years old, her mother had betrothed her to a rich astrier man ten years her senior. She was expected to wait seven years, to marry, and then begin bearing children. A great swarm of children: astriers—those who followed any of the Edeic religions —were required to conceive as many children as possible, to ensoul as much consciousness as possible, miraculously transmuting dead matter into human beings so that, at the end of time, the entire life consciousness of the universe would be united and vastened in Ede the God. By fleeing to the Society of Courtesans, Tamara had escaped this fate of "cancerous motherhood." The very idea of marriage aroused in her intense anxiety and dread, and she usually avoided talking about it. And so, for the first time, as she clutched at Danlo's hand and gulped her tea, she spoke in her sad, bittersweet voice, and she told him why she could never marry him and be his wife.

"Marriage is the most horrible of all traps," she said. "Once a woman begins having babies, there are *too* many details to attend to, and no time for ecstasy."

Danlo stroked her hand and said, "But doesn't it seem to you that astrier marriages . . . are extreme."

"Marriage is marriage," she said. "Even your Alaloi bear a good many children."

"Yes, they do," he said. He touched the scar above his eye as he thought about the Alaloi tribes. "But many of the children die before they are named."

"And so the women continue having more babies."

"Yes . . . but not to replace those who have gone over. At least, not *just* to replace them." He held his hand over his forehead, remembering. "The women of my tribe were very passion-

548

ate. Their cries, coming from the snow huts deep in the cave—this could keep us awake all night, especially in deep winter when there is almost no end to night. The wives of the men—they knew about ecstasy. They did not need religion to encourage them to lie with their husbands."

Tamara pulled at the dark hairs on his forearm, then she said, "Did the Devaki marry for life?"

"They married for *eternity*," he said. As he ate succulent pieces of bloodfruit, he told her something of the Alaloi beliefs concerning the world of spirits. A man's spirit, he explained—his first self—came into the world naked and alone, cut off from selves of all living things. But each man had a *doffel*, an other-self, a special and magical animal that he was not permitted to hunt. It was a man's first duty, when his membrum was cut and he first became a man, to enter into the dreamtime and identify this other-self. If he were a full man, his spirit would merge with that of his other-self, mystically, and he would become his deep self, his true self that lived in eternity. He would become a part of the World-soul. Only then could his deep self seek out that of the one woman fated to be his wife. How an Alaloi woman became her deepest self was a secret that he did not know. He knew only that the completed spirits of man and woman would share eternity together, and they would give birth to other spirits, the spirits of their children, and in this way life went on.

"The Alaloi theology is complex but very beautiful," she said. Her face was glowing and her eyes were alive with interest. "Your Alaloi are a romantic people."

"Yes . . . they can be," he said. He listened carefully to the way she said the word "romantic." He sensed that, at heart, she was a romantic woman who had concealed many of her desires.

"You're still an Alaloi man in your soul, aren't you?" she asked. "A wild, wild man."

In truth, Tamara Ten Ashtoreth loved men as she did life, and for many years she had dreamed of making a marriage based on the merging of two souls. She had even dreamed of bearing children, two children, a boy and a girl. She had kept this dream a secret; she regarded it as a silly notion of her childhood self, and she was ashamed of longing for a kind of union that her mother would have called "a selfish desire and really quite impossible." In an age when few married for love, and fewer still for life, this was certainly an impractical desire, if not quite impossible. She must have dreaded that Danlo would reawaken this desire in her, only to abandon her, perhaps for the sake of his various quests, or to become a god, or because he had found something coiled in the secret part of her: a ravenous and terrible beauty that one day might quicken into life and devour him.

"You really wouldn't want to marry me," she said.

"I think . . . I do," Danlo said.

Slowly, she ate a slice of bloodfruit as she looked at him. "Would you give up your quest, the whole Vild mission, to marry?"

The room was quiet for a long time before he finally said, "Yes, I think I would."

"Well, you shouldn't even consider such things," she said. "You shouldn't ever abandon your dreams."

"But I have . . . another dream, now."

"And your people? The Alaloi?"

"*Lalashu,*" he said, "the blessed People . . . are doomed. I think I have known that for five years."

"But could you just abandon them without being certain?"

Danlo stood and paced around the room then. The wooden floor tiles squeaked in rhythm with his heavy footsteps. After a while he paused before the window and stared out at the frozen sea. "No," he finally said, "I could not abandon them. Even if they are doomed. Especially . . . if they are fated to die."

"And I couldn't turn away from the Society," Tamara said. She stood up and came over beside him. "Not now."

"Because you have a calling," he said. He licked his teeth, which were coated with the bittersweet taste of bloodfruit.

"I'm *involved* with the Way of Ringess," she said. "Many of us are."

Danlo laughed softly, then said, "It is ironic: Bardo thinks he is converting the courtesans . . . but it is really the reverse, yes?"

"We don't try to convert anyone."

"Hanuman believes differently."

"Hanuman," she said. "He's such a difficult man."

"Is that why you avoid him?"

"But he's impossible to avoid, I think. He's quite insistent about what he wants."

"He wants to make a new religion," Danlo said.

"But we're all making this religion, aren't we? All of us who are involved in the Way. Even you, Danlo. We can make it a living religion, or let it die, like so many others have died."

550

"And then?"

"What do you mean?"

"If I completed my quest," he said, "and if your calling were successful and you awakened every Ringist in the galaxy . . . what then?"

"Then it would be *then*," she said.

"If I quit the Order, would you quit the Society?"

"To marry you?"

"To marry . . . yes."

She faced him and reached out to stroke the long hair behind his neck. She kissed his lips, then she smiled and said, "I can't look into the future the way you can. Now it's *now,* and that's all that really matters. It's very late, you know. Why don't we sleep now and forget about things that may or may not ever happen?"

She took his hand and led him back into the fire room, which doubled as her sleeping chamber. The fires had burned down to red embers, and the room was now almost dark and much too cool for sweating. In fact, it was quite cold, and they needed to pull sheets and blankets over their bottom fur to keep warm. They lay holding each other in their silky bed, and soon Tamara was asleep, breathing softly over his face as he watched her breasts rise and fall. He lay awake watching her for a long time as he thought about the way that nowness would always become thenness, as surely as day followed night, on and on through a universe without end.

For the next couple of tendays, even as others were contemplating new doctrines and technologies that would forever change the Way of Ringess, Danlo could not forget his dream of marrying Tamara. While drinking coffee in the morning, or learning his mathematics, or, as an exercise, interfacing his lightship where it rested deep within the Lightship Caverns—many times each day he thought of his conversation with her. He concluded that she must have regarded his talk of marriage as insincere. And, in a way, he *had* been insincere. He had given her no promise to marry, no ring or disk or firestone, or other pledge of his devotion to her. He had learned enough of civilized customs to know that such pledges are not always given, that people often marry as easily and unceremoniously as they might walk into a café and place an order for roasted meatnuts. But, as

Tamara had observed, he was still an Alaloi in his heart, and Alaloi men always give pledges to the women they intend to marry. They give them alaya shells or amethysts or rings of carved ivory. Sometimes they give them pearls. Danlo remembered quite clearly the night he had met Tamara, the way he had blurted out his desire to give her a pearl to wear around her neck. She had thought him insincere then, too. But he was not insincere. Nor had he spoken idly. He was the poorest of men, much too poor to buy pearls or gemstones, but since the moment he had first seen her, he had been thinking of a way that he might give her a real pearl.

On the morning of the sixty-first, he went down to the Quay where the ice schooners were harbored in neat, colorful rows along West Beach. He arranged with the boatmaster to take a sleek, red schooner out onto the ice. From a supply hut near the mooring slips, he picked out the few supplies that he would need for a brief journey: sleeping furs; a heated tent; a cooking stove and steel utensils; ropes and climbing paraphernalia; a compass, sextant, and maps; a hammer, ice drill, shovel, chisels, knives, and heat jet; and enough food—mainly baldo nuts, dried snow apples, and cheese—to last twelve days. He planned to be gone no more than four days, but when traveling in deep winter, it was always wisest to apply the rule of three: that one should always carry three times as much food as should be needed. No one knew better than Danlo what it was like to starve while waiting out a storm far from shore. The boatmaster, when he saw the quantity of stores that Danlo was stowing into the schooner, warned him of the dangers of sailing alone in deep winter. He was a thin man with a high, reedy voice nearly lost to the early morning wind that whipped along the beach. "I shouldn't let you go, but you're a journeyman, and there's no telling journeymen what to do. Especially you pilots—what's the saying in your college? *Journeymen Die*—is that right? Be careful, Young Pilot. The sea is more dangerous than deep space. Stay close to the coast, and keep the mountains in sight. I don't imagine you could know what it's like to be lost out on the ice."

It might have been safer for him to take a dog sled instead of a schooner. As Danlo had walked down the beach, he had passed snow-covered sleds and kennels full of soft, whining dogs. He had not liked the look of these dogs; the city people used them only for sport and recreation, and he did not wish to entrust his life to ill-trained dogs whom he did not know. In truth, ever since his journey to Neverness, he could not look at a dog without his stomach knotting up tight and hard as a baldo nut. And so he balanced his gear in his schooner, and he hoisted the bright blue lateen sail. He put on his goggles and said farewell to the boatmaster, and then he was off, running before the wind. The towers of the City vanished behind him, gray stone points lost into a gray-white glare; ahead was deep blue sky and hard air and open ice that went on mile after mile. And always there was the wind that blew at his back and filled his sail and set the spun-diamond mast singing. The wind blew him due south. Most icemen who took out schooners sailed north across the Sound and then tacked against the cold, constant wind, slowly working their way up the west side of the island. The west coast of Neverness Island, cut with fiords, glaciers, and green-fir mountains, has long been known for its beauty. But that day Danlo was seeking beauty of a different kind, and so he sailed south across the open sea where the people of the City were not permitted to go.

He traveled very quickly. That is the charm of these graceful, delicate boats, to be able to move quickly across the ice. Some iceboats, the smaller skeeters or skimmers, when sailing over glass ice can reach a speed three times that of the wind. Since the wind blowing out of the northwest in deep winter is a fast, murderous wind, Danlo's concern was not keeping up his speed but controlling it. To be sure, his schooner, with its flat, skilike runners in place of steel blades, was the slowest and steadiest of all icecraft, but it was still no vehicle for the weakbrained or the cowardly. He sat low in the schooner's cockpit, clutching at the tiller as it leapt at every rill and bump. He pushed it left or right, at an instant's warning, to swerve the boat and avoid the fissures that opened in the ice just ahead of him. Very often, it was hard to see, with particles of spindrift rattling against his face mask and goggles. It was hard to breathe; he thought that everything about ice schooning was hard and cold and utterly exhilarating. The seascape, in its colors of white and silver and aquamarine, flew past beneath him at tremendous speed. The steering blade vibrated like a saw catching at the ice; the scrape of the runners over the ice shivered along his legs and up through his scrotum. More than once, the wind shifted suddenly, stealing his breath away and nearly flipping the schooner end over end. As he pulled farther away from the shore, the ice grew faster, and in places even rougher. He schussed across sets of frozen waves called *sastrugi,* and the quick stuttering bumps hurt his teeth and pounded at his spine. Ten miles out, the sea was covered with hard-packed snow, *safel*, as the Alaloi call it, the fast, smooth snow that is good for sledding. It was good for schooning, too, and in little time Danlo reached the thirty-mile markers that demarcate the boundary of Neverness Island. Ahead of him, planted in the ice at intervals of a thousand feet, was a line of red poles curving off to either horizon, east and west. The poles were bent before the wind, pointing south, as if beckoning for him to continue his journey. Long ago the lords of the Order had made a covenant with the Alaloi people that no civilized person would venture beyond these bounds. Except for the island that Neverness is built upon, the whole of the planet named Icefall was to be touched by none but the Alaloi, forever. Because Danlo would always think of himself as one of the People—and because he intended to touch land forbidden to those of the City—he sailed past the poles with the speed of the wind, and he said the prayer of all travelers setting out for unseen islands: *"Ali alli-lo kiro lisalia."*

Seventy miles south of Neverness there is an island famous for the profusion and fecundity of its bird life. The Alaloi call it "Avisalia." It is a small island of mountains, cliffs, and wide, sandy beaches. It stands between Neverness Island and the Great Southern Ocean. There, where the warm Mishima current flows close to the land shelf, the seabirds come to feed upon vast schools of herring, shoko fish, and arctic cod. Each winter, flocks of birds numbering in the tens of thousands migrate from the northern islands and build their nests there. The air above Avisalia, in deep winter, is often white with clouds of puffins, thallows, ospreys, shirkirts, and terns. And kestrels, skuas, and loons, and twenty other species of birds. The thunder of their wings and their harsh hunting calls can be heard from miles away. Most of these birds overwinter on the island's sunny southern slopes. They bask in the low, slanting sun, and they fly out over the beaches, and they use their talons or beaks to pluck silvery fish from the ocean. On the southern side of the island, the ocean flows fast and warm and it rarely freezes. On the island's northern side, however, there live different birds. There the kitikeesha come to eat the snow atop the frozen sea, and the snowy owls come to eat the kitikeesha. The gulls—the snow gulls and hunting gulls—make their roosts on the steep gray cliffs above the sea. In deep winter, when they cannot get at the meaty treasures locked up beneath the shore ice, they scavenge the leavings of bears or of other birds, or if they get hungry enough, they turn on their own kind and peck each other to death. But each year, in false winter when the ice breaks up, the shallow seabed yields up an abundance of food, and then the gulls feast. The shallows along Avisalia's north shore teem with ice crabs, spirali, and with tens of species of mollusks. And, of course, with palpulve. At low tide, the wide beach is carpeted with millions of purple-shelled palpulve. The hunting gulls like no other food better; it is their instinct to grab up a living palpulve and soar high into the air, only to drop it and dash it on the rocks below. In this way, the gulls break open the shells to get at the meat inside. In hatching season when their young constantly cry for food and give them no peace, the gulls fill their crops with the meat of hundreds of palpulve each day.

Perhaps one palpulve in ten contains a shiny bit of matter walled off from its living tissues: a pearl that grows inside it like a gleaming, stony egg. The gulls, rapacious animals that they are, gobble down palpulve meats like candy, and they make no complaint if they also swallow a pearl. It is these lustrous silvery or black pearls of the palpulve that are prized across the Civilized Worlds as the second most beautiful of all pearls. For generations, wormrunners from Neverness had flown their windjammers out to Avisalia to poach these pearls. Each false winter, they would use diamond knives to open thousands of palpulve and cut the pearls free, leaving the meat for the gulls. Each season the gulls gleefully await the coming of the wormrunners, for it saves them the work of opening the palpulve themselves.

Had Danlo sailed to Avisalia in false winter, it is likely that he would have been greeted by hungry gulls circling above his head and crying out their raucous cries. Had he gone crunching across the tidal flats in search of palpulve pearls, it is also likely that the wormrunners would have greeted him with laser fire or quick diamond knives slipped between his ribs. But he came to the island's north shore in the deepest part of deep winter, when all the world was frozen and peaceful. His journey from Neverness had taken less than a day. A hundred feet from the beach, he struck his sail and anchored his schooner onto long screws that he twisted into the ice. He erected his heated tent. Out of nostalgia for his youth, he considered building a snow hut to sleep in, but he had no ice saw for the cutting of snow blocks, nor did he have the tools to make such a saw. In truth, a heated tent was much roomier and more comfortable than any snow hut, and so he hauled his sleeping furs inside his tent, and he spent the night listening to the clary fabric flapping in the wind and to the gulls calling to each other on the cliffs high above the beach. The next morning he ate a cold, quick breakfast of cheese and flat bread, and he went to work.

Onto a small red sled, the kind a child might use to slide down a snowy hillside, he lashed his shovel, buckets, heat gun, knives, and other gear. He faced south, toward the cliffs where the gulls roosted. Their cries rose high on the morning wind. He could see them at the edge of the island, thousands of little white specks against the broken rocks. He counted ninety thousand of them before he gave up and began surveying the cliffs. The cliffs were a dark gray wall that ran along the beach for two miles. Above the cliffs there were snowfields and shatterwood forests and the dark blue sky. He looped a rope around his mittens and pulled the sled straight for the cliffs. He pulled it across frozen waves and thick-ribbed snow. Below him, beneath twelve feet of ice, were millions of palpulve, hibernating through the winter. He might have chopped through this ice and brought them up in buckets; he might have used his knife to cut them open, but that would have killed them, and this he could not do. From his early years of watching seabirds, he knew of another way of finding pearls. He pulled his sled across the shoreline, up across the frozen sands and dune scarp. Now he was closer to the foot of the cliffs, and now the screaming of the gulls drowned out all other sound. Despite the bitter cold, the rich nitrogen smell of bird droppings was overpowering. There were droppings everywhere. The whitish guano was spattered over rocks, and streaked against the cliff face, and piled up in great stinking mounds many feet thick. Up and down the beach, there were miles of guano mounds that had accumulated in layers over the years. The topmost layer was as thin as a sheet of skin; it was moist and slimy, and it was being laid down by the birds above him even as he stood there. Fresh bird droppings fell over him like warm rain, smearing his furs, spattering the lenses of his goggles. He dragged his sled across the mounds, and his boots made a *squelch-squirch* sound as the gooey new guano sucked at them and made for perilous walking. Closer to the base of the cliffs, he picked up his shovel and began digging. He cleared away the surface droppings to reveal the permanently frozen guano below. He used his heat jet to thaw this guano, layer after layer, and he dug it up and sieved through it for the pearls. Over the next two days he found many pearls. He filled his buckets with them. Each of these pearls had passed through the gizzard and vent of a palpulve-eating gull. Most of them were of poor quality, too small or misshapen or scoured by the stomach acids of the gulls. He examined and discarded 1,038 pearls before he found one that he liked. After cleaning this pearl with fresh snow, he held it up to the sunlight. It was a large pearl the size of his thumb tip; it was of an iridescent, purplish-gray color that the Alaloi call *lila*. It was not a perfect pearl, neither perfectly round nor uniform in hue. The Alaloi mistrust perfection in pearls; perfect pearls they find coldly beautiful but uninteresting. Danlo's pearl was shaped like a teardrop, and in various places, around its smooth surface, it gleamed with soft pink undertones. As the jewelers in the Diamond District say, it was "the kind of pearl you can look into forever and it will never end."

After looking at it through most of an afternoon, Danlo decided that he had found his pearl. He used a laser drill, then, to burn a tiny hole through the narrowest part of it. Through this hole he threaded strands of his long black hair that he had plucked from his head and twisted into a string. He cemented the ends of the string together with some shaving glue, and when he was done, he had a pearl pendant that Tamara might slip over her head and wear around her neck. He dropped the pendant into a silk bag, the kind that Bardo employed to distribute strands of toalache or triya seeds. He pulled tight the bag's drawstrings and put in his pocket. And then he prepared to return to Neverness.

His journey back across the ice was uneventful, though it took him two full days. The wind blew mostly from due north, and he had to tack against it, beating northeast or northwest, or sometimes due west when the wind shifted suddenly. He paused once to explore a tiny, nameless island equidistant between Avisalia and Neverness. On this island he came across the naked white bones of a walrus washed up on the rocky beach. He was lucky enough to find one of the walrus's tusks whole and undamaged. He scavenged this tusk and stowed it in his schooner. The best part of his expedition had been the rediscovery of his natural passion for making things. The moment that he saw the tusk, he devised a plan to carve it, into rings and a pipe and animal sculptures and, most of all, into an ivory chess piece to replace the missing god in Hanuman's set. It was his hope that he might heal the wounds in their friendship by giving him a gift that he had made himself. And so he returned to the City, full of his success and dreams of the future. He burned his ruined furs, and he spent half a day in the hot pool of his dormitory, cleaning himself of guano and showing the pearl pendant to his friends.

After sleeping for a night and a half the next day, he made arrangements to visit Tamara late in the following afternoon.

He met her in her tea room, where they sat together as she served him coffee and grilled breads. It had been a day of bright, clear air and high spirits and sunlight streaming golden through the windows. Tamara basked in the last of this sunlight, naked as an animal, with only her long golden hair covering her. She liked to watch the play of the light rays through her lace curtains as the sun fell slowly into the west.

"I have been away from the City these past days," Danlo said to her.

"In the lightship of yours that you call *The Snowy Owl*? Have you taken it into the manifold?"

"No," he said, "I took a schooner out onto the sea." He quickly told her of his journey, and then he pulled his silk bag from his pocket and set it on the table. "I have brought you something . . . to wear around your neck."

She picked up the bag and used her long fingernails to tease open the drawstring. She spilled the pearl pendant into her hand, and her eyes jumped with light as she looked at it. "Oh, it's very beautiful!" she said. "I've never seen such a beautiful pearl."

She looked at him and smiled, and then they were both laughing together as if they had just tasted some new, euphoric drug. She held the black pearl in her hand, and the contrast it made with her ivory skin was striking.

"It should slip over your head," Danlo said to her. "I made the string long . . . so that it would slip over easily."

"I can see it's thoughtfully designed," she said. She rubbed her finger up and down the shiny string.

"I made the string . . . with my own hair. It is a custom of the Alaloi."

"It's beautiful," she said. She reached out to stroke the hair on his head. "I suppose I guessed that you made it that way. You have such beautiful hair, so long and thick. I've always thought that hair like yours shouldn't be wasted on a man."

"Someday I might be old and bald," he said. "But if I have a wife . . . she would still wear this pearl."

Tamara smiled as she set the pendant atop the table, next to her coffeepot. She stood up and said, "I've something to show you." She stepped into her meditation room, for a moment, and then returned carrying a long, flat shatterwood box. It was hinged at the back, and it opened like a palpulve shell. "This

558

came for me this morning," she said. "I thought you might like to see it."

Danlo took the box and sat looking at her.

"Why don't you open it, please?"

He opened the box and peered inside. There, against a padding of black velvet, was a necklace of creamy pearls. The pearls were graded by size and matched by color, and each pearl was a work of perfect symmetry. There were thirty-three pearls along a strand of platinum. Danlo knew nothing about modern jewelry, but he suspected that the necklace must be very valuable.

"They are . . . splendid," he said.

"They're Gilada pearls," she said.

Of all the pearls of the Civilized Worlds, Gilada pearls are the most prized. They are fabricated on the artificial world of Gilada, which lies at the edge of the Vild. They are assembled molecule by molecule in a vacuum without light or sound or any vibration. There, deep in space where there is no gravity to deform the iridescent nacre as it is layered down around a single seed molecule, the Gilada jewelers make perfectly spherical pearls. The making of a single pearl can take more than a year. Gilada pearls are famed for their perfect beauty, but also because no one except the perfectly rich can afford them.

"This must have come from a merchant-prince," Danlo said.

"No, I've never consorted with Trians," she said. "It's from Hanuman."

"Hanuman! Hanuman . . . li Tosh? But how could he get the money to buy such pearls?"

"I don't know," she said.

Danlo rubbed his finger over the largest of Hanuman's pearls, accidentally leaving skin oils to smear its perfect surface. "It is a remarkable coincidence that Hanuman sent you these pearls . . . this morning."

"Did you tell him you were going to give me a pearl?"

"I never . . . talked to him. We do not talk anymore. But I showed the pearl to my friends. It is possible one of them told him."

"Then there's the secret of your coincidence."

"Yes, it must be. But why would Hanuman give you *pearls*?"

"Well, he's been wooing me since the night we met."

"Wooing you . . . to marry?"

"I don't think so. But there are many ways of wooing, you know."

"The night at the party, do you remember?" Danlo said. "The way Hanuman looked at you—it was obvious that he burned for you."

"Oh, the poor incandescent man!"

"You say that so coldly."

"Do I? I don't mean to."

"You do not like Hanuman very much, I think."

"It's not true that I don't like him," she said. She looked down at the box that Danlo was holding, at the strand of pearls. "I'm afraid of him."

"Because he is a cetic?"

"Because he's so *controlled,*" she said. "I've never known anyone to have such control of himself."

"But the cetics strive to master all their emotions. All their thoughts . . . what they call their programs."

"It seems he's succeeded too well."

"Perhaps he only wants people to think that."

"And people do," she said.

"Hanuman has his passions like anyone else. But the greater the passion . . . the greater the need for control."

"Do you remember what he said during the sermon? 'Only by becoming fire will we ever be free from burning.' I don't think his passion is women, not anymore."

Danlo smiled to himself, and he thought that he understood a thing about her. He saw her as a completely beautiful woman, the kind of woman who had always commanded the affections of men. Such women, he supposed, naturally mistrusted any man over whom they had no sexual hold. That Hanuman could cut himself off at will from all sexual desire must have horrified her and insulted her sense of her own special powers.

"You would never consider making a contract with him, then?"

"Oh, I've considered it," she said. "A courtesan has to consider such things, even if it's quite impossible that she'd ever carry through with such considerations."

"Of all the men in Neverness," Danlo said, "who else has need of your art as Hanuman does?"

"Aren't you jealous of him even slightly?"

Danlo smiled and shook his head. "When I was a boy, my found-father taught me that jealousy is *shaida*. It poisons the soul."

"But Hanuman is so dead inside. He's all coldness and ashes."

"You could wake him up," Danlo said. "Make him alive again, yes?"

Tamara tapped her fingernail against the rim of her coffee cup. She seemed to be contemplating the patches of light that floated atop the coffee's dark surface. "You must love him very much, to say such a thing."

"I love him . . . as I would love my brother," Danlo said.

"Would you give me away so easily?"

"When an Alaloi hunter visits another tribe," Danlo said, "often he must leave his wife at home. He makes his journey across the ice, alone, many miles and many days. When he arrives at his destination, he is cold and hungry. Often, one of his near-brothers will lend him his wife for a few nights. To warm him inside and ease his hunger."

"But we're not Alaloi," she said. "At least, *I'm* not."

"No, that is true."

"And I'm not yours to give."

"Even among the Alaloi," he admitted, "the wife must make a gift of herself, or else the hunter must bear the cold."

"I could never give myself to Hanuman," she said. "Any other man, but not him."

Danlo rapped his knuckles against the wooden box that Hanuman had sent her. He looked at the necklace of Gilada pearls, glittering in the light. He said, "Then you will send back the pearls?"

"I wish I could," she said. She sighed and ran her fingers through her hair. "I wish things could be so simple."

"Is it that you do not want to wound his heart?"

"Oh, I think his emotional organs are beyond such delicacy."

"No . . . never beyond."

"The truth is, I can't risk offending him," she said. "He's not wooing me simply for himself."

"For your society, then?"

She nodded her head. "He's sent gifts to other courtesans. Nothing so exquisite as this necklace, but he's wooing my sisters, too."

"All this wooing must irk Bardo . . . endlessly."

"Well," she said, "Bardo *is* a jealous man."

"It is unseemly . . . to fight over women."

"At least Bardo appreciates us for who we really are. My

sisters have told me that they've never known a man who loved women as he does."

Danlo smiled as he remembered a story he had heard about Bardo: that the huge, prepotent man had once swived nineteen women in a single night.

"Would you rather it was Bardo who sent you the pearls?"

"I'd rather not be sent gifts that I can't return." She lifted Hanuman's necklace out of the box and held it away from her as if it were a dead snake. "I *can't* return this, you know. The Mother wouldn't want me to."

"The Mother . . . is the head of your society?"

Again, she nodded her head. "The Mother, at this time, wishes none of us to offend either Bardo or Hanuman."

"I see," he said. "The Mother is a courteous woman, yes?"

"She's the wisest woman I've ever known."

"Then she is watching our church, yes? Watching and waiting."

"You're not so naive about politics as you'd like everyone to think."

"I know . . . hardly *anything*," he said. "Only that Bardo has charisma and power, but Hanuman is more willful. It is impossible to say who will prevail."

"And whom do you wish to prevail?"

At this simple question, Danlo stood and began pacing around the room. "I am not sure," he said. "I am not sure that either of them could make the Way of Ringess . . . into something worthwhile. Something blessed. I am not sure that anyone could make it so."

"We could," she said softly.

"There speaks your pride," he said, and he sat down next to her and kissed her forehead. "There speaks your love."

"Should we let Hanuman's vision sweep everyone else's aside?"

Danlo looked at the pearls dangling from Tamara's hand. They were perfect and beautiful and utterly cold, and he suddenly remembered Hanuman's universe of dolls, which had been too perfect as well.

"Hanuman has his vision," he said. "But we have ours, too."

"And that's why we should preserve it while we can."

"What do you mean?"

"Haven't you received your invitation to copy your remembrance?"

"What do you mean? How could my remembrance . . . be copied?"

"Then you haven't heard? Hanuman has asked some of us to copy our remembrances into a computer that he's made."

Now quite alarmed, Danlo was up off the cushions again, pacing back and forth, rubbing his finger along his forehead. "But our remembrances cannot be *copied*! Why would Hanuman say he could do such a thing?"

Tamara replaced Hanuman's necklace in its box. She stood up and placed her hand on Danlo's chest. "Everyone knows how hard it is to remembrance the Eddas," she said. "Many of the godlings have never had a clear memory, let alone an inkling of the One memory."

While Danlo stood staring out the window at the silvery ice of the Sound, she told him about Hanuman's plan to perfect the remembrance of the Elder Eddas. Three days ago, she said, Hanuman had begun inviting Ringists of the inner circle to copy their memories into a computer. He promised that he could record whole sequences of memories as one might record musical notes on a synthesizer. It was his plan to edit and enhance these memories, to merge them into what he called an "essential remembrance." A perfect remembrance—Hanuman claimed that any godling or new Ringist, upon interfacing his computer, would experience a perfectly vivid remembrance of the Elder Eddas.

"This is very bad," Danlo said.

"Do you think so?"

"Yes."

"Well, Bardo has consented to Hanuman's plan."

Danlo covered his face with his hands and began rubbing his eyes. Then he looked out the window for a long time, watching the moons come out against the twilight sky. He finally said, "Yes, Bardo has feared the remembrancing of the Eddas, too. He is the founder of a new religion—what if someone remembrances a truth that this religion calls false? What if a person of vision sees falseness . . . in all that Bardo holds as true?"

"But, Danlo, what is truth?"

He smiled and said, "I have wondered this all my life."

"Whatever truth really is, don't you think that we should allow Hanuman to copy our remembrances? So that *our* truths can be incorporated into this essential remembrance?"

"Are our truths so truthful, then?"

"Oh, I think they are," she said. "You've had a great remembrance, as everyone knows, and you've described it so beautifully, even if you always claim that you're clumsy with words. And I've seen such miraculous things, too. What are the Elder Eddas but a way of waking ourselves up? *All* of ourselves. To let the energy of consciousness consume us, atom by atom, cell by cell—there's an utterly ruthless force inside each of us that destroys and creates and destroys and creates, and it's all there waiting for us to let it be born, if only we could bear all the blood and the terror and the screaming. It's the most beautiful thing in the universe. I'd *die* to see this vision made true."

He rubbed his head and sighed. "Then you have decided to copy your memories into Hanuman's computer?"

"Won't you?"

"No," he said.

"Of course not—you're not afflicted with pride as I am." She turned away from him and stared at the polished stones lining her windowsill.

"Tamara," he said. He looked at the blond hair hanging down her long, lithe back. He touched her shoulder and said, "I love this pride of yours."

"You do?"

"As I love the wind."

She turned to face him then, and she locked eyes with him. "Didn't you tell me that the wind almost killed you once?"

"Yes, that is true," he said. "But it is also true that the wind is the breath of the world. Just as your pride is your strength and your life."

"Do you really think so?"

"Yes," he said.

"I was told once that my pride was an ugly program that would destroy me."

"No, it is a blessed thing."

"When I was a child," she said, "the readers in my church tried to cleanse me of pride and other sins but they never really succeeded."

"If they had, then you would not be who you are."

"No, of course not," she said, and she laughed nervously. "I've often wondered if all the efforts to cleanse my pride only made me more vain."

"What is it that the Architects teach? 'Vanity is insanity'?"

"I suppose you must hate me for being so vain."

"No, it is just the opposite," he said softly. "Each of your vainglories is like a pearl—unique, splendid, blessed. And beautiful."

"It's you who are beautiful," she said. She gazed at him for a long time. "I've never known anyone like you before."

He bowed his head once, then looked at her.

"No one has ever really *seen* me as you have," she said. "I don't think anyone ever could."

He searched her dark eyes then, looking for the deepest of all her vainglories. At last, he thought he saw it, gleaming like a natural pearl, this vision that she had of herself as a goddess of terrible beauty, the embodiment of all life's energies as well as the urge to death. *She is terrible beauty,* he thought. Ever after, he would love her for this deep, primeval beauty, and he would cherish this quality above all others.

"Yugena los anasa," he said.

"What does that mean?"

"It means," he said, " 'To see deeply is to love deeply.' "

She smiled as if she were a little girl again, then she stepped over to the table. She picked up the box containing the string of Gilada pearls. With a flip of her hand, she snapped shut the box. The sound of wood against wood resonated through the room. "I suppose I should keep these," she said. "I really wouldn't wish to offend Hanuman. But I'll never wear them, I could never wear them, now."

She scooped up the pendant that Danlo had made, and she let it dangle from her fingers. The tear-shaped black pearl caught the colors of the night as it swung back and forth in the air. "Men have given me many things, but no one has ever given me anything like this," she said.

"I made it . . . for you to wear," he said.

"I wish I could wear it," she said.

"I wish that as well."

"If I *did* wear it," she said, "I suppose there would be a meaning to my wearing it?"

"Only the meaning we would give it."

"But don't the Alaloi view the giving of a pearl as a promise to marry?"

"You could wear this as a troth, if you would like."

"A troth between both of us?"

"Your promise to marry me, and mine to marry you."

"But what would I give you?"

"The pleasure of seeing this pearl close to your heart."

"But would we have to appoint a time for the fulfillment of

this troth? I still have my calling, you know. You still have your quest."

"Any troth we made would be . . . timeless. We have all the time in the universe."

She looked down at the pearl, and she said, "I've never seen anything so beautiful before."

Seeing his moment, he stepped forward to take the pendant from her. Although his whole body vibrated with excitement and he could scarcely breathe, he moved quickly, deftly. With his fingers, he spread out the pendant's black string and slipped it over her head. This trapped her long hair against her neck and shoulders. As he pulled her hair free, the pearl fell into place between her breasts.

"Oh," she said, "I hadn't expected it would be so heavy."

"The pearls of the palpulve are very large," he said.

"I didn't think I'd like wearing it so much."

"You were made to wear it," he said.

"I didn't think I'd ever marry anyone."

"I have always hoped . . . that I might marry you."

"Well, I think I'd love to marry you," she said.

"I have dreamed that someday, this will be our greatest joy."

"Oh, but we'll always have joy," she said. "We were made for joy."

He looked at her, and in her eyes there was nothing but joy, a pure, golden joy that spread out like light and warmed him inside. She kissed him then, and she led him into the fire room. That evening they practiced none of the exercises of her art, nor did they take care who lay atop whom or for how long. They fell into an easy and natural love play that went on and on until they cried out in joy and clasped each other in exhaustion. For a long time, he lay next to her, holding her so tightly that his chest was crushed against hers. He felt the hardness of the pearl pressing his breastbone, cutting into the skin above his heart. The entire universe, for him, had narrowed to the immediacy of deep breathing and the thick salty scent of her neck and this little pain that gave him so much joy. He was full of joy, full of pride in finding a wife who would someday bear his children. Although he feared this fierce pride more than he feared death, he could not remember having ever been so happy.

CHAPTER 24

THE CEREMONY OF REMEMBRANCE

After the Holocaust, on Old Earth and across the Civilized Worlds, there arose universal religions seeking to unlock and explain the mysteries of life. There were Logism and The Passion and the Science of God. And Edeism, and Zanshin, and the Way of the Serpent. And so on. All told, during the Fifth and Sixth Mentalities of humankind, there have been 223 such religions. And all of them, in order to unleash the so-called spiritual energies, have institutionalized the use of drugs: sex, music or word drugs, or plant drugs such as the sacred teonanacatl, or synthetic drugs, or the most potent drug of all, which is the interface of the human mind with the cybernetic spaces of the accursed computer.

—*from* A Requiem for Homo Sapiens,
by Horthy Hosthoh

The next day Hanuman li Tosh invited Danlo to meet him in the computer room of Bardo's cathedral. To call it "Bardo's cathedral" was misleading, for although Bardo oversaw everything that happened within that great heap of stones, he did not own the building, nor did the Way of Ringess. The Timekeeper, remembering too well the history of Old Earth, long ago had delimited the power of all organizations within the City. (Excepting the Order, of course.) The Timekeeper had decreed that the societies, cartels, associations, and religions seeking to

567

establish themselves in Neverness should have no legal status nor should they be able to own property. In keeping with the covenants between the Order and the City, Bardo's cathedral was owned in condominium by the many Ringists who had paid for its purchase. These Ringists, toward the latter third of deep winter in the year 2953, numbered at least four thousand. And there were more of them every day. Since Hanuman's Fire Sermon, the evening joyances inside the cathedral were swarmed with men and women wishing to begin the great journey toward godhood. There were so many new Ringists that Surya Lal, who had become Bardo's confidante and administrator, had to use a computer to enroll their names.

"If this growth continues, we'll have to hold two joyances daily," Bardo was heard to tell Surya. "There are so many of these new godlings. Too many to know by name and face, too bad. Even for one with a memory such as mine. And if they don't know *Bardo,* by God, why should they be loyal to Bardo? It's my thought that we should require the new Ringists to take an oath, along with their profession of the Three Pillars. An oath of loyalty and obedience to *me.*"

On a cold day, late in the afternoon of the sixty-sixth, Danlo made the short journey through the streets of the Old City to the cathedral. The Old City is full of fine old buildings, some of them quite tall, some of them graceful, glittering sweeps of organic stone. Bardo's cathedral stood out among them not because of its height or its splendor, but because of its quaintness (as well as its beauty). It occupied most of a block just south of Danladi Square. Because most of the streets in that part of the City parallel the Old City Glissade, which runs straight from the Hollow Fields to North Beach, the blocks around Danladi Square are oriented from northwest to southeast. But Bardo's cathedral had been built on an exact east-west axis; thus, unlike any of the hotels or towers nearby, it sat on the block obliquely, at an odd angle. The makers of the cathedral— they were Kristians of the Society of Kristoman The God—had built it that way because the cathedrals of Old Earth that were the glory of their religion had each been laid out east to west. Bardo's cathedral followed this ancient design; as seen from deep space, it was laid out as a cross, a shape and symbol known to be sacred to all sects of Kristians. The head of the cross pointed east toward the Academy; the foot of the cross was practically planted in the heart of the Old City. In between was eight hundred feet of graceful stonework, long windows, and great flying buttresses made of granite blocks. Where the arms of the cathedral met the building's main body, above the crossing, a magnificent tower had been built. This central tower rose up 150 feet above the rest of the cathedral, and it could be seen from the Academy. With its intricate traceries that seemed to drip across the granite facing like icicles, with its arched windows and delicate aretes pointing toward the heavens, it was considered one of the most beautiful structures in the City. Bardo, however, thought that the tower's sharp angles and recticlinearity made for the wrong shape with which to surmount his cathedral. (Curiously, he did not mind holding his joyances in a building shaped like a cross. As a student of symbols who had once considered becoming a notationist, he knew that the cross was one of the oldest of symbols, much older than any church or religion. The cross—according to the notationists—is the great Tree of Life which stands at the center of the universe. It is the bridge over which the soul makes its crossing in order to reach God. The most ancient meaning of the cross is that of life's suffering. Two kindling sticks crossed together and rubbed, as a man rubs against a woman, will ignite the terrible fire that is all life.) And so Bardo had plans to pull down the tower and to replace it with a golden clary dome. He wanted to open the cathedral's ceiling vault, so that from inside, the heavens could be seen in all their glory. Bardo had other plans as well, as Danlo discovered that day when he skated off the gliddery and approached the cathedral's western portal. There, Bardo stood beneath the great center archway. Although he was busy directing the refurbishing of the cathedral's facade, he noticed Danlo skating up the ice and called to him.

"Hello, Danlo!" his voice boomed out. "Well, Little Fellow, how do you like our little stone hut?"

Danlo skated up to him, and he bowed. Then he glided back a few yards, the better to see the changes that Bardo was carving into the cathedral. Three doorways opened out of the western front; although the center doorway was much the largest—even Bardo seemed small standing next to the massive double doors—they were each of a similar design: they were set into huge, pointed stone archways that opened up and out toward the street. At the center of the main archway, above the doors, was a circular window of stained glass. This lovely, light-filled archway was really a series of nine nested arches, each arch surmounting and projecting out from the one below it. The rims of the arches had been carved with stone saints and prophets, and other personages dear to the Kristian religion. Indeed, these icons fairly festooned the entire facade, and the largest of them could be seen staring out with stony eyes from the statue niches above the archways. Bardo, of course, as the founder of Ringism, could not countenance these icons. And so he had determined to remove them. The cathedral's entire western face swarmed with robots accomplishing this program. There were thousands of robots, each the size of a furfly. They clicked and scurried over the archways like a furious moving carpet, chewing at the stone with tiny diamond chisels. The air was full of their scraping and hammering and crunching, and full as well with stone chips and dust that fell down over Bardo and powdered his curly black hair. Soon, he told Danlo, every icon in the cathedral, inside and out, would be gone. He said that other robots would lay down organic stone in the icons' place. From this stone would emerge sculptures of Katharine the Scryer, Balusilustalu, Shanidar, and others who had guided Mallory Ringess along the path to godhood.

"And we'll have to rip out the windows, too bad," Bardo said. "But we can't have the godlings dwelling on ancient superstitions and miracles, can we?"

"But the stained glass . . . it is so beautiful."

"Ah, but we'll replace the glass, of course. Actually, I've already begun replacing it, as you'll see when you enter the cathedral."

They stood there for a while exchanging pleasantries and bits of gossip. Bardo, pretending to a sternness that lines of his fat face could never quite hold, asked him why he had absented himself from all church functions since the Fire Sermon. Danlo told him that he had spent his time perfecting his lightship and making mathematics. He had to raise his voice above the whine of the robots to make himself heard. And all the while Bardo nodded his head as he snorted and coughed at the stone dust raining down upon him.

"Ah, of course," Bardo said, "you're a pilot and pilots must make mathematics. I, myself, once found mathematics to be the most beautiful of all creations. Your father and I used to joke that each of the theorems we made was like discovering a beautiful pearl."

He emphasized the word "pearl" with a plosive rush of breath, accidentally spraying droplets of spittle out into the air. He shot Danlo a pointed look, and a huge grin split his face.

"I think . . . you must know every secret in the City," Danlo finally said, and then he was smiling, too.

"Have you given your pearl to Tamara?" Bardo asked. "By God, she's the most beautiful woman in the City! Have you promised to marry her, yet?"

"Am I so easy to read, then?" Danlo asked. "Has Hanuman taught you face reading?"

"No, he's taught me nothing, too bad. At least, he's taught me nothing *explicitly*. He likes his solitude, now that he's become famous."

"You cannot forgive him . . . for what he did during the Fire Sermon?"

"Forgive him!"

"You do not trust him, I think."

Bardo sneezed and rubbed the stone dust away from his eyes. Then he pulled Danlo deeper into the recess of the archway so they might be shielded from falling debris. "Do *you* trust him, Little Fellow?"

"He is my . . . deepest friend."

"Well, he's my friend, too, or he used to be before he began posing as a goddamned prophet. Can one trust a prophet? Ah, *do* I really trust him? Should I? A difficult question. I trust him to attract people to the Way. I trust him to give great sermons and inspire them. I even trust him to show them something of the ineffable, these goddamned Elder Eddas that everyone thinks they want to remember. He's a religious genius, by God! and I trust him to do what all geniuses do, which is to glory in their genius and let it shine so that others can glory, too."

With these words, Bardo might have been mocking himself, for as he grinned at Danlo and pulled at his mustache, his eyes were full of light.

Danlo met his gaze and said, "But you trust Hanuman . . . to cark our remembrances into a computer?"

"Ah, I wondered if you would ask me about this."

"Is it true, Bardo?"

"Seven years I've known you now, and you're still questioning me!"

"But why shouldn't I question you?" Danlo said, and there was a smile on his lips. "If I desisted, I would ruin your pleasure of delivering your answers."

"True, true," Bardo said. "Then let me answer this one question, and we'll both be content. You know I've said before that the kalla is a dangerous drug. It's too, too dangerous, and therefore we've decided to disband the kalla ceremony. No one is to drink the kalla anymore. At least, no one is to drink it *publicly*. But the godlings must have their remembrances, and so we've instituted another ceremony. That is, tonight we'll institute it. We'll hold a special joyance—I'll guide the ceremony, and Hanuman will be seen to *assist* me, do you understand?"

"I think I do," Danlo said.

"There will be a thousand people in the nave tonight," Bardo said. "And each of them will have remembrances they've never had before. *My* remembrances, some of them. Thomas Rane's. And yours, too, I hope."

"My . . . remembrances," Danlo said, closing his eyes.

"You did receive Hanuman's invitation?"

Danlo said nothing, and then he nodded his head.

"Excellent! I'm glad you've agreed to record your remembrances."

Danlo, who had agreed to no such thing, opened his eyes and looked inside the cathedral. He felt Bardo's gaze burning his cheeks, and he said, "Hanuman has promised me that my first remembrance . . . can be perfectly preserved."

"Like a firefly preserved in ice," Bardo said. "And we've little enough time to preserve it. I'd like to, ah, *incorporate* your great remembrance with the others and use it for tonight's ceremony."

"You would use my memories . . . so soon?"

"We have to move quickly," Bardo said. "Ah, but that's the hell of guiding the manswarm into the mystic pools of enlightenment: if we don't move quickly enough, events will rise up like an ocean and sweep us away."

He proceeded to give Danlo directions to the computer room, then he excused himself and returned to supervising the renovation of his cathedral.

When Danlo passed through the doorway into the great nave, he was immediately swept away by memories that welled up within him. He had never been inside a cathedral before, neither this one nor any other. He knew this as surely as he knew that he had never climbed the ice mountains of Agathange's moon, yet, as he stood looking off into the fountains of light pouring through the windows, he felt as though he had stood there a thousand times before. Despite the robots swarming over the outside walls, inside all was calm and quiet. Cold currents of air sifted through the deserted nave, and through the transepts that gave out onto the crossing. On either side of him, the walls and the windows and the multiple columns supporting the ceiling vault rose up in uninterrupted vertical lines. High above him, great fingers of stone splayed out from these columns in long, graceful arches that met each other along the center line of the vault. It seemed that these sweeps of stone had been flung up and magically suspended in space. The whole design of the cathedral bespoke a desire to cancel gravity and elevate matter toward the heavens. Everywhere Danlo looked, it was as if the fundamental religious feeling of man had been frozen into stone and colored glass. The pillars and the pinnacles, even the ornaments of stone, he thought, bore memories of ten thousand years of chants and incantations. The windows —the long mosaics of stained glass that were the cathedral's glory—bore scenes of miracles that Kristoman the God was said to have worked. Already, ten of these windows had been knocked out and replaced with bits of new glass. A little drama cut in colors of blue, green, yellow, and deep red had been set into the arched mosaics high above. The low afternoon sunlight illuminated the great figure of Bardo as he opened his mouth in a silent scream and shook his fist at the sky. A long spear stuck out from his chest, and blood spattered his white furs. It was one of the great moments in Bardo's life, when he had died his first death. As Bardo never tired of telling people, he had given his life so that Mallory Ringess might live, and now he had worked the truth of this moment into stained glass for all to see. He had plans for replacing all the old stained glass with new glass depicting great moments in the life of Mallory Ringess. (It never seemed to embarrass Bardo that he confused his best friend's greatness with his own.) As Danlo walked deeper into the nave, he looked from window to window, and he wondered what these moments might be. He marveled at the play of light through the windows, the way the colors deepened or brightened at the passing of every cloud. The whole cathedral was brilliant with blue and golden light, and everywhere he looked, he was reminded of all life's aspiration toward light. It amused him that this light was everywhere dazzling and lovely, no matter that it streamed through windows new or old.

He walked through the nave and past the chancel, where red-carpeted steps led up to a simple altar. In preparation for the night's remembrance, the altar had been set with golden candelabra, the golden urn and blue bowl used in a hundred kalla ceremonies, and with 1,089 freshly cut fireflowers. Past the altar, down a quiet aisle lined with statues and columns, he came to a door that led into a passageway. The computer room, Bardo had told him, lay outside the cathedral proper. Adjacent to the cathedral's north side was a collection of small buildings connected by a maze of roofed passageways, walled gardens, and cloisters. Down this dim passageway Danlo walked, past the sacristry and the library until he came to the doors of the chapter house. Once, this lovely building had been used as a meeting place for the luminaries of the Kristian church on Neverness, but now it had been converted into a workplace and a storeroom. He knocked on the door, and it opened, and there stood Hanuman straight and proud in his cetic's robe.

"Hello, Danlo," he said.

"Hello, Hanuman."

He invited Danlo inside, and to thaw the instant chill that fell between them, Hanuman talked about the various objects of the room. It was a large room full of many objects, most of them computers of one sort or another. The upper half of the chapter house was a granite dome cut with long windows between the stone ceiling ribs; it was all open space and light, but the lower half was all clutter. Scalloped arches and false pillars formed a stone paneling around the room's perimeter. Originally, circles of chairs had been set beneath this paneling, but they had been ripped out and replaced with tall wooden cabinets. Between the cabinets and the room's center, set out on tables above the checkered floor, were computers, and the neurologics of computers, and tools used to disassemble, heal, or grow new computers. There were mantelets and sulki grids and hologram stands. Hanuman had recently become a collector of archaic and unusual computers, which he had put into display cases as if they were jewels. (In fact, one of these computers *was* a jewel, an antique Yarkonan firestone whose lights had long since dimmed.) Danlo walked around the display cases, looking inside. He saw electronic computers, and an optical computer, and computer cubes, chips, disks, and even a computer whose graphics were projected inside a clear diamond ball. Hanuman, it seemed, was especially fond of his various mechanical computers. One whole case was taken up with a difference engine of brass gears and gleaming chromium switches. He opened another case and removed a Japanese abacus, and he began snapping wooden beads along various wires with a blur of his little fingers. He showed Danlo two kinds of quantum computers, and a glowing gas computer, and then he pointed at a brilliant Yarkonan tapestry hanging on the wall, and he said, "This is the showiest of computers, of course. The Yarkonans embroider the logics and circuitry directly into the fabric."

They chatted for a while about Bardo's refurbishing of the cathedral and other things of little matter. Although Danlo wanted to tell him of the pearl that he had discovered and of his promise to marry Tamara, he could not. Their mutual wooing of Tamara was like an open wound between them. It was like a canker on an autist's face: out of politeness and embarrassment, they refused to look at this festering hurt or to comment on it, but they could not forget it for a moment.

"You look well," Hanuman said at last.

"You . . . you have shaved your head," Danlo said softly. "You have sworn to wear the skullcap, yes?"

Hanuman snapped his finger and began spinning red beads around the wires of the abacus. He looked off above him, and Danlo thought that he was not really looking into the sunlit, open space of the dome, but rather into other spaces that burned with a different kind of light. Covering most of Hanuman's naked head was a gleaming skullcap, the kind the cyber-shamans wear. It was a shell of clear diamond, inside of which the purple neurologics had been woven to simulate the branchings and wispy sub-branchings of human nerves. Hanuman's entire head seemed to be wrapped in a network of electric nerves. It was a showy thing, this master computer, and many cyber-shamans loved displaying it, even though of all the cetics, they have always been the most secretive.

"We call it the clearface," Hanuman said. He smiled, and his face seemed to be all glittering teeth inside a ghastly, glittering skull. "Some people think it's silly for a man to shave his head like a novice, but that's the only way it will fit tightly enough."

Indeed, the clearface fit his head like a second skin. It had been cast and molded to conform with the bones of his skull. A glue called gimuk held it in place; the glue and the constant pressure of this profound computer had irritated his scalp, for along the rim of the clearface, across his forehead and temples, around his ears, the skin was red and inflamed.

Danlo looked at him, trying to keep his eyes fixed on Hanuman's eyes rather than on the clearface. "I have heard that only the higher grades of the cyber-shamans wear the skullcap . . . continually."

"Are you asking if I've been initiated into the higher grades?"

575

"I have heard there are grades . . . that even cyber-shamans of the higher grades know little about."

"Are you speaking of *secret* grades?"

"Not quite . . . secret," Danlo said, and then he smiled. "How could they be secret if I have heard of them?"

Hanuman looked at him but said nothing.

"I have heard that there are *neurosingers* who use the skullcap to interface other computers . . . continually."

Hanuman smiled to himself as he looked up into the dome. His eyes were bloodshot as if he had not been able to close them for a long time. His eyes were frozen open, but they seemed empty of normal sight. He stood motionless as a sleekit on the snow, and all the while, his hollow eyes haunted his face. Danlo knew that he must be interfacing the skullcap, or perhaps one of the room's many computers. Which one he interfaced was impossible to determine. The skullcap—the clearface—was like a window into the cybernetic spaces of all common computers, and into many that were uncommon, as well. Hanuman stared off into space, as eyeless as any scryer; he might have been interfacing a quantum mechanical computer, or the wall tapestry, or even the very walls themselves.

"Hanu, Hanu, what are you doing?"

As if in answer, Hanuman turned his gaze to a computer in the exact center of the room. There, resting on a plain shatterwood stand at the level of Danlo's eyes, was a black crystal sphere. It was as large as the head of a walrus, and Danlo immediately recognized it as a much larger version of Hanuman's universal computer, the one that he had used to create his universe of dolls.

"Excuse me," Hanuman said, "I was only completing an experiment."

Danlo turned his head left and right, looking for the square table that Hanuman had kept in his room after his great remembrance. But Danlo saw no such display table, nor any other kind of screen or monitor that might be used to display the dolls.

"I left the table at Bardo's house," Hanuman said upon reading Danlo's puzzled expression. He tapped the diamond clearface covering his head. "Now that I wear this, there's no need for such vulgar displays."

Hanuman turned to look at the sulki grid against the wall. He said, "That is, there's no need for myself. But you'll want to see how my dolls have evolved these last hundred days."

Without waiting to see if that was indeed what Danlo really

wanted, Hanuman nodded his head, and the sulki grid flared into life. Instantly, the whole chapter house from the floor to the dome above filled with glowing silver shapes the size of large seals. These images of dolls were all around Danlo, floating through the air, perching atop the cabinets, floating *through* the cabinets and other objects of the room as if such constructions of common matter could never impede beings made of pure light. Again, he had to remind himself that the dolls were only information structures stored in Hanuman's universal computer; the hologram projected through the room was only a representation of this artificial life.

"Please, no," Danlo said. "No more."

While Hanuman stood there motionless, Danlo jumped back as one of the dolls darted through the air and hovered in front of him. In the way this great silver being oriented itself toward him, it seemed to be studying him. Although none of the dolls had eyes or faces, as humans or even seals do, there was something facelike about each of the dolls, as if each one possessed a unique personality and expression. The patterns of light composing the dolls were unique in each one, and the shifting bands of silver-blue and aquamarine seemed responsive to stimuli that Danlo could only guess at. And each doll seemed responsive to every other. The dolls twisted and quivered, and Danlo imagined that he could see the very air molecules vibrating as with speech or some other kind of information wave. He had an eerie feeling that the dolls were talking with each other in strange and complex ways, perhaps even discussing him or laughing at him. Perhaps they were pitying him. Somehow, he thought, the dolls were aware of all that occurred between him and Hanuman. It horrified him to think that these dolls might manifest themselves in any part of the real universe as easily as Hanuman might enter theirs.

"Hanu . . . please."

As suddenly as they had appeared, the dolls vanished. The pretty lights that had made up the dolls were gone, and the computers and cabinets stood out plainly in the unmoving air, and the chapter house suddenly seemed too dark, too quiet, too real.

"Have you ever wondered about memory?" Hanuman asked. "These dolls have evolved a perfect memory."

"A computer's memory of information . . . is not the same as a man's."

"Are you sure?"

Danlo rubbed his eye and said, "I did not come here to see your dolls."

"Are you sure?" Hanuman repeated.

"Once, we used to know each other's thoughts, almost without talking."

"Shall I tell you what you're thinking, Danlo?"

Danlo shrugged his shoulders and said, "If you would like."

He was aware of Hanuman's eyes picking over his face, and he expected him to utter some witticism or piercing truth about the paradoxical nature of his quest to become an asarya. But Hanuman turned facing the center of the room, and he said nothing. Then Danlo became aware of his own mind, of his wild, churning surface thoughts: he was praying that Hanuman would look away from him and keep his silence.

"You used to know me as a friend, not as a cetic," Danlo said.

Hanuman stepped close to his universal computer, and he said nothing.

"And I used to know you," Danlo continued. "I thought I always would."

Hanuman pressed his forehead to the gleaming black sphere, and there was a clinking sound of crystal against the diamond clearface, and still he said nothing.

"Hanu, Hanu—why did I ever come to this insane City?"

At last, Hanuman deigned to speak, saying, "If you hadn't come to Neverness, I would have frozen to death in Lavi Square."

"Why speak of that now?"

"Because there's a life between us. There always will be."

"Yes . . . a life."

"And now there's something more between us," Hanuman said. "This way of the gods that we've seen more clearly than anyone else."

"But the Way of Ringess . . . is not my way."

"No?"

"No."

"Would you renounce the very religion you've helped create?"

"I? But what about you and Bardo, then?"

"Let's never forget," Hanuman said, "that your remembrance has been the inspiration of thousands."

"But I—"

"Soon they will be millions."

"So many—"

"And someday, millions of millions. There's never any end to humanity's swarms, is there?"

With slow, tense steps, Danlo paced around the room. Finally, after considering his words carefully, he drew up close to Hanuman and said, "The Way . . . is not what it used to be."

"Everything evolves, of course," Hanuman agreed.

"But now Bardo is practically selling memberships to the godlings!"

"So?"

"You cannot buy remembrance."

"Perhaps not," Hanuman said. "But if the godlings don't sacrifice something dear to themselves such as money, they won't value the privilege of becoming Ringists."

"Privilege?" Danlo cried out. "I thought the Way . . . was supposed to be a way for everyone."

"And it will be. It is. Only, for some of us, it will be a more glorious way than for others."

"I see."

Hanuman steepled his fingers beneath his chin and said, "Some of us have been chosen to copy their remembrances; others have not."

"Who are these chosen, then?"

"Do you want to know their names?"

"Yes."

"Well, there's Bardo, of course. You, me, Thomas Rane. Kolenya Mor."

"And?"

"And, as I'm sure you know, I've asked Tamara, too. And the brothers Hur and seven others of the kalla fellowship. And Surya has consented—"

"Surya Lal!"

"She's a brilliant woman, you should know."

"But she has opposed the kalla ceremony almost from the very beginning!" Danlo said. "I think she is afraid . . . of the memories."

"Nevertheless, it seems that she's had an important remembrance."

"Truly?"

"Would you wish to judge, yourself, the truth of her remembrance?"

Danlo looked up into the dome, at the windows which had

fallen dark and reflective of the room's little lights. He shook his head and asked, "What . . . remembrance?"

"She's remembered a simple thing, really, a truth that should be important to any who follow the Way: that someday a god would arise among human beings and lead us to our destiny. This god's name is Mallory Ringess."

"She says that she . . . remembranced this?"

"Of course."

"But how could she?"

"She says that this is one of the racial memories of the Ieldra."

"But the Ieldra," Danlo said, "abandoned this galaxy fifty thousand years ago. How could they have known the name . . . of my father?"

Hanuman looked at Danlo and smiled. "Perhaps the Ieldra were the greatest scryers of all time. Their memories: memories of the future. You, yourself, have said that in deep remembrance, there is no time."

"That is true."

"Then the Ieldra must have carked all their memories, future and past, into the human genome. It's there, coiled up in our chromosomes, these brilliant memories. You've seen them, as have I. What else are the Elder Eddas, if not the memories of the gods?"

Danlo walked past a few cabinets and rickety tables until he came to the room's curved wall, which was thick and ornate with granite paneling. He leaned against one of the false pillars there. High above his head, the wind drove through the cracks along the iron window frame and fell down over him like an icy waterfall. The dense air had chilled the wall so thoroughly that he instantly felt the coldness of it pierce the layers of his kamelaika and his undergarments. He looked at Hanuman and said, "I think the Elder Eddas are something more than genetic memory. The Eddas are . . . something other."

"What, then?"

"The One memory, this life shimmering in all—"

"The One memory! Oh, Danlo, I think you're the only truly religious person I know."

Because his head was beginning to throb, Danlo rubbed his eyes and temples. "It is ironic you should say that. I think I am done . . . with all religions."

Hanuman walked over to Danlo and stood facing him. "Even Ringism?"

"Especially Ringism. There is no joy in it anymore . . . for me."

"No joy? You, of the great remembrance?"

"The kalla ceremony," Danlo said. "It is empty . . . of true remembrance. It is like a thallow egg whose yolk has been sucked out."

"Which is why it has been disbanded."

"Is that really why, Hanu?"

"Well, tonight we'll have a new ceremony of remembrance."

"Yes . . . another *ceremony.*"

Hanuman looked up suddenly, as if he had just seen a dagger suspended above his head, and he told Danlo, "It would be a tragedy for you to leave the Way."

"But I must."

"Are you sure?"

"Yes."

"And when did you make this silly decision?"

Danlo did not want to speak, but his pride cried out that truth was blessed and must be told, and so he said, "Before I came here tonight, I was not sure. I did not know . . . what I would do."

"And now you know?"

"Yes."

"And what will Danlo the Wild do, then?" Hanuman looked straight into Danlo's face, but his eyes were far away. "A cetic wants to know."

With his hand pressed against his aching head, Danlo told Hanuman that he would never attend another joyance nor any kind of religious ceremony. However, each evening he would practice the remembrancing art, privately, under Thomas Rane's guidance. He would spend his days studying mathematics. It was still his intention, he said, to join the second Vild mission and find a cure for the great plague that had killed his people.

"You've accounted for all your time except your nights."

"You must know where I spend my nights," Danlo said softly. Then, because he had fallen so deeply into truth that evening, he told Hanuman of the pearl and his betrothal to Tamara.

This happy news did not seem to surprise Hanuman. He just stood there, his eyes full of mockery, and full of pity, too.

"She'll never marry you, of course. Please believe me—I know about these whores."

Neither Danlo nor Hanuman moved; the silence in the chapter house was now oppressive and ominous, and it seemed that it would never end.

"I should go now," Danlo finally said. The pressure inside his head was sharp and intense; when he looked suddenly toward the door, a quick pain sliced through his eye, deep into his head.

"Now I've offended you," Hanuman said. "I'm sorry— please don't leave yet."

Danlo rubbed the scar along his forehead, saying nothing. Then he started toward the door.

"You can't just betray your friends like this!" Hanuman said.

As if his muscles had been touched with an electric current, Danlo whirled about and pointed his finger at Hanuman. "*You* say that?"

"If you leave the Way, you harm all of us."

Out of pure frustration, Danlo clawed the air, then clenched his fists.

"Well, whatever you do, please don't betray our secrets to anyone."

"A secret is a secret," Danlo said.

"Of course, but please don't speak to anyone about the Way. Please don't tell anyone you've left us."

"You want me to keep . . . a silence?"

"Is that so hard to do?"

"Not so hard. So . . . wrong."

Hanuman flashed Danlo a quick look, and he said, "Don't let your love of truth destroy everything you love."

"I do not know what you mean."

There was a moment of silence as Hanuman worked his eyes over Danlo's face. "You've already decided to speak against us, haven't you?"

"I . . . do not know."

"Please tell me the same truth you'd tell everyone else."

"What truth?"

"The truth your face affirms and your lips deny."

Danlo sighed, then said, "You must know what I will say."

"Yes, you'll keep our secrets, but you'll speak against us— you'll tell everyone that Ringism has been corrupted beyond redeeming. You're contemplating telling Tamara this half truth tonight. But you mustn't. You mustn't speak to Tamara about what you've seen here. Please don't."

"But we tell each other everything."

"If you tell her, you'll destroy her," Hanuman said. His voice had fallen deep and ragged, as it used to get after a spell of coughing.

"You think it is so easy to destroy a person, then?"

"Listen to me—Tamara is enchanted with the idea of creating a religion after her own image. It's what she lives for."

"No, you are wrong."

"Please believe me. I've seen what I've seen."

"You are a cetic, and you have seen her face. But you have never seen . . . anything deeper."

"I'm a cetic," Hanuman agreed. "And it's as a cetic that I'll tell you this: If you malign the Way to her, you'll destroy whatever there is between you."

Danlo did not like the faraway look that fell over Hanuman as he said this. He hated the paleness of Hanuman's eyes, the self-absorption, pity, and dread there. These, he thought, were the attributes of a scryer who has seen some tragic and inevitable future, not the silent face of a cetic.

"I understand," Danlo said. "You would not want me to alienate a . . . *courtesan*."

"Don't say anything to her, please."

"I should go now," Danlo said again.

Hanuman smiled, and then he spoke, and his words were as cool as quicksilver, "But we haven't recorded your memories yet."

"I . . . cannot let you do that."

"Please, Danlo."

"How can you ask me this?"

"Because you're my friend."

"Would a friend ask his friend . . . what is impossible to do?"

"You've had a great remembrance," Hanuman said. "I should think you'd want to share it with others."

"But it cannot be shared!"

"No?"

"No."

"But if you *could* share your memories, would you?"

"I . . . do not know."

"Would you at least face one of our remembrancing computers? Would you face the memories we've chosen to record?"

"Why?"

"To see for yourself."

Danlo rubbed the scar above his eye, then slowly nodded his head. "If you would like."

"We'll need a heaume, then."

So saying, Hanuman crossed the room and stood in front of a deep mahogany cabinet nearly twice his height. As he swung open the doors, the hinges squeaked and groaned. Inside, at the bottom of the cabinet, as Danlo could see, were many skull-like heaumes stacked atop each other in a mound. They looked like trophies collected by some ancient warlord. Hanuman ignored these heaumes and turned his attention to the many shelves of heaumes above them. His little fingers danced along a shelf of heaumes, tapping over the silvery shells until he came to one that apparently satisfied him. He nodded his head and used both his hands to lift it up, and then he gave Danlo the heaume.

"I have never seen one like this before," Danlo said. He ran his fingers across the heaume's curved, chromium surface. The metal was quite cold; looking into its mirror finish, he could see a distorted reflection of his face.

"What's wrong?" Hanuman asked.

Danlo looked back and forth between Hanuman and the gleaming heaume. He remembered that one of the first things a novice is taught is never to put a strange heaume on his head.

"This was made on Catava," Hanuman told him. "It's beautiful, don't you think?"

Just then, Danlo heard light footsteps along the corridor outside the chapter house; he thought that someone must be stalking closer to the room, perhaps to press his ear against the door and eavesdrop on their conversation. Hanuman, intent on examining the heaume's silvery striations, seemed not to notice this faint sound. Then the door suddenly banged open, and Bardo blundered inside. He wore a bright, formal, golden robe and a gold ring around the little finger of his right hand. His beard and hair had been freshly cut, combed, and oiled; he smelled of sihu perfume, the kind that he wore when he wished to inspirit himself to lead some great ceremony. He glanced at Danlo, then at Hanuman, and his voice came rolling out like winter thunder: "Haven't you copied his goddamned memories yet?"

"No," Hanuman said. He seemed both surprised and dismayed to see Bardo looming above him like a mountain about to explode. For a moment Danlo wondered if Hanuman had secretly summoned Bardo to reinforce his arguments, but if there was any truth written on his delicate, white face, clearly this could not be so.

"Well?"

"Danlo doesn't want his memories copied."

"By God, why not?"

"You should ask him that," Hanuman said.

Bardo pulled at his beard and looked at Danlo. His eyes were soft and sad, and he asked, somewhat rhetorically, "Why should I have to stand here dreading you're about to tell me bad things?"

While Danlo explained his reasons for deciding to leave the Way, taking care to choose words that would not give too much offense or lay too much blame on others, Bardo walked over to Hanuman and plucked the heaume away from him. He held it cupped, upside-down, in one of his huge hands. The heaume's smooth metal seemed welded to his fingers. *"You,"* he said to Danlo, "every Ringess I've known—why do you have to be so willful?"

"I am sorry," Danlo said.

"Ah, I should have seen your disillusionment," Bardo sighed. "But I've been too damn busy."

"I am sorry," Danlo repeated.

"Well, you can't simply abandon us. How can I persuade you of the, ah, advantages of being a prophet among godlings?"

"I do not think you can," Danlo said.

"But have I explicated how great these advantages might become?" Bardo turned the heaume around and around slowly between his fingers. "Have I . . . By God, what's this?"

His great voice suddenly filled the room as he stabbed his finger against the base of the heaume. There, stamped into the curved band of metal that would have fit over the back of Danlo's neck, was the seal of the Cybernetic Reformed Churches: a simple string of Edic lights twisted once so as to resemble a figure eight lying on its side.

"This isn't one of our heaumes!" Bardo shouted.

Hanuman smiled, then said, "No, it's a cleansing heaume."

"A cleansing heaume! Why do you have a *cleansing* heaume?"

"It's silly of me, but I collect such things," Hanuman said smoothly. He moved over to a row of ten steel cabinets. He opened the door of the first cabinet. Inside were ten shelves and ten heaumes lined up on each shelf. Each heaume appeared identical to the cleansing heaume that Hanuman held in his hands.

"But *these* are our remembrancing heaumes!" Bardo said, pointing.

"They *do* look alike," Hanuman said. He lifted out one of the remembrancing heaumes and tucked it into the crook of his right arm. He carried it over to Danlo and Bardo. "But of course there's no insignia on the remembrancing heaumes."

Bardo grabbed the remembrancing heaume away from Hanuman. He chewed his mustache as held the heaume up to the light of the flame globe, and he traced his finger over its base. As Danlo could see, the smooth metal bore neither stamp nor seal of any Cybernetic Church.

"We bought a thousand of these from the Catavan Architects," Bardo admitted to Danlo. "And we've ordered ten thousand more."

Danlo looked back and forth between the two heaumes in Bardo's hands; they seemed more like each other than any two thallow eggs taken from the same nest. He looked at Hanuman, smiling his empty smile, and he thought of the old saying: "Catava makes the holiest computers."

"The damn Architects like to mark everything they make, but we've bribed them to leave their seal off these computers," Bardo said. "Naturally, it would be best if the godlings didn't suspect they were wearing Architect heaumes."

Danlo paid scant attention to his words. He was staring at Hanuman now, and Hanuman was staring at him; while Bardo cleared his throat and muttered something to himself about the high cost of dealing with Architects, Danlo and Hanuman locked eyes together in a way they had not done for a long time.

Then Bardo pointed his chin at Hanuman and demanded, "Why did you design these heaumes thusly?"

"As a joke, of course," Hanuman said. His eyes were as pale as chalk ice. As pale, Danlo thought, and as cold and clouded.

"A *joke*!"

"Well, the Architects use the cleansing heaumes to mutilate people's memories. I thought it would be ironic to design a similar-seeming computer. In order to *give* the people the deepest memories in the universe."

In the time it took for Danlo's heart to beat nine times, nobody spoke. Then Hanuman continued, "I was only going to show Danlo the difference between these heaumes."

Hanu, Hanu, are you telling the truth?

Danlo watched Hanuman watching him, and his eyes ached at the coldness he saw there, and he did not know the answer to this question. A voice inside him cried that Hanuman would never harm him, that it was unthinkable Hanuman should ever place a cleansing heaume upon his head. No friend could do this to another, no matter if their friendship were cracking like old sea ice which has borne a heavy weight too long.

Oh, Hanu, Hanu.

As Danlo gazed at his best and deepest friend, he thought it was possible that Hanuman, himself, did not know what he had intended to do.

"Ahhh," Bardo said. He tossed the cleansing heaume directly at Hanuman's face, and he seemed startled at the quickness of Hanuman's hands jerking up to catch it. "You should lock this away with your other collectibles. It wouldn't do for some poor godling to put this on her head by mistake."

While Hanuman locked the cleansing heaume in one of his cabinets, Danlo glanced at Bardo. His fat cheeks were puffed out into something resembling a smile. Clearly, Bardo accepted Hanuman's explanation, though it was also very clear that Hanuman's "joke" had disturbed him. *He is afraid of Hanuman,* Danlo thought. *Afraid for himself.*

"Now," Bardo said to Danlo as he drummed his fingers along the crown of the remembrancing heaume, "what we would like from you is your sense of the Eddas. We'd especially like to preserve the, ah, *mystical* element of your remembrance."

Danlo noticed that Hanuman was standing next to his universal computer; his head was rigid as if he were deep in thought. Danlo turned back to Bardo and said, "Even if you could copy the exact state of my mind, now, here . . . it would not help you. Tonight I am far from any of the remembrancing attitudes."

"Well, I don't suppose that really matters," Bardo said.

"But only in the One memory, in the experience of it, in the Now-moment when time comes to a stop . . . it is only during remembrance that there is any mystical element worth preserving."

"So you think you know what's worth preserving and what's not?"

"All I have now," Danlo said, "is a memory of the Eddas. A memory . . . of the One memory."

"Ah, but who has a finer memory of this state than you?"

Danlo looked over at Hanuman, and he thought that *he* had a fiercer memory of his remembrance, if not a finer one. "Nothing in my memory can bring anyone closer to the Eddas," Danlo said.

"Then why have you spoken so freely of your remembrance?"

"I . . . do not know."

Bardo rubbed his beard and said, "You've spoken so eloquently, too—it's because you have this habit of telling the truth, even to those who don't deserve it. Will you listen to a friend who's only slightly less eloquent than yourself? Words are like jewels in the night. Words are like constellations of stars pointing the way when one is lost. Words can evoke the mystical feeling, as I well know from listening too attentively to *your* goddamned words. I, myself, mistrust this feeling, as you must know, but others crave it. For them, your words are golden. It's your words we want, Little Fellow. Hanuman tells me you have a nearly perfect memory for ever word you've ever spoken."

From a pocket in his robe Bardo removed a golden clock studded with twenty diamonds, a little piece of forbidden technology of a kind that had proliferated in the City since the Timekeeper's demise. He held up his hand and motioned Hanuman nearer. He gave Hanuman the remembrancing heaume and said to him, "We've a ceremony to lead in less than two hours. I haven't time to persuade Danlo to copy his memories. You persuade him. Please."

He turned to Danlo, reached out and rumpled his hair. "And if *he* fails to illuminate you as to the advantages of doing what you should do, I'll have to speak with you privately. Do you understand? Good. Well, now, I must attend the placement of the sulki grids. With all the harassment the Order has been inflicting upon us, we'll have to hide them—or at least be more discreet."

So saying, he bowed perfunctorily and then sauntered out of the room. After the door had banged shut, Danlo and Hanuman were left alone with each other.

Hanuman held the remembrancing heaume out to Danlo; although he spoke not a word, his eyes beckoned as if to say: Don't you trust me? Or more pointedly: Can it be that Danlo the Wild is afraid of a computer?

In truth, Danlo *was* afraid of computers, and it was precisely because of this fear (and out of his friendship for Hanuman) that he forced himself to take the heaume. With a quick motion, he pulled the heaume over his head, trying to smooth his hair out of the way as the chromium earpieces squeezed over his temples. The fit was not good. His hair, though swept back behind his neck, was too thick and unruly to allow a tight fit between the logic silk and his skull. Hanuman told him that it did not really matter, that the silks lining the remembrancing heaumes generated a more powerful field than did common silks. Danlo, who had always had misgivings about encasing his brain in any kind of logic field, powerful or weak, was not comforted by this news. Indeed, in what he was doing, there was no comfort at all. The base of the heaume cut against the back of his neck, compressing the muscles and arteries there, aggravating the pain in his head. Even though the interior of his eyes throbbed so sharply he could hardly see, he looked at Hanuman and smiled. He nodded once, then shut his eyes as he waited for the computer to fill him with remembrance.

The images, when they came, were much like those of any other surreality or simulation. Interfaceing the memories that Hanuman had recorded was something like entering a library's cybernetic spaces—even more like being part of a fabulist's drama. In fact, in the design of the remembrancing program, Hanuman had solicited the aid of both a cartoonist and a master fabulist. It amazed Danlo to witness the great events from his father's life. In a stream of blazing images, he "followed" his father to the planet Agathange, where he had been brought after dying his first death. The Agathanian engineers—who were in truth more like gods than men—had restored his father to life. As if Danlo were a jellyfish floating in a tropical sea, he "watched" as the Agathanians touched Mallory Ringess's proud and noble face and disassembled his ruined brain, neuron by bloody neuron, and healed him, and remade him into a man who might become a god. He also "listened" to private conversations between Mallory Ringess and Bardo; he "walked" across a cold beach noisy with barking seals, and he listened to these two great men speak of programming the self, of mastering the biological programs that lead to rage, hatred, and ultimately death. Everything about the life of the Ringess, according to the memories that Danlo reviewed, was a way of escaping the meaninglessness of death.

The highest art is self-creation.

The heaume infused remembered words into Danlo's inner ear, and he marveled that his father's voice was much like his own, or rather like his voice might someday become: deep, rich, tender, passionate, and pained. The irony in this voice amused him; its willful, fated quality brought to mind remembrances of faraway stars and galactic wonders (and tragedies) he had never seen. The image of his father inside him spoke of compassion, *with* compassion, and each of his noble words was an inspiration and a pleasure to hear. It was Danlo's way to cherish pleasure as an indicator of good and blessed things, but *this* pleasure he mistrusted as he did the *morasha,* the deadly, crumbling snow that covers an invisible crevasse. He knew too much about cetics and their arts. He knew too well how the cyber-shamans use computers to control the brain. And now, when he looked away from the dark, compelling image of his father—when he looked into his own shimmering awareness—he could almost see the heaume's manipulation of his mind. He could feel it, as exhalation and quick euphoria, the spray of endorphins through his brain's neurons. Timed to each of his father's perfect words (and at each mention of the name "Ringess"), he experienced a moment of opiate intoxification. The heaume stimulated the release of peptides and other twisted-up proteins specific to certain moods. Standing beneath this hard shell of metal that cut against his spinal cord, he fell through a quick succession of moods: wonder, awe, curiosity, even joy. He astonished himself laughing out with joy so hard that tears came to his eyes and he could hardly keep his feet. Then came other, deeper moods: the mystic upwelling of the serotonin flows, cool, quick, and sublime; and the rush of noradrenaline that brought a marvelous clarity and concentration, opening him to new ways of seeing things, speeding up his mind.

The image of God is found essentially and personally in all humankind. Each possesses it whole, entire and undivided, and all together not more than one alone.

It came to him, suddenly, that he could understand great things. Godly things. There was no lack of things to be understood and remembered. Hanuman and Bardo had recorded many images, words, ancient writings, musics, and simulated miracles—as well as doctrines they had invented to explain how one man had become a god, and how others might join him in godhood. Danlo should have absorbed this information easily, as dry snow sucks up water. His brain had been beautifully prepared for such veneration and false remembrance. Even now, the heaume was pulling at his neurons, programming his brain stem to pump out ever more noradrenaline and other chemicals that would enhance his memory. Only, his memory needed no enhancement. In truth, because he had been born with such a clear and deep memory, it was always easier for him to remember than to forget. To purge from his mind anything at all, even such minutia as the pattern of pimples on Pedar's face the night that he had been killed, always required from him a tremendous act of will—as well as the use of certain techniques that Thomas Rane had taught him. It was this will and these mental tricks that now inoculated him against the stream of images pouring into his brain. Thus, with smiling lips and tightly closed eyes, he faced the remembrancing heaume gladly, and he was not afraid of falling into the trap that Hanuman had prepared for him.

Man is a rope, tied between beast and god—a rope over a bottomless crevasse.

Of course, Hanuman was not the first to use mind machines to wash the brain with religious sentiments and dogma. Nearly three thousand years earlier, Nikolos Daru Ede had authored the first four books of *The Algorithms,* and in many ways, Hanuman's interpretation of the Elder Eddas copied the architecture of this monumental work. Hanuman's "Eddas," as he called them, were structured even more tightly than the *Visions* or the *Iterations* or any of the later books of *The Algorithms.* In putting on a remembrancing heaume, as Danlo found, there was little freedom of movement among the recorded memories. In this respect, it was nearly the opposite of facing a library's cybernetic space: there was no soaring among the lovely information storms and crystalline knowledge structures, no true sense of fractality or fugue or sudden discoveries that the librarians call gestalt. He did not need his shih sense to find his way among the images that Hanuman had assembled into movements and transhuman dramas, because a way had already been prepared for him. Programmed for him. It was being programmed now, as he smiled and sweated beneath the hard silver heaume.

You have made your way from worm to man, and much in you is still worm. Once you were apes, and even now, man is more ape than any ape.

He opened his eyes, and he faced away from the remembrancing heaume. It was a difficult thing to do. Near him stood Hanuman with his tight lips and unseeing eyes. Around Hanuman's shaved head, the clearface was lit up, thousands of strands of neurologics glowing bright purple. Danlo realized that Hanuman had chosen certain Eddas to infuse into his brain; very probably Hanuman was editing these memories moment by mo-

591

ment. It occurred to Danlo that the program calling up the memories, whether in private sessions such as this or in mass public ceremonies, would be rewritten to provide each person's "remembrance." And it would always be Hanuman (or Bardo or some other cyber-shaman) who wrote these programs.

The universe is a machine for the production of gods.

The memories that came to him then were not quite like the Elder Eddas, not like true remembrance as he had experienced it. They were other people's memories. They were words and pictures that a fabulist had put together. All these memories had come from people whom Danlo knew very well, and he found that Bardo and Surya Lal and others had stamped them with their individual concerns and conceits, much as a tiger leaves distinctive prints in the snow. There was one "Edda," cold and hard and clear, that he was sure Thomas Rane must have remembered. Danlo could see this memory as an image just behind his closed eyelids, where points of red and blue light sparkled across his visual field. There, an image of an organism appeared. It was as vast and beautiful as a whale, only it lived far above the seas of any planet, and its skin shone like gold against the blackness of space. Mathematical formulas appeared then, indicating that for evolving organisms adapting themselves to new environments, the rate of energy metabolism varies according to the square of the temperature.

Because low temperature favors order, the coldest climates are potentially the most hospitable for complex forms of life.

Whole sequences of memories came quickly now: Old Earth before the agricultural holocaust, Bardo's vision of a world of primeval green forests, blue oceans, and white clouds as pure as snow; Hanuman's prophecy of the dead god in the 18th Deva Cluster and his account of the great war that the gods waged across the stars; there was even something from Danlo's first remembrance, words that he had spoken immediately afterward: "By none but a god shall a god be worshiped, and we are all potentially gods." He laughed silently to himself because he knew he had never uttered the phrase: "and we are all potentially gods." He thought that Bardo or Hanuman must have added on this bit of doctrine, as a virus adds new information to a computer program, or to a living cell. He laughed to see his memory of the Elder Eddas embroidered so easily, and then he shook his head and ground his teeth in despair.

It was the Agathanians who first recognized Mallory Ringess as a potential god. They healed him of his mortal

wound and showed him the path toward the infinite things. **The Ringess made himself into a god, and then he went out to heal the universe. Someday, he will return to Neverness.**

Danlo might have thrown off the heaume and fled from the room then, but a sudden image compelled his attention: his father as a noble-looking young man, with his black and red hair, the strong, predatory face, the cold blue eyes that seemed to grow larger as they fixed on the stars above Neverness. It was a famous, noble pose out of the mind of some fabulist, only now this glittering image filled Danlo's mind, and it transformed itself into something vast and glorious, even as Danlo clamped his teeth together so that his jaw muscles popped in sudden pain. He looked behind his eyes, inside himself where his father's image was becoming his own; it was the image he might see reflected in a common silvered mirror. Hanuman, he guessed, was playing with the heaume's program, morphing and melding Danlo's bearded face with that of his father, much as a cartoonist blends together different visages to invent new characters. The eyes of this new image were dark blue like liquid jewels; soon they had grown huge and mysterious as moons. His eyes were blue-black windows full of stars, opening outward in every direction, drinking in all the universe.

Each man, woman, and child is a star, and all human beings can shine with the light of gods.

Now it comes, Danlo thought. *Now he will use all his skills to spring the trap he has prepared.*

The path toward godhood lies in remembrancing the Elder Eddas and following the Way of the Ringess.

The memories flickered inside so quickly that they would have overwhelmed him if he hadn't used his time sense to speed up his mind. As if he were floating in the pit of a lightship in deep space, almost by instinct, he fell into slowtime, and he reached out with his thoughts and entered the computer's electron flows. Single moments of time seemed to come apart and last forever, as a silken strand from a worm's cocoon unravels endlessly. He entered into electronic samadhi, and the computer's memories became *his* memories, and his mind raced along strands of endless circuitry all frenzied and electric with information. He should not have been able to do this. No heaume should have been programmed to allow this kind of dangerous merging. Many were the pilots who had lost themselves into their computers. (Almost as many as the poor harijan who put illegal mind machines on their heads and die forever to the outside world.) Danlo, himself, loved mystical states of consciousness—even those induced by computers—and there had been a time in his life when he had sought such ecstasies wherever he could. He thought he understood the nature of Hanuman's trap; he thought that Hanuman was tempting him with the promise of easy electronic samadhi, as if to say: Behold, each time you go beneath my heaumes, all memory and mind will be yours.

For an endless moment of time, this seemed to be true. His mind seemed to extend itself, to become one with that of the computer. To *become* the computer. He, himself, whoever he really was, made no effort to run the computer's programs. He let himself be swept away by the ecstasy of pure computation. His awareness spread out into a nearly infinite field of on-or-off voltages, trillions of sparks of light twinkling in total blackness. Brilliant patterns formed themselves up momentarily only to be broken apart an instant later and replaced with others just as beautiful. All computation was the asking of a single, eternal question: yes or no? This question was asked about every aspect of shape, color, sound, number, idea, or emotion. He asked himself this question a million million times each second, yes or no, and his computational self coded information into memories, the pattern of yeses and noes making the pictures that were memories. Mechanically, something inside moved these memories from one place to another, sorting, comparing, negating, adding memory to memory so quickly that they filled an entire memory space. Thus he could see Hanuman's Eddas from a coign of vantage that was wholly new; he gazed at these bright memories as if he were a god peering through a microscope at all the features of the world, all at once, and he let his vast, new mind make sense of all that he beheld. It came to him that he had never understood so many things. He wondered if the heaume was faced with some larger computer, or perhaps whole arrays of computers that Hanuman had hidden from view. As he had done many times before, he wondered at the nature of the mind-computer interface, the very nature of mind itself.

Hanu, Hanu, how is it possible that the mind can know more than itself?

He felt the blood racing through the arteries of his throat, and he knew much about other people's memories that he had thought it was impossible to know. He wondered, then, if he truly might copy something of his great remembrance into Hanuman's heaume; he wondered if together they might create a remarkable likeness of the Elder Eddas.

Gods create; creation is everything, and you are God.

This calling to create, he thought, was the whole of his temptation; he thought he could reach out and touch the icy, translucent walls of Hanuman's trap, and if necessary, break his way out at will. He thought he had seen all there was to see. And then the heaume looked through his mind and touched it with a pale fire. There was a sudden frenzy of neurotransmitters that made his brain cells rush with wild, electrochemical storms. It was a pleasure beyond pleasure, a greater ecstasy of the mind than anything he had ever known. He stood there swaying, drunk with this mind fire, and there came a moment of illumination so intense it seemed his interior world had been lit up by a flash of lightning.

Where is the lightning to lick you with its tongue? Where is the frenzy with which you should be inoculated? Behold, I teach you the god within: he is this lightning, he is this frenzy.

He stumbled about blindly, afraid that he might fall over and knock into one of Hanuman's cabinets. He struggled to control his breathing, to calm the fiery waves of bliss pounding through his brain.

So this is the real electronic samadhi, he thought. *The samadhi that the cyber-shamans keep for themselves.*

As he grimaced and ground his teeth against the intense pleasure of the moment, he thought that nothing in the universe could be so marvelous as this samadhi. And then, as if a light had been turned off, he fell out of samadhi and stood there panting. He remembered something that he should never have forgotten. He remembered the true Elder Eddas. True remembrance was not the same as entering electronic samadhi. The sudden heaven of the cyber-shamans was like standing at the top of a mountain, and looking down to see each crack and glittering fleck of mica in every pebble and stone in the world; it was seeing broadly and more intensely the analysis of each wavelength of light reflected off all the crevasses and snowflakes and ice, out to where the world curves off into infinity. But true remembrance was like looking inside all things, into the interior light that makes all things reach out toward life. True remembrance was *being* lightning itself, not merely being dazzled by its flash. He remembered, for a moment, what it was like to see clearly and deeply, to be one's deepest self, and then he thought back upon something that Old Father had once said: *Surfaces glitter with intelligible lies; the depths inside blaze with unintelligible truths.* And surely Hanuman must have known this. He must have known that it was only himself he had trapped in his glittering cybernetic heaven.

"No, Hanu, this is not the true Eddas—it is only a simulation," Danlo said aloud. His words vibrated between heaume and the bones of his head. To him, his voice sounded too tender, too passionate, too pained. He should have taken off the heaume immediately but instead he opened his eyes to look at Hanuman.

He saw only blackness. For a moment he was light-headed and disoriented and sightless in his mind. He felt his brain fall electric and strange, tingling with an aura of sick anticipation. And then suddenly there was light. That is, he was blinded by a stroke of lightning that tore straight through his eyes to the back of his brain. Lightning is always just lightning, but this time he felt the heat of it rather than the illumination. Raging through his brain cells was a storm of neurotransmitters, dopamine and taurine and norepinephrine, this time of a slightly different concentration and mixture than before. This time, there were no beautiful visions; there was no sense of making connections with a mind greater than his own; there was no pleasure, but only pain. All the pain in the world.

"Hanu, Hanu!" he cried out, but no one seemed to hear him. He knew that it was only Hanuman who programmed these chemicals of consciousness; he knew that he might escape this torturous interior landscape merely by facing away from the computer. And yet he could not face away. He felt himself caught, as in a whirlwind of flames, a hideous space more akin to an epileptic fit or madness than it was to any kind of samadhi. He threw his hands to his head then, and he bruised his fingertips against the hard metal heaume. As if a giant hammer had smashed both his knees, he fell writhing to the floor. He cracked his elbow against the floor tiles and bit his tongue, but the agony of bruised bone was nothing against the fire inside his head. He burned with the dread and despair of utter neverness, all the neurons of his brain, all the cells of his body. He trembled to tear himself into a trillion bits and parts, to scatter every burning piece of himself in the icy sea, if only this would extinguish the terrible fire. But the fire grew hotter and hotter, and he burned in the pain of himself, a pain inside pain that would never end.

Danlo, Danlo, you must wish to consume yourself in your

own flame. How could you wish to become new unless you had first become ashes?

All things, however, must finally end. Danlo managed to claw the heaume off his head, and he lay crumpled on the floor, sweating and panting. He became aware of Hanuman, who was kneeling above him. Hanuman looked down at Danlo as he grasped a folded white linen and wiped the blood from Danlo's lips. He looked into Danlo's eyes and made sure that Danlo had returned to an even consciousness, and then he helped him sit up. He hurried to ease himself away from Danlo, to stand and keep a proper space between them. His hand was trembling, slightly, as he gave the linen into Danlo's hand, and he said, "Here, you've bitten your tongue."

"Oh," Danlo said. He used the linen to clean his mouth. His tongue was raw and bleeding, and he could hardly speak. "Why did you do that, Hanu?"

Hanuman stood close by, fingering the diamond clearface on his head. He bent down to pick up the heaume that Danlo had taken off. He looked into its shiny chromium surface, which was now scratched and dented. Then he dropped his eyes and smiled at Danlo coldly. "This was only a simulation, too," he said. "Would you give the people the *true* Eddas?"

Danlo looked up at Hanuman, and the muscles along the back of his neck were stiff and aching. For the first time he could almost see Hanuman's real pain. Just as electronic samadhi was only a glittering reflection upon the surface of the One memory, the fiery simulation that had raged through Danlo's brain was only a shadow of what Hanuman must have felt the night of his first remembrance.

Oh, Hanu, Hanu, I truly did not know.

Danlo inclined his head toward the heaume that Hanuman was holding. He said, "I did not know the memories . . . would be so consuming."

Hanuman was still smiling, but there was no humor in him. "It's a clever program. Lord Pall helped design the heaumes, you should know."

"But he has been against the Way from the very beginning!"

"That's true," Hanuman said.

"You have made an accommodation with him? With the Order?"

"We've reasoned with him," Hanuman said. "We've shown

597

him that it would be silly to continue this ill feeling between the Order and the Way."

"I . . . see."

"Lord Pall is the greatest of cetics. He's taught me much of what I know."

"Have you suborned him or has he suborned you?"

"No one has suborned anyone," Hanuman said. "We've merely reasoned with the greatest lord of the Tetrad."

Danlo rubbed his elbow and asked, "But what of Lord Ciceron, then?"

"I'm sure that Lord Pall will reason with Lord Ciceron. They're both reasonable men."

"I see."

"It's quite reasonable, don't you think, that all Ordermen should be allowed remembrance?"

After rubbing his neck, Danlo pointed at the heaume. "That," he said "is no remembrance."

"No? But we've given the people the best of the Elder Eddas."

"*Your* Eddas," Danlo said. "Your interpretation of them."

"In truth, it's Bardo who's authored most of our doctrines. I've merely edited the memories to fit these doctrines."

"But what about *your* remembrance, Hanu?"

Hanuman drew his finger along the inflamed skin of his forehead that edged the clearface, and he said, "We'll give them my words from the Fire Sermon. That should be enough. There's no need to torture the poor people."

"As you tortured me?"

"I only wanted to show you that the memories we copy into the heaume must be selected carefully. I'm sorry if I caused you any pain."

Danlo looked at him and said, "It does not matter."

"We must give the godlings the best memories, not the worst."

"And you would sweeten these memories with electronic samadhi, yes?"

"It would give them something of the mystical."

"Yes, *something*," Danlo said.

"Please don't look at me that way," Hanuman said. "You should know, too great a pleasure is as dangerous as too much pain."

"Dangerous . . . to whom?"

"Dangerous to us, of course. Dangerous to the godlings. Which is why we must control these remembrances."

"But you are not just *controlling*, Hanu. You are making a counterfeit of true remembrance."

"What's true, then?" Hanuman asked. "Do you mean *your* vision of what you call the One memory? How can we make people see that? Not everyone has your talent for miracles, you should know."

Danlo touched the feather dangling from his hair, and he said, "I believe . . . that everyone does."

"No, they don't, which is why we must give them your words, your memories, your understanding. We'll even give them a little cybernetic samadhi—we'll give them a taste for the miraculous."

"No," Danlo said, "you will give them sweetness instead of honey; glitter instead of gold. Your simulation of the Eddas . . . will never be real."

Now Hanuman's smile was no longer empty; now his face was full of cold, cruel amusement. "But no one wants reality," he said. "Reality is much too real—why else do you think people always hate anyone who'd show them the truth?"

Seeing that Danlo made no move to stand up, Hanuman knelt down in front of him, and he sat back on his heels, politely, and quite formally. He held his little hands folded in his lap as he talked of people's need to enter deeper modes of consciousness and go beyond themselves—but not *too* deep or too far beyond. He told Danlo that most people, when they knelt beneath the remembrancing heaumes, would be satisfied with only the slightest taste of cybernetic samadhi. It was his duty, he said, to measure out this bliss, much as a chef carefully adds garlic essence to a tableful of frying kurmash. Danlo thought he was both cynical and sincere, too aware of the darkness that everywhere permeated the universe and yet strangely innocent, almost like a bright-eyed altar boy who stands before the Edic lights at a vastening ceremony and is forced to ponder mysteries he is too young to comprehend. Danlo sat there listening, and the floor beneath him was cold as ice. There was something eerie and foreboding about them sitting together on uncovered floor stones, while the wind blew sheets of spindrift against the windows and screamed through the cathedral's spires. These sounds sifted through stone walls into the open spaces of the chapter house; there were other sounds, too: quick steps up and down the hallway outside the door; excited, muffled voices;

599

swishing silk. In the distance, far above the cathedral and the City, the thunder of rockets fell deep and smothered out of the night. Listening to the lightships leaving Neverness for the stars near the Vild, Danlo fell into remembrance. After a while he pulled out his shakuhachi and held it lightly in his hands. He held it to his lips, but he did not play it. Hanuman eyed this length of bamboo with longing and fear, and hatred, too. He hated Danlo's ease with mystical music, just as he obviously hated it when Danlo told him that the imminent remembrancing ceremony was a betrayal of everything natural and blessed. Danlo regretted the rebuke in his own voice, for he still clove to the Fravashi ideal of becoming a perfect mirror of all things, and he would have liked to have reflected the best part of Hanuman's selfness, not the worst. But his higher duty was to truth, or so he thought, and thus he spoke of the great wrong that Hanuman and Bardo were about to inflict upon the people of the City. He spoke of electronic samadhi, of how the yogin had coined this expression—derisively—to refer to an artificial state that merely imitated true samadhi. Because he wanted to lay open his heart, he admitted that he cherished electronic samadhi, for what it was, but he also warned that using it to facilitate the veneration of Hanuman's Eddas was the worst kind of manipulation, akin to slelling someone's DNA and fashioning viruses with which to infect the brain.

"It is *shaida* to give children sweet things," Danlo said, "all the while knowing . . . that it will ruin their hunger for what is truly blessed."

And what was most blessed, according to Danlo, was the One memory, this marvelous shimmering consciousness that could never be simulated because it was not an experience of the senses, nor a mentation, nor any emotion; it was neither a subjective ecstasy of the mind nor the vistas of the objective universe that the gods observe when they open their vast, ancient eyes. The One memory, Danlo said, was the natural state where every atom of one's body "remembers" its connection with all the elements of the universe. Thus reality (and truth) is something created between the universe and each living thing.

For what seemed a long while, Danlo sat there in the shadow of a computer cabinet, talking about the mystery of memory. Hanuman's eyes were like pools of pale blue fire burning out of the darkness; he watched Danlo with an intensity that annihilated all time, and yet they were both aware that time was passing too quickly, that the appointed hour of the new remem-

600

brancing ceremony was drawing nearer. Everything about this exchange of urgent words had the bittersweet thrill of a last conversation. Danlo saw that the more he spoke of the One memory, the more uneasy and desperate Hanuman became. Soon the fire in Hanuman's eyes quickened to a terrible apprehension. There was a falling away of years from his face. His fine cheeks, usually so pale and hollow, were now bright with blood. He squinted in pain as if he were coming into the moment when he had first beheld the sun. He might have been a child again reliving his fear and love of light. His mouth opened in what was almost a scream; he threw his hand up against his tightened brows, shielding his eyes from Danlo's eyes, from the look of compassion that Danlo flashed him. *How he hates to be loved,* Danlo thought. In truth, Hanuman hated Danlo's love of remembrance, his love of life, this rare and wild love that Danlo himself called *anasala.* Above all other things, Hanuman hated the naturalness with which Danlo opened himself to the One memory. And so, because he had found the part of Danlo that he could hate, sincerely and utterly, he suddenly turned away from Danlo. He sat like a statue of a neurosinger, still and remote, staring into himself. Around his head, the clearface was all glittering lights and hard, reflective surfaces. This diamond shell cut him off from any words or compassion that Danlo might have given him. Hanuman retreated into the private universe that only he could know, and Danlo hated him for isolating himself this way. Danlo looked at Hanuman's smooth, silent face, and now he could see only their hatred for each other. Since the day of their first meeting, these hatreds had always been present and growing, but now, like drill worms chewing free of the body when an infected hibakusha has died, their darker passions emerged into the light for them both to see.

He burns and he burns, but he hates burning alone.

Danlo suddenly understood Hanuman's deeper reasons for taking him into such a hellish simulation of remembrance; he felt too keenly the twisted compassion that Hanuman bore for him and bound them to a single fate. He closed his eyes then, remembering something that Tamara had said to him: that Hanuman would always destroy the object of his compassion before losing himself in bondage to it.

When he could stand it no longer, Danlo sprang to his feet and said, "I should go."

Hanuman stood up, too, and he faced Danlo. In his left

hand, he gripped the remembrancing heaume. He bowed to it and asked, "Will you help me?"

Something in Hanuman's voice made Danlo suspect that he was being asked to do much more than merely record his memories. In Hanuman's eyes, there was a dread of some great event or crime yet to be committed, and so Danlo shook his head and whispered, "No . . . I cannot."

"Please, Danlo."

"No," Danlo said, and his own voice was full of dread, too.

Hanuman's face emptied of all hope, but one more time he looked at Danlo and asked, "Will you help me do what must be done?"

"No," Danlo said, and after he had spoken there was a silence almost without end.

"You should go now," Hanuman finally said. His face was drained of all emotion, as dead as a moon. "Please, go."

Danlo hesitated a moment, then said, "Good-bye, Hanu. I wish you well."

He almost ran to the door, but before he could open it, Hanuman called out, "You should be careful of the truth, you know. Bad things always happen to those who think they must bring the truth."

Without plan or destination, Danlo left the chapter house and walked back through the long corridors into the cathedral. He passed several godlings who were busy making errands for Bardo. They were dressed in formal robes, and the golden cloth they wore in devotion to the ideals of Ringism creased and crinkled as they bowed low to Danlo and hastened out of his way. When Danlo entered the cathedral proper and stood inside the nave, many more godlings were completing the preparations for the night's ceremony: setting up candelabra stands, lighting candles, laying out many rows of little red rugs for people to kneel upon. Because Danlo was grieving over what had just occurred between him and Hanuman—and because he was curious—he decided to watch the remembrance. He walked through the nave and passed through a great archway where he found the stairwell leading up through the central tower. The doors to the stairwell, however, were guarded by a surly-looking godling whom Danlo did not know. But the godling knew him, and he allowed him to pass without explanation. Danlo would have raced up the stairs three at a time, as he had learned to do in Perilous Hall, but every time he tensed his arm muscles, a wicked pain shot through his injured elbow, and so he climbed the worn steps carefully, as if he were a farsider from some made-world who had never negotiated steps before. His footsteps echoed through the empty stairwell, and he made his way up to the mezzanine level. Much farther above him, he had heard, at the top of the tower was Bardo's sanctum, a room of great arched windows which looked out on the four points of the City. He wondered if Bardo was in his sanctum now, perhaps rehearsing a sermon for the ceremony, perhaps swiving some bright-eyed godling whom he was personally instructing in the delights of submitting to the Way. He smiled and shrugged his shoulders then, and he entered a dark corridor that smelled of ashes and old stone.

Soon he found the central loggia overlooking the nave. He stepped out onto a narrow balcony; it was as if he were stepping out into space. The cathedral's glorious interior opened up before him. On either side of him, and above, great pillars flared outward into the granite ribs that made up the cathedral's vault. Below was the main body of the nave, which was now golden in the light of thousands of candles. He placed his hands on the balcony's railing and leaned out to get a better view. The fine stonework on the outside of the balcony's parapet, he noticed, was carved with Kristian angels and other godlike beings. He could clearly see every detail of the windows and walls around him. He looked across the nave at the pinnacles and pretty wall ornaments where Bardo had cunningly hid his sulki grids. He looked straight down below him. There, godlings scurried about the chancel, arranging vases of fireflowers around the altar. One godling, a devout-seeming woman with a gold ring in her ear, approached the altar table and filled the familiar golden urn with what looked like plain seawater. From the aisles behind the nave, other godlings appeared pushing steel carts over the bumpy floor stones. Each cart was stacked full with remembrancing heaumes. The godlings laid these out in front of the altar, one silvery heaume precisely placed in the center of each red rug. When they were done, Danlo quickly counted the heaumes. There were a thousand of them arrayed in rows between the altar and the cathedral's great double doors.

Oh, Hanu, Hanu, why have you done what you have done?

Because he did not wish to be seen, Danlo moved back into the loggia's shadows. He waited there while the cathedral began to reverberate with a lovely, godly music. He stood listening to the music that the sulki grids made, listening and remembering. After a while, the doors were opened, and people submitted their steel invitation cards as they poured inside, and they took their places by each of the rugs. There were a thousand people, many of whom were godlings wearing golden formals or other gold-colored articles of clothing. Many were newcomers attending their first remembrance. Bardo had even invited a few masters and lords of the Order who had hitherto been scornful of Ringism: the Sonderval, Elia li Chu, Mahavira Netis, and, most surprisingly, Lord Mariam Erendira Vasquez, the fourth lord of the Tetrad. They knelt on their rugs like everyone else and sat holding the gleaming heaumes in their laps. Then, from a doorway behind the chancel, Bardo stepped out into the light and took his place at the center of the altar. He was splendid in his golden robe, to which he had fastened a great, flowing cape of black velvet. He was all magnanimity and grandness, and he cleared his throat and delivered a grand sermon that boomed like thunder through the nave. After he was done, he directed Surya Lal and other highly placed Ringists in pouring water from the golden urn into blue cups. There were many of these cups, which were passed up and down the rows of godlings kneeling on their rugs. Danlo watched the thousand people place their lips to the cups, and he lamented that this ritual drinking of water was all that remained of the kalla ceremony. He listened with regret as Bardo sipped from his own gleaming cup and then announced: "It's known that Mallory Ringess became a god and will return among us. Soon, sooner than you might expect. If you would follow his way toward the infinite things, you must renounce your old ways of thinking and remembrance the Elder Eddas."

Upon these portentious words, the sulki grids bent and twisted the light waves streaming through the cathedral, and on the altar next to Bardo, an imago of Mallory Ringess appeared. Many had never seen a sulki-made imago, and there were many gasps of amazement. Although the imago's eyes were too bright a blue and it wore a formal pilot's robe (which Mallory Ringess had rarely worn), it seemed very real. The imago looked out over the people kneeling before him, and it smiled. It stepped down from the altar. Among the people it walked, smiling, beaming peacefulness and great power, and speaking in a wonderfully rich voice of the joy of becoming a god. At last it paused and held out its finely made hands, beckoning to the heaumes that almost all of them were clutching. It invited the people to put on the heaumes and remembrance the Elder Eddas.

Danlo watched as a thousand people lifted up their heaumes and a thousand heads disappeared into these glittering metal shells. He looked through the rails of the balcony to the altar below, and he watched Hanuman emerge from the chancel's doors. That night Hanuman wore no toque or hat of any kind; the clearface covering his head was lit up brilliantly, and a ghastly purple light spilled down over his face. He bowed to Bardo, to the imago of Mallory Ringess, and he bowed to the thousand seekers whose eyelight had disappeared into a world that Danlo had come to know too well. There were rows of seekers kneeling dead-eyed and motionless. The polished heaumes along one row reflected the empty faces in the row behind, row upon row all through the nave. Hanuman looked up toward the loggia and smiled as if he knew Danlo was watching, and he bowed deeply without mockery or shame. Then he turned his attention to directing the remembrance. He faced himself into the computer that he wore, and his eyes turned inward upon himself, and then he was gone, too.

THE CATAVA FEVER

We classify disease as error, which nothing but Truth of Mind can heal.

—*from* Science and Health, *by the Eddy, founder of Kristian Science*

And so Danlo, true to his word, spoke out against the Way of Ringess. During the darkest days of the year, when the first *sarsaras* blow white and deadly out of the north and sweep the citizens of Neverness off the streets, he went about the colleges of the Academy, speaking to friends, explaining to masters and his fellow journeymen why he had decided to renounce Ringism. He spoke passionately, lucidly, and sincerely. But as Old Father was fond of saying: "Truth disappears the moment it is told—like steamy breath into air." Thus Danlo discovered that for every academician he persuaded against attending a remembrance, three more were excited to apprehend the Elder Eddas in any way they could, and they were all too eager to kneel beneath Hanuman's heaumes. To counteract this mass religious fervor, Danlo began to speak cleverly, even cunningly, in a way that was not natural for him to speak. He gave tongue to the verbal razors of the logicians in order to cut away at unreason wherever he found it; he used secret cetic techniques to play upon others' doubts and alarms; into the tender ears of his listeners he even injected Fravashi word drugs, carefully designed memes and phrases that would inoculate them against the temptations of an explosive new religion.

In little time, people began to listen to him. To all devoted Ringists, he became a nuisance, and then more than a nuisance.

He was, after all, Danlo wi Soli Ringess, he of the great remembrance, son of a god. Everyone knew that Hanuman and Bardo were his friends; why, they wondered, would a friend speak against the way of his friends, unless that way were indeed tainted and twisted with lies? Ironically, Danlo's growing influence upon the members of the Order won the approval of Chanoth Chen Ciceron, whom Danlo detested as the most insincere of men. When Lord Ciceron made overtures of friendship—or rather alliance—Danlo politely demurred, citing his mathematical and remembrancing studies as reason for rejecting numerous dinner invitations. For a young pilot who had not yet taken vows to rebuff his Lord Pilot was unheard of. Danlo worried that Lord Ciceron might find a way to deny him his full pilotship, but this was a vague and distant worry, as nothing next to his despair over Hanuman.

This despair was almost total. Not since the Devaki had died—not even when he had learned that it was his father who had brought the slow evil to his tribe—had he suffered such abandonment of hope for another human being. Despair colored all his words and each of his acts, and its color was as black as the oil that the scryers rub into their empty eye sockets. His face bore the stark lines of sleepless nights and forgotten meals; his body fell gaunt like that of a wolf at the end of midwinter spring. He had a presentiment of disaster, and all his visions of the future revolved around the image of Hanuman li Tosh, with his diamond skullcap and his lifeless eyes. He tried to communicate something of his foreboding to Tamara. One night, over a late meal of bloodfruit and cheese, he talked about Hanuman's love of power, and he asked her not to record her memories. With clear, calm words, she promised to reconsider her appointment with Hanuman. But then she laughed, as if to say, I'll do whatever it pleases me to do, and her laughter was full of dark music and pride. When he left her house the next morning, a blizzard was beginning to blow, a great mother storm of furious winds and blinding particles of ice. He hoped this bitter weather might keep her inside next to her fireplace where she would be comfortable and safe from harm.

It is an historical curiosity that the *sarsara* of 2953 raged for sixty-six days, more or less continuously, far into midwinter spring of the succeeding year. It was the longest storm ever recorded in Neverness, and in many ways it was the worst. Considering that it was very cold, there was a good deal of snow, and the wind blew at a deadly speed of a hundred feet per second, instantly icing the flesh of anyone foolish enough to expose her face. The cold wind killed people: hibakusha huddled over their street fires; harijan beggars without family or shelter; autists, of course, and even a few farsiders who lost their way along the paths and the snowdrifts of the Gallivare Green and froze to death only fifty yards from the Yarkonan embassy. It was a grim, dark time, made all the darker by the blowing spindrift and the endless snow clouds that lay over the streets blocking out the sun. And then, on the seventy-fourth of deep winter, there came news that numbed the people of the City and made them eye their neighbors with suspicion and loathing: Chanoth Chen Ciceron and two other members of the Order had fallen ill with a disease that seemed to mimic the depredations of the Catava Fever. When a master virologist examined Lord Ciceron's brain tissues for evidence of infection, it was discovered that he had indeed contracted a rare form of the Catava virus. It was a memory virus, a bio-weapon made on Catava long ago and long thought to be extinct, and no one could guess how it had found its way into the gray matter of Lord Ciceron's brain. But it had, and shortly after falling down into a screaming, foaming fever, Lord Ciceron began to forget things. The first part of his memory to be lost was his mathematics, followed by his grasp of the universal syntax and other huge blocks of knowledge. He forgot his history, just as he forgot all about the politics of the Order. Then he forgot his name, the name of his father and mother, the names of such common items as razors, bars of soap, or mantelets. After three days of spitting at the novices who attended him and changed his bed linen, he completely forgot how to control his bladder and bowels. When the virus attacked the stem of his brain, the virologists said, he would forget how to breathe, and that would be the end of Lord Ciceron. The other infected professionals—Angela Nain and Yang li Yang—did not forget so much so quickly. There was hope for their lives, even for part of their memories, if not their professions. As there was neither an immediate vaccine against the virus nor a cure, they were kept isolated in the Academy's hospice in comfortable little rooms next to Lord Ciceron's. Much to everyone's horror, the virologists singled out semen and vaginal secretions as the vectors of infection. This determination sent the staid academicians into a panic. It was discovered that the crusty Lord Ciceron had had many lovers: Angela Nain and Yang li Yang were only two of the young women and men he had taken to his bed. After a quick inquisition in which all members of the Order were made to reveal their sexual liaisons, the virologists constructed complicated trees diagramming who had swived whom. At least half of all Ordermen, of course, had kept vows of celibacy, but of the remaining half, almost all were connected by unbroken chains of sexual fluids to Lord Ciceron.

"This virus goes through the membranes of a pessary like a drillworm through bone"—this was the rumor that spread through Borja and Resa more quickly than any plague. But it was not so. The virologists determined that the preparations that prudent peope made before coupling were usually sufficient to maim the virus, or at least to stop it from spreading. During the worst part of the storm, when everyone at the Academy was required to submit bits of tissue for examination at the virologists' tower, only four other people were found to be infected. This good news touched almost everyone with an unreasonable joy. (It is curious how deliverance from disaster will elevate human beings to the highest of spirits, even though their day-to-day lives remain as dull and arduous as ever.) Danlo, even though he scorned the fear of disease for himself, was nevertheless relieved that none of his friends or colleagues would fall to the memory virus. He had been especially concerned for Tamara, who, after all, had made a career of swiving the lords and masters of the Order. He decided that she should be told the news immediately, and so he braved the snow-packed streets and made the short, frigid journey to her house. He was surprised to find her not at home. Six times over the next three days, he crossed the City into the Pilot's Quarter, but her house remained as dark and empty as an abandoned cave.

"Most likely she's taken shelter at a hotel," Thomas Rane said to Danlo when they met for their evening remembrancing work. "Or perhaps she's cloistered in some master's apartment and hasn't wanted to get her feet cold. There's no reason to worry."

But Danlo did worry, and as the storm continued to blow, his worry deepened to dread. Then, on the eighty-second, there was an interlude in the *sarsara*'s ferocity; the wind died to a low howl, the snow stopped, and the temperature rose almost to the melting point of mercury. And still Tamara did not return home. On a hundred other planets, of course, Danlo might have signaled her instantly by fone or radio, but this was Neverness and no such devices existed. (That is, they did not exist *legally*.) Finding a lost or hidden person in a city of so great a size was nearly an impossible quest, but Danlo was certain that something terrible had befallen her, and so he set out into the snowy streets on his skis, searching every place he could think to search. First he went to the Hollow Fields to make sure she had not left the City. After the Port Master assured him that no one like Tamara had taken passage on any shuttle or other vessel leaving Neverness, he skied back along the almost abandoned Way to the center of the City. Just south of the Street of Embassies, he turned off on a broad sliddery that ran past the grounds of the Courtesans' Conservatory. He stopped before the gates of the Conservatory, and he implored the gatekeeper to tell her superiors that he requested an audience. Few men, of course, had ever been admitted into the Conservatory. Danlo might have been turned away, but he vowed to wait outside in the cold until the gates were opened. He stood there with his back to the wind as patiently as a hunter crouching over a seal's hole. Seeing that he might freeze to death on the Society's property, the gatekeeper took pity upon him. At last, she let him in. She ushered him into the gatehouse, where a harridan was summoned to talk to him. The harridan—a once-beautiful courtesan wearing embroidered red pajamas—questioned him about his precise connection to Tamara. When he revealed that theirs was a great love match, possibly the greatest the universe had ever known, she made a sour face as if she had been made to chew on the fruit of a lemon. But then she assured Danlo that the Society was as concerned with Tamara's disappearance as he was. She agreed to help him. She would send messengers to the City's pleasure domes to query courtesans who might know her whereabouts. She would review the list of Tamara's most recent assignations and make discreet inquiries of the Order's lords and masters. "I promise she'll be found if it's possible," the harridan said sternly. "But when she's found, I can't think she'll be allowed to continue a liaison with a pilot who hasn't even taken vows."

The next place Danlo journeyed in search of Tamara was to her mother's house. Although it was unlikely she would have returned to her family home, he thought that if Tamara were sick or dying, she might desire a reconciliation with her mother. And so he went down into the remotest part of the city, where the Ashtoreth District overlooks the open sea. On huge, tree-lined blocks stood the houses and apartments of the many Ashtoreth families, and Danlo knocked on five doors before he found a matron who directed him to Tamara's mother's house. This was an ugly and soulless mansion just off the Long Glissade. Victoria One Ashtoreth received him in the mansion's outer hallway, which was all heating grates and bare stone, and quite cold, scarcely above zero temperature. In truth, it was more of an air lock than a place for human beings to meet and converse about important matters. But the Worthy Victoria did not invite him into the inner hallway, nor into the house proper. She stood before him in a voluminous furgown, puffing out steamy breaths of air as she ascertained his mission. Despite the shapelessness of her furs, it was obvious that she was pregnant, as he remembered, with her thirty-third child. She stood tall and aloof, with her hands folded across her swollen belly. Hers was a suspicious, calculating face, plumped out with maternity fat, but still lively and beautiful, in many ways more beautiful than Tamara's. She looked Danlo up and down with the kind of disdain one usually reserves for autists or itinerant maggids. As a pilot in a city where pilots are elevated to an almost godly status, her dismissive manner might have irked (or amused) him, but he was too desperate to indulge such emotions, and so he merely stood before her scrutiny, waiting for her to deny that she had seen Tamara. This she soon did. In fact, she denied Tamara altogether, patting her belly and saying, "This boy will be named Gabriel Thirty-three Ashtoreth, but he'll only be my thirty-second child. My tenth child no longer exists. She's been forgotten. In answer to your question, I must say I don't know anyone named Tamara Ten Ashtoreth. I *must* say this—do you understand? None of my kinsmen will know her either. You may ask for her in any house on any street, but the woman you seek would never return here. Never."

Although the Worthy Victoria must have perceived that Danlo was hungry and cold, she offered him neither food nor hot drink. As an Architect in good standing—and he being one of the Unadmitted—she was forbidden to extend this simple courtesy. But she was not a cruel woman; when Danlo opened the door letting in a frigid blast of wind, she offered to send for a sled. As Danlo had no money, she even offered to pay for it. For a matron of a sect renowned for chariness with money, this was an unusual grace. Danlo thanked her but shook his head and bowed, and then he went out into the storm. Because he had made a practice of unbelief, he went up and down the street knocking on doors and asking if anyone knew Tamara Ten Ashtoreth. But no one did. She truly had been forgotten, it seemed, banished willfully from people's memories.

On the eighty-fifth of deep winter, snow began falling again and it grew colder. As it happened, in the year 2953, this was also the first day of the Festival of the Broken Dolls. It was a dangerous time for anyone to be out on the streets. Although the Festival is held to memorialize and mourn all artificial life wantonly erased over the centuries, there are always a few aficionados of terror who use this holiday to make human beings mourn their own lives. There are slel neckers who steal upon the unwary at night, who jab needles into necks and fract DNA with terrible little viruses; they do this to "break" human beings at random so that people might understand the pain of all the dolls broken in all the cybernetic spaces of computers throughout the Civilized Worlds. It was a dangerous time for Danlo to go about the Old City glidderies searching for Tamara, but he had no thought—then—of slel neckers.

Late on eighty-fifth night, after he had spent many cold and fruitless hours exploring the hospices near the various cemeteries, he returned to his dormitory rooms. There, in the inner hallway standing next to the fireplace, a messenger was waiting for him. A young novice from the Society of Courtesans informed him that Tamara had been found. Tamara was alive and waiting to meet with him. The novice had been sent to escort Danlo back to this meeting at the Courtesans' Conservatory.

Upon hearing this news, Danlo beat the air with his fists and cried out in joy. He did not care that his shouts likely would awaken his entire dormitory. Then he looked at the novice all grim and earnest in her flawless furs. His face fell hard as iron, and he asked the question that he did not want to ask: "Is she well or . . . ill?"

"She's ill," the novice said. "I'm sorry."

"Please tell me . . . how ill?"

"I don't know. If you'll come with me, everything will be explained."

Pausing only to grab a fresh face mask from his room (the mask he had worn all day was stiff and caked with ice), he accompanied the novice across the Academy's deserted grounds to the west gate. Then they skated up the old sliddery that leads from the Academy straight to the great circle outside the Hofgarten. It was very late, too late and much too cold for anyone to be about. But the street was not wholly empty of people. They passed quite a few festival-goers returning from parties. Despite the cheery voices and puffs of toalache smoke, an air of menace overlay the street. It was impossible to make out the features of the people's faces, covered as they were with masks or hoods. And it was too dark. The flame globes had all been extinguished so that their light would not interfere with the glow of the ice lanterns. Hung from each building were ice lanterns fashioned in the shapes of little houses or temples or other types of dwelling places. They were delicate constructions of sheet ice and light, the faint light of the blue or green or scarlet flames burning inside. These flames were meant to symbolize the life of all artificial organisms, and the street should have been glorious with light. Only, it was snowing and the wind was up, and too many of these lights had been snuffed out. Danlo marveled at the trouble the people took to renew the lights, night after night, year after year. He thought deep, troubled thoughts then, and he despaired over the inherent fragility of flame. He was very glad when they turned off the street and passed through the gates of the Courtesans' Conservatory. No matter how ill Tamara might be, he thought, it would be good to smile at her again, to press his lips against her forehead and listen to her rising breath.

"Please follow me," the novice said as they entered the grounds of the conservatory. "And please keep a silence—we're not supposed to talk while the novices are doing their midnight exercises."

She led him past dark buildings rimed with driven snow. He had no difficulty keeping a silence. He listened to the novice's chattering teeth and the whoosh of his own breath inside his face mask. The wind had died, momentarily, and the conservatory was oppressive in its silence. He expected to be taken to a hospice or cryologist's station, but the novice surprised him by showing him to the door of the great house at the center of the conservatory. "This is the Mother's house," she said. "You're the second man today she's asked inside."

Without knocking, the novice opened the door and escorted him through various hallways into a gowning room. She took his furs, his face mask, and his boots, and she stowed them neatly on drying racks. She gave him a pair of knitted house boots to wear over his cold feet. Then she helped him pull a black silk gown over his head, and she told him, "You may dress in this house as you wish, but you must be gowned if you're to talk with the Mother—she's asked to meet you before you go in to see the Ashtoreth."

Danlo nodded his head, and he followed the novice into a fire room rich with beautiful furniture and other finely made things. Although the room was much too luxurious to suit him, it was a luxury of good taste and perfect proportion; he thought he had never been in such a lovely room since coming to Neverness. He sat at a marble chess table which had been cleared of chess pieces and set with a tea service. He rubbed his head as he watched the novice pour a fragrant cha tea into his blue cup. She bowed to him, smiled shyly, and she went to inform the Mother that he was prepared for their meeting.

He waited through three cups of tea. To him, this seemed quite a long time, but it was actually not since he gulped his tea like a thirsty wolf, burning his mouth and throat. At last he heard sounds outside the room, and then the door opposite the fireplace opened. Two harridans in red pajamas stood supporting an old woman between them. It was the Mother, he thought, the famous harridan who was the head of the Society of Courtesans. She wore a gown of black silk over her pajamas. The whole of the gown, front and back, was covered with crewelwork and other embroidery; the scores of harridans who run the Society had each stitched this exalted fabric with jewels and lovely designs, as a pledge of their devotion to the Mother. The harridans helped the Mother into a soft couch next to Danlo. They made sure that her legs were properly cushioned and elevated. They poured her tea. After plumping out her pillows and arraying her gown so that it spread out like a giant fan, they bowed to Danlo and left him alone with her.

The Mother inclined her head toward Danlo, and she said, "My name is Helena Turkmanian, but you may call me Mother, if that pleases you."

Danlo smiled and he bowed to her. It pleased him indeed to regard her as a most motherly woman, for she seemed aglow with life and tenderness, despite her great age. In truth, she was late into her final old age; she was old beyond old in a way that the women of Danlo's tribe had never been. Her skin hung freely from her bones and smelled sweet as a good leather. She was frailer than any bird, yet she still possessed the strength of a great energy, which seemed to well up inside her and concentrate in her eyes. She had lovely eyes, clear and infinitely kind, though hard as diamonds. Looking at her as she looked at him, he thought that she would be completely generous in her devotion to others—and completely selective of those upon whom she bestowed this rare gift of love. At last, he said to her, "You are Mother to the courtesans, yes?"

"I am."

"And Tamara called you this, too?"

"Since she was a novice—she was always the most polite of girls."

"Does she still call you Mother, then?" Danlo asked this question softly as he stared into his empty teacup.

"She still does," the Mother said, and she smiled sweetly. "She's not as ill as you might have feared."

Danlo put down the cup and then touched the white feather dangling from his hair. He was very aware of the Mother studying him, listening to his uneven breathing, perhaps even counting the pulses of the great artery that throbbed along his throat. "I have been . . . very afraid for her," he admitted.

"I'm sorry," the Mother said. "And I'm sorry to tell you that Tamara is not as well as you will have hoped."

Danlo pressed the scar above his eye as he looked at the Mother and waited for her to say the terrible words, the words he had dreaded hearing since Tamara had disappeared.

And the Mother said, "It seems that Tamara Ten Ashtoreth has lost part of her memory. Two days ago, one of our voluptuaries found her wandering about the Street of Musicians."

"Two days ago! Why didn't you send for me sooner?"

"I'm sorry, but our first concern was for Tamara. She'd suffered dehydration and frostbite, and it's possible she'd been raped before—"

"Oh, no!" Danlo cried out as he leapt to his feet. "Oh, no."

The Mother leaned forward upon her couch and covered his fist with her soft, old hand. This was not an easy act for her to manage, and the strain of it made her gasp. "Please sit down, Young Pilot. Would you like another cup of tea? It would be my pleasure to make your cup, but my days of pouring tea are past."

Danlo sat down and filled his cup with steaming tea. He held it to his lips, but he did not drink it. The Mother was smiling at him, in a kindly way, as if to reassure him that everything would be well. He looked down to see his hand squeezing hers, then he closed his eyes because it hurt to keep them open.

"The tragedy," she said, "is that we may never know what happened to Tamara. She's forgotten certain incidences in her recent past."

"Is it the Catava Fever, then?"

The Mother nodded her head. "It would seem so."

"A manufactured virus," he said. "A weapon made on Catava six hundred years ago."

"Are you familiar with these weapons, Young Pilot?"

Danlo opened his eyes, looking at nothing in particular, remembering. "Yes," he said. "Such a virus once killed people . . . who were near to me."

"You mustn't be afraid for Tamara's life—she won't die from what's happened to her, you know."

"But if her brain is infected—"

The Mother clapped her hands together softly, once, and then looked at Danlo with a mixture of sternness and compassion. "It might give you hope to know she's not presently infected. The virologist we summoned could find nothing in her body or brain. The blood bears *antibodies* to the virus. Only antibodies. It's possible the virus was destroyed immediately upon entering her. Such miracles are possible. There are a few people—a few billion people, most of them descendants of Architects who survived the War of the Faces. Their bodies are almost immune to bio-weapons. The Ashtoreths, for instance—there are so many Ashtoreths. Tamara is an Ashtoreth, after all, and I've never known her to be sick, not even a flu or a cold. The virus did no detectable damage to her brain. This is certain. I've had three akashics paint her brain, neuron by neuron—they've found nothing. She should be as well as you or I."

"But she has forgotten . . . things?"

"She really hasn't forgotten very much," the Mother said. "It would seem that the virus fracted only select parts of her memory."

"But how is that possible?"

"That's the mystery—no one really knows. Too little is understood about memory. Not even the remembrancers can explain how this filthy virus did what it did to Tamara."

Danlo was quiet for a moment as he looked down at the scars on his hands. Then he asked, "And what did it do?"

"That's hard to say."

"Please tell me."

"There are so many memories," the Mother said.

"Please tell me what has happened to Tamara."

With a wave of her graceful hand, the Mother indicated various items about the room: the golden alaya shells set out above the fireplace, the Fravashi carpet, the ice sculptures kept clear-cut and cold inside refrigerated clary vaults. She sighed and said, "If a wormrunner were to enter this house and ransack it before stealing things, it would be difficult to tell at first sight what was missing. But it would be obvious that many things were gone. Only after the rooms were put together again and an inventory made would it be possible to determine which things these were."

"Has Tamara's memory been ransacked, then?"

"No, it has not. And that was the difficulty. It took us most of a day to discover that there was a problem with her memory. Talking with her was like entering a room from which one or two items of great value had been stolen, with quiet and great cunning. Little things that might appear as trifles or curios to outsiders—but to Tamara they would be the most priceless of memories."

Danlo sat completely still, as an Alaloi man sits beneath the falling stars and awaits the coming of his ancestors. Although he heard no voices nor saw any visions, he sensed that the memories lost from Tamara's mind concerned him deeply. Despite this overpowering presentiment—the absolute coldness of knowing that locked open his eyes—he was unprepared for what the Mother said to him next.

"Young Pilot, I'm sorry to tell you, but Tamara has forgotten who you are."

Danlo's eyes were wide open, but he could see nothing. Or rather, he could see nothing more than the objects of the room dissolving into a dazzling blackness that took his breath away. The sound in his ears was like the ringing of a great bell that drew out long and high until it hissed and burned inside him. After a while, he became aware that the Mother was looking at him, leaning nearer, reaching out her trembling hand to touch his face. She touched his lips with infinite gentleness, and he was aware of her old, quavering voice, this golden instrument of compassion that pulled him back into her presence.

"She's forgotten meeting you," the Mother said. "She's forgotten your time together, the words you spoke together when you were alone."

He thought the Mother might break into weeping then, because her eyes were shiny with tears. But she kept her composure. Some deep part of her seemed to be watching herself; it was as if she were playing at life's tragedies with all the power of her soul—despite the pain, always playing and ultimately finding the game to be sweet and good.

"She's forgotten even your name. Oh, not your last name—she knows about *the* Ringess, of course. But she doesn't remember he has a son."

"Has she forgotten . . . everything?"

"I'm afraid so."

"Unless she had died, I would not have thought that was possible."

"I know," the Mother said.

"I cannot see . . . how it must be for her," he said.

"It's not well, you know. She's not at all well."

"It must be terrible . . . to forget."

"Yes, it is." The Mother said this with the certainty of an old woman whose memory was not as keen as it once had been. And then she smiled and said, "But it's the most marvelous thing to suddenly remember what only seemed to have been lost."

Danlo nodded his head as he thought about this. He asked, "Has she been told about me? About . . . us?"

"I talked with her myself this morning. Nirvelli was with me. Naturally, since I hadn't been aware of your liaison, I could only tell her what Nirvelli had told me about both of you—and that wasn't very much."

"No," he said, "we tried to keep things secret."

"Well, at least Nirvelli knew that Tamara was liaising with a journeyman—actually she said that Tamara had fallen into love."

"Yes," he said. "She had fallen. We did . . . fall together."

The Mother smiled at Danlo as if she knew very well how such a thing could be possible. It was obvious she favored Danlo, as a mother does a favorite child—and in other ways, too.

"When I told Tamara about this *love,* she was astonished. Oh, not because you're just a journeyman—she's accepted that she might have broken our rules. Just as, seeing you, I've forgiven her for breaking them. The astonishing thing is the depth of this love. Nirvelli said that she saw it in Tamara, once. I see it now. It's astonishing that Tamara could forget the 'greatest love match the universe has ever known.' No, please don't be angry, I'm not quoting your words sarcastically. I believe there's something great in this love. Isn't love what we all live for? A remarkable kind of love. *This* is what Tamara was trained for. This waking up of the whole organism, the deepest parts, out of love. The possibility of creating a new being. This was her calling, her dream. The dream of many of us. Astonishing that she might have come so close—and then nothing. How must it be for her to know that she might have lost the most priceless thing in the universe—and have no memory of what that thing felt like or meant to her? I believe there's a black hole of memory in the

618

center of her mind. It draws her inward. Looking at this hole, she grieves. We all grieve, Young Pilot. For her. And for ourselves, of course, for what might have been."

Danlo bowed his head, trying to imagine what it would be like to forget what had passed between him and Tamara. He could not. After a while, he looked at the Mother and said, "Surely you have reminded her that she had . . . a calling."

"You don't understand. Such things can't simply be reminded. They can't be told."

"No," he said, "I suppose not."

"Tamara has lost a good deal of our art, as well. Not just the dream—but knowledge of the body, there are techniques that she once knew, her flair for passion, all gone, now, completely gone. She can't practice our art as she is now."

"But she can relearn these things, yes?"

The Mother's face fell mournful and her fingers played over the fine wrinkles around her eyes. She seemed to reminisce about the keenest of her memories, for her face was alive with old hurts and pleasures. Then, in a soft, musing voice, she said, "Considered against all the things we learn in a lifetime, what is this knowledge of ours but a grain of sand? Against the tapestry of our whole selves, what is our sacred art but the smallest of threads? So very little has actually been taken from Tamara. And yet, everything."

"It must wound her very deeply," he said.

"It's killing her," the Mother said. "Killing her soul."

Danlo shook his head. "No, that is not possible."

"Nevertheless—"

"Did you know that the remembrancers have a saying?" he asked. "They say this: 'Memory can never be destroyed.' "

The Mother suddenly flashed him a lovely smile. "This is our hope."

"Then it must be my hope, too," he said. And then he thought: *Hope is the right hand of fear.*

"You must be impatient to see her."

"Yes," he said. "I am."

"Very well, you must go to her now, if you're ready. Talk to her, Young Pilot. Help her remember."

That was all the Mother said to him. They drank their tea in silence, and there was an understanding between them. Soon the two harridans came to take the Mother away. Danlo bowed to her, and she to him, and she took his ungloved hand in hers and squeezed it so hard that the flesh along her arm jiggled and shook. In her ancient eyes, there was contentment, even happiness. He sensed he would never see her again, so he said, "I wish you well."

Then he turned to study his teacup, at the bits of greenish leaves floating through the last unfinished dram of tea. He wondered what it would be like not to remember, and he took a swallow of tea, and he was not surprised that the taste of it was stringent and very bitter.

THE GIFT

Memory is the soul of reality.

—saying of the remembrancers

After what seemed a long while, the novice returned to lead him down a dimly lit hallway to the guest room. In the Mother's house, on the first floor, one room was always kept ready for honored visitors, or for harridans returning to Neverness from missions across the Civilized Worlds—or for simple courtesans such as Tamara who required the Mother's attentions. The novice stopped before a plain wooden door and looked at Danlo. She used her little, white knuckles to knock at the door, and she announced, "My lady, your visitor has arrived."

The door opened, and Danlo heard the novice say, "My lady, may I present the pilot, Danlo wi Soli Ringess?"

He heard her say this, but the words made no impression upon his mind because suddenly Tamara stood before him in her red robes and long golden hair. He drank in, all in a moment, the darkness of her eyes, the quick embarrassment, the livid wounds on her face and hands. Out of joy and good manners, he rushed forward to embrace her in the Alaloi way, with his arms thrown wide as a thallow's wings. But she held up her hand and backed away. "Please, no," she said.

She bowed to the novice and told her, "Thank you, Maya, I'd like to be alone with the pilot."

The novice returned her bow, cast Danlo a nervous glance, and then retreated down the hallway. Danlo followed Tamara into the room and shut the door behind him. The sound of it closing was of metal clicking into metal. He looked around the room, which was full of plants native to Old Earth: araucaria and cactus and wandering Jew, and other green plants whose names he did not know. They gave off a light oxygen smell at odds with the heaviness of sweat clinging to Tamara's robes. It was really too warm for her to dress so formally, but clearly she was not comfortable receiving him in pajamas or unclothed, as was her wont. Looking at her, at the patches of red skin regrown across her frostbitten face, he was uncomfortable, too.

"Tamara, Tamara," he said. "I looked for you . . . everywhere."

"I'm sorry," she said. "If only I'd known. Please, would you like some tea or ice wine? Would you sit with me, for a while?"

The Mother's guest room was bright, cheery, and furnished for the convenience of old women. There was a raised bed covered with knitted shagshay spreads; there was a multrum in a closet with gleaming steel handrails; there was a robot that one could summon or send scurrying about the wall shelves or vanities to fetch various things. At the far end of the room, by the window overlooking the conservatory grounds, there was a little tea table and two high-backed chairs. She motioned for them to sit, facing each other, in these plush chairs. Of course, he would have preferred sitting cross-legged on the carpet by the fireplace; he could scarcely believe that she seemed to have forgotten this.

"I'm sorry," she said as she gripped her hands together. "I'm sorry, but this will be difficult. You have me at a disadvantage. I've been told so many things about us—you'll be thinking about these things while I try to remember."

"You do not remember anything?"

She shook her head. "No, nothing."

He stared at her in disbelief, and his breath quickened, and he had the strange feeling of the hairs along the back of his neck pulling up, tingling. There was a tightness in his chest, a fiery knot in his throat that no amount of swallowing would undo. He had hoped that seeing him would help her remember, instantly, the way the shock of a sudden wind might recall cold, happy nights spent around the oilstones, talking with friends or playing with lovemates. He had hoped this too desperately, and clearly, so had she. Hope was written across her lovely, damaged face. They met eyes, and she must have expected to see something familiar and comforting in this encounter, for suddenly she looked away, and her eyes were black and bitter with disappointment. *There is nothing there,* he thought. And this was an astonishing thing; this was a truth that made him want to scream and pull his eyes out of his head. They should have recognized each other, as they had at their first meeting and all their times together since then. Even if both their memories had been lost, it should have been as if they had known each other for a billion years and would honor this bond for ten billion years more. Only now there was nothing. Looking at him, he thought, she could not see him. Something inside her (perhaps in him, too) was blind.

She has been blinded, he thought, and with this turn of his mind, he began to rage against a universe that could engineer such a tragedy.

"Pilot, are you all right?"

He sat in his soft chair, knuckles pressed to his head. After a while, when he had caught his breath and could see again, he choked out, "You . . . were right. This will be hard."

"I can only imagine how painful this must be for you."

"And for you," he said, "isn't there a similar pain?"

"No, I don't think so. Mine is only the emptiness of forgetting. While you—what could be more painful than remembrance?"

He smiled and shook his head. "Everything I remember about us is blessed. Truly. Shall I tell you the things I remember?"

"You have a remarkable memory, it's said."

"Sometimes it is hard . . . for me to forget."

"Then tell me," she said.

He swallowed three times, then said, "There was a game you taught me, an art, a kind of telepathy like face reading—but not really like it at all. The object was to open the cells to signals from the cells of the other. After joining, for half a night in the lotus position, always looking into each other's eyes . . . this *becoming* of the other person's cells. To become the other. We did this, once. Do you remember? It was the ninth of winter, and it was snowing all night, and when morning came you kissed me and said—"

"No, please." Tamara held up her hand and shook her head.

"We found the place," he said, "where the thoughts stream before they become words, and our thoughts were the same, for a moment, then for half the night. Like two rivers flowing together. Wordless. But endless, too. When morning came, you said a thing to me that only I—"

"Please don't say any more."

At the sound of panic in her voice, he suddenly paused. "But why not?"

"I've decided it would be best if you didn't *tell* me anything."

"But you must want to know," he said. "It must be terrible, not knowing."

"Of course I want to know. But it's tiresome being told. I want to remember, for myself, if I'm to remember at all."

"But that was my intention. To help you remember."

"I don't think anyone can help me, after what's happened."

"There are ways," he said. "The memories are always there. Onstreaming, like light. But with our minds, we close doors to them. We stand with perfect vision in darkened rooms. This is called forgetting."

"Well, I suppose some doors are locked shut—forever."

"No, that is not true. There is always a way to open a door. To find the key. The problem is finding the key."

"If only I could believe that," she said. "I wish I had your faith."

He smiled and said, "Faith—I have been accused of being too much a disbeliever to have any place left for faith."

"Have you?"

"Don't you remember?"

"Well," she said, "you must be the most faithful of all disbelievers."

"You used to tell me that very thing."

"Did I?"

"Yes, you did," he said. "I think you are remembering, now."

"No, I'm observing."

"Just that?"

"If I'm remembering at all, it's only what others have told me about you."

"Are you sure?"

She cast him an icy look, then said, "This is very tiresome, you know."

"I am . . . sorry. It is late and—"

"Please. *I'm* not at all tired. It's just that these remembrancing tricks have all been tried and nothing has worked."

"Has a remembrancer attended you, then?"

"Of course. Thomas Rane—I believe you know him quite well. He was here this morning."

"Looking for keys, yes?"

"Isn't that what remembrancers *do*? He tried his word keys, of course. And olfaction and gestalt, association memory, too. He even had me face a simulation that some cartoonist had made—a little vignette of you and me doing our work together. I'm sure it was meant to shock me into remembrance. It *did* shock me, but not as Master Rane had wished."

As Danlo nodded his head, he happened to look down at the tea table. It was as black and polished as an obsidian mirror, though besmeared in many places with fingerprints. He saw his reflection there, dark, troubled, and faint. Although it usually amused him to look at his own face, the sight of himself brooding over Tamara's disfigurement annoyed him, so he covered his reflection with the palm of his naked hand. Instantly, the top of the table began to change colors. It swirled with bands of indigo, chlorine, and puce. He realized that this was probably a Simoom antique, a frivolous piece of technology designed by cetics to read the simpler emotions. Its surface was of pure chatoy, and it ran with colors as extravagantly as did the eyes of a Scutari. In a moment one color settled out and spread across the whole of the table. It was grege, the ugliest of all the yellows. He could not know which colors were coded to which emotions, but he knew what he was experiencing at that moment, and that was a blend of frustration and disgust.

He lifted his hand up from the table and watched it return into blackness. He said, "In order to make his simulation, the cartoonist must have captured our basic images and voices, yes? Before permuting them."

Tamara, he saw, had been staring at the table as a hunter studies the sky for signs of changing weather. He noticed that she was careful to keep her hands away from it.

"You're a beautiful man," she said. "And I'm a . . . I'm a courtesan. The outlaw cartoonists are always slelling images of people like us to make their little simulations."

"But Thomas Rane is no cartoonist."

"Of course not. But who knows who he knows?"

"It is possible," he said, "that Bardo has recorded the images of various persons who have entered his house."

"*That* shouldn't be a surprise," she said.

"No," he said. And then, "But you say that even this simulation failed to excite . . . your memory?"

"It failed utterly."

"Perhaps there is some key element missing from these images."

"Thomas Rane suggested the same thing. He thought it would be best if I saw you in person."

"I had hoped . . . that you would recognize me," he said. "That my voice would be familiar."

"I wish I could say that it was."

"Then . . . I have failed, too."

His voice, he thought, his true voice that vibrated from his throat as naturally as any animal's, should have been the simplest of keys. It should have unlocked her memory, or at the very least, the sound of it should have touched off inside her the deeper emotions.

She is deaf to me, he thought. *Something has deafened her.*

Tamara smoothed her hair away from her face and said, "Thomas Rane even tried giving me kalla, but that did nothing to help me—it seems impossible to me now that I was ever enamored of that particular drug."

"Yes, you once had a taste for kalla."

"No more."

"But kalla brought you . . . your first clear sight of the One memory."

"I know," she said. She closed her eyes and pressed her knuckles to them. She was on the threshold of tears, but like an astrier mother attending her child's funeral, she would not allow herself to cry. "I know that I once had this unitary memory that everyone talks about. *Saw* it, quite clearly. I could hold it, relive it again and again. But now it's slipped away. I've only the slightest memory of the memory. It's very faint, like the glow left in the sky after the sun has gone down. I know it was important—the most important thing in the world. But I can't see why. I can't see it, and that's what bothers me. Because I really don't miss this memory, even though I know I should. *This* is what frightens me, Pilot. If I've lost this marvelous thing, I should mourn its passing, shouldn't I? What's the matter with me that I don't care? That I don't *care* that I don't care?"

He watched her press her fist into the pit of her belly. Her face had fallen waxy and white, as if she had eaten from a cache of rotten seal meat. He engaged her eyes, then. He smiled and said, "I cannot believe . . . that you do not care."

"But I *mustn't* care, don't you see?"

She let her hand fall to the table, and its surface warmed to the color of steel. Then Danlo touched the tabletop and it vibrated up into a pearl gray. He reached out his hand to touch her fingers. She left her hand motionless to be touched. There should have been a connection between them, electric and instantaneous, the sure knowledge that the cells of his body were meant to join with hers. But her palms were cold with moisture, and her fingers were stiff and unalive as if they had been caught in the open wind, and there was nothing between them, nothing at all.

Tamara, Tamara, he silently lamented. *What wind could ever blow so cold?*

Now the table was as gray as ashes; they both stared at it, saying nothing.

After a while, she withdrew her hand from his. She sat quietly with her hands folded, resigned to her fate, looking very much like an image that Danlo had seen on one of Bardo's stained-glass windows. It was an image of one of the Kristian martyrs about to be burned to death out of pride for her faith.

Not wind but fire, he suddenly thought. *Not coldness, but burning.*

Though her hands had suffered frostbite, they were as red as if she had plunged them into a pot of boiling water. He asked her if she remembered wandering the streets during the storm, and she nodded her head.

"I remember thinking I should find a warming pavilion or go inside. The snow was blinding me, and it was so cold my face was burning."

Fire is the left hand of wind, he remembered.

"Of course, when I finally realized I had frostbite, it was too late. In another place, I might have lost my fingers and my nose. But the City has the best cryologists in the universe, if one can afford them."

He drummed his fingertips against the table as he stared at her. He asked, "Is your memory complete since you were brought here?"

"I'm sure it is."

"But what do you remember in the period just before you were found?"

"I don't remember anything," she said. "There's a hole there—missing time."

"How much time?"

"I really can't say."

His fingers drummed faster, in waves from right to left.

"But on the other side of this hole—there is more memory, yes?"

"Of course there is."

"What memory?"

She sighed and clutched the sleeve of her robe. "I know what you're doing. But it's hopeless—Thomas Rane has already tried reconstructing the chronology. There are too many holes. Too much time has passed. Even in the best of times, of course, I could never have remembered my day-to-day activities over more than half a year."

Danlo, who sometimes recalled every day of his life since he was four years old, could only bow his head in respect for her debility. In a low, solemn voice, he asked her, "The holes in your memory go back more than half a year?"

"At least that far."

"There must be a . . . first thing that you have forgotten."

"I believe the first hole has obliterated much of the night of Bardo's party."

"The night we met?"

"It would seem so."

"Strange," he said. The table beneath him, he saw, was now turquoise on the verge of deepening into blue.

"It was the third or fourth time I'd been to Bardo's house," she said. "I remember drinking a glass of wine and chatting with a holist I'd once had a contract with. I remember the triya seeds popping and the smoke, and I remember meeting Hanuman and—"

"You remember meeting Hanuman?"

"Of course I do."

"But he met you . . . only minutes before I first saw you."

Tamara squinted and rubbed the back of her neck. She seemed confused. "I'm sorry, I don't remember seeing you."

"With our eyes, we found each other," he said. "And then Hanuman presented us."

She shook her head slowly back and forth. "I remember looking at Bardo's bonsai trees and thinking how ill they seemed, and then, when I turned around, Hanuman was standing next to me. *He* presented himself to me. Which was really a courageous thing for a journeyman to do; most journeymen won't even talk with a courtesan. But Hanuman was different. I've never met anyone with a better sense of himself. He was quite charming."

Danlo waited a moment before saying, "And then?"

"After that, nothing. I suppose I met you and we . . . I've been told we went off together. I'm sorry, Pilot."

"You remember nothing more of that night?"

"Only fragments. It's as if I'd drunk too much wine. Well, no, it's really not like that at all because my memories aren't at all hazy. They're clear as glass, but they're all broken apart into thousands of pieces. I remember Hanuman reading faces, little things he said. He was quite brilliant."

"You remember him reading faces." Danlo said this flatly, without emotion, though it surprised him to see the table changing colors to a rich aquamarine.

"Yes, I've said that I do."

"Nothing more?"

"What do you mean?"

"You do not remember we were standing together while he did this?"

"Is that true?"

"We were holding hands," he said.

"I'm sorry, no."

"Do you remember Hanuman reading Surya, then?"

"Only that Surya was thinking of the Ringess. She was almost worshiping, really. And after Hanuman read her face, she practically worshiped *him*."

"Strange that you should remember this much but no more."

"I'm sorry."

"Then you have no memory of warning me about Hanuman?"

"Why should I do such a thing?"

"Because Hanuman frightened you that night. And other times since."

Tamara covered her face with her hands, and she pressed her fingertips against her closed eyes. She sighed and then looked at him. "I can't imagine being frightened of Hanuman," she said.

"You have . . . no dread of him?"

"No, I don't think so. Most of my memories of him are favorable."

Suddenly the drumming of Danlo's fingers stopped. "Is it possible," he asked, "that you have forgotten certain things about him?"

"That would be only natural," she said. "Since many of my memories of him must have been connected to you."

How is memory connected to memory? he wondered. And then: *Hanu, Hanu, what is this fate connecting us like two hands joined together?*

Without warning, a coldness and clarity came over him, and he sat utterly still. He was distantly aware of the table's surface falling away into a deep blue color, and then into a luminous blue-black that swallowed up his outspread hand. His field of vision widened to include many things at once: the snow-encrusted windows; the plants hanging from the ceiling in brilliant cascades of green; Tamara's lovely face, full of perplexity and pride; and the other thing that was not of fiber or flesh or material substance, but was nonetheless just as many-textured and real. This other thing was composed of plots and aspirations and jealousies (and love), of strands of fate woven together as tightly as a tapestry, and of real events that had occurred in spacetime, in chambers and houses that human beings had made, and out in the pure, frigid air that circles the world. What he saw was not a dreamscape nor of the universe of conjecture, but rather a perfect visualization of reality, whatever reality really was. It came to him in an instant, fully formed, like a jewel falling out of the night. It was faceted with ten thousand surfaces and angles; he had a sure knowledge of only a few of these parts: Tamara's loss of fear for Hanuman; a memory virus made hundreds of years ago on Catava; the cleansing ceremony of the Cybernetic Universal Church. To see the whole structure of Tamara's disfigurement from these parts astonished him. And more, it sickened him to know that what he saw so completely must be true.

The universe is like a hologram, he remembered. *Every part contains information about the whole.*

All his life he had sought a new way of seeing, and now, here, in a secluded room closed in by a raging blizzard, his eyes were beginning to open. In truth, he should have seen it sooner, but his love for Hanuman had blinded him. But now there was no love. Or rather, love had been joined—right hand to left—to that terrible emotion that he feared more than any other thing.

"Please, Pilot, have I said anything to anger you?"

He sat staring at his clenched fist as it trembled atop the table, which now ran with the darkest of red colors. His head hurt, and his throat, and he was afraid the blood vessels behind his eyes might burst. There came a moment when he saw that he might actually pass into unconsciousness or stroke of death. It would be an easy thing to do. He was very close, walking for the first time this particular razor's edge. He was very close, as well, to cooling this deadly rage, but he allowed himself, for a single moment, the luxury and satisfaction of pure righteous anger. And then he fell—instantly, dizzyingly—far beyond mere physical emotion into that other place which is all nightmare and torment. Terrible images burned through his mind. There was a moment of sickening freedom in which anything was possible and all things permitted. He wanted to murder a man. He wanted to crush the breath from the throat of his best friend. He wanted this more than he wanted life, and there was a moment when he would have died to accomplish it. Then he looked down at the table reflecting a dark image of his face. The chatoy finish was now purple-black, the color of a bruise where the blood has clotted deep in the tissues. He suddenly raised his arm and punched downward, smashing this hard surface with his fist. He gripped his damaged knuckles and watched the colors in the table die.

No, I won't.

"Pilot, Pilot."

When he looked up, Tamara was standing next to him, resting her hand on his shoulder. She touched his face, slowly, carefully, as a zoologist might touch a sleeping cobra.

"No, I will not," he whispered to himself. "Never again."

"Pilot, I'm sorry. I'm sorry."

Never hurting another, not even in one's thoughts.

He rubbed the knuckle of his ring finger. It was bleeding and already swollen; probably it was broken. He promised himself, then, that he would never again allow his hatred for Hanuman to overcome him. If he could not purge this ugliness from himself, he would bury it deep inside and build a wall around it. As an oyster surrounds an irritant grain of sand with layers of pearl, he would build walls and walls around his urge to kill, only each wall would be as pure and adamantine as diamond.

"I've never seen anyone so angry," Tamara said.

"I am . . . sorry," he said. The coolness of her hand against his temple was a marvelous thing. He covered her hand with his hand, then he smiled. "But I have never had any anger for you."

"No?"

"No, never."

He wondered if he should tell her what he had seen. How could she believe the accusations he would direct at Hanuman? That Hanuman was both a murderer of minds and a slel necker? How could he believe this himself?

These are things that I cannot know, but nevertheless I know them.

Later, with logic, with knowledge, with all the resources of the Order, he would analyze the events leading up to Tamara's memory disfigurement. But now there was only the certainty of this new way of seeing.

"Your face," she said. "There was so much hatred there."

"Yes, hatred," he said. He peeled her hand away from his cheek and looked at her.

"I've never seen anything like it before. At least, I don't remember."

"Anyone can hate," he said. "A child can hate."

"From what the others told me about you, I'd never have imagined that you could hate anything."

"I was . . . thinking," he said. "Thinking about what happened to you."

Even now, as he squeezed her hand tightly and clenched his teeth against the popping of his knuckle, he was brooding over Hanuman's maneuvers to ruin her, seeing the whole of this scheme from beginning to end. In the beginning, there was pride, pain, and immense ambition. In the beginning, in secret, in a locked room deep within the cetics' tower, Hanuman had approached his Lord Cetic, the very private and unapproachable Audric Pall. The two men had conspired to gain power over the Order. And over the Way of Ringess. Hanuman had promised to aid Lord Pall's ascendency within the Tetrad, if only the Lord Pall would promise to use his position to stop the Order's harassment of the Way, and eventually to support the growth of Bardo's church. And so, promises had been made. Never saying a word, Lord Pall made signs with his fingers and face, and he came to an understanding with Hanuman. Only, Hanuman understood much more than did Lord Pall. Hanuman could see that Lord Pall was entranced with the temptation to manipulate and make a new religion. Lord Pall would use his—and Hanuman's—immense cetic skills to accomplish this. He, the powerful and wise Lord of Cetics, would impose his will upon Ringism, and he would use its wild, religious energy to revitalize the Order. He told himself that he would do all this unselfishly, legally, if secretly. He would become Lord of the Order and the secret master of a new universal religion. And he would continue to guide and control Hanuman li Tosh—or so he thought.

Oh, Hanu, Hanu, how clearly you understand that the whole question of power always turns upon who has fear of whom.

After this conclave—recorded neither by machine nor the minds of men, save the two cetics—Hanuman had gone down into the Farsider's Quarter where he knew many people: worm-runners, warrior-poets, even a few slel neckers were among the more dangerous of his acquaintances. He solicited the services of an outlaw splicer, a smug little man with drooping mustaches and ugly, jeweled eyes. For a huge sum of money, the splicer procured for Hanuman a vial of viruses made six hundred years previously on Catava. Like a bottle of Summerworld wine, it had been passed from collector to collector, gaining value at each passing. Hanuman was the first of its owners to make use of the virus. With sweet ruthlessness, he seduced one of Lord Ciceron's lovers, a young man named Yang li Yang. He infected him with this virus. And Yang li Yang had passed this virus to Chanoth Chen Ciceron, and on to three other academicians who immediately had commenced the forgetting of themselves. Hanuman had done this in fulfillment of his promise to aid Lord Pall; as well, he had done this to unnerve and warn his Lord Cetic, and for deeper reasons.

Danlo suddenly stood up, and he asked, "Tamara, do you remember going to Hanuman . . . to record your memories?"

She looked at him sadly as she shook her head. "No, of course not."

"It would have been . . . just before you began to forget things."

"If I'd gone to Hanuman, I suppose *he'd* remember that I'd visited him."

"Yes, that is true."

"Well, he's your friend—presumably, when you discovered I was missing, he would have told you that I'd recently been to see him."

"It is possible . . . that you presume too much."

"What do you mean?"

Danlo came closer and lay his hands atop her shoulders. He said, "We are not the same friends . . . that we used to be."

"I'm sorry, Pilot, but why should it matter if I went to Hanuman just before this virus destroyed my memories? Are you afraid that I've somehow infected *him*?"

"No," he said, "I am not afraid of that."

"What, then?"

"Do you remember *resolving* to record your memories? Your experience of the One memory?"

She backed away from him unexpectedly and said, "I suppose it's possible I would have wanted to record whatever understanding I had of the One memory. Do you think that's too vain of me? Well, I'm told that I used to be afflicted with this sin of vanity."

Yes, he thought, she was vain and proud, and Hanuman knew this as well as he did. Hanuman, ever a man of multiple purposes, had kept this vanity in mind even as he designed his remembrancing computers. He had schemed to lure her into the chapter house where he kept his gleaming heaumes. He had issued an invitation to her—and to the best minds in the City. How could she resist such a compliment to her talents and accomplishments? She could not, and so late one night she had gone to Hanuman, out of will and pride, knowing that she was doing a dangerous thing. When Danlo closed his eyes, he could see this encounter with a perfect clarity: Tamara, stepping through the doorway into the cavernous chapter house, standing nervously in her snow-dappled furs as Hanuman politely bowed and offered her a cup of hot tea. Her face was all curiosity and resolution as she forced herself to trust Hanuman. And with his sweet, silver words, Hanuman flattered her, and she betrayed an instant delight at this good news of herself, though she was instantly embarrassed at being so easily manipulated. And then there occurred the crime that no one in the universe knew of except Hanuman and Danlo.

Danlo watched this crime as it unfolded; he might have been a bird perched on a windowsill high inside the chapter house. This image burned in his eyes: Hanuman, lowering a mirrored, metallic sphere over Tamara's head as she fairly trembled with anticipation. Hanuman told her that it was a remembrancing heaume, but it was not. It was a cleansing heaume, stamped with the seal of the Cybernetic Reformed Churches. With this unholy machine meant to free the sinful of their negative programs, Hanuman laid bare her memories and her mind. He painted a computer portrait of a woman's selfness and soul, and when he was done, no part of her remained a secret to him. It was an easy thing for him to remove her memories, as easy as editing an erotic cartoon of unwanted scenes. The heaume's invisible field propagated through her brain, ripping electrons away from their mother atoms, dissolving dendrites, erasing the pattern of synapses that was uniquely her own. It was the opposite of an imprinting, and it did not take very long. Several times, she cried out, "Danlo, Danlo!"—he could hear this as closely as if her lips were pressed to his ear. She called to him as she remembered many moments for a last time, and then she was silent in unconsciousness, and only the air molecules and wall stones carried the memory of the words she had spoken. When Hanuman faced away from the ruins of her mind, he was horrified with himself, yet pleased that he had finished a nearly impossible task. It only remained for him to slip a tiny needle into the back of her neck. He did this smoothly, injecting killed viruses into her blood. Then he helped her walk through the deserted chapter house into the main body of Bardo's church. He left her there, in the cold nave, wounded and groping for consciousness and completely alone.

"Tamara, I think you began to forget things . . . in the cathedral." Danlo said this with all the gentleness he could find.

"Did Thomas Rane tell you this?"

"Yes," he said, bowing his head, lying. "Master Rane said that you remember being alone in the cathedral."

She took a deep breath before saying, "Sometimes, after I'd completed a contract, when I was too tired to skate home, I liked going to the cathedral. Late at night when no one was there. Bardo had arranged with the godlings to let me in whenever I wanted. It was a good place to think, to be with myself. I remember lying on one of the rugs, looking up at the windows. Which was quite unusual, because I never allowed myself to fall asleep there—I always sat when I meditated, you know. I remember looking at the new window Bardo had put in, the one where the Ringess has his head broken open and dies his first death. That *horrible* window. And suddenly I couldn't remember how I'd come there. I had a sense of missing time—it's the most horrible thing, like dying a little, in parts. Then, when I tried to remember other things, going back, there was nothing. All these parts. All these moments that should have been there. That I *knew* had been there. And I couldn't remember. I think I panicked, after that. I couldn't catch my breath and I was so dizzy I could hardly stand up. For a while, I forgot who I was. No, I don't mean I couldn't remember *things,* about myself—in a way, I had too many memories. But I had no sense of myself. Of *why* I existed, why I was even alive. I think that's when I started skating the streets. I couldn't go home, don't you see? I didn't want to be around anything familiar until I found out who I really am."

Danlo met her eyes then, and he wanted to tell her that she was Tamara Ten Ashtoreth, his betrothed, his joy, the woman with whom he would someday create many children. He wanted to tell her many things, but he just looked at her, and he clenched his jaws, and he said nothing.

"If ever I'd resolved to record my memories," she said, "after I'd been alone on the streets, there was no more possibility of *that*. It's too bad that Hanuman didn't find me before the virus did its work—something might have been preserved."

Danlo found his lip between his teeth, and he had an urge to bite at it until he tasted blood. But then he said, "Tamara, this virus—"

"This virus," she interrupted, "was such a bizarre chance. Who ever dreams of such things happening? It was just fate, I suppose. Everyone has her own fate."

Yes, he thought, fate. Her fate intertwined with his, and his fate joined with Hanuman's. He was certain, then, that the memory virus had not touched her brain. It was a killed virus, as harmless as any inoculation; Hanuman had murdered these little bits of protein and DNA solely to create inside her particular antibodies. Detectable antibodies. Hanuman knew that when she began forgetting, virologists would examine her for the existence of the Catavan Fever. They would find the antibodies, and they would presume she had been infected. No one would suspect that she had been tricked beneath a cleansing heaume. People would pity her as just another victim of the virus—along with Yang li Yang and Chanoth Chen Ciceron.

As Danlo looked at Tamara, at the way she searched his eyes for pieces to the puzzle of her own fate, he knew that Hanuman's destruction of Lord Ciceron was the least of his objectives. In truth, it was little more than a diversion concealing his deeper purposes.

Why, Hanu, why?

Because, he thought, because Tamara dreaded and mistrusted Hanuman—therefore he had cleansed her of her fears. Tamara had the respect of the highest courtesans, and so Hanuman had disfigured her mind so that she would not speak to the Mother against Hanuman or the Way of Ringess. Hanuman still hoped to win over the Society—this was the first of his hidden plans.

Looking past Tamara at the snowflakes breaking against the dark window, Danlo said, "I cannot believe in fate. You are still . . . who you are. Nothing has changed."

Truly, he thought, she seemed much the same as the Tamara he had loved. He knew that Hanuman had not wanted to destroy her—only certain of her memories. This was the sec-

636

ond part of his plan, to remove from her mind any thought or image of Danlo. Truly, Hanuman loved her, too, and he had continued loving her since the night of Bardo's joyance. He still hoped to make a contract with her and, more, to preserve the best part of her for himself.

"The memory virus," he said, "cannot have touched your deepest self."

"I wish that were true."

"You have only forgotten . . . a few things that have happened."

"Parts of my *life*, Pilot."

"But these parts could be remade."

For a moment her face brightened, and she said, "It's kind of you to say that. I must have loved this kindness in you."

"It was more than that," he said.

"I'm sure you have many traits that anyone would love. You're so—"

Danlo rubbed his eyes and shook his head. "It was not just a matter of us loving certain traits in each other. It was more—there was something between us, *imaklana*, this love magic that is instantaneous. Eternal, too."

"Are you speaking of falling into love? It's always so dangerous, to fall."

"Dangerous, yes. But also *halla*."

"Halla?"

"Have you forgotten . . . this word?"

"It would seem so."

"*Halla* is . . . the interconnectedness of things. The secret fire that all things share."

"No, I don't remember."

He closed his eyes for a moment, then said, *"Halla los ni manse li devani ki-charara li pelafi nis uta purushu."*

"I don't remember this language at all."

He touched her hand, and he said, " '*Halla* is the man and woman who light the blessed fire inside each other.' "

"Oh, no," she said. She pulled her hand away from him and dried her palm on the side of her robe. "It's just this burning we must avoid."

"But loving another . . . there is nothing more blessed than this, yes?"

"But falling," she said, "isn't really love for another. It's only love of love. Of the state of *being* in love."

637

"Love is . . . love," he said. He did not want to admit that he understood the distinction she was making.

"It's curious, but my mother used to warn me against falling. Falling into 'love drunkenness,' as she called it. It's like drinking yourself into blindness: when you fall, you can't see anything. You don't even *want* to see what's inside the other. All that matters is being near each other. Together, being aflame."

With his forefinger, he touched the line of her jaw where the skin had been badly frostbitten. He said, "It might be hard for you to hear this but . . . I am still drunk with this fire."

"Yes, I know."

"But not blindly drunk," he said. "It has never been like that between us. We could always see . . . each other."

"Do I see the same man now that I used to know before I fell ill?"

"Yes," he said. "I am still myself."

"But do *I* see you differently?"

"I do not know—what do you see?"

"Just a few moments ago, in your eyes, so much hatred. And despair. I don't think I could ever bear to be close to this kind of despair."

He closed his eyes, sorting through images of all the tragedies he had seen during his life. Then he looked at her and said, "Everyone has the capacity for despair."

"Perhaps they do," she said. "I know *I* do. Which is why it's difficult seeing you like this—in you, it's all so *desperate*. So total."

Again, he moved to touch her, but she stepped backward and shook her head.

"Please," he said.

"I'm afraid, Pilot."

"No, no," he whispered.

"I'm afraid of you."

There was a stab of pain just above his eye, the place where his headaches always came, suddenly, as lightning wakes up a sleeping city at night. He pushed the palm of his hand against his head, and he understood the third and final of Hanuman's purposes, the end toward which all his schemes had pointed. He, himself—Danlo the Wild—was this end. Hanuman wished to give him the most precious of gifts. He wanted to share with Danlo a part of his soul, to make him see, to burn into Danlo's brain the wound that will not heal. Out of love, out of hate, out of his twisted compassion, he had annihilated the best parts of

638

Tamara's memory. He had done this terrible deed because he wanted Danlo to suffer the universe the way it really was.

Hanu, Hanu, no.

He heard himself murmuring, "No, no, no," and he wanted to touch Tamara's fingers, her hair, her dark eyes which were filling up with tears. But he could hardly move because he suddenly lost his wind; it was as if a mallet or flying elbow had caught him in the soft spot beneath his heart muscle, knocking his breath away. He staggered, then threw out his hand to steady himself. He stood with his head bent down, trying to get his breathing right, and the weight of his hand fell hard against the tea table. There was light, then, a blinding white light that flashed from the chatoy finish and filled the room. Tamara gasped at its intensity, and she flung her hands over her face and turned her head away. He squinted and shielded his eyes; he might have been an infant left alone on the frozen sea, a lost manchild looking beyond the ice's dazzling light for any sign or hope of rescue. And then he *was* a child again, and his vision fell off toward an infinite horizon. He was two years old, almost, and he stood alone on the burial grounds above the cave. He stood on the hard, squeaking snow totally alone, and that was strange because Haidar, Choclo, and Chandra—the whole of the Devaki tribe—were gathered all around him. In the center of the circle that his people made, on a bier of whalebone and white shagshay fur, lay the body of his favorite brother, Arri. During the night Arri had died of a belly fever; now he lay here beneath the harsh blue sky, naked and alone. A short time ago Chandra had anointed him with a rank-smelling seal oil so that the whole of his little brown body shined like polished wood. Artic poppies, red-orange like the sun, had been scattered across his head, chest, and legs. Haidar and all the others were praying for Arri's spirit, putting voices to words and concepts that Danlo could not comprehend. After the prayers were finished, Haidar leaned against Choclo, weeping, and he spoke of how he had loved his oldest son. And all the time, Danlo stood close, listening, learning a strange new word, *anasa. Anasa:* loving and suffering—it was all the same thing, and somehow Danlo understood this. We love most fervidly that which is separate from ourselves, but being apart, we suffer. When his turn came to put fireflowers in his brother's hair and to say good-bye, Danlo fell across his cold body, clutching at him as if this were just another wrestling match that Arri had let him win. He was too young to understand that sometime, beyond years and seasons, their spirits would walk together on the other side of day. At last, Haidar had to pry his fingers away from Arri's arms. The air was so cold that the tears would have frozen in his eyes, if he could have kept them open. But his eyes were tightly closed and burning, and now he stood over the chatoy tea table with his head bowed down, unable to bear the blazing white light. He straightened up, then, and removed his hand from the table. The room was now dull and flat with washed-out colors; outside the window, snow was still falling. He looked at Tamara. Her eyes were wet and inflamed, and her chest was trembling. In another place and time, it would have been easy to console her, but now she crossed her arms over her breasts and stood as stiff and cold as an ice sculpture. He could not touch her, even though he burned to lace his fingers through her hair and kiss her head. At that moment, it was all he ever wanted to do. *To love is to burn,* he thought, *anasa,* and as long as lovers could be together, this burning was the sweetest pain in the universe. But if they were kept apart, it was pure flaming agony. Tamara, at least, had been spared this pain. (That is, she had been spared the *consciousness* of it.) But Hanuman had given him the gift of fire, and now and always he would burn for something impossible to ever hold.

"Tamara," he said, "this does not need to be."

Moving very carefully not to touch the table, she sat back down in her chair and tried to smile at him. "What has happened has happened. You can't change the past."

"No, but I can remember it."

"It might be better if you could forget."

"No, it is just the opposite," he said.

She must have seen a flash of hope in his eyes, for she asked, "What do you mean?"

It is one of the ironies of existence that each human being, once in his life, will come to think thoughts which were once unthinkable. One day each of us will do the very thing he had thought impossible to do. Danlo stood with his knuckles pressed to his lips, and he burned with desperate dreams, so he said, "There might be a way to remake your memories—have you considered this?"

"No, I won't consider false hopes," she said.

"Every word you ever spoke to me," he said, "the temperature of your skin every time you touched me . . . I cannot forget. It should be possible to copy these memories into a computer. And then to make an imprinting. There is a woman I know, an imprimatur who helped me when I first came to Neverness. She could help you."

Tamara stared at him in disbelief, shaking her head. "You want to *cark* your memories into my mind?"

"It would be a way . . . to remember."

"Are your memories that good?"

His memories, he thought, were flaming crimson. His memories were ten billion fiery jewels spinning in the center of his mind. He looked at her and said, "Thomas Rane has told me that my memory is nearly perfect."

"Perfect for you, perhaps."

"Tamara, I will—"

"If it were you who'd lost your memory," she said, "would you let someone cark you this way?"

"I . . . do not know." In truth, he could not imagine parts and pieces of his memory simply vanishing. "What else can we do?"

"But there's nothing to be done," she said softly. "Everything that you remember, the way that you remember things— these are your memories, not mine."

He moved around the table, over to the window. The clary panes were rimed with frost, and he dragged his fingernail over them, etching and scraping, seemingly in random lines. It was only when he stepped back a pace and focused his eyes that he realized he had absentmindedly cut out a picture of a silver thallow. It occurred to him then that Hanuman might have preserved the memories that he had cleansed from Tamara's brain. This was much more than a false hope. Why should Hanuman cast away something so valuable? Perhaps he had incorporated Tamara's memories into his Elder Eddas. Certainly he would want to know whatever secrets Tamara had discovered about him, Danlo the Wild. Hanuman collected knowledge and secrets the way some aficionados of art selfishly hoard rare paintings for their own pleasure—he might wish to gaze at the scenes he had stolen from Tamara's mind, again and again, in the privacy of whatever computer space they had been hidden.

He turned to her and said, "But what if it were possible to recover *your* memories? To put them back into your mind?"

"*My* memories? But it's all gone."

He did not want to tell her about Hanuman, not yet, so he said, "Suppose—this is just a thought game—suppose the Architects are right and the universe is really a computer. A computer that records every event in spacetime. What if the events of your life could be recovered from this computer? If God were really computer who could restore—"

"But how could that be possible?" she quickly asked.

Because, he thought, *the memory of all things is in all things.*

Before he could answer her, she smiled to herself, then said, "No, I can't play these kinds of games."

"But all memory is—"

"Pilot, Pilot," she said, "please, no."

She got up from her chair and came over to him. She covered his hand with hers. It was obviously a difficult thing for her to do, because her hands were trembling, and her eyes were full of hurt and uncertainty. But then she forced herself to a sudden decision; she squeezed his fingers, gently, and she said, "Oh, Pilot, you don't understand. You've been so kind to try to help me—I think I still love you for this kindness. But I don't really want any more help with this remembering. That's not why I asked you here tonight."

"Then . . . why?"

"To say good-bye. I wanted to tell you that I can't make any more liaisons with you."

He grasped her hand and looked down at her fingers as they reddened with blood. He stared at the whorls and lines of her fingertips, burning this unique pattern into his memory. He looked at her fingers and hands; it was as if he hoped some unexpected and favorable future might suddenly reveal itself there. For a long time, he scryed like this, and he wanted to ask her, "Why? Why?"

"This will be hard to explain," she said. "But I can't live for whatever has happened. I can't mourn myself, not while I'm still alive. I *won't.* What I am now, tonight—shouldn't that be enough? I'm always *I.* I always will be. My memories, myself. *This* is the real marvel, don't you see? I mustn't ruin this by hoping I'll wake up someday and remember things that I've forgotten."

Danlo thought deeply for a while, then said, "I have dreamed . . . that we would live our lives for each other."

"I'm sorry, Pilot."

"But if we could meet each other every night then—"

"I'm sorry but it would be best if we didn't meet again."

"Never . . . again?"

"No, never."

So saying, she undid the collar of her robe and reached down between her breasts. There was a scraping of chafed skin against heavy silk. She slowly drew out her hand, which clutched the palpulve pearl he had given her. Then, with a single, sweeping motion, she pulled the necklace over her head.

"I wanted you to see this," she said. The tip of her finger played over the pearl's teardrop surface, lingering.

He looked at the pearl as she spun it between her fingers. He always liked the way it caught the light and changed colors, from silver to deep purple to iridescent black. "It is splendid," he said.

"It's very unusual, too—I don't have any other jewelry like it."

"No," he said, "I wouldn't guess you would. These pearls must be rare."

"Did you give it to me?" she asked.

Without waiting for him to reply, she pulled at his fingers, opening up his hand. She dropped the pearl down against the center of his heart line. Strangely, it was heavier than he had remembered.

"I am only a journeyman pilot," he said. "How could I afford such a gift?"

"I didn't know."

"I have never seen it before," he said.

"Oh, I'm sorry, then." She studied the string of the necklace dangling from between his fingers. She touched this string, made of a twine of shiny black hair. Then she looked at his hair, hanging long and wild halfway down his back.

"Does it please you?" he asked.

"It's lovely," she said. "I found myself wearing it when I began forgetting, in the cathedral. I couldn't remember who gave it to me."

He looked up at her dark, liquid eyes. There, in the center of each pupil, he saw a tiny reflection of the pearl. "Perhaps someday . . . you will."

"Perhaps," she said.

Suddenly he closed his fingers around the pearl, making a fist. He squeezed this hard little teardrop of nacre, feeling the hurt of it against his skin; he squeezed it as long as he could, until the muscles of his forearm began to tremble and ache. Then he reached out with both hands and slipped the necklace back over her head.

"If you like it, you should keep it."

She bowed her head, once, then looked at him. "I should send for the novice—she'll show you the way out."

"I think I can remember the way."

"But that wouldn't be decent," she said. "In the Mother's house, nobody goes to the door alone."

"Why don't you accompany me, then?"

"Very well."

Because the outer hallway would be frigid, she went over to the closet to find a houserobe to wear. While she was pulling on this musky new fur, Danlo bowed his head, looking down at the tea table for a last time. He spread his fingers out, then slapped his hand down against the cold finish. The layers of chatoy remained dead and black, devoid of all color. And then Tamara announced, "I'm ready," and he couldn't imagine never seeing her again, and suddenly, strangely, the whole plane of the table warmed to a faint golden hue.

Together they walked through the quiet hallways of the house. Neither of them spoke; neither of them looked at the other. She led him back to the gowning room, where he dressed for his return to his dormitory. He put on his furs and boots, for the moment leaving his face uncovered. Then she showed him through the final hallway to the outside door.

"I should say good-bye now," she told him.

He looked at her for a long time. And then he said, "Good-bye."

With difficulty, she forced the door outward against the raging wind and struggled to hold it open. In mere moments, the hallway filled with clouds of snow.

"Farewell, Pilot. I wish you well."

He paused, standing in the doorway, leaning his shoulder against the heavy door. He wanted to tell her an important thing. He wanted to unglove his hand and touch her blinking eyes, and he wanted to tell her that they were fated to meet, again and again. But he did not really believe this would be true. He *could not* believe it, and he looked at Tamara's cold, white face, and he remembered that flesh once frostbitten was forever more susceptible to freezing. So he bowed, once, deeply. He smiled at her and said, "Farewell, Tamara."

He stepped out into the screaming storm, and instantly needles of ice were breaking against his face. Then, with a harsh and hollow sound, the door slammed shut behind him. He stared at this dark, massive door, and he said, "Farewell, farewell."

A PIECE OF IVORY

Self-creation is the highest art.
        —from Man's Journey, *by Nikolos Daru Ede*

In deep winter, the light over the city of Neverness falls weak and strange. On cloudless days—the brief, tenuous periods of illumination when the sun is little more than a red glare staining the horizon—the sky is half the color of night, and there are many stars. Some say that if it chances to storm during this darkest season, then there is no true day. Certainly there is no daybreak, for how can light break through layers of cold nimbus clouds and swirling snow and a blackness that is nearly total? When the *sarsaras* blow wildly through the streets, there can never be a clear demarcation between darkness and day, and so it is hopeless to stay awake all night and await the coming of morning. Only the most tenacious or foolish of people would attempt such a thing. In the bleak, desperate hours after saying good-bye to Tamara, this is what Danlo wi Soli Ringess did. He skated about the Old City until he was exhausted and lost, and then he stumbled half-frozen into a warming pavilion on a nameless gliddery. There, in this miserable little shelter, with the wind shrieking all about him, he waited for the air to lighten through the shades of sable and slate and silver-gray. He waited endlessly. He thought he was near Bardo's cathedral; it was his resolve to race through the cathedral doors the moment they were opened, to find Hanuman, to reason with him, to plead with him or shame him—anything short of physically harming him, as long as he would promise to restore Tamara's memories.

But all his waiting was in vain. When day finally came—a

cold, gray chaos of clouds and blowing snow—Hanuman refused to see him. And on the days that followed, Hanuman remained locked in the chapter house of the cathedral, and he refused to see anyone: neither Danlo, nor Bardo, nor any of the godlings who approached his door with trays of food and drink. Danlo might have broken down this door, but two godlings always stood outside it, guarding Hanuman's privacy. The godlings were new converts to Ringism, and they were not friendly to Danlo. They informed him that Hanuman had entered into the memory space of one of his computers; he was experiencing a great remembrance, they said, possibly the greatest remembrance that any human being had ever known.

"By God!" Bardo announced on the fourth day that Danlo had come to visit Hanuman, "if Hanuman won't open the goddamn door, *I'll* break it down!"

But Bardo did no such thing. He seemed reluctant to oppose Hanuman openly, especially at Danlo's behest. Although he obviously was still quite fond of Danlo, it embarrassed and outraged him that Danlo had quit his church.

"Perhaps you shouldn't come here anymore, Little Fellow. This cathedral is for *Ringists,* or for those wishing to become so. You're a *Ringess,* it's true, but this is not the same thing, eh?"

"No," Danlo admitted, "it is not the same."

"Why are you so eager to see Hanuman—may I ask?"

"I have . . . news to tell him."

"About Tamara?"

Danlo wiped a clot of snow from his hair and said, "Yes, how did you know?"

"Nirvelli told me she'd been stricken," Bardo said. "I'm sorry, Little Fellow. Oh, the poor woman—she was so bright. It's too bad, so undeservedly bad. But tell me, please, why would you wish to give this bad news to Hanuman? I've heard that you're no longer the closest of friends."

Danlo protested that they *were* still deep friends, while Bardo listened with all the suspiciousness of someone buying a firestone from a renegade programmer. Danlo considered telling him the full truth, that Hanuman had stolen Tamara's memories, but he no longer completely trusted Bardo. Bardo, at the moment, was too caught up in the dreams of Bardo. Even if he were willing to risk a schism within his church, he was incapable of coercing Hanuman into restoring Tamara.

"I would hope you're still friends," Bardo said. "Friendship is golden. We shouldn't give up our *friends* so easily, eh? As one friend speaking to another, I should advise you to leave Hanuman alone—for now. Let there be a space of time between you and those you are close to. A time for, ah, *appreciation.* For reconsidering, perhaps. Do you understand? You're a Ringess, and you belong with us—it would be too sad if we had to close our doors to you."

Later that day, Danlo considered seeking the advice of a master akashic. He considered revealing that Hanuman had used an Architect's heaume to cleanse Tamara's memories, which he had most likely preserved in one of his computers. He wanted Hanuman to submit to an akashic's reading; he wanted the akashics to use *their* computers to lay bare Hanuman's thoughts and make him reveal where he had hidden these pearls stolen from Tamara's mind. But, in truth, it seemed a lowly and faithless act, to enter the akashics' fortresslike building, to bow before some strange master and accuse Hanuman of crimes. Even though Tamara now took refuge in an old woman's room that smelled of auracaria and frostbite ointment, even though he burned for redress, even though Hanuman had betrayed *him,* he could not betray Hanuman this way.

Of course, Danlo knew very well that both Hanuman and Tamara had been born into Architect families; therefore they both had the right to cleanse and be cleansed. This issue had been settled a thousand years ago. Properly, it was a religious matter. If the akashics construed this cleansing strictly, they would declare that Hanuman had committed no crime at all. They might even chastise Danlo for involving himself with a courtesan and a strange, new religion. The akashics, as everyone knew, were opposed to all religions.

"But, Hanu, you put *viruses* into her blessed body!" Danlo told himself. "And you put viruses into the Lord Pilot, too, and this is a crime that is *shaida* inside *shaida!*"

Slelling, the act of injecting strange DNA into the human body, is in fact the worst of crimes. But the laws of the Order stipulated that only a master pilot (or other master) could force someone before the akashic courts with so little evidence of crime, and Danlo had no real evidence at all. He had only the sudden knowledge that had come to him during his meeting with Tamara. And what, after all, had really happened that night? Had he been possessed of an hallucination or some terrible vision? Had it been only a waking dream or some unbidden simulation of his mind? Or had he entered into some marvelous new mode of perception that was perhaps akin to scrying or remembrancing? He did not know. He knew only that this perception was real and true; he *knew* that he was right about Hanuman, but what if he were somehow wrong?

Oh, Hanu, Hanu, what is the truth?

In the end, Danlo did not go to the akashics. Not even the Lord Akashic himself could make Hanuman restore Tamara's memories. Only Danlo could do that. Somehow he must ease the hurt between him and Hanuman and move Hanuman toward true compassion, or else Tamara would never remember her life and who she really was.

And so Danlo returned to his dormitory room. He spent most of a day and night thinking and brooding. He ate no food; he drank neither tea nor water. Atop his matted furs he lay nearly motionless, and his eyes were open, unblinking. A visitor peering in his frosted windows would have guessed that he was dead. Indeed, a part of him *had* died, and another part did not want to live. But a third part whispered that Tamara might be healed. Even as the darkness inside him deepened, in the terrible time between death and morning, this whisper grew louder. It grew into a roar more urgent than the storm beating against the windowpanes. He recalled, then, something that Jonathan Hur had said to him two days earlier, a random piece of news tossed out as casually as a snowball. Jonathan had told him of a celebration that Bardo had decided to hold at Year's End. It would glorify the final journey of Mallory Ringess, and it would be a great event—for those who followed the Way. For those who did not (or for such mavericks as the brothers Hur), Bardo's grand joyance would mock the ceremonies marking the end of the Festival of the Broken Dolls. "Is it a coincidence that your father left Neverness on the ninety-ninth?" Jonathan had asked him. "Certainly it's no coincidence that Bardo has called for a gift exchange—didn't you know that *our* holiday must outshine all others?"

So, on the holiest day of the Festival of the Broken Dolls, a day in which Architects of the Infinite Life presented each other with rich gifts wrapped in colored papers, the followers of the Way would appropriate this ancient ceremony. They would do this to symbolize the gift that Mallory Ringess had brought to humankind: this promise of becoming godly which almost no one understood. The idea of giving gifts was like a star exploding inside the depths of Danlo's mind. It immediately roused him from despair. He recalled, then, the walrus tusk that he had found on his journey to Avisalia. It had been his intention to carve this tusk into a chess piece, and then to give it to Hanuman as a gift. For thirty days this plan had remained only half-formed and uncertain; at times he had forgotten it altogether. But now he fairly leapt out of bed and laughed with the thrill of anticipation. Now, inside him, an image stood out as clearly as a yu tree against the sky. He beheld this image from many angles, all at once, and he seared it into his memory. He decided to make this image real. Out of a simple piece of ivory, he would carve a god. It would be more than just a replacement piece for the missing god of Hanuman's chess set. He would create a tangible figure that would embody all the pain and passion of the gods. Hanuman had given him the gift of fire; in return, at the great joyance, he would give Hanuman a solution to the fundamental problem of life, a way that all burning finally might be quenched. When Hanuman held this gift in his hands, he would feel the true weight of love, and his heart would break open. He would restore Tamara's memory, and he would restore their friendship—this was Danlo's last desperate hope.

After making himself three cups of tea (he was very thirsty), he set to work. He didn't care that it was the middle of the night; his was one of Resa's few private rooms, so a little banging about would disturb no one. It was a tiny room, just big enough for his sleeping furs, drying rack, tea service, and his wooden chest. Beneath the window sat the plain, deep chest that he had been given as a novice. He stepped over to it and grasped the steel handle. The top swung open on well-oiled hinges. Inside were all his possessions, which were few enough considering that he was now a journeyman pilot. Beneath his spare furs, robes, skate blades, and kamelaikas, he kept the only things that he valued: his mother's diamond ball; the two books that Bardo had entrusted to him; the carving of the snowy owl he had made on his journey to Neverness; the point of his old bear spear; and sometimes his shakuhachi. At the very bottom of the chest, inside an old seal leather bag, were his carving tools. Except for the white feather that he wore in his hair, nothing was more precious to him than these tools, for they connected him directly with his childhood, with his people, and with the world of rocks and animals and trees in which they had lived. He pulled out the bag and opened the drawstring. His tools clicked and rattled together as he rummaged about. Onto his sleeping furs, as neatly as a jeweler setting out firestones, he arrayed his scrapers and burins, his gouge, graver, and adz. He lifted out his saw and ran its glittering teeth lightly across his thumb. Then he set out his chisels. He had five chisels, and they were his glories. Two of the chisels Haidar had given him on his eleventh birthday; his found-father had made them of rare diamond stones set into hafts of whalebone. He, himself, had made the three other chisels, originally from lengths of shatterwood and flint blades. The blades were of varying widths and could be easily sharpened or replaced as they wore out. When he had entered Resa, he had replaced two blades, not because they were chipped or worn, but because he had found a finer material for carving than flint. On the day he started to grow his beard, he had taken his shaving razor (the same diamond-edged razor he had used to shave Pedar's face), and he had carefully broken it into pieces. He had refit his chisels with two of these pieces and used another to make a wickedly sharp round knife. The simplest of his tools was a little mallet: a smooth river stone that fit snugly into the palm of his hand. He would accomplish much of his carving with this stone, tapping it against the hafts of his chisels. And when he was done chiseling and scooping and graving, there would come the polishing. For this tedious work, he had many bits of fine sandstone and a rough oilskin. No piece of ivory, it was said, could come alive until it was polished as smoothly as new white ice.

When he was ready to begin the actual carving, he said a prayer to the spirit of the ivory, and he removed the tusk from the chest. It was as long as his arm, with a good, dense weight and a rich smell that recalled the sea. It was old ivory, well seasoned in salt water; its color was of dark cream streaked with amber and gold. He picked up his adz and began stripping off the tough enamel husk. The flint blade made a high-pitched rasping sound as it cut. With long, quick strokes, pulling the adz in toward his body, he worked down the length of the tusk from tip to root so as not to split the ivory. He sat cross-legged on his furs with his tools close at hand. In little time, his lap and his furs were covered with long ivory splinters. After the tusk was well cleaned, he paused to wipe the sweat from his forehead. He knocked away the splinters, careless of where they landed. Then he used his saw to cut the tusk into five sections of equal length. Although he would make only one chess piece, he had never attempted such an intricate carving. It was possible that he would ruin one or two pieces of good ivory before the god took shape.

In fact, he ruined four pieces before going to work on the last one. The first two pieces split apart, almost as soon as he put

650

a chisel to them. Ivory is the loveliest of all materials to carve; it has a quality of aliveness that only improves with age, but as it ages it hardens, and the flaws inherent in all living things often grow into deep cracks. The trick of carving is to work around these flaws, not excising them, but cutting so that the natural strength of the ivory can support them. It might have been better if he had found a tusk of new ivory, all soft and white and easy to work. New ivory, after a year or so exposed to the air, will develop veins of color which grow and merge until the whole surface gleams like a seal milk spread over ice. It was just this pure coloration, however, that Danlo did not want. His task was to make a chess piece to match the rest of Hanuman's set. The other pieces—the pilot, the alien, and the cetic—were ancient; they were lined and cracked and seamed with subtle golden hues. His god must resemble these pieces, not only with regard to weathering and proportion, but according to style, as well. It would be hard enough to duplicate the Yarkonan style: detailed but not ornate, realistic but with a transcendence of emotion that hinted at the ideal. The sculptor of the original set was quite accomplished; she had endowed the black god and both goddesses with various combinations of serenity, compassion, joy, and power. The black goddess was particularly striking, for her face was cut with both wrath and rapture, and she seemed all-wise, like the statues of Nikolos Daru Ede that stand outside most of the Cybernetic Churches. While Danlo could find no fault with this beautiful work, he was seeking something more, a rendering of a face inside him that might be impossible to bring to life. Certainly, after ruining the third and fourth pieces of ivory, he began to despair of ever creating his god. These pieces did not split; he solved the splitting problem by roughing out their shapes, not with mallet and chisel, but with the rasp and whine of his skate file. When it came time to begin the fine carving, however, he gouged the god's eyes too quickly and too deeply, and so twice he had to abandon the work. He picked up the last piece of ivory, then. He promised its spirit that he would cut more slowly. He would visualize the exact shape and size of each particle of ivory before removing it—either that or he would not cut at all.

Thus he began to carve his final god, and the carving seemed to have no end. Moments flowed into moments and accumulated until whole days had passed, and Danlo took no notice of time. Occasionally, when his eyes burned with fatigue and his hands began trembling, he lay back against his furs and dozed, holding the ivory close as a child does a doll. Once every day, perhaps, he left his room to eat a large meal. And then he would return refreshed and strengthened for more carving. For long periods, he would sit hunched over with his naked feet clamped like a vise around the motionless god as he cut and trimmed. Using one of his chisels, he chipped away at the ivory bit by bit until his back knotted in pain and his feet were blue with cold. During his worst moments, he thought of abandoning the carving as hopeless. The sheer effrontery of what he was attempting to create daunted him. Sometimes, it amused him. But always, it astonished him, and so he kept carving, on and on. He knew that if the image inside him were true, if he could see it exactly, then he could make it be. It was only a matter of freeing the god from his ivory prison. Somewhere within the shrinking block of ivory dwelt his god. Indeed, all gods and goddesses dwelt there, and all species of humankind, every child, woman, and man who would ever live. He could see them all, with a carver's eye, nestled inside each other, the way the dour body of an Architect matron contained the smiling, newlywed woman, and countless younger versions of herself. All men, if you looked at them just right, were much like each other. One might have curly hair, a bellyful of sorrows, and believe that Ede was the sole God of the universe; another might possess the other-worldly beauty of the Elidi birdmen, but between the two there was a commonality and connection. And how simple it was to make one man into another. How hauntingly easy the transformation of a thoughtful child into one who was sad. With a press of his graver, he could cut grief into a contented face. He would scrape away a creamy white fleck, scarcely larger than a nail clipping, and a billion trillion atoms of ivory would tumble to the floor, thus changing the face of his god, subtly, irrevocably. If he could carve with some finer tool, removing a single atom with each stroke, might not all possible forms and things inevitably be revealed?

He thought about this as he marveled over the mystery of identity and consciousness. As the lights in his room burned on and on through many nights, he wondered many strange things. What if some great god such as the Solid State Entity, with technologies known only to the gods, could carve *him*, atom by atom? What if she could slowly alter the pigmentation of his hair, the length of his bones, the contour of his teeth against his tongue? Would he still be *he*? Why wouldn't he? Yes, but suppose she could cark his mind with a new memory. What if the sensa of his eating kurmash at his last meal were replaced with the aftertaste of saffron rice and garlic—would this change anything significant about him? No, he was certain it would not. But suppose she could replace *all* of his memories, one by one, as minerals migrate through a fallen log to create petrified wood. Suppose he remembered eating cultured kid and wearing a clearface over his head. If, with divine subtlety, the goddess could transfigure his flesh and mind through an almost infinite succession of forms, perhaps into someone more willful and self-contained, then couldn't she cark Danlo the Wild into an entirely different person? What, after all, was the essential difference between himself and a man such as Hanuman li Tosh? In his darkest nightmares, he had dreaded becoming more like Hanuman; he had long suspected that Hanuman's pale, anguished face was somehow a reflection of his own. Now, as he hammered a thin blade of diamond against ivory, he could see how this might be so. He could see the truly marvelous thing about mind: that if he were to become Hanuman or some other being, gradually, an atom of consciousness at a time, then at no point would he ever feel very different or that anything important about himself had perished. But one day he would wake up and behold himself against the mirror of the universe, and he would *not* be he. What, then, could have happened to his true self, his deepest self that could not die? Would it still live, somehow, inside whatever dread shape he had become? Inside an alien, or a crab, or a worm twisting through lightless tunnels beneath the snow? Inside all things? What was the true, unchanging essence of anyone? And more to the point, what was the soul and fate of this godly animal that some called man?

He had no final answer to these questions, or rather, no neat aphorism that he cared to formulate as a philosophical truth. He had often argued with Hanuman over such conundrums, ultimately to no end. Now he must present his friend with a different kind of argument, cut out of ivory instead of words, which would appeal to the hands and eyes and heart. And so he worked his hard, sharp tools against a cold chunk of ivory. He worked for seven days with the sound of ice particles pinging against the windows, knocking away invisible molecules of glass. By the eighth day, his god was almost finished. It was a noble creature arising out of a pedestal of flames; so skillfully had he carved the base of the chess piece that it was difficult to tell whether the tongues of flame wrapped around the god's legs or flowed *into* them, becoming flesh, animating the god with the essence of fire. The whole pose and expression of his carving was directed toward one question: What survives when a man becomes a god? The answer was cut into the knotted muscles of the god's body, from the open hands to the tormented, twisted neck. It was an answer that Hanuman would understand in each cell of his body. *Pain is the awareness of life,* Danlo thought, and gods were the most completely aware creatures that the universe had ever known.

All of history had pointed toward this awareness. In the beginning, at the birth of the universe, all things were concentrated into a single point, infinitely heavy, infinitely hot. There was neither joy nor pain nor darkness nor light. And then, in less than a trillionth of a trillionth of a second, there was everything. The fundamental particles of matter—the strings and infons and other noumena—fell out of the primeval cosmic energy like snowflakes crystallizing from a cloud. Very quickly, in an ageless, eternal second, as the universe exploded outward at the speed of light, the plasma of matter cooled and combined into larger units, into quarks, into electrons, photons, and neutrinos. But it would be a half million years before the first stable atoms evolved, and billions of years more before these atoms learned how to join into the molecules of life. It was the most astonishing phenomenon that randomly moving atoms of hydrogen could eventually come together to make a creature who would love and laugh and suffer. Who might laugh at his own suffering, or suffer the love of life. All of history was the cooling of matter and the falling away from the fiery primal unity, but history was also the rise of the consciousness of life. And now the number of galaxies was uncountable, and in the Milky Way galaxy alone, there were a hundred billion stars blazing in the stillness of the night. And now there were human beings. How many, no one really knew. Each man and woman was a cold island of consciousness adrift in space. Each was afflicted with the alienation from other life, with despair, with loneliness and the keen knowledge that his sufferings could end only with death. This was the doom of self-awareness, the disease of man. Animals—a wolf or an owl absorbed into the sounds of snow-covered forest —might enjoy a simple health and ease with life, but never a man looking toward the future for hope of joy. It was thought that gods had transcended all human suffering. Gods, it was said, possessed minds as vast and perfect as computers, and they could not fall mad over hunger or jealousy or the shame of watching their bodies decay with age. Danlo was sure that he had never seen a god, in the flesh, but he could see their predicament in a way that others could not. Gods could die—the Sonderval's discovery of the dead god out near the star named Hanuman's Glory had proved this beyond dispute, but even the eschatologists had not understood what this might mean. With all the universe beckoning, gods must fear death more than any human ever could. To a being who might live a million years, death is the supreme tragedy, to be avoided at any cost. Gods dread death as mere nothingness, the annihilation of the infinite possibilities that lay before them. This was the *meaning* of becoming a god: immortality, power, the vastening of the self. No living being has a greater sense of selfness than does a god, nor understands better what it is like to be truly alone. Some might imagine that the gods, in their quest for life without boundary or end, are the closest to God of all creatures. But it is just the opposite. A snowworm is closer, a grain of ice crunched beneath a harijan's boot is closer. All of history is the flight from death, and none flee more quickly than the gods. They flee outward toward the Virgo group of galaxies and the Ayondela Cluster, and beyond, where the stars surge like an ocean against the universe's cold, shimmering edge. But no god has ever found a way out of suffering in this direction. And none, though many try, has ever completely abandoned the body or escaped the pull of matter. For gods, too, are made of atoms, and each atom inside them once experienced the splendor and ecstasy of the universe's birth, and they never forget. Inside all gods is a burning for the infinite, for the moment of creation where death and life are as one. *This* is the pain of the gods. This is their eternal longing and torment. It is the burning awareness of life that grows and grows, without limit, on and on without end.

Danlo was one of the first men to understand this, as a man. With the cold edge of his chisel, he tried to grave awareness into every part of his god, especially into its deeply flawed face. But this was not enough. In many ways, Hanuman understood the suffering aspect of godhood better than he did. And so Danlo worked other passions into the god's face, guiding his round knife and shaver with all the care of a tightrope walker placing his feet. *Face is the doorway to the spirit*—thus say the Alaloi mothers to their children when they wish to discourage the more selfish emotions. Danlo knew something about spirit that Hanuman did not. Yes, there would always be pain, and none could escape the flames of hatred, sorrow, lamentation, and despair. But everyone carried inside the memory of the ancient heavenly fire so brilliant that it was beyond all burning. The fire whose touch could cool the spirit and quench the most raging thirst. Hot and cold, fire and ice, beginning and end—it was Danlo's gift to see the identity of opposites and to wed them together in his carving. The god's finely cut lips were pulled back both in ecstasy and anguish. It was the look of a man in the throes of sexual fever, or of a father who stands with his face toward the sky as he holds his son's cold, broken body in his arms; it was the pleasure of a god who has created life around a million planets, and the pain of watching a billion stars burn out and die. Danlo carved and carved, and his god's eyes twinkled with both laughter and madness, and with the utter awareness of a love beyond love or hate. It took all of his skill to reveal these passions. In truth, he had doubted that his hands were capable of such work, and in all his exhaustion and rage to carve, sometimes, he wondered if the spirits of the Old Ones might be guiding him. As a boy, sitting by the oilstones on deep winter nights, he had watched the grandfathers of his tribe cut animals out of ivory or wood. Now he emulated the ease of their callused old fingers, their sureness and strength, and most of all their patience. He took infinite pains with the god's face. With his sharpest graver, he did the delicate work around the eyes, and he cut these fine lines between heartbeats, to keep his fingers free from the slightest of tremors. He worked with infinite slowness to bring out the god's most vital aspect, which he thought of as terrible beauty. Hanuman must behold the god and be soulstricken with this beauty. He must take the chess piece in his hands and say: This is a god who drinks continually from the deep well of fire inside until he overflows with the power to nourish other life. He is the one who demands life despite all suffering and evil, and he shines with a terrible will toward all that is fertile, wild, and strong, and his face is my own.

When Danlo finally finished carving, he picked up his polishing stone and began rubbing the body of the god. He was uncertain, at first, how closely this chess piece approached the image he had seen. But the more he polished, the more satisfied he was with his work. Of course, he had not realized this interior image perfectly, but then no creation can ever be perfect. He hoped the god was "just as it is," or *lowalosa*, which is an Alaloi compliment for a carving that has revealed the true spirit of any animal or being.

He was very tired, but with his sandstones he polished and polished for most of a day, pausing only to blow away the fine ivory dust that accumulated in the folds and fissures along the length of the god. He tested the smoothness of this polishing with his eyes only. The Alaloi consider it childish to put finger to a carving before it is finished. But after he had rubbed it from pedestal to brow with his finest oilskin, he pronounced his labor done. He looked around the room for a place to put the god; the entire floor was carpeted with ivory shavings and white dust. Moving like an old man whose limbs are crippled with pains, he set the god on the chest beneath the window. He touched it, then. He pressed his hot, blistered fingers to the ivory, which was now icy cold from the drafts of air falling all around. He marveled at the god's creamy smoothness, the lustrous beauty of old ivory. He touched the eyes, the long nose, the coiled muscles of the throat. He smiled just before collapsing against his furs. The god returned his smile, or so he imagined, and the god laughed at him and wept for him, even as he fell into a dreamless sleep that went on and on without end.

THE BROKEN GOD

You are what your deep, driving desire is.
As your desire is, so is your will.
As your will is, so is your deed.
As your deed is, so is your destiny.

—from the Brihadaranyaka Upanishad

Danlo would never know how long he slept, for he had lost all measure of time. When he awoke, the lights still burned in his room, and it was dark outside. The storm had mostly stopped; down through the trees and glidderies, the wind whooshed weakly, like a sick child's breath. Without looking at the thermometer outside the window, he knew that it was warmer. Some would hope that the *sarsara* was dying, but he recognized this almost-quiet as only a period of recuperation, when the wind rests for its sudden and murderous return. It was a time for waiting, a time of chilblains and delusions and the nursing of old wounds. He dreaded going out in such weather, but he had to face the streets, and soon, because he had learned from one of his dormitory mates that it was early evening on the ninety-ninth of deep winter. Bardo would be conducting the great joyance even now, as he stood in his quiet little room, gazing at the god that he had made. A part of him insisted that he should heave on his furs and rush across the City to the cathedral. But, like a man preparing for his wedding, he dallied. Because his beard and hair were powdered with ivory dust—and because he stank of old sweat and seal oil—he used up long moments cleaning himself and drying his hair beneath the hot air jets in the bathing room. He combed his thick, tangled hair—for him an unusual act of grooming. After making sure that Ahira's feather was bound tightly and properly displayed, dangling curved side out between his ear and shoulder, he put on a clean kamelaika and his furs. He sharpened his skate blades. He pulled on his cold boots and spent much time walking back and forth, crunching ivory chips against the hard wooden floor. Then he wrapped the god in a newl skin, a beautiful piece of white leather that his found-mother had once chewed and worked into a lovely, clinging softness. He stowed this package in the inner pocket of his furs. Each of his motions he savored as if he were watching a drama that some master cartoonist was programming, moment by moment. At last, when he could think of nothing else to do, he opened the door to the hallway, then went out into the storm.

His journey to the cathedral was short, cold, and memorable. It was the last and holiest night of the Festival of the Broken Dolls. Fourteen nights ago he had gone out to see Tamara, and the streets had been splendid with tens of thousands of delicately glowing ice lanterns. And now the lanterns were still lit, only there were not so many of them because the yearly ritual of their destruction had begun. Gangs of red-masked Architects from the orthodox churches roamed the streets, using hokkee mallets or sticks to smash any lantern they could find. Danlo tried to avoid these gangs, but they were everywhere, in groups of three or four or forty. The whole of the Old City rang with cries and shouts and the tinkling sound of broken ice. Lights died all around him, one by one, making the skating treacherous. He kicked and stumbled and grated over ice shards; every third building, it seemed, had been vandalized, the pretty lanterns smashed into piles of crystal. On one or two streets, the air was black and stank of alcohol—not the kind of alcohol that one might drink as skotch or beer, but the pure methanol that the outlaw Architects use to douse the robes of the dead. That night, Danlo was to shun all violence, but in other districts of the City, Architects of the Infinite Life would die defending their ice lanterns, and their enemies would burn their bodies with blue alcohol flames. For any Architect, from any of the numerous Architect sects, this is the most horrible of fates, for once the brain has been boiled into a red jelly, it is impossible to preserve the mind in an eternal computer. Architects dread dying such an irredeemable death, but each year, on the morning after Year's End, six or seven charred bodies are found in alleys or out-of-the-way glissades. Although Danlo was lucky not to intrude upon any such religious struggle, at various intersections of the darkened glidderies, he smelled the sick scent of burnt flesh. He could not tell which direction this stench emanated from, for the wind was fickle and cruel, blowing now from the east, then a moment later from the south or north. Frigid gusts of air surprised him and cut him, like drunken knives out of the dark. It was this inconstant wind, he remembered, that had frozen Tamara's face and nearly killed her. The wind followed him down twisting streets, growing stronger at each skate stroke and turn. By the time he reached the cathedral steps, he was cold to the quick, and one eye was frozen shut. It occurred to him, then, that his plan to redeem Tamara (and Hanuman) was truly hopeless. He might have traced his way back to his dormitory, but the screeching wind kept him from returning there. The wind was a wall of ice and memory and sound that drove him up the steps three at a time, in through the great western doors of the cathedral.

Immediately, two godlings stopped him. They were handsome young men too impressed with the gold robes they wore, and they pushed the palms of their hands toward Danlo and asked to see his invitation. When he admitted that he had none and then gave them his name, it was as if a magic word had been spoken. The shorter godling examined Danlo's wind-burnt face and said, "We're honored, Pilot. The Bardo has hoped that you would return. We're sorry you missed the joyance, but the Bardo is still inside, and many of your friends. If you please, we'll take your furs."

Danlo slipped the god from its pocket, then shrugged off his furs. He stepped into the nave, which was ablaze with light from thousands of candles. Although there were many people—perhaps two hundred men and women milling about in their golden formals—they seemed small and insignificant beneath the vast sweeps of the stained-glass windows. Bardo had finally completed his scheme of replacing the old glass with new; even the lovely stonework lining the walls had been resculpted, with figures of Bardo and Leopold Soli and Dama Moira Ringess, with Balusilustalu and other Agathanians whom some people believed to be nearly as godly as Mallory Ringess. Danlo thought that this robot-made sculpture was poorly executed, but then, he was the only person in the cathedral whose attention was turned in this direction. All the others stood in groups of five or ten, deeper inside the nave, in the paper-strewn area around the chancel. Indeed, there were papers everywhere, ten thousand squares of gold foil carelessly cast against the bare floor stones.

660

They made a gleaming, crinkling carpet beneath his boots. He realized then that he had missed not only the joyance but the gift giving that followed. While he had been combing his hair, Ringists from across the City had unwrapped their presents and departed. Now only the elite members of the Way remained. As he walked down the nave, he could see the faces of those he knew very well: Thomas Rane, the brothers Hur, Surya Surata Lal, Kolenya Mor, Nirvelli, and Mariam Erendira Vasquez. And Sherborn of Darkmoon, Lais Motega Mohammad, and Delores Lightstone, and many others. Some he did not recognize, such as the Trian merchant-prince and the alien courtesan who stood next to Bardo. In truth, there were too few people. He had hoped to present Hanuman with the god just after the joyance, in the great confusion of giving gifts that had filled the cathedral. He had wanted to catch Hanuman by surprise, perhaps behind one of the pillars of the dark aisle, to speak with him privately and watch his face as he unwrapped the newl skin. But now Hanuman stood at the center of a circle of his admirers, and it would be impossible to slip through unobserved and take him aside. And so Danlo walked straight ahead, the sole figure in the cathedral who was dressed in black. He stepped over mounds of rustling foil. It was probably the crunching of this golden paper that caused Mariam Erendira Vasquez to look his way. Suddenly ten others followed her gaze, and then two hundred more, as everyone turned to watch him approach. They were strangely quiet, as if they had been caught talking about him. But that seemed unlikely because their eyes were soft and happy with the remembrance of Hanuman's Elder Eddas. In their hands, they clutched jewelry or boxes of triya seeds or purlets or other coveted things. All of them, around their fingers, wore a golden ring that Bardo had given them earlier. Bardo had given rich gifts to every Ringist, and he seemed well pleased with his munificence. He was drunk with the splendor of the moment. (And stupefied with the afterglow of electronic samadhi.) In a golden robe studded with black diamonds, he stood above all the others as he laughed and waved his arm and called out, "Danlo wi Soli Ringess! You've returned to us!"

Danlo walked into the crowd of people standing below the altar. He might have been a stone falling into the sea, for as he moved forward, men and women hurried out of his way, and then, in golden waves, closed in behind him. He heard Bardo bellow, "What a night this is, by God!" The word "God" rolled over him and echoed from window to window high above; it filled all the cathedral, and Danlo wondered if Bardo had chosen this ancient structure in order to glory in the sound of his magnificent voice. "But it's too bad you missed the joyance," Bardo continued. "It's been a brilliant night—a night of true remembrance."

The last of the people stepped out of Danlo's way, and Bardo was waiting with his arms held wide to welcome him. But Danlo kept a distance; he bowed politely and looked past Bardo to the altar stairs. There, standing on the plush red carpet of the second step, was Hanuman. He was dressed out of color in a new golden robe, and he wore the diamond clearface like a second skin molded to his naked head. He bowed to Danlo. When he straightened up, due to the added height of the steps, his head was just higher than Bardo's. "Hello, Danlo," he said.

Inside the clearface, the neurologics were lit up like millions of glowing drillworms. They cast a nimbus of purple light around Hanuman's head. His face was lit up, too, but not with electronic samadhi nor any kind of cybernetic bliss. He stared at Danlo with complete concentration, and his pale purple eyes burned with a terrible awareness. Instantly, he knew that Danlo had uncovered his rape of Tamara's memories. He looked at Danlo, and he knew, and he knew that Danlo could see this sudden knowledge running wild in his eyes.

"Hello, Hanuman," Danlo said. He bowed, never taking his eyes away from Hanuman's. Inside the black centers of Hanuman's eyes, he saw fear, as intense and dark as holes in space. There were no secrets separating them anymore, only the truth of what Hanuman had done. And then Hanuman's gaze closed in upon himself, and Danlo could see nothing there except hatred—but hatred for whom he did not know.

Hanu, Hanu, he thought, *I must not hate you.*

"I'm sorry for Tamara," Hanuman said. His voice was warm, sweet, and gentle; many people pressed closer to hear his words. "We all share your grief."

A nearby mechanic smiled at Danlo, but he would not meet his eyes. It was that way with the others, too. Although they offered quick and easy sympathies, they were suspicious of him for suffering such a bizarre misfortune, and they regarded him as if tainted with a secret disease. For a moment Danlo dwelt in memory of his last conversation with Tamara, then he turned to Hanuman and said, "You speak as if . . . she is dead."

"No, it's just the opposite," Hanuman told him. "A part of

662

er—the deep, mysterious part—has been preserved. Tonight, we've all witnessed this miracle."

Danlo took a quick breath of air, then asked, "What . . . miracle?"

"Ah," Bardo said. He stepped closer, and his great belly was like a weapon forcing Danlo backward and upward, up upon the first step of the altar. "Ah, Little Fellow, but you should have been told. Hanuman was able to record a few of Tamara's memories before her affliction. She remembranced the Eddas with a beautiful passion—tonight we've all tasted of this passion. You were lucky to have known such a woman, too bad."

Danlo did not want to look at Bardo just then. He rubbed his forehead, and he said to Hanuman, "You say that she came to you . . . and you recorded her memories?"

"Yes," Hanuman said. He smiled, and his face was like a closed door. "She had a beautiful soul—it was always her pleasure to share the best parts of herself with others."

He is afraid, Danlo thought. *He is afraid of something, but he has no fear that I will accuse him of his crimes, here, now.*

"I know how you loved her," Hanuman said softly. "Losing her must be like losing the whole world. Like losing your life."

"Yes," Danlo said. He pressed his fingers against his eye, the one that always ached with the beginning of a head pain.

"If only you had attended the joyance," Hanuman said. "You've been wounded, I know. I'm sorry, Danlo, but it might have helped to hear Tamara's voice inside you, to see the Eddas with her eyes. You should know, there's a part of Tamara's soul that can never die, now."

Hanuman smiled at the people edging the bottom of the steps, and his voice flowed out like honey: "What is the Way of Ringess if not the way to heal humanity of its wound?"

The wound that will never heal.

Danlo peered into Hanuman's eyes, looking for this wound, but he saw only the reflection of his own anguished face. He promised to restrain himself, then. He resolved that his anger and hurt should flow out of him, despite all Hanuman's mockery and twisted compassion.

Danlo rubbed his aching throat and said, "I think that parts of Tamara are gone."

"But, Danlo, what parts?"

Danlo gripped the god in his fist and looked about him. There were too many people standing too close. He was too aware of their muffled voices, their curious eyes, their sweet, meaty breaths. He moved closer to Hanuman so that he could talk more privately, but Nirvelli and Bardo and five others followed him up the steps. "Parts . . . of her character," he forced out. His words sounded bare and hollow to him, and he could hardly speak. "Her emotions, her ideals . . . the way she sees herself."

"Aren't these the parts of the self that you once called 'face'?"

"Yes," Danlo said.

"And isn't this just the illusory sense of identity that you've always disregarded?" Hanuman was speaking for the benefit of his audience—and all the while aiming his words like a dagger at Danlo's heart. "Isn't this just the 'I' that dies when the body dies, while the deeper self lives?"

"Yes," Danlo said. "I never saw face . . . as it really is."

"But now you do?"

Danlo looked at Hanuman; despite the press of bodies nearby, it seemed they were the only two people in the cathedral. "Death is death, and there is nothing to fear," Danlo said. "Truly. But as long as life is in life . . . face is precious beyond words or reckoning."

Standing one step lower than Hanuman was Surya Surata Lal, with her tiny red eyes and ugly mouth. She beamed a smile of adoration at Hanuman, and she said, "Someday, we'll preserve ourselves from every possible disaster. This is what gods must do: preserve."

"As memories are preserved . . . in a computer?" Danlo asked.

Hanuman nodded to Surya, then to Bardo. He said, "Danlo has always doubted that memories could be thus preserved."

"I have doubted . . . many things," Danlo admitted.

"He doubts," Hanuman said to Nirvelli and to the others standing below him. "He of the great remembrance, Danlo wi Soli Ringess—even he doubts. Yet he would like to believe. But what is the truth of what is preserved?"

Yes, Hanu, what is the truth?

"Everything is preserved," Nirvelli said. With her dark beauty and lovely voice, she was beloved of other Ringists, and it seemed that she was speaking for everyone around her except Danlo. "That's the Way of Ringess, to preserve."

Bardo, posing with one foot against the steps while he pointed toward the vault of the nave, caught the attention of those around him as he said, "Someday, the Ringess will return to Neverness. If only he'd return tomorrow, he would restore Tamara's memory. He's a god, by God! She would look at him, and the Ringess would look into her goddamned brain, jiggle a few neurons, and—instantly!—she'd remember herself."

"That's the Way of Ringess," Surya said.

With a wave of his hand, Bardo beat the air as if to dispel any doubts he himself might have about the dogma he was delivering. "It's the Way of Ringess to relieve human beings of their suffering. It's the Way of Ringess to become a god without flaw or bound. Who of us hasn't seen this in the Eddas, tonight? Someday, when we've attained our godhood, there will be no more suffering—we'll cure the whole damn universe of its evils and pains."

Danlo looked around him to see who accepted Bardo's words and who did not. Thomas Rane, of course, was cool and aloof and imperturbable; he stood tall and grave in his gray robe, and what he was thinking, not even a cetic might know. And the brothers Hur, with their impish faces and eyes aglow with kalla—certainly neither they nor the thirty members of their fellowship took Bardo's pronouncements very seriously. They gathered as a group away from the altar, and many of them were smiling or suppressing laughter. But Mariam Erendira Vasquez and Rafael Mendeley and all the others seemed to be waiting for Bardo or Hanuman (or even Danlo) to say more; they drew in closer, like a school of paka fish around some bright stone or bit of shell cast into the water.

"No," Danlo said suddenly.

"What?" This came from Bardo, who was standing below him on the third step of the altar, sighing and pulling at his beard.

"What did the young pilot say?" Surya asked.

Hanuman had now worked his way up the steps, and he stood alone on the altar. All around him were thousands of fireflowers in their blue vases. He pointed at Danlo and said, "I suppose Danlo views godhood otherwise than we. After all, we must remember who his father is."

Do I remember who my father is?

Danlo wondered about this as he stood on the top step, looking down at all the people spread out below. They cast uneasy glances at each other and traded quick, nervous words. There was an air of uncertainty about them, as if they regarded Danlo as an incarnation of his father, or at least as a messenger that he had sent to them. From the center of the altar, Hanuman was staring at him with a fey intensity. Danlo sensed that future of Ringism might somehow revolve around this moment, so he chose his next words with infinite care. "Truly," he said, "the gods are sick with their suffering. It maddens them. You cannot imagine their pain."

Hanuman made a slight motion with his thumb, a bit of the cetic's hand language that spelled out a single question: Can *you*?

Surya Lal must have caught sight of this silent communication. Her mouth turned down as she looked at Danlo and said, "I suppose the young pilot will tell us what it's like to become a god?"

With his finger, Danlo made a series of signs down by his right side so that no one could see them except Hanuman. Then he said, "To a god, the worst agony of a man is no more than the sting of a single snowflake breaking against the eyelid. It is a drop of water in an infinite sea."

Hanuman nodded his head as if he had been waiting for his moment. He stepped over to the altar table where the golden urn gleamed as brightly as a mirror. He looked out over his fellow Ringists, and he smiled the smile of a cetic about to share a great secret with them. With quick, precise movements, he pulled up the sleeve of his robe. Then he plunged his naked arm down into the urn. When he drew it out, his hand was dripping with water. He held his finger to his open mouth and let a single drop roll off onto his tongue. From the people crowding the altar steps, there were gasps and cries of alarm; many of them, obviously, had forgotten that the urn contained only seawater and not kalla. Now Hanuman held the urn in both hands as he brought the rim of it to his lips. He tilted his head back and drank deeply. Bardo, naturally, was outraged and envious at this act. He must have viewed it is as one more of Hanuman's brilliant symbolic gestures (if not a sacrilege altogether). But before he could stomp up the steps to offer a rebuke, the urn was back on its table, and Hanuman was pointing his finger at Danlo as he called out in his silvery voice, "Why have you come here tonight? Do you wish to discourage us from our destiny merely because it is painful?"

"No," Danlo said. He stood listening to the wind as it roared through the cathedral spires. High above him one of the new windows was poorly seated in its metal casement, and it rattled and shook with each violent gust. "No, I only wanted . . . to give you something."

So saying, Danlo gripped the god and stepped onto the altar. All this time he had been holding his carving down by his left side. If Surya or anyone else had taken notice of what was in his hand, she must have thought it a bunched-up cloth or chamois used for wiping down skate blades. Even Hanuman, who missed few details about human beings' mannerisms or accoutrements, seemed surprised. Danlo walked deeper onto the altar, and his boots sank into the soft red carpet. With each step he left imprints behind him and little chunks of slush. All around him—on both sides of Hanuman—fireflowers burst from their vases in lovely scarlets and tones of flaming pink. Their scent was heavy, pungent, and sweet. At the center of the altar Danlo froze into motionlessness. His arm was outstretched as he stood with the god in his open hand, wondering what Hanuman would do.

"He's brought him a gift!" he heard someone say.

Cautiously, slowly, Hanuman approached him. He looked at Danlo's eyes and then at the lump of newl skin in his hand, back and forth. Then, like a squirrel snatching up a baldo nut, he took the god and retreated back a few paces nearer the altar table.

"What is it?" Bardo said.

"Look," Hanuman said to Bardo, who was standing at the edge of the altar, ahhhing and mmming as he pulled at his mustache. "Danlo has brought me a gift."

For a moment Hanuman's composure melted away, and he seemed both abashed and secretly delighted at Danlo's gift. He looked at Danlo sadly, all the while clutching the newl skin in his hand.

"Open it now!" Bardo called out.

"But it's too late," Hanuman said. "I exchanged all my gifts earlier. I've nothing to give Danlo."

"Oh, but you have already given me the most precious thing," Danlo said. Although he spoke without irony, he was aware that his voice sounded deep, angry, and pained. "You have given me your friendship. Your love. Your . . . compassion."

The wound that will not be healed.

They locked eyes, then, and a deep knowledge flowed between them. It was as if their brains were connected along the firing of their optic nerves. In that moment, Danlo thought it

667

would be impossible for Hanuman to conceal the truth from him. And he could keep nothing from Hanuman, least of all his awareness of the purpose of Hanuman's crime.

I know why, Danlo thought. *I know that you know that I know that . . .*

Hanuman stood holding the gift in his hand; apparently he could not decide if he should open it. Then, under the gaze of two hundred other Ringists crowding the altar steps, he gently peeled back the wrappings of newl skin. Soon the god was revealed in its creamy ivory perfection, and he stared at it for a long time.

This is what you fear: that I know why.

"What is it?" someone asked.

"It looks like a chess piece," Bardo said. "Perhaps a god."

"Hold it up so that we can see it!"

Hanuman cast the newl skin away from him. Then he gripped the god by its fiery pedestal and held it above his head.

"It is a . . . replacement," Danlo said. "For the missing god of your chess set."

Bardo stepped onto the altar to take a better look at the god. He was always interested in expensive, finely made things. "Ah, but where did you buy it? It's Yarkonan, isn't it? This is marvelous work—it must be priceless."

Many of the people standing around the altar began remarking upon exquisite qualities of the chess piece, while many more remained silent as they stared at the god's beautiful face.

"I . . . made it," Danlo said. "I found a piece of ivory and carved it. The Devaki fathers taught me how to carve."

Hanuman, too, was staring at the god. He could not take his eyes from it. He turned it around and around in front of the candles that flickered in their golden stands. Tongues of flame illuminated the cool, subtle contours of the ivory as Hanuman watched the firelight dance across the god's terrible face.

"Oh, Danlo," he said.

Danlo watched him examining the god. Did he understand that it was meant as both a peace offering and a synthesis of two ways of viewing the universe? *He must know,* Danlo thought. He must see that there was a connection between the passion for burning and the quest for remembrance. Ultimately, life's terrible fire and clear waters of the Elder Eddas were made of the same substance, and Hanuman must take the god in his hands and accept this final paradox of existence.

"I've never seen anything like this," Hanuman said. His

knuckles were hard and white from gripping the god so tightly. He should have smiled and bowed to Danlo, but the sight of the god struck something deep inside him, and his face fell hateful and furious as if Danlo had dropped a hot coal into his hand.

"I had hoped that it would match . . . your other chess pieces."

"Can we take this as a hopeful sign that you've returned to the Way?"

Danlo swallowed against the dryness in his throat and said, "No, I am sorry. It is just a gift."

"Well, it's quite beautiful."

"I had hoped . . . that you would like it."

"It's more than beautiful, really. It's inspired work."

Danlo saw the old madness come into Hanuman's eyes; instantly his belly muscles tightened up as if expecting a blow.

"The god *looks* something like your father," Hanuman said.

"My . . . father."

"Mallory Ringess. *The* Ringess, whose inspiration we all must follow."

From ten feet away, Danlo peered at the god from a new angle. He looked at the long nose, the deep-set eyes, the sensuous mouth open to both cruelty and compassion. Suddenly he saw what Hanuman saw: the chess piece resembled Mallory Ringess as a young man, before he had been sculpted into the form of an Alaloi. Without realizing what he was doing, almost by chance, Danlo had carved this image of his father.

"I . . . did not know," Danlo said. He looked down at his fingers, which were red and pocked with blisters. It was strange, he thought, that during all the days he had worked on the god, his hands might have recognized what his mind did not.

"You've been inspired," Hanuman said. "But your inspiration is false."

"But, Hanu—"

"As a *man*," Hanuman interrupted, "Mallory Ringess was the most passionate of men. When he loved, he loved. When he wept, his tears would have scalded the eyes of a lesser being. We all know this. But *the* Ringess is far beyond such emotion. He's left all suffering behind him. Can't you see this, Danlo? You've given us the man, not the god."

"No, no, Hanu, you do not—"

"*You* don't understand," Hanuman said. "You never have."

They were now shouting at each other, trying to make

themselves heard above the wind which fell over the cathedral like an ocean. The wind roared and shuddered and beat against the windows; at any moment, it seemed, the panes of colored glass might slam against their casements and shatter inward. But Danlo was only distantly aware of this potential disaster. All his senses concentrated on Hanuman. Because Danlo's words were lost into the larger sound of the storm, he stopped shouting. His voice fell to a whisper. Hanuman would not be able to hear this whisper, but he might read the shape of Danlo's lips and finally understand what he was saying.

"If gods truly have the powers that you say, then restore Tamara."

"Am I a god, Danlo?" Hanuman whispered this question so that no one could read his words except Danlo.

"But she suffers—she tries to remember herself and she cannot."

"I know."

"Help me," Danlo said. "Please."

Hanuman's cheeks suddenly flushed red as if Danlo had slapped his face. "Three tendays ago I asked for your help," he said. "But you wouldn't help me."

"I . . . could not."

"And I can't help you."

"You could let an imprimatur copy Tamara's memories. From your computer. There could be an imprinting, and Tamara might remember."

"No," Hanuman whispered. "That's impossible, now."

"But, Hanu, why?"

"Because her memories have all been destroyed. I never saved them. You *know* why."

Hanuman pointed the god's head at him and shook it as if to accuse Danlo of a worse crime than slelling memories. Danlo knew then that all his hope had been false, just another way of facing the universe with dreams rather than grasping the reality of the present moment. Now, there was only the wind streaming against the fragile windows and cold, falling air. Now he hated a man. He looked at Hanuman, and Hanuman looked at him, and something dark and primeval flowed between them, back and forth, back and forth.

I must not hate him, Danlo thought. *I must not hate.*

But he did hate; it was there, inside, indestructible, surging up toward his brain with each contraction of his heart. He'd thought that he had built a wall around this hate, but now it was breaking out of him like a wound bursting open with poisoned blood. He shook his head back and forth while his fingernails clawed deep into his palms. Bardo, who was standing nearby, looked at him strangely. He heard Bardo bellow out: "What are you saying? By God, what's going on here?"

There was a swirl of golden silk from his side, but Danlo stared straight ahead. Even though he was aware of Bardo bearing down on him, he could not break eyelock with Hanuman.

"What have you done?" Hanuman whispered. He stood facing Danlo, and he gripped the god with both hands. He held it in front of him as if he were about to snap it in two.

"No!" Danlo cried. His voice spilled out and vanished into the hollows of the cathedral. For a moment he felt himself falling through an emptiness as vast and black as an underground cavern. All he could hear was the murderous wind pushing through cracks and shrieking over scooped stone. Although many people crossed their arms over their chests against this bitterly cold air, Danlo was burning like a child with fever. His hands were hot and inflamed, and his belly, and his head; his eyes stung from staring at the lustrous piece of ivory that Hanuman held in his little hands.

No, no, no, no.

It appeared that Hanuman was hardening himself to break the god. His hands were tightened into fists. There were tears in his eyes, and love, and madness, as if he could not bear looking at Danlo—but neither could he look away. All his life he had tried to create around himself a perfect sphere of self-will, and he had almost succeeded. Only one connection with the universe outside himself remained.

"What are you *doing*?" Bardo shouted from a million miles away.

Hanu, Hanu, no.

There was an endless flow of hate and love between them, and this love beyond love was the one thing that Hanuman could not bear. For a moment his eyes burned into Danlo's, and he saw the universe as Danlo saw it, and he willed himself to break the god. His will was very strong. If there had been a cleansing heaume at hand, he might have used it to destroy his own memories of Danlo. But there was only a simple chess piece carved out of ivory, six inches of a walrus's tusk that Hanuman held near his body as his fists clenched and trembled.

"He can't break it, can he?" someone shouted.

Danlo watched Hanuman struggling against the tough, old

671

ivory. To Bardo and the other Ringists, it must have seemed impossible that he could gain enough leverage to break it. But Hanuman's hands were hard and strong from years of practicing his killing art, and there was a flaw at the god's center. Danlo, in his carving, had tried to hide this long, twisted crack through the ivory, but he knew it was there.

"Look!"

With a sudden jerk and snap, Hanuman broke the god in half. It divided along a jagged crack through the god's belly. Something broke inside Danlo, then. He watched tiny ivory splinters flying out from the break at the god's center, and he stepped toward Hanuman in order to kill him. There was a roaring in his ears louder than the wind. Something was calling him to lay his hands about Hanuman's throat and squeeze until he was dead. The memory of Tamara was inside him, whispering terrible things. And then he heard the voice of his father, and his father's father—all his ancestors, male and female, back to the first bacteria which had fought their dark and desperate battles in the oceans of Old Earth. There were billions of voices inside him, screeching and crying and laughing, spread through the tissues of his heart and brain. And all these voices together were just the sound and the memory of life. The love of death. Each cell of his body burned with a will toward destruction and death. He felt this terrible will flow like molten stone into hands he was aware of it as a flash of lightning behind his eyes. For a moment he was almost blind. His field of vision narrowed so that all he could see was Hanuman, grinding his teeth together, bearing down with all his strength against the ivory god as he looked at Danlo and despaired. He saw Hanuman holding the pieces of the god in his hands; Hanuman's face shone with astonishment, hatred, triumph, and shame. And then other voices began calling Danlo: the scream of his young son; his daughter's quiet whimpering; the laughter and weeping of a billion billion granddaughters waiting forever to be born. This memory, too, lay inside him. It was the memory of a future that only he could create. He saw his hands circling Hanuman's throat to choke off the flow of air and blood. He saw Hanuman writhing like a fish between his hands, spitting and thrashing in his death agony. And Hanuman dead with a broken neck, and Hanuman lying on the altar, his head broken open upon the bloody golden urn that Danlo held in his hands. Danlo began to take a step toward Hanuman, and a thousand times Hanuman died with his eyes wide open, gazing at him in love and fear. I

672

was impossible to escape these deaths, or any death, for it was all around him, frozen into an instant of time. All things, even as they quivered and swelled with life, were really quite dead. The tribes of the Alaloi were dead—he could see their twisted bodies abandoned in their snow huts, or bleeding inside bright caverns, or spread out in their thousands and thousands across the winter ice of the world. Out toward the Vild, where the stars burned so brilliantly they were sick with light, in each second of time, a million human beings cried out and died. Soon all the stars would burn out and die, and each man and woman across the galaxy would be burnt and broken and dead. There was nothing to save them, neither medicines nor meditation nor belief in the redemptive technologies of the gods. This was the way the universe was. This is the way it always would be. And now a little piece of the universe named Hanuman li Tosh stood before him, looking at him with fury and hate. Hanuman twisted his hands, suddenly, forever, and a little piece of ivory broke in two. And so Danlo would kill him now. In an animal rage, he would rip out Hanuman's throat or break open his brains. Out of pure hatred and will to destroy, he would hurry Hanuman on to his inevitable death. It was right that he should do this. The wind was calling him to kill Hanuman, and the stars, and each atom of each living thing across the universe.

NO!

Danlo took a step across the altar, and he became aware of himself as a bringer of death. He wondered, then, how he could hate so deeply and completely, yet see himself hating so clearly.

I am not I. I am the one who sees myself, who sees that he sees.

With this thought, his field of vision opened as if he were a bird breaking through a layer of clouds below the sky. He saw Hanuman trying with all his might to break the god; and Hanuman, beholding the wildness in Danlo as he stared at him with his love of fate; and Hanuman, hardening himself to kill Danlo the moment that the god snapped and Danlo rushed upon him. He saw many things at once. Now Bardo sighed and moved toward him, and the fat along Bardo's belly rippled like the waves upon the ocean. Now, in the vase nearest Hanuman, a petal from one of the flowers separated from the stem and fell in a scarlet flutter through the air. Now there was light everywhere, photons from the thousands of candles pinging against stone pillars, reflecting into dark corners, falling upward in golden streams toward the cathedral's windows. He was suddenly very

673

aware of these windows. There were eighty-two windows spaced evenly around the nave, but one window in particular called to him. It was the scene of Mallory Ringess saying farewell to Bardo before his leaving Neverness and his ascent to the heavens. His hand was laid across Bardo's forehead and tear-streaked cheeks, and his eyes, cut of gray-blue glass, bathed Bardo in a silent blessing of light. The body of the Ringess was made of bits of glass of every color, and each time the wind gusted, the glass fragments strained against each other, and the whole window bowed inward.

No!

At last the god that Hanuman was holding snapped. At the same moment, a blast of wind blew in the great window, ripping the casement entirely away from the stone wall. At first no one was aware of this disaster except Danlo. High above the chancel, he saw bits of violet and blue and gold burst into a shower of glass. Many of these bits were still glued together and fell in glittering shards and sheets. The heavy steel casement, still supporting whole sections of the scene between Bardo and Mallory Ringess, fell like a giant hammer directly toward the altar. Danlo watched as the wind destroyed the window; this took only a moment. But it would be a tenth of a second before the sound of breaking glass and the sudden storm reached the ears of the people below, and longer still before their nerves fired and caused them to lift their faces upward.

"No!" Danlo cried out.

He took a step toward Hanuman. He saw the window break, and he waited an eternity to hear the sound of it. He saw himself standing on the altar, lost into his hatred, raging like a bird of prey. It was as if his center—the seeing part of himself—was no longer located behind his eyes or in his belly, but rather inside the stone wall ornaments, or along the ribs of vault, or circling through the cold space of the nave itself. Ten thousand bits of glass fell through the air, describing lovely parabolas of sapphire and rose. The window casement dropped in a perfect parabola toward the altar; Danlo did not need mathematics to see that this rectangle of heavy metal would exactly bisect the space occupied by Hanuman's head. In twenty-seven tenths of a second, it would crush Hanuman's brain into jelly and he would die.

Hanu, Hanu, you must die.

For part of a second Danlo waited, and then the sound of death exploded through the cathedral, and two hundred pairs of yes snapped toward the falling window above them. Only Hanuman, of all the Ringists, did not look up. He held the broken rod in his hands, and he never stopped staring at Danlo.

Danlo, Danlo.

It was a truth of the universe that Hanuman must die. Danlo knew that his own will toward hatred was a truth, just as it was true (or would someday become true) that the galaxies out beyond the Canes Venatici and many others would die. All these truths he saw for the first time, and he knew he was very close to the affirmation that he had been seeking for so long. But then, unexpectedly, there came the flash of another truth that he did not want to acknowledge. It was written in Hanuman's face, in his death-haunted eyes, in the way that Hanuman would never stop looking at him.

I have created him, Danlo thought.

With every word that he had ever spoken to Hanuman, with each act, ideal, and expression of faith, he had created in Hanuman the desire to be more. With love, with wildness—even with the sound of his shakuhachi which Hanuman could never bear listening to—he had driven Hanuman to the dark interior door that opens out onto the universe. Danlo, himself, had flung open his door as if he were a child careless of the wildest and worst storms. And Hanuman, for fear of freezing to death, had been forced to slam it shut. Danlo looked at Hanuman waiting behind his closed door, waiting for Danlo to step closer and open it one more time, and he wondered how could he murder this broken-souled man that he had created with so much love and pain.

"No, I won't," he whispered. "No."

Upon this single word the universe turned. The hatred suddenly left Danlo, or, for the moment, transfigured itself into a deeper emotion. He took a step toward Hanuman, and then ten more blindingly quick steps. He practically flew at Hanuman in his urge to preserve his life. There were only tenths of a second before the window casement crushed them both, but this was time enough to change the future forever. He collided with Hanuman in a shock of fists and knees and exploding breath. He bore him backward, even as Hanuman tried to grapple with him. Then, just behind Danlo, the window crashed into the altar, throwing out bullets of glass, tearing a gaping wound in the red carpet and pulverizing the stone beneath. The whole cathedral shook as if a bomb had exploded. Everywhere glass was falling in showers, even as he fell against Hanuman to push him out of the way. With difficulty, through the shriek of broken steel and

Danlo's wild rush, Hanuman kept his feet. He jumped backwar
and struck out, with his knees, with his eyes, with the pieces
the broken god that he still grasped in his fists.

"By God, you'll kill him!"

Danlo was falling toward Hanuman, and he saw a gleam o
jagged ivory sweeping up toward his face. He might have caugh
Hanuman's fist in his hand or at least twisted his head away, bu
he was still trying to take hold of Hanuman, and his balance wa
gone. As he fell over Hanuman, he waited for his head to ex
plode into light. But the blow never came.

"Be still, now, easy there!"

Bardo had stepped behind Hanuman, and he had his hug
arms wrapped around him. Hanuman's arms were pinione
against his sides. Although Hanuman stamped his boots agains
Bardo's feet and drove his diamond-covered head back agains
Bardo's chin, he could not make him let go. He twisted an
writhed and beat the pieces of the god against Bardo's robe
tearing open great rents. Danlo fell against him, pressing him
back into Bardo's belly. For a moment the three of them stoo
welded together, struggling. Danlo grasped Hanuman's wrist
and pulled his hands up against his chest. Hanuman could barel
move. His face was up against Danlo's; his breath fell ove
Danlo's face in hot, urgent bursts. Danlo waited a long time fo
the madness to leave Hanuman's eyes. Then he let go of Hanu
man and stood back, waiting to see what Hanuman would do.

"What's wrong with you?" Bardo's voice thundered out
He let go of Hanuman and stood looking about him at the ruin
of the altar. Broken vases and crushed flowers were strewn a
about, and there was glass everywhere. At the center of the alta
lay the golden urn, dented and leaking seawater onto the carpet
Many people had been cut by bits of flying glass; they stoo
about, moaning or screaming or looking back and forth betwee
Danlo and Hanuman, and they seemed utterly confused.

"Oh, my poor window," Bardo said. "This is too bad.
Then he remembered his compassion and called out, "Is anyon
injured? By God, is everyone all right?"

As it happened, miraculously, no one was badly injured
But due to the missing window, everyone was instantly shiver
ing. The storm roared in through the opening in the cathedral
walls. The north wind was bitter and deadly cold, and it droppe
clouds of snow over the Ringists crowding the altar.

"Ah, but it's cold in here," Bardo said. "Perhaps we shoul

adjourn for the evening and go to the tower and take some refreshment."

But no one, at that moment, was in the mood for food or drink. With the breaking of the god, the great joyance had come to an end. A few Ringists began edging toward the doors, while others were speaking in low, nervous tones.

"Danlo wi Soli Ringess!" This came from Hanuman, who had regained his quickness of mind. He approached Danlo holding his hands open so that he—and everyone else—could see the two halves of the chess piece. "I can't accept your gift: you're not a Ringist any longer, and this thing that you've made is no expression of the Way of Ringess."

So saying, he cast the pieces down to the altar. They bounced and clicked against pieces of glass; they rolled over and over before coming to a stop. Bardo, who was horrified to see such a treasure so badly treated, huffed across the altar. With much sighing, he bent over and scooped up the pieces of the god.

He turned to Hanuman and said, "But Danlo saved your life!"

Danlo waited motionless, letting plumes of snow fall over him. Although he never stopped looking at Hanuman, he was aware of Surya Lal and others talking among themselves, trying to explain what they had witnessed: ". . . has taken a vow of ahimsa . . . yes, but what a coincidence that Hanuman broke the god exactly when the window fell . . . I don't believe in meaningless coincidences."

In fact, Ringists across the Civilized Worlds would see the hand of a god in the breaking of the great window, as if Mallory Ringess were somehow displeased with the composition of his image and had somehow willed its destruction. People would talk about the miraculous coincidence of the broken god for many years to come. But now Hanuman was addressing Danlo, and Bardo, and they turned their attention toward events of more immediate concern.

"Danlo has saved my life," Hanuman said. He looked at Danlo as though he hated what Danlo had done. "I'll never forget this—I can't forget he's been my friend."

"He saved your *life*!" Bardo repeated. Then he pressed the pieces of the broken god into Hanuman's hand. "He might have died in your place!"

Hanuman turned to Bardo and pointed at the pieces of the window scattered across the altar. He said, "If this window had

677

been mounted properly, Danlo wouldn't have needed to demonstrate such self-sacrifice. Such faithfulness to his vow of ahimsa. But, no, you wanted the window ready for the joyance, even though many of us thought that the portrayal of the Ringess was poorly done."

Bardo's face fell purple-black then, but he said nothing. He stared down at the altar, muttering, "Ah, too bad. Too bad."

With a few words, in front of two hundred stunned people, Hanuman had shamed Bardo. And he had made a connection, however false, between Danlo's carving and Bardo's monumental effrontery in mounting a window that glorified Bardo as much as it did Mallory Ringess. This was Hanuman's genius, to make such connections, to construct in the minds of those who admired him a reality that he wished them to believe.

I have created him, Danlo thought. *This is the future that I have made.*

He shut his eyes, brooding over the cruelest of truths: that time is like a river flowing in only one direction, and that the future, once it arrives, can never be unmade.

Hanuman nodded at Danlo and said, "In my hurry to escape the window, I tried to knock it away and nearly struck you. I'm sorry."

Most of the Ringists, Danlo realized, had been too panicked by the exploding window to notice what had occurred between Danlo and Hanuman. But a few of them must have understood. Even now, Hanuman was beginning to edit the memory of what they had seen.

"Danlo, I'm sorry," Hanuman repeated. He held up the pieces of the god so that everyone could see them. Then he brought them together, fitting them like pieces of a child's puzzle. Although Danlo was standing close to him, it was difficult to see the crack that divided the god in two.

Hanu, Hanu.

Hanuman's face was full of emotion as he called out: "The distance between the love of two friends is as small as the space between the two halves of this chess piece."

Suddenly, as if he were executing one of the motions of his killing art, he jerked his hands apart. High above his head, the two halves of the gleaming god were now separated by three feet of air. "But the distance between one who follows the Way of Ringess and one who does not is as wide as the light-years between the stars."

I have let him live, Danlo thought. *I cannot be sorry for that.*

678

"Danlo," Hanuman said. He moved forward and gave the pieces of the god into Danlo's hands. "I'm sorry I can't accept your gift."

"I am sorry, too," Danlo said. His breath burst into steam the moment it touched the cold air falling over him. Tiny snowflakes broke against his eyes, and his face was burning with cold. Every cell of his body was cold, yet burning, too, with Hanuman's secret gift that he would never forget.

"You should go now," Hanuman said. He covered his face against the snowy air sifting down over the altar. "The storm has returned—this late it might be difficult to call for a sled."

"What do you mean telling Danlo that he should leave?" Bardo suddenly asked. He glowered at Hanuman, then sighed with great force. "Is it upon you to ask him to leave?"

Hanuman gestured toward Surya Lal and Mariam Erendira Vasquez; he bowed to all the Ringists. To Bardo he said, "Do you think it's appropriate that they should have to share this night with someone who doesn't follow our Way?"

Everyone was now looking at Bardo. Hanuman was concentrating his whole awareness on Bardo's soft eyes, staring at him as a cat stares at a mouse. "Ah, no," Bardo said. "I suppose it's inappropriate."

"Then perhaps we should ask Danlo to leave."

Bardo hesitated as he rubbed his beard. Then he said, "Ah, why don't you ask him?" He smiled at Danlo weakly, distantly, as if to say that he was sorry, and Danlo wondered what spell Hanuman had cast over him.

"All right," Hanuman said. He turned to Danlo, and his eyes were full of light, full of himself. "Please leave."

Danlo bowed and said, "If you would like."

"Never return here. It would be wrong for you to do so."

"You should leave, too," Danlo said. He looked at Lais Motega Mohammad and Thomas Rane and Rohana Chang; he had everyone's attention, so he spoke the truth of his worst fear. "All of you. The Way of Ringess . . . is like a fever waiting to break out upon the universe. It will destroy you. You should leave before it is too late."

Danlo moved down the altar steps, and his boots sent pieces of glass tinkling against each other. As before, people moved out of his way, allowing him to pass. They regarded him with something like awe, but there was also guilt and anger in their admiration for him, as if they sensed they should turn their backs on him and not meet his eyes. Some, with cotton swabs and tubes of glue that Bardo sent for, were wiping drops of blood from their robes and tending each other's wounds; many more were looking toward Hanuman, wondering what to do. Just before leaving the cathedral, beneath the nested arches of the doorway, Danlo turned and looked back behind him. Hanuman stood alone on the altar. Snow swirled around him and broke up the radiation of the candles so that he seemed enveloped in a sphere of golden light. His face was hard and implacable, and it shouted, "Never return here, never!" Danlo looked deep into the nave then, and he looked through time as well as space. The nave—the whole cathedral from wall to wall—was full of thousands of people, all of them facing the altar, all of them swaying and chanting and shouting in ecstasy. There was light everywhere, coming not from candles set afire, but streaming in through the windows in lovely parallel lines of emerald and blue. He saw himself standing on the altar next to Hanuman, bathed in this beautiful light. He saw himself dressed in black pilot's robe, tall and powerful and burning with compassion—yet it was not himself but only some other man who bore slight resemblance to the person he knew as Danlo the Wild. Even as he fell out of this moment of scrying—in the suddenness of broken glass and wind—he thought that he would never set foot inside the cathedral again. One last time, he bowed to Hanuman. But Hanuman did not see him. Around Hanuman's head the clearface shone like a glowing skull. Now and forevermore he would be imprisoned inside his own skull; he was like a brilliant star about to begin the final collapse into himself, into the crushing singularity of consciousness from which there is no return.

I have created him, Danlo thought.

As he turned to pass through the cathedral's great doors, he felt the jagged pieces of the broken god cutting his hand, and he wondered why he had done what he had done.

DANLO PEACEWISE

Before, you are wise; after you are wise. In between you are otherwise.

—Fravashi saying (from the formularies of
Osho the Fool)

The first day of midwinter spring in the year 2954 arrived inauspiciously in a fury of snow and darkness that seemed would never end. None—except the scryers—might have foreseen that this new year would be a glorious and fateful time in history, as crucial to the evolution of the Order as had been 908, or the Dark Year, or 2326, when Dario the Bold discovered the dead stars of the Vild. Not even Danlo could have known that the strange happenings in Bardo's cathedral would set off an avalanche of decisions leading the radical historians, eventually, to rename 2954 as "First Year," and to remake their calendars. The great changes began with a seemingly minor event: Lord Pall, upon the urging of alarmed academicians in both the Masters and Lords' Colleges, banished Hanuman li Tosh from the Order. With the breaking of the god, Hanuman at last had flouted too many people's sensibilities and had compelled too much notice. He had violated several canons as well as betraying his cetic ethics, and so Lord Pall forbade Hanuman to use any of the Order's libraries or to dine at any of the Order's restaurants, and most importantly he forbade him ever again to cross the Academy walls. In spirit, of course, Hanuman had long since left the Order, so his dismissal caused him no real regret or shame. He must have been secretly glad to be free of his vows, free to imprint his designs on a new religion. Although he pretended to outrage, he and Lord Pall were still playing a deep game with each other. It is impossible to say whether they intended, at this time, to make Ringism the religion of the Order; but certainly they conspired to bring down each other's enemies. On tenth day—while Bardo was preoccupied designing the window that would replace the one broken on Year's End night—Hanuman approached Bardo with a simple, if subtle, plan to reorganize their church.

Hanuman proposed formalizing the status of the Way's inner circle. All Ringists who had recorded their remembrances of the Elder Eddas into one of Hanuman's computers would henceforth be known as "Elders." While Bardo naturally mistrusted any scheme springing from Hanuman's lips or brain, this appealed to his vanity. Bardo would be seen as the great priest of a universal religion, the bestower of the titles and boons upon those who had been most faithful to him. It never struck him as absurd that very shortly young journeymen, with their golden robes and pimply faces, would skate about the City demanding to be addressed as "Elder Lais" or "Elder Kiku," and that they would make these demands even of older masters who had lived several lifetimes. And so Bardo approved Hanuman's suggestion and went back to choosing plates of glass for his window.

So it happened that Lord Mariam Erendira Vasquez, one of the finest lords ever to serve the Order, came to be called Elder Mariam. This title was to ruin her. The Order's forty-fourth canon, while allowing choice of religious belief, prohibited all who had taken vows from holding formal position in any religion, cult, or ideological movement. In a ruthless act that stunned the whole Order, Lord Pall invoked the letter of this canon and banished Lord Vasquez, along with Thomas Rane, Huang li Wood, and several other prominent masters whom he must have regarded as stones in his boot. Of the four original members of the Tetrad (Chanoth Chen Ciceron died quietly in his bed shortly after the Festival of the Broken Dolls), only Lord Nikolos now remained to oppose Audric Pall's lordship of the Order.

Then the Lord Cetic delivered his final, brilliant stroke. On nineteenth day, he convened the entire Lords' College and called for a vote over the final planning of the Vild mission. For years, the faction of lords who were loyal to him had forestalled this planning. They—the score of old, fearful lords who were loath to divide the Order and throw it into chaos—had voted repeatedly against provisioning the many lightships and deep ships such a mission would require. But on eighteenth night, in a secret meeting in the cetics' tower, Lord Pall plied them with rare and potent teas, and he soothed their fears. He reasoned with them; he made them promises. He pointed out that the Vild mission would attract the Order's malcontents and mavericks, and many disruptive personages whom they would be well rid of. In fact, he requested the old lords to present him with lists of those they considered most worthy of the honor of risking their lives in the perilous journey to the Vild. This purge would cleanse the Order, he said, not weaken it. Just as it would strengthen their eternal Order if there was again a single lord who ruled over it. And so the next day the Lords' College convened in their cold, drafty building to decide the fate of many billion stars and the billion billion human beings who lived around them. By secret ballot, the 119 lords cast their votes, and at last the great Second Vild Mission came to pass. While the lords sat around their tables and exchanged quick words of jubilation and surprise, Lord Pall stood to address them. For the first time in fifty years, he deigned to speak without hand signs in his natural voice. "My lords," he gasped out in a stream of breath that rattled and hissed, "I would like to propose that Nikolos Sar Petrosian be installed as Lord of the Mission. There is no one more able to lead it than he."

To lead the mission, of course, Lord Nikolos would have to quit the Tetrad. This he soon did. Although he must have dreaded leaving the Order to be ruled once again by an ancient, autocratic lord—after all it was he who had organized the schism against the Timekeeper twenty years previously—it had always been his dream to establish a second Academy among the shattered stars of the Vild. He completed the final plans for the mission with the same speed and decisiveness that had ultimately brought down the Timekeeper. For seventy days the sky above the City was full of rocket fire and thunder as the ferries lifted factories, robots, computers, libraries, diamond tunnelers, and other tools of assembler technology—and a million other things—up to the ten deep ships that orbited the planet. Beside them, floating in the darkness of nearspace above the atmosphere, three great, gleaming seedships awaited their passengers. To fill these ships and make the long journey to the Vild, Lord Nikolos chose eschatologists, mechanics, holists, historians, and even cetics—a thousand masters and adepts from among all the professions. Many of these men and women, during the schism of the Pilot's War, had left Neverness once before. Many more were put forth by Lord Pall, who had compiled a long list of notorious Ordermen, including famous pilots who once had followed Mallory Ringess to war: Helena Charbo, Aja Richardess, Alark of Urradeth, and perhaps the greatest living pilot of all, the Sonderval.

First on Lord Pall's list, however, was a young pilot as yet untested as a pilot. Lord Nikolos must have wondered why the name of Danlo wi Soli Ringess appeared before all others. He must have hesitated in choosing Danlo for such a mission, for Danlo was only a journeyman and therefore deemed too inexperienced to pilot a fragile lightship through the deranged and unmapped spaces of the Vild. But three things weighed in Danlo's favor. First, he was almost a full pilot; at times of crisis according to a precedent established during the War of the Faces, a promising journeyman could be elevated before his formal convocation. Then, too, Lord Nikolos liked it that Danlo had spoken so fiercely and eloquently against the Way of Ringess. Lord Nikolos had a mind as flawless and clear as winter air; he might have been better off born thousands of years earlier into the Age of Reason, so keenly did he mistrust man's dark, moist, intuitive energies. Ironically, he regarded Danlo as a champion of the rational and, like himself, as a hater of all that was religious or that hinted of the occult. The Vild mission would be, essentially, a war of reason against the galaxy destroying doctrines of the Architects of the Old Cybernetic Church. Danlo, steeped in the Fravashi language philosophy the enemy of all beliefs or belief systems, was a man whom Lord Nikolos thought he could trust. Lord Nikolos also assumed that since Danlo was the son and grandson of great pilots, one day he would be a great pilot, too. And so in the end he approved Danlo as a member of his mission. In this way, through chance through fate, through fundamental misunderstandings, after eight years of waiting to journey to the stars, Danlo at last prepared to leave the city of Neverness.

He took his vows on the second of false winter. Since he was the only journeyman to be elevated that day, the ceremony was held privately inside the Hall of the Ancient Pilots, in a little room without windows or furniture. The floor, save for a single old carpet laid out like a beggar's bed, was bare stone. The walls were cold and gray, broken only by portraits of the men and women who had served as Lord Pilot. On the room's north wall the likeness of Mallory Ringess hung between those of Leopold Soli and Chanoth Chen Ciceron. Next to Lord Ciceron's nobly (and falsely) rendered face was only empty granite; someday this space would be filled by the portrait of the new Lord Pilot, Salmalin the Prudent. Salmalin was a spare, laconic man who had been installed as Lord Pilot only ten days earlier. One of his first duties was to preside over Danlo's elevation. Attended by only two other pilots as witnesses, he performed the ceremony quickly, as if he were a guest at an alien banquet forced to make a speech or eat a distasteful dish. He stood all stiff and sullen in his black robes while Danlo knelt on the carpet and made his vows. Then Lord Salmalin presented Danlo with a black diamond ring and told him, "With this ring, you are a pilot." That was all he said. He offered neither congratulations nor encouragement. He bowed, turned abruptly, and left Danlo musing that he had finally accomplished his dream of becoming a full pilot.

Over the next ten days, as the storms of midwinter spring gave way to warmer and fairer weather, Danlo went about the City saying his farewells. He had many people to visit: Madhava li Shing, Rihana Tal, and Jonathan and Benjamin Hur, and many other friends. During his years of religious exploration, he had met autists, nimspinners, ronin warrior-poets—women and men of a dozen sects. He found most of these people down in the Farsider's Quarter, and he told them that he would soon be leaving the City for a long time, possibly forever. It surprised him how difficult this leave-taking proved to be. Seeking out his old masters, such as Master Jonath who would not be making the journey to the Vild, he skated across the Academy from hall to hall, and he savored the play of sunlight off the spires, the cut and set of each building stone, the music of the novices' skate blades ringing against the ice. From a friend, he learned that Thomas Rane would be moving into one of the apartments adjacent to Bardo's cathedral. Therefore he made his last journey to the Tower of Remembrance where he watched Master Thomas pack various drugs, gyres, attitude pins, and other belongings into a plain wooden box. His final meeting with him was awkward and sad. Danlo showed him his pilot's ring, and Master Thomas said, "Congratulations, Danlo. But I hope you'll continue learning the attitudes, even if I won't be there to teach you. You would have made a fine remembrancer, don't you know?"

Danlo said good-bye to him then. But he did not tell him that since the night in Bardo's cathedral, he had lost his passion for remembrance. In truth, during the dark and endless days of the great storm, the golden door to the One memory had slammed shut with such force and reverberation that he thought he would never again find the key with which to open it.

On the twelfth of false winter he met Bardo down on the Street of a Thousand Bars. Because Bardo did not wish to be seen talking to Danlo, for their rendezvous he chose a dark bar that was more like an animal's lair than a place in which two friends might enjoy conversation. Over cups of tarry, licorice coffee, as they stood side by side at the ancient bar, Bardo professed that they *were* still friends, even if their friendship had suffered over his founding the Way of Ringess. He made no apologies to Danlo. He hinted that he was caught up in momentous events, or rather that he was playing some sort of cosmic chess game too important for him to simply knock over the pieces and quit. That he *could* still quit, at will, Danlo doubted, even though Bardo pretended to a control over himself that he had never possessed. Indeed, his words that night were full of pretension, self-deception, and lies. He blamed the difficulties of his church on Hanuman's overweening ambition instead of looking into the smoke-stained mirror on the wall behind the bar (or any other mirror) for the source of his woes. If only Hanuman could be whipped and disciplined like a sled dog, he said, the Way of Ringess might achieve true salvation for all people.

"It's Hanuman who's ruined everything," he said. Although he had sipped only coffee for his beverage, he seemed half-drunk. "Ah, but what can I do? Threaten to excommunicate him? Yes, yes, of course, the thing to do—except I've already done it. Threatened him. And his response was to threaten *me*. No, don't be alarmed, there's no need. I hope. I mean, he threatened to leave the Way. To found his own goddamned church and take half my Ringists with him. Half? Three fourths. Nine tenths—does it matter? He threatened to ruin what I've created. And so I must find a way to control him. His genius—he's a goddamned religious genius. Did you know that the courtesan's have finally agreed to follow the Way? The whole damn Society! Because of him. How can I do without him? How can I *not*? Ah, Bardo, Bardo—whāt has Bardo done? you may wonder. Are you listening, Little Fellow? I remember that I once warned you not to make friends with him. I should have heeded my own advice. Too bad. There's something wrong about Hanuman, I think. Something ill-fated, even sinister. Did you know that he was seen with Tamara the night before she supposedly con-

racted the goddamned virus? Before this virus supposedly
ped her of her memories? *Supposedly*—what a weight of
eaning I impregnate that word with. Do you understand? You
? Ah, you do. Now *I* understand. It's clear what happened in
e cathedral. You could have killed him. Yet you saved him.
hy? Because of your vow? Or because you had no proof of his
thy crime? No proof. But somewhere there has to be proof.
o you think I won't find it? And then. And then. Ah, and then
u don't care, do you?"

"It is not that," Danlo said. He sipped his coffee while he
cked at the steel footrail and listened to it ring. That Bardo
d ferreted out evidence of Hanuman's crime surprised him
nly slightly.

"You've no taste for revenge?"

"No," Danlo said.

"Too bad. And it's too bad what's happened to Tamara."

"Have you seen her, Bardo?"

There was a long silence as Bardo pulled at his mustache.
hen he sighed and said, "Listen, I bring you heavy news. I've
eard from the courtesans that she's left the City. She's re-
ounced the Society, abandoned her calling. She's gone, and no
ne knows where. Out to the stars. I'm sorry—you'll have
anted to call on her before your journey."

Danlo shook his head and looked at Bardo. "No . . . we
ave already said good-bye."

"Well, perhaps she'll return, someday."

"Perhaps."

"Ah, poor Tamara. Poor Danlo." Bardo turned to preen his
eard and study his reflection in the dark mirror behind the bar.
is face fell sad and dreamy, full of self-pity. Then he mumbled,
Poor Bardo. What shall we do? Do you think it doesn't mat-
r? No, it *matters*. Everything. I, you, Hanuman li Tosh—the
Vay. Have you ever doubted there's truly a way for us to be-
ome gods? There *is* a way. I've seen it, the Elder Eddas. Mal-
ory Ringess. His genius. His life. His fate. *His* way. Have I ever
nderstood why he did what he did? No. Did he instruct me to
ound a goddamned religion? If only he'd remained in Never-
ess. But someday he'll return. I have to believe that, don't I?"

Danlo smiled at him through a haze of smoke and steaming
offee. "Oh, Bardo . . . I shall miss you," he said.

"Well, it's all too damn bad," Bardo said. He banged his
offee mug down on the bar, then embraced Danlo and

thumped his hand against his back. "Little Fellow, Little Fellow."

"Good-bye," Danlo said.

"I wish you well," Bardo said. He squeezed Danlo's hand and looked down at the black ring circling his little finger. "Fall far and well, Pilot."

It was three days after this that Danlo made a brief journey across the City. With a symmetry he found pleasing, his final farewell was with the master who had first greeted him upon his arrival in Neverness: the Honored Fravashi called Old Father. This wise, ancient alien—ever one to savor irony—suggested they meet on the very beach where Danlo had almost speared him so many years before. On a cloudy false winter day, Danlo went down to the Darghinni Sands and waited by the ocean for Old Father's arrival. He stood on hard-formed sand shingle with chunks of pack ice, and he stared out at the dark waters of the Sound for a long time. Then, from behind him, far off, he heard a faint whistling as of air flowing through fipple pipes. He turned to see a small white figure trudging across the dunes. It was Old Father, of course, dressed only in his body's silky white fur. As he drew nearer, Danlo could see that Old Father's arthritis must have worsened, for there was little grace left in his long alien limbs, and he moved carefully across the black and white sands as if stepping over shards of broken glass. Although he was obviously in pain, his mouth was shaped into a deep smile; his marvelous golden eyes shone down upon Danlo like double suns.

"Ah ho!" he said, "it's Danlo the Wild, not so wild any more, I think. You've changed—you're a man now. So, it's so."

Indeed, Danlo's appearance had recently changed. He had shaved his face until it was as smooth as the skin of a baldo nut. He had trimmed his long fingernails. Then, after unfastening Ahira's white feather and storing it inside his chest along with the broken chess piece and his mother's diamond sphere, and other mementos, he had cut his hair. Despite these mutilations, however, despite all that had happened to him since the Devaki had died, he could not think of himself as a full man.

To Old Father, Danlo said, "It is good to see you, sir. You seem . . . much the same."

"Ahhh," Old Father said, "ohhh—the same, only more so."

"Perhaps we should have found a meeting place closer to your house. It must be hard for you . . . to walk this far."

"Oh ho, it is hard," Old Father said. With his black finger

ails, he scratched the great double membrum dangling between his legs, then touched his hips. "When I was younger, I tried to flee the pain by sitting and doing nothing. But that only made me more aware of it. Therefore, let us walk down by the water, and you will tell me about *your* pains so that I may forget about mine. It's a lovely day for walking, don't you think?"

Together, arm in arm, scuttling along like two crabs who had locked claws, they walked down by the water's edge. There was a brisk wind blowing off the sea. The air was heavy with salt and the reek of rotting wood. And with other smells, too: bird droppings and crushed shells and old, wet fur. They stepped over strands of crackling seaweed and driftwood bent into deranged shapes, and Danlo told Old Father all that had happened between him and Hanuman li Tosh. He had much to tell. Even at their crustaceal pace, they walked a long way, almost to the end of the Darghinni Sands where the dunes gave way to the rugged shoreline of Far North Beach. It was an afternoon of darting clouds and wind. Snow fell in sudden flurries followed moments later by bursts of sunshine. Delicate little snowflakes—which Danlo once would have called *shishay*—hung suspended in the air only to be vaporized before striking the ground. Faced with this uncertain weather, Danlo could not decide if he was hot or cold. But Old Father seemed completely in his element. Neither the snow nor the spray off the breakers dismayed him. He liked to dig his furry feet into the hardpack, leaving footprints larger than a bear's. As Danlo told him how Hanuman had broken the god that he had carved, Old Father played in the sand and his little black nose quivered happily.

"Ah, oh, you were right to keep your vow of ahimsa," Old Father said.

Danlo listened to the waves breaking against the shore, and he said, "Every moment since I gave Hanuman the god . . . I have wondered if that is true."

"Aha, never harming another, not even in one's thoughts."

"But I *did* harm him," Danlo said. "I saw him . . . dead."

"Oh?"

"I wanted to kill him."

"Ahhh, but instead you saved his life. So, it's so."

"Yes," Danlo said, "it is so."

Old Father smiled as one of his eyes shut halfway. He whistled and said, "You shouldn't judge yourself, oh, no! You saved his *life*. In the field of action, you were a man of ahimsa, and I honor you for this."

689

Old Father's insistence that he had saved Hanuman's life did nothing to ease Danlo's doubts. In fact, his words were like salt in the open wound that divided Danlo in two. With his thumb, he massaged the bone above his eye; there was an aching in his head, now, nearly all the time. "I think it is still your delight to inflict the holy pain," he said.

"Oh, ho, the angslan!" Old Father said. "Am I not still a Fravashi?"

"More so than ever, sir."

"And you're still human, I see. This new religion of yours has done nothing to change that." Old Father's face was radiant with sunshine, and both his eyes were now wide open. "It's a tradition that we Fravashi give gifts to *human beings*. Once, on this very beach, I gave you a gift. Do you remember?"

Danlo nodded as he reached down to slip the shakuhachi from his pocket. He held up the bamboo flute so that the sunlight glinted from it.

"Aha!" Old Father said. "And now I wish to give you another gift."

Except for his shining fur, Old Father was completely naked, and he held nothing in his long, fine hands. His gift, then would be no musical instrument or other thing wrought of wood or ivory or stone.

"There's a title," Old Father said, "by which certain of the Fravashi Fathers are known. This I give to you, from my lips to your ears: I shall call you Danlo Peacewise. Oh ho, you are wise in the ways of peace, and you'll wear the name well."

"Thank you," Danlo said. "But I do not feel very wise."

"Ahhh."

"Nor am I at peace."

"Ohhh."

"At least, I cannot be at peace . . . with what I have made."

"Do you mean with this religion that everyone is calling the Way of Ringess?"

Danlo hadn't meant precisely that, but he said, "I have spoken against the Way, you know."

"I would imagine so. Many of the Peacewise are great speakers."

"But I am afraid what I have said has caused . . . great harm."

"Never harming *anyone*—this is ahimsa," Old Father said.

Oh, ho, but freeing others from their beliefs—this is the holy task."

"This *belief* in the way my father became a god—I would destroy it if I could. All beliefs. All . . . religions."

Old Father stood quietly with both his eyes nearly closed. It seemed that he was staring out across the Sound at the mountains, whose white peaks were now lost into layers of puffy white clouds. "Oh, Pilot, you must be careful," Old Father finally said. "There is a union of opposites: the stronger your will to destroy a thing, the more tightly you'll bind yourself to it."

"But it was you who taught me," Danlo said. "To oppose all beliefs, yes?"

"Ha, ha, I think I taught you too well."

Danlo stood watching the waves come and go. The tide was going out, moment by moment, slipping away into the deeper parts of the sea. After a while, the sky fell cloudy and gray, and the waters of the Sound were as dark and turbid with sediments as old wine. As he listened to the far off barking of the seals and the gulls screaming and circling above the waves, he was aware that a whole part of his life was ending. He could no longer be a student of alien philosophies, or dreamscapes, or techniques of remembrance. Here, on this cold beach, he would try at last to find beneath the universe naked in the mind without beliefs. He would *will* himself to do this, even if Old Father thought that such a way of living was impossible for any man.

"Danlo, Danlo."

He turned to see Old Father standing next to him, touching the shaft of his shakuhachi. Old Father smiled at him as if he were reading his thoughts.

"You can't give up everything," Old Father said. "What of your devotion to ahimsa?"

"But there is no devotion," Danlo said. "Ahimsa is not what I believe. It is . . . what I am."

Old Father whistled sadly and said, "At our first meeting you told me that you wished to journey to the center of the universe. A noble conception, don't you think?"

Danlo shook his head. "No, it is . . . a childish view. The universe goes on and on. There is no center."

"But you will go to the Vild?"

"Yes."

"Oh, ho, to find a cure for the plague that killed the Devaki?"

With an uncharacteristic urgency, Old Father hummed a

strange little melody that Danlo had never heard before. O
Father's right eye was entirely closed while the left searche
Danlo's face with the intensity of a moonlight.

"Once, I believed the slow evil could be cured," Dan
admitted. "I believed the Alaloi could be saved."

"Once it was also your desire to become an asarya."

"That is your word," Danlo said. "Affirming ever
thing . . . is a Fravashi ideal."

"Ah, oh, then it's no longer *your* ideal?"

Danlo stepped out a few paces toward the water until th
surging waves began lapping at his boots. "The problem," h
said, "is to affirm *anything*."

"So, it's so."

"Do you see?" Danlo said. He pointed toward the offsho
rocks that pushed like granite needles into the sky. Sheets
feather moss covered them in green. Everywhere, they we
speckled white with snow gulls resting or making their nests. "
is all so beautiful. But so flawed. With *shaida*. The mountain
myself. Even you, sir—we are all a part. There is no escaping
I think that Hanuman understood this more clearly than anyo
should."

"And you can't forgive him for this, can you?"

"No . . . I cannot forgive myself."

"Ahhh."

"I used to hope that there was a way out in remembrancin
A way toward . . . an innocence."

"Then you never found the answer in the Elder Eddas?"

"Once, I thought I did," Danlo said. "I was so clos
But . . . no."

" 'Shaida is the cry of the world,' " Old Father said, quoti
a line from the Song of Life that Danlo had once taught hi
"Aha, but you didn't make the world."

With a habitual motion, Danlo reached up to touch th
feather in his hair, but he found that it was gone. He bowed
Old Father, then said, "Shaida is the way of the man who ki
other men. There was a man who Hanuman might have becom
A truly splendid man. And I . . . killed him."

"And you find it impossible to accept this murder."

"I am sorry, sir. I must . . . disappoint you."

Old Father smiled mysteriously and said, "No, it's just th
opposite."

They stood there in the wet sand, looking at each other a
smiling. It was now past late afternoon; in the west, out whe

e ocean ran fast and deep, the clouds had pulled back to real the blazing sun as it spread out along the horizon. The sky
as on fire, melting, and the waters burned with crimson and
ld. Because it would soon be dark and the Fravashi do not
e to be outside at night, Old Father made ready to leave. He
aced his fingers on Danlo's flute one last time. He whistled a
ick song of blessing. (Or perhaps it was a ribald aria—with
e Fravashi, one never knew.) And then he opened both eyes
mpletely and said to Danlo, "But how will you live now, Pi-
t? Oh ho, what will you *do*?"

Danlo pointed toward the eastern sky, at the night's first
ars twinkling between the breaks in the clouds. "There are
ds out there," he said. "Perhaps my father still lives . . .
mewhere. I would find him if I could. Any god. There is a
estion that Hanuman once asked me—my question, now: I
uld ask the gods if the universe could have been made differ-
tly. *Halla,* not *shaida.* The gods know. The gods create, on
d on, and so they must know."

Soon, he said, he would go out into the universe, not to find
center nor to discover a cure for a disease that had no cure,
t simply because he was a pilot of the Order on a desperate
est. The stars were dying, and even if there was no help for
e world's evil, at least the destruction of the entire galaxy
ight be averted.

Old Father's response to Danlo's words was strange. His
es were open yet devoid of light, as if his consciousness had
pped away from him and flown up toward the sky. Although
stood three feet away on the sand of a darkening beach, he
emed to be looking down on Danlo, even while looking in-
nsely at himself. His mouth was set into a sad smile that told of
inful and elusive memories, or perhaps a vision of a future
at had never been. There was a vast coldness about him. It
emed that he wanted to tell Danlo something. But for once—
d only for a moment—this Old Father of the Fravashi race
uld not speak.

"Sir . . . it is falling late," Danlo said.

At last, the great tide of consciousness rushed back into Old
ather's eyes, and he whistled softly. "Ohhh, very late—we
ould say good-bye. It may be a long time before we walk here
ain."

Danlo bowed his head, looking down at the tiny black and
hite grains of sand beneath his boots. "I think . . . I will
ver return," he said.

"Then I must ask you to give me a gift before we go," O
Father said.

"But what do I have to give you?"

Old Father looked at Danlo's flute. "Why not a song?"

"What . . . song?"

"Something that you've composed yourself. Somethi
strange and wild, yet peaceful. Oh ho, you are Danlo Peacewis
are you not?"

Danlo smiled as he shrugged his shoulders. He held t
shakuhachi's cool ivory mouthpiece to his lips and began
play. A stream of long, low notes flowed out over the beach. H
had to play strongly with much breath or else the music wou
have been lost to the wind. It was a simple song, really, a so
that returned to itself over and over with subtle variations
each round. He might play it forever and not reach any concl
sion or climax, yet, in the poignant passages and movemen
there was a progression toward a completeness of sound th
hinted of infinite possibilities. Old Father listened to this so
with his head held rigid and his eyes nearly closed, in the at
tude of a Fravashi who wishes to remember a piece of mus
perfectly. He appeared well pleased with the composition. A
last, realizing that Danlo had no intention of stopping, duri
the pause between rounds, he reached out to touch Danlo
forehead. And then he announced, "Oh ho, I must go now, b
you must play. Ha ha, oh ho, you were born to play."

In this way, Old Father said good-bye to his favorite st
dent. He whistled and smiled and laughed, and then he turn
to make the long walk back to his home. The sound of his laug
ter—rich, compassionate, and overflowing—rang out above t
beach sands for a long time. Strangely, it did not interfere at
with the music that Danlo made.

All during twilight Danlo stood alone by the water's edg
playing his shakuhachi. After a while it grew dark and cold. T
wind blew the clouds away, and the sky fell through the colors
deep blue until it was as black as a pilot's robe. In a great circ
all around him, from east to west, north to south, the stars gl
tered in the heavens. He looked up at these cold, bright sta
and the sound of the song that he played was lost into the i
mense light-distances. The familiar constellations that he h
known since childhood were impossibly far away, yet they a
peared very near, almost as near as the luminous waves rushi
at his feet. He played and played, and Old Father's last questi
reverberated inside him: What would he do? He listened to t

an's long, dark roar as he waited for an answer. He might
t forever, for that was the marvel and mystery of the ocean,
way it shimmered in the starlight, always waiting, always the
ie, yet always moving, always calling, always astonishing with
w sounds and creations. Although it was now full dark, he
ened for the cries of the various seabirds, the loons and gulls
l puffins, and the silver thallows and other hunters who liked
ly at night. He listened for the rare song of the snowy owl. At
:, in the neverness of this one sound that he longed for above
others, in the thunderous silence of the sea, he had his an-
:r. He would continue to play his own song and no other. He
uld look clearly upon all that he had done. He had created
numan—this was a truth of the universe too terrible to deny.
d Hanuman had created him. The difficulty now, as it ever
uld be, was in saying "yes" to such broken, hateful creations.
t if he was strong enough, if he was wise enough, he could do
: simple thing. He could affirm the act of creating, in itself.
: miracle of simply living. Life, he remembered, was every-
ig. One day he might laugh again, or find completion in love,
now it must be enough for him to live, on and on without
l.

And so on a lovely night he stood alone by the water's edge
he lifted his face to the stars and played a song on his
kuhachi. And he played and played and played.

About the Author

DAVID ZINDELL's short story "Shanidar" was a prizewinning entry in the Writers of the Future Contest. In 1986 he was nominated for the John W. Campbell Award for best new writer. His
first novel, *Neverness* was nominated for the Arthur C. Clarke
Award. He lives in Boulder, Colorado with his wife and children, where he is at work on a new novel.

Only once in a great while does a writer come along who defies comparison—a writer so original he redefines the way we look at the world. Neal Stephenson is such a writer and *Snow Crash* is such a novel, weaving virtual reality, Sumerian myth, and just about everything in between with a cool, hip cybersensibility to bring us the gigathriller of the information age.

SNOW CRASH

NEAL STEPHENSON

"A cross between *Neuromancer* and Thomas Pinchon's *Vineland*. This is no mere hyperbole."
—*San Francisco Bay Guardian*

"Fast-forward free-style mall mythology for the 21st century."—Wiliam Gibson

"Brilliantly realized...Stephenson turns out to be an engaging guide to an onrushing tomorrow."
—*New York Times Book Review*